Sister Magdalena

A Novel by Michael Converse

SISTER MAGDALENA

ISBN-13: 978-0692442739 (Michael R. Converse)

ISBN-10: 0692442731

Published by Michael R. Converse

Printed in the United States of America

THIS BOOK IS DEDICATED TO MY FATHER,

J. LEON CONVERSE,

A MAN WHO ALWAYS KEPT HIS WORD.

DISCLAIMER

This is a work of fiction. Characters in this book may share names with figures from history, but they are in no way meant to represent actual fact. I have taken some creative freedom with the geography and history of Spain. In this book, actual history is only a guideline to a story about the undead.

The religious ideas put forth by Sister Magdalena are by no means condoned by the Catholic Church or any right thinking person. With the Afflictor Cult, I have attempted to take actual scripture and twist it into something that could only be described as evil. These ideas should never be thought of as truth and under no circumstances should anyone attempt to follow them. That being said, I welcome you read this dark tale.

PRELUDE

Sister Magdalena ascended the stairs which spiraled up from the dungeon. Our Lady of Repentance was completely devoid of life. The only sound was the echo of her footfalls upon the concrete stairs. The stench of the crematorium had soaked into the walls. The rest of the nuns, both living and dead, were sent ahead to join the Afflictors. The destruction of The Chapel would give them ample time for the flight to Spain.

As she came to the top of the steps, Sister Magdalena could hear the wind howling outside. She walked down the long hallway which led to the foyer. There were four couches surrounding a low table where the nuns would sit and discuss their faith. The couches were now covered with white sheets. Soon there would be nothing at all. She passed the sitting area and continued up the enclosed wooden staircase that led to the second floor of the convent.

The Mother Superior's room contained little more than a small bed and a plain wooden desk. It was here that Magdalena had composed many letters on devotion. There were similar authors from the Spanish Inquisition, but Afflictor doctrine is principally the work of Sister Magdalena. Most such works have been lost to the fires of time. Pope Innocent III condemned them all as heresy.

A sheaf of parchment paper was laid out on the desk, along with an ink pot and several feather quills. A lantern sat off to one corner of the desk. The lantern was little more than an iron candle holder with glass walls. The white candle inside was not lit. Over the desk was mounted an iron crucifix. Isabel knelt down next to her simple bed. She reached underneath and grasped the handle of an old wooden chest.

The chest was made of heavy oak which had been stained black. The family crest of Montenegro was carved into the surface of the lid. The image of a stallion rearing up on its hind legs was to either side of the crest. The chest had once contained a wedding dress, the deed to Black River

Ranch, and a dowry of gold and jewels that would have made any woman desirable.

The contents of the chest were much different in the 21st century. There were several black dresses and the black and white nun's habits that went with them. Also in the chest was a wooden rosary, several iron scroll cases, and a silver reliquary for Holy Communion. Yet one more item was hidden beneath the folds of black cloth. It was a marble box with the image of the cross etched into the lid.

Magdalena carefully removed the lid of the box to reveal her most prized possession. She stared down at a very old Bible underneath the thin sheet of glass inside the marble. It was from this very book that her father had taught her to read. She had been called Isabel in those days. In the years since, she had carefully oiled the leather and had it taken to specialists several times to preserve it. The verses were all written in Latin. The calligraphy had been painstakingly transcribed by hand by Dominican monks. There were many beautiful paintings illustrating the scriptures inside and the first letter of each chapter was its own work of art.

Sadly, Sister Magdalena would not be able to look at these paintings as the pages were far too old and delicate. She sighed as she looked down and closed her eyes. What she could not see with her eyes, the nun could imagine from her memories. Time seemed to run backward as the snow fell outside her window.

Part 1

The Heiress of Montenegro

CHAPTER I

"The Lord giveth and the Lord taketh away."
(Job 1:21)

"Do you like it mija," her father asked? Rafael Montenegro was a broad shouldered man and quite tall for a Spaniard. To Isabel, he was a giant. His head was clean shaven and he had a thick moustache which hung down slightly at the corners of his mouth. If one looked closely, they would see that his baldness was a product of his age as well as his choice. Lord Montenegro was a mountain of a man with features like chiseled granite. When he looked at his daughter, it was as if nothing else mattered in the world.

"Oh yes," Isabel exclaimed, "I like it very much!" It was the most beautiful book she had ever seen in all her ten years. The black leather of its cover was softer than any she had ever touched. The inscription on it read, 'Biblia Sacra,' which meant 'Holy Bible' in Latin. The inscription was made of gold leaf that had been worked into the surface of the tome. Isabel gasped with delight as she opened the Bible and saw that there were several masterful oil paintings scattered throughout the pages. These pages were a little thicker than the rest. Each one seemed more beautiful than the last.

"The paintings are the work of the late Brother Claudio," the priest told her. "May God rest his soul." The priest was a grey haired man in a long black robe. There was a black tunic over the robe. The tunic had the symbol of the cross embroidered into its surface in red. The robe had red piping around the sleeves and the hem. He also wore a silver crucifix over his neck.

"They're wonderful," Isabel breathed.

"But you would have to be very careful to keep it safe," Rafael cautioned.

"I will Papa," she promised. "I will treasure it always."

"Forever is a long time for a little girl," he said smiling. They looked at each other for several seconds before Rafael began to laugh. Isabel joined him. Lord Montenegro pounded one fist on the table wherein the priest had laid out several Bibles for his perusal. "We'll take this one," Rafael said.

"Right away my Lord," the priest said. He wrapped the bible in fine black cloth and handed it to Lord Montenegro. Rafael then handed the precious bundle to his daughter. She hugged it to her chest as if it were gold. Rafael kept one arm on Isabel's shoulder as they left the Great Cathedral of Teruel. It was the most majestic structure in the city. It was crafted of rose colored stones that sparkled in the sunlight. The architecture was greatly influenced by the Moors who had once ruled the city in years past. The Cathedral was massive in size with sweeping arches and finely crafted domes. The domes were painted green and had iron crosses at the top of each. The entrance was a circular archway over twenty feet high. The heavy oaken doors stood below the arch and looked out on a courtyard of white cobblestones.

In the center of the courtyard was a marble fountain. The fountain bore a statue of Saint Christopher carrying an infant on his back. Isabel paused to look at her reflection in the pools below the statue as they waited for Lord Montenegro's carriage to come hither. Her blue black hair had been braided and wrapped into a coil that rose from the top of her head. Strings of pearls were woven through the coil on silver chains. Her dark brown eyes were shining with happiness. She adjusted her lavender shawl over the violet hued gown that her father had purchased for her the night before. The pearls belonged to her mother, the Lady Priscilla. Priscilla was visiting Isabel's aunt, Lady Imelda, in Zaragoza.

The trip to Teruel had been necessary in order to sell a score of stallions. Each of them had been trained to carry a man in heavy armor. Their hooves were deadly instruments. They would perform magnificently, even in the chaos of war. Pope Innocent III was calling for a crusade against the Moors and Spain would surely answer. Rafael, having once led the Spanish Army, was well trusted by the nobility. Lord Marcilla had overpaid for the war horses, and he had requested that two of them be sold to Lord Enriquez of Morera. Morera was just west of Huesca, which Isabel and her father would have to travel through anyway on their return trip to Montenegro. Rafael had graciously agreed. The trip to Teruel had afforded Lord Montenegro the opportunity to take his only daughter to the Convent of Saint Mary the Mother of God. The nuns of Saint Mary's put on liturgical dramas several times a year for audiences from across Europe. Seeing one of their great musical plays was something that Isabel had dreamed of for several years.

The idea had started when Lord Manuel Barillos had come to visit her father's court. In his entourage was a singer from the Parisian court. She had performed a beautiful aria for Lord Montenegro's assembled guests. The aria awakened a longing in the child. Isabel wanted very much to perform in the theatre. It was all she could talk about for months, much to Rafael's chagrin. At the urging of Lady Priscilla, he was convinced to hire a music instructor to help his daughter develop her talent. A lady would never be allowed to perform in a theatre, but singing was a desirable quality for noble women. In less than a year, it was Isabel who sang for Lord Montenegro's court.

Their first night in Teruel, Lord Montenegro and his daughter visited a tailor who had altered the violet gown that Isabel now wore. Isabel was sent to her quarters in the estate of Lord Marcilla while her father conducted business. They were provided with a sumptuous meal before turning in for the evening. That morning, they had eaten breakfast and strolled through the streets of Teruel before making their way to the Great Cathedral.

The nuns had performed the Drama of the Resurrection. To pretend to be Christ, even in a play, was unthinkable. So it was that the story began after Jesus had left the tomb. It was a beautiful story and the nuns told it perfectly. The finale was a sorrowful song performed by the character of Mary Mother of God. The actor really seemed to feel pain as she told of how Christ suffered on the road to Calvary. Isabel cried and even her father's eyes grew misty.

Once the carriage pulled up in front of them, Lord Montenegro helped his daughter up the step which led inside. She kissed him on the cheek before seating herself on the leather cushions. Most nobility would have traveled inside the safety of the carriage. Lord Montenegro rode with the soldiers. Isabel was not afraid to be alone. She knew she had nothing to fear as long as her father was close by.

It was late in the spring of 1169A.D. The air was cool and the mulberry trees were blossoming as they rode up the path to Lord Enriquez' manor. Isabel was seated in front of her father. He held the reins with one hand and used the other arm to encircle her. Off to either side of the path was a vast orchard where mulberries were being harvested. The trees were covered in white flowers. A blue bird was singing in the branches of one as the carriage passed by. The bird puffed up his feathers and fanned out his tail to attract a mate. Isabel giggled at the bird showing off. "Look at the bird Papa," she cried! Rafael smiled and glanced over.

"We're almost there," he said. The manor house was a huge gabled structure with white washed walls and dark brown roofing. A low wall surrounded the courtyard. It too was made of white colored wood and had a dark brown rail over the top of it. Two servants in blue livery threw wide the iron gates into the courtyard. Isabel and her father were led inside the estate, while the soldiers remained outside.

They were received in a private dining room. A feast of roast duck had been laid out on the table. The knives and spoons were made of silver. The rest of the dishes on the table were made of silver also. There was a round loaf of bread baked with oil and rosemary on one platter and a round of cheese on another. There were also bowls of fresh greens and bowls of rice set by each place. A large window looked out on the courtyard and the trees beyond. The sun was dying in the western sky.

"Lord Enriquez is currently indisposed, but he will be joining you very soon," one of the servants told Rafael. He encouraged them to begin dining and then quickly left the room. The duck was succulent and the sweet plum sauce was perfectly offset by the slight bitterness of the asparagus spears. Isabel was very mindful not to spill any food on her new gown.

After the sky had faded to grey, Lord Enriquez entered the room in a red velvet cloak with gold embroidery along the neck and cuffs. His white hair was drawn back into a pony-tail. His eyes were sharp but his flesh was sagging with age. Rafael stood up from his chair as the man came in. Lord Montenegro's dark brown tunic was obviously of expensive cloth, but not as extravagant as the other man's garb.

"Good evening," Rafael greeted the other Lord.

"Lord Montenegro," Enriquez began, "it is an honor to receive you as a guest.

"It is an honor to be here," Rafael replied graciously. "This is my beloved daughter Isabel." He motioned to her as he spoke.

"She is quite lovely," Enriquez remarked. Isabel could see the pride in her father's face as the other man spoke well of her. She stood and curtseyed to Lord Enriquez. They were all seated once more. The men talked idly of the weather and the Moors while Isabel finished her meal. A servant was called to bring desert. A silver bowl of cherries was set next to Lord Enriquez and he took a handful of them for his plate. "I love cherries," he said as he looked at the young heiress. "Would you like some?"

"I would be delighted," Isabel replied with perfect manners. She averted her eyes when she spoke and succinctly pronounced every word. The servant bent over to pick up the bowl again, but Lord Enriquez held up a hand to prevent him.

"I will serve our charming young visitor," Enriquez told his servant. The serving man stepped back while his lord picked up the bowl of fruit. Enriquez swept over to where Isabel was seated and stood beside her. He was positioned such that Isabel was between the two lords. He set the bowl down on the table next to her plate. He selected one of the cherries and plucked it out by the stem. This he held before Isabel's face. Isabel reached up with her left hand to accept the fruit but Enriquez pulled it out of reach. "No, no, no," he chuckled. "There is no need to stain your delicate fingers, just take it from mine." Isabel paused. There was confusion written on her face.

"Be still my daughter," Rafael interrupted. He looked then at Lord Enriquez. "You forget yourself," he said unkindly.

"Do I," Lord Enriquez asked. There was feigned hurt in his voice but challenge in his eyes.

"My Isabel is not a dog that she should perform tricks for you," Rafael said angrily. "Continue with this foolishness and I will kill you where you stand!"

"You dare threaten me in my own house?" Lord Enriquez asked with disdain. "It is you who forget yourself Lord Montenegro. Your sword was left with my steward…and your men wait outside these walls."

"Not all men die by the sword," Rafael suggested. He cast a meaningful look at the large knife that had been used to carve the duck.

"Do not press me to summon the guard," Enriquez threatened.

"They should never arrive in time," Rafael said with a terrible calm. "Rather than start a war between us, I recommend that you beg my daughter's pardon and send us on our way. As for the horses, buy them or no. I came here only as a favor to Lord Marcilla."

"But of course," Lord Enriquez replied acidly. "Young lady, I beg your pardon."

"I humbly accept," Isabel replied. Lord Enriquez reached into his pocket and drew out a rawhide bag. He tossed it onto the table before his guests. Some of the coins spilled out of the top.

"The horses remain," Lord Enriquez snapped. "Remove yourselves now from my house." Rafael rose from his chair and straightened to his full height. He towered over the other man and glared down at him. Isabel stood as well.

"Come now," Rafael said as he extended an arm toward her. "Let us depart from this place." He returned the stray coins to the bag and placed it into the pouch on his belt. He did not bid Lord Enriquez farewell. Putting his arm around Isabel's shoulder, Rafael led her out of the manor. The soldiers were not pleased to leave so soon, but they adjusted quickly.

The iron gate shut behind as Lord Montenegro's band departed. They traveled at a leisurely pace down the path through the cherry trees. Once back on the road, Isabel's father shut up the windows of the coach. He instructed her to leave them closed. By the motion of the carriage, Isabel knew that they rode swiftly toward the River Ebro.

They were forced to break camp for several hours once they reached the river. The horses would die if they were not allowed to rest. The men were tense and their mood rubbed off on Isabel. "What is the matter," she asked her father? "Are they chasing us?"

"If they are, then they are far behind," he assured her. "Get some sleep Isabel. We are not stopping for long."

"What if they catch up to us?" she asked nervously.

"Then they will wish they hadn't," Rafael replied. "Don't fear. No one will touch you."

"Why did Lord Enriquez wish to feed me with his hand?"

"There is something wrong with him," Rafael replied stonily. Isabel wanted to ask why it had made Rafael so angry, but she knew better than to question her father. She would be much older before she came to realize why her father had become enraged.

"Will you lay down with me Papa?" she asked.

"Of course," her father replied. They curled up together in the front half of the coach which contained a bed instead of a bench. Rafael hummed a familiar tune while he stroked her hair. It was the lullaby he had sung to her as a baby. It was not long before Isabel's fear subsided and she found sleep. Rafael floated in that state, halfway between slumber and wakefulness, which is so familiar to men of war. His sword was propped between the mattress and the wall of the carriage. All he would need to do was draw it out.

†   †   †

They left long before the sun broke over the horizon. Isabel slept straight through. It wasn't until her father was shaking her awake that she opened her eyes. The carriage door was open and she could see her father's stables through the opening. The familiar smells of hay and manure came on the breeze. Isabel yawned and stretched out her arms. "Are we home already?" she asked, but she knew the answer.

She could hear the sound of the chains as the gate of Montenegro's Keep was being lowered. There was a gorge that separated the keep from the path which led up to it. The gate connected them when lowered. Rafael closed the door and the carriage traveled over the path which led up the mountain to the keep. The black granite walls of the keep rose out of the side of the mountain and towered over all else. Twin towers were positioned on either side of the edifice. The eastern tower contained the aviary. It was from there that Lord Montenegro could survey all the surrounding lands. The western tower was a prison. Iron bars extended out from each of its four windows. An iron cage was suspended from each of these bars, but it had been years since any of them were occupied.

There was also a pulley system going down to Black River from the western tower. The river was so named for the black rocks underneath the clear water. The water was collected from a spring that flowed down from the Pyrenees Mountains. The pulley ensured that those inside would have fresh water, even under siege. The mountain upon which the keep was situated was steep and rocky. It left no room to enter except by the path that ran up to the drawbridge. The river passed down by the stables and traveled for several miles before it joined with the larger River Ebro.

A walk connected both towers to a central platform. The platform was the resting place for the large ballistae. The ballista on top of Montenegro's Keep was capable of launching a volley of one hundred arrows at a time. The siege weapon was mounted on a smaller octagonal shaped platform. The octagon could be rotated to allow defenders to fire in six different directions. In time of war, barrels of oil and torches would be brought up. Rags would be saturated and then wrapped around each arrow. Hundreds of flaming bolts would rain fiery death on anyone foolish enough to lay siege. Although Rafael ensured that the machine was well oiled and tested periodically, there had been no need to fire it in anger during Isabel's lifetime.

The stables were contained in a large two story building at the base of the mountain. There was space within for some one hundred animals, an enclosed room for the tack and harness, and a massive hayloft that was the entirety of the upper floor. Several ladders led up to the loft at intervals from the ground floor. The openings for the ladders were large enough that stable hands could drop down bales of hay with little danger of hitting those climbing up. A well had been dug in the center of the stable. Therefore, it was no trouble at all to bring fresh water to the horses. A far smaller stable existed inside the walls of the keep, but Rafael's success at the horse trade had warranted much more space.

The land below the keep was made of softly rolling hills. The forest had been cleared for several kilometers around the base of the mountain. It would be nearly impossible for an enemy to pass unnoticed over the grasslands. There were several outlying farms and a small cluster of dwellings for the peasants, most of which were employed at Black River Ranch. These houses were built around a small market square with a church dedicated to Santiago, (Saint James the Greater). The western edge of the village was along the bank of the river and the forest which stretched out into the horizon.

Isabel could hear the soldiers on the walls after the carriage passed through the gate. She let her father help her down. She could have done it herself, but her mother had taught her to always be a lady, especially in public. Isabel carried her new Bible in her hands. It was still wrapped in the black cloth from the Cathedral. "See that my horses are fed and well rested," Rafael instructed the stable hands. There were bows and murmurs of assent before the men went forth to do his bidding.

Father and daughter ascended the three stone steps that led into the keep itself. The doors were made of heavy oak and curved upward like a pair of praying hands. Pilar, whose job it was to care for Isabel, was already waiting inside the door. Pilar was an elderly woman with grey hair that hung in a single braid down her broad back. She was short and squat with a simple woolen dress the color of earth. Over this she wore a white apron which was nearly always clean. She had a warm smile and eyes that shone with a light that defied her age. "My Isabel," the old woman said with delight. "I am so happy you are back safe."

"I missed you as well Little Grandma," Isabel replied. Pilar was no blood relation, but Isabel had called her Little Grandma for as long as she could remember.

"Come now," Pilar said. "I'll have a bath drawn for you. You must tell me all about Teruel!"

"It was more beautiful than I imagined," Isabel said wistfully.

"Come, come... Tell me upstairs," Little Grandma said. She practically herded the girl up to the third floor. Isabel looked back questioningly at her father.

"Go along now," Lord Montenegro chuckled. "I'll see you at dinner. You and Little Grandma have a lot of catching up to do. Don't forget to show her you're new Bible."

"Oh my God," Pilar exclaimed. "He takes you to the liturgical drama and he buys you this wonderful book? How spoiled you are!" Rafael went down a side corridor which led to his sitting room while Isabel rushed upstairs with Little Grandma yapping at her heels.

The wash room contained two large ceramic tubs. Each had rose designs carved around the rim with swirling stems that connected the flowers together. A small armoire rested in one corner of the room. Inside it was a wealth of towels and cloths for washing. There were also salts and oils for the bath water, and plenty of soap. Though most people during that time bathed infrequently, Isabel's mother couldn't get enough of it. She had passed on her penchant for cleanliness to her daughter. Servants were called to bring boiling hot water up from the hearth. They filled one of the tubs and left the room to Isabel and Little Grandma.

While they waited for the water to cool, Isabel told Pilar all about the liturgical drama at the Convent of St. Mary. She showed the older woman the 'Biblia Sacra' as well. Pilar fussed over it and sighed over the paintings within. Little Grandma said it was the most beautiful thing she had ever seen. Isabel happily agreed. After Pilar left the room, Isabel lowered herself into the steaming water. She was still sore from sleeping in the carriage as it jounced along the road home. The hot water felt marvelous.

Isabel had not told Little Grandma about Lord Enriquez. Neither did she mention the cherries. In truth, she was hoping to forget about it herself. The way Enriquez had looked at her was like a dog salivating over a piece of meat. She pushed the man from her mind and let the bath soothe her thoughts as well as her muscles.

Later that night after the evening meal, Isabel and her father were gathered in his private sitting room. They were each sitting in an overstuffed brown chair facing the fire place. Isabel was reading aloud from the Bible that he had purchased for her. Rafael's eyes were closed in relaxation but Isabel knew that he was not asleep. He would correct her whenever she mispronounced any of the Latin.

The scripture reading was interrupted by the Master of Servants clearing his throat. Eubasio's hair was salt and pepper gray. He wore the plain grey cloth that was common to Montenegro's servants. Unlike the others, he had black leather bracers with the family crest engraved into each one. His brown eyes reflected a cool air of authority even though his fingers were curled with arthritis. Rafael opened his eyes and Isabel looked up from her reading. She didn't need much instruction, but her father's vision was not as it once was. He could only read for short periods of time before his vision began to blur…and then the headaches would start.

"Pardon my intrusion," the Master of Servants said respectfully, "but Lord Barillos awaits in the courtyard."

"Has he no concept of day or night?" Rafael said irritably.

"He says that it is a matter of some urgency my lord."

"Very well… Send him up, but delay him for a short time."

"What shall I tell him?" Eubasio inquired.

"I'm sure you'll think of something Eubasio," Rafael replied.

"Of course," Eubasio said as he backed out of the chamber.

"I suppose that must be good enough for tonight," Rafael sighed. Isabel carefully closed the Bible. She shrugged her shoulders and sighed as well. "Let me see it," Rafael said. Isabel dutifully carried the Bible to her father and gave it into his hands. "Who is my favorite little girl in all the world," he asked?

"Me," Isabel asked as if she didn't know the answer?

"That's right," he smiled. "Now kiss your father goodnight." Isabel giggled and leaned forward. She planted a kiss on her father's cheek as he inclined his head toward her. "I'll see you in the morning mija. Don't neglect your prayers."

"I will not," Isabel promised. She never felt so cherished as when her father smiled at her. It covered his entire face. "Goodnight Papa," she said. She then hurried up the stairway that ran along the east wall of the room. She went down the hallway which overlooked the living room. Her bed chamber lay at the end of the hall. She paused when she reached her doorway. Eubasio had said it was a matter of urgency. Isabel knew that her father would be angry to catch her eavesdropping, but curiosity won over good sense. She slowly crept back up the hallway and sat against the wall before it gave way to the railing.

"Lord Manuel Barillos," Eubasio announced from below Isabel's position. Through the miniature balustrade that held up the railing, Isabel could see that her father was standing to receive his guest.

"Good evening Lord Barillos," Rafael said. "You are welcome in my house, but I am eager to know what brings you at this late hour."

"It is only a matter of business my Lord Montenegro," Lord Barillos replied quickly, "and nothing to cause alarm. Unfortunately, there is little time to act on this opportunity." The two lords clasped hands and Rafael directed his guest to the chair that Isabel had been sitting in.

"You may leave us," Rafael told the Master of Servants. The lords seated themselves as Eubasio left the room. Manuel Barillos was a skinny little man with a moustache and brown hair that barely touched his shoulders. He was dressed in green velvet and his fingers were covered with jeweled rings. Isabel could hear Eubasio's retreating footsteps as her father spoke once more. "So what is this opportunity that you speak of?"

"The Knights of St. John are currently camped around my estate on their way south. They are in need of at least seventy war horses," Barillos said excitedly!

"I take it they leave in the morning?" Rafael asked.

"It is the truth. Now do you see why I come at night?"

"I do," Rafael agreed, "but seventy is far too many."

"They are fat with gold my lord!" Barillos insisted.

"It doesn't matter," Rafael explained. "I do not sell war horses until they are fully trained. I have more than seventy animals but not seventy war horses. I can sell forty and no more." Before Barillos could protest, Rafael continued. "There is also the matter of breeding stock. I need my best mares if I am too turn a profit. For the same reason, my three best stallions are not for sale. You have to understand the horse trade my lord."

"Oh I do Lord Montenegro; I do," Barillos soothed. "Hear my plan if you will and then decide."

"I am listening," Rafael said guardedly. Lord Barillos grew more fidgety and he licked his lips nervously before speaking.

"Do you remember Master Diego?"

"A good man," Rafael replied.

"He is involved in the horse trade also."

"True...but Diego deals in work animals."

"He has over three score horses," Barillos said conspiratorially, "and that only accounts for the stallions."

"I fail to see whatever insight you are trying to show me," Rafael replied.

"Let us brand Diego's animals with the mark of Montenegro. I'll put up my six chargers as well!"

"Surely you jest," Rafael said with growing distaste.

"I am quite serious," Barillos assured him. "You would only have to sell thirty five animals. You were willing to sell forty. Therefore, this bargain presents no danger to your breeding stock. Through me you will purchase his stallions."

"They are work horses," Rafael interrupted. "They are not meant for the battlefield."

"Exactly," Barillos continued, "which leaves a huge profit which you and I can divide among us!"

"Barillos," Rafael said loudly, "A work horse is ill equipped to carry a man into battle. They'll spook. Men will die because of it. This plan of yours will bring disgrace to us all. Whatever the Crown of Aragon was to decide, we would deserve execution!"

"You must see the beauty of my plan," Lord Barillos implored. "The knights are leaving for the Holy Land on the morrow. Men are dying by the thousands in the crusades. No one will live to blacken your name. Those who die will die. Those who live will be too thankful for their lives to think about whether the fault lay with the horse or the rider."

"I see," Rafael sneered. "Horses don't talk and neither do dead soldiers."

"That is exactly the reason this is such a sound plan!" Barillos exclaimed. "Just hand over one of your branding irons and I shall see to everything."

"Get out," Lord Montenegro said coldly.

"Of course," Barillos said furtively as he rose to his feet. "I was never here." Rafael stood as well. Isabel edged farther back along the wall as her father turned round to face the exit. He might see her if he looked up. She prayed that he had not seen her already. Even still, Isabel peaked through the first set of posts that made up the balustrade.

"Once I have your branding iron," Barillos began.

"You are lucky to leave with your life intact," Lord Montenegro said angrily. "What you suggest is no less than treason: to his majesty, to his holiness the Pope, and let us not forget God!" Lord Barillos blanched at her father's tirade.

"I beg your forgiveness Lord Montenegro," Barillos said hurriedly as he edged toward the door.

"What you were handed at birth, I earned with blood; yet even this is no excuse. Have you no honor, no shame, no pity?"

"I misspoke," Barillos said with his hands held out imploringly toward the larger man. "Let us forget..."

"Faithless dog," Rafael roared! He took a menacing step toward Barillos and grabbed the smaller man by his velvet tunic. Isabel stifled a gasp.

"Mercy," the smaller man pleaded.

"I tell you this," Rafael spat from between clenched teeth. His face was mere inches away from the other man's. "Were it not for your blessed mother, I would destroy you now! Your death would surely bring her down to the grave in sorrow." Barillos squirmed in the larger man's grasp but could not break free. Rafael held his shirt so tight that it was starting to gag the smaller man. Rafael opened his mouth to speak again. Instead, he threw Lord Barillos to the floor. As the cravenly man picked himself up, Rafael glared down at him with restrained fury. Barillos turned and fled through the door under the walkway. "Pray that she lives long," Rafael muttered to himself.

Lord Montenegro dropped down into his chair once more. He held his head in one hand as he stared into the fire. Isabel remained in the hallway for some time after. Her heart was fluttering like a bird. She had overheard some unsettling stories of her father in the Spanish Army, but she had never seen him look so. There had been an awful edge to his voice and murder in his eyes. His anger when Isabel misbehaved was nothing compared to this and the encounter with Enriquez.

After a few minutes, Isabel's heartbeat slowed down and she crept quietly to her feet. "Go to bed Isabel," her father said crossly. His voice echoed up from below. Isabel ran to her bed and quickly pulled up the covers. Some time later, she slept.

It was nearly ten days later when Isabel's mother returned from Zaragoza. The hum of the cicadas in the trees dulled the staccato of the horses' hooves as they came over the drawbridge. The wooden carriage pulled behind them was treated with a dark stain and trimmed in black. The wheels and axles were of wrought iron. The horses were sepia colored mares with blond manes and tails. Tiny braids of turquoise rope were braided into their coarse hair. The crest of Montenegro was carved into the door of the carriage. It was stained many times over to be darker than the rest of the wood.

Isabel had been playing in the aviary when her mother arrived. By the time the gate was completely lowered, she had run out onto the walkway between the towers. A grey liveried servant rushed to open the carriage door while her father came out into the courtyard to greet his wife. Isabel could see the glint of silver from her mother's circlet as Lady Priscilla ducked her head to exit the carriage.

Unlike Rafael, Lady Priscilla of Aragon came from old blood. She had very fine blonde hair that was braided in the Parisian style and hung to the small of her back. The pastel green of her gown matched her pale green eyes. The fabric of the gown was tied loosely around her waist to accentuate her hips and the sleeves flared out at the cuff as was the fashion of the day. The neckline was sewn with soft white rabbit fur. A short train of white cloth hung in a wide arc from her shoulders and waist.

Lord Montenegro's face lit up when he saw Lady Priscilla. Here was the father that Isabel was accustomed too. The unpleasantness of the trip home from Teruel was like a distant dream. Though her father had caught her eavesdropping, they had not spoken of it since. Isabel was glad that he had chosen to forget as she was not eager to be punished. Years later, Isabel would wish that she had spoken to her mother about it. Perhaps things might have been different.

Lady Priscilla was followed by Alejandra her chambermaid. Her servant was dressed in a pastel pink gown and a coif that covered her dark brown hair. Rafael embraced his wife and together they walked back into the keep. Alejandra was close behind. Isabel admired the way her mother carried herself. When she walked it seemed that she was floating on air. She wanted to cry out excitedly, but

Priscilla would certainly chastise her for behavior not befitting her station.

Isabel flew down the stairs of the east tower. She stopped her self before very nearly colliding with her parents as they traveled upward. "Mother," she said breathlessly. After several seconds, the girl curtsied and Lady Priscilla curtsied in return.

"So well to see you Isabel," her mother said warmly. Priscilla held out her arms and Isabel stepped into the embrace.

"I have so much to tell you of Teruel mother! Did you enjoy your visit to Zaragoza?" Isabel asked.

"It was divine," Priscilla sighed. "I shall tell you all about it this evening. Right now I feel tired from the journey." Isabel squeezed her mother tighter and then disentangled herself.

"Alright Mother," she said. "Father, will you come to the stables with me?"

"Not today mija," Rafael answered. "Your mother and I have much to talk about."

"Do we?" Priscilla asked with one eyebrow raised. A hint of a smile touched the corners of her lips. Rafael just winked at her and stepped aside so that their daughter could go down the spiraling stairs.

"Take Rosita for a few turns in the training yard," Rafael told Isabel. "I don't think anyone rides her while your gone."

"They're too big for her," Isabel said knowingly. "I will take her now!" Her face brightened at the idea of riding her pony. Rafael kissed her on the forehead before she hurried past. Her parents continued up to their bed chamber.

Rosita was penned inside the private stables within the keep's walls. The white pony was contentedly munching on oats when Isabel arrived. When Rosita dipped her head to eat, her blonde main nearly touched the ground. Her stall had just been cleaned and Isabel was satisfied that the pony was being cared for.

Raul and several other stable hands were feeding and grooming her mother's horses. Isabel thought that they must all be tired from the trip home from Zaragoza. "Raul," she called out, "I should like to take a ride in the yard." The stable master wore loose brown clothing and leather bracers that denoted his station.

"I am sorry young mistress," he answered, "but we are very busy with your mother's horses. Perhaps we can ride later, no?"

"Perhaps," Isabel sighed. She noticed that the troughs for her mother's mares were getting low. She walked over to a hay bale that had been set out and locked her fingers around the twine that held it together. She tried very hard to move it toward the pens before the stable master noticed what she was doing. Raul rushed over and removed her hands from the hay.

"Let me do the work," Raul said as he prodded her out of the way.

"I am quite capable of doing it," she said. "I only want to help so that I can take out Rosita."

"I know," Raul said, "but I don't want to anger Lady Priscilla."

"Neither do I," Isabel said with resignation. She had watched the men tend to the horses enough times. She was certain that she could do as good a job as any of them, but her mother would be furious. "You mustn't pick up the hooves from the back," she told one of the new boys. "You have to come from the side and keep your head clear of them."

"As you wish young mistress," the boy said nervously. He dropped the hoof he had been cleaning and rose to obey. He looked at Raul for direction as he moved around to the side of the mare.

"A horseshoe print might make little difference to that face of yours," Raul chastised the stable boy, "but I'll wager you don't want to be kicked. Do as she says."

"Yes master," the stable boy replied with color rising in his cheeks. Raul gave Isabel an approving nod while the stable boy rushed to correct himself. Isabel smiled wanly. She could have been done already.

When the work with Priscilla's horses was nearly finished, Raul grabbed the saddle and other accoutrements for the pony from off the wall. He opened Rosita's pen and set the saddle on her back. Isabel placed the bridle and reigns over the pony's head and fastened the buckles. This was also man's work, but Raul did not protest. "The rest of you finish up while I take our young mistress to the yard," the stable master told the others. Raul led the pony out and Isabel followed. Raul handed her the lead rope and they walked out into the courtyard.

Isabel felt a slight pang of jealousy as she mounted her pony. It would have been much easier if she were not required to ride side saddle. She would have dearly liked to jump her pony. As it was, she had a difficult enough time with a fast trot. Still, Isabel loved to ride and she spent the better part of the afternoon doing so.

Dinner was still about an hour away when Isabel returned Rosita to her pen. She carefully dismounted and handed the reigns to the stable hand that assisted her. She dusted off her dress and then hurried up to Lady Priscilla's sitting room. The curtains and the fabric which covered the furniture was all of turquoise damask. Two couches and a divan surrounded a low cherry wood table. The open side of the table faced a large window with billowing curtains.

On the same wall as the archway which led into the sitting room, there was a large fire place with metal doors. The doors were thin sheets of beaten metal that had been carved through with flower designs. These cut outs would cast dancing shadows on the wall when the hearth was lit. A line of iron worked horses ran along the mantle. Their heads were held forward and their tails streamed out behind so that they were all of one piece.

Isabel's mother was reclining on the divan with a glass of white wine while Alejandra played the harp in the background. The serving girl was on a low platform surrounded by gauzy curtains that broke up her features.

She was seated on a black wooden stool behind a harp that was almost as tall as she. "Good afternoon mother," Isabel said sweetly as she curtseyed.

"Come in child," Priscilla said as she beckoned with one hand. Isabel hurried over and sat on one of the couches near her mother. Her feet hung above the floor as her legs were too short to reach. Lady Priscilla cast her critical gaze over her daughter. "You've taken some sun," she said at last.

"I was riding my pony in the yard," Isabel explained quickly.

"I wish you would not spend so much time with the horses," Priscilla sighed.

"But I love to ride," Isabel protested.

"I know…but not so much. Your cheeks are red from the sun. Tomorrow they'll darken. You must remember to have a care for your appearance," Lady Priscilla said.

"I know," Isabel sighed. "How was it in Zaragoza?"

'The weather is always lovely at the summer cottage. Your cousin David is barely walking. He has the most precious curly hair."

"Does he fuss much?"

"No," her mother replied, "David is very well behaved. He's an absolute joy!"

"How is Aunt Imelda?"

"She is well but I believe she is going to worry herself sick."

"Whatever is the matter," Isabel asked with concern?

"She's trying to direct the King's attention toward Catherine. Your cousin isn't really doing her part either," Priscilla sighed.

"She can be quite cross sometimes," Isabel agreed.

"God forgive me for saying it," Priscilla said, "but she is a far cry from Helen of Troy. An opportunity such as that comes only once." Isabel nodded her head but she was terrified of marriage. She never wanted to leave her father's house. Priscilla was telling her about the cottage and her various relatives, but Isabel was too busy worrying about getting married to listen. "What is that?" her mother asked. "Isabel...I am talking to you. What is that?"

"What," Isabel struggled, "what is...what?"

"That smell," Priscilla said with irritation. "Let me see the bottom of your shoes." Isabel bent her left foot to one side. She was trying to catch a peek before showing her mother. "Now Isabel," her mother commanded. Isabel lifted both feet up for inspection. "Insufferable child," Priscilla cursed, "you've stepped in it!"

"I am sorry," Isabel began.

"No time for apologies," Priscilla interrupted. "You shall go wash up and change immediately. I won't smell horses at the dinner table. Take your shoes off and carry them with you. I don't want that mess on the floor!" Isabel's cheeks were burning as she removed her shoes. "My goodness," her mother lectured, "God has blessed you with a comely appearance and a beautiful voice. Suitors should be lining up in no time. Who, I ask you, is going to want a girl who smells like a horse corral?"

"I don't know," Isabel said as she stood up carrying her dirty shoes.

"No one is," Priscilla finished. "You do want to marry well don't you Isabel?"

"Oh yes mother...I do."

"Run along then," her mother said with one hand pinching her nose, "and be quick about it." Isabel tried to curtsey at the doorway before her mother raised her voice again. "Just go Isabel!"

Little Grandma was trying to hide her smile while she helped Isabel prepare for dinner. "I should dance in the horse stalls every morning if I thought it would help me stay here with you!" Isabel said petulantly. Then Little Grandma did laugh. "What is so amusing about it?" Isabel demanded.

"Perhaps you'll find a man who likes that sort of smell," Little Grandma replied mirthfully. They both shared a good laugh over that. Isabel told her mother about Teruel at dinner that night. She forgot all about the fact that her time at Montenegro's keep was limited.

CHAPTER II

Days turned into weeks, months, and years. Isabel the child blossomed into a beautiful young woman. Her talent for singing increased into an art. She would have been delighted to perform in a theatre, but it was not to be. In those days, stage performers were in the same social class as prostitutes. Sometimes the line between the two professions blurred. Isabel was to be a lady.

By the age of fifteen, Isabel had been approached by many suitors. She was still not betrothed, however. Most of the young men came on their own. Some of the meetings were engineered by her mother. Like Rafael, Isabel was a keen judge of character and she soured many courtships before they had really begun. Those who seemed good enough for the young heiress were never good enough for her father. The reverse was also true. Lady Priscilla could often be heard chastising one or both of them for ruining a perfectly good match. Nevertheless, she deferred to her husband.

As the years wore on, Priscilla became more and more desperate to bear a male heir. Yet try as they might, the couple could not manage to succeed. It seemed that Priscilla's womb had run dry after Isabel was born. There was talk among the servants. When a lord's wife could not bear him a son, it was customary for the lord to take a mistress. Although doing so would assure the continuation of his family name, Rafael had never taken up this practice. He found the custom revolting and sinful. Suggesting that he take a mistress was akin to challenging Lord Montenegro to a duel. Wise men kept their opinions to themselves.

Even when Priscilla herself suggested that a concubine might be necessary, Rafael was unmoved. Isabel had eavesdropped on one such conversation. Her mother was near tears and she could hear her father's comforting voice. "Priscilla," he said, "even if the name dies, it will still be our blood that rules this land. If God does not see fit for you to bare a son, than it will be Isabel's son that one day rules. What name he bears is of no consequence." Priscilla kept apologizing but Rafael shushed her and held her close. Isabel had begun to feel like an intruder and so she crept back to her bed. Whatever else her parents shared was between them.

Although Rafael had not planned to train Isabel in manly pursuits, the lack of a male heir did necessitate some exceptions. She already knew a great deal about horses, but in her twelfth year; her father began to bring her along when he had to conduct business. Though some men took offense to the girl being present during their dealings, Rafael would not be moved. "My daughter only leaves when our business is concluded," he would say. Those were the only two options.

Isabel learned that haggling was a battle of its own. The men were very clever in the way they played the game. Buyers would try and portray Montenegro's horses to be little more than nags. Rafael would pretend to be insulted. Then he would extol the virtues of his trainers. If that didn't work, then he might tell them the long history of Montenegro's stallions as an asset to Spain. Sometimes he would make the buyer feel guilty by citing favors he had done them in the past. If the buyer agreed, then money would be exchanged for horses. If they were not convinced, then the dance would start all over again. The steps were only limited by one's imagination.

After a deal had succeeded or failed, father and daughter would discuss it in the carriage. They would talk about what had worked and what could have been done differently. They would also run scenarios with Rafael as the buyer and Isabel as the seller. Isabel found it all quite fascinating and she learned quickly.

Lord Montenegro was quite taken with his daughter's singing voice. While he would never allow her to perform in a theatre, he did not hesitate to show off her talent to his guests.

1174 A.D.

In Isabel's fifteenth year, word of her singing had somehow reached the Crown of Aragon. So it was that the entire family was invited to the royal palace in Zaragoza. After reading the invitation, Lady Priscilla was on the moon! Even Little Grandma was swept up in the excitement. To hear the two of them carry on, it would seem that the widowed King had already chosen Isabel to be his bride. Isabel was terrified of the idea. Nevertheless, she smiled and laughed in all the right places when her mother spoke of it.

Isabel let them fuss over her and how they did fuss! In the weeks leading up to the trip to Zaragoza, Isabel was forever being fitted by the local seamstress. There was one particular day that she swore she must have changed her clothing a hundred times.

Priscilla became even more watchful than usual. It was as if there was nothing Isabel could do that couldn't be improved upon. She must walk straighter, bat her eyelashes more when she smiled, practice a more ladylike laugh, (hers was too loud), eat smaller bites, avoid the sun, and avoid the rain as well, (she might catch cold). The only thing Priscilla did not criticize was Isabel's makeup. There would have been little point. Isabel was a natural beauty. Yet even this was a burden, for her mother used it as an excuse for why everything else should be the easiest thing in the world. By the time they got into her mother's carriage that spring, Isabel couldn't wait for the whole thing to be over. Rafael looked exhausted as he rode close by. Isabel guessed that her mother's determination for all to be perfect had tired out her father as well.

The women were all dressed in fine clothing for the palace, even Little Grandma. No one would be permitted to outshine Isabel in any way while they were in Zaragoza. Isabel's beauty was beyond compare and her dark brown eyes still reflected the innocence of youth. Alejandra's beauty was that of a woman, sultry and full of mystery. Her clothing and jewelry were more understated than usual, however. Priscilla had even made sure that her own accoutrements were not as dazzling as those with which she adorned her only daughter. Her eyes were a bit misty on the way to Zaragoza, but she would not say what was upsetting her.

The retinue of soldiers that surrounded the carriage was smaller than usual. There were always a number of them required to guard the keep, but a great many had gone off to the crusades. Although Rafael's experience would have no doubt been of help in the Holy Land, King Alfonso had not summoned him to war. Rafael had spent decades of his younger years soldiering and he was still without a male heir. The king had made it easier on Lord Montenegro's conscience by telling him how invaluable his trained stallions were to the armies of Christ. Rafael was satisfied. He had played with fate enough times and was not overly eager to leave his wife and daughter.

The Summer Cottage was hidden in the forest outside Zaragoza. The great city was clearly visible in the distance. Rafael directed his entourage off the main road and onto a dirt path that led into the trees. The path was lined by large sycamores. Their canopy spread out so that it was completely shaded. There were several white tailed rabbits that had chosen to congregate on the path, but they scattered into the brush as the horses approached. Here and there, beams of sunlight penetrated the leaves above and shone down onto the hard packed earth.

As the carriage traveled further inward, the dense underbrush gave way to tall grasses. Bluebells and snowdrops grew wild by the roadside. Their collection of leaves looked like a star filled sky to Isabel. Honey bees traveled among the flowers. The trees began to thin out also. Soon the stretches of grass were long and wide and the trees were few. Isabel could see the line where the wild grass ended and the lawn began. Beyond this, one could see the white wooden walls of the Summer Cottage off to the right side of the path.

The cottage was at the top of a wide hill with a huge olive tree growing up from the slope. There was a rope secured to one of the higher branches that Isabel and her cousins had often used for a swing. The olive tree had once been two trees. Their trunks had grown together and formed a cradle that a child could sit on like a throne.

The trail curved around the house and two massive sycamores flanked the far side of the path at its highest point. There was a massive wooden porch off the front side of the house. The trail ended in front of the porch. The lawn spilled down from there to a single line of trees. Many different kinds of flowers were planted between their trunks. On the far side of the trees was a sizeable garden. It was filled with rows of vegetables. Several women in long skirts and loose blouses were tending the gardens.

Lady Imelda was already standing on the porch to greet them. She was flanked by her ten year old son David. Catherine stood there as well. She was only a year older than Isabel. Imelda wore a high necked gown of dark blue fabric. Today, her black hair was woven up into a bun and her eyes shone with excitement. She broke into a smile as Lady Priscilla stepped down from the carriage. Isabel and Alejandra came close behind, followed by Little Grandma.

David was wearing black trousers and a loose white shirt that was mostly open at the neck. His hands had been freshly washed but Isabel thought she saw a smear of dirt on the side of one sleeve. "Isabel!" he shouted as they approached. "I found out where Grandfather Frog lives! It's on the far side of the pond. Want to help me catch it?"

"Please David," Lady Imelda chided gently. "Isabel has only just arrived." David was grinning from ear to ear. Isabel could not stop herself from joining him. Catherine looked even more sour than usual. She gave Isabel a withering stare. Isabel ignored her and threw her arms around her younger cousin.

"Look how big you are!" she exclaimed. "The last time we were here you only came to my waist."

"You look nice Isabel," he said. "Your almost a grown up right?"

"Not yet," Isabel laughed. Then Aunt Imelda was hugging her and telling her what a beautiful woman she had become. As she returned her aunt's embrace, she noticed that Catherine was still glaring at her. When Lady Imelda broke away, Isabel curtsied to her aunt. She even managed a pleasant hello for her sour faced cousin.

"So nice to see you," Catherine responded. "Was it very sunny in Montenegro?" she asked too sweetly.

"Not very," Isabel replied. She started talking about the weather at home until she realized that Catherine had been making fun of her. Her cousin was trying to suggest that Isabel's face looked beaten by the elements...indirectly of course. Imelda maintained her smile even as she pinched her fingers down on Catherine's collar bone.

"That hurts mother," Catherine whined.

"Of course it doesn't," Imelda replied crisply. "Now be a dear and help your cousin Isabel up to your room. You'll be sharing it as you know." Catherine rubbed her shoulder and turned back toward the house. She walked in and Isabel followed. Isabel wished that she could have stayed in David's room as she had in the past. Propriety now dictated otherwise.

Catherine had long, straight hair the color of which reminded Isabel of a chestnut mare. She had on a lavender gown that was tied about the waist with a reddish brown cord that matched her hair. She was comely and developing the features of a woman much faster than the younger Isabel. However, Catherine's beauty was sullied by her sulky demeanor and constant unpleasantness.

The door to the Summer Cottage opened directly into the breakfast room. The table had already been set in anticipation of their arrival. Each place was decorated with a turquoise napkin. No doubt the napkins had been chosen to reflect Lady Priscilla's favorite color. The bustle of the servants could be heard in the kitchen through a doorway to the right. The two cousins went left and down the hallway that led out of the back corner of the breakfast room. The first door on the right contained a narrow and creaking staircase. The upstairs hallway went around the top of the stairwell and had access to all seven bedrooms. The hallway had windows on both sides and warm light poured through onto the wood flooring.

Catherine and Isabel's room would be the first one. It was the only room on the left side of the stairwell. Most of the stairwell was encompassed by a railing to avoid mishaps. The hall wrapped in a J-shape around to the rest of the bed chambers. Lord Vasquez and Lady Imelda's room was also on the left side, but the door was at the top of the hall beyond the stairwell. The rest of the doorways were on the east wall.

As they entered the bedroom, the first thing Isabel noticed was that there was lace everywhere. The canopied bed that dominated the left side of the room was now covered in gauzy pink curtains. The curtains had swirling white designs on the fabric that could barely be seen. The wood of the frame and the bedposts had been painted white. The goose down pillows and white sheets were still where they belonged, but the old comforter had been replaced with a pastel pink blanket.

The right side of the room contained an armoire for their clothing and a vanity. The armoire was quite large and its doors stood open. Catherine had a vast wardrobe and Isabel could see that no expense had been spared. There was a vanity next to the armoire. The vanity's reflective surface was a pounded sheet of metal. The image was a bit distorted but the sheet had been carefully worked into the wood backing of the piece. Brushes, combs, powders, and various other cosmetics covered the surface. There was a small platform in front of the armoire that seemed to serve no purpose at all.

"What is this for?" Isabel asked.

"For dressing of course," Catherine replied as if it were the most obvious thing.

"You have so many beautiful things," Isabel breathed as she examined all the clothing and jewelry inside the armoire.

"Try not to look all at once," Catherine remarked. Isabel frowned.

"Why must you be so cross with me? I haven't done a thing to deserve it."

"I'm not being cross Isabel," Catherine said soothingly. "I just don't want you to strain yourself. I'll have some pillows put over in that corner so that you'll have a place to sleep."

"On the floor," Isabel asked with rising irritation?

"No silly," Catherine laughed. "The pillows go on the floor. You sleep on top of them."

"The bed is large enough for both of us...David too if it were necessary. Ladies don't sleep on the floor," Isabel snapped.

"That is precisely why I will sleep in the bed," Catherine said unkindly.

"You may take either side as you prefer," Isabel replied. "I shall not sleep on the floor and I am certain that this is your horrible idea, and not your mother's."

"Well there is no need to get so upset," Catherine said as if she felt injured. "I was just making a jest and...you thought I was serious didn't you? I would never let my cousin sleep on the floor. Now do let's be friends."

"Alright," Isabel sighed. "It's been a long trip. I almost feel like sleeping already."

"I don't think my brother will allow it," Catherine said. "He's determined to show you some frog out at the pond." She rolled her eyes to show her disdain for the idea.

"It doesn't bother me," Isabel explained. "I'll look at it. He can do the touching."

"Yes, that's it exactly!" Catherine said.

"Last time we came up to the cottage, David caught a frog," Isabel remembered aloud. "He insisted that I hold it. The little thing peed in my hands!"

"Oh that is foul," Catherine said with disgust.

"It was," Isabel agreed, "but he means well."

"David loves you," Catherine said in a low tone. Isabel thought she detected a hint of jealousy.

"That's only because we can't see each other all the time," Isabel replied. "I'm sure if we did, we would be quarrelling constantly. Don't you think?"

"I suppose," Catherine replied absently. "I trust the servants have set out our food by now. Let's go down. I'll have them take up your things."

"That sounds lovely," Isabel said. "I should like to eat very much." She followed Catherine down the stairs. The food was indeed laid out on the table. There was a loaf of fresh baked bread that was moist from the olive oil the cooks had added into the flour. An omelet had also been prepared with tomatoes, garlic and onions. Isabel was famished after the journey, but she was careful to eat slowly as Lady Priscilla had taught her.

By listening to the adults' conversations, she learned that her uncle Jaime had already gone on to court. Lady Imelda told stories of how King Alfonso had eyes only for Catherine. She expected a courtship to be initiated in no time at all. "That's wonderful," Lady Priscilla replied, but her eyes told a different story. They narrowed slightly, but only for a second. Isabel guessed she was the only one at the table to notice.

Rafael spoke briefly of the horse trade, but he mostly let the others talk. He always seemed a bit uncomfortable around Priscilla's family. Lord Jaime Vasquez had been born to nobility. Both of their wives were second cousins to the King. Rafael had grown up as a common peasant. He was glad for the delicious food which gave him an excuse not to speak.

Eventually, David asked to be excused. Isabel and Catherine followed suit. Before Isabel could take two steps away from the table, David was already tugging on her sleeve. "Come on Isabel," he said conspiratorially. "Grandfather Frog will never see us coming!"

"I have to change my clothing David," Isabel said, "but I'll hurry!" Priscilla looked like she was going to disagree, but Rafael held up a hand.

"They are children," he said. Priscilla silently acquiesced by forcing a smile. Isabel ran upstairs and opened her trunk that the servants had brought up. She changed into a plain, tan-colored dress and black, flat-bottomed shoes. It was almost the same outfit she used for riding in the yard in Montenegro. The fabric was soft and well-worn. She chased David out through the gardens and down the small dirt trail that led back into the forest.

The pond was in a secluded clearing in the woods. Much of the pond was bordered by bull rushes, except for the side that faced the end of the trail. Here a small dock stretched out over the water. The dock ended in a finely crafted gazebo made of mahogany wood. The dome of the gazebo had a hexagonal shape. There were several benches inside where one could look out on the tranquility of the water.

Dust motes sparkled in the sunlight as they floated through the air. A flock of geese swam on the far side of the pond and the water reflected gold from the sun. This was Isabel's favorite place. She sighed as her eyes took it all in.

The pond was quite usual for David, however. He was taking off his boots and creeping around the bank toward the far side. He beckoned for Isabel to follow. No one would criticize her in this private sanctuary. Isabel removed her own shoes and cinched up her skirts. She walked closely behind David in the reeds. The muddy bottom squished through her toes.

A blue dragonfly whizzed past them. It hovered near the surface of the water to drink before flitting off. As they reached the other side, they could hear a deep croaking sound. The frog fell silent as they drew closer.

David put a finger to his lips and then snuck off to his left. Isabel stayed to the right and closer to the bank. Something moved in the water and David plunged his arms in after it. A frog the size of two man's fists launched its fat body out of the water and toward Isabel. She let out a cry of surprise as the frog swam past her. She made a dive to catch the fleeing amphibian and fell into the muddy water. They chased the frog on either side. David almost caught it as it leapt toward the deep water. The frog slipped out of his grasp and left behind nothing but a ripple.

"You almost had him," Isabel said breathlessly.

"I thought I was going to get him for sure," David said. There was no disappointment in his voice. The thrill was in the hunt and there would always be tomorrows. Isabel didn't notice how filthy she was until they were halfway back to the cottage. She tiptoed quietly toward the stairs, but her mother came out into the hallway before she could reach them.

"Really Isabel," her mother said disapprovingly. "Go wash up."

"Yes mother," Isabel replied. She ran up the stairs before Priscilla could get another word in. She hurried into her room and began to disrobe.

"You're a mess," Catherine remarked from her perch on the bed.

"I know," Isabel replied. She quickly stripped down. "Who do I ask to draw me a bath?"

"I forgot how much the Montenegro's love baths," Catherine said sarcastically. "In this case, I suppose it's justified. I'll get someone." She rolled her eyes. "Don't leave your clothes in here. They stink."

"I won't," Isabel conceded. The steaming bath felt wonderful and Isabel lingered until her fingers and toes were water-logged. She finally returned to the bedroom in a cloth robe that the servants had provided. She guessed that it belonged to Catherine.

Pilar was in the room when Isabel returned. Little Grandma was making space in the armoire for Isabel's clothing. Catherine hovered close by. The elderly woman looked vexed as she hung up the dresses. "Be careful with that pink gown woman!" Catherine complained. "It's satin you know?" she said as if explaining to a fool.

"I'll take care my lady," Pilar replied tersely. Her face brightened when she saw Isabel come in. "I'm putting your things on the left toward the front," Little Grandma explained. "Why don't you wear the white gown today? We can save the nicer ones for court."

"That sounds reasonable," Isabel agreed as Pilar removed the bathrobe. Little Grandma helped her into the plain, white gown and brushed Isabel's hair in front of the reflective metal of the vanity. Pilar used a silver hair pin to bring all of Isabel's hair to the left side where it spilled over her shoulder.

"You have such fine and beautiful hair," Pilar sighed. "It's fit for a queen."

"Stop it," Isabel chided.

"Oh, but it is true," Pilar insisted. "Isn't it true Catherine?"

"I'm certain that there is none better in all of Montenegro," Catherine quipped.

"Or anywhere else," Pilar finished the sentence so that it wasn't an insult.

"Of course," Catherine said smugly. Isabel remained uncomfortably silent. Once Pilar had finished, the two cousins were left alone in their bed chamber.

"Did you know that King Alfonso favors me?" Catherine asked.

"I hadn't given much thought to who the King favors," Isabel replied, "but I think that's wonderful. Your mother must be so pleased. You could not ask for a better prospect."

"No, you could not," Catherine bragged.

"I'm afraid of marriage," Isabel confessed. "When will you be betrothed?"

"Soon," Catherine answered. "We haven't officially started the courtship, but he promised to visit me this Friday afternoon. I'm certain that it will be then."

"That is wonderful!" Isabel exclaimed. What was wonderful, however, was that she would have one less suitor to worry about.

"Yes," Catherine said nonchalantly. "He'll ask me to marry and I shall be queen."

"Won't that be strange?" Isabel chuckled.

"What do you mean," Catherine asked indignantly?

"You'll be in a higher station that Aunt Imelda," Isabel explained. "She'll have to do whatever you say!"

'That is true, isn't it?" Catherine said thoughtfully.

"Go straight to bed Catherine," Isabel mimicked her aunt. "No mother…you go to bed!"

"And not a bit of supper," Catherine added imperiously. This sent both girls into gales of laughter. When their merriment died down, Catherine looked seriously at her younger cousin. "Aren't you the least bit nervous about singing at the Royal Court? There will be so many people watching."

"I'm completely distraught," Isabel replied honestly. "I have had practice at my father's court, but it is far smaller. I'll do my best. I can't imagine the shame it will bring my father if it's not good enough."

"I would be terrified," Catherine admitted.

"Then you know exactly how I feel."

"Would you like to practice?"

"Right now," Isabel asked?

"Yes. I'm just one person after all."

"I suppose it might help," Isabel said, "but you must tell me honestly what you think."

"What will you sing?" Catherine asked.

"It is called the Road of Suffering. I first heard it in Teruel," Isabel replied.

"I am ready," Catherine said as she sat up straighter on the bed. Isabel took several seconds to compose herself before stepping onto the platform by the armoire. Her voice was low and tentative at first, but it gained strength as she lost herself in the music. Isabel's clear tenor filled the room and floated out into the hallway. Her eyes were closed as she finished the last verse. When she opened them again, Catherine looked stunned. "That was perfect," Catherine said at last.

"Do you truly think so?" Isabel asked with color rising in her cheeks. Compliments from Catherine were so rare.

"I do," Catherine replied. Isabel was flattered. It wouldn't be until later that she would recall the tension in her cousin's voice. In those days, it was Isabel's way to forgive and forget quickly.

The remainder of the day passed easily enough. Whenever Isabel began to get nervous, David would interrupt her thoughts with a stream of endless chatter or some new thing he had to show her. David's near constant attention made her forget her anxiety. He was so good natured and excited about every little thing. The beautiful thing about David was that he could turn anyone into a child by his mere presence. Things that might seem immature suddenly became acceptable because David was there also.

Isabel's nervousness returned when she lay down to sleep that night, however. She tried to focus on the compliment she had received from Catherine. Eventually, sleep overtook her. Isabel did not dream.

The next morning, Isabel awakened early while the rest of the house slept. Still in her nightgown, she left the Summer Cottage and walked to the secluded pond. The water was smooth and still in the grey light of pre-dawn. There was a bird heralding the approach of daylight in a tree close by. A light mist covered the pond and clung to the edges of the reeds on the bank.

Isabel's steps creaked on the wood as she walked out to the gazebo. She knew that the journey to Zaragoza would immediately follow the morning meal. She needed to collect her thoughts. Here was the perfect place. A heron flew over the water and up into its roost in the trees. There were ripples on the surface of the pond where its feet had skimmed the water, but they were quickly swallowed by the mist.

Isabel closed her eyes and began to sing. Her voice echoed out over the still water. Even the lark stopped his song long enough to listen. Isabel's confidence grew and she was satisfied as the song ended. She remained in the gazebo for some time, enjoying the solitude and the peace of nature. The sun broke over the trees in the east. It stained the clouds first red and then pink. When the clouds began to whiten, Isabel rose from her seat and returned to the cottage.

The rest of the family was already gathered around the table. Little Grandma was in a flurry when Isabel came back through the door. "My goodness child," she scolded, "we all thought you had run off!"

I'm sorry," Isabel said as her mother and aunt looked at her with disapproval. "I was only down at the pond."

"Did you catch Grandfather Frog?" David asked with interest.

"No," Isabel said as her mother frowned. "I just needed some air."

"Eat your food and drink with haste," Priscilla said curtly. "Go up to your room as soon as you are finished. You must be prepared for court."

"Yes mother," Isabel replied. She hurried to the table and quickly ate what she could. Wolfing down the entire meal was no option for a lady. Therefore, Isabel left a large part of her breakfast untouched. Little Grandma came right behind her as Isabel hurried up to her room. The gown which Isabel's chamber maid had laid out for her was a deep maroon color with black material in the midsection. The black material went just under her bosom and just above her waist. The maroon fabric was sewn through with golden threads that shimmered when struck by the light. Little Grandma tied the back of the dress securely. The crest of Montenegro had been embroidered in gold over the black cloth which clung to Isabel's body.

Pilar tied Isabel's bangs into two thin braids. These she secured behind the young woman's head, giving the appearance of a circlet. Over this she placed a hat of the same maroon material bordered in black. The cloth hat rose to a point, not unlike the helmets of the Spanish soldiers. Little Grandma lightly dusted Isabel's cheeks with a red powder to bring up their color. The girl's dark eyelashes and full lips needed no improvement.

Last to go on was the jewelry. Pilar adorned Isabel's earlobes with golden teardrops. Around her neck, the chamber made fastened a beautiful golden choker. There were tiny rubies at intervals along the chain. In the center of the chain was a large opal. It was framed in gold and hung down over Isabel's slender neck. When this was done, Isabel stepped into a pair of black shoes that pointed at the toes.

Isabel looked critically at her distorted reflection in the metal. She sighed nervously before Pilar embraced her from behind. "Don't give it another thought," Little Grandma told her. "You look beautiful and you'll do fine."

"Thanks," Isabel smiled as she held on to Little Grandma's forearms with her hands. "You always know just what to say." Pilar squeezed the young woman tighter and then drew back.

"Run along," the old woman said emotionally. "Lady Priscilla is waiting." Indeed, the carriages were prepared by the time Isabel came onto the wooden porch of the Summer Cottage. Isabel and Little Grandma hurried toward Lady Priscilla's carriage. Lord Montenegro and the soldiers were already on horseback. Rafael looked down proudly at his daughter as she passed. "Who is this beautiful lady," he asked Pilar, "and what have you done with my little Isabel?"

"Thank you my lord," Little Grandma said modestly. Isabel smiled up at her father as her cheeks burned. They climbed into the carriage where Priscilla and her chamber maid were already waiting.

"Hurry and sit down child," Lady Priscilla commanded, but Isabel though she saw approval in her mother's eyes. Priscilla's blonde hair was pulled up into a bun and wrapped through with strings of pearls. They were the same pearls that Isabel had worn to Teruel so many years past. Her mother wore a high necked gown of turquoise cloth. It had long sleeves and silver hemming around the bottom of the skirt. Alejandra was dressed rather plainly. Her gown was black and she had a white head covering that tied below her chin. It was the same outfit as the matronly Pilar was wearing.

There was a quick jerk as the driver of the carriage set the mares into motion. Isabel could hear the iron wheels crunching over the path that led away from the Summer Cottage. The clopping of the horses hooves seemed to keep time. Lady Imelda's carriage followed close behind and they were both surrounded by soldiers. Rafael wore the same dark clothing as his guards with nothing to denote his station. He would change into his finery after they arrived in Zaragoza. The soldiers were all garbed in leather armor with metal helmets and swords belted at their waists.

After the journey was well underway, Isabel's mother closed the curtains over the windows. "There are many things you need to know before we arrive at court," Priscilla told her daughter. Isabel looked up expectantly and her mother continued. "You're a very honest and sensible child which has made raising you a bit easier than some I've seen. You are about to travel into a nest of vipers. I really should have prepared you for this. Most of the women you encounter in the royal court will be horrid. At times, you will not believe the things that come out of their mouth! They will try to cut you down with words. Most of their insults will be so subtle that you will not be able to accuse them of anything. You must learn to speak to them in their own tongue." Priscilla sighed. "I hoped that you would learn more from Catherine. She seems to do quite well at it."

Isabel just nodded her head. She didn't know how to respond. "You mustn't help Pilar or Alejandra with anything," her mother continued. "Doing so will be a sign of weakness. You have a good heart Isabel, but I have failed by allowing you to become accustomed to following it. What is acceptable in Montenegro will not do in Zaragoza. Also, you will refer to your chamber maid only by her name…Pilar. Little Grandma is too familiar."

"I shall do as you say," Isabel promised.

"I know you will," Priscilla replied. There was pain in her voice as she spoke once more. "You must not be discouraged or let any hint of discomfort show when they unleash their wicked tongues, even if their words cause laughter at your expense. However, you must not remain silent to their barbs unless I speak for you. You must always beat them at this game. I will help as best I can, but you must maintain your composure. Do you understand?"

"Yes," Isabel answered, "but why do they do this? Aren't we all under the Crown of Aragon?"

"It is not that simple," Priscilla replied. "Position in the royal court is everything. If they aren't directly competing for the King's eye, they will attempt to insult you anyway just to show who is the more clever. For every potential bride, there are twenty old maids that will discredit you to heighten the chances of some other worthy young woman. You must be careful."

"But that's not an issue," Isabel said. "Catherine told me that King Alfonso already favors her. She said that the courtship is certain to begin within the week.

"Whether your cousin really believes that or not is up for questioning," Priscilla answered. More likely is that she worries that the King will favor you over her. She is counting on your honesty. She hopes you will be a good cousin and step back if he should show any interest. Catherine may consider you her greatest opponent."

"Aren't you and Aunt Imelda on the same side? She is your sister," Isabel said incredulously!

"We are not on the same side when it comes to the crown. Trust only your father and those who are now inside this carriage," Priscilla told her. "All of our futures depend upon it." Isabel nodded. "Don't worry Isabel," her mother said as she placed a hand the girl's shoulder. "I won't let you navigate this storm alone."

"Thank you mother," Isabel said nervously. The apprehension she had felt about coming to the royal court before was like nothing to the fear that now gripped her. She did her best to appear confident as the towers of the Basilica loomed over the river in the distance.

CHAPTER III

The sprawling city of Zaragoza carpeted the countryside below. It was magnificent and just as Isabel remembered it from previous trips to the Summer Cottage. Massive edifices of stone rose up out of the city. Farther in, one could see the steeple of the Catedral de Seo. The Castle Aljaferia, where the Crown of Aragon rested was farther still. Most visible was the Basilica del Pilar which was both a fortress and a cathedral for the Roman Catholic faith. The stone bridge that spanned the River Ebro would bring travelers right in front of its huge stone walls. Below the battlements were narrow windows that jutted out from the upper floor. From these and from windows that were narrower still below them, defending archers could safely send their arrows toward oncoming foes.

A high tower stood at each corner. The parapets of these towers were at least as tall again as the wall itself. The first level of each parapet had a tall window on each of four sides. The upper levels were hexagonally shaped and had tall windows on each side as well. Every parapet ended in a corniced dome with a black cupola on top. Each cupola had a steel cross superimposed over a sun rising out of the steel ball at its apex.

There were eleven domes rising over the cathedral within the Basilica's walls. Ten of these were smaller and had diamond shaped tiles of white, blue, yellow, and green. All of the tiles together gave the appearance of successively smaller diamonds expanding out from the center of each formation. A massive dome rose up out of the center of the structure. It was the same ruddy tan color as the rest of the Basilica. Each of the eleven domes was topped with cupolas identical to those on the four parapets. Isabel could hear the voice of a priest inside the Basilica as they passed. His loud prayer was in Latin, which was known to nobles and merchants as an international language. Peasants were generally not versed in Latin. Isabel had learned it well from her father.

Rafael had served as General of the Army under King Ramon Berenguer IV. Aragon now belonged to Berenguer's son, Alfonso II. Alfonso was once more a bachelor because his wife had died in travail. She had given birth to a daughter, Teresa. They had not been blessed with a son. Every mother with a daughter of marriageable age had a dream, a wish, or a plot to take the throne. Alfonso's lack of male heirs meant that his next wife's son would one day be the ruler of Aragon.

As the carriages clattered over the streets of Zaragoza, they were assaulted by the cries of dozens of street vendors. Booths lined the main street as they came closer to the plaza in the center of the city. The booths were covered by brightly colored canvas in every imaginable hue. Here was a man selling poultry. All sizes and types of foul were hung by the neck from the rafters of his booth. On the counter below were knives and cutting boards used for dividing the animals into portions. There was a large wooden bowl filled with salt as well.

Another booth contained a wide assortment of blades. Most were daggers or knives to be used in the home, but there were a few swords set up on a rack behind the counter. There was also a great stone wheel for sharpening. Yet another booth contained wooden toys and another had expensive fabrics. It was all quite dizzying to the senses.

It wasn't much longer before the towers of Castle Aljaferia came into view. The castle was built of stone with a dull rose colored hue. It set on a massive foundation of the same material. It was surrounded by a wide moat that was crossed by a stone bridge to the main gate of the castle. If the drawbridge were not lowered, the stone bridge only spanned half the length of the moat. The main road wrapped around the side of Castle Aljaferia and up to its entrance.

The oldest piece of the Castle was a huge square shaped tower that faced to the north. It was a Moorish structure that dated back to the 9th century. The stone of this tower was grey and there were many small windows and arrow slits for defense. On top of this tower flew the red and yellow flag of Aragon. Slightly lower flew a black flag with the crest of the Berenguer family upon it. The front of the structure was on the eastern side. It had six cylindrical towers with battlements running along the walls between. The towers at the corners were slightly lower than the battlements, while the inner towers rose above them. Castle Aljaferia was by far larger than Montenegro's keep, but Isabel did not think that the walls were as heavily reinforced. Once they passed over the drawbridge, the stone path led into a grand courtyard. The stone walk that bordered the courtyard was visible through the many archways that led into it. Smaller paths within encircled extravagant gardens with olive trees and flowers of all kinds. Soldiers lined the walls of the courtyard. They lifted their swords in salute as Lord Montenegro passed.

Servants assisted the nobles out of the carriages once they came to a halt. Rafael had donned a dark red cloak of velvet. The cloak was fastened with a brooch depicting the Montenegro crest. These, along with a golden signet ring were the symbols of his power. He took Priscilla by the arm and led her up to the steps of the palace. Isabel followed behind them with the chamber maids coming last of all.

King Alfonso II waited at the top of the steps to greet them. He was a handsome man with long brown hair and a full beard. His royal robe was of the deepest black velvet with white fox fur at the sleeves and neck. Underneath this was another robe of crimson fabric secured by a thick belt. A golden crown adorned his brow and he carried a thin golden scepter topped with the symbol of the cross. He was flanked by his bodyguards, advisors, and his younger brother; Ramon Berenguer the Count of Provence. Ramon also had long brown hair and dark eyes, but his face was kinder and his beard not as full as that of the king. He wore a black cape over his orange robes and a red hat instead of a crown.

Many lords and ladies were gathered to watch behind the arches of the courtyard.

"My liege," Rafael said as he lowered himself to one knee. He placed his fist over his heart in salute.

"Your majesty," Priscilla said as she knelt as well.

"Rise Lord and Lady Montenegro," King Alfonso said as he extended his scepter toward them. Each kissed the scepter and then rose to their feet. "It is an honor to meet one who led my father's armies to so many decisive victories," he said to Rafael.

"Your majesty does me great honor," Isabel's father replied, "but I have heard of your own great victories for the Armies of Christ. It is I who am in awe."

The King nodded in acceptance of the compliment and then continued. "We pray fervently for a male heir to the line of Montenegro," he told Priscilla. "Make haste so that your husband's skill in directing battle may once more be put to use against the Saracens."

"Yes, your majesty," Priscilla answered as she curtsied and lowered her eyes. "The prospect of my lord going off to war is hardly an attractive one for me, but let me assure his majesty that we are doing our level best." Alfonso paused for a few seconds before Priscilla's words sunk in. He laughed out loud. "I am certain that you are milady!" he chuckled.

"Your majesty," Priscilla said as she reached one hand back and pulled Isabel forward. "May I present to you my daughter...Isabel Montenegro. There was a hush amongst the crowd of onlookers as Isabel's name was mentioned. Many had heard of her coming, and all were eager to see the King's reaction. Most were hoping for something ranging between disgust and dismissal, but the girl's beauty did not make either of these seem likely.

Isabel maintained perfect poise as she knelt before the King. "Your majesty," she said. When she brought her gaze back up, King Alfonso was quite obviously staring at her. This time, she met his gaze and did not flinch away. Instead of his scepter, King Alfonso offered his hand and helped

Isabel to her feet. He brought her more delicate hand to his lips and lightly kissed it.

"You are welcome here Isabel Montenegro," he said. There were murmurs of approval from the crowd, but their faces were not so gentle. Alfonso's eyes never left Isabel's and she could feel a flutter in her breast. He let go of her hand and she curtsied.

"Thank you your majesty," she said.

"I am sure that my subjects are eager to hear you perform," the King said. "There are rumors that your voice is more beautiful than the nightingale."

"His majesty flatters me," Isabel said.

"It is only flattery if the stories are not true," he answered.

"Then I shall have to live up to them."

"Indeed you shall, but come now all of you. My servants have prepared quarters so that you may stay within the Castle. Let us go inside."

"Lead the way your majesty," Rafael said. They were all ushered inside the entry hall where tapestries lined the walls. The tapestries showed kings of Aragon from ages past and some illustrated battles with the Moors. They were led from there up to the apartment that the king had prepared for them. The main door opened into a sitting room with two bedrooms adjoining either side of it and two off the back wall. Aunt Imelda and Uncle Jaime would share one bedroom and her parents would share another. Catherine and Isabel would once more be stuck together. Their chamber maids would share a bedroom and David would have a room all to himself.

They all settled in quickly while the servants brought up a light afternoon meal. Lord Vasquez was reliving the siege of his fortress in Castile. The story that Uncle Jaime told was much different than the one Isabel's father had told her long ago. In Jaime's version, the brave soldiers of Lord Vasquez took the field against a Frankish army. Though outnumbered, Vasquez' troops held their ground until reinforcements arrived. Rafael nodded his head agreeably and supplied details from the battlefield that Jaime could not.

In Rafael's version of the story, Isabel remembered that Lord Vasquez had sent an urgent request to Queen Petronilla for reinforcements. The Queen had responded by sending General Montenegro and his great army. As Rafael and his men were preparing to envelop the enemy troops, the gate of Vasquez' fortress lowered and an untrained band of guardsmen came charging forth.

Rafael was appalled at the foolish move. 'Those fools put their women and children at risk for no reason," he had told Isabel. "They had plenty of provision in their larders and they knew that we had arrived. All they had to do was wait for the victory. Dozens of your Uncle's troops were slaughtered before we could intervene. I don't know what he was thinking, but I hope that it wasn't to make a name for himself. I suspect that to be what happened, however. It was too bad for all those brave young men, but it did give me the good fortune to meet your mother!"

Isabel supposed that Uncle Jaime was trying to find some common interest with her father. He probably thought that Rafael would be interested in talking about war. He didn't realize that he would have done better to talk about horses. Her father was quite gracious and he did seem to be interested. He never spoke to her about his military exploits unless asked, and then only rarely. Isabel also suspected that there was much he left out of such tales.

Lady Imelda and Isabel's mother were talking about their daughters. It seemed that each was trying to outdo the other in praise for their particular child. It was then that Isabel remembered Priscilla's warning. Aunt Imelda was not an ally, not when it came to the crown.

When Isabel retreated to her room, Catherine's chamber maid was already combing her hair. Isabel submitted to the same treatment from Little Grandma. The two servants fussed over their mistresses. At the same time, they gave compliments which were really just a continuation of the rivalry between Lady Priscilla and Lady Imelda.

After some time, the girl's mothers came in to make sure the servants had done everything to perfection. Isabel felt exhausted by the time Pilar was tightening the strings of her gown. Lady Priscilla had insisted that they were too loose. "Remember to keep your head about you," Priscilla whispered to Isabel before they left the apartment.

"I will," Isabel whispered back. Their voices weren't as soft as they thought, however.

"I'm sure I don't need to tell you to do the same," Aunt Imelda told Catherine proudly.

"Please," Catherine replied with a roll of her eyes. Imelda's face was smug as she smiled at Priscilla.

"Of course," Priscilla replied. The four of them gracefully descended the stairs and made their way out to the courtyard where the wolves were waiting to tear them apart. They walked out amongst the gardens. People were strolling here and there in small groups. There were few men in the courtyard beyond the occasional guard. Most of the men were inside discussing business, politics, and war. Some of the ladies were looking at them with suspicion…at Isabel most of all.

The Heiress of Montenegro was very conscious of herself as she walked with her mother. Priscilla was telling her the names of the beautiful flowers that were growing in their stone beds. Isabel was trying to be interested in them, but she was too distracted. There were dozens of eyes judging her and looking for weakness. "Pay attention to the flowers," Priscilla whispered. "Your nerves are showing. Forget about all of them."

"Why must we be out here at all?" Isabel replied softly.

"Because we must," Priscilla answered. It took several minutes, but Isabel was finally able to focus on the flowers. She had never seen yellow roses before and she allowed herself to be swept away by their beauty. She was watching a honey bee working its legs in the pollen of one such bloom when the silence was broken.

"A pleasant afternoon to all of you," said the voice of an older woman behind them. She was wearing a blue colored dress with lace around the collar. She wore a matching blue cap. A peacock feather stuck pretentiously out of it. Her grey streaked hair was drawn up underneath and her pale skin and accent proclaimed a Russian heritage. She was accompanied by a cluster of women in equally ostentatious fashions with equally pale skin.

"Good day to you all," Priscilla replied.

"Good day," Imelda echoed. Isabel and Catherine remained silent.

"I am Queen Richeza of Castile," the elder woman told them.

"Ahh...," Imelda replied. "I am your cousin Lady Imelda of Castile. I don't think we have yet had the pleasure of meeting your majesty. This is my beautiful daughter Catherine." Catherine curtsied when her name was mentioned.

"This is Lady Aurelia Ignacio," the queen continued, "also of Castile. This is Lady Marta Ramiro of Barcelona, and my beautiful daughter Infanta Sancha. Sancha was darker skinned than the others, but still pale in comparison to Isabel. She wore a canary yellow gown with many layers of brocaded lace. She was blessed with the most beautiful blonde hair that was nearly white. Her bangs were tied back and hung in three loose curls over the rest of her flowing hair. Her earrings and necklace were gold adorned with sapphires. Her green eyes shimmered like the surface of the River Ebro. Sancha curtseyed, but she did not lower herself as far as Catherine had.

"I am Lady Priscilla Montenegro, wife to Rafael Montenegro," Isabel's mother said proudly. "This is my Isabel."

"A pleasant day to each of you," Isabel said sweetly. She curtseyed lower before Queen Richeza than the rest.

"I saw you admiring the yellow roses," Richeza said. "They are beautiful are they not?"

"They are indeed," Isabel answered.

"Oh no," Richeza said with a tragic glance downward.

"What is it," Isabel asked with concern.

"There at the base of the stone," Richeza replied. The queen pointed a finger at the bottom of the stone flower bed. A dandelion was growing out of one of the cracks. "It's a weed," she said with disappointment. One could almost believe that the sight of the dandelion hurt her feelings.

"It's only a dandelion," Isabel said without thinking.

"It is, isn't it," the queen answered. Its petals are almost the same shade as the roses…a little darker I think. Poor dandelion…it will never be a rose."

"What will happen to the dandelion," Sancha asked with feigned concern. "Won't someone get rid of it?"

"After a time," Richeza answered. "It will remain in the garden as an eyesore until someone comes along and plucks it out!"

"What a mercy to the roses," Sancha said with relief. Priscilla narrowed her eyes, but her voice was sickeningly sweet when she finally spoke.

"That does seem to be the probable outcome your majesty," Isabel's mother agreed, "but what if the roses are infected?"

"By the dandelions," Sancha asked?

"No," Priscilla replied, "something else I think."

"What could these roses possibly be infected with Lady Priscilla," the queen asked unkindly.

"When people talk unpleasantly around flowers, it is said that the flowers may react to it. They may even die. If there is naught but unpleasantness among the roses, the gardener will have to remove them. It is very much like when a man courts a maiden with a sour disposition. The courtship dies. The man will cast out this harpy before her foul manners infect everyone around her. So too must the gardener cast out the dying flowers, no matter how well-bred they may be."

While Queen Richeza was formulating her reply, Isabel joined the fray. "Once the roses are removed," the heiress said, "then the beauty of nature will reclaim the garden. I don't imagine it would be more than a few months time before the dandelions had multiplied to cover the entire courtyard!"

"What a novel idea my daughter has," Priscilla laughed. "Imagine…the Crown of Aragon spread through with dandelions!"

"Thank you mother," Isabel said sweetly. She had to restrain herself from laughing at the faces of Queen Richeza and the rest of them. They were as sour as any she had ever seen on Catherine.

"Of course dear," Priscilla sighed. "Now as I was explaining earlier, people are often afraid of roses because of their thorns. But no matter how the rose may cut you, they can not move from their spot in the ground. Once you see through the deception they are really quite harmless."

"Do you suppose his majesty might allow us to pick some of them out?" Isabel asked hopefully.

"For you Isabel," Priscilla finished grandly, "I am certain that the whole lot of them could be uprooted!"

"Well I am sure that we don't need a lesson in gardening do we ladies?" Queen Richeza asked her flock. They shook their heads. "Farewell," the queen said to Priscilla's party.

"Farewell your majesty," Priscilla answered pleasantly. Then they were all curtseying as the Queen of Castile departed. Priscilla looked triumphant. She gazed down proudly at her only daughter. "You were marvelous my dear," Isabel's mother whispered. Isabel simply smiled and basked in her mother's approval.

They shared other small conversations, but none as directly offensive as the first. All were drowned in innuendos and insinuations, however. Eventually, Catherine complained about the heat and they all moved back into their apartment. The men were gone. David was no doubt with them.

Aunt Imelda decided that a short nap was in order. Priscilla agreed. "You girls lie down also," Imelda ordered.

Isabel looked questioningly at her mother. Priscilla simply nodded and so the two girls retired to their bedroom. Catherine disrobed and crawled into bed immediately. Isabel could not do the same. She paced back and forth across the floor.

"Oh do quit pacing," Catherine groaned. "You're bothering me!"

"I beg your pardon," Isabel said absently. She sat down on her bed but had no intention of sleeping. Pilar had spent far too much time on her appearance already. She did reach back and loosed the strings of her gown, however. She thought about how much had changed since she walked up the steps to the palace.

King Alfonso had been handsome and eloquent. He was much older than she, but his air of command reminded Isabel of her father. She had told Catherine that she never wanted to leave Montenegro. She had told herself the same thing, but now she was imagining herself as Alfonso's bride, Isabel the Queen of Aragon.

It was a much idealized fantasy as only a young girl can dream up. She would forever be surrounded by beauty. She would have an entire library of illuminated manuscripts like the Biblia Sacra that her father had purchased for her. She would hang great tapestries from the wall showing her father and the saints. To Isabel, her father was just as noble as any of them. Her court would be filled with troubadours and poets. Jesters and acrobats would amuse the children. There would be many children.

Because of the love she had seen between her parents, Isabel imagined that Alfonso would cherish her always. She would put her father in charge of the Queen's Guard and Little Grandma would live forever as her chamber maid. As if thinking of Pilar could conjure her up, it was just at that moment that Little Grandma came into the room. "Isabel," she whispered. "What are you doing awake mija? Your mother told you to go to bed."

"I cannot," Isabel replied. "I am far too nervous about the coming night."

"You sing like an angel. There is nothing to worry over."

"Well, I..." Isabel began.

"Well...what then," Little Grandma asked. "You must rest if you are to perform well."

"I am worried that his majesty the king..."

"Yes?" Pilar prodded.

"He is supposed to be calling on Catherine this Friday, but the way he looked at me on the steps..." Isabel trailed off.

"Oh," Pilar said excitedly, "your fond of him aren't you?"

"He's too old," Isabel protested. "He must be at least twice as old as I am!"

"I saw him looking at you as well," Little Grandma told her. "There could be wedding bells in the future, God willing."

"He is far too old," Isabel insisted, but then she dropped the façade, "but he is quite handsome, no?" Pilar began to laugh and she rung her hands as she crossed the room to where Isabel sat. She put her arms around the heiress and made a fuss over her. When this subsided, Isabel looked up at Little Grandma with a serious expression. "How do I draw his attention?" she asked.

"That is the beauty of it mija," Pilar whispered. "You already have. Tonight, when you sing; you must also touch his heart."

"And then..."

"And then he will come to you."

"Do you truly think so?" Isabel asked hopefully.

"I know so. Get some rest will you?"

"I'm just going to sit down for a spell," Isabel decided.

"Yes, yes, but make sure that you are quiet. I must get back to my own bed now. I love you Isabel!"

"And I love you," Isabel smiled. Little Grandma gave her a little wave before she crept back out of the room. Isabel set back on the bed with the pillows propped between her back and the headboard. She dozed off a little but she never did lie down. When the others awakened from their rest, Isabel was up already. The servants had to once more dress and beautify their mistresses in preparation for the appearance at court. Pilar finished in no time at all. All she had to do was tighten the straps of Isabel's gown.

Rafael and Jaime, (with David in tow), came up to fetch their women for the evening meal. "I have to stay here," Isabel told her father.

"You cannot," Rafael replied. "It would be very embarrassing to the King and I if you did not perform."

"I will perform father, but after dinner. I simply cannot eat right now," Isabel explained.

"Perhaps, after her performance, we could have food brought up to the room," Lady Priscilla suggested.

"I suppose that would be acceptable," Rafael conceded.

"Thank you both," Isabel said respectfully. "Little Gran...I mean Pilar. Will you fetch me a pitcher of water?"

"Of course my lady," Pilar answered.

"See if there is lemon to be had," Priscilla added.

"I will do as you say," Pilar agreed.

'Thank you mother," Isabel said.

"You are welcome child," Priscilla replied. "I shall send Pilar for you when the time is at hand." Isabel nodded and the rest of the family left her alone in the sitting room. She practiced only twice; once before the water, and once after. She didn't want to become hoarse before being put on display before the entire royal court. She felt nervous. Time seemed to crawl at a snail's pace. Finally, Little Grandma came to get her.

"It is time Isabel," Pilar said. She was out of breath as she hurried into the room. "Tell me you're ready."

"I am," Isabel confirmed. It would have to be the truth. They nearly flew down the stairs to reach the entry hall. They slowed their pace after that and walked down the western corridor. It was little time before they reached the huge double doors that led into Castle Aljaferia's banquet hall. A servant waited by the door. He was wearing red leggings and a red tunic underneath a white surcoat. The royal crest was embroidered on the front of the surcoat. His face was clean shaven and he wore a black hat with a ridiculously large feather hanging off of it. He held a long silver trumpet that was nearly his equal in height. The sling that was attached to the trumpet was of red cloth with balls of fabric hanging from tiny strings along its length. His shoulders were slumped as they approached, but he straightened up as Isabel drew near.

"Good evening my lady," he said. His voice was slow and onerous. He bowed with a grand flourish after speaking.

"Thank you good sir," Isabel replied.

"May I have your name?" he asked.

"I am Isabel Montenegro," she told him.

"It is you," he said with eyes widening. "Please wait here while I announce your coming."

"Is that necessary," she asked peevishly.

"By order of his majesty," the herald said. He threw open the doors and lifted the trumpet to his lips. He blew three long notes and four shorter ones. "Lords and Ladies," his voice boomed across the hall, "your majesty. I present now to the court of King Alfonso, Isabel Montenegro, heiress to the house of Montenegro!" There was a hush as Isabel glided into the room. Pilar waited outside.

Five long tables formed a large rectangle around a huge rug that was no doubt used for performers. The side of the rug facing the doors was open and free of furniture. The rug was woven from a scarlet material. Intricate designs were worked into it with white and gold thread. The chairs were only placed on the outside of the tables so that the entirety of the rug was bare. Alfonso was flanked on the left side by his younger brother Ramon and his mother Petronilla, (the former Queen of Aragon), on the left. Next to Ramon were seated Isabel's parents as the guests of honor. Lord and Lady Vasquez sat after them, followed by Catherine and then David. Queen Richeza sat to the left of

Petronilla, followed by her daughter Sancha and several nobles Isabel did not recognize.

Noblemen and their families filled the rest of the seats in the banquet hall. Their plates were mostly picked clean though the wine was still flowing freely. A pig had been roasted on a spit for the occasion. The pig now sat on a silver tray on the table just to the right of the King's table. Isabel could not help thinking what a macabre spectacle the animal presented. Its body was still intact, except for the midsection and hindquarters which had been carved free of meat. The finishing touch was the apple that was firmly set between its teeth. It was almost as if the pig were eating and being eaten at the same time. Isabel found it quite revolting, but none of the guests seemed to mind. Their eyes were all on her.

Isabel had rehearsed what she was going to say. She was supposed to thank King Alfonso for inviting her and her family to the palace. She would then tell a little bit about the song she had chosen. All the strange eyes on her left the young woman dumbstruck. Instead of her practiced speech, Isabel curtsied low before Alfonso. "Your majesty," she said simply. She closed her eyes to black out the stares of the nobles. She took a deep breath and opened them once more.

Her eyes found the King's and lingered there. It was as if he were the only other person in the banquet hall. The beauty and emotion she poured into the Road of Suffering can scarcely be described in words. It was divine. Isabel clutched her hands over her breasts as she sang of the suffering of Christ on the road to Calvary. One could almost believe that it was Isabel's son that had been crucified.

There was awed silence as her voice faded. Tears stood in the eyes of Petronilla. Rafael beamed with pride and Priscilla looked exultant. David was the first to rap his silver cup on the table and then the entire hall was filled with thunderous applause. Isabel felt herself blushing as she curtseyed once more. She made her way off the rug and towards the exit. The applause did not abate.

The hem of a crimson robe protruded out of the deep shadows by the left side of the door closest to the corner. As Isabel drew closer, the man who wore the robe seemed to materialize out of the dark. The staff he leaned upon was of purest silver, all save the Iron Christ that was crucified on the silver cross at the top of the staff. The pointed hat that he wore on his brow marked the man as a Cardinal of the Holy Church. There was a large signet ring on his left hand which showed that he was a man of considerable power. She could not see his eyes at all. They were completely obscured by the pools of shadow that had formed around them. Even when Isabel was close enough to touch him, she could not penetrate through the shroud of darkness. He was more like a statue than a real man. That was how still his form seemed to the child as she drew near.

Just as Isabel was about to pass through the doors, the Cardinal's head jerked to the right and glared down at her. Defying logic, the shadows still obscured his eyes even though the light from a chandelier was falling on his face. Isabel could not stifle her gasp and she hurried out of the banquet hall. There was something unnatural and terrifying about the man that Isabel could not understand. Her heart hammered in her breast as she hurried down the corridor. Once she reached the stairway, Isabel ran.

Isabel was still in a panic when she burst through the door of the apartment. Her breath came shallow and fast as she seated herself on one of the couches near the fire place. She held a hand to her lips and then to her heart until finally the pounding of her heart subsided.

"Isabel…mija?" Pilar called from the door to the servants' bedroom. Little Grandma came quickly to her side. "Isabel…whatever is the matter child?" Isabel tried to articulate her terror, but found that she could only stammer in half words. Little Grandma held her close and whispered words of comfort in her ear. "Oh Isabel, it was too much for you wasn't it?" Pilar asked as she cradled the young woman on the couch.

Pilar assured Isabel that she had sung beautifully and that the King had clearly taken notice of her. This was the farthest thing from the girl's mind. She eventually calmed down enough to eat the sumptuous meal that Little Grandma had brought up from the kitchens. She was famished and devoured most of the contents of the plate. She could not eat the pork. The image of the beast's exposed spine and hind legs filled her mind every time she looked at the cut of meat. Little Grandma encouraged her to eat it, but Isabel complained of feeling feint.

Before Pilar could protest further, Isabel's parents and the rest of the family came rushing in to congratulate her. She thanked them modestly but their words were all blurred together. Lord Montenegro called for a bottle of wine to celebrate. Isabel was allowed a small glass for the occasion, but the new experience was lost on her. She gulped it down and set the glass back on the table. The alcohol only seemed to heighten her fear. "She drinks like you Rafael," Uncle Jaime joked. Rafael laughed heartily.

"That's my girl!" he said proudly.

"You act as if you're dying of thirst," Priscilla chided. "Wine is to be sipped." There was a smile on her face, however. She was too pleased to give much effort to rebuking her daughter. The reverie became too much for Isabel. She was the first of them to turn in for the night. She immediately regretted her decision. Sleep was long in coming and her dreams were worse still. She was haunted by visions of the man in red cloth…and the darkness from whence he came.

Isabel was still tired when Little Grandma dragged her out of bed the next morning. Everyone else was in high spirits and it didn't take long to rub off. She forgot all about the Cardinal who had so upset her soul. In later days, she would rationalize the event as a trick of the shadows. Her nerves had already been stretched to the limit that night.

However, the night at Castle Aljaferia was only to be their first meeting.

Pilar formed Isabel's blue-black hair into one long braid that hung down her back. She then attired the heiress in a lavender gown with a white cord tied below the breasts. She used the same jewelry as the night before, but added a golden circlet on Isabel's brow. Her mother was still talking animatedly with Aunt Imelda about the previous evening. She spoke of how impressed the King had been. Imelda just smiled. After a few seconds, Isabel realized that there was no joy in her aunt's face. It was only a blanket to cover much darker sentiments. It was the same smile Catherine wore. It made the familial resemblance all the more striking.

Isabel was certain that her cousin was harboring some sort of jealousy, but Catherine's words caught her by surprise. "Do you suppose that Isabel and I could travel back together...just the two of us?" Catherine asked Aunt Imelda.

"Well," Imelda began.

"Oh please mother," Catherine begged, taking Imelda by the hand.

"I don't see why not dear," Imelda conceded. "What say you my sister?"

"I am certain it will be no bother," Priscilla answered. "Doesn't that sound like fun Isabel?"

"That will be...great fun," Isabel replied hesitantly. Servants from the palace carried out all of their things from the apartment and loaded them onto the carriages. King Alfonso was waiting in the entry hall to bid them farewell. A cadre of servants, body guards, and hangars on stood behind him. Ramon and Petronilla stood by his side.

"It was good to see you again Lord Montenegro," the King said as Rafael approached.

"Likewise your majesty," Rafael replied. The two men clasped arms in farewell.

"You must be very proud," Alfonso said to Priscilla, "your daughter has the voice of an angel."

"Thank you your majesty," Isabel's mother said respectfully.

"It is I who must thank you for bringing her before me," he replied. "Will all of you be heading back to your summer home?"

"We will," Priscilla answered.

"How long will you be there I wonder?"

"At least a week your majesty," Isabel's mother replied.

"Then I trust that you shall be there when I come to visit later this week," he concluded.

"I will make sure of it," Rafael told him.

"You have my thanks," the King said. Though he spoke to her father, Alfonso's eyes were on Isabel. The King bid them all farewell. Everyone seemed to reply at once, all save Catherine. She waited until the end before curtseying low before the man. She looked up into his eyes as she spoke.

"I shall never forget this meeting your majesty...or the last," Catherine said suggestively. Alfonso coughed uncomfortably at Catherine's display.

"Yes," he replied, "well then until next we meet Lady Catherine." Catherine curtseyed once more and then strutted toward the door like a peacock.

"Coming Isabel?" she asked sweetly.

"Coming," Isabel replied. She spared one last glance at the King before following Catherine out of the courtyard to the waiting carriages. Servants helped the two of them into Lord Vasquez' carriage. The cushions and upholstery inside were white and Isabel could see that they were already becoming soiled. There wasn't much talk as the carriages rolled down the Via Palacio and out to the main road of Zaragoza. The Basilica del Pilar was beautiful in the early light of morning. Isabel could see the statues of angels over its massive doors from her window as she passed.

Once out of the city, it was Catherine who broke the silence. "I didn't know that you were such a skillful liar cousin," she said.

"Surely you have an explanation for such an accusation," Isabel answered tersely.

"An explanation," Catherine scoffed. "You must think me very stupid."

"Since you are accusing me of being a liar, I see few alternatives," Isabel shot back.

"You said you were terrified of marriage," Catherine answered.

"I am," Isabel said.

"That did not stop you from making eyes at King Alfonso, did it?"

"I made no such expression," Isabel said angrily. "I am not a whore!"

"No, of course not; but you worship him with your eyes. That is just what you were doing!"

"He was flattering me. What you think you saw was actually my embarrassment. I do not want to marry and I never wish to leave Montenegro again!"

"Liar," Catherine seethed.

"Just because you're feeling second rate," Isabel said with rising temper, "that does not make it acceptable for you to take out your pitiable fears upon me! Maybe a new gown or some jewelry would bring a sparkle to that horrid face of yours!"

"Pitiable," Catherine asked in disbelief, "pitiable?" She gnashed her teeth before speaking again. "You are the one who is pitiable Isabel Montenegro!"

"I am certain that enviable is what you really meant to say," Isabel said coolly.

"Hardly…why…if your father hadn't married Aunt Priscilla, you would be nothing at all…a commoner."

"Well how fortunate for me then," Isabel replied sarcastically.

"Quite," Catherine replied smugly.

"If you think for one second that I am ashamed of my father, than you are much more the fool than I imagined!"

"You are the fool Isabel," Catherine retorted. "They can give a commoner a plot of land and some servants, but it won't breed the peasant out of him. Your father is very crude. He even dresses like the common soldier he is when we travel. He knows his place."

"At least my father is brave enough to lift a sword. They are used for more than directing other men you know?" Isabel snapped.

"Spoken like a true peasant," Catherine said with contempt.

"You may insult me as much as you desire," Isabel said, "but if you continue to disrespect my father; I will show you just how common I can be."

"You wouldn't," Catherine scoffed, but Isabel detected fear in her cousin's eyes. Isabel settled back on the bench and stared at her cousin. Her eyes dared the other girl to speak. They rode in silence back to the summer cottage. Isabel's gaze was locked on Catherine. Her cousin seemed to be looking anywhere else.

CHAPTER IV

Isabel was relieved when the carriages came to a halt in front of the Summer Cottage. Although Catherine had held her tongue for the remainder of the trip, the damage had already been inflicted. Isabel was furious and eager for some time alone which might help her calm down.

Catherine called for the servants to help her out before the wheels even came to a complete stop. Isabel followed her. She noticed that Catherine was already half way to Aunt Imelda before her foot even touched earth. *"Let her hide behind her mother's skirt,"* Isabel thought angrily. *"I shall be happy to be rid of her!"* She had a strong desire to hurt Catherine. Isabel decided to remove herself from temptation.

"I'm going out to the pond for a while," Isabel told Little Grandma. "Have my things taken up to the room. I shall see you at supper."

"As you wish mistress," Pilar answered. It was not usual for the heiress to give orders, but the chamber maid obeyed. Isabel left her family behind and walked out the dirt trail to the secluded waters. She seated herself inside the gazebo and let the tranquility of the pond soothe her anger. There was a splash on the surface of the pond. Whatever creature had made the splash disappeared below the surface before Isabel could see it. She spent the next several hours sitting by the pond or strolling around it.

David came to join her in the late afternoon. He was dressed only in his undergarments. "Want to help me catch Grandfather Frog?" he called out to her.

"I cannot," Isabel replied with regret. "My gown will get dirty."

"Alright," David said with disappointment.

"I will cheer you on from here," Isabel offered.

"Here I go!" David said excitedly. He ran down the dock toward the gazebo. Before he reached it, David jumped off into the water.

"David," Isabel laughed, "all that noise…you'll scare him away!"

"Aren't I a good swimmer?" David shouted as he paddled toward the other side.

"The best," Isabel shouted back. "You are the best, David," she said quietly. Isabel watched David as he swam toward the far bank. He tried very hard to catch the elusive 'Grandfather Frog', but was not successful. The fact that he kept shouting to Isabel may have had something to do with it. He quickly grew bored with the hunt.

"Look at me!" David cried. "I am David the Frog!" He squatted down in the shallow water among the reeds and made loud croaking noises. After that, he hopped about on all fours. Isabel laughed out loud. Her cousin alternated between hopping and croaking until that too lost its novelty.

"Now be a fish," Isabel called out over the pond. David lowered himself into deeper water and swam out toward the middle. He sunk below the water again and resurfaced next to the gazebo.

"Watch this," David yelled up at her. He coughed a little as he choked on some water but it was soon over. He dived below the surface and came up only moments later. He was laughing wildly. "Did you see me?" he asked excitedly.

"I did," Isabel lied. David broke into laughter once more and Isabel joined him. He went back under to do another fish impression and came up sputtering for breath. When he regained his wind, David gave Isabel a big smile of anticipation. Isabel clapped her hands and laughed at the boy's comical expression. Soon David was giggling too. Time passed quickly and soon they could hear Imelda's voice calling out to them from the house.

David picked up a stick on the way back. He proceeded to swing it at whatever he could find: trees, bushes, flowers, tall grass, and whatever else presented itself. Nothing went unscathed. "Give me the stick," Aunt Imelda said before allowing them inside. David sighed and handed it over. He looked sad to see it go, but only for a second or two.

"I was a fish today!" he told his mother proudly.

"Were you?" Imelda asked.

"Yes. I was swimming around like this," David said as he puffed out his cheeks and wiggled his whole body. Isabel stifled her laughter which made it sound like she needed to blow her nose.

"That is wonderful David," Imelda sighed. "Go inside to dinner...the both of you." Isabel and David ran down the hallway, past the stairs, and into the dining room. The dining table was centered underneath a large chandelier. The chandelier was covered with thick white candles, but there was no need for them in the day. The dining table was surrounded by wooden windows on three sides. The windows opened outward like doors, letting in the sun and the summer breeze. The smell of the snow drops came in from the fields below.

The others were already settled. Uncle Jaime was at the head of the table with windows surrounding it. Imelda sat to his right and Catherine to the left. Rafael was on the opposite side with Priscilla at his right side. Isabel sat in the chair to the left of her father. David sat between her and his mother which left an empty chair between Priscilla and Catherine.

The plates were empty, but each had a bowl of fresh greens next to it. The vegetables were fresh from the garden. Carrots had been arranged over the lettuce like spokes on a wheel. Pieces of onion and tomato rested between the spokes. No sooner did Isabel sit down than she felt instantly famished. She could smell the red vinegar that had been poured over her salad. She took a sip of water on the sly and waited for her uncle to pray over the food.

Isabel would have loved to stuff her face. David did just that when Lord Vasquez finished praying. There were too many eyes on her. She did not want to embarrass her mother or provide Catherine with material for future insults. She took time to savor the crisp vegetables before the servants brought out the main course. The steaks had been blackened over the fire and they tasted heavenly.

Isabel was quite satisfied when she got up from the table. She was spared Catherine's sour looks for the evening because her cousin was still fearful. They all retired to the living room after dinner. It was filled with straight backed couches and chairs. The cushions were of a royal blue material. The room was dominated by a huge fireplace. The servants brought more wood and soon the room was filled with warmth.

While their fathers discussed matters of state, Isabel made shadow creatures on the wall to amuse David. "Lord Enriquez has ignored the call to arms by His Holiness the Pope. He has not sent any of his men to the Holy Land to fight for the Armies of Christ," Uncle Jaime told her father.

"Not even one man to spare," Rafael asked incredulously?

"Not one," Lord Vasquez replied as he shook his head. "I have sent several men from my house. I don't think there are any houses but his who have not."

"We've had so many noble lads volunteering that I have had to deny some of my men the right," her father said. "I was proud of their willingness to serve God, but the keep must have defenders also."

"Too true," Jaime replied. "I wonder what lack of faith afflicts Enriquez that he cannot spare a single man. Has he no honor?"

"Perhaps it is not a matter of faithlessness," Rafael mused.

"I keep expecting his majesty to conscript some of Lord Enriquez' men, but that has yet to happen," Jaime said angrily. David was giggling at the shadow of a lizard's head that Isabel's hands were casting on the wall. Isabel chuckled as she switched from one shadow to another, but she was really paying attention to her father's conversation.

"I wonder what that old dog is up to," Rafael said. "He must know that he loses face with his refusal."

"He's an imbecile!" Jaime scoffed.

"No...I don't think that is the case. He plots something," Rafael frowned.

"Surely he would not start a war within Aragon!" Jaime exclaimed. "We are in enough danger from the Moors!"

"That could be the very reason he will not spare a man for the crusades," Rafael replied. "There are darker possibilities."

"What do you mean?" Jaime asked with alarm.

"Perhaps Enriquez is the only one of our countrymen to know about an impending attack from the Moors."

"That would be treason!"

"I've seen worse," Rafael said gravely. "Lord Enriquez may have sided against Aragon."

"I'll have his head on a pike," Jaime spat.

"Do not be hasty," Rafael cautioned. "There is nothing proven. If you attack Enriquez on a hunch, you'll no doubt be crushed by all of Aragon's armies."

"What would you suggest?" Isabel's uncle asked.

"Have him watched," Rafael advised. "Liars always make mistakes."

"That is true," Jaime agreed. "I'll put a man on it presently."

"You must send word to Montenegro if anything should arise. We are more formidable together than apart."

"Do not worry yourself on that account," Jaime chuckled. "I remember well how your men carried the day in our last conflict!" Rafael nodded. "You will know what is afoot as soon as I," Jaime promised.

"Good," Rafael said. "In the meantime, I'll see what I can do to improve the size of your cavalry."

"That would be greatly appreciated," Jaime said sincerely.

"I would say good riddance, but Priscilla would be quite sorrowful if she were to have to go to your funeral," Rafael said with a twinkle in his eye. Jaime's jaw dropped and his face reddened with anger. Rafael laughed out loud.

"I cannot believe how you insult me!" Jaime said

stiffly. This made Rafael laugh even harder and then both men were laughing. Jaime called for more wine. Aunt Imelda suggested that the children be off to bed. Catherine whispered something in her mother's ear while David and Isabel headed for the stairs. After a few moments, Catherine followed. Isabel turned into the bedroom but Catherine kept walking with David.

"Where are you going?" Isabel asked.

"Never you mind," Catherine said without looking back. Isabel bid David goodnight and prepared herself for bed. Some time passed and Catherine never returned to the bedroom. Isabel finally blew out the candle that burned in its holder on the bedside table. She crawled beneath the covers and breathed out a sigh.

Isabel was long used to sleeping alone, but this was not her bedroom in Montenegro. The night sounds were different here and she found that she missed the comfort of having another person in the bed with her. It was a clear night and the moon cast a bluish glow through the open window. Isabel rose from the bed and crossed over to it. She closed the wooden doors that covered the window and latched them together.

The floor creaked and the latch of the window banged against itself when the wind struck it. Isabel climbed into bed and pulled up the blankets. Just as she was finally going to sleep, she began to hear the yelping of wild dogs afar off. Their barking grew more feverish as they closed in on whatever animal had the misfortune of being their prey. Isabel guessed that the prey was a rabbit. Her father had once told her that a rabbit's death cry sounds almost identical to that of a woman or a small child. This was what she heard now from outside. Isabel covered her head with the pillow to drown it out. She could hear the dogs growling as they fought over the remains.

Eventually the sounds of the dogs receded into the night. Isabel had the urge to run to the servants' quarters and crawl into bed with Little Grandma, but what would Catherine say? In the end, fatigue won out. Isabel's heartbeat slowed with her breathing and she finally found rest.

† † †

The next morning, Isabel saw Catherine coming out of her parent's room. It therefore stood to reason that she had slept there. Isabel felt a sense of victory that she had so unnerved the other girl. That would teach her to insult Isabel's father! Catherine could not spend every night in her parent's bed. She avoided Isabel and remained silent for the next several days thereafter. This was no bother to Isabel. She spent the interlude relaxing at the pond and playing with David.

King Alfonso II and his retinue were not scheduled to arrive until Friday. So it was that everyone in the Summer Cottage was surprised to see him arrive a day early. It was just past midday when the first of Alfonso's soldiers could be seen riding up from the trees. The flag that the first rider bore contained the royal crest of Aragon. Like the other soldiers, he wore a chain shirt, leather gauntlets, and a steel helmet. The next rider bore the banner of House of Berenguer. Several more mounted soldiers broke through the tree line before Alfonso's carriage appeared. It was drawn by six Arabian chargers. The reins were bright red like the plumes that stuck up from each horse's head. There were many horses and they brought a cloud of dust with them up to the edge of the house.

Isabel had still been at the pond when she first heard the approaching hooves. She emerged from the trail that led back through the trees to the pond and saw the carriage as it wrapped around to the front of the Summer Cottage. She saw two men atop the King's carriage. One remained seated while the other got down to the ground.

Isabel watched the sun gleam off the trumpet in the man's hands that had come down off the carriage. She could not make out his face, but she surmised that he must be a herald from the palace. She stepped off and walked quickly toward the cottage. The sound of the trumpet confirmed her suspicion. The servants in the field dropped to their knees as the herald made an introduction for the King of Aragon. The occupants of the house filed out of the front door and formed a line facing the carriage.

When Alfonso stepped out, the servants bowed low with their faces pressed to the ground. Isabel's family members knelt down and bowed their heads as well while King Alfonso stepped up onto the wooden porch. Isabel joined the line at the last minute. She could hear the servants bustling in the kitchen behind her. She almost tripped herself as she knelt beside David. She could see Alfonso's brother Ramon getting out of the carriage as the King went down the line to make his greetings. "Please rise, daughter of Montenegro," Alfonso said as he came to her at last." Isabel stood and King Alfonso took her hand. He looked deep into her eyes and pressed the back of her hand to his lips. She felt herself blushing as Alfonso stepped back and was replaced by his younger brother, the Count of Provence.

Ramon greeted each of them pleasantly. He was very similar to his brother in appearance. They both reflected confidence and an air of command, yet only Alfonso's eyes suggested that he might be dangerous. "You are as beautiful as ever, Lady Isabel," Ramon said as he kissed her hand. He did not linger or stare as his brother had done. When Ramon stepped back, Lord Vasquez spoke.

"Please be welcome in our house," Uncle Jaime said. "We shall have food brought for you and your men presently."

"You are most gracious, Lord Vasquez," the King answered.

"Let my men take your horses to our stables," Rafael offered.

"Thank you Lord Montenegro," Alfonso replied. "My men are weary from the journey."

"It is our pleasure," Isabel's father replied. He signaled for several of the servants before leading Alfonso and his brother inside. Imelda snuck past them and hurried into the kitchen. She closed the door behind her, but they could still hear her shouting out orders to the kitchen staff on the other side.

King Alfonso was placed at the head of the table with his brother at the opposite side. The two lords were placed to either side of the King. The ladies sat next to their respective lords. Catherine and Isabel seated themselves next to their mothers. David protested when Aunt Imelda made him go eat in the breakfast room, but there were only eight chairs at the dining room table.

The servants brought out a simple meal of bread, cheese, and fruit. "His majesty is early," Imelda said tensely as the food was laid out.

"I beg your pardon Lady Vasquez," Alfonso offered. "I meant no inconvenience."

"Oh it is no trouble your majesty," Imelda hastily replied. "It is only that I would have had a much more sumptuous meal prepared."

"Sometimes the simplest things are the best," Alfonso replied graciously.

"Thank you your majesty," Imelda replied.

"That will not be necessary my lady," Alfonso said. They all ate heartily. The bread was still warm from the oven and the cheese had a slight hickory flavor. It was while they were eating that Catherine decided to break the silence.

"I am delighted to receive a visit from your majesty," Catherine said sweetly. "Perhaps he will walk with me in the garden after the evening meal. It will feel marvelous in the cool of the day." She batted her eyes flirtatiously at the King as she finished speaking.

"I am happy to be here Lady Catherine," Alfonso said politely.

"You are so early," Catherine said with a triumphant look at Isabel. "I am ever so happy to have you here now."

"Thank you," Alfonso said, "but I have not come early."

"Our meeting was to be on Friday your majesty,"

Catherine reminded him.

"That is correct my dear, but today I come to see Isabel. Tomorrow I shall see you as promised." Catherine looked about as pleased as if someone had served her a bowl of her own vomit! Isabel looked down at her food. "Isabel and I shall walk in the garden tonight," Alfonso said, and then as an afterthought, "if it should please Lord Montenegro."

"Nothing should please my house more," Rafael replied. With the meal concluded, the women and children were excused while the men remained to discuss the concerns of state. As Isabel turned into the bedroom, her angry cousin stormed in on her heels. Catherine was positively seething when she closed the door behind them.

"Isabel," she said tersely, "I insist that you stand down at once. You must refuse to walk in the garden tonight." Isabel turned back to face Catherine.

"Why does this upset you?" Isabel asked.

"You have no interest in his majesty, true?"

"True," Isabel agreed.

"Then you must step back and allow me to charm him," Catherine explained with a false smile.

"Step back?" Isabel queried. "I have made no advances on the King."

"You must refuse," Catherine insisted.

"How can I refuse the King of Aragon?"

"There are a million ways a lady may refuse: headache, faintness, food that sets ill in your stomach. Pick one!"

"I am a horrible liar Catherine," Isabel protested. "He'll see through it."

"You must not go!" Catherine said menacingly.

"I will not insult the King!" Isabel shot back. Her anger was rising.

"You are right cousin," Catherine hissed. "You are a horrible liar!" Isabel inhaled and exhaled slowly before speaking again.

"My taking a walk with his majesty is no threat to

your schemes," she told Catherine. "Have you never considered that I might not wish to give my power to a man?"

"Your power," Catherine scoffed.

"Yes," Isabel answered. "I know that King Alfonso's mother ruled Aragon for many years alone. Even when she married Alfonso the first, she was still Queen of Aragon and he only the Count of Barcelona. Queen Petronilla only married Berenguer so that she might have an heir to her throne. I am not yet ready to bare children, nor would I marry one of such high station."

"You think to rule Montenegro in your father's stead?" Catherine asked with contempt.

"He has already taught me the business of horses and how to deal with men," Isabel said proudly. "If my mother bears no son, than why should I not take control? I am as able to do it as any man."

"You cannot fight with a sword," Catherine pointed out.

"Nor can most lords," Isabel replied. "They have other men do it for them. I am no danger to you, but I will not slight King Alfonso in any way because of your fears. I would rather he consider me with respect in the future."

"So you are going?" Catherine asked as she glared at Isabel.

"I am."

"You lying whore," Catherine growled, "I shall not let you take him from me!"

"I told you," Isabel began.

"You told me nothing Isabel," Catherine interrupted. "Even if I were to fall for your fanciful deceptions about ruling, I still would not believe you. You say that your father taught you how to deal with other men but he hasn't. He doesn't even know how to deal with them, not the nobility anyway."

"Mind yourself," Isabel said from between clenched teeth.

"You see?" Catherine balked. "You're angry because

it is the truth! He can only deal with other men because of their gratitude for the victories he brought to Aragon. You see how he skulks about and doesn't know how to act around my father and mother. Your father has no culture, no breeding… What makes you think you are fit to rule? Your blood does not run true. What have you ever done for Aragon?

"This," Isabel said. It was at that precise moment that she balled up her fist and planted it into Catherine's glaring right eye. Her cousin staggered back from the blow. The skin around her eye was red and swollen. Neither of them spoke for several moments. They stared at each other.

"Stupid peasant girl," Catherine said at last. "I shall…"

"Do nothing," Isabel finished for her. "You were told not to insult my father. If you will not mind your tongue, then I shall help you to discover what the taste of the floor might be like." The silence after this being said was much longer. Catherine backed up from Isabel. She slowly and nervously opened the door behind her. She never turned her back until she was safely out into the hallway. Catherine bolted and Isabel could hear her cousin's footsteps loud on the stairs. Isabel sighed as she heard Catherine screaming for her mother.

As expected, it was little time before Aunt Imelda came bursting into the room. Isabel's mother was close behind her. Catherine stood outside the storm and watched from the hallway. She was holding a hand to her eye which was starting to turn purple. "How dare you strike my child like that?" Imelda demanded.

"You had better have a good explanation for this!" Priscilla added.

"She should not have said those things about my father," Isabel answered.

"What could she possibly say to warrant such awful behavior?" Priscilla asked.

"Let her tell you," Isabel said, "but not in my presence."

"What did you say to your cousin?" Aunt Imelda asked Catherine.

"I didn't say a thing," Catherine sobbed.

"Take her away," Isabel said with disgust, "for I promised to do worse if she should insult my father again!" It was then that Priscilla slapped her daughter across the face. Isabel's cheek stung from the blow.

"We have not come to hear demands from you child," Priscilla said sternly. Isabel looked down at the floor and did her best to contain her anger.

"Why did you hit Catherine?" her mother asked again.

"I already told you mother," Isabel replied.

"Tell us what she said," Priscilla commanded.

"If I tell you, then you will tell my father," Isabel said.

"Most likely," Priscilla agreed. Isabel sighed heavily before speaking again. She knew that her answer would not please her mother or her Aunt. Unfortunately, love left her few options.

"That is exactly why I must refuse to tell you," Isabel said nervously.

"Do as I say," Priscilla fumed.

"I cannot," Isabel said firmly.

"She is obviously lying," Catherine chimed in from the hallway.

"Be still Catherine!" Imelda said as she shut the door.

"Tell us Isabel," Priscilla said once the door was completely closed.

"I am truly sorry mother," Isabel said. "I should never have acted in such a common way. Whatever she said, it is no excuse for what happened. I shall gladly accept your punishment, but I could never repeat what she said. Ask her if you will. I cannot do it."

"She won't say Isabel," Priscilla objected. "She's already claimed innocence and your silence only justifies her."

"Presuming you are not at fault," Imelda added. "Now is your time to speak." Isabel shook her head.

"So then you are confined to this room until morning," Isabel's mother decided. "This is your fault so remember that you have chosen it."

"Yes mother," Isabel said humbly.

"Very well then," Priscilla sighed. "Let us go then Imelda. Isabel is obviously unfit for any company other than her own."

"What a pity," Imelda agreed. The sisters left the room. The door shut behind them and Isabel was left alone. She didn't even wait by the door to hear what Catherine might say. Instead, she walked across the bed chamber and opened the window to the outside. She watched the servants working in the garden rows. They were weather-worn women, bent and stooping to harvest vegetables from the earth.

At times; Isabel could see a bird or an insect flitting about, but mostly she watched the servants. She wondered if what Catherine said was true. Would she be one of those women if not for her mother? She decided that it didn't matter. If it had been her lot to pick vegetables then she would have picked as many as she could.

It was nearly dark when a servant brought up a tray of food. Isabel found that she was ravenous. She devoured the meal almost instantly and had the servant bring more. Some time later, there was a knock at the door. Isabel opened it and was surprised to see her father standing there. "Papa," Isabel asked confusedly?

"Your mother thinks you should stay in here all night," he said. "I agree with her. However, King Alfonso is determined to see you and so I am compelled to grant your release."

"Thank you father," Isabel said.

"I heard what happened today," Rafael said. "Whatever did Catherine do to anger you so?"

"Nothing of significance," Isabel sighed.

"I am pleased to know that you defend my good name," he told her, "but there is no reason that you should lose control."

"I know," Isabel said with eyes downcast.

"Well…go on then." Rafael gestured toward the door. Isabel slipped around her father and made for the stairs. Everyone was gathered in the living room where the fire in the hearth was burning bright.

Alfonso stood as Isabel entered the room. "There she is," he said. "I was beginning to think you were avoiding me."

"Perish the thought your majesty," Isabel said as she curtseyed before him. "I was feeling faint this afternoon and had to lie down. Please forgive my absence." Catherine was glaring daggers at Isabel from the chair she had seated herself in closest to the fire. Her right eye had swelled and discolored with bruising.

"Shall we go?" Alfonso asked.

"Of course," Isabel replied. The king offered his arm and together they left the cottage. Arm in arm, they strolled down to the garden. An evening mist had come in from the River Ebro. It obscured most of the smaller plants and gave the rows of flora a surreal quality. The water brought up the smell of the vegetables, interlaced with the flowers that grew round about. Several soldiers had posted themselves at the edges of the garden in order to watch the king. They were close enough to respond in an emergency, yet far enough away to appear impersonal. Each of them carried a long torch in addition to the sword on his waist. The torches were like beacons to guide Isabel and the King in the gathering darkness.

They walked in silence for several minutes until Alfonso finally spoke. "This is a pleasant night for a walk. Do you not think so?"

"It is quite pleasant," Isabel said amiably.

"The torches break up the mist so we can make our way. Is there always so much of it?"

"Usually," Isabel replied. "It comes up from the river. I like the way it blankets everything in grey. It's almost like two different places from day to night."

"You are right," Alfonso agreed. "It is beautiful…and who better to share it with?"

"His majesty flatters me," Isabel blushed.

"I am so pleased that Lord Montenegro agreed to bring you to Zaragoza," he continued. "Your singing left me enchanted."

"You barely know who I am," Isabel gently chided.

"As you barely know who I am," Alfonso smiled.

"Catherine speaks very highly of you."

"Does she," Alfonso asked? Isabel thought she detected a note of apprehension in his voice.

"Yes. She tells me that the two of you are sure to begin your courtship tomorrow. I am certain that you will enjoy each other's company very much. Catherine is very…cultured…a real lady."

"And you?" Alfonso asked.

"I am my father's daughter," Isabel replied.

"A rather evasive answer," Alfonso chuckled.

"I am truly grateful to have been given the opportunity to visit the royal court," Isabel told him, "but my place is in Montenegro. I have very little in common with the women I met in Zaragoza. They all seem to be playing an elaborate game. It is one that I want nothing to do with."

"What game is it that the women of my court play? Do let me in on it," Alfonso said with a grin.

"It is a contest really…to see who can keep her dignity. They are all trying to embarrass the others and make veiled insults," Isabel explained. "I just don't have the stomach for it!"

"Who is winning, do you think?"

"No one," Isabel replied vehemently. "They all look like fools!" Alfonso laughed out loud. "What is it?" Isabel asked as the king continued to laugh. "Have I said something amusing?"

"Forgive me," Alfonso said as he caught his breath. "It is only that I have often thought the same thing." Isabel let herself laugh then too.

"They do look silly do they not?" she asked mirthfully.

"Indeed they do," he replied. After several more steps, the king spoke again. "Does Catherine play this game?"

"Everyone does your majesty," Isabel sighed.

"Does she play on your side...or against?"

"Well..," Isabel began. She was at a loss for words. She did not want to say the truth of what she thought.

"She must play against you then," Alfonso concluded. "Is that what blackened her eye?" Isabel was not skilled at lying and so she had to look away when she made her answer.

"Perhaps she fell and hit herself on a bedpost," Isabel suggested with a hint of a smile.

"Really," Alfonso said with disbelief.

"I should not like to speak of it if it pleases your majesty," she implored him.

"What shall we speak of then?" Alfonso asked.

"Tell me about the crusades," Isabel blurted out before she could stop herself.

"Surely you do not wish to know about such a harsh subject," Alfonso said. "We do our best to reclaim Jerusalem, but the work is...messy."

"Tell me about my father then," Isabel requested. "Was he as great a general as they say?"

"Lord Montenegro is a great man and he was a superb military commander under my father," Alfonso began. "I could list his accomplishments, but I'm sure you have heard them already. Instead, let me tell you about the battle in which we two fought together."

"Would you?" Isabel asked excitedly.

"It was the Battle of Al Qadir. Has he never told you?"

"He tells me what is seemly for a woman to hear. My father is not given to boasting."

"By the time I arrived," Alfonso said, "your father was laying siege to the Fortress of Kamil al Zaim. It had been a month since he had routed Al Zaim's army. With the supply lines cut, it was only a matter of time until the Moors would be forced to meet us on the field of battle once more. However, we had no way of knowing how much food they might have in reserve. We had enough food to last only one more week. We had received word that our own supply lines had been raided. There was no knowing when we would receive more food for our own hungry men. The scarcity of lumber in the desert was slowing down the making of catapults and other siege weaponry. On the thirty fifth day of the siege, we saw one of the Saracens step off the rampart of the fortress and plummet to his death!"

"Why would he do such a thing?" Isabel asked.

"That is what your father and I were wondering. The Moors are known to fight relentlessly. They do not surrender. Your father had never seen one of their men commit suicide. Therefore, he sent four men to retrieve the body under cover of night."

"Why would he want the body?" Isabel wondered aloud.

"It was really quite ingenious. Your father wanted the dead man in order to gauge how much food our enemies had left. From the look of him, the Saracens had already been starving for quite some time," Alfonso told her. "I'll spare you the details."

"Go on," Isabel encouraged as they made another go round of the garden.

"You can imagine that we were pleased," Alfonso continued. "The men were getting bored and picking fights with one another. We were very relieved that the siege was coming to an end. I slept quite well that night. I slept late in fact. By the time I came out of my pavilion, the men had finished building the one and only catapult we used for the battle. I remember thinking that the general had ordered a feast because I saw half a dozen hogs being slaughtered. The cooks were butchering them right near the newly constructed siege weapon. They were draining the blood of the animals into huge earthenware pots. They were making a grand display of it too. Your father launched the first volley himself. It was all very ordered. You can imagine my surprise when I realized that he had launched one of the hogs instead of a stone!"

"He did what?" Isabel asked incredulously.

"I remember watching the first one sail over the enemy battlements. I kept expecting to hear the pig squeal as it flew through the air, but of course it was already dead." Once the initial shock wore off, I became furious! I went down to where the general, your father, was overseeing the launch of the remaining hogs. I told your father that he had lost his wits. We needed those animals to feed our men. He looked back at me with this ridiculous grin which I thought confirmed my suspicion."

"What did he say?" Isabel asked.

"He said, *They are unclean your highness.*" By this he meant the hogs. He seemed to think it was quite amusing and I demanded an explanation," Alfonso said. "Apparently, your father had become quite familiar with the Moors' culture in all his years of making war against them. General Montenegro told me that our enemies were forbidden by their religion to touch swine. The flesh of the swine was unclean. He also said that they believed that dying in Jihad would guarantee their place in heaven."

"What is Jihad?" Isabel asked.

"A holy war," Alfonso answered," but the Saracens must purify themselves for it. If they touch anything unclean, then their death does not guarantee salvation. I still thought he had lost his mind. He must have noticed the look on my face, for he quickly added that hunger would drive the enemy to eat the hogs. *"They're not going to eat pork just because you're delivering it to them,"* I said. *"You're wasting food that could fill our bellies!"* Your father said, *"They starve your highness. It is either the pork or each other.""*

"How gruesome," Isabel said with revulsion.

"I beg your pardon," Alfonso said.

"Please go on," Isabel said after a few seconds.

"I do not wish to disturb you."

"Do continue," Isabel reassured him.

"You must understand milady," Alfonso said, "war only offers death…be it yours or that of your enemy."

"I understand," Isabel shuddered, "but please tell me the rest of the story."

"Alright," Alfonso agreed. "I still wasn't convinced of your father's soundness of mind. I ordered him to quit wasting time. The enemy was slightly outnumbered and very weak from starvation. *I'll have that wall knocked down tomorrow*," I told him. Your father was actually pleased with this because he had planned the same thing. I went to bed irritated and in a foul temperament."

"The soldiers had risen before dawn," Alfonso continued. "They were all formed in their ranks to the rear of the catapult. Your father was barking out orders and moving his men around in preparation for the coming assault. I heard him telling the men on the catapult to aim for the courtyard first because that would be where the enemy would have their siege weapons. The Saracens' arrows came as soon as our men moved the catapult into position. The cart that held our catapult was constructed quite well. The sides of the cart were much higher than is usual and there was a wooden ledge over their heads that protected from the arrows. What the ledges could not stop was deflected by shield bearers that marched next to each man who pushed the cart."

"Once in position, Montenegro's soldiers knocked out the wheels of the cart and began the second phase of the General's plan. Instead of launching boulders, your father was first launching the earthen pots filled with blood. I ordered him to stop it at once," Alfonso told her. "I thought we should be firing boulders. Your father yelled at his men to continue launching blood. It was a risky move for all of them, but the soldiers obeyed their commander rather than their prince. I was furious! I had planned to have your father beheaded after the battle was over."

"Why?" Isabel asked with amazement.

"A prince cannot be disobeyed if he is to be king. In this case, however, your father's decision was the right one. After the first few launches of pig's blood, the enemy stopped their own attacks. Fortunately our catapult was not hit. Once the blood pots were exhausted, your father launched boulders at the Fortress of Kamil Al Zaim until a large piece of the wall fell crumbling to the sand. The hole was big enough to move an army through."

"I was pleased," Alfonso continued, "and I directed the General to begin the attack. He requested that we delay the attack just a short time further. We waited for a few moments that seemed like an eternity. Your father yelled for the archers to loose. Arrows rained down on the fortress as the infantry were commanded to charge forth! The Saracens began to pour out of the hole that our catapult had made. The gate was lowered also and our enemies came out of it."

"Montenegro ordered his cavalry to horseshoe out to the left side and then envelop the enemy from the flank. He began to ride off with them and I called for him to stop. "Where are you going, General?" I shouted. I shall always remember his answer. "Battles are won on the field," he called back. "Better to die with my men than hope for mercy once I am overrun!" He spurred his horse forward and I lost him in the throng. I did not follow him," Alfonso said regretfully. "As fate would have it, there was no need. The white flags began to go up all through the enemy ranks. The Saracens surrendered that day. Lord Montenegro had defeated them with hunger and their own superstitions."

"The enemy was spattered with blood, but most of it was not their own," the King continued. "Neither was it our blood." There were huge streaks and puddles of pig's blood inside the fortress. One could not have ventured far without stepping in it. Al Zaim ordered them to kneel and surrender their weapons. It was a decisive victory for Aragon, not just because we had taken the fortress, but because your father showed mercy."

"He didn't...kill them," Isabel asked. "What did he do with them?"

"He branded them," Alfonso replied.

"Like animals?" Isabel asked incredulously.

"Yes," Alfonso replied. "He told them that if they ever again carried a sword against us, than they would be slaughtered without question or mercy. The branding would mark them as having given up. Your father was certain that their countrymen would not welcome them back. Word of his mercy spread across Arabia. There have been some few surrenders since that time. There have not been many, but before the Battle of Al Qadir, a Moorish surrender was unprecedented.

"That is magnificent," Isabel said breathlessly.

"That is why the soldiers of Aragon still revere your father," Alfonso told her. "Do you recall how my soldiers raised their swords when you first came to Castle Aljaferia?" Isabel nodded. "It was for your father that they raised their salute. Lord Montenegro is a great man," the King said. "You can be proud to bear his name."

The walk did not end there, but the rest of their conversation was of little importance. They were the meaningless words that come before a courtship. Alfonso was quite charming. He gave Isabel the strong impression that he was interested in her without being overly direct or vulgar. "Will I see you tomorrow?" he asked when they had come back to the house.

"Of course," Isabel giggled. "Where would I go?"

"We could take a ride into the country," Alfonso suggested. "Would my lady join me for a picnic?"

"I would be delighted to," Isabel replied. Her heart was aflutter. All those words she had told her cousin about marriage seemed very far away. "I shall look forward to it."

"As will I," King Alfonso said as he released her hand. He was smiling and his eyes danced. Isabel felt herself grinning back. They went inside the house and into the hallway. Isabel shot him a backward glance as she went up the stairs to her bed chamber. Alfonso remained at the bottom of the stairway and watched her go.

CHAPTER V

When Isabel crept back up the stairs, she was very careful to remain silent. She winced as the door to the bedroom creaked on its hinges. She did not want to wake Catherine. Isabel felt like she was floating on air. She was certain that her cousin would ruin the mood were she to wake up. Isabel was, therefore, quite relieved when she found the bedroom empty. Catherine had gone to sleep in Aunt Imelda's bed once again.

It took Isabel some time to fall asleep. She was imagining herself as the Queen of Aragon. It was all quite lovely as fantasies usually are. She would vacation with her parents in Montenegro. She and Alfonso would come to the Summer Cottage to get away from the Royal Court and all of its troubles. She imagined a son, Rafael II, which she would raise to be King.

Isabel awakened the next morning feeling refreshed. Catherine came into the room just after she had removed the sleep from her eyes. Catherine was silent at first, but Isabel could read a thousand accusations in her gaze. She knew that her cousin would speak as surely as a boiling kettle will eventually whistle.

Catherine's movements were short and seemed to come in spasms. Isabel silently joined her cousin at the wardrobe. When they were forced to share the same reflective piece of metal, Catherine could hold back no longer. "You are no cousin of mine," Catherine said crisply.

"Anger won't erase lineage," Isabel said with a sigh.

"Look at my face!" Catherine nearly shouted. Isabel paused in combing her hair to turn toward her cousin. The black eye was much more noticeable than it had been the day before. The black and purple bruise covered the entirety of Catherine's right eye. It reminded Isabel of a spotted dog she had once seen running around the stable yard in Montenegro. "Well?" Catherine demanded.

"I am looking," Isabel said dismissively.

"You may think you have won, but you have not!" Catherine exclaimed. "I shall take back what is mine, even with this dreadful mark on my face! The King and I are to go on a picnic today. You will see upon our return. He will have forgotten all about little Isabel from the country."

"I doubt you will be going anywhere today," Isabel said with disdain. "Perhaps after I leave you may succeed, but not while I am still here."

"I knew it! I knew you had designs on the crown!" Catherine screeched. "That was the whole reason your family came here!"

"Maybe it was," Isabel replied with deliberate antagonism.

"All those lies about ruling Montenegro alone… I knew it!"

"That was no lie," Isabel said. "I really did not want to leave Montenegro…but now…"

"Oh, what now?" Catherine seethed.

"Now I have changed my mind," Isabel answered. "Things change you know."

"What has changed?" Catherine asked. She was trying to conceal her nervousness but not doing a particularly good job.

""Well, his majesty is quite charming and even were he not; I now have reason to enjoy watching you squirm." Isabel looked Catherine in the eye as she spoke as if daring a reaction.

"Bitch!" Catherine cursed.

"I knew there was a bit of peasant girl hiding in there all along," Isabel said smugly. She then turned her attention back to her hair.

"I will do whatever it takes to win his majesty's hand," Catherine promised. "Just because you fight like a man does not mean you can defeat me as a woman!"

"Better take some extra powder to cover that eye of yours," Isabel suggested. "On second thought, the whole of your face is unpleasant. Perhaps you could borrow some more from your mother."

"We shall see," Catherine said threateningly. Isabel allowed her cousin the last word. She braided her hair back into one thick coil that hung down her back. She made two tiny braids to hang from the center of her bangs down past the front of each ear. The white gown that her cousin selected was dazzling. Isabel remained in her night gown for the time being. She had other plans.

Isabel left the bedroom and crossed hurriedly to that of her parents. She did not want the King to see her in her bed clothes. She let herself in without bothering to knock. Rafael and Priscilla were still asleep. Her father slept on his back. Priscilla lay on her side with one arm over her husband's chest. Isabel tried to be very quiet shutting the door, but it wasn't enough. Isabel cringed as the door shut loudly and she could hear her mother's gasp from behind her.

Isabel looked back long enough to realize that Priscilla was unclothed. She quickly faced back toward the door. Her face was flushed with embarrassment. "Isabel Montenegro," her mother hissed, "whatever are you doing sneaking up on me like this?"

"I am sorry mother," Isabel gulped. Her father groaned in his sleep and rolled over onto his stomach. He was unclothed also, but the bed sheets thankfully covered the parts that Isabel least wanted to see.

"I need a moment," Priscilla sighed. Isabel could hear the rustling of fabric as her mother located her night gown. "Now then," Priscilla whispered several seconds later, "what is it?" Isabel turned around to face her mother. She walked over to the bed so that she could hear more easily.

"The King has invited me to dine with him today," Isabel whispered.

"Oh mija.., is it true?" her mother exclaimed. Priscilla covered her mouth with her hand when she realized how loud she was. Mother and daughter looked at Lord Montenegro to see if he was disturbed. Rafael slept on. "Where will you go?" her mother whispered. "Will it be the palace?"

"No," Isabel whispered back. "It is to be a picnic in the country."

"That is wonderful."

"I have a favor to ask of you."

"Just name it," Priscilla replied. Her eyes were positively glowing.

"I want to borrow your gown."

"Which one?"

"The turquoise gown," Isabel answered, "the one without sleeves."

"With the train," Priscilla asked?

"Yes…the little white train," Isabel agreed.

"That dress is very special to me," Priscilla said apprehensively.

"I know."

"Do you know why?" Priscilla asked.

"I know only that it is your favorite," Isabel replied.

"I met your father in that dress," Priscilla explained. "I should be devastated if it were ever marred in any way. I love that dress more than my wedding gown."

"I will be so careful," Isabel promised.

"I know you will," Priscilla said. She stroked her daughter's face with one hand. "My little girl," she sighed.

"Thank you mother," Isabel said. She kissed Priscilla's cheek and then they both tip-toed over to the armoire that contained Lady Montenegro's clothing. Priscilla sorted through several sets before she selected a light blue night gown. Isabel was about to protest, but then she saw the turquoise neckline peeking out from the top of it. The white train hung down from the bottom. The night gown was only used to protect what was inside. Priscilla handed the gown to her daughter as if it were gold. Isabel accepted it in kind.

The young heiress took several steps toward the door, but she could hear others moving about beyond the walls of her parents' bed chamber. She looked back at her mother with indecision. Priscilla pointed to a hand carved, wooden screen which had been crafted to look like there were vines crawling up it. Here and there, flowers crafted from a darker wood seemed to bloom from the vines.

There was a small wooden platform behind the screen, much like the one in Isabel's own bedroom. Isabel stepped upon it. She was expecting her mother to call for Alejandra, Little Grandma, or both of them. Although it was uncharacteristic, Priscilla dressed Isabel herself. She would leave nothing to chance.

Priscilla made sure that the tiny rope was set perfectly around Isabel's waist. The trains had to hang just so and she even placed her own gold circlet on her daughter's head. She rubbed scented oils into Isabel's skin and brushed her cheeks with red powder. She painted her daughter's lips with a tiny brush. "How do I look?" Isabel asked anxiously when her mother was done.

"Beautiful," Priscilla replied. Isabel could see that there were tears standing in her mother's eyes. "Run along before your father awakes." Isabel hugged her mother and left the room more quietly than she had come in.

Isabel could feel the jealous gaze of Catherine as they passed each other in the hallway. All eyes were on Isabel at breakfast. The men seemed a little more polite than usual and all wished her a good morning in some fashion. Alfonso scarcely took his eyes off of her. His younger brother was looking also, but Ramon had the decency to look elsewhere when their eyes met. The Heiress of Montenegro was radiant.

The meal was nearly concluded when Catherine spoke up. She had made a valiant attempt to cover her bruise with arsenic, but it only gave her eye a bluish appearance instead. "I beg his majesty's pardon," Catherine said as she stood and curtsied.

"Please speak freely, Lady Catherine," Alfonso replied, turning his eyes upon her for what Isabel thought might be the first time that day.

"I only wondered where and at what hour his majesty should like to meet before our departure," Catherine said.

"Oh Catherine," the King said with feigned concern, "you cannot go anywhere this day. A woman must rest and recover when she has had such an ordeal."

"What ordeal?" Catherine asked with anger creeping into her voice.

"I told him about your mishap with the bedpost," Isabel explained.

"A terrible tragedy to be sure," Alfonso said. "We shall all pray for your speedy recovery."

"But," Catherine stammered.

"I am certain there will be another opportunity when you are feeling better," Alfonso said consolingly. Catherine looked then at Isabel. There was a message written clearly in her eyes.

"*I shall never forgive you*," those eyes seemed to say.

"As his majesty wishes," Catherine faltered. She managed one more curtsy before hurrying up the stairs to her bedroom. A pang of regret passed through Isabel, but she would not allow herself to feel pity. The fury in Aunt Imelda's eyes was terrible to look upon. Isabel focused instead on Alfonso. He was so handsome and vibrant, even if he was twice her age. The King stood then and addressed Isabel.

"My lady," he said, "meet with me just before mid-day if you will. My carriage shall be prepared and waiting in front of the house." Isabel stood gracefully and curtseyed.

"I shall be there your majesty," she said demurely, but she smiled at him before leaving the room. She wanted the man to know that she was open to the idea of a courtship. Her heart fluttered as she returned to her parents' quarters. She did not want to risk a confrontation with Catherine just then.

Priscilla and the servants fussed over Isabel to remove every crumb of food that had made it onto her dress. She listened while they each gave her advice on the coming venture. They all seemed to have differing opinions on most everything, (though they ultimately deferred to her mother). Everything from poise, to conversational topics, to meal etiquette; they filled her head with more than she could remember.

As the sun approached its highest point in the sky, Rafael arrived and dismissed everyone else from the room. "Leave me alone with my daughter," he told them. The other women filed out and Rafael closed the door behind them. He walked over to the couch where Isabel was already settled and sat beside her. "I want you to be careful today," her father said seriously.

"Have I cause to fear?" Isabel asked him.

"Perhaps and perhaps not," he answered, "but one ought to remain vigilant."

"What shall I watch for?"

"Just remember that Alfonso is King. His word is law."

"I will remember," Isabel interjected quickly, but her father held up a finger for silence.

"Yet no law is higher than the Law of God," he reminded her.

"You must not worry," Isabel assured him. "I would never…"

"I have complete faith in you," her father said. "You are a lady. You will be responsible to conduct yourself as such."

"I will," Isabel promised.

"You had better go," her father sighed. Isabel stood and smoothed down the folds of her gown. She curtseyed to her father and turned to leave. "Isabel," he called to her as she broke the plane of the door. She looked back over her shoulder. "From now on…do not curtsy so low. You are Montenegro!" Rafael smiled and held one hand up in a fist as he said this last.

"Montenegro," Isabel echoed, holding her own small hand in a fist and smiling back at him. Rafael gave her a wink and she left the room. Isabel walked out the front door and stood on the wide porch of the Summer Cottage. It was a beautiful day with the sun shining down from between fluffy white clouds. The sunlight made the wood seem to glow and the slight breeze animated the diaphanous white trains hanging from the back of Isabel's gown. The trains bowed out from where they were connected to gold bracelets that rested below her elbows.

Alfonso's carriage pulled up before the house. His horses' bodies had been brushed and oiled so that their black fur seemed to sparkle in the sunlight. A guardsman opened the door of the carriage and the King stepped out. "I can hardly believe my eyes," Alfonso exclaimed! "Lady Isabel, you are simply breathtaking." Isabel curtseyed. It was not as low as the day before, but Alfonso did not seem to take notice.

"Good afternoon your majesty," she greeted him.

"It is a good afternoon indeed," he replied. Alfonso bowed with a flourish and then held the carriage door for her. Isabel approached slowly, making sure to walk with grace and poise as her mother had instructed her.

"Thank you my liege," she said as the King helped her inside. Alfonso entered behind her and sat on the opposite side of the carriage so that they might face each other. The carriage started with a jerk and soon the horses were clopping down the path to the main road.

The carriage turned away from Zaragoza once they emerged from the tree line. There was a large basket of food on the bench next to the King. A white cloth covered its contents. Alfonso reclined on the bench with his arm resting on the back of the seat over the basket. Isabel sat straight with her legs crossed neatly. "Did you sleep well?" the King asked her.

"I managed passing fair," Isabel replied.

"Did Catherine keep you awake?"

"Not at all," Isabel answered.

"Then what was it?" Alfonso asked.

"I was looking forward to right now," she smiled.

"As was I," Alfonso agreed. They looked at each other for several seconds more before Isabel broke the silence.

"It is a perfect day," she said as she ducked her head to peer out the window. Isabel could not remember much of what was said in the carriage. What she saw in the King's eyes seemed to say so much more than the idle chatter that passed between them.

They took lunch in a grassy meadow not far from the road. It was only slightly obscured by the trees, but there were few passersby. A pair of ground squirrels skittered up and down a nearby trunk. High in the branches of one tree was a cardinal. The cardinal puffed out his red feathers and sang a song that echoed through the forest. The guards laid out a white blanket and then positioned themselves with the carriage by the side of the road.

Alfonso sat down on the blanket and Isabel sat opposite him. He removed the cloth over the picnic basket with an exaggerated flourish. Isabel laughed at the expression on the King's face as he set the cloth down. "This is no laughing matter," Alfonso said with mock seriousness. Then they were both laughing.

The King had brought sweet breads made with honey, a large round of cheese, and sweetened meats with caramelized sugar upon them. When the meal was done, Alfonso withdrew a smaller basket of strawberries and a bottle of white wine. Isabel remembered little of their conversation, but she did remember how enchanted she was with Alfonso. She became giddy from the wine. She told Alfonso that she was unaccustomed to drinking, save the smallest sip of Holy Communion. The King did not seem to be concerned and so Isabel allowed herself to relax.

At one point, their eyes met and they became engaged in a kiss. The kiss seemed to be the culmination of all that had passed between them. Isabel lost herself in it. Alfonso was not timid or blundering the way many of her previous suitors had been if given the chance.

They leaned upon one another on their way back to the carriage. Alfonso still managed to trip on the grass, nearly taking Isabel with him. She laughed out loud and then helped him to his feet. He then offered to help her into the carriage. "Better let the guardsmen take care of this your majesty," she chuckled. As it turned out, the guardsmen had to assist Alfonso in as well.

The King shut the door and they were instantly in each other's arms once more. Isabel could barely breathe and her heart beat like a humming bird. Had it ended there, it would have been beautiful. Isabel felt Alfonso's fingers loosening the straps of her gown. She pushed away at his chest but he would not let go. She breathed in sharply as she finally broke free of his lips. "Let me be!" she said loudly. She felt so insulted.

"Come now, Isabel," Alfonso said soothingly, "We both knew how this day would end from the start. Why not enjoy yourself?"

"Let me go now!" Isabel shouted as she worked one arm up. Her elbow was now keeping the King's face away from her breasts. Alfonso persisted in trying to remove Isabel's clothing. She twisted and turned to avoid him and finally had to clutch the fabric in her hands to prevent him from having his way.

"Do not resist me girl!" Alfonso growled as he grabbed hold of the dress once more. There was the sound of ripping cloth as the neckline was stretched to breaking. Her breasts were exposed for only the time it took to slap Alfonso hard across the face. Isabel clutched the ruin of her mother's gown to her bosom. Alfonso leaned forward to have another go.

"Touch me not!" Isabel hissed. Alfonso sat back as if considering but did not seem fully convinced. He smiled at her.

"Look at you," he sneered. "You should feel fortunate that I have an interest in you at all. Your cousin is not so ungrateful."

"Then take her," Isabel snapped. "I will not be shamed."

"You will do as I tell you," Alfonso said with a cruel smile. "I have had women beheaded for less." Isabel was terrified but she held on to the last of her composure. She knew that if she showed any weakness, than this horrible man would ruin her forever. She felt betrayed and near tears but she would not falter.

"You can do as you will your majesty," she said furiously, "but you will pay dearly."

"What can you possibly do to strike at me?" Alfonso laughed. "I am Aragon!"

"You think me to be a foolish child," Isabel said tremulously, "not unlike your other conquests to be sure."

"Ha," Alfonso jeered. He made a play grab at her arm and Isabel yanked it away.

"You yourself told me how my father is so loved by the men of your army. They respect him."

"That matters little," Alfonso scoffed.

"It matters most of all," Isabel corrected him. "His majesty can ill afford a revolution when he is at war with the Saracens."

"You seem to have a very high opinion of yourself," Alfonso said, but Isabel saw that she had struck a chord.

"My father left the world of bloodshed for me," Isabel said proudly. "You are indeed a fool if you think he would not take up a sword again. I tell you this. You should kill me if you are going to do anything, for the result will be the same!"

"That will be enough, Lady Montenegro!" Alfonso barked. His face was sullen.

"It is not enough," Isabel declared. "If you harm even a hair on my head, my father will hound you to the ends of the earth. He will not rest until you are dead. All the victories my father gave to Aragon can be laid to waste. He knows enough to give your enemies an advantage I'll wager."

"Your father would never ally himself with the enemy," Alfonso interrupted her.

"Unless you make yourself the enemy," Isabel finished. "You have damaged my mother's clothes. The suspicion in this act alone could be enough to enrage my father."

"You shall not start a war with a lie," Alfonso snarled. "I won't stand for it!"

"No," Isabel replied. "I shall lie to prevent a war." Alfonso glared at her but he held his tongue. "I should like very much to go home now if it pleases your majesty," Isabel said curtly. Alfonso rapped loudly on the wall of the carriage and set the driver in motion. They rode in silence. Isabel could see the King's angry stare out of the corner of her eye, but she would not look at him directly. She knew that she was teetering precariously on the edge of death.

When the carriage finally came to a stop, Isabel looked finally at the man who was now only a man. "I am in need of a cloak," she said flatly. There was a pause while Alfonso tried to formulate an answer. In the end, he did as she bade him. Isabel covered herself with the cloak that was given her by one of his majesty's servants. It was an effort, but she managed to hold the cloak around her so that the damaged gown did not show through. She was so upset that it took all of her concentration to appear calm.

Isabel ascended the stairs and entered the room where Pilar and Alejandra were quartered. She did not bother to knock or announce her presence. "Leave us," she told Alejandra.

"As my lady wishes," her mother's chamber maid replied. Alejandra curtseyed and left the room without another word. The door banged shut. Little Grandma walked quickly to where Isabel was standing.

"What is the matter Isabel?" Little Grandma asked with concern. "Are you feeling ill? Here…let me take your cloak." Isabel allowed Pilar to take the cloak. She was then exposed with one hand holding up Priscilla's ripped gown. "Oh my God," Pilar exclaimed! "That is your mother's prized possession!" Isabel opened her mouth to reply, but found that she couldn't even speak. She felt a tear sliding down her cheek. "Isabel?" Pilar asked as she put a hand on the girl's shoulder. "What is it mija? No.., do not tell me that the King has hurt you."

"Oh my Little Grandma," Isabel sobbed, but she could not continue. Pilar put her arms around the heiress and Isabel cried into her shoulder.

"There, there child," Little Grandma soothed. "You are safe now." Pilar let Isabel cry. When they drew apart, Little Grandma looked furious. "Your father will destroy him!" she fumed.

"No!" Isabel stopped her. "I did not let him. He wanted to but...I still have my virtue."

"Oh thank Heaven," Pilar breathed. "What did happen?" Isabel told her everything. The more she told the angrier Little Grandma became.

"I believed him," Isabel finished her story. "He seemed like a good man and my father likes him."

"Your father will kill him now!" Pilar said vehemently.

"You mustn't tell him," Isabel pleaded.

"Why not?"

"It would start a war," Isabel cried. "I would die if my father were to be killed! Please Little Grandma..."

"Isabel," Pilar began harshly, but then her face softened. "You swear that he did not..."

"I swear it!" Isabel insisted.

"Alright my child," Pilar sighed. "For you I will say nothing."

"Thank you," Isabel said with relief.

"Let me see the dress," the elder woman said. She looked critically at the damage. "It could be worse," she concluded.

"How do you mean?" Isabel asked.

"It's ripped at the seam," Pilar explained. "I should be able to fix it. The maker of this dress used white thread. That should be easy to find."

"Oh I am so relieved," Isabel sighed.

"I think you should be," Pilar said with a hopeful smile. "Stay here while I steal something to wear from your chamber."

"I will," Isabel replied. She waited while Little Grandma left the room. Pilar returned shortly with Isabel's lavender gown. She helped Isabel out of the damaged gown and into the other. She redid the braids in the girl's hair and put her makeup back in order.

"Go and settle yourself in your room," Pilar suggested. "You cannot maintain the charade if you miss the evening meal though. I will do my best with Lady Priscilla's dress. Do not worry yourself."

"I will not," Isabel promised, but she did not sound sure of her answer. She left the servants' quarters and went back to her own bed chamber. When Isabel opened the door, she realized that relaxation was not going to be part of the plan. Catherine waited for her on the bed.

"Look who it is," Catherine said resentfully.

"He's all yours cousin," Isabel declared.

"What?"

"I was cross with you before because of what you said about my father," Isabel said, "but I truly have no desire to leave Montenegro."

"But the King," Catherine protested, "he only has eyes for you now and…"

"I can assure you that this is no longer the case," Isabel interrupted her.

"Truly," Catherine asked with disbelief.

"See for yourself," Isabel said with a sigh. "I wish to be alone now."

"I told you though, did I not?" Catherine said smugly. She gave Isabel a crooked grin as she waltzed toward the door. Isabel sat down in one of the two cushioned chairs by the window. She did not answer Catherine's question. There was no use in doing so. She could have warned her that Alfonso was a rogue, but Catherine would never have listened. Also, Isabel suspected that her cousin had already squandered the gift that can only be given once.

Isabel planned to relax in her bed for a spell until she realized how impossible that would be. Her mother would be along any minute and what would she tell her? Priscilla was so in love with the idea of Isabel being queen. Would her mother believe her about Alfonso's crude behavior? Isabel suspected not.

The Heiress of Montenegro left the bedroom and stole away to the hidden pond. Only David might bother her at the gazebo. He would not be entirely unwelcome. Unfortunately, David never came. Isabel spent the afternoon watching the geese floating lazily on the surface of the water.

When she finally made her way back, she saw a tall figure stalking toward her from the direction of the house. It could only be her father. They met half way between the Summer Cottage and the tree line. She could tell by the stony look in his eyes and the set of his brow that he was angry. "Isabel!" he barked as they came together. "What are you doing out here?"

"I..," she stammered, "I needed to be alone."

"Well you are definitely that!" Rafael retorted. "His majesty has departed for Zaragoza. He said that he no longer feels welcome." Lord Montenegro clenched and unclenched his fists. "Your mother and I have done everything possible to make him feel welcome, but you…"

"It was no fault of mine," Isabel protested.

"Of course not," her father said sarcastically. "It never is. The two of you go away and everything is fine. Upon your return, the King acts as if he has been spat upon!"

"Let me explain Papa!" Isabel pleaded.

"Explain it to your mother!" Rafael snarled. "I am too angry to listen to your excuses." The look on her father's face brooked no argument. "Get you back inside!" Isabel led the way and her father came behind her. When she turned up the stairway, Rafael continued on toward the sitting room.

Isabel walked with light steps toward her parents' bedroom. She expected every creak of the wood below her to summon an angry Priscilla out into the hallway. She barely knocked on the door, hoping her mother would not hear. "Come in," Priscilla said from the other side of the door. Isabel entered. Her mother was reclining on a divan when Isabel came in. Priscilla's eyes glared angrily up at her daughter. "Sit down Isabel," Priscilla said icily.

"I should prefer…" Isabel began.

"Sit down Isabel!" Priscilla interrupted sharply. Her mother closed her eyes and her lips moved as if speaking. No sound issued forth, however. Isabel sat down on the bed, opposite her mother. Finally, Priscilla opened her eyes and spoke. "Are you feeling well, Isabel?"

"I am in perfect health," Isabel answered nervously.

"Then you must have lost your wits," Priscilla said with a forced smile.

"You do not understand."

"I understand," Priscilla shouted. "There is no man on this earth good enough for my child!"

"But…"

"But nothing," Priscilla screamed. "I have been very patient with you where I see that I should not have. If you were a hideous girl than I could pity you. I could forgive you. I could pray every night that God would bless you with beauty as you grow older. This is not the problem with you though, is it? You have had many suitors…many worthy suitors!"

"They have nothing for me," Isabel shot back.

"Grow up," Priscilla snapped. "Marrying for love is the stuff of stories. No one marries for love in real life."

"Except that you did," Isabel argued.

"My marriage was arranged," Priscilla corrected her. "I came to love your father only after years of being together."

"You told me that you were smitten by him from the start," Isabel replied.

"Do not quarrel with me Isabel," Priscilla warned.

"I am not quarreling."

"Even the King of Aragon is not good enough," Priscilla asked? Her eyes burned. "Have you not noticed that you are an only child? You have been alive some fifteen years. In all this time I have been unable to bear another. Soon I will be incapable of it. The future of Montenegro lies with you Isabel. Do you not understand?"

"He is no good mama," Isabel cried!

"Who is then," Priscilla retorted? "If God himself sought your hand you would reject him as well!"

"I do not need a man," Isabel shouted. "I can rule Montenegro by myself!"

"Oh is that it?" Priscilla asked. "You are such a foolish child."

"Alfonso's mother had no difficulty," Isabel shot back.

"Petronilla's blood goes back to the first conquest of Aragon and beyond. Yours ends at your father," Priscilla explained.

"Your blood is old too," Isabel argued. "Does that count for nothing?"

"Nothing," Priscilla said. "When I married your father, I became Lady Montenegro. Your father has become landed nobility only through his service in war, but common folk will not be ruled by one as common as they. His prestige will die with him if a son is not born. Therefore, you must marry and marry well before that day comes. My womb has dried up Isabel. It must be your son that carries our name! You mark my words," she said with emotion creeping into her voice, "the King will not leave us to rule Montenegro. You will destroy us with your stubbornness! I am a lady. I cannot be a peasant Isabel. Perhaps you would enjoy seeing your mother as a servant. Can you see me slaughtering chickens?" Priscilla's face pinched up as she began to weep. "All their filthy blood...I should sooner die!"

"I am so sorry," Isabel said as she reached toward her mother.

"No," Priscilla said as she quickly regained her composure, "touch me not."

"But mother," Isabel implored. "He wanted...he wanted too..."

"To what Isabel," Priscilla asked as she dried her eyes, "he wanted to what?"

"He wanted to deflower me as he has no doubt done to Catherine!" Isabel sobbed. "I am so sorry mother. I do not want you to be a servant. I just…I just couldn't. I liked him at first." Isabel's chest hitched as she continued. "We had the most beautiful day. I should have known when I saw that he had brought wine. No, no…I should have let him. He is the King and I…"

"Priscilla wrapped Isabel in her arms. There were tears in her mother's eyes too. "Hush child," Priscilla soothed. Isabel cried into her mother's bosom. "You did right Isabel. I am sorry for doubting you. I should be proud of you this day."

"Thank you mama," Isabel said as her tears began to subside. She looked up at her mother then. "But what will you tell Father?"

"I shall handle your father," Priscilla replied. "I just have to find a way to tell him that will not result in him doing something rash."

"I should never forgive myself if he should go off to die because of me," Isabel said fearfully.

"Do not worry for that," Priscilla said comfortingly. "I am rather fond of him as well. I will not let him run off waving a sword about in the air." Her mother smiled.

"That is why I love you mama," Isabel said as she hugged Priscilla tight. "You are so wise."

"It will be well," Priscilla said, "but never let it cross your lips again. Catherine would be ruined. I pray that she is not with child already."

"I shall never…" Isabel began.

"Shhh," Priscilla hushed her daughter with one finger held to her lips. "I know that you will not. Now go back to your room. I shall send Pilar up with food. I need time to contemplate what I will say to your father. Until then, it must appear that you are being punished. You are excused Isabel." Isabel stood up and curtseyed low before her mother.

"I love you," Isabel said sincerely.

"Yes and of course I love you as well," Priscilla said quietly. Then she screamed at the top of her lungs, "Go to your room you wicked child!" Isabel fled instinctively at the sound of her mother's anger. She ran up to her bedroom and shut the door hard.

The remainder of the day Isabel spent in her bed chamber. Catherine did not join her until much later in the evening. Her cousin was in high spirits and kept looking at Isabel to detect some sign of emotion. Isabel simply rolled over so that her back was facing her cousin. "Good night cousin," Catherine said sarcastically.

"Good night," Isabel replied. This seemed to satisfy Catherine's need to gloat and so they both slept. Isabel awoke the next morning with a start. She was breathing rapidly and it took some time to calm herself. She had been having a nightmare, but she thankfully could not recall it. Her parents gave her the silent treatment at the breakfast table. Isabel said her goodbyes to Uncle Jaime and Aunt Imelda. She embraced David. "I shall miss you so," she told him. She even managed a farewell for her older cousin.

Once inside the carriage, Isabel relayed all the sordid details of the picnic to her mother. During this time, Little Grandma and Alejandra were made to ride on top of the carriage with the driver. Together, mother and daughter concocted the story they would tell Lord Montenegro. The glossed over version was that the King had tried to kiss Isabel but she had not felt ready for it. Rafael was not completely happy with this excuse. He suspected that his daughter had kissed other suitors. He was displeased that she had left King Alfonso on such a bitter note, but there was little he could say to rebuke his daughter. Chastity and purity were both desirable traits for a young woman. Isabel was well within the bounds of being a good Christian.

Master Eubasio did not look at all pleased to see them returning early. There was something in the Master of Servants' eyes that Isabel could almost call suspicion. Her father must have noticed it also for he inquired after the man's health. Eubasio said something about the keep not being yet clean to his standards. Rafael assured the old man that everything would be fine and so Isabel gave it little more thought.

CHAPTER VI

As the weeks wore on, Isabel's life fell back into its normal routine. Most mornings she spent in the yard. While she still had affection for her pony, Isabel had progressed to riding horses. In the afternoons, she might learn courtly etiquette from her mother, dance from Alejandra, or simply relax. She would often practice her singing, and even wrote a few songs of her own. Most nights after the evening meal, Isabel would read the Bible to her father. In so doing, her command of Latin was growing stronger by the day.

Isabel's bedroom was located on the third floor of the keep as were all such rooms. There were no windows on the first floor and the second only had slits for arrows. She was sitting on a cushioned bench that had been crafted as part of the alcove below the large window of her room. The heavy curtains were drawn back on gold hued ropes. The drapes were made of the same royal blue material as the cushions on the bench. The curtains of Isabel's canopy bed and the comforter on top of it were made of a similar fabric. The curtains over the bed and window had thinner curtains underneath. These were of translucent chiffon and were colored like the blue of the sky.

The darker curtains of the canopy were drawn up around the bed posts. The lighter curtains gently rippled in the cool breeze. The wind would cause them to open briefly as they moved back and forth. The under-curtains of the window bowed inward like sails, but it was more the lightness of the chiffon than the strength of the wind that moved them.

Isabel sat in a loose white gown secured by a simple leather cord below her bosom. Her back was propped against the alcove by the window and her feet were up on the cushions of the bench. Her long black hair hung down over her shoulders and back. She had been reading to herself from her father's Biblia Sacra. The bible sat by her on the bench. Isabel had her eyes closed and she was enjoying the feel of the sunlight and the breeze coming in off the river.

A soldier on the battlements over the gates of the keep started yelling down to someone below. Isabel could not make out what either of them said. The soldier looked down over his shoulder to yell at one of the servants in the courtyard. This time the heiress could hear them both perfectly. "You," the guard shouted at a young man below, "go and tell his lordship that Count Ramon Berenguer of Provence has come up from Zaragoza!"

"Yes sir!" the voice of the servant came up faintly from below. The young man hurried inside and returned almost immediately. "Lower the gate," he shouted as he came out of the main doors of the keep. He repeated Lord Montenegro's orders several times over even though the soldiers were already complying.

The Count's carriage rumbled over the drawbridge and through the gate. The moat in Montenegro was a deep gorge spanned by a bridge that came up from the path below. Black River fell down from the mountain on the western side of the keep. A pulley system ran from the western tower down to the river before it plunged into the ravine.

The carriage was surrounded by a contingent of soldiers. Once the gate was closed, the soldiers broke off and formed ranks along one side of it. The ranks were facing the door of the carriage and the soldiers saluted as Count Berenguer stepped out. These same soldiers saluted once more when Lord Montenegro came out to greet their master. They knew Rafael from the stories told by the eldest of them.

Count Berenguer clasped hands with Lord Montenegro and the two of them entered the keep side by side. The soldiers followed shortly thereafter. Isabel frowned, why would the younger Berenguer come all the way to Montenegro? She suspected that something evil was brewing and she prayed that it was not a war. Her father trained his men on every day other than the Sabbath. Isabel had never imagined that these exercises might one day become real.

Isabel remained in her room where she fretted over what might be happening below until dinner. She could have come down stairs if she had wanted too, but Isabel did not want to see anyone from the Crown of Aragon. Nevertheless, she worried herself sick wondering why they had come.

Over much protest, Little Grandma redressed Isabel in the lavender gown and tied up her hair. Much like her father, Isabel's fears usually translated into anger. So it was that she was in quite a foul disposition when she came down to the dining hall. Her parents looked in very high spirits when she entered. She curtseyed toward them and then to the Count of Provence. Ramon stood and bowed slightly in return. "My lady Isabel," he said respectfully.

"Your grace," she acknowledged. Isabel then took her place beside her mother at the table. There were larger tables in the dining hall reserved for the servants and soldiers, but this one was reserved for the nobility. Master Eubasio, who was standing close by, clapped his hands and the servants promptly brought out a meal for them all. Rafael had spared nothing and soon the tables were heavy with food. The Count exchanged pleasantries and small talk with Isabel's parents but there was little that was actually said. Rafael and Priscilla kept staring at Isabel as if to see what she might do or say. The Count seemed to be looking at her also. It was all quite uncomfortable. Isabel was wondering if they were all expecting her to grow feathers or something.

When she had finished eating, Isabel politely interrupted her father's conversation. "I beg your pardon father," she said, "but might I be excused?" Rafael frowned. Before he could reply, Priscilla answered for him.

"The Count has come all the way from Zaragoza my dear," Priscilla said. Her eyes made it very clear that she meant for her daughter to stay.

"It will only be for a moment," Isabel said. Priscilla smiled approval at her daughter for correcting the social blunder.

"Go right ahead my daughter," Lord Montenegro said.

"Thank you," Isabel replied. She rose from the table and went up to her room. She stared out into the darkness and tried to make sense of things. Her thoughts were interrupted by a knock at the door.

"Isabel," Pilar's voice came to her from the other side of the wood.

"Yes?"

"Shall I call for a servant to remove you're…um…"

"I am not doing that," Isabel called back, casting a glance at the empty chamber pot. Little Grandma opened the door and entered Isabel's bedroom.

"What are you doing up here child?" Little Grandma asked.

"I needed some air," Isabel said weakly.

"You cannot stay up here mija," Pilar insisted. "The Count of Provence has come all this way just to see you!"

"What? I thought he came to see father. Surely you cannot be serious?"

"He came to see you. I swear it," Pilar said as she made the sign of the cross to lend credence to her words.

"Why would he come here?" Isabel asked crossly. "I do not wish to see him! Why me?"

"I do not know," Little Grandma replied, "but you had best take yourself down before your mother comes looking for you!"

"I suppose you are right," Isabel sighed. She turned around and left Pilar to follow behind as she exited the bed chamber. She felt much more conscious of herself knowing the real purpose of the Count's visit. She made an effort to smile and give pleasantries as she re-entered the room and took her seat.

For the remainder of the evening, Isabel said little and heard less. How could her parents do this to her? She had told her mother everything. Perhaps it was her father's doing. Isabel wished that she had told him everything as well. These were selfish thoughts but she could do little to stop their coming. "Isabel," the Count's voice broke through her thoughts.

"Pardon me your grace," Isabel blushed. "I could scarcely hear you over the ugh..."

"I should like to walk with you in the courtyard tomorrow if it should please you."

"Nothing would please me more," Isabel lied. She did not raise her eyes to look at the man as she spoke. Some would see this as a sign of respect, but it was really because lying did not come naturally to the young heiress. "When shall I await his majesty?"

"Let us go following the morning meal," he decided. "Then neither of us shall have to wait." Isabel rose and curtseyed toward Alfonso's brother with her eyes still lowered.

"If your grace would please excuse my absence, I am in need of rest," Isabel requested.

"I shall see you on the morrow," the Count smiled as he spoke. Isabel returned his smile out of decorum, curtseyed once more, and then left the dining hall. Anger, confusion, and even some guilt roiled within her from the memory of her short lived courtship with King Alfonso. Did Ramon intend to succeed where his elder brother had failed? Like any good Catholic girl, Isabel had vowed to maintain her chastity. That gift would only be given to her husband. She was fuming by the time she pushed open the doors to her room.

Little Grandma was in front of Isabel's wardrobe which was wide open. She was going through the various ensembles. Isabel had no doubt that the older woman was pre-selecting her attire for the next day. "Leave me be," the heiress said unhappily.

"Why the long face?" Pilar asked.

"You should know already!" Isabel replied crossly. She began to let her hair down as Little Grandma walked over to her.

"You cannot be so unpleasant all the time," Pilar began. "Your mother…"

"Leave me be!" Isabel snapped. "That will be all."

"That will be all?" Pilar asked with her own ire rising. "You listen to me child!" Isabel glared at the older woman and spoke before she could continue.

"You will leave now," Isabel commanded.

"I have raised you from a baby," Little Grandma said with indignation.

"A servant must do as she is bid," Isabel said quietly. "Now…that will be all." She looked away from Pilar then and tried to concentrate on her hair. There was awkward silence that hung in the air between them for some time.

"As my lady wishes," Pilar finally said in a very small voice that was thick with emotion. Isabel did not respond, but waited for Little Grandma to leave. She felt some remorse for speaking to the old woman so, but she could not abide her company just then. If she allowed Little Grandma to keep lecturing her about the Count, only God knew what horrible things might come out of Isabel's mouth. Had everyone gone mad? Of anyone, Isabel would have expected Little Grandma to understand.

Sleep did not come easily that night. Isabel's emotions were in an uproar. A wind had risen from the south and Isabel smelled rain. She closed the wooden shutters against the night. She pulled the ropes and let down the heavy curtains as well. The rain came. The staccato of water droplets hitting the top of the keep eventually drowned out Isabel's thoughts. The heiress of Montenegro drifted at last into unconsciousness.

It was a somber twosome that stood in front of Isabel's wardrobe the next morning. Gone was Little

Grandma's usual chatter. When she did speak, it was as if they had never known each other. "I believe this should be suitable," Pilar said as she held up a light green gown.

"That will do," Isabel agreed. Little Grandma helped her step into the dress and tied up the strings in the back. She worked in silence braiding Isabel's hair. "I apologize for my behavior last night," Isabel finally said.

"It was I who overstepped," Little Grandma replied flatly. "You have nothing to apologize for my lady." The silence continued after that. Pilar's feelings were hurt and Isabel was not prone to begging for forgiveness. When the preparations were complete, Isabel walked from the room without a backward glance. She went down to the private dining room instead of the main hall. There was no privacy to be had, however. Her parents were already seated and Count Berenguer came shortly after.

"Did it rain last night," the Count asked?

"It did," Rafael replied.

"I thought so," the Count answered. Isabel stopped paying attention to the conversation. It was without substance. Nevertheless, she hoped it would last a long time. She was dreading the coming walk in the courtyard. Her mother looked just as enchanted with this Berenguer as she had the other. It was all quite sickening.

Inevitably, the morning meal ended and the Count walked over to where Isabel was seated. She rose before he could get close and curtseyed as was proper. "Are you ready, your grace?" she asked. The question was just as pointless as the one he had asked about the rain.

"I am," Count Berenguer said eagerly. He offered his arm which Isabel reluctantly took. She smiled and inclined her head toward her parents. Rafael nodded and Priscilla positively beamed at her. The two of them walked out into the courtyard. It was not as grand as the one in Zaragoza. It consisted of a grey cobblestone walk around a rectangular yard that Lord Montenegro used to train his soldiers in close combat. There was no training today. It was not the

Sabbath so Isabel concluded that her father had canceled it because of her.

The guards on the battlements and the servants that occasionally appeared did their best to appear nonchalant. Isabel knew they were being watched. This caused her some discomfort at first until she realized that it afforded her more safety. "I suppose you are wondering why I have come," Ramon began.

"I suppose," Isabel replied defensively.

"You must forgive me," the Count said, "but ever since I laid eyes on you...standing on the steps of the palace; I have known that you are the one whom I have tried for so long to find." Isabel looked away so that Count Berenguer would not see her rolling her eyes. She looked back with her face carefully composed.

"Surely there are more qualities than beauty that need be present in the one you speak of," Isabel told him. "I am certainly not she."

"Your song broke my heart," Ramon said passionately.

"Your brother said the same thing," Isabel replied with a forced laugh.

""I am not my brother," Ramon answered. Isabel made no response. They walked in silence until he spoke again. "You do not understand Lady Isabel," he said. "Your face haunts my dreams. I am smitten...I love you!" Isabel frowned and walked on. "It is the truth," Ramon insisted. "You are all I think of from day to night!"

"Oh do stop it," Isabel scoffed as she extricated herself from the Count's arm.

"How can I?"

"Oh foolish love," Isabel replied. "I just hope your grace lies to himself and not to me."

"My lady I lay my heart at your feet," Ramon said earnestly.

"I am not a game to be played," Isabel snapped at him. "Do you think to succeed where your brother failed? I took my vows for myself and for God, not just for my father!"

"My intentions are not so base," Ramon said quietly.

"I should really thank your brother the King for making me wiser."

"My brother is a fool," Ramon frowned.

"Quiet," Isabel hissed. "Someone will hear you!"

"I do not care!" Ramon exclaimed.

"You will when they put your head on the block!" she whispered. This sobered the man's declarations and they walked quietly for a few more minutes together. "This is madness," Isabel said finally. "Let us not waste any more time with these games. I am not a girl to be tricked and I'm sure that your grace has a host of others to choose from..."

"Isabel," Ramon interrupted her, "you have a right to be wary, but will you not give me a chance? I promise to go nowhere with you privately."

"I shall never drink wine or listen to fools again," Isabel said icily.

"I shall never offer wine," Ramon promised. Isabel knit her brow in consternation. The man was very convincing, but so had his brother been. "Let me show you that I am a man of honor," Ramon pleaded.

"I will not be made a fool of," Isabel said emphatically.

"If you ask me to leave, then I shall do so," Ramon sighed, "but I pray that you do not ask." Isabel raised an eyebrow in disbelief. "Meet with me once more," the Count blurted out.

"Again," Isabel asked?

"Yes, tomorrow... Walk with me here tomorrow."

"And if I refuse?"

"If you refuse..," Ramon struggled for the words. "If you refuse, than sit by your mother at breakfast. If you say yes, than sit by Lord Montenegro. If I find you by Lady Priscilla, I will know that I must return home. I will not pressure you by asking anything in the presence of your father."

"I shall think on it," Isabel said at last. Ramon's face lit up. "What is it?" Isabel asked, trying not to smile herself.

"My lady did not say no," Ramon replied with a smile.

"I said I shall think on it," she reiterated.

"Than I shall await the morning and your decision," the Count said happily. He bowed with a flourish. Isabel curtseyed in return and the Count went back into the Keep. There was a spring in his step. Isabel watched him go. She wondered if the man were truly sincere.

"I do not even desire a husband," she told herself. The rest of the day passed like so many others, but not entirely. Count Berenguer would scarcely take his eyes off Isabel at meal times. She also thought she saw him in one of the upper windows when she was riding one of the larger brown mares in the yard.

Isabel gave her decision a great deal of thought. She kept herself up for some time after blowing out the candles by her bed. Eventually she slept. She had decided not to meet with the Count again.

She came to breakfast with her mind made up. Seeing Ramon sitting at the private dining table changed everything. The Count of Provence looked positively fearful. His eyes were filled with an anxiety that bordered on desperation when she approached the table. Isabel paused…and then sat next to her father.

When Ramon smiled, Isabel could see the relief in his eyes and then the unabashed joy. She could not stop herself from smiling back at him. It was a much more willing Isabel that took the arm of Ramon Berenguer that morning. "I am so pleased," Ramon told her when they were back in the courtyard.

"Why," Isabel asked?

"Here we are," he replied.

"Yes," she agreed. She looked away so that the man might not see her grinning. They walked a few steps more and then Isabel spoke. "Why did you not speak to me in Zaragoza?"

"Alfonso had already declared his interest to me. What could I do?"

"You could have spoken ill of me to dissuade him."

"Not convincingly," he chuckled.

"It would not have hurt," she smiled.

"No, I suppose not," Ramon replied. Isabel closed her eyes and lifted her face into the sun. It was warm and tingled on the skin of her face.

"Is it difficult," Isabel asked, "to live in the palace I mean?"

"I generally do not stay there if I can help it," he answered.

"Where then?"

"When Alfonso was crowned King of Aragon, he named me Count of Provence."

"Do you like it there in Provence?"

"The people are hard working and the land is fertile. I have little to complain over, but... it would be much more pleasant if I had someone to share it with." Isabel smiled but said nothing. "How is it for you here in Montenegro," he asked?

"I love Montenegro," Isabel said honestly. "I never wish to leave this place."

"How will you marry if you never leave?"

"I am not certain that I want to marry," she replied.

"Then what," he asked incredulously?

"I suspect your mother had the right idea in ruling Aragon as Queen."

"My mother also grew old quickly."

"Was she made happier with your father?"

"I do not know," Ramon admitted. "I wasn't around before to compare the difference. How fare your parents?"

"They are very much in love," Isabel told him. "My father does not defile himself by taking mistresses as I have heard many men of power are wont to do."

"The rumors are unfortunately true," Ramon sighed.

"Yet another reason to avoid marriage," Isabel decided out loud. "I cannot abide a liar. I would sooner run away to live in squalor than live with such a man."

"Perish the thought," Ramon said.

"What is it you are doing here," Isabel asked pointedly?

"I have already told you," Ramon answered.

"A count with old blood must join in marriage with a lady of old blood. There are alliances to seal and reputations to uphold. Here in Montenegro, we are nobles only by virtue of my father's service. Surely you must know this."

"I have the utmost respect for your father," Ramon said. "Aragon needs such men to survive. I would be proud to have such qualities passed down to my son."

"What qualities are you speaking of?"

"Strength, honor, bravery, perseverance, loyalty…"

"Have you none of these qualities yourself," Isabel asked. Ramon sighed and put a hand to his head. "Forgive my rudeness your grace," Isabel implored him. "I only meant…"

"I should like to think I have these qualities," Ramon said sincerely, "but I have never had my mettle tested in war."

"You needn't run off and risk your life to prove yourself brave," Isabel told him.

"If my brother continues his operations in Italy, than I will not have to worry about it," Ramon said unhappily.

"What do you mean?"

"We cannot both go to war at once," Ramon explained. "Neither of us has any sons."

"I see," Isabel said. "Are there daughters?"

"Alfonso has one, but the mother died in travail. I have not yet been married," Ramon replied.

"Why not? I should think Aragon would be eager to secure its lineage."

"I have yet to find a woman acceptable. With Alfonso married, the pressure to wed was removed for some time."

"And now things are different," she asked him?

"Yes, but that is only a small part of why I am here. As I said, I have never found a woman possessing the right qualities."

"Are you so discerning?" Isabel asked.

"The women I have met thus far were sorely lacking. It is not all their fault to be sure. They have been so trained to deference that they can scarcely think for themselves. I speak to them and there is no substance beneath. They are surely beautiful."

"Is that not enough?"

"No," Ramon said emphatically. "Beauty fades with age. Perhaps that is why so many noblemen take mistresses."

"Why?"

"A pretty fool grows into an old and wrinkled fool. What is there to entice a man after that?"

"Another woman," Isabel answered.

"Precisely," Ramon replied, "that is why I must wed a woman of substance; intelligent as well as charming. Beauty is not so important in the grand scheme of things."

"How flattering," Isabel replied sarcastically.

"Do not misunderstand me Lady Isabel," Ramon said quickly. "Your beauty is beyond compare. That is the reason my brother pursued you. For me, it is merely a blessing that you should also be lovely to look upon."

"Now you flatter me indeed," Isabel blushed.

"I only speak the truth," he replied. They walked arm in arm and whiled away the hours until the sun was high in the sky. Isabel would have stayed longer, but Ramon insisted that she would become faint from the heat. Isabel allowed herself to be coddled.

They met again that afternoon in the stables and rode together in the yard. As the Count talked, Isabel noticed how critical he was of himself. She found his honesty a refreshing change from the boasting that was so common in other men. They sat side by side at dinner that evening and tarried long after the meal was over.

Duty required the Count to return to Zaragoza in the morning, but he promised to return as soon as he was able, and hopefully within the week. He kissed Isabel's hand before his departure and she watched his carriage from the battlements of Montenegro.

✝   ✝   ✝

So it went for the next year. Ramon would call on Isabel once each month. There were many occasions when he came twice in that length of time. The more they were in each other's company, the longer it seemed to Isabel until their next meeting. Sometimes she would mope around for weeks until his return, but it was not entirely unpleasant. She had never felt that she needed a man beyond her father, nor had she ever felt so needed in return. It was therefore a sweet melancholy that befell her between visits.

That year seemed to go on forever, except for the days that Isabel and Ramon spent together. Those would pass in what seemed like an instant. Eventually, summer gave way to fall and then the winter set in. Ramon's visits became less frequent because of the cold weather.

On one cold December evening, a coach arrived from Provence accompanied by a contingent of soldiers. Isabel watched it enter the courtyard from her bedroom window. She recognized the crest as soon as it became illuminated by torchlight. She rushed down the stairs and into the entry hall. Her anxiousness gave way to disappointment when she realized that Ramon was not among the men in the carriage.

Isabel did not notice the approach of Eubasio until she heard his voice behind her. "Your gentleman sends only his carriage young mistress," he said. There was something in the man's tone that Isabel did not care for.

"I am certain there is a good explanation Eubasio. You may retire. I have no need of you," she said coolly.

"Of course," Eubasio answered. He was quite good about minding his tongue. The Master of Servants disappeared up the stairway. Isabel guessed that he would inform her father within the minute. She opened the main doors and waited as the men from the carriage approached. Although she did not know their names, Isabel recognized some of the soldiers as members of the Count's personal guard. They were dressed heavily but their faces were red from the harsh cold of the Pyrenees winter. One of the men stepped forward and bowed low before Isabel. He had long black hair and not a hint of a beard on his face.

"Please rise," Isabel said uncomfortably. "She was not accustomed to such gestures. One would have thought she were a queen by the way the man had knelt before her.

"My lady I am Captain Quintero of Count Berenguer's personal guard. He asked me to deliver this to you personally." The soldier rose up and handed her a sealed parchment with the symbol of Berenguer pressed into the wax. "Break the seal," she told him. The captain drew out a small dagger and carefully obeyed her command.

"My dearest Isabel," he began.

"No, no," she admonished him. "I only meant for you to open it."

"I beg my lady's pardon," Quintero replied as he stepped back away from her.

"All is well," she assured him. Isabel opened the letter and began to read…

My dearest Isabel…,

I have sent my most trusted men to bring you with all haste to Zaragoza. I pray that you will join me for the coming feast of Saint Nicholas. I have sent my own servants to attend you at your family's cottage. Please tell your esteemed father of my request. With his permission, my men will ensure your comfort and safety for the journey.

Ramon Berenguer, Count of Provence.

Isabel sighed with delight and hugged the letter to her breast. She turned around to find her father. Rafael had just entered the room and Eubasio was close behind him. "Isabel," Rafael said suspiciously, "what goes on here?" His eyes lingered accusingly on Ramon's guardsmen.

"The Count of Provence requests that I join him for the Feast of Saint Nicholas," she replied innocently.

"Let me see the letter," he demanded as he strode toward her. He grabbed it from her hand and unfolded it quickly. The sound of the parchment was audible in the silence of the entry hall. Rafael frowned as he read the letter. When finished, Lord Montenegro glared down at his daughter. "Well, he said when Isabel did not speak up. "Will you go to Zaragoza?"

"Can I?" Isabel asked hopefully.

"Should you," her father asked with one eyebrow raised.

"My lord," Eubasio interjected, "I must advise against it."

"I am speaking with my daughter," Rafael said. Eubasio pursed his lips and faded back behind the larger man.

"I believe that I should go," Isabel replied.

"Why," her father asked?

"Because I believe that Count Berenguer is an honorable man with only the purest of intentions," Isabel answered proudly.

"My lord," Eubasio interrupted.

"Enough," Lord Montenegro said over his shoulder. "Leave us."

"As you command," Eubasio replied. He bowed slightly at the waist and left the room. Rafael looked back down at Isabel.

"Oh father, I must go," Isabel cried!

"Go then," he told her. "I know that your loyalty to me is only superseded by your loyalty to God above. If there is anyone in this world in whom I trust…it is you." Rafael smiled. "Go mija."

"Thank you Papa," Isabel said with emotion. "That was the most beautiful thing you have ever said to me!"

"Then do not forget it," her father replied. "Prepare your things while I speak with your mother."

"I go," she nearly shouted as she hurried up the stairs.

"You men come and warm yourselves at the fire," she heard her father say as she ran up to her room. Isabel sang to herself as she packed one of her trunks with clothing from the armoire. She was still singing when Pilar came into her bed chamber.

"My lord, your father, tells me you are off to Zaragoza," Little Grandma said.

"It is the truth," Isabel gushed! "I am meeting Ramon at the Summer Cottage!"

"Lady Priscilla insists that I accompany you," Little Grandma said sternly. "We are to leave at first light." She looked with apprehension at the young heiress as she waited for a reply.

"Wonderful!" Isabel said happily. "That is a splendid idea!"

"You...want me to come," Pilar asked?

"Of course," Isabel replied. "Do you not want to?"

"No...I mean yes," Little Grandma struggled. "It is just that I thought...I would love to go to Zaragoza with you!"

"No time to waste," Isabel sang out happily as she trailed one of her scarves across the older woman on its way to her trunk. Pilar smiled and packed what little she owned for the journey. She then helped Isabel finish with the rest of her things.

"We have never been to Zaragoza in the winter," Little Grandma remarked excitedly as they worked. "I have heard that the whole city will be strung with wreaths and garlands for Christmas and the Feast of Saint Nicholas. A great tree will be cut and brought to the Plaza del Seo. I can hardly wait to see how they decorate it!"

"I know it will be gorgeous," Isabel said as she folded her black and maroon gown with the embroidered crest. A shadow moved out on the battlements at the edge of Isabel's vision. She turned and looked out.

The figure wore a dark hooded cloak against the cold and carried a long bow in one hand. There was no quiver on his back, but only a single arrow in his right hand. The cloaked man looked furtively down into the courtyard. When he was satisfied that no one was watching, the man knocked the arrow and loosed it high into the night sky. The cloaked man watched the arrow fly for several seconds before hurrying back down the stairs that led up from the courtyard.

Little Grandma," Isabel said sharply! "Who is that man?" Little Grandma hurried over to the window.

"I cannot see for the hood," Pilar answered.

"Nor I," Isabel said with uncertainty. As it so happened, the man lowered his hood as he traversed the courtyard.

"What is the matter?" Pilar asked.

"I do not know," Isabel frowned. As the man came into the torchlight, the two of them could easily see his face and the bracers marking his station. The long bow was no longer in his hand.

"It is Master Eubasio," Pilar whispered.

"What is he doing," Isabel muttered? "Find out what he is doing," she told Little Grandma.

"He is the Master of Servants," Little Grandma protested. "He will not tell me!"

"Then I shall ask him myself!"

"No child," Little Grandma said. "I am sure he knows what he is doing. I am sure that it is nothing mija." Isabel was not convinced. She stalked down the stairs and met up with Eubasio in the entry hall. He was just preparing to go down the west hall toward the servant's quarters when Isabel called out after him.

"Eubasio," she said loudly. The Master of Servants paused in the archway. He slowly turned around and faced her. There was irritation in his countenance but his voice was cordial.

"Lady Isabel?" he said questioningly.

"What are you doing?" she demanded.

"It is late," he replied smoothly. "I was about to retire."

"No," Isabel said. "What are you doing skulking about on the battlements? I saw you."

"I am sure you saw nothing," Eubasio replied. "Now if you will excuse me..."

"I will not!" Isabel shouted. "Father!" Eubasio grimaced but he did not move from the spot wherein he stood. They could hear Rafael's heavy footsteps as he hurried up from the eastern hallway. He pushed his way past Isabel. A large sword was unsheathed and gripped in his right hand. There were several chips in the blade and it was obvious that it was not merely for show.

"What goes on here?" Lord Montenegro thundered. Eubasio sighed.

"My lord," the Master of Servants began.

"He was sneaking about on the battlements with a bow and arrow," Isabel interrupted. "He shot an arrow down the mountain. He looked down to make sure no one saw him before he did it!"

"Explain," Rafael said darkly as he tightened his grip on the sword handle.

"My lord," Eubasio said in a placating tone. "I have ever served you faithfully. What your daughter saw was nothing more than your humble servant trying to protect the aviary."

"Why does my aviary need protecting," Lord Montenegro asked suspiciously?

"I saw a night owl swooping close by and I feared for the safety of your pigeons. I grabbed the long bow from one of the guardsmen and rushed up onto the battlements!"

"And the owl?"

"I confess my shot did not strike true. The owl escaped into the darkness. I beg my lord's pardon," Eubasio implored him. Rafael relaxed his grip on the sword.

"All is well," Rafael sighed. "He will not escape you again Eubasio."

"I shall leave the hunting to your lordship's archers next time," Eubasio chuckled nervously.

"Well and good," Rafael replied. He turned back toward his daughter. "Isabel," he said with a frown, "Why do you not finish preparing for your journey. Quit jumping at shadows. There is no need for me to charge with sword in hand at my own servants."

"I apologize," Isabel said with embarrassment, "and to you as well Master Eubasio."

"There is no need my lady," Eubasio replied. "With your permission my Lord," he said to her father, "I should like to retire for the evening."

"Of course," Rafael agreed. Isabel returned to her room where Little Grandma was waiting.

"What was it?" the older woman asked.

"It was nothing," Isabel mumbled. They packed the last few things in silence. Isabel bid her Little Grandma goodnight before snuffing out the candles that lit her bed chamber.

CHAPTER VII

Isabel was so excited the next morning that the events of the previous night were easily forgotten. She said her goodbyes to her mother and father and then hurried into Count Berenguer's carriage. Little Grandma joined her shortly thereafter. The servants had packed their things onto the top of the carriage before first light. Ramon's soldiers fanned out their horses around the carriage and they were soon on their way.

Isabel and Little Grandma talked excitedly about the coming festival. They spoke of the courtship, of the possibility of marriage, and all manner of things as the wheels kept turning toward Zaragoza. As the day wore on, Little Grandma dozed off. Isabel soon joined her.

The carriage came to a quick halt which jolted its occupants into wakefulness. "Have we arrived already," Isabel asked? Her voice was heavy with sleep.

"I…suppose," Little Grandma said without much confidence. There was a loud knock on the wooden shutter that covered the window on the right side. Pilar opened it. The captain who had delivered Ramon's message was standing next to it. The rest of the men were still on horseback.

"We are about to have a problem," Quintero said tensely.

"What is it?" Pilar asked with concern.

"Bandits," the man said gravely. "They have gathered across the roadway ahead of us." Isabel leaned her head out of the carriage. In the distance, she could see several horses gathered across the road.

"How can you tell they are bandits," she asked as she squinted into the sun.

"Get your head back inside!" Pilar exclaimed as she yanked the heiress back by the arm.

'Trust me," the man told her. "Keep the windows closed. I have dealt with men like these before."

"But there are only three of them," Isabel protested, "four at most."

"Those that you can see," the Captain replied. "They are counting on the fact that we will stop to see what the matter is. That is when they will strike."

"What will we do?" Isabel asked anxiously.

"We will charge straight through," Quintero explained, "run them down if need be." He sighed as he looked down at the ground. "Close all the windows," he said as he looked back up.

Isabel closed the wooden shutter and drew down the latch. Little Grandma was doing the same thing on the other side of the carriage. There was no battle cry to spur the soldiers into action. The carriage jerked to a start and then the sound of the horses outside was like thunder on the dirt path!

Isabel held tight to the rail next to her seat. Her upper body was pressed up against the wall for support and her feet were braced against the opposite bench. From the motion of the carriage and the sound of the wheels bouncing over rocks, Isabel worried that the whole thing would come to pieces! The rocks would have been inconsequential if not for the breakneck speed of the horses pulling them on.

The young heiress screamed as the tip of an arrow punched through the wall directly in front of her eye! She pushed herself up and tried to switch her grip to the back of the bench. The carriage bounced hard and Isabel ended up on the floor. She could hear the shouts of the bandits and then the first clash of steel sounding outside. More followed. There was a great rending noise and the whinnying of the horses as a tree was felled. The branches scraped loudly on the back of the carriage as it narrowly escaped the trunk of the falling pine.

The men outside were yelling and urging each other to go faster. Isabel could hear arrows whizzing by and impacting the back of the carriage behind her seat. After several minutes of fleeing at full tilt, Isabel could hear the sound of a horn from close by. Seconds later, the attacks of the bandits ceased. The sound of many more hooves surrounded the carriage.

"They are behind us!" Captain Quintero cried.

"To arms, to arms," the voice of another soldier shouted. The thunder of hooves receded north as the reinforcements from Zaragoza gave chase. Berenguer's carriage continued to flee south toward the capital. The driver did not stop until they reached the safety of the Summer Cottage.

Ramon was waiting on the wooden porch when Isabel arrived. She stepped down from the carriage and nearly fell into his arms. The horses were exhausted. Spittle covered their mouths and their breath ran ragged. One of them collapsed. The others whinnied and struggled against their yokes. The servants came and unhitched the horses from the carriage and led them back to the stables.

Isabel was shaken. When Ramon held her close, she began to cry. "There, there," the Count said as he stroked her hair. "You are safe now."

"Will Captain Quintero be alright," Isabel asked hopefully, "and the rest of your men?"

"They will be fine," Ramon reassured her, but he did not sound confident. "The bandits will be outnumbered."

"Why would bandits go about in the dead of winter?" Isabel asked with indignation.

"Maybe they are hungry," Ramon mused. "Come inside the both of you." He looked back into the darkness of the trees with apprehension before ushering Isabel and Pilar inside. He sighed heavily after closing and bolting the front door. "I am so glad that you are safe," he said with relief. "How I have missed you!"

Isabel rushed into his arms once more. "There is nothing without you Ramon," she cried. "Let us never be apart again!"

"Better words were never spoken," Ramon said. His voice was heavy with emotion. He kissed her then. It didn't matter if the servants were watching. After a time, Pilar cleared her throat.

"I shall take my lady's things to her bed chamber," Little Grandma said. She put emphasis on the word 'her'. Ramon and Isabel drew back from each others arms and lips. They both stood in the glow of the other's adoring eyes. "Let my servants tend to the luggage," Ramon said without looking away from Isabel. "You take my Isabel to her bed chamber. I shall have food brought up for both of you."

"Will your grace be joining us?" Pilar asked.

"No," Ramon frowned, "at least not immediately. "I must wait for Quintero to return."

"Oh do be careful my love!" Isabel exclaimed.

"I shall be very safe," Ramon promised. "Go up now. I will surely join you very soon." Isabel nodded. Little Grandma put a hand on her shoulder and gently led her up the stairs. They went in to the bedroom that Isabel normally shared with Catherine.

The servants brought up a lovely dinner but Isabel was worried to distraction. She kept pacing back and forth or looking out the window. She looked down to where the path disappeared into the trees. By day, the canopy was vibrant and beautiful. The darkness muted all colors to grey. The place where the trees grew together over the path appeared quite ominous. The grey leaves of the trees softly rustled around a black hole that looked as if it could lead into a nightmare.

Isabel gasped when the first outline of a horseman seemingly spawned out of the darkness of the tree line. "They are coming," she cried! Little Grandma rose and hurried to the window.

"Come away," Pilar hissed. She grabbed Isabel and began to tug her out of what would certainly be plain view. They were relieved when they heard the shouts of the men outside. There were cries of, "for Aragon" and "God be praised! Isabel could wait no longer. She hurried downstairs to greet the men who had defended her. Captain Quintero and several other officers were gathered with Count Berenguer in the breakfast room. Ramon was clapping them on the back and congratulating them.

Captain Quintero was the first to notice Isabel as she entered through the hallway. "My lady," he said as he bowed toward her.

"Thank you Captain," Isabel said. "We all prayed for your safe return. How fared our enemies?"

"They are routed," the captain replied. "Their band is much smaller now. They will trouble us no more."

"Praise be to God," Isabel said with relief.

"Indeed," Ramon agreed with her. "Captain Quintero is, as always, a credit to his station." He then turned and addressed the captain directly. "There is a meal prepared in the dining room. My servants will bring food out to your noble soldiers. Let them eat before they return to Zaragoza."

"Your personal guard as well?" Quintero asked with confusion.

"Certainly not," Ramon answered. "You will remain here with me. Let us dine."

"My thanks great Count," Quintero said humbly.

"It is the least I can do," Ramon laughed. "You all kept my Isabel safe from harm. I can scarcely describe my gratitude!"

"We are happy to serve," the captain replied as he bowed to Ramon. Ramon nodded his head and let the officers into the dining room. He held a hand back to Isabel. She took it and followed him. They all ate heartily. Ramon whispered something in one of his servant's ears and sent the man scurrying out of the room. The air was filled with laughter and the boasting that is the reward of victorious men. They relived moments from the evening's events as well as conflicts past.

After the soldiers had departed, Ramon led Isabel onto the porch of the Summer Cottage. Their breath was visible in the cold night air. A line of torches was stuck into the ground leading off to the trees that led into Isabel's sanctuary. Each torch was taller than a man and burned brightly in the darkness. Ramon put an arm around Isabel and held her close to his side. They both wore heavy fur cloaks over their clothing. Ramon's cloak was fashioned of grey fox fur. Isabel was wrapped in the white pelts of snowshoe hares.

"What is the meaning of these torches?" Isabel asked as she stared out over them.

"Perhaps we are meant to follow them," Ramon replied innocently.

"A lady knows when you are up to something," Isabel smiled.

"I would be disappointed if you did not," he replied with a wink. The Count led her down the line of torches until they reached the path through the trees. More torches were burning by the secluded pond. Isabel could see their orange flames flickering through the trees.

Ramon's servants had attached a torch to every post that held up the dock. This illuminated the walk to the gazebo and cast orange reflections on the ice below. It rarely snowed in Zaragoza, but the frosty air had created a light powder and a thin sheet of ice that covered most of the pond.

The gazebo had been filled with pure white camellias and tiny branches of red witch hazel. There was just enough room at the far side of the gazebo for the two of them to sit down. "It is ever so beautiful," Isabel sighed as she reached out a finger to touch the petal of one of the camellias.

"Do you like them?" Ramon asked.

"They are gorgeous," she answered. "I love them."

"Will you sit down?" Ramon invited. Isabel settled herself onto the bench. The wealth of flowers in the gazebo filled the air with their sweet cloying fragrance.

"Will you join me?" she asked as she looked up at him.

"Soon," Ramon replied. There was silence for a moment as they stared into each other's eyes. A cold breeze stirred the leaves of the trees. "I have something to ask of you," he began.

"Yes?"

"I thought it could wait until the spring…but after what has happened tonight…"

"Yes," Isabel encouraged. She felt breathless.

"I just realized how fragile life is," Ramon replied. "We are here now. It is uncertain what may befall us tomorrow…but one thing is sure."

"Yes?" Isabel could barely contain herself.

"I love you," he said simply. Isabel could see the truth written in his eyes.

"I love you as well," she said. Her eyes were misty and her heart fluttered.

"If you were my wife," Ramon told her, "I would make certain that you would never want for anything. I would do nothing to dishonor the vows sworn before God. I would never breathe a single word to your detriment. There is nothing I would not do for you Isabel. Do you believe what I am telling you?"

"Yes," Isabel nodded.

"I would treat you as my wife and my lover, but my feelings would be so great to equal the love of a father to a child. If you will only consider…"

"Yes," Isabel interrupted him.

"Please be patient," he implored her. "My words are difficult to compose and…"

"Yes," Isabel cried with tears forming in her eyes. "Ramon I am saying yes!"

"You are," Ramon asked hopefully. He lowered himself to one knee and withdrew an ornate wooden box with leaves carved into its surface. He held the box out toward her. "Isabel Montenegro," he said, "will you do me the honor of being my wife?"

"Of course I will," Isabel said happily. She extended her hand down toward him. He gave her the box and she opened it so that the light of the torches would illuminate the inside of it. It was lined in red velvet. There were indentations for thirteen coins which were arranged in a circle. The coins were made of the purest gold from Byzantium. The surface of each one was engraved with the likeness of Christ. In one hand, the Son of God held the gospels and the other was raised in benediction.

"They are beautiful!" Isabel cried. "Come," she said as she reached for him. They were in each other's arms as the sound of a night bird echoed across the water. His kiss was like fire. Isabel could have remained in the warmth of that embrace forever.

Isabel clung to Ramon as they made their way back through the trees. "How long shall we wait until we are wed?" she asked him.

"How long must we wait?" Ramon answered with a smile.

"Oh…I do not know," Isabel said. She smiled as she snuggled her cheek into the sleeve of his coat. They walked down the line of torches toward the cottage.

"Let us do it now!" Ramon said suddenly.

"Tonight," Isabel asked with happy disbelief.

"I am Count of Provence," he said. "I can surely find a priest when I want one."

"But I have sent no word to my father," Isabel chided. "Surely you will ask Lord Montenegro for his blessing."

"We will have another wedding in the spring so that our families can attend," Ramon insisted. "I know how important that is for you."

"Yes," Isabel agreed. "My mother would be devastated if I did not wear her wedding gown and mantilla for my wedding." (The mantilla is a lace veil that covers the bride from head to toe.)

"I should not be the one to upset Lady Priscilla," Ramon laughed. "What a temper!"

"She would have us both strung up by our toes," Isabel chuckled.

"It is not too soon for you is it my heart?" Ramon asked seriously.

"I would rather this than too late," Isabel replied. "I do not want to lose you."

"You will not," Ramon promised. "I will always be yours." They shared one last kiss on the wooden porch before retiring to their own beds. Isabel wanted very badly to tell Little Grandma everything, but the elderly woman was already fast asleep when she tiptoed up to the room.

† † †

The next morning dawned cold and crisp. The chill air made Isabel's skin feel alive and she had never known such excitement. She hurried over to the other bedroom to awaken Little Grandma. "Grandma…my Little Grandma," she sang out. "It is time to get up." Pilar groaned and rolled over as she clutched the pillow closer to her face. "Wake up," Isabel chuckled as she shook the old woman by the shoulder.

"It is still so early Isabel," Pilar complained as she rubbed the sleep from her eyes.

"Ramon has asked me to marry him!" Isabel exclaimed.

"Oh my God," Little Grandma said as a smile covered her aged face. "I am so happy for you!"

"I have prayed so long for this," Isabel cried.

"When did he propose?"

"Last night," Isabel told her, "in the gazebo."

"I hoped that was the reason for all the torches," Little Grandma said happily. Isabel sat down on the bed next to her chamber maid who was still under the covers. She told the elder woman everything and Little Grandma listened with rapt attention.

"What about your mother and father?" Pilar asked when Isabel had finished.

"The Count says we shall have another ceremony in the spring. The oranges will be blossoming and it will be a perfect time for everyone to gather in Provence."

"You will be the most beautiful bride," Little Grandma said wistfully.

"I want you to be there by my side," Isabel said, "as the maid of honor!"

"Oh no mija," Little Grandma protested. "I am not a lady. You will have to be surrounded by nobility to make it proper."

"There will be time for that in Provence," Isabel protested. "Oh please say yes Little Grandma. It will only be the three of us and the priest."

"Oh," Pilar said longingly.

"Little Grandma please," Isabel begged.

"Your mother will be angry if she learns of this," the old woman said apprehensively.

"Mother is still in Montenegro. You must be there Little Grandma. My heart will be broken if you are not.

"Oh mija, of course I will go," Little Grandma gushed. "How could I not?"

"Thank you," Isabel said tearfully. She wrapped her arms around the elder woman and hugged her close. "I am so happy!"

"Then I am happy too," Pilar sighed. They spent the next few days in preparation for the wedding. With Little Grandma's instruction, Isabel embroidered the collar and cufflinks of Count Berenguer's white tunic. Using green and white threads, she created camellias that were connected by vines. With black threads she brought out the details of the leaves and petals.

The bridal gown and all of its accoutrements were brought up from Zaragoza. As was the custom of the day, the gown was cut from a soft black material. A glossy black cord ran through small loops over the hips of the dress and tied loosely in the front. There was a tall, rectangular comb made of ivory for Isabel's hair. There was a fan which was likewise made of ivory with white fabric between. An artist had inked the image of swans in flight across the top of the cloth. The mantilla was delicately crafted white lace, sewn at the edges with gold fabric. The lace was so thin that one could see through it and so long that it would cover Isabel's entire body and then some.

Isabel became distraught when she tried the wedding gown on for the first time. The tailor had cut the sleeves too short, exposing her forearms a full four inches up from the wrists. "Do not worry yourself mija," Little Grandma reassured her. "I will fix everything!" Pilar shortened the length of the mantilla and used the extra lace to extend the length of Isabel's sleeves. The finished product was beautiful and one would have thought it designed that way from the beginning.

By night, Isabel and Ramon sat in each other's arms before the great fireplace. They spoke of the future and the children they would have one day. Ramon welcomed Isabel's plan to bring the arts to Provence. "You shall be most beloved by my people," he said with a smile, "Isabel the Countess of Provence." Isabel laughed and kissed him.

It was only three days until all was in readiness. The clouds were low in the sky on that Saturday afternoon. Beams of golden light shot down through the grey cumulous clouds and sparkled on the surface of the pond. The gazebo was once more filled with pure white camellias. The small branches of witch hazel had been replaced with the tiny pink blooms of winter heath. Strings of camellias ran between the dark posts along the sides of the pier, blossoms frozen in time by the cold.

Ramon and the priest waited inside the flower strewn structure while Isabel walked slowly down the dock toward them. Little Grandma walked a few paces behind her in a beautiful gown of lavender hued lace. Her hair was covered by a scarf of the same material. Captain Quintero followed next to Pilar. He was dressed in brown leggings and a fine white tunic. Ramon was very handsome in his black coat and leggings and the white tunic that Isabel had embroidered for him. There was a gold circlet on his brow and he radiated such joy that it was surely felt by everyone around him. Isabel was the happiest of them all.

The bride wore the beautiful black wedding dress underneath the diaphanous lace of the mantilla. Her hair was drawn up by the comb into a long rectangle that ran along the back of her head. The mantilla hung down over her face. The sides of it hung to the floor and covered all but the smallest line down the front of her gown. In her hands, Isabel carried the box of coins that symbolized Ramon's promise to always take care of her.

Pilar and the Captain Quintero remained in the archway that led into the gazebo while Isabel stepped forward to join her husband to be. The priest set a hand on each of their shoulders and said a prayer in Latin. After the prayer was completed, the priest looked up at the bridal couple and the two gathered behind them. "Dearly beloved," the priest began, "we have gathered here in the sight of God to join Ramon Berenguer and Isabel Montenegro in holy matrimony. This is an honorable state, one instituted by God into which these two come now to be joined. Therefore, if any man has a just cause by which they may not be lawfully joined together, be it the law of God or the law of Aragon; let him now speak or forever hold his peace."

With no dissent, the priest continued on. "I charge you both," he said, "for you will answer at the Day of Judgment when the secrets of your hearts will be laid bare, that if either of you know any reason why you may not lawfully be joined in matrimony, that you confess it now. For if such reason exists and you not confess it, you cannot be joined by the law of God." After a moment of silence, the man spoke again. "Count Ramon Berenguer, will you have this woman to be your wife, to live under God's ordnance in the state of holy matrimony? Will you love her, comfort her, honor, and keep her in sickness and in health; forsaking all others and cleaving only unto her as long as you both shall live?"

"I will," Ramon answered.

"Isabel Montenegro," the priest said, "will you have this man to be your husband, to live under God's ordnance in the state of holy matrimony? Will you obey and serve him, love, honor, and keep him in sickness and in health; forsaking all others and cleaving only unto him as long as you both shall live?"

"I will," Isabel replied happily. Ramon smiled back at her as if nothing else existed but that moment. The priest motioned to the black wooden bench before them. They knelt on either side of it. Isabel placed the box of coins down on the bench next to her before taking Ramon's hands. They were facing each other with their folded hands touching in the center. The priest withdrew a beautiful rosary from the folds of his robe. It was crafted of finely cut rubies linked together with gold. He wrapped the rosary around both of their hands as a symbol of their union under heaven. He sprinkled their bowed heads with holy water from a silver vial and waved a cruciger made of silver over them.

"Oh merciful God," the priest prayed, "Creator and preserver of all mankind, send your blessing upon these your humble servants, this man and this woman whom we bless in your name. Bless them that they may keep the vow and covenant that is here made. Let this rosary be a symbol of their pledge, that looking upon it, they may live according to your laws and remain together in perfect devotion. We pray in the name of Jesus Christ, the savior of all men...amen." The priest then put his own hands around theirs which were joined by the rosary. "What God hath joined together, let no man put asunder."

The priest withdrew his hands and slowly unraveled the rosary from the bridal couple's hands. Isabel picked up the box of coins and opened it so that the man could gently deliver the rosary into the box as well. She closed the lid and stood with the box in her hands. Ramon stood also. Little Grandma came forward and took the box from Isabel. She then returned to her place next to the Captain. Isabel and Ramon faced each other and the priest spoke again. "Forasmuch as Ramon Berenguer and Isabel Montenegro have consented to join in holy wedlock before God and those assembled, and have given their pledge of fidelity unto each other, and have declared the same by the wrapping of the rosary and the joining of hands; I pronounce them Man and Wife, in the name of the Father, the Son, and the Holy Spirit...amen."

The priest looked at Ramon and said quietly, "take her in your arms." Ramon put his arms around Isabel's waist and she in turn wrapped her arms about his shoulders. "Oh God," the priest prayed heavenward, "bless them, keep them, and look in mercy upon them; and so fill them with all spiritual grace, let them live together not only in this life, but in the world to come, give them life everlasting…amen." The priest opened his eyes and then looked down at Ramon and Isabel. "You may kiss the bride," he said with a smile.

Isabel looked up as Ramon lifted the mantilla from her face and set it back down on her head just in front of the ivory comb. She stared into her husband's eyes and caught her breath. Ramon smiled down at her as the sun sank below the trees. Their kiss was long and passionate. When they came apart, Little Grandma was smiling and congratulating them with tears in her eyes. Captain Quintero clapped Ramon on the back and wished them well. Isabel was glowing as they all walked back to the Summer Cottage. Isabel gasped as Ramon swept her off her feet and carried her over the wooden porch and into the house.

The four of them shared an intimate meal in the breakfast room. The cooks had prepared a large platter of paella, (a rice dish with many different kinds of seafood). Small pieces of sourdough bread were topped with slices of tomato and olive oil. There was a beautiful cake with white frosting and almond cookies arranged around it.

After they dined, Ramon paid the priest and asked Pilar to retire for the evening. "This was such a beautiful day Ramon," Isabel cried. "It is the happiest day of my life! I wish I could live it again forever!"

"So do I," Ramon agreed. He leaned over and tenderly kissed her lips. "Come now my beautiful wife," he said. His eyes burned with passion. "Let us go up to our bed chamber." Isabel could not reply but she followed him up the stairs of the cottage and into the bedroom normally used by her aunt and uncle. There were several candles which provided a dim and flickering illumination.

Ramon removed the mantilla and carefully freed Isabel's blue-black hair from the ivory comb. He slowly undid the laces of her black gown while pressing his lips to the smooth flesh of her back. With his hands, he pushed down the sleeves of the gown until her breasts were uncovered to the night air.

Ramon removed first one sleeve and then the other completely from her wrists. The gown fell to the floor and Isabel caught her breath as his hands cradled her breasts and his lips softly kissed her neck. She slowly turned around in his embrace and kissed him deeply. She removed the embroidered tunic by pulling it up over his head. Ramon gently lifted Isabel up from the floor and placed her onto the bed.

Although there was some pain at the beginning, Ramon was gentle with her. Their lovemaking was like an ocean tide, crashing softly into the shore. When Isabel finally slept, she was cradled in the embrace of her husband's strong arms.

† † †

When Ramon and Isabel awakened as husband and wife, their passion rekindled and they lingered in bed far into the morning. That night, they traveled by carriage to the great city of Zaragoza where the Feast of St. Nicholas was already underway. The dwellings of the city were decorated with wreaths and garlands made of pine boughs and red berries. Iron torches wrapped with garlands were posted all along the main roads and their fires lit up the night.

The Feast of St. Nicholas was being held in the Plaza del Seo in front of the Catedral de Seo. The people were being fed from large tables laden with a bounty of food. A great pine tree had been set up in the middle of the square. Strings of gold and silver colored beads were wrapped around the length and breadth of the pine. A small statue of an angel was perched at the top. There were large ornaments made of red threads stretched over balls made of several rings of wood connected together.

The carriage continued on to Castle Aljaferia where the nobles were having their own feast. The clatter of silverware and the conversations of the revelers filled the air. The herald was about to announced their arrival, but Ramon pulled him back by the arm and whispered in his ear. "The Count and Countess Berenguer!" the herald proclaimed. A hush fell over the room. King Alfonso stood with a look of shock on his face. Infanta Sancha, (now made queen), put a hand to her lips and Alfonso's mother, Petronilla, gasped in surprise.

There was an elderly French gentleman at the royal table who ground his teeth when the announcement was made. He stood up from his seat and nearly shouted at Alfonso in his native tongue. Isabel was not certain what was being said, but it sounded like an accusation.

Alfonso answered in French and made a motion with his hand for the Frenchman to sit down again. The old man obeyed as Alfonso stalked across the dining hall with anger written on his face. "Follow me now!" he told Ramon. Isabel and her new husband followed the king into a small antechamber in the east hall.

Small torches hung in sconces along the wall to light the room. Crimson couches lined the walls. Ramon and Isabel seated themselves while Alfonso remained standing. The King's eyes smoldered as he peered down at his younger brother. "This is an outrage!" he said. Ramon did not reply. "You are to marry Adelaide, the daughter of Lord William of Montpellier! You know this! Our mother had it arranged. The two of you were to be wed in the spring. What are you trying to do…start a war?"

"I was made aware of my mother's scheme but never consulted," Ramon replied. "I told both of you many times that my heart belonged to Isabel Montenegro. Surely you could not have believed that I was lying."

"This cannot be," Alfonso nearly shouted! "I will summon a priest and have the annulment performed at once!"

"Summon whom you will," Ramon snarled, "I will have no part of it!"

"I am King," Alfonso roared!

"King...but not God!" Ramon shot back. "I love Isabel. You are wasting your breath. You cannot deny the law of God and you know it!"

"Ramon," Alfonso said soothingly, "Surely you will not risk a war with France?"

"I would sooner risk that than be known as the man who dishonored the daughter of one of Aragon's greatest generals!"

"My God you will ruin everything," Alfonso fumed. "How will I soften this blow?"

"I cannot say," Ramon replied, "but Isabel is and shall remain my beloved wife."

"You will leave me to unravel this mess," Alfonso asked with exasperation? Ramon held out his hands to signify a lack of concern. "Very well," the king spat. "Take you back to your rooms and I will give you my decision by morning."

"We are staying at my family's cottage your majesty," Isabel said.

"I thought as much," Alfonso muttered. "I heard rumors of your purchases brother...and to think it was my decision that you should rule Provence!"

"I have never failed your trust on that account," Ramon replied.

"Be gone," Alfonso said with disgust. "I have to think my way out of this problem that you have created." The latter he said while glaring at Isabel. Alfonso turned and left the room, letting the door slam closed as he went.

"What will happen now?" Isabel asked nervously.

"Now we go back," her husband replied. He looked at her then and stroked the side of her face with one hand. "Do not worry my love," he said. "Even my brother cannot defy the will of God." Ramon walked Isabel back to the carriage which carried them back to the Summer Cottage.

Their lovemaking was just as passionate as it had been the night before, but there were new emotions now: nervousness, fear, and desperation. Isabel did not mention these things because she did not want Ramon to be alarmed. In later years, she would imagine that he had done the same.

✝   ✝   ✝

The next day dawned too early. A currier from the palace arrived before the newly weds had yet awakened. "Your Grace," Pilar called through the door. "You're Grace…"

"What is it?" Ramon yawned.

"A message from your brother the king," the old woman answered. "His servant waits in the breakfast room."

"I come," Ramon sighed.

"Do not go," Isabel said before opening her eyes. "I need you here."

"I could let him wait," Ramon suggested. Isabel opened her eyes and looked up at him. She could see that he adored her, but there was anxiety in his face as well.

"You could," Isabel sighed as she pulled herself upright, "but it would not be proper." She rose from the bed and paused to lean over and kiss him. Ramon tilted his head up and received her lips. "I will join you very soon," she promised.

"Oh alright," Ramon said with disappointment. He hurriedly dressed and left the bed chamber. Isabel did her best to be quick. At the same time, she felt that she must not show her worst side to Alfonso's servants. When Ramon started shouting, Isabel abandoned her preparations and hurried down the stairs. She had dressed in a flowing white gown, but her hair hung loose down her back like a child. "I will not!" Ramon shouted. "This is madness! Shall I be left without an heir? I refuse. I outright refuse!"

"I beg Your Grace's indulgence," the currier said apprehensively, "but I do not believe his majesty will accept your refusal."

"Alfonso be damned!" Ramon shouted as Isabel walked with tentative steps toward the breakfast room. He noticed her coming and thrust out his hand toward her. It was holding a rolled piece of parchment. "Look at this," he nearly shouted! Isabel took the parchment and opened it toward the light. It read…

To the Count of Barcelona, Ramon Berenguer…

We all understood your infatuation with Isabel Montenegro was to be simply that. You alone did not understand. It angers me greatly that my hands are tied in this matter. This is what you have done. Inasmuch as I know that you will never consent to an annulment, I have arranged a plan which will attempt to salvage our relations with France and Lord William.

I first explained to Ambassador Laurent that my herald had indulged in alcohol and made a grievous error. As a matter of course, that herald has been publicly flogged. Your marriage to Lady Isabel must be kept secret for a year's time. She will be safe in her father's care.

During this same time, you will join the Knights of St. James in Italy. Conduct yourself with honor and noble accord. I wish for you to take the city of Nice from Genoa. You will come back a hero and then be publicly married to Isabel Montenegro at the Basilica del Pilar. I will find another suitable match for Adelaide while you are away. Perhaps we will make it appear that you are dead for a time.

In any case, one year is a small price to pay for peace with France. Do not fail me in this. My servant will take you immediately to Zaragoza where you will continue your journey to Genoa by ship. I have explained to Ambassador Laurent that you were only escorting Lady Isabel so that she might perform for my assembled guests. I have described your great desire to serve God in Italy. You must write a letter in this regard to Adelaide. She must believe that you plan to marry her on your return.

The news of your supposed death will be devastating to her. I will then have her married to another before the time when you come back from the dead. I do not expect you to obey happily, but I do require obedience. Remember that it was your doing that led us to this unfortunate charade. May God go with you.

Signed...

King Alfonso II
Ruler of Aragon

Isabel looked up thoughtfully when she had finished reading. "Oh Ramon," she said sadly.

"I will not go," he declared! "My place is with you." Isabel began to cry. "No Isabel," Ramon said as he put his arms around her. "I shall not let this happen."

"But you must," she replied. He tried to reassure her but she would not be comforted. "You must go," she said finally. It was all she could do not to weep. Her mind conjured up all the worst outcomes of war.

"I cannot," Ramon insisted.

"It is only a year," Isabel said with a forced smile. I shall miss you like life itself, but think how wonderful our reunion will be."

"Isabel…"

"Come with me now to the gazebo," Isabel interrupted him. "I have something for you before you depart."

"I will remain," Ramon disagreed.

"You cannot my love," Isabel replied. "You will force your brother to do worse still, and then what shall become of us?" Ramon looked down at the floor in resignation.

"Why must you be so wise?" he asked. His eyes were beginning to fill with tears.

"Follow me now," Isabel said softly. They walked together through the trees to the secluded pond. The sky was clear and the sun shone brightly on the water. Ramon had to steady his wife as they walked out onto the dock. Standing in the shade of the gazebo, Isabel kissed him. They lingered long and Ramon would have tarried longer. It was Isabel who pushed away at last. "While I waited for you in Montenegro," she said, "I composed a song." Her eyes were misty but she managed to keep smiling.

"Why did you never share it with me?" he asked.

"I was worried that it might not please you."

"How could it not?"

"I do not know," Isabel replied, "but I mean to share it with you now. It gave me comfort when you were gone. I want you to take this song with you to Genoa…and think of me."

"I shall never stop thinking of you," Ramon promised.

"Hush now," Isabel said as she put a finger to his lips. She inhaled deeply and closed her eyes. Her voice was sweet and filled with passion.

El Río

Aquí sentado
Ala orilla del río
Mis lágrimas caen hasta el lugar donde te encuentras

Te echo de menos
Tú estás tan lejos
Pero sé que mi amor volverá en días mejores.

(Chorus)
El tiempo pasa
Llega el invierno
pero mi corazón arde por ti como el sol
El sol de verano

Aquí hace frío
Aquí estoy vacío

Regresa y llena mi alma con la pasión de tu amor.
Extraño tus manos
Extraño tus besos
Desearía que pudieras ver que sin ti estoy perdido

=(repeat chorus)
Aquí sentado
Ala orilla del río
Mis lágrimas caen hasta el lugar donde te encuentras.

The River

Here I sit
On the bank of a river.
My tears fall down to the place where you are.

I miss you
You're so far away
But I know that my love will come back in better days

(Chorus)
And time goes by
And the winter comes
But my heart burns for you like the sun
The Summer sun

Here it is cold
Here I am empty
Return and fill my soul with the passion of your love.

I miss your hands
I miss your kisses
I wish you could see that without you I am lost

(repeat chorus)

Here I sit
On the bank of a river.
My tears fall down to the place where you are.

When Isabel finished singing, there were tears in both her eyes and those of her husband. "That was beautiful Isabel," Ramon finally said.

"I shall send the words to you so that you will not forget," Isabel smiled.

"I will not," Ramon promised. Isabel kissed her husband one last time. She forced herself to gently remove herself from his embrace.

"Go now," she told him.

"Will you not walk with me?" he asked.

"I cannot," she said sadly, "else I will beg you to stay...and so wretched will be my pleading that you will be forced to remain out of decency alone." Isabel forced a chuckle as she wiped the tears from her eyes.

"I would stay," Ramon said seriously.

"That is why we must say our goodbyes here," Isabel answered. Ramon kissed her again, and again she had to push him away. "Please Ramon," she implored, "I cannot bare it."

"Then I go," he said bravely.

"Farewell," Isabel said in a small voice.

"I love you," he told her.

"Promise me something," she said.

"Anything..."

"Promise you will not be brave."

"I promise," he vowed.

"I will pray every day you are gone," she said tremulously.

"For that I shall have to return," Ramon said. "Farewell my love."

"Farewell," Isabel replied. She could barely speak. Ramon turned and trudged away from her. He looked back over his shoulder and waved when he reached the trees. Isabel waved back with her white scarf in hand. She then held a hand to her face. It was too much to bear.

Ramon left through the trees and soon had disappeared from view. Isabel continued to look anyway until she heard the cry of the driver to spur the horses on. Isabel sat down as the wheels of the carriage and the horses hooves sounded on the path leading away from the Summer Cottage. Isabel wept when she could hear the horses no longer.

CHAPTER VIII

Captain Quintero returned to the Summer Cottage after accompanying Count Berenguer to Zaragoza. He and his men escorted the bride back to her father's keep. It was past nightfall when they arrived. Isabel was heart broken and clung to Little Grandma as they walked up the main steps.

Her parents greeted her warmly in the main entry hall. Quintero and his men were taken to the quarters where they would sleep for the night. Isabel managed to remain poised while her mother hugged and kissed her on the cheek. Her father came next. "It is good to see you Papa," Isabel said as they came together.

"There's my girl," Rafael said as he embraced her. We missed having you here for Christmas. How was it in Zaragoza?" Silence hung in the air and Isabel looked up at him.

"It was...it was," she stammered. Her father's eyes held only love and concern and Isabel could hold back no longer. She buried her face in Rafael's chest and wept.

"Isabel what is the matter?" her mother wanted to know. Priscilla came closer and rubbed her daughter's back.

"What has happened?" Rafael asked with panic growing in his voice. "Did he hurt you?"

"Papa," Isabel began but her voice escaped her.

"He will pay," Rafael snarled. "They shall all pay!"

"No Papa," Isabel interrupted him. "Ramon has done no such thing." Priscilla shot Rafael a disapproving look that seemed to urge him to calm down.

"What is the matter dear?" Priscilla asked gently. Isabel told them the story of her wedding.

She told them of King Alfonso's anger and Ramon's forced journey to Genoa and the Knights of St. James.

"Why did you not tell me?" Rafael demanded when she had finished. "Why did you not tell either of us?"

"If we had not married, Ramon would have been forced to wed Adelaide of Montpellier. "We had to do it father," Isabel explained. "How I wish both of you could have been there, but there was no time."

"We could have journeyed to Zaragoza in three days time," Priscilla objected.

"But we would not have approved," Rafael said sternly.

"Father," Isabel said with amazement, "surely you cannot mean that?"

"Every word," Rafael confirmed.

"But why," Isabel cried?

"To avoid this," Lord Montenegro answered harshly. "Ramon had no business courting you if he was engaged to someone else. He had even less justification for making you his bride! I would not have given my blessing for such an affront to the Crown of Aragon!"

"But he loves me father," Isabel sobbed. "Surely you know this is the truth?"

"That makes it all the more unpleasant, but my duty to the Crown would still compel me to refuse. I am done fighting wars Isabel."

"I cannot listen to this," Isabel shouted as she pulled away from her father's arms. "I cannot!" She did a poor job of concealing her tears as she ran up to her bedroom and closed herself in. She let herself cry into the pillow and would let no one enter.

Several minutes later, Isabel heard the sound of a key in the lock and her father came quietly into the room. He shut the door softly behind him. After this, he came over to her bed and sat down next to where his daughter lay. He balanced himself with one hand and stroked Isabel's hair with the other. "Don't worry mija," he comforted, "Count Berenguer will be kept far away from the fighting."

"Are you certain," Isabel asked hopefully. She turned her head around to look up at her father.

"I am," Rafael promised. "He will return before you know it."

"I hope so," Isabel said.

"We will have words he and I," Rafael said sternly.

"It is not his fault Papa," Isabel pleaded.

"Yes, but we have business to conclude," Rafael told her. "I will not be cheated. I am your father and it will be I who walks beside you in the Cathedral."

"Oh Papa," Isabel said happily, "I knew you would understand!"

"Love and understanding are two separate things," Rafael replied. "You need your rest." He leaned down and planted a kiss on her cheek. "A year will seem to be a long time, but it is truly nothing." Isabel smiled up at her father.

"I love you Papa," she told him.

"And I you," he answered. Rafael snuffed out the candle beside her bed and let Isabel sleep. She did not dream.

It was a lonely winter in the snow-capped peaks of the Pyrenees Mountains. Isabel sent letters by currier almost every week. The currier would travel to Zaragoza where her letters could then be put out to sea. There was nothing back from her husband. When pressed, the currier explained that travel in Genoa was difficult due to the weather and the danger involved. This gave Isabel hope and worry at once, but she was continuously disappointed when the currier arrived empty handed.

One evening in the early spring, Isabel was alone in the aviary. The night air was calm and the sounds of the forest were audible, even from the lofty height of Montenegro's Keep. Isabel had gathered some grain in an apron and brought it with her. She tossed handfuls of it through the bars of the pigeon coop. The pigeons flitted down from their perches and began to jostle each other on the floor of the cage.

The Countess Berenguer walked over to the huge window where the birds would sometimes be released. There was nothing stopping the homing pigeons from leaving during such times, but they inevitably returned. It was their nature.

Isabel looked down over the battlements. She could see the dark outline of Black River Ranch down at the base of the mountain. Fainter outlines highlighted the village. Moonlight danced on the surface of Black River as it rushed down into the gorge. From there it would wrap around the mountain until it joined with the River Ebro and flowed down by the village. From thence it would travel south to the Mediterranean Sea. Isabel imagined that somehow after that, the water would find its way to Nice.

As she was watching the silver reflections on the river, Isabel heard two male voices coming from the prison tower. "Have mercy," the first man begged.

"Mercy," the other spat, "do you even begin to understand the damage you could have done?" Isabel thought she recognized the second man's voice, but she could not place it.

"It shall never happen again master," the first said desperately.

"Well of course not you fool," the other man sneered. There was a loud slapping noise and Isabel heard the first man cry out. "Now get back to your bed chamber and remain there," the second man hissed! Isabel stayed still and listened for several seconds more, but nothing more was said. Her gut instinct was to run and tell her father, but she wondered what he might say. The conversation had made little sense to her and she would not be able to name either of its participants. The last time she had made accusations, they had been unfounded. Isabel remembered the anger and embarrassment she had caused her father and so decided not to act.

The moon hung low and swollen in the night sky. Two thin clouds partially obscured the glowing orb. Isabel was left with only the sounds of falling water and the darkness. She returned to her chambers and slept fitfully.

Isabel was startled from her sleep by the sound of the bell tower from the Church of the Greater St. James. The bell echoed up from Black River Village to the open window of her bedroom. A chill crept over her neck and she sat up quickly in her bed.

"Alarm...alarm!" shouted a watchman from the battlements of the keep. The fortress came alive with the sounds of soldiers shouting to one another. It wasn't long before Isabel smelled smoke coming up the mountain as well. Shouts and screams joined the church bell which tolled on into the dark.

"To arms," Isabel's father shouted as he rode his black stallion into the torch lit courtyard. He was quickly joined by several other men on horseback. The drawbridge lowered and they charged out of the keep. Isabel could hear the clashing of steel from the village as her father rode down toward the ranch house. The main body of Montenegro's soldiers was garrisoned in a barracks adjacent to it.

Isabel ran up into the aviary so she could see what transpired below the mountain. Fires had blossomed up from the village. There were small fires up and down the streets and byways. These would be torches. The larger flames would be the dwellings of the people. The fires spread and lit up the town with a lurid orange glow. Isabel thought she could make out the outlines of horsemen. The distance to the village was too far for her to be certain. Her heart beat rapidly as she watched the spectacle unfold.

The men on the wall closed up the gate quickly after Rafael and his captains had departed. The night was soon filled with the shouts of men and the sound of steel on steel. The battle seemed to go on forever as Isabel watched fearfully from the tower. At last, she heard cheers rising up from the village. Her father did not return, however. The villagers and soldiers formed lines out to the river. Buckets were passed between them to bring water to the burning buildings farther in. Finally, the fires began to dwindle until they were no more.

From her vantage point, Isabel could see the wounded being carried to the Church of the Greater St. James. There was no way to tell whether or not her father was among them. Her mother began to shout for her from the stairwell. "I am here!" Isabel called out. Lady Priscilla appeared in the doorway moments after.

"What are you doing up here?" Isabel's mother demanded. She was still in her night clothes.

"I was…feeding the pigeons," Isabel said weakly.

"We have servants for that!" Priscilla said sharply. "Come out of there!" Isabel followed her mother back to her bedroom. "Stay in your room unless your father or I tell you different," her mother instructed. "No one else…If you feel that you absolutely must leave your room, then come with haste to mine. There is a panel behind our bed which leads into the mountains. You will have to move the bed aside or crawl beneath it to open the panel. Be sure you are not seen and be sure that you close it up to cover your passing."

"Yes mother," Isabel said nervously. "Do you think they will come into the keep?"

"No dear," Priscilla answered. "I do not; but if they do, God forbid, then you must know what to do." Isabel nodded her head. "Don't worry mija," her mother assured her. "It appears that your father has already routed them."

"Is Papa well then?"

"I am sure that he is," Priscilla replied. "It would take more than that rabble to hurt my Rafael. Stay here. I will send Pilar up to keep you company."

"Thank you Mama," Isabel said. Priscilla nodded.

"I have to go now. I have to make sure that these men are doing their jobs correctly." Priscilla turned and walked swiftly out of the room. Isabel was still trying to forget about the worry in her mother's face when Little Grandma arrived.

Isabel's window was not so high that one might see over the wall. She and her chamber maid sat by the window and waited for Lord Montenegro to come riding through the gate. They hoped to hear cries of victory. Instead, the two could hear screaming coming from the town afar off.

Minutes later, the thunder of many hooves sounded on the trail up the mountain. Isabel saw the archers on the wall tensing in preparation for the worst. "Open the gate!" her father's voice echoed from below. The gate was quickly lowered and landed on the bridge with a crash. The men who worked the crank had to press themselves up against the wall to avoid being trampled by the horses that charged through.

Isabel watched with baited breath. Rafael looked over his shoulder once and then wheeled his grey stallion around. He now faced the one opening into Montenegro's Keep. 'Close it now!" he yelled after the last rider was through. The guardsmen quickly obeyed. "Loose," Rafael shouted to the men on the battlements, "loooose!" The air came alive with the whizzing sounds of their long bows. Lord Montenegro quickly rode across the courtyard to the wooden stairway that led up along the side of the wall. He dismounted quickly and ran up onto the battlements.

Isabel could see her father's face illuminated from below by the torches in the courtyard. He stared back at the keep in disbelief. At first, Isabel though he had seen her by the window. She quickly removed herself and pressed up to the wall at the edge of it. Rafael was not staring at Isabel, however.

"What in hell are you waiting for?" her father thundered. "Loose!'

"My lord," said a terrified voice from above Isabel's room, "the rags are too wet and will not light!"

"What happened to the tar?" Rafael asked incredulously. With no reply coming he continued in frustration. "Then do not light them. Loose them now!" Rafael's voice was moving. Isabel guessed that he was coming toward the western tower. "Loose you damnable fool!" Rafael screamed. His voice sounded closer still. Isabel heard the door of the west tower bang shut. She peeked out of her window. The captains on the ground and many of the men were yelling at whoever was manning the porcupine. By the sound of their angry shouts, Isabel guessed that he was not doing as told.

"Get out of my way," Rafael thundered from directly above. The platform for the porcupine was located there. There was a grunt and then a loud thud as the man was knocked clear. A clink of steel was the first warning that Rafael had loosed the machine himself. Scores of wooden shafts whistled up into the night and arced down toward the trail leading up from Black River Ranch. "You," her father directed, "bring more arrows now. Get help with it! There were no cries of assent but the sound of boots running above told Isabel that her father was being obeyed. "Why in God's name have the reserves been moved?"

"We do not know my lord?" said the voice of one of the retreating soldiers.

"Just go!" Rafael shouted furiously. When the footsteps returned, he began barking out orders once more. "The two of your reload this thing," he shouted. "Get off your back soldier!" he roared at the one who had disobeyed. "You help us replace these arrows!"

"Yes...my lord," came the timid squeak of the offender.

"Hurry before I throw you down to the stones!" Rafael threatened.

"Yes," the man said quickly. It was not long before another volley of arrows was loosed.

"Come away," Little Grandma said nervously. The older woman's concern reminded Isabel of her own mortality. She obeyed. They sat on the floor with the bed between them and the window. Isabel leaned against Little Grandma who held the younger woman while the battle raged outside.

They could hear the sound of infantry marching across the stone bridge toward the gate. This was broken by the sounds of the enemy soldiers who were impaled by Montenegro's arrows as they walked forward. "Where is the oil? Bring the oil!" shouted one of the guards.

"Here it is," another said loudly. There was a thunderous crash as the enemy's battering ram struck the gate. "Now!" the first man shouted.

"Get down!" Pilar exclaimed as Isabel rose to look. Isabel ran to the side of the window anyway. She couldn't help herself. She wanted to know if the gate would fall. Otherwise how would they know when to flee into the mountains? Three men were gathered around the center of the battlements over the gate. Isabel had often wondered at the horse shaped gargoyle that was mounted directly over it. The stone stallion seemed to balance a steel beam between its head and the walls. The reasoning behind this construction became immediately apparent as the three men hoisted up a large wooden barrel. The sides of the beam were raised up to allow the oil to pour down over it without spilling prematurely. More soldiers brought additional barrels to go behind the first.

"Isabel heard screams and cries of terror as the boiling oil poured out and down onto the bridge below. The bridge was built at an upward angle to allow the oil to flow down and coat it entirely. Barrel after barrel was poured over the beam with no slowing of the archer's attacks. One archer worked furiously to wrap a long strip of cloth round and round one of his arrows. He dipped it in one of the barrels along the assembly line and then lit it with a torch that had been placed nearby. He stood up above the safety of the wall long enough to fire this flaming shaft down toward the bridge.

The screams of the enemy as they were struck with the scalding liquid had been unnerving enough, but now they were on fire! Their cries were terrible and echoed far into the night. "No, no...," Isabel heard one of the enemy soldiers say fearfully. "Get away from the battering ram! No!" His words became incoherent as the flames consumed him. It was surreal. Cries of victory rose up from the men on the walls to join with the dying men's pitiful wailing.

"Run you dogs!" one of the archers shouted down at them.

"The Lord is with us!" Rafael shouted over the din. Pilar made the sign of the cross and Isabel sighed with relief. She ran down the stairs and met her father as he came down from the western tower.

"Papa!" she cried. Rafael held out his arms and Isabel ran into the embrace. "I was so worried," she said with her face pressed against his chest.

"Everything is fine now mija," he assured her, "but come...I must go down." Isabel released her father and followed close behind as he descended.

"Are they gone?" she asked.

"No," Rafael sighed, "but I do not expect they will be back tonight. You should go on up to bed."

"I will never be able to sleep," Isabel protested as they came into the entry hall. "May I stay with you please?"

"Of course," Rafael answered as he ran a hand over her black hair. "Follow me." The two of them went quickly into Rafael's study where he also held audience on occasion.   A map of Montenegro and the surrounding countryside was spread over the large table that dominated the room. Two wooden chairs set behind the table. Lord Montenegro pulled out the chair that was normally reserved for his wife. "Sit here," he told Isabel. "Stay quiet and you may learn a few things."

"I will," Isabel promised. Lord Montenegro groaned as he seated himself beside her.

"Papa?" she asked with concern. Rafael shushed her and then waited expectantly for his officers to arrive. The three captains filed in and stood before the table. "Gentlemen," Rafael greeted them, "give me your reports."   As he spoke, Rafael opened a long wooden box that held the map down on one side of the table. Inside were many small wooden figurines. There were soldiers on foot, soldiers on horseback, archers, and even a few siege weapons. The wood came from acacia trees and was divided between a dark stained legion and a lighter army that was not stained at all. The darker figurines represented the soldiers of Montenegro.

"I have ordered my men to protect the village," the first man said. He was a handsome man with blue eyes, dark hair, and the ghost of a beard on his face.   "Our enemies are camped back behind the trees. My guess is that they have bedded down in the meadow by the riverbank. Their arrows came from that direction after the first attack."

"True," Rafael agreed. "We would have noticed earlier if they had begun to clear the forest of trees, although they are probably doing that now. Thank you Captain Pascual." The first man nodded and stepped back. Rafael placed three archer figurines on the battlements of the keep. Two cavalry units he set in the diagram of the courtyard. The porcupine he put in its place on the platform between the two towers. "Captain Aquinas?" he asked as he placed one cavalry unit onto the diagram of Black River Village.

"My Cavalry are also inside the village," Raul reported. Isabel had not realized that the stable master was also an officer in her father's army. "Captain Pascual and I intend to have a roving patrol set along the perimeter. They should have already departed our lines."

"Very well," Lord Montenegro replied as he placed one of the horseman figurines outside the village. "Captain Jinosa?" The last officer stepped forward and reached his hand into the box of figurines. Jinosa was an older man with brown hair streaked grey. The numerous scars that covered his face were only partially obscured by the long beard he wore. There was defiance about him that Isabel found unsettling, but her father seemed to pay it no mind. Jinosa removed six infantry and placed four of them throughout the village. He placed one each at the stables and at the barracks next to it. The other two men looked uncomfortably at each other and at their lord. Rafael was not bothered in the least by Jinosa's boldness, however. He simply looked on as the Captain positioned his troops.

"Fifty men stationed here," Jinosa said as he pointed between the stables and the barracks. "Half are standing guard while the rest are asleep. Another two score men are asleep in the Church of St. James. The same number guard it or are patrolling close by. This unit guards the main road and the last is patrolling through the dwellings of our people."

"And the scouts," Rafael wanted to know?

"I expect to receive word very soon," Jinosa replied.

"How is the changing of the guard?" Rafael asked.

"It will be three times daily my lord," Jinosa replied. "Two asleep and four awake at all times.

"Very good," Rafael replied, "and the cavalry?"

"Two awake and one asleep," Aquinas supplied. The cavalry inside the keep will sleep while the rest patrol."

"Glad to see you all still know what you are doing," Rafael said. "There is one other matter I think."

"The traitor," Jinosa said knowingly. There was disgust written plainly on his face.

"Indeed," Rafael replied.

"Master Eubasio has locked that man in the dungeon," Captain Aquinas reported.

"Have him brought up," Lord Montenegro commanded. Aquinas pounded his fist on his chest, turned sharply on his heel, and departed the room.

"This may not be the best sight for you," Rafael warned his daughter.

"I can bare it," Isabel replied stoically. Before Aquinas returned with the prisoner, Lady Priscilla arrived. She had managed to dress herself, but little effort had gone to her hair and her face was bare.

"Isabel," Lady Priscilla said with confusion, "return to your room." Isabel rose from her seat and curtseyed toward her mother.

"Stand beside me," Rafael contradicted her. With an apologetic look at her mother, Isabel obeyed him. Her mother took the empty seat but did not neglect to glare her disapproval at Rafael. Her parents had never disagreed before the eyes of others.

Moments later, Captain Aquinas returned. In his hand was a brass ring connected to a chain that was functioning as a lead rope. The chain was attached to either side of a yoke that ran underneath the prisoner's arms and behind his back. His hands were manacled onto the yoke also. A chain went down from the wood to manacles that locked over his ankles.

The young man had been stripped of all clothing save his loincloth. His eyes were filled with fear and Isabel could see several bloody marks on his shoulders where the bite of a whip had struck him. Behind the prisoner came Master Eubasio whose countenance could only be described as malevolent. A more discerning eye might have noticed the tension in his eyes, but they were all afflicted with anxiety over the impending conflict.

Eubasio stood with his hands behind his back. Isabel thought she could see the coil of a whip protruding out into view from behind one side of him. "Here is the dog you sent for," Aquinas said gruffly.

"How do they call you?" Rafael asked sternly.

"Marco," the man answered quickly, "your humble servant!"

"Would you care to explain why you disobeyed my direct command?" Rafael inquired.

"I was afraid to die," Marco replied fearfully, "much to my shame."

"So you were afraid," Rafael asked with disbelief.

"Yes…yes my lord," the man squirmed. Aquinas jerked him forward with the brass ring and caught him before he could fall to the floor.

"Stay still," Aquinas said flatly.

"Yes master," the man replied enthusiastically. Captain Aquinas just shook his head.

"You are afraid now," Rafael said. "That much is certain."

"Yes my lord," Marco agreed as his eyes shifted nervously between his captors.

"Why do you suppose we had no arrows to reload the porcupine?" Lord Montenegro inquired.

"I…I do not know," Marco stammered.

"You know I have not the stomach for torture," Rafael said as he looked into the man's terror stricken eyes, "but Master Eubasio has no such aversion. Is that not the truth, Master Eubasio?"

"I am always willing to do what must be done your lordship," Eubasio replied smoothly.

"What must be done in order for us to hear you speak truth?" Rafael asked the prisoner.

"I tell you the truth," Marco said desperately! "I had no hand in removing the arrows and I…" Marco was interrupted by Eubasio's boot crashing down into the back of his leg just below the knee. He crumpled to the ground and would have smashed face first into the table had Master Aquinas not pulled him back by the yoke. Isabel saw her mother wince as the man was jerked back.

Eubasio noticed Priscilla's discomfort and grinned widely. Isabel wondered if the man was actually enjoying himself but she dared not speak. "Perhaps our friend needs to be relieved of one of his fingers," Eubasio suggested. "He may then decide to tell my lord the truth."

"How many fingers will it take?" Rafael asked coldly.

"One…two…two at most," Eubasio replied, "but there will yet be eight more if he is not so compelled." Lady Priscilla paled at the man's words.

"Surely this is too much for her," Priscilla whispered to her husband.

"Is it?" Rafael frowned. As he contemplated what to do, Eubasio spoke up.

"Let me take him back to the dungeon," the Master of Servants offered. "I shall have him singing in moments." He then whispered into Marco's ear. The prisoner trembled visibly.

"Take him away," Rafael agreed. "Some things are better left unseen." Aquinas handed over the brass ring to Eubasio who dragged Marco from the room. Isabel found it odd that Marco should not protest or confess whatever he might be hiding immediately. Rafael sat back and sighed heavily once the two men had departed for the dungeon. "You gentlemen should return to your commands," he told the captains before him. The three officers saluted and left the room one by one as they had entered. Aquinas was the last to go. "Hold," Rafael said as the man was just under the doorway.

"My lord," Aquinas asked as he turned back?

"Send a rider to the Crown of Aragon immediately," Rafael instructed. "We could use reinforcements and we may not get another opportunity."

"Yes my lord," Aquinas replied as he bowed slightly and inclined his head.

"I'll send word by pigeon as well," Isabel's father decided out loud.

"It would not hurt," Aquinas agreed.

"After you send the rider you need to get some sleep," Rafael ordered. "I need you to be fresh for tomorrow."

"What happens tomorrow?"

"The Lord only knows," Rafael answered, "but there was not much dedication in that first attack was there?"

"No," Aquinas frowned.

"I think they were testing our defenses."

"You must be right," the captain agreed.

"Ensure that you do as I have commanded," Rafael reminded him.

"That was unnecessary my lord," Aquinas replied. "I have never failed you thus far."

"I am talking about the part where you get some sleep," Rafael grinned.

"As you command," Aquinas grinned back. He pounded his fist over his heart and exited the chamber.

"I think we should all retire now," Rafael told his family. Isabel noticed how tired her father looked.

"Where do the enemies come from?" Priscilla asked him.

"They had no standards or uniforms," Isabel's father replied. "I suppose they were mercenaries."

"Who would dare such a thing?" Priscilla cried with indignation.

"I do not know," Rafael answered," but I'll wager we shall know by morning."

Isabel slept poorly that night. She could not quiet her fears about her father being killed by the enemy soldiers. Despite his skill, how could he know where every arrow and sword strike would come from? The wind carried the stench of smoke and burnt flesh.

✝   ✝   ✝

As the sun's rays barely broke over the Pyrenees, a lurid crimson was cast onto the bottom of the dark grey clouds. The cavalrymen in the courtyard would soon be waking. Some of the archers slumbered on the battlements, but more were awake and looking down at Black River Village with red rimmed eyes.

While Priscilla and Isabel eventually found sleep, Lord Montenegro had not been so fortunate. He had lain beside his wife for some time. Once satisfied that she was unconscious, Rafael had risen from their bed. Taking up his sword and armor from the stand beside the bed, he carried it all quietly from the room. Once girded in heavy chain mail, he returned to the bed chamber and retrieved a black cape from the wardrobe. The crest of Montenegro was embroidered upon it in silver thread. He fastened the cape to the plates on his shoulders and left Priscilla to her sleep.

Rafael paused when he passed by his daughter's open doorway. She lay in her bed facing him. Isabel slept on her side with her head on one pillow and the other held between her arms in front of her. He remembered the first time he had seen her lying in her crib. She had been so tiny, laying in much the same position as she was now. The only difference was that baby Isabel would have had her arms wrapped around a rag doll that Priscilla's midwife, Pilar, had sewn together.

Rafael remembered how perfect his child had seemed, a little angel with her tiny mouth open and eyes closed. Her body rose and fell with her steady breathing. He had run his fingers over her little head and down her arm. Isabel made a soft, "ooh" sound and then clutched the end of his finger in her tiny hand. That was when he had fallen in love with her.

For the first time since childhood, Rafael felt the icy hand of fear crawling up his spine. There was always some degree of nervousness before a battle, but this was different. Now Rafael had something to lose. "I will not let them touch you," he promised in a whisper. He said a prayer to the Archangel Michael for her safety before continuing on to the east tower.

Lord Montenegro looked down at the damage that had been inflicted by the invaders. Many of the village houses had been burned and gutted. There was a hole in the roof of the Church of the Greater St. James, but the bell tower still stood. These heathens had no respect for the House of God. They would pay.

Fire had burned most of the tar off the bridge that ended a stone's throw away from the keep. The enemy had not bothered to recover their dead for burial. Rafael would have allowed it as long as the litter bearers had been unarmed.

The attackers had not been well organized. Some of them didn't even speak the same language. Rafael thought he had heard French spoken several times during the fight. A great number of his foes had been fellow Spaniards. Rafael had never before put his own countrymen to the sword. They had died just as easily as the Saracens. There was nothing glorious about death, not like they told in stories.

Rafael waited in and out of consciousness in the east tower all night. The scouts never returned. That meant that the enemy was probably still awake. That meant they were preparing for another attack. In the pre-light just before dawn, it almost seemed that the tree line around Black River Village was expanding. Rafael knew better. The main body of the enemy army had arrived at last. "To arms," Lord

Montenegro shouted down to the soldiers below. He was first echoed by several archers and then the cavalrymen joined in as well.

Lord Montenegro looked again. He thought he could see the colors of Aragon on one of the standard bearers. It was impossible to be sure from the great distance between them. He hurried down to the private stables where the stable hands were trying in vain to saddle his horse, Santiago. "Get away from him!" Rafael shouted at them. Santiago was a grey, foul tempered beast who would only be controlled by Rafael. His years in combat had made an overly aggressive stallion even worse by wars end. Now it was time to make use of his full potential once again. Rafael quickly saddled Santiago and rode out into the courtyard. The war horse tossed his head in anticipation and Lord Montenegro took a tighter grip on the reins.

The rest of the cavalry unit inside the keep fell in behind their Lord as he rode out. The horses' hooves thundered over the drawbridge. They galloped down the mountain in two columns following behind Rafael. The standard bearers rode in the first row. One carried the yellow and crimson flag of Aragon. The other held the black flag of Montenegro aloft with the white crest emblazoned upon it. They were quickly joined by the other two cavalry units once inside Black River Village. The forces of Montenegro formed a defensive line on the side of town facing the trees where the enemy had gathered in a similar formation. Rafael could see the tops of the catapults being wheeled up the road that led to Zaragoza and points south.

Rafael rode behind the ranks of cavalry and infantry until he met up with his captains. It was a grim faced trio of officers that stood waiting on horseback when he rode up. "No word from the scouts?" Rafael asked, but he already knew the answer.

"None," Captain Jinosa said angrily, "but I think we can all see the truth in front of the trees." He glared at the enemy soldiers with one hand resting on the pommel of his sword.

"We are outnumbered," Captain Aquinas said gravely, "two, maybe even three to one."

"Where are their standards?" Rafael frowned. "I thought I saw the flag of Aragon on the ride down. Now I see nothing."

"Sell swords," Jinosa replied in disgust.

"No you are right my Lord," Captain Pascual spoke up. "I saw it as well, but...here they come." Three riders broke ranks and came forward into the clearing between the two armies. As they did, their standards were raised up for all to see. The rider on the left bore the banner of Aragon. The rider on the right bore the violet flag of Morera with its dueling white dragons fighting above a large tree. The rider in the center wore a violet cape which set him apart from the rest of the soldiers.

"Jinosa...control the line," Rafael commanded, "the rest of you with me!" Captain Aquinas and Captain Pascual fell in beside their lord as he rode out to meet the enemy envoy. The two groups of riders came to a stop in the center of the field. The rider in the violet cape was not Lord Enriquez, but only one of his officers. "Tell me why Lord Enriquez has sent you all to die in Montenegro?" Rafael asked without waiting for introductions. The officer cleared his throat and smiled before speaking.

"I am Captain Vidana, commander of Lord Enriquez' army," he said.

"That does not answer my question," Rafael interrupted. "Let us skip the formalities. You already know who I am."

"I do," Vidana agreed. "Lord Montenegro, you stand accused of high treason and are summoned forthwith to the Crown of Aragon for trial. Allow yourself to be taken and no blood will be shed."

"Except those who died last night," Rafael contradicted him. Vidana held his hands out with a smirk.

"You know how ambitious mercenaries can be," he said.

"Your paying for these dogs says a lot for the quality of your own troops, commander," Rafael sneered.

"They are the best money can buy," Vidana quipped. "Will you surrender?"

"Hardly," Rafael scoffed.

"You would disobey the direct order of your king?"

"Never," Rafael grinned.

"Then you must give yourself up," Vidana declared.

"You are a liar," Rafael replied with disdain.

"Am I?" Vidana asked.

"If someone has charged me with treason, King Alfonso would have simply to summon me to court. I would have obeyed instantly."

"Perhaps he was afraid you might flee," Vidana suggested.

"No," Rafael shook his head. "He would not have been required to tell me the reason for the summons. There was no need for this."

"Rest assured Lord Montenegro," Captain Vidana said, "the summons is legitimate."

"I will surrender," Rafael conceded. Captain Pascual's jaw dropped and he shifted uncomfortably in his saddle. Captain Aquinas grinned.

"A wise decision," Captain Vidana said smugly.

"Before my arrest," Rafael continued, "there is but one more thing you must do."

"And what is that?" Vidana asked condescendingly.

"Your mercenaries have unjustly killed citizens of Aragon, which includes not only the peasants but my soldiers as well. For this they must be executed."

"You wish for me to make an example of their leaders then?" Vidana asked.

"All who have committed offenses must pay," Rafael explained. "It is written in law."

"Surely you are not suggesting…" Vidana hesitated. Rafael grinned and nodded his head in the affirmative.

"The soldiers of Montenegro will assist you if need be," Rafael said with a predatory smile, "for the honor of Aragon."

"I will not execute half my army," Vidana said angrily!

"Then you support their crimes which means you must all die," Rafael concluded. "Montenegro takes no prisoners."

"Treason," Captain Vidana hissed!

"Not treason," Rafael corrected him. "When I answer King Alfonso's summons; I will expose Lord Enriquez as the real traitor, but before I go…I will stain the earth red with your blood."

"Here, here," Captain Aquinas said with a tone of quiet menace.

"Perhaps an agreement could be reached," Captain Vidana hedged. There was a nervousness creeping into his voice that Lord Montenegro immediately picked up on.

"What is the matter commander?" Rafael sneered down at him. "You are eagerly anticipating your return to the safety of your Lord's army, true?" Vidana looked over his shoulder quickly, but then steeled himself and glared up at Rafael.

"I have nothing to fear from you," he scoffed. "Your men are greatly outnumbered."

"But it is a very long ride back to the line," Captain Aquinas grinned, "a long ride indeed."

"These negotiations are concluded," Rafael said loudly. "As long as you and your men remain on my land, your lives are forfeit! We will show no mercy nor accept surrender. Your only salvation will come when you flee from this place. Tell Lord Enriquez that his death has been decided!"

"History is only written by those who conquer," Vidana sneered. "We will not surrender!" the man shouted.

"The dog finally speaks the truth, if only to us," Rafael joked to his captains. Pascual laughed without humor. Aquinas gave a toothy grin. Lord Montenegro looked back down at the enemy commander. "Challenge me to single combat," he shouted across the clearing, "or get you back behind those you would have die in your stead!"

"There is nothing to prove," Vidana said as he wheeled his horse around. He spurred the animal on toward the trees and his waiting army. His standard bearers moved their horses at full tilt behind him.

"Do not let them carry our flag!" Rafael roared. Captain Aquinas quickly lifted up the medium crossbow that rested on his hip and aimed in. The bolt spiraled through the air and punched through the back of a man's skull. This man was the same one who carried the standard of Aragon for the enemy. The dead man slid off the horse and crumpled to the ground. His flag went with him.

Captain Aquinas galloped forward and leaned off his horse to retrieve the red and yellow flag. "Back to the line," Rafael barked as his captain returned to the group. The two officers obeyed and soon they were all three galloping back to the rear. Once behind friendly lines, the three men reined in.

"We should have killed their commander," Captain Pascual remarked. Captain Aquinas, a veteran of many battles, (most of them under Rafael's command), just shook his head.

"It was the symbol that needed to die," Lord Montenegro explained. "Captain Vidana is just a man. Our troops need to see these men as the dogs they are, not as brothers."

"I understand," Captain Pascual said. Santiago whinnied as Rafael turned him sharply about. "Aquinas…envelop left! Pascual…envelop right! Jinosa…set your pike men!" Rafael galloped down the line between the archers to the rear and the cavalry to the front. The infantry was still farther forward and were even now setting up their staggered lines of pikes to await the charge of the enemy horses. "Archers loose!" Rafael screamed. Arrows filled the sky as he yelled out the last of his commands. "To me," he shouted at his own mounted soldiers.

Montenegro's preemptive volley of arrows filled the air with the whistling of wooden shafts. Enriquez archers returned in kind. The majority of Montenegro's archers were able to flee back out of range and into the shelter of the city before impact. Enriquez archers had the relative safety of the trees to fall back to. Unfortunately for them, Vidana's delayed order to loose arrows cost many a man his life. In war, timing can be everything.

Vidana had positioned his cavalry in front of the rest. They charged forward as soon as Montenegro's arrows were loosed. The cavalry of Montenegro were able to avoid the first volley of arrows by charging forward. Captain Pascual went out wide to the right flank before turning toward the charging horsemen of Morera. They smashed into the sides of the oncoming foes.

Rafael and Aquinas took their men out to the left flank. Rafael's men were more toward center. He raised his sword at an upward angle and his men followed suit. Rafael then veered his riders left and struck into the enemy cavalry who had not been broken by Pascual's charge. Captain Aquinas and his men continued on toward the enemy line.

In the rear, Captain Jinosa ordered his men into a hasty phalanx which repelled most of the arrows from Morera's forces. The enemy infantry ducked behind their own shields, but did not cooperate to protect each other. There was little unity among them and less with the mercenaries.

"Kill them all!" Lord Montenegro shouted as he and his men burst into the flanks of the advancing enemy. Rafael's sword caught one of the mercenaries through the side of his face, punching through the rider's cheek and breaking teeth on the way to his skull. Rafael quickly pulled back the blade as the enemy fell from his mount. Out of his peripheral vision, Rafael saw another horseman dodging the attack of one of Montenegro's riders. Though he had not been killed by the sword, the man had lost his balance. He slipped from the saddle with a startled cry. With no urging from Rafael, Santiago reared up and trampled the man beneath his iron shod hooves.

Rafael's size gave him a much greater reach with the sword. This was a definite advantage. He pushed Santiago hard into the formation and cut the men down like wheat! Rafael felt as though he were in a dream. Hovering outside his body, he watched the horrors it inflicted on the enemy soldiers, some of them barely old enough to leave their father's house. The sounds of steel and the screams of the dying seemed as if they were coming from very far away. Despite Rafael's distaste for killing his own countrymen, it did not affect the speed or the voracity with which he laid them to waste.

While the cavalry of Montenegro was successful in breaking the enemy's charge, it did not stop it entirely. The infantry had set their pikes and braced themselves for the coming attack. They were well trained, but a poor match for mounted aggressors. Rafael was about to lead his men back to aid them when a ram's horn echoed across the field of battle.

Aquinas and his men would never reach their objective. Vidana's infantry split into three groups and rushed forward to join the melee. The reason for their division became immediately obvious as a horde of cavalry galloped en masse out of the forest and rode through the newly formed gaps. Aquinas' charge was broken and the rest of the enemy horsemen moved swiftly into the fray.

All of the enemy cavalry were wearing the colors of Morera, but these riders traveled in perfect columns five abreast. Rafael cursed himself for not having seen the ruse. Now that Montenegro had expended so much effort on the mercenaries, the army of Morera would come in and take advantage of their fatigue. Seeing that his men were outnumbered as well, Rafael called a retreat. The soldier who had carried the horn for Rafael's cavalry men had been cut down and so he was forced to give his orders by shouting. Captain Aquinas and his men were too far forward to hear the call. Rafael could only hope that they would notice before they were overwhelmed. Aquinas and Rafael had been through countless battles and they had a strong bond of friendship. If Montenegro's men stayed on the field, then they would surely be defeated. This was one of those decisions that officers and Lords never speak of.

Rafael rode Santiago hard back toward the village. The enemy was closing in fast behind him. "My lord," Jinosa called over the thundering hooves! Rafael looked just long enough to see his captain waving at him. "Through Beggar's Alley," the man shouted! Beggar's Alley was the narrowest alley in Black River Village. They would only be able to fit two horses side by side if nothing was in the way. In war, one cannot afford to hesitate. Rafael decided to trust Captain Jinosa.

"To Beggar's Alley," Rafael shouted. His riders formed into two columns behind him as they rushed at breakneck speed into the village. Fortunately, the alley had been mostly cleared of obstacles. Rafael had just enough time to register the ropes that were laid across the alley between slats that had been removed from the buildings that walled it in. There were more removed slats and another rope between them at every forty paces through the alley. Captain Jinosa had served him well.

The cries of both men and horses rose behind Rafael and his fleeing cavalry. The peasants had pulled up the ropes and sprung the trap. Horses crashed headlong into the cobblestones and each other. The riders fared no better. With pikes, pitchforks, and sharpened sticks; the people of Montenegro lashed out at the topped riders from the slats that had been removed from their homes.

Jinosa had sent archers back to the rooftops. From there, they rained death on the advancing enemy. The peasants helped also with bricks, stones, and anything heavy that they could cast down.

Rafael joined up with Captain Pascual's men on the other side of the village. Together they fled up the mountain trail and into the keep. They left the drawbridge down as long as possible for stragglers and some few did make it back. Rafael hurried up into the east tower so he could see what was happening beyond the walls of the keep.

When the enemy began to form in ranks on the near side of Black River Village, Rafael realized that Captain Aquinas and Jinosa were lost. They had stayed behind to halt the enemy's advance and protect their lord. "Raise the drawbridge!" Rafael shouted. As the soldiers worked the crank to close the gate, Rafael looked down at the carnage. Even the peasants had joined in to defend him. Now they would be held at the mercy of Captain Vidana and his loathsome mercenaries. Silently, Lord Montenegro wept.

CHAPTER IX

When Isabel rose from her bed, her father and the cavalrymen were already departing. She wanted very much to go up to the aviary and look down on the battle, but she had been ordered quite explicitly to stay in her room. The uncertainty was wearing on her nerves. Nevertheless, Isabel obeyed.

Little Grandma waited with her. This made the tension only slightly more bearable. They could only see the courtyard from Isabel's window. Everything beyond the walls was a mystery. Sometimes, Isabel could hear soldiers on the battlements calling out to one another. She was certain that she had heard one of the men saying that Montenegro was outnumbered. Little Grandma must have heard it too for she gave a start. Rising quickly from where she sat on the bench by the window, Pilar hurried toward the door. "Where are you going?" Isabel asked nervously.

"I have to go and check on your mother," Little Grandma answered, "to see what she would have us do."

"What do you mean?"

"Just wait here child," Pilar answered. "I will return swiftly." Isabel nodded and watched the old woman leave the room. Isabel's hands fidgeted with her dark green dress as she waited for what would happen next. Moments later, the door to her room reopened. It was not Little Grandma who came through, however. "Master Eubasio?" Isabel said questioningly.

"Lady Isabel," the Master of Servants replied deferentially. He sounded out of breath and his eyes were frightened. His gaze darted around the room quickly before falling once more upon her.

"What is it Eubasio," she asked him? "What is the matter?"

"Your father commands me to take you up to the western tower," Eubasio told her as he wiped a hand over the side of his face.

"What of Pilar and my mother," Isabel queried, "I am to stay with them am I not?"

"No no no," Eubasio interrupted, "follow me."

"I am to go nowhere unless..," Isabel began.

"There is no time!" the man spoke over her. "Your mother and chamber maid are in the western tower already. Now do as I tell you...for your own good!"

"Alright," Isabel said confusedly. She followed close behind the man up to the tower. She did not see her mother, (or Pilar for that matter), in the hallways which lent credence to Eubasio's demands. He opened the prison tower's door with the master key and practically shoved Isabel inside as he helped her along.

Isabel quickly realized that the prison was empty, not just empty of prisoners but empty of anyone. She heard Eubasio locking the door and wheeled around to face him. He was in the tower with her. "What do you suppose you are doing?" she asked crisply.

"Fighting a war," Eubasio sneered. He was grinning as he looked her in the eyes.

"Where is Pilar," Isabel demanded, "and where is my mother? I will see them now!"

"I would say it does not matter where they are," Eubasio chuckled.

"Out of my way," Isabel ordered as she strode toward him!

"The door is locked," he answered with amusement as he stepped aside.

"Give me the key!" she ordered. She reached her hand out to grab it from his belt, but Eubasio slapped her so hard across the face that she fell back and nearly lost her balance. There was a hiss of steel as the master of servants drew a short sword from the scabbard on his hip. "Guards," Isabel screamed!"

"That is not going to help," Eubasio sneered as he came forward.

"You will be killed," Isabel assured him with panic rising in her voice.

"No, Eubasio shook his head. "By the time they break this door down; I will be down the pulley and into the river. It is you," he said as he tightened his grip on the sword and raised it above his head, "you who will be killed…and I cannot say that I will not enjoy it!"

Isabel was slowly backing away as the man advanced. She gasped as her shoulders bumped against the mantle of the prison's fireplace. "Mouthy little bitch!" Eubasio cursed as he struck down with the sword. Isabel cried out with fear as she ducked down and to the right. The sword echoed loudly on the stone mantle behind her. In that instant, Isabel spied one of the irons for the fire. She grabbed hold of the poker with its spike and curved hook. She brought the implement up just in time to parry Eubasio's sword as it swung toward her face.

While Isabel spun out of the traitor's reach, she brought the poker down across his kneecap. The strike did not break flesh, but it did cause Eubasio to grunt and stagger back. Isabel took a ready stance with her new weapon. She had no training…only watching her father instructing his troops in the courtyard. Eubasio tisked and wagged a finger at her. "That was your one shot," he chided. "You should have made it a good one. I will not be surprised again."

"Lady Isabel," a man's voice shouted from the other side of the door!

"Help me!" Isabel screamed at the top of her lungs.

"Lady Isabel," the man's voice came again as if to confirm that she was indeed behind the door. The handle twisted back and forth as her would-be savior tried to get in.

"Break it down," another man shouted. The door to the prison shuddered as the first man kicked it with all his might. The door held.

"Too late now," Eubasio said as he lunged forward. Isabel jumped back and the man's sword thrust came just shy of penetrating her bosom. Steel clashed on iron as Eubasio drove Isabel back with a flurry of slashing blows. The girl was terrified and her hands were already sore from holding on to the poker. Eubasio's strikes threatened to knock it from her grasp...or worse.

"Watch your step," Eubasio grinned. His eyes seemed to look beyond her. Isabel couldn't help but look back and see that she would soon reach one of the large openings of the tower. The sound of rushing water became louder as she drew nearer to it. If this kept up, she would either die on Eubasio's sword or plummet to her death on the rocks of Black River.

Where Eubasio had been alternating his attacks from the right to the left side and back, he suddenly reversed the blade and came from the left a second time! Isabel shrieked as she brought up the poker to block the deadly steel. The impact caused her to stumble.

Suddenly, it seemed as if the whole world was underwater. It was amazing to Isabel how time seemed to move in slow motion and she could see so much detail in what she would later realize was only an instant. She had fallen to one knee. She could see the gleam of bloodlust in Eubasio's eye as he drew back to thrust the short sword into her. She could see the reflection of the iron bars from one of the cells in the blade. She also took note of the new position of her own weapon. Where the point of the poker had been above both of their heads for much of the fight, it was now only inches below Eubasio's chin. The flesh of his chin was whiskered and he probably hadn't shaved in several days. Isabel remembered overhearing her father talking to Master Aquinas about "the eye of the storm," a calm in the midst of battle. Now she understood completely. There was no time to hesitate.

Isabel drove herself up with all of her might. She rammed the point of the fire iron into her enemy's throat. The poker pierced all the way through his neck and scraped along the bottom of his skull. Isabel could see the blood on the other side of the poker as it burst forth from the flesh next to where his spine and skull met. Eubasio made a tortured sound and blood began to leak from the side of his mouth. The short sword clattered to the floor, startling Isabel who leapt clear of it and her attacker.

Eubasio struggled to retain his feet for only a moment. His hands reached up as if to clutch at his neck but never quite made it. Isabel watched in horrid fascination as the blood leaked out around the iron and down toward the neckline of his tunic. Eubasio's eyes rolled heavenward and he fell, spinning in the air as he dropped out by the pulley system and fell quickly toward the river below. His back arched as his body was broken on the rocks. The poker was pushed back through his neck until it was only hanging onto the wound because of the curved hook.

In moments, the powerful rapids carried Eubasio's body down river. The poker went with him for a time before falling free and sinking below the water. The corpse disappeared as it plunged into the gorge around Montenegro's Keep. A smear of the traitor's blood was left behind on the rock where he had come down. This too was soon washed away. Isabel stood gasping over the opening. She leaned on the wall for support as her stomach threatened to revolt.

The door finally cracked in and Montenegro's soldiers flooded the room. Isabel could faintly hear the voices of these men searching the chamber for her attacker. Some of them were perhaps inquiring after her welfare, but there was nothing for her to say. It was over. The Heiress of Montenegro allowed herself to be taken to her mother's bed chamber. Priscilla was quite unnerved and she held her daughter tight. Isabel was grateful for her mother's arms.

When Rafael returned from the battlefield, he came immediately up to his wife and daughter. "My angels," he said as he entered the room. He drew them both into his strong embrace. Priscilla was crying and trying to tell her husband what had almost happened. "They told me Priscilla," he shushed her. Isabel held on to her parents for all she was worth.

After a time, Lord Montenegro had to extract himself and return to his duty. He began barking orders as soon as he entered the hallway. "I want six guards on this room," he shouted, "two within…four without. No one is to enter but myself and Pilar. Execute anyone who disobeys!"

Two guards entered the bed chamber immediately and posted themselves at either side of the doorway. Isabel could see the others taking position in the hall as the heavy wooden door swung shut. She could still hear her father's voice on the other side. "Captain Pascual," he shouted, "too my study!"

Little Grandma and Lady Priscilla were intent on comforting their little girl. Isabel was grateful for the attention, but all she really wanted was to know that her father would be safe. The thought of losing him terrified her like nothing else.

In Rafael's study, which was now the war room, Lord Montenegro and Captain Pascual stood over the large map that was still spread out over the table. Rafael somberly removed Aquinas and Jinosa's troops from the table. "How goes it," he asked his last remaining officer?

"Not well," Pascual answered. "The enemy has taken over Black River Village and is even now staging their siege weapons at the base of the mountain."

"It is an impossible angle," Rafael said. "I should be surprised if they can launch anything that comes close to us. I chose this place quite deliberately. Wait for them to get everything in place and then we shall rain fire upon their heads. By the time they rebuild, we should be able to get our own catapult set up in the courtyard. They will not be able to touch these walls."

"Perhaps they will starve us out," Pascual mused.

"This keep has a tunnel leading back into the mountains. Very few know about it. We shall not starve."

"Will not the enemy see us moving goods in and out?"

"Not unless they know our secret," Rafael replied. The tunnel goes back to a sheep ranch. The ranch is high up in the Pyrenees and all but invisible from below."

"Praise be to God," Captain Pascual said with relief.

"But our people will suffer," Rafael frowned, "those who did not make it up to safety in time." His own bitter childhood was the last thing Rafael wanted to cloud his mind, but memories are not wont to ask permission.

A hot wind stirred up the dust on the streets of Valencia. On the Sabbath, the Montenegro family would normally be preparing to go to mass at the Church of St. Michael, but not this day. Rafael and his father Luis were getting ready to go to work in the stables of Lord Francisco. Luis Montenegro was the stable master and Rafael was being apprenticed to do the same sort of work. Now even that was in question. Lord Francisco had been killed by the occupying army of the Almovarids.

Marisela, Rafael's mother, had gone out to the small chicken coop on the side of the house to fetch eggs for their breakfast. "Just because there will be no mass today does not mean that it is not still the Sabbath," she had told them with a brave smile.

"Do not trouble yourself," Rafael's father implored her, "just stay inside." Marisela looked out through the window at the dark skinned troops that were moving through the streets. She looked down at her son. Rafael was only seven years of age.

"I will be right back with your breakfast mijo," she said with a smile. Rafael didn't know what to say. He didn't have the words to articulate his fear of what might happen to her. He was not the sort of boy who questioned his parents either. He smiled back at her the best he could and made a wish in the form of a silent prayer that she would be safe.

Marisela walked out the front door of their small dwelling for the last time. When she did not immediately return, Luis hurried to the window. "Marisela!" he called out. Rafael saw his father's face darken before the big man left by the front door also.

"Give them back!" the boy heard his mother's voice from outside. He ran to the door and peaked out. Several of the enemy soldiers had gathered around his mother. One of them was amusing himself by playing tug-of-war with her egg basket while

the others laughed. The soldier finally yanked the basket from his mother's grip. When she came forward to try and regain what was stolen, the soldier raised his arm and backhanded her across the face. Marisela did not cry out but she put a hand to the bruise that was forming on her cheek.

"Hey!" Luis barked. The soldier had not seen Rafael's father walking up behind him. He turned around just in time to see Luis' massive fist crashing into his face. The force of the blow knocked the man down. Luis stood menacingly over the one who had raised a hand to his wife.

"Leave him alone Luis," Marisela begged. The soldier picked himself up from the road and stood with one hand held to his mouth. Behind the man's hand, Rafael glimpsed a mess of blood and broken teeth. His father was breathing heavily, but Rafael knew that it was from anger and not exhaustion. The other soldiers had drawn their swords, but were still hesitant to advance on the towering Spaniard.

At the same time, a mounted patrol of the occupying army was coming up the road from behind Luis. One of the horsemen took notice of the confrontation and separated himself from the rest. "Papa, look out!" Rafael shouted, but Luis either did not hear or did not understand. Marisela, who was trying to pull Luis back toward the house and away from the soldiers, did notice the rider. The rider swung down with a heavy horseman's flail toward Rafael's father. Luis didn't have time to look back before the flail smashed into the back of his skull!

Blood gushed from the wound as Rafael's father crumpled to ground. His mother gave an agonizing cry and fell to the earth beside him. She knelt over his body. Her hands were feeling his face and she was begging him to wake up. "Papa!" Rafael cried. He ran out of the house and toward his parents.

"No Rafi!" his mother screamed as she noticed her child running out into the open. One of the soldiers on foot grabbed Marisela by her hair and jerked her head back. "Run mijo!" she shouted through her tears. Rafael hesitated. The soldier plunged his curved blade through Marisela's breast. He grinned as he yanked the blade out of her...and her life along with it. Rafael's mother fell dead on top of her husband.

The child knew he should not attract attention to himself, but nothing could stop the inarticulate cry of pain that burst forth from deep in his lungs. The soldiers took notice of him then. They conversed with each other rapidly in Arabic and began to advance toward him. "Come here boy," one of the soldiers commanded. Rafael turned and fled.

Rafael's childish instincts told him to run to the safety of his room, but something else sent him between the houses and back to the alleyways behind. He turned many corners to avoid pursuit. He kept running long after the soldiers had given up chasing him.

For nearly two years, Rafael lived in the streets, stealing whatever scraps of food he could to live. When Valencia was finally retaken by the Armies of Christ, Rafael was taken in by the Orphanage of St. Jude. Several years later, a scout for the army of Aragon came to the orphanage. Taller and stronger than most of the other boys, Rafael was a likely candidate for conscription. It was not necessary to force the lad, however. Rafael volunteered.

"How wonderful," Father Lysandro said with obvious pride.

"He seems healthy enough," the Spanish officer agreed. "So young man, you wish to do your part for Almighty God?"

"No," Rafael replied. "I just want to kill them." Father Lysandro had been quite upset with the boy's answer, but it suited the officer just fine. Rafael's sheer physical power and his burning desire for revenge carried him quickly up the ranks of Queen Petronilla's army. He was valued by his commander because he always had a cool head and an eye for strategic maneuvering. The men around him respected his strength and fearlessness. Many would conclude that it came from his size and skill, but this was not the case. Rafael did not fear death because it would only end the pain he felt over the loss of his parents. His marriage to Priscilla would change that. The birth of Isabel would change it completely.

✝   ✝   ✝

Lord Montenegro's arms were crossed and he held his chin in one hand as he glared down at the map. It was Captain Pascual who eventually broke the silence. "It appears that we are left to wait for the Crown of Aragon to send reinforcements," he said.

"Unless Captain Vidana was telling the truth," Rafael replied.

"That is doubtful."

"True," Rafael agreed, "but still a possibility. Lord Montenegro let out a snarl as he pounded his fist on the table. "My God we cannot afford to wait!"

"We are outnumbered my Lord," Pascual reminded him.

"I know," Rafael said angrily, "and we may be even more so when Aragon's troops arrive. I hate to admit it, but we have to act first."

"How can we? Even if we attack by night, we are not likely to overcome them."

"We have to strike at their heart," Rafael replied. "Lord Enriquez must die. Get me a man in the city. I need to know where his lordship is staying."

"I could send a man out through the secret entrance you spoke of," Captain Pascual suggested. "I am certain that it will then be easy to acquire the information you seek."

"Good."

"I must inform you that we have no professional assassins in our employ, and..."

"I know," Rafael interrupted him, "but we shall have to make due."

"I will find a man presently," Captain Pascual said.

"Thank you Captain," Lord Montenegro replied. "May God help us all." Rafael remained in his study after his officer had left. He spent a large part of the day brooding over the darker possibilities that might lie ahead. One of the kitchen servants brought him a meal but he barely tasted it. His mind was preoccupied with death and the horrors that were no doubt being inflicted upon the brave common folk. He felt guilty for sitting safely behind the walls of the keep.

When it was nearing dusk, Rafael led Captain Pascual and the soldier he had selected up to the bed chamber where his wife and daughter were waiting. Captain Pascual's scout was an older man with short grey hair and a face weathered by the elements. Rafael pulled the bed back from the wall and removed a panel that had been hidden behind it. "Once you discover where Lord Enriquez is making his bed, you will not return to the keep," Rafael instructed the man. "You will wait until tomorrow night when the moon is high in the sky. At that time, you will make haste to Lover's Rock. Do you know it?"

"Every man who grew up in Black River Village knows it my Lord," the man grinned.

"Excellent," Rafael replied. "Off you go then. See to it that you are not captured."

"I will see to it," the man replied. With that, he got down on his hands and knees and crawled through the space that had been opened in the wall. There was a tunnel of rock behind it. Rafael replaced the wall panel as the soldier got to his feet on the other side. He then pushed the bed back into place. This time Captain Pascual assisted him.

"All will be lost if he is captured," Lady Priscilla said nervously.

"That is why I told him not to let that happen," Rafael answered her. "Do not worry my dear. He is dressed as a peasant. No one will pay him any mind." Priscilla did not look comforted, but she nodded her head in understanding. "Let us go," Rafael told his captain. "I will explain the next part of my plan." Captain Pascual nodded and followed Rafael back to the study. Once the two men were closed inside, Rafael laid out what would take place.

A small unit of men would meet the spy at the appointed time. These men would then lead a daring assault on Lord Enriquez as he slept. They would ensure that his body would be seen by the mercenaries. This would put the matter of the sell swords' compensation in question. "With no leader, and no idea whether or not they will get paid," Rafael explained, "my hope is that it will cause them to disburse."

"That could actually work," the officer said with approval.

"Let us pray that it does," Rafael suggested. The two men bowed their heads over the map while Rafael sent their hopes heavenward. He prayed to God for success in the coming endeavor. He prayed that the Holy Spirit would be with them. He prayed also to Christ and many of the Saints. "And watch over us oh God," he said in conclusion, "that we may live and that the traitors may at last find repentance in the flames of perdition...amen."

"Amen," Captain Pascual echoed. They stood for several more moments in silence before leaving the war room. The next several hours were spent selecting the twenty men who would be part of the mission. Captain Pascual assumed that he would be leading it. It would have been safer to wait out the siege, but every time Rafael was tempted to do this, his mind would replay the sword thrust that ended his mother's life. Thus, Lord Montenegro was resolved to his course.

Rafael had his wife and daughter moved to a different bedroom for the evening. He did not want the men to see his wife in any state of undress and God forbid they should lay their eyes on Isabel! He decided not to tell Priscilla that he planned to lead the mission himself. It would only cause her to worry needlessly. If he were to die, Priscilla could mourn him then...not before. In any case, the both of them would be taken care of by the Count of Barcelona upon his return, living or dead.

When darkness set in, Rafael and his family gathered before the hearth. Isabel read the 23rd Psalm out of the Biblia Sacra that he had purchased for her in Teruel all those years ago. There were tears shed by those he loved, but Rafael made sure to keep a brave face on. He would not dishearten them by showing his own apprehension. Death was now something to fear for it meant losing them. He feared even more what might happen if the keep was taken.

If Rafael had known what was to transpire that evening, he might have spent more time with his daughter.

He had told Priscilla not to worry. He would always love her and he would always be there for her. If he had known, he might have made love to her one last time. Unfortunately, Rafael was not a seer that he could divine the future.

When the time was at hand, Lord Montenegro was gathered with Captain Pascual and the twenty soldiers who had been selected to perform the raid. Rodrigo the archer was among them. He was a young man with long brown hair tied back into a pony tail. He had sharp eyes that seemed to be in a constant state of alertness. He carried a long bow and had a full quiver of arrows on his back.

Several of the men had torches, but only one was lit. Two of the soldiers pushed the bed aside and Rafael removed the panel which covered the tunnel into the mountain. He knelt down in front of the tunnel and motioned for the men to gather round. "Let us pray," he said. The men bowed their heads and closed their eyes as they knelt around their lord.

"Oh God," Rafael prayed. "We come to you your humble servants. We ask for your guidance as we prepare to engage the traitors who are encamped around us. Send Michael to watch over us and protect us from harm. Let the Holy Spirit sharpen our eyes, empower our hands, and strengthen our resolve to do your will. Be with the women and children of these brave men who kneel before you. Be with the people of Montenegro who even now are suffering under this army of sinners. Protect them and give them hope that your servants are coming to their rescue. Let the death of Lord Enriquez be swift and merciless oh God. Let it break the enemy's will to fight. We pray all this in the name of the Father, the Son, and the Holy Spirit…Amen"

"Amen," the soldiers said as one.

"This is it," Rafael told them. "Are you all prepared to fight for our homeland?" Their answers were many but they were all in the affirmative. "Some of us may die," Rafael said, "but our sacrifice will not be in vain. Think of your wives…your children. This is why we fight. Are you with me?"

"We are with you my Lord," one of the soldiers said stalwartly. There were murmurs of approval and echoes of the first man's declaration. "Captain Pascual," Rafael said as he turned to face the man.

"Yes my lord?" the officer answered.

"You are to remain here and defend the keep."

"Who will lead the raid," the man protested.

"I will," Lord Montenegro replied.

"But my lord…"

"But nothing Captain," Rafael cut him off. "I cannot remain here while the children of Black River Village are in danger. I will hear nothing more of it. You are to remain here."

"As you command," Pascual said heavily.

"I entrust you to protect my child…and my wife."

"With everything I have," Captain Pascual promised.

"I will return Captain," Rafael said. "Await my coming. The rest of you are with me." Rafael ducked down and crawled into the tunnel that had been carved into the rock. His men followed and his captain closed up the wall behind them. They could hear the scraping noise as the bed was pushed back into place. Rafael took the lit torch from the soldier who carried it and led his men forward. The tunnel widened the farther in they traveled until they were walking through a huge cavern under the mountain. Water dripped down from the stalactites and echoed on the face of the granite floor below. The cavern was vast and it took them almost an hour to traverse from one side to the other. When Rafael's torch began to gutter out, he would use it to light one of the unused torches.

Partially hidden behind a huge stalagmite at the end of the cavern was the tunnel that would take them up into open air. The tunnel ended in a forested area of a saddle high up in the Pyrenees. It was a clear night. The stars shown brightly in the sky and the full moon bathed everything in a pale glow. Rafael put out the torch he was carrying in the damp earth at the mouth of the tunnel. He led his men into the trees. The sounds of the forest were amplified by the night air. Rafael's men were trying very hard to be quiet. One of their boots snapped a branch and the sound of it echoed through the darkness.

"No matter," Rafael said out loud at the men who were whispering to one another. There is no one that can hear this far. They resumed their march and eventually heard the bleating of sheep in the distance. The trees opened up on a clearing in the center of the saddle they were walking over. There was a small log dwelling near the edge of the clearing but no light shone from within. Next to the house was a covered pen for some forty sheep. As they drew closer, the growl of a large dog echoed across the open field. The men put their hands to their weapons but Rafael motioned for them to stand down. "All is well," he admonished them. "We are still among friends."

Rafael went forward, leaving his men following behind. The shaggy grey dog by the sheep pen began to bark loudly and the sheep voiced their own fears as the men approached. The door of the cottage opened. An old man stood there in his night robe. He had a lantern in one hand which illuminated his grey bearded face. The other hand bore a large hatchet. "Don't come any closer," the old man warned them. The herding dog seemed to agree as she growled and barked by her master's side.

"It is only I Javier," Lord Montenegro called out.

"Rafael?" the old man queried. "Who have you brought with you?" Javier asked as he squinted into the darkness.

"These men are my soldiers," Rafael replied.

"You promised I would be left alone," the old man grumped.

"That is why you are out here old friend," Rafael agreed as he drew closer. The Spanish water dog had stopped barking, but still stood protectively by her master's side.

"You said you would not come out here unless there was a war," Javier said accusingly.

"There is a war," Rafael confirmed.

"So what do you need me for General? I am a cripple."

"We are just trying to sneak up on them," Lord Montenegro explained. "We need to get down the back way."

"So you're not starving?"

"No."

"I suppose you want me to show you where the goat trail is. Did I not show it to you already?"

"That was a long time ago. It was also in the middle of the day."

"In a moment," the old shepherd grumbled. "I have to get dressed." He slammed the door behind him as he and the dog went back inside. Several minutes later, Javier reappeared in a course woolen tunic and leggings. He leaned on a crooked staff for support and a sword was girded on his belt. "You kids follow me," he said unceremoniously. Rafael motioned for the men and they all followed.

The old man led them to a narrow trail that hugged the backside of the mountain. "There it is," Javier pointed at the treacherous path. "Take care that you do not get killed."

"Farewell," Rafael replied. The trail was barely wide enough to fit one man and so the going was slow and arduous. In places, the trail narrowed to the point that they had to sidestep to avoid falling down the steep drop that would certainly lead to an unpleasant end.

Once off the trail, Rafael's band traveled through the dark forest until they had walked all the way around the mountain. They found themselves at the waterfall that spilled down into the gorge from beside Montenegro's Keep. Rafael and his soldiers walked along the riverbank. The river flowed around another mountain before reaching the flatlands.

Rafael knew that they would find Black River Village about a league downstream on the opposite shore. This was not their initial destination, however. Staying within the safety of the trees, they made their way toward Lover's Rock. They crept quietly through the forest when they drew near to the docks. They could see enemy soldiers patrolling on the other side of the water.

When one of the men stepped on a dry twig, they all froze. Rafael made a motion with his hand for them to get down. Each of the men crouched down slowly and waited. "You hear something?" one of the enemy soldier's voices floated across the river to the spot where the men of Montenegro were hidden.

"I heard nothing," another man answered. Rafael kept his men still until the soldiers resumed their patrol of the docks. Even then, they waited some time before moving again. While he was waiting for the enemy to calm down, Rafael noticed a sailing vessel moored next to the dock by Black River Village's shipping yard. The vessel had two sails, neither of which bore the standard of Montenegro. They were not colored with the violet hue of Morera either. This ship was not docked next to the side of the pier as was usual, but positioned at the end of it. The vessel was facing down river and there were two soldiers guarding the dock that led out to it. Another odd thing about the sailboat was the rudder. It was made up of the pintel and gudgeon that would normally be seen on a much larger ship. Rafael had never before seen its like.

Storm clouds were quickly rolling in from the east as Rafael and his men made their way down river. Lover's Rock jutted out on the opposite bank. It was a large shelf of stone that rested along the shoreline. It was higher on the side facing the village and sloped down to form a flat surface on the other. It was here that young lover's often came to hide from view.

When Rafael came out of the trees, Pascual's scout stood up from where he was hiding against the rock. The man picked up an arrow that was attached to a length of rope. This arrow he knocked in his long bow and shot high out over the water. The arrow stuck into the earth on Rafael's side of the river. "Secure that rope," Rafael told Rodrigo. The young archer picked up the rope and the arrow with it. He removed the arrow and tied the rope securely to a tree. On the other side of the river, the scout was doing the same thing.

One by one, Rafael and his men pulled themselves across the swift current until they reached the other side. Rain began to fall as the men gathered on top of Lover's Rock. The scout came very close to Rafael so that he could be heard above the rain. "Lord Enriquez is inside the warehouse at the bank of the river," the scout reported. "There are six sentries within and ten to fifteen without. Change of the guard has been going at midday and midnight.

"What of the sailing vessel by the dock?" Rafael asked the man.

"It belongs to Lord Enriquez. I assume it is staged for a hasty retreat. The prow faces down river and the pier is always guarded."

"I saw it as we passed the village," Rafael told him. "Unfortunately, I could not see a good avenue of approach to the warehouse. We need the element of surprise for this to work."

"I have taken care of that," the scout said proudly. I have acquired over a score of the short white tunics that the dock workers wear."

"Where did you get so many?"

"From the dock workers themselves," the scout answered. "Enriquez has them working day and night to gather up the goods looted by the soldiers and prepare them for transport to Morera. The dock workers will change shifts at midnight also."

"And we are to take their places this night," Rafael finished for him.

"Precisely," the scout agreed.

"What about our swords?"

"We will smuggle them in with the loot from the village…trunks, rolled up cloth, anything that will hold a sword."

"Perfect," Rafael grinned. "They shall never see us coming!"

"Except..," the scout trailed off.

"Except what," Rafael said impatiently?

"You cannot be among them my Lord."

"Why not?"

"How many men in Black River Village have your stature?"

"Damn," Rafael cursed! The scout was right. "Very well, all of you change into your disguises. Rodrigo and I will lie in wait for Lord Enriquez to flee." The scout hefted a bundle of white cloth. When he tore the red twin that held it together, the bundle revealed itself to be the aforementioned tunics. The men gathered round and each took one. They changed quickly into their new disguises. "You shall take command of the raid," Rafael told the scout. "It is your operation after all."

"Yes my lord," the man said proudly.

"Do not bring them all into town at once," Rafael warned.

"We will be very discreet," the scout assured him.

"God be with you."

"And also with you Lord Montenegro," the scout replied. He led the men into the forest while Rafael and Rodrigo re-crossed the river. The rain was coming faster and with it the current. Rodrigo was almost lost to it, but Rafael pulled him back to the rope in the nick of time. The two men traveled upriver to the ambush site across from the docks. As they passed a sharp bend in the river, an idea began to from in Rafael's mind.

"Stay here," he told Rodrigo when they were almost in position. Rafael then began to strip off his chain mail armor.

"What are we doing my lord?" Rodrigo inquired.

"I am going swimming," Rafael replied. When he had stripped down to his undergarments, he looked back again at the archer. "Give me your dagger," he said.

"The dagger is my last defense," Rodrigo protested.

"Do what I tell you," Rafael commanded. "I will return shortly. I am your last defense."

"Your will be done," Rodrigo said with uncertainty. He handed the long dagger over to Lord Montenegro.

"Go down river and lie in wait just up from the bend we passed earlier. Give sufficient distance that you will be allowed several arrows before the boat goes around the turn. You are to kill whoever is working the sails."

"I will," Rodrigo agreed.

"Make sure you do not miss."

"I do not miss," the archer said with confidence. Rafael nodded and left the man to wait for him in the forest. The wind, rain, and the motion of the ship would all be working to Rodrigo's disadvantage. He prayed that the man's skill and confidence would be enough.

CHAPTER X

Rafael kept a low profile as he crept through the forest toward the village. Stealth was not his specialty, but the darkness and the rain made up for his short-comings. The clouds were now dumping down water in great sheets. The sound of the rain hitting the river drowned out all else.

The two sentries protecting the boat remained miserably in their assigned position. The rain did not allow torches to burn. Rafael could only see his enemies in the brief flashes of lightning created by the thunderstorm. The patrols and the rest of the men had taken shelter inside the warehouse. At the end of one particular illumination, Rafael broke from his hiding place. He quickly ran to the water's edge. He did not leap into the river but lowered himself slowly so as not to startle anyone.

The current of Black River was swift and made stronger by the rain. It took all of Rafael's might to swim upriver to the boat that waited at the last dock. He came up gasping for breath on the side of the boat facing away from the warehouse. He edged around the sailboat until he reached the rudder at the back of the vessel. Holding onto the rudder allowed him to both hide and rest behind it. If the weather were not so intense, one of Enriquez' guards might have noticed his fingers curling around from the other side.

Once he had caught his breath, Rafael plunged back down into the dark water. He had to feel rather than see the place where the two pieces of the rudder came together. He took Rodrigo's blade and inserted it through this narrow space until the thickest part of the dagger was stuck between. He yanked up as hard as he could on the handle until the dagger was completely secured between the pieces of wood. The ship's ability to turn was now gone without the proper wind.

Rafael came up for one last breath of air before swimming down river. He swam below the churning surface of the water. This time the current was working with him and he washed out onto the opposite shore far away from the sight of the guards. He fled immediately into the trees and made his way quickly back to where Rodrigo was yet hiding. "I do not like this visibility," Rodrigo commented when Lord Montenegro returned.

"There is not much of a choice," Rafael answered. Rodrigo just shook his head. The padded shirt that went under Rafael's armor was soaked through from the rain. It felt heavy in his hands. While Rafael had to ascertain whether he should wear the armor at all, they heard shouts coming from up the river. The faint sounds of clashing steel told them that the attack on the shipping warehouse had begun. It did not seem to Rafael that enough time had passed but there was no way to tell with the moon obscured behind the black clouds. "Remember your mission," he told the young archer. "All of Montenegro depends on this day." He did not wait for Rodrigo to reply, but ran through the drenched forest.

There was no time for the armor. Rafael had to reach the bend in the river before the ship. His heart was pounding from exertion when he finally reached his destination. He quickly scooped up some of the river water in his hands and drank before hunkering down behind some bushes between the soaking wet trees.

After what seemed like a long time, the sailing vessel materialized on the river in front of him. Rafael had just enough time to see the dead man at the helm before he was forced to leap out of the way. The navigator was slumped over the wheel with an arrow sticking out of his chest and another that had punctured through his neck. The boat crashed up onto the riverbank and lodged between the two trees where Rafael had been hiding. He made a crouching run toward the side of the sailboat and pressed himself up against the now exposed underbelly. He drew his sword. The sails were creaking in the wind and rain as Rafael prepared himself for whatever might come.

There was the sound of the cabin's door opening from above and boots coming up onto the deck. Rafael could feel the vibrations in the wood. He tightened his grip on the long sword and waited. "They shot him through the neck," a man's voice called over the din.

"Well, I do not pay you to stand there gaping like children," Lord Enriquez shouted! "Get this thing back on the water!" Out of his peripheral vision, Rafael saw a leather boot coming down over the side of the prow. Lord Montenegro side-stepped toward the front of the ship. He was almost within reach when the guard leapt down. Rafael did not hesitate. The man's knees buckled slightly as he landed on the muddy earth of the forest floor. Before the guard could rise from his semi-crouching position, Rafael brought his sword down with both hands.

The blade of the long sword cleaved through the man's neck and severed his spinal column before ripping out the other side. The disconnected head fell into the mud and the decapitated corpse quickly followed. Blood pooled in the mud even as the rain diluted it. Something else happened as well. The skin of the dead guard shrunk inward and blackened as it rapidly decomposed before Rafael's disbelieving eyes.

There was no time to marvel over it. "We are under attack!" shouted a third man's voice. Wasting no time, Rafael ran back to the side of the ship. He had to duck to avoid running into the tree branches which were pushed up against it. He sheathed his sword and pulled himself up onto the deck. The remaining body guard noticed the intruder as he came up over the side. Lord Enriquez' guard already had his sword drawn and rushed toward Rafael.

Rafael was not given enough time to draw his own blade before the other man struck out at him. Rafael rolled off onto the deck to avoid the attack and rose up to his feet. In the same motion of drawing his sword, Lord Montenegro brought the handle crashing up into his enemy's ear. The man staggered back as his vertigo was turned upside down. Rafael held the blade of his sword low as he circled toward the body guard. The other man was having trouble keeping his balance and held his bloody ear with the free hand.

Lord Montenegro stepped forward with the blade held out horizontally before him. This forced his enemy to parry. As Rafael had hoped, the man brought his sword out vertically, blocking the attack with the part of the sword closest to the hilt. As soon as the two blades came together; Rafael pressed the attack by shoving his opponent forward, putting the man even more off balance. At the same time, he brought up his boot and stomped down hard on his enemy's kneecap.

Enriquez' guard grunted in pain and fell to one knee. Before he could rise again, Lord Montenegro plunged his long sword into the enemy's throat. There was a gurgling noise from the dying man as blood filled his mouth. Rafael planted his boot in the man's chest and pushed him off the sword. He twisted the blade which tore the wound even wider as the sword came free.

The man fell hard onto the deck of the sailboat. Rafael could actually see the flesh of the man's throat reconstructing itself! Rafael's mind was trying to sell him a comforting story about the heavy rain and that it was just a trick of the light. The warrior instinct told him otherwise. Rafael brought the long sword down quickly across the guard's neck. It had worked on the first guard. Once severed, the head shriveled in on itself. This man's corpse did not completely decompose but went from that of a youth to an old man in seconds. Rafael kicked the head away in horror. It sailed through the air and off the side of the ship, landing on the earth with a wet thud. Rafael shoved his boot hard into the crotch of the man's remains, sending the body to join the head in the mud. He only succeeded in shoving it against the side of the ship, however. He looked then at the door leading down into the cabin. "It is finished Enriquez!" he shouted over the driving rain.

The door to the sleeper hold was thrown open and banged against the sides of the boat. The wind bashed the door against the wall several more times as Lord Enriquez ascended the few short stairs. Lightning illuminated the two lords starkly against the night. Enriquez wore a dark suit of leather armor with a violet cloak. The cloak bore the white crest of Morera upon it. In his hand he held a thin saber and there was a look of cool arrogance upon his face.

Rafael wore only his boots and brown pantalones. He had left his tunic and armor in the forest. His arms and chest rippled with muscle as he gripped his sword. Water ran in rivulets over his bare skin. "Montenegro," Enriquez sneered. "What a pleasant surprise! I never expected to see you here."

"I imagine not," Rafael replied. "Your guards are dead. That leaves you."

"You risk much by coming here," Lord Enriquez scoffed. "Have you no one left willing to undergo such a mission?"

"I have many brave men remaining. I simply choose not to hide behind them until I am forced to beg for my life. You are welcome to do so, but I would spare yourself the humiliation. Begging will not change the fact that I have come to execute justice upon you."

"Begging," Lord Enriquez asked with dripping sarcasm, "is that what you imagined would happen now?"

"You could have come to your men's aide. You did not. This shows you a coward."

"You have not the smallest idea of whom you are dealing with," Enriquez chuckled. The men were slowly circling each other with blades drawn.

"This will spare you the indignity of facing trial," Rafael told his opponent. "The king would surely drag you in front of…"

"I am king," Lord Enriquez snarled. "You are simply the only one in Aragon fool enough not to know it!"

"Your men died together," Rafael said accusingly. "They were soldiers. You shall die alone…a traitor…and a coward."

"You cannot kill that which has transcended the grave," Enriquez grinned. The enemy lord began to laugh as lightning forked across the sky afar off. Rafael could see the sharp canine teeth inside the man's mouth. The creature charged forward with the saber raised high over his head.

As soon as Lord Enriquez brought his thin blade down onto Rafael's larger sword, he became a blur of motion! Rafael was being driven back by the man's quick and relentless strikes. He drew first blood with a wide but shallow gash into Rafael's chest. Rafael grunted but did not cry out. His wrists were sore already from parrying Enriquez' attacks... (attacks which were delivered at dizzying speeds). He had never before fought a man who could move so swiftly, but this was not a man. It was something else.

"You cannot hope to win," Enriquez sneered as they circled each other once more, "but perhaps if you take an oath of vassalage; I could be moved to show mercy." They circled for another few moments. Rafael did not answer. He needed to save his strength. Thunder rolled and lightning crashed down from the sky. The lightning went to ground through a nearby tree. The bolt split the tree in half and lit it on fire! The flames were quickly doused by the rain.

"I know not from what pit you were spawned," Rafael breathed as another shaft of electricity lit up the night sky, "but I shall return you to hell!" The sound of their blades rang in Rafael's ears as they fought across the deck of the derelict ship. Enriquez opened several ribbon cuts across Rafael's arms and upper body. The smaller man had been forced to give ground as Rafael's determined attack began, but now it was Rafael who was being driven toward the edge.

They locked swords as Rafael's backside was pushed up against the side wall of the ship. Enriquez used his greater strength to push the larger man toward a fall. Before he could succeed, Rafael used his own head to smash into his opponent's face. Enriquez fell back a mere second, more from surprise than injury. Rafael feinted right with his sword. Enriquez brought the saber up to block. There was a thin trail of blood from his broken nose, but the bone itself was rapidly healing.

With Enriquez attention locked on the sword, Rafael seized the opportunity to smash into the creature's jaw with a powerful left hook! While Enriquez' head was being rocked by the blow, Rafael rammed his sword between the joints of the dark leather armor. The blade entered through the man's left armpit and the point stuck up from the back of his left shoulder. Rafael twisted the blade as he forced it back out. A spray of blood followed.

The fight should have been won. Rafael had struck a major artery. Instead, he found himself blocking another barrage of sword strikes. Enriquez attacks felt increasingly more powerful as the fight continued. Rafael knew that his enemy was not growing stronger. That would be impossible. In actuality, Rafael's wrists were weakening from having to hold up against him. He had used this very thing to his own advantage against skilled opponents in the past. Rafael had to change tactics or else he would be defeated.

After blocking another of Enriquez' wrist jarring blows, Rafael brought his sword up in both hands as if to do a vertical overhand strike. Enriquez raised the saber to ward off the attack. Instead of steel meeting steel, Rafael let his legs drop out from under him. He landed in a low crouch, all the while swinging the blade horizontally with all his might. The long sword sliced through flesh and bone; shearing off one of Enriquez' legs just below the knee, and ripping through the other all the way to bone!

Enriquez cried out in pain as he lost his feet. He spun to the left as he fell; tearing more of the flesh from his remaining leg before hitting the deck face first. A mortal man would surely be defeated by such a savage wound. Rafael knew that this was no man of flesh and blood. There was no time to hesitate. Rafael pressed the attack!

Launching himself up into the air, Rafael raised his sword high. He reversed his grip on the handle so the blade pointed downward. As he landed, Rafael planted one boot on the deck of the ship and the other onto the base of Enriquez' spine. He used the momentum of the jump, his full weight, and all the strength he could muster to drive the long sword down into his enemy's skull! There was a satisfying 'thunk' as Rafael's blade bit into the wood of the ship.

Enriquez' head was now stapled to the deck with blood pooling below it. Rafael breathed raggedly as he leaned on the hilt of his weapon. He had been cut many times by the saber and his wounds seemed to burn as the rain washed over them. The fear that Rafael had put aside now came heavily upon him. Had he been doing battle with devils? He looked around nervously as he struggled to catch his breath. Were there more? Father Lysandro had taught the children that the devil's angels were everywhere. Back then it had seemed like mere words to scare them into obedience.

Rafael made the sign of the cross before grasping his long sword with both hands. "God, give me the strength to protect my family," he whispered into the darkness. Another bolt of lightning crashed and the scene was briefly illuminated by its brilliance. Rafael yanked the long sword free and raised it high above his head. There was just enough time to see the creature that called itself Enriquez starting to move. Its hands clutched in spastic motions before the blade fell.

A great cry burst forth from Rafael's mouth as he removed the demon's head from the rest of its body. The decomposition of Enriquez was almost instantaneous. The flesh shriveled up and flecked away like ash. Not even bone remained. Lord Enriquez had turned to dust. Rafael felt suddenly light headed. He dropped to one knee as darkness filled his vision. "Thank you," he whispered toward heaven, and then he saw no more.

Isabel awakened to a loud scraping noise coming from behind the bed where she and her mother were slept. She sat up and shook her mother as the scraping continued. "What is it?" Lady Priscilla asked drowsily. There was a loud bang as the panel behind the bed fell from the wall and landed on the floor behind the head board.

The two guards stationed inside the room were already positioned to either side with their swords drawn. "Lady Priscilla," Rodrigo called through the opening. "It is I…Rodrigo…an archer of Montenegro." Isabel and her mother had already risen from the bed and moved behind the guards. The additional soldiers posted outside the door had moved into the room as well. "I have Lord Montenegro," Rodrigo shouted. "He needs a doctor! Move this accursed thing out of my way!"

"That is Rodrigo," one of the guards said. "I recognize his voice!"

"Move the bed," ordered another. Four of them set to work shoving the heavy bed away from the opening. One propped up the panel beside the opening.

"Fetch us a doctor," Priscilla screamed out into the hallway. Rafael was unconscious as they pulled his body through the opening. He entered head first and on his back and was quickly lifted up by the six soldiers in the bedroom. Isabel saw an old man with the younger Rodrigo inside the tunnel. The grey bearded shepherd turned around and left as soon as the soldiers had taken Rafael's body from their hands.

"Thank you," Rodrigo called after him. There was some muttering from the other man as he departed, but Isabel could not make out what was said. Rodrigo crawled through into the bedroom and helped one of the guards replace the panel in the wall. The rest of them carried Lord Montenegro to his bed. Rafael moaned as they hoisted him up and onto the sheets.

"Be careful," Priscilla nearly shouted as they pushed the bed back into place!

"Lady Priscilla," Pilar called from the doorway. Priscilla looked back as Isabel was stroking her father's forehead. "We do not have a physician." Pilar's face looked stricken.

"Oh my God! Why not," Priscilla asked? Her voice was sick with worry.

"The doctor," Pilar faltered; "he was in town tending to the injured when… Black River Village now belongs to Lord Enriquez."

"Oh my Rafael," Priscilla sobbed as she turned back toward her husband. She rubbed her hand across one of his massive arms. The ribbon cuts were now swollen and angry looking.

"You know more than the rest of us," Isabel told the old woman without looking back. "You have to help him."

"Oh I do not know mija," Pilar said as she wrung her hands nervously.

"We have no time for your indecision!" Isabel shouted. "Help him now!"

"Alright, alright," Little Grandma told herself more than Isabel. "I can do this." She came over to the bedside and took charge. "Help me take off his wet clothes," she told Isabel.

"I ought to do that," Priscilla said nervously. Isabel did not like the panic in her mother's face.

"It is alright mother," Isabel said as she worked off one of her father's boots. "I am quite capable."

"If my lady would have hot water and dry clothing brought to us," Little Grandma requested.

"Right away," Priscilla answered. She quickly retrieved a tunic from Rafael's wardrobe and placed it over the foot of the bed. She then left the room and began shouting orders to the servants. The cloths were brought up and with them a tub of steaming water. Little Grandma dunked one of the cloths in the hot water and used it to clean Rafael's wounds. Isabel followed suit. When it was done they used still other cloths to pat him dry. The inflammation of the wounds gave Isabel cause to worry but she pushed that to the back of her mind. The last of the cloths they tore into strips to make bandages.

Together, they used the long strips of white cloth to bind Rafael's wounds. He began to shiver violently as beads of sweat formed on his brow. Isabel put one slender hand on her father's cheek. "He is so cold but his head is burning up!" she told Pilar.

"Get his bed clothes," Little Grandma replied. It took some effort, but they eventually got Rafael into a night robe and bundled him under the blankets. Little Grandma put a wet cloth on his feverish brow. The shivering did not subside. "Lay down with your husband," she told Isabel's mother. "The heat from your body will warm him. Priscilla quickly crawled into bed.

"I can help too," Isabel volunteered. She got under the blankets and lied down on the other side of her father.

"What now?" Priscilla asked nervously.

"Just wait," Pilar said. "We must pray that the fever will break. I will come back to check on him from time to time. Try and get some rest."

"Alright," Priscilla replied. She snuggled close to Rafael and looked into his face with worry. Isabel nuzzled her cheek up to her father's arm and closed her eyes. She looked to be the calmer of the two, but her mind was wracked with fear. The candles were snuffed out and the soldiers were made to wait outside the room.

Isabel eventually fell into a fitful slumber. She was awakened by her father talking in his sleep. "They are everywhere," Rafael was muttering to himself. Everywhere," he then said loudly!

"It is alright Papa," Isabel shushed him. "You are home now." Her mother was sleeping soundly. "They are everywhere," he whispered, "all around us!"

"Who is?" Isabel asked him.

"Devils," Rafael replied with agitation.

"They are gone now."

"No," Rafael mumbled fearfully. "Sharp teeth...too fast...too strong..." He looked wildly around the room before shouting, "God protect my family!"

"I am right here beside you Papa," Isabel said comfortingly. She wasn't sure if her father was awake or not. His eyes were half lidded and she was not certain if someone who talked in their sleep could also respond.

"Heads...have to cut them off, cut their heads," he mumbled. Isabel opened her mouth to speak but she was cut off by her father's screaming. "Cut their cursed heads off," he shouted at the top of his lungs. Priscilla moaned and stirred in her sleep but did not awaken.

"Shhhh," Isabel hissed. "You are safe Papa!"

"Take off their heads! Take off..," he trailed off. Rafael began to breathe easily, but then snorted and opened his eyes. "Mija," he asked groggily, "what are you doing here?" Did you have a bad dream?"

"No," Isabel said. She was so relieved to hear him speaking naturally. "You are sick. Mama and I were trying to keep you warm." Rafael looked over at Priscilla who slept on.

"So you are," he smiled. Isabel put a hand to his forehead. It was still warm, yet not as hot as before. "I think the fever is breaking," she said happily.

"I feel so tired," Rafael sighed, "like I had been up for days."

"Get some sleep Papa," Isabel told him as she snuggled once more to his side.

"No," Rafael said with some confusion in his voice. "I need to talk to you."

"Alright," Isabel agreed, "but then you will go to sleep."

"Yes," Rafael said, "I will try to be quick." Isabel waited for her father to go on. "You should comply with Alfonso's request."

"What?" Isabel asked with displeasure creeping into her voice.

"Let them perform the annulment."

"Do not be silly," Isabel whispered. "I love Ramon more than anything!"

"More than your father," Rafael asked?

"Almost," Isabel said, "but I will not leave him. I cannot."

"That will not end well," Rafael sighed.

"How do you know," Isabel asked skeptically?

"The same way I know that you are to take my place."

"What?"

"I saw it in a dream. I was speaking with an angel."

"It was just a dream," Isabel told him.

"Priscilla is a great woman and a perfect wife," Rafael said as if he was not listening to her, "but she will not be able to do it on her own. There are things she cannot do…things a man should do."

"You are going to be fine," Isabel said. "Mama has you for those things."

"Now she'll need you," Rafael said sadly.

"You should try to sleep," Isabel said gently.

"I am not finished Isabel," he replied. "Oh…my head feels like a heavy weight. This cannot happen just yet."

"I will call Little Grandma," Isabel said worriedly.

"No."

"Can I do something…anything?"

"Just listen," her father told her. Rodrigo has Lord Enriquez´ cloak. It is covered in his blood."

"You do not have to tell me of this," Isabel interrupted.

"I do," Rafael said angrily, "and you need to listen as I told you!'

"Sorry Papa," Isabel said worriedly. She could see that yelling put a strain on the man.

"The catapult in the courtyard should be constructed soon. Press upon your men to finish it." Isabel did not like the way her father referred to the soldiers as hers. "As soon as it is done, launch the cloak down at the enemy. Tie the cloak around a rock. The enemy must know he is dead. You have to make certain of it!'

"I will," Isabel said nervously.

"My little girl," Rafael smiled. His voice was coming short of breath. "I always knew you were the one." Isabel did not understand what her father meant but she caressed his head with one hand until his breathing became even. Her own eyes grew heavy and her hand seemed to lose its strength as sleep overtook her as well.

Isabel drifted off with her hand resting on her father's chest. His arm encircled her and held her close, much as he had done when she was a small child and had awakened from a bad dream. As Isabel slept, the poison from Lord Enriquez' blade ran its course. Rafael gave up the ghost...and was no more.

Part II

The Tragedy Of Isabel

CHAPTER I

Isabel awoke to a stale odor and the sound of her mother's frantic screams. Lady Priscilla was crouched over the lifeless form of her husband. Her tiny fists were beating on Rafael's chest as her tears flowed freely.

The sentries rushed in from outside the door. They came in with swords drawn but quickly sheathed their weapons. The spectacle of their dead lord and his grieving widow played out on the bed before them. Isabel felt numb. She watched her mother as if she were but an observer in a dream. Her father's head lolled to the side. His dead eyes seemed to stare at Isabel as his mouth dropped open.

Isabel rose from the bed and backed up quickly. She kept telling herself that this could not be real. She reached out and held onto her father's hand. There was no warmth in it. Rafael was dead.

The Heiress of Montenegro began to tremble as the weight of what had happened settled upon her like a millstone. Quite uncontrollably, Isabel began to weep. She made no sound, though her chest hitched and tears fell from her eyes. She could barely swallow for the lump in her throat.

At some point, Pilar and Alejandra were pulling Lady Priscilla from the bed. Her mother's face was a mess of anguish and loss. The two chambermaids gently led her from the room. The soldiers stood in uncomfortable silence as Isabel's body shook with sorrow. Slowly, she crawled back into the bed and laid her head down on her father's chest. Her crying became audible as she pressed her cheek up against Rafael's cold flesh.

Isabel did not know how long she lay there crying, but eventually a priest entered the room to give Lord Montenegro his last rites. Captain Pascual escorted the man in. It was he who propped up Isabel's sobbing mother in the background. When the funeral rites were concluded, Isabel still lay there holding onto her father. There was none in the chamber who had the heart to remove her.

Finally, Captain Pascual came forward and held out a hand. His face was stricken with grief. Isabel took his hand and allowed him to pull her up from her father's death bed. She wiped the tears from her eyes as her father's last instructions came back to her. "Where is the one called Rodrigo?" Isabel asked. It took all her efforts to retain her composure.

"Rodrigo the archer," Captain Pascual queried? "He is no doubt on the battlements my lady."

"Bring him up to the east tower," Isabel commanded. "Bring cloak of Lord Enriquez as well."

"It will be done," Captain Pascual agreed with some confusion. He looked at Priscilla for a contradiction but none came. Rafael's widow could barely stand, much less give orders. He gave Isabel an awkward bow and left the room. Isabel walked over to where her mother was leaning on the priest. She embraced Priscilla who then wept into her shoulder. Isabel wanted to cry with her, but she had to be strong now for her father.

She left her mother in the care of the priest and the chamber maids. Isabel left the bedroom and made her way to the east tower. She forced herself to hold back the tears as she ascended into the aviary. She looked down at the enemy soldiers camped at the bottom of the mountain. They seemed to crawl around their siege weapons like so many scurrying insects.

Pascual arrived several minutes later with Rodrigo and the requested item. "Thank you for your swift obedience," she told the captain.

"Of course," he said uncomfortably.

"Before he died," Isabel said, "my father instructed me on the next part of the war." The men made no reply and so she continued. "You are to lash Lord Enriquez' cloak to one of the rocks. Launch it into the enemy camp so they may know he is defeated."

"Yes my lady," Captain Pascual answered. "Lord Montenegro suggested a similar course to me last night before his departure." Isabel looked down at the catapult that was being constructed in the courtyard below.

"Is the catapult ready," she asked rhetorically.

"Not yet my lady," Pascual answered.

"Then I charge you to have your men make haste. We cannot bury my father until they are gone."

"What shall we do with his body until then?" Pascual mused. Isabel swallowed hard before answering.

"Wrap him in cloth and place him in the western tower."

'The prison," Captain Pascual asked with disbelief. "May I ask why?"

"Because my mother will not go there," Isabel snapped. "Do not trouble me with questions when there is work to do!"

"Yes my lady," the captain answered. "I will go now to prepare the catapult."

"Do so," Isabel agreed curtly. "Take that foul pig's cloak with you."

"As you wish," the captain replied as he collected the cloak.

"Wait," she said. "Cut off the collar of the cloak and give it to me." The collar was embroidered with symbols from the crest of Morera. This gave Isabel an idea.

"As you wish," the captain answered. He took out his dagger and unceremoniously ripped the collar free of the cloak. He handed the blood stained collar to the Heiress of Montenegro.

"Leave Rodrigo with me," she added. "I will release him shortly." Captain Pascual almost saluted before he remembered who he was speaking too. Instead, he bowed and left the room. Isabel looked out the large window as she spoke once more. "I should like to thank you Rodrigo," she said.

"Please my lady," Rodrigo protested. "I have failed your father. If only I could have arrived faster."

"It was not your fault," Isabel explained. "Please accept my gratitude. I know you did everything in your power. Montenegro will be forever in your debt for…bringing him home."

"My lady is too kind," Rodrigo said wryly. "We shall all miss Lord Montenegro."

"As do I," Isabel said with great effort. "Please go now. I wish to be alone." Rodrigo left quietly. When she could no longer hear his footsteps on the stairs, Isabel allowed herself to weep. Eventually, there were no more tears to shed. She had an ink and parchment brought to her. She also had her father's signet ring removed and brought to her with some paraffin wax from his study. She seated herself on the wooden stool before the table upon which the pigeon coop rested. She dipped a quill into the inkpot as the sun broke out from behind the clouds. This is the letter she wrote for her father.

To the enemies of Montenegro...

Let it be known that your lord, the traitor Enriquez, has fallen to capture. The penalty for betrayal in Montenegro is death. Lord Enriquez has paid for his crimes. Your service to this man dictates that all among you shall share in his punishment.

However, I am not without mercy. Therefore, remove yourselves from my lands forthwith. All those who remain shall be put to death. Do not tempt my anger, but depart with all haste.

I entreat each of you to think upon the swiftness with which your Lord met his fate. He was the most protected man among you. How much easier than shall it be for justice to reach the least of you?

Any man who styles himself an officer or a leader among you shall be quickly destroyed. The rest of you have until nightfall. Disobedience will bring death with the coming dark.

Given by my hand...

Lord Rafael Montenegro

After the forgery was completed, Isabel melted the paraffin wax onto the parchment and then imprinted it with her father's seal. She took the rolled up letter and carried it with her as she walked out onto the bridge between the towers. She crossed the platform containing the porcupine and continued on into the western tower. Once inside the stairwell, she made her way down to the next landing which opened on a narrow bridge connected to the battlements.

The archers looked at Isabel as if she was a curiosity, but none objected to her presence. Captain Pascual was harassing the men in the courtyard to work faster. Isabel was not sure, but it looked like it would be ready very soon. With all the men in uniform facing outward, she could not be certain if Rodrigo was among them. "Fetch me Rodrigo," she said loudly.

"He is on the other side my lady," one of the archers told her.

"Well," she said to the man who had spoken. He hesitated a moment, but Isabel's stare made up his mind for him.

"Of course," he said. "I will fetch him at once!" Isabel simply waited. In moments, the archer returned with Rodrigo in tow.

"I am at your service," Rodrigo said with a bow.

"What are you doing here?" Isabel demanded of the other man.

"I..," he stammered. "I have brought Rodrigo as commanded."

"Does that not leave a gap in our defenses," Isabel asked imperiously? Before the man could formulate a reply, the heiress shouted at him. "I did not command you to escort him back. Take his place at once!"

"As you command," the archer said hurriedly. He turned around and moved quickly to the position Rodrigo had so recently occupied on the other side.

"I need this message sent to our enemies," Isabel told Rodrigo. "Your arrow must fall as close to the command tent as possible." Rodrigo looked critically down at the enemy camp.

"It is very far," he said as he peered down. "I think it will barely reach the catapults."

"So be it," Isabel said as she handed over the parchment. Rodrigo cut a small length of twine from a larger length of it that he kept in his belt pouch. With this, he fastened the letter to an arrow from his quiver. He had to break the seal before he could roll the parchment tightly around the shaft of the arrow. The twine he used to secure it firmly in place. "Wrap this around the arrow as well," Isabel said. She handed the bloody collar of Lord Enriquez' cloak to the archer.

Rodrigo did as he had been commanded. He then drew back and loosed the arrow high into the sky. It sailed at an upward angle before gravity plunged it down toward the enemy camp. It was too far a distance for Isabel to see where it had landed. "Did the arrow make it?" she asked with uncertainty.

"It must have," Rodrigo answered, "but near the catapults as I said.

"Thank you."

"It is my privilege," Rodrigo replied. Isabel left the battlements by the narrow wooden stairs that led down the wall and into the courtyard. She walked up behind Captain Pascual who was overseeing the construction of the catapult.

"How much longer" she asked him?

"Not long," he answered.

"Will it be ready by nightfall?"

"Well before…"

"Send word to me when it is done," she commanded. "I go now to be with my mother." Isabel left the courtyard and went back up into the keep. It was very difficult, but she managed to retain her bearing as Lady Priscilla wept into her arms. She held her mother tight; not knowing what might be in store for them.

Some time later, Captain Pascual sent one of his soldiers to inform Lady Isabel that the catapult was completed. "Tell him to meet me by the porcupine when dusk is upon us," she told the man. "Ensure that the weapon is properly loaded."

"Yes my lady," the solider answered crisply. He turned on his heel and left the bed chamber.

"What are you doing Isabel?" Priscilla asked with some confusion. Her voice was heavy and her face was red from crying.

"Papa told me last night what must be done," Isabel answered. "I am only making sure that it is."

"You are so brave," Priscilla complimented her. "What did your father say?"

"That I am to launch Lord Enriquez' effects into the enemy camp… It will let them know that their lord is defeated."

"What else?"

"That I am to take his place," Isabel answered apprehensively, but her mother did not seem to take offense.

"He must have known how much this would hurt me," Priscilla said sadly. "I have not the stomach for soldiers just now."

"Leave it to me," Isabel reassured her mother. "Papa told me everything. I will make sure the Captain does it exactly as he would have."

"Did he say anything else?" Priscilla asked desperately.

"He said that he loves you very much," Isabel lied.

"Oh why," Priscilla sobbed. "Why could you not have awakened me?"

"I did not know," Isabel answered. It was difficult for her to speak and she could feel the tears welling up in the corners of her eyes. "He seemed well. I thought he would sleep and I thought…he would wake up."

"Oh Isabel I am sorry," Priscilla cried. "Come here mija." Isabel let her mother embrace her as the tears fell freely. She did not try to hold them back.

When the sun hung low in the sky, Isabel made her way to the platform where Captain Pascual was waiting. The smell of tar hung in the air. Several wooden barrels had been filled with the boiling black liquid. These had been placed close to the porcupine. There were also many quivers of arrows that were waiting to be coated.

Clay pots of tar were being hauled into the courtyard to provide ammunition for the new catapult. "Look," Captain Pascual said as he pointed to the enemy camp below. Several of the formations of both cavalry and infantry were departing down the road that would take them out of Montenegro altogether. "They are retreating," Captain Pascual said with happy relief.

"It worked," Isabel thought out loud.

"What worked my lady," the captain asked?

"I sent a message by way of Rodrigo's arrow," she explained.

"What sort of message," the man asked uncomfortably? He was unaccustomed to taking orders from a woman, much less being kept in the dark by one.

"An ultimatum," Isabel answered. "I told them that their Lord had been executed and that they must all leave before nightfall or suffer his fate."

"Nicely played," the captain said with approval, "but we are still outnumbered."

"Perhaps when you give them his cloak it will convince those who still have doubts."

"I pray that you are right."

"Why do they not use their own catapults," Isabel asked?

"They have," Pascual answered, "but they have also discovered what your father already knew when he built this place."

"Which was?"

"The angle is impossible and there is not enough purchase to be had on the trail up the mountain."

"What do you advise?"

"I agree that we must send Enriquez' cloak to them," the captain replied, "but we should also set their catapults to burn."

"You said the catapults cannot reach our walls."

"They cannot," Pascual agreed.

"Then why destroy them?"

"Because they are made of wood," the man answered. "They are so tall that the fires will burn for all to see."

"Making their cause even more hopeless," Isabel finished for him.

"Precisely," the captain answered.

"Make it so," Isabel told him.

"Shall we wait until dark?"

"No," Isabel decided. "There must be a worse fate if they are still here after nightfall."

"Well said," Captain Pascual replied. "Send what is left of their Lord!" he shouted down to the men below. He hurried toward the west tower and out onto the battlements over the gate. Enriquez cloak was lashed to a boulder with long pieces of rope. The soldiers loaded the bundle onto the catapult.

"Ready," one of the men shouted up to Captain Pascual with one hand cupped to his mouth.

"Loose!" the Captain yelled back. The man by the rope swung down with his sword and cut the rope that was putting tension on the siege weapon. The boulder was thrown high into the air and then began its descent toward the camp. Isabel watched as the rock slammed into the ground and sent up a cloud of dust. She could see the enemy soldiers scurrying about and could only imagine what they must be saying to each other. The ranks of men reformed themselves far behind the line on which the useless catapults were standing. "Can we still hit them that far," she called over to Captain Pascual?

"We can!"

"Destroy the catapults!" Isabel shouted. The men loaded one of the bubbling pots onto the catapult. One man touched a torch to its surface. Igniting the tar before another soldier released the deadly missile toward the enemy. The first launch did not strike true. Isabel could see the curl of the fire as it spread over the grass where the pot had impacted. Some of the pots did hit their mark and others did not. Nevertheless, Captain Pascual called down the adjustments that inevitably got the weapon on target.

The resulting fires burned high into the air like three great charnel pyres. "Destroy the commander's tent!" Isabel screamed. Captain Pascual nodded before staring down at the chaos below. "Move it left," he yelled down to the soldiers in the courtyard. A group of them grunted and struggled to push the weapon. "That's perfect," Pascual told them, "now angle up!" A swarm of soldiers lifted up the front of the catapult while others placed blocks of wood underneath. They set the weapon down loudly on top of its new braces. It would shoot farther now.

"Ready," one of the men in the courtyard shouted.

"Loose," Isabel and Captain Pascual yelled as one! The flaming projectile arced high into the air and then crashed down on top of Captain Vidana's tent.

"Direct hit," Captain Pascual yelled excitedly.

"Launch another," Isabel shouted. "Be sure that whoever leads them now is dead!" The men obeyed and another pot of fire descended on the already burning remains of the enemy commander's tent. "They are fleeing!" Isabel yelled triumphantly. It was not a full retreat, but the departure of the mercenaries paired the enemy down to but a third of their former strength. Cheers rose up from the men on the battlements. They clapped each other on the back and praised God as the sell swords abandoned the soldiers of Morera.

Isabel watched as they departed. Her exaltation was soured by the remembrance of her father. Rafael was gone. She would never hear his deep voice again. She would not be held by those strong, loving arms. Tears fell from her eyes as she watched the mercenaries go. She pointed one trembling finger at those soldiers who remained. "Kill them!" the Heiress of Montenegro screamed across the battlements. "Let no enemy of Montenegro draw breath on my father's land!"

"Loose," Captain Pascual shouted to the men in the courtyard. The first flaming pot was airborne before the word could fully escape his lips.

"Loose," Isabel barked at the men behind her. One of the men operated the crank of the porcupine. This pulled down the paddle until the rope was taught and the paddle bent. Another man touched the flame of his torch to the tar-soaked arrowheads that stuck out of the front of the siege weapon.

"Loose," the soldier in charge barked loudly. A third man cut the rope, sending scores of flaming arrows into the gathering dusk. The soldiers of Morera scattered as fire rained down upon them from the keep. Every time the porcupine was reloaded, the soldiers would adjust the angle of the platform to fire in a new direction. The battlefield was soon blazing and the screams of the dying could be heard even from where Isabel stood.

Captain Pascual ordered the men to lower the gate. He rode out with the soldiers of Montenegro. "Let none live!" Isabel shouted after them.

"Kill them all!" Captain Pascual shouted as he raised his sword. A loud cry went up from the soldiers as the horses thundered down the mountain toward the fleeing men of Morera. Isabel was numb. The taste of victory was like bitter ash in her mouth. She left the soldiers to do their work. She did not care to see how it ended.

Isabel did not feel rested the morning after. She had cried herself to sleep the night before. Her heart was weighted down with sorrow. "Close the gate!" she heard someone yell from outside. There was the sound of chains scraping as the soldiers worked the crank to raise the drawbridge. Isabel hurried up to the aviary to find that Captain Pascual was already there. "What is it?" she asked as she crossed over to the opening.

"The army of Aragon comes," Captain Pascual answered uneasily as he stared down toward the village. The army of the previous day's battle seemed insignificant compared to the horde that now came forth. Using the corpses of Morera as a guide, Aragon's army formed a line out of reach of the siege weapons of Montenegro.

"They are raising the white flag," Isabel said as she looked down. Three riders were coming swiftly toward the mountain trail. The rider on the left bore the white flag. This flag he raised higher than the flag of Aragon which was born by the man on the right. The rider in the center did not carry a standard. The three men rode up the path and across the stone bridge that led to the keep. They stopped just short of the spot where the bridge ended at a drop into the gorge.

"We come to parlay," the man in the center shouted. "We bear you no malice!" Captain Pascual looked questioningly at Isabel.

"Let them enter," she shouted! The men below obeyed and the delegation from Aragon rode over the drawbridge and into the courtyard. Priscilla was already in the entry hall when Isabel made her way down. "The envoy from Aragon has arrived," she told her mother.

"I know," Lady Priscilla replied. She was dressed in all black and her face was covered by a veil.

"Will you stay with me while I decide what to do with them?" Isabel inquired.

"While you decide," Priscilla asked as the servants looked on? "You may go up to your chamber. It is not for you to decide."

"Father said I am to take his place," Isabel said disagreeably. The day's events had worn her patience thin. "That is what I am doing, and have been doing since yesterday!"

"Do not use my husband's death to feed your own desire for power," Priscilla corrected her. "Your mother still lives."

"He told me…"

"Your father only meant for you to pass on his orders child," Priscilla said curtly. "He certainly did not intend for you to rule over your mother."

"I am only reporting what was said," Isabel disagreed.

"What was said was not as important as what was intended," Priscilla explained patiently. "There are things the two of you shared that I was never privy too. I will thank you for any advice you may have when it pertains to the business of horseflesh. Montenegro is grateful to you for carrying out my husband's military strategy. Now that it is concluded, it is your duty to obey my commands." Isabel frowned. She was almost certain that her father had meant for her to take the reigns of command. Priscilla was very convincing, however, and Isabel was long used to obedience. "Go up now to your room my daughter," Priscilla said. "Focus instead on the position you will surely hold in the coming year."

"Yes mother," Isabel said meekly. She curtseyed and left the entry hall as the three men from the Crown of Aragon entered, accompanied by several of the soldiers of Montenegro. What Priscilla told her made perfect sense. Isabel would be Countess of Provence in less than a year's time. It would not be seemly for her to usurp her mother's authority, only to return it to her several months later. She put what Rafael had predicted about her marriage far from her mind.

Several hours later, Priscilla entered her daughter's bedroom without knock or introduction. "Be at peace," she told Isabel. "The war is over."

"That is well," Isabel replied. "I am terribly ashamed to have argued with you before the servants. I beg your forgiveness."

"I forgive as God forgives," Priscilla replied, "but let it never happen again."

"It will not," Isabel promised. Lady Priscilla crossed over and set next to her daughter on the bed.

"Your father's name has been vindicated," her mother said.

"Does that matter," Isabel asked morosely?

"For us it does," her mother replied. There was sadness in her voice also. "We shall not be at war with the rest of Aragon."

"That is well," Isabel said again.

"King Alfonso sent word that they discovered a spy for the French among us."

"Who was it?" Isabel demanded.

"The dog Eubasio," Priscilla said angrily. "Lord William was slighted by your husband's marriage announcement at the Feast of Saint Nicholas as well."

"So the French know that we are wed," Isabel asked?

"I am certain they do," Priscilla answered. "They might desire your death simply to avoid the scandal."

"Does life mean so little," Isabel shuddered.

"Despite appearances, most rulers are Godless." Lady Priscilla sighed heavily and then continued. "So Eubasio convinced Lord Enriquez that your father was planning on betraying his country... He had convinced him that my Rafael was planning to help the Saracens wage war upon Aragon."

"But father was famous for defeating the Saracens," Isabel said. "How could Lord Enriquez believe such a lie?"

"In the same way that your father believed that he could trust Eubasio," Priscilla answered. "He deceived us all."

"He did," Isabel agreed sadly.

"The King has expressed his great sorrow at your father's death. We will hold the funeral in five days time so that he may be in attendance," Priscilla told her. Isabel just hung her head. She had no words to reply. "You will surely sing for your father one last time, won't you mija?"

"Of course I will," Isabel answered.

"You have been a good daughter to him. He was always so proud of you."

"I shall never feel joy again Mama," Isabel said brokenly. She fell into her mother's arms and wept into her embrace. Priscilla also was moved to tears.

†   †   †

Tiny drops of blood welled up in Sister Magdalena's eyes and spilled over onto her cheeks. The only sound she could hear was the roar of the jet engine as the Boeing 757 sailed over the Atlantic Ocean. Her coffin was nailed inside a crate which sat in the belly of the beast. The memory of her father's death still caused her pain as if it were only yesterday. She did not precisely remember the details of Rafael's funeral. It had been held at the Church of the Greater St. James and well attended. Many of the officers of his majesty's army had spoken before those assembled. Lords of several neighboring lands came to pay their respects. Even King Alfonso said a few words.

Soldiers of Montenegro carried the fallen Lord through Black River Village and back to the cemetery behind the church. The women of the village followed and their wailing filled the streets. Isabel had walked in silence, supporting her mother who could barely stand.

For the next several nights, Isabel and her mother slept in the bed they had shared with Rafael on that fateful night. During the day, Isabel could barely stomach the thought of food. What little she had eaten was only at Little Grandma's insistence. She kept the Biblia Sacra hugged to her breast for much of the time, although she could not bring herself to read it.

Most vampires measured their age by the anniversary of their own death. For Sister Magdalena, it was measured by the death of her father. When Rafael Montenegro died, Isabel's spirit died with him.

CHAPTER II

Several months after the death of Lord Montenegro, Lady Priscilla began to travel away from the keep with increasing frequency. She went mainly to Zaragoza. As for what it was she did there, Isabel could only guess.

With her father and Master Aquinas dead, Isabel busied herself with the running of the stables. Her father had taught her well. She would keep her promise to take care of those things which her mother could not.

Isabel's letters to her husband decreased in frequency. She would send them with Lady Priscilla so that the Crown of Aragon could send them on to Ramon in Genoa. There was still no reply and Isabel feared the worst. This only deepened her depression. Some days she never left her father's bed. She found comfort from Little Grandma. The old chamber maid was always there to lend an ear or a shoulder to cry upon.

Isabel guessed that her mother was dealing with Rafael's death in her own way. She did not ask questions. It came, therefore, as a complete surprise when she was called away from the stables to meet Lady Priscilla in the sitting room. It was the same one where Isabel had so often read to her father. "Sit down Isabel," her mother invited her. Priscilla was sitting on the high backed chair that her husband had once been fond of.

"Yes mother?" Isabel asked as she took the chair next to it.

"I have decided to marry Lord Manuel Barillos," Priscilla said matter-of-factly. Isabel's jaw dropped.

"Surely you must be mistaken," Isabel said with shock written all over her face.

"I am not," her mother replied. "We are both without an heir and he has been quite the gentleman…very comforting to me as a widow."

"How could you love a man like Barillos? He is nothing like father was. You must not marry him mother! The man is a cretin."

"Do not speak so of him," Priscilla said angrily.

"I am speaking the truth Mother," Isabel insisted. "Why not consider Captain Pascual? He lost his wife during the battle with Morera. He is a good man and very loyal to us."

"He is a good man," Priscilla agreed, "and will make someone a fine husband should he choose to marry again."

"Then you will consider" Isabel asked hopefully?

"No," her mother replied. "I must marry a man of noble blood. Captain Pascual is only a commoner."

"So was my father," Isabel answered furiously, "or have you already forgotten?"

"Your lack of understanding does not give you the right to speak to me so," Priscilla said coldly. "Remove yourself from my presence!"

"I will," Isabel said crisply. She rose from her seat and stalked quickly out of the room. She went straight up to her chamber and locked herself in. Her heart was filled with rage and sorrow. Her mother's behavior was appalling.

"He will be the ruin of her," Isabel thought aloud. "See what you have done," she demanded of her dead father? "Oh Papa, why did you have to leave us now?" Tears stung Isabel's eyes. There would be no reply from Rafael. If his spirit was nearby, it made no attempt at manifestation. Isabel was alone.

It was a fortnight before Lord Manuel Barillos arrived with a small retinue of body guards. They were greasy men and had not the disciplined look of soldiers. They more closely resembled highwaymen. At her mother's request, Isabel made a token appearance to greet the man. They exchanged pleasantries which were composed of lies. Lord Barillos then went up with Isabel's mother to her private sitting room. The way he looked at everything in the keep was most disturbing. It reminded Isabel of a child looking at forbidden sweets. She could almost imagine him salivating.

With Lord Barillos taking up residence in one of the guest rooms, Isabel became more and more furious by the day. He was very attentive and charming toward Lady

Priscilla, but Isabel could see through it. The man seemed nervous much of the time and there was the hint of desperation about him. Unfortunately, Isabel could see also that her mother was quite enchanted.

Isabel did her best to avoid both of them until the day that Lord Barillos first visited Black River Ranch. She and several of the stable hands were overseeing a breeding. They were letting nature take its course. If the mare was unwilling, than they might have had to step in... Fortunately, everything seemed to be going well.

Isabel did not notice the man's approach until he was almost upon her. "All goes well I see," Lord Barillos remarked. The tone in his voice made what they were doing seem less like a profession and more like perversity.

"Lord Barillos," Isabel said with a bite in her voice, "to what do I owe this pleasure?"

"I have been looking forward to meeting you but you have been so far unreachable."

"I have been busy."

"I never expected to find you here amongst the animals," he said with a chuckle.

"So why have you come?"

"As I said Lady Isabel," Barillos replied; "I came to see you."

"It ill befits a man of station to tell lies," Isabel said icily.

"Leave us," Barillos said loudly to the stable hands. Before they could react, Isabel gave them an order to the contrary.

"Stay where you are," Isabel told them. "Lord Barillos and I shall leave. This is an important match. We must be certain it succeeds." She turned back to Barillos with an affected smile. "Shall we take a walk together my lord?"

"Yes," Barillos answered slowly. They walked in silence until they reached the courtyard. Isabel let the man squirm as they walked around the perimeter. She would not speak to him at first. This forced Manuel to reopen the conversation. "An apology is in order young lady," Barillos said furiously!

"I owe you nothing," Isabel retorted.

"I think you do."

"You said you would never expect to find me in the stables. Therefore; your reason for being here could not possibly be to see me. Unless you are without sense, you must agree."

"Your reasoning is sound, but I have been looking for you nonetheless. There is no call for you to question my honesty."

"Your honesty," Isabel repeated sarcastically. She shook her head in disgust.

"We are concluded," Lord Barillos said angrily. "I think I shall relay your sentiments to your mother. Such insolence deserves a whipping. Unless you are without sense, you will apologize and never let such things pass your lips again!"

"Tell my mother everything that I have said," Isabel challenged him. "I will do the same for you. Perhaps she will be interested to know about the last exchange you had with my blessed father?"

"My last conversation with Lord Montenegro," Barillos asked guardedly?

"Why yes," Isabel said as she clasped her hands together! "Remember how wretchedly you begged for your life?" Manuel gave her a stony glare but Isabel would not let up. "He found you to be so reprehensible that he threatened to kill you. What was it he called you again my Lord?"

"That will be enough," Lord Barillos declared!

"I remember now," Isabel continued as if the man had not spoken at all, "a faithless dog!"

"I will not tolerate such talk from a woman," Barillos shouted!

"Why not," Isabel asked? "You sounded like a woman when you were begging my father and it is because of a woman, (your mother), that you yet live." Lord Barillos struck her hard across the face with the back of his hand.

"Silence," he screamed! Isabel held a hand to her face and glared hard at the man with malice in her eyes.

"You shall not marry my mother," Isabel promised. "I will never allow it!"

"I take what I want girl," Barillos retorted. "You can only make it worse for yourself." Isabel spat on the ground and walked back further into the stables of Black River Ranch. Lord Barillos did not chase her, but stood there smugly as if he had attained some sort of victory. Isabel saddled one of the brown mares and rode out toward the keep. She galloped past Lord Barillos without a second glance.

Once in the courtyard, Isabel called for one of the stable hands to take her mount. A young man came running out of the private stables to help her down from her mount. By the time he got to Isabel, all he could do was take the reins. She walked quickly up to her mother's room and burst in without bothering to knock. "We have to talk mother," Isabel announced. "It is far too important to wait.

"You must give warning before entering my quarters," Priscilla said.

"Forgive me," Isabel replied, "but we must talk."

"Very well," her mother replied. "What is it?"

"I did not want to upset you before because I assumed that Lord Barillos would reveal his character in time. Now I see that you are enamored of him. It is my duty as a daughter to inform you…"

"What Isabel?" Priscilla asked with irritation. "What could it possibly be?"

"I remember overhearing a conversation he had with Papa," Isabel told her mother. "Barillos wanted to brand common work horses with the symbol of Montenegro. He was going to sell them to the knights of St. John as if they were trained war horses!"

"Isabel," Priscilla cut her off, "I miss your father as well. That is no reason for you to tell lies!"

"I do not tell lies," Isabel retorted. "Papa was so angry with Lord Barillos that he threatened to kill him if he should ever set foot in our house again! This is the man you mean to marry?"

"That is quite enough."

"Are you not hearing me?" Isabel demanded. "I am trying to prevent a serious mistake!"

"I suppose you would have me all by myself," Priscilla replied. "It will not be long before you leave for Provence. What will become of me then? The world is a dangerous place without a man."

"The man you wish to replace my father with is a sneak and a Godless pig," Isabel cursed! "I do not know what he says that you find so appealing, but I am sure that it is a lie. You are being deceived!"

"Silence," Priscilla spoke over her! "I am not replacing your father! Rafael is gone. He will never be coming back! You will be gone too before winter comes again. It is no business of yours whom I choose to marry. I only thought to tell you out of courtesy. I do not seek your permission!"

"He will destroy Montenegro," Isabel cried! Horses are the life's blood of this land. Barillos will sell nags as if they are trained stallions. Our reputation will be ruined. The breeding stock will become polluted. You will have nothing!"

"I already have nothing," Priscilla said unhappily. "I do not understand why you are doing this to me."

"I am trying to help you!"

"Telling these terrible lies will not bring back your father," Priscilla cried! My husband is dead!"

"Mother please," Isabel began. She was crying now also.

"Get away from me," Priscilla screamed! "Get away!" Isabel's heart was torn. She wanted to say more against her mother's suitor but Priscilla was in so much pain. Perhaps now was not the time. When would the right moment come? "Get away from me!" Priscilla's scream broke through Isabel's thoughts. The door of Priscilla's chamber swung wide and Manuel Barillos entered. The door slammed shut behind him.

"Get out now," Lord Barillos said angrily.

"I go as my Mother bids me," Isabel replied contemptuously.

"Get out!" Priscilla screamed. Isabel departed. She looked over her shoulder once as she left. Her mother's face was a red mess of tears. Manuel Barillos was watching her go. He winked when Isabel caught his eye. He was smiling at her. As Isabel closed the door, she wished that her father would have killed the man, instead of merely threatening.

Over the next few weeks, Isabel tried many more times to convince her mother to listen to reason. Priscilla was unusually moody and Lord Barillos was never far from her. Isabel wondered if her father's death had driven her mother mad. Having a conversation with Priscilla was like talking to a stranger. She could not ever recall seeing her mother so irrational. It got so bad that Isabel could not even walk in the room without her mother's face darkening.

Lord Barillos presented himself as the soul of charm and concern. Isabel was certain that the man was feeding into her mother's paranoia when she could not be around. The heiress found it curious that Manuel should visit so long. Were there no matters in his lands that needed tending to?

One morning, Isabel awakened to find her mother gone. Lord Barillos was likewise absent from the keep. "Where is my mother?" Isabel demanded of Little Grandma.

"I do not know mija," Pilar sighed.

"Well she has to be found," Isabel exclaimed! "That rotten Lord Barillos must have taken her. I will summon Captain Pascual immediately!"

"She went quite willingly," Little Grandma said.

"You said you did not know where she went!"

"If my lady would let me finish," Pilar replied, "I would tell her that the two of them left early this morning. They told the Captain that they would be returning in a week's time, but they would not say where they were bound."

"Oh, all is lost," Isabel said morosely.

"Whatever is the matter?"

"They are going to marry," Isabel explained in defeat.

"So soon," Little Grandma asked? "Surely not..."

"They will," Isabel cried, "and he will ruin her!"

"'It will not be so bad mija," Little Grandma reassured her, but her voice betrayed her lack of confidence.

"Do not tell me he has fooled you as well," Isabel asked angrily.

"I know not what to make of him."

"I will tell you." Isabel told Little Grandma everything there was to know. The chamber maid's face became more and more horrified with each word.

"Why did you not tell me," Pilar asked with amazement? "I would have spoken to her."

"She would not listen. If you had told her, she would have known that it was at my behest. There would be no difference."

"I could have tried," Pilar argued.

"You are right," Isabel wept. "She might have listened to you. I am only a girl!" Little Grandma embraced her and let her cry. They retired to Isabel's room where the older woman undressed her and hung her gown carefully in the armoire. Isabel lay down as Pilar left the room. Only unconsciousness could spare Isabel from the worry that now plagued her mind.

As Isabel had predicted, her mother returned as Lady Barillos. Manuel was with her and he made a grand show of helping her down from the carriage. Isabel came out to meet them so she could hear the truth from her mother's own lips. "We are married," Priscilla said happily as Isabel approached them in the courtyard. Isabel's face dropped along with her spirit.

"Congratulations mother," Isabel replied flatly.

"Is it not wonderful?" Priscilla said dreamily. Isabel could not answer. "Manuel will be your father now!"

"I could not be happier," Lord Barillos chimed in.

"I shall respect him as your husband," Isabel said tensely, "but my father is dead."

"Oh Isabel I know," Priscilla said sadly as she pressed a hand to her daughter's cheek. "It will get better. You will see."

"Alright Mama," Isabel agreed as she forced a smile. Priscilla let her hand drop but Isabel could feel her concern. She could have used this side of her mother before. It was now too late.

"Let me help you inside Lady Barillos," Manuel offered.

"Oh thank you Manuel," Priscilla breathed. "I have been feeling so faint lately.

"You need your rest my love," the man said, "come." Priscilla leaned on her new husband and he led her dutifully up to her bedroom. Isabel remained in the courtyard. She was stunned. There was nothing more she could do. Her attempts to save Montenegro had failed. She exhaled heavily and looked up at the sky. The grey clouds that rolled overhead offered no answers.

"A storm is coming," Isabel shouted to Rodrigo who was up on the battlements.

"Yes my lady," Rodrigo called down. "Do not worry yourself. It will be warm and dry inside!"

"And you Rodrigo," she called back, "how will you fare?"

"I will be relieved before long," he replied. "Congratulations to your mother!"

"Yes…thank you," Isabel said half-heartedly. "She is very happy." Isabel could not hear what the man said next. She nodded her head as though she had heard and smiled before going inside.

An awkward silence hung in the air as the three of them ate dinner that evening. Priscilla was the first to speak.

"I know that the two of you have had a rough start," Priscilla said as she looked at her daughter, "but I think we can make the best of it, true?"

"Of course," Isabel agreed, "just leave the business of horseflesh to me and all will be well."

"There is much for me to learn from you," Barillos added. "Surely you will pass on your father's wisdom."

"I will," Isabel said critically, "if you truly wish to learn."

"I do," the man insisted!

"That will be wonderful," Priscilla exclaimed!

"Yes," Manuel agreed. Isabel frowned and set to eating her meal. Surely the man was lying…but perhaps not. If he could learn the horse trade, then he might see that the largest profit would be turned by dealing honestly. If she could teach him this, than perhaps Montenegro would have a chance of success after her departure to Provence. It would have to be enough. Isabel resolved herself to instruct the man, however unpleasant it would be.

"This food feels so heavy in my stomach," her mother complained. "I feel faint again as well." Manuel rose from his seat and went quickly to Priscilla's side. He fussed over her and then half carried her from the room. By the sound of their footsteps, Isabel guessed they went to her mother's bedroom. After several minutes went by, Manuel returned alone.

"Your mother is not feeling well," he said.

"Do you truly love her," Isabel asked pointedly?

"She makes a good wife," the man replied. "Of course I love her."

"Hmmm," Isabel mused. "Will you not be offended by the stables being my domain? Can you defer to a woman on this matter for a time?"

"I am eager to learn all that you know," Barillos replied evasively. Isabel frowned.

"I want my mother to be taken care of when I am gone," Isabel said. "Perhaps my lord will meet with me in the stables of Black River Ranch tomorrow morning?"

"I will," Manuel smiled. How Isabel hated that smile. There was something ugly about it that made her flesh crawl. The next day, Isabel met with Lord Barillos as planned. She had rode Santiago down from the keep much earlier. Lord Barillos arrived by carriage when it was almost mid-day. Isabel had no love for the way the little man strode in like he owned the place. He looked down his nose at the stable hands that made an effort to look busy, (if indeed they were not).

It was then that Isabel was reminded that Lord Barillos did in fact own it. He owned all of it. For her mother's sake, Isabel put on an air of respect. She curtseyed to the man as he approached. "Young lady," he said with approval.

"My lord," she responded. "Welcome to Black River Ranch. Allow me to show you around."

"Please do," he replied smugly. She started by introducing the individual stable hands, but her step-father grew impatient.

"Yes-yes," he interrupted her, "let me see the horses."

"Of course," Isabel replied with irritation. She sent the men back to work and walked Barillos down the line of stalls. "In Montenegro we breed for size and aggression," Isabel explained. "Our stallions typically do not get along because they all want to be the alpha male."

"This is the one I have often seen you riding. Is it not?" Lord Barillos asked as he reached a hand out toward the large grey stallion in the stall beside him. Santiago snapped his massive teeth at the interloper. Manuel pulled his hand back in the nick of time. The horse stomped his hoof in anger and whinnied his displeasure.

"Woe," Isabel said disapprovingly. Santiago nickered.

"It tried to attack me," Manuel said as if he had already been injured!

"You are too nervous," Isabel told him. "You cannot be afraid around them. They will sense it."

"I am not afraid," Barillos said petulantly. "I will ride this one…this Santiago," he said with false bravado.

"No," Isabel answered quickly. "He only lets me touch him now that my father is gone. Besides, you have spooked him already."

"Nonsense," Lord Barillos said dismissively. "Have him made ready at once!" Isabel sighed heavily. This was not going to be easy.

"My Lord," she said patiently. "Santiago is spooked. See how he stands toward the back of his stall? See how he keeps stomping at the floor?"

"If the horse is afraid then why should I be?" Barillos argued. He reached a hand toward the latch on the stall door.

"He is not afraid," Isabel exclaimed with alarm! She hurried to grab the man's wrist before his fingers could reach the latch. "He is warning you. I cannot allow you to ride him my lord. Even if we should manage to get you in the saddle, the horse will rear and buck until you are thrown."

"Why would he do that exactly?"

"Because the ground is the easiest place for him to kill you…my lord," Isabel told him. Barillos gulped and drew his hand back quickly away from Santiago's stall.

"I see," the man said nervously as he backed away. Santiago stomped his hoof and flared his nostrils as Barillos retreated from the wooden rails that separated them.

"Does my lord ride?"

"I know how to ride," Barillos replied as if he had been insulted.

"That is not what I meant," Isabel said. "Let me be plain. Do you ride often?"

"There is no need. I have a carriage."

"We shall have to change that. I will start you on Violet. She is a good horse." The man did not argue. It was not long before Isabel had Manuel riding around the training yard. He was not a natural but he learned well enough. Over the next few weeks, Isabel taught her stepfather to improve his skill in horseback riding. Their tense relationship improved initially, but soured when it was discovered that Manuel would never be able to command a warhorse. He simply did not have the courage. Isabel did her best to soften the blow but there was no way to tell the man and avoid an embarrassing situation.

After being thrown from horseback several times and nearly trampled on one occasion; Lord Barillos was more than happy to concede leadership of the stables to Isabel. He could not bear being around the stable hands after they had witnessed his ineptitude first hand. Inwardly, Isabel was quite pleased at this turn of events and began grooming one of the stable hands to take her place. Paolo was the oldest of them and he showed much promise.

In the fifth month of that year, Isabel made a trip down to the Summer Cottage. Her mother could not come. She was becoming increasingly faint and stayed in bed much of the time. Despite her illness, she would let no one but Manuel come near to her. Isabel was not going to the Summer Cottage for relaxation alone. She planned to go also to Zaragoza and petition for an audience with King Alfonso. It had been nearly six months since her husband had set sail for Italy and still no word. She was fearful for him and wanted answers.

Isabel took only Little Grandma for company. Captain Pascual insisted on sending a contingent of soldiers to protect them. Rodrigo was among them and Isabel was comforted by their presence. There were no bandits to waylay them, however.

As always, the Summer Cottage looked just as it had when Isabel had last departed. The beauty of the surrounding land was timeless. The rabbits still congregated under the canopy of trees that covered the path in from the main road. The lilies were once more in bloom and there before the cottage was the tall sycamore. Even though Isabel lived primarily in Montenegro, this place always gave her the feeling of coming home.

Isabel left the business of unpacking to the soldiers and house servants. She walked out to her sanctuary beyond the trees. The water was still and beautiful. The croaking of a frog sounded on the opposite bank and Isabel found herself longing for the company of her little cousin. *"If only David were here,"* she thought, *"he would cheer me up without even trying."* There was the hum of the cicadae in the trees and the soft breeze was cool on her skin.

The heiress walked out over the pier and sat herself down in the gazebo. On the floor beneath one of the benches, she could see a handful of dry twigs. Looking closer, she realized that they were tiny, dead stalks of witch hazel. She could almost hear her husband's voice in the wind. *"There is nothing I would not do for you,"* he seemed to say. She looked out over the water with an ache in her heart. She prayed that Ramon would return safely.

The next morning, Isabel and her retinue made their way to Zaragoza and the Crown of Aragon. The carriage clattered over the stone bridge that spanned the River Ebro and passed by the massive Basilica del Pilar. They traveled across the breadth of the capital city until they arrived at Castle Aljaferia.

Isabel exited her carriage inside the grand courtyard of King Alfonso's castle. The gardens were filled with yellow roses in bloom. Bluebells carpeted the soft earth below the rose bushes. Isabel ignored the groups of nobles who walked in the garden and headed straight for the main entrance. She could feel the eyes of the other ladies upon her. It was irritating the way they talked to each other in whispers while obviously staring at her.

Isabel walked through the great halls with their vaulted ceilings and ornately sculpted archways. She came at last to the Hall of Audience. There were soldiers standing guard around the closed doors that led inside. She did not see the Harold as she had on her previous visit. "I need an audience with his majesty," Isabel told one of the guards.

"Of course my lady," the man answered. "Go down this hallway." He pointed with one finger. "You will find a scribe there who will show you where to wait."

"Thank you," Isabel told the man. The guard bowed slightly and Isabel curtseyed in return. She traveled down the hall until she came to a man in deep blue robes. A red strip of cloth was sewn into the fabric. It formed a 'V' below the man's neck and went up over his shoulders and down to the hem of the garment. His face was mostly covered by his white beard and the floppy red hat that set on top of his head. He stood behind a wooden lectern whereon a leather bound ledger sat open. The scribe was writing names into it with a large white quill. There was a line of common men along the wall that came to see him one by one. Isabel looked down the line to see where it began.

"Please come forward my lady," the scribe said from behind her. Isabel approached the lectern and looked down at the scribe who was bent over behind it. "Your name my lady," the scribe asked? There was a large white quill poised in his right hand.

"Lady Isabel of Montenegro," she answered. The man wrote her name into the ledger and then peered at her from beneath his hat.

"What business," he asked.

"I want to talk about the whereabouts of my husband," she told the man. The scribe notated this in the ledger next to her name.

"Please make yourself at home in the room here on my left." The scribe made a sweeping gesture with one hand as he spoke. Through the door was a luxurious sitting room. Many rust colored couches surrounded a low table upon which sat a carved chess board, several flagons of wine, and pewter goblets. There were more chairs and couches along the walls of the room as well.

An older gentleman was hunched miserably over the table where he had spread out several business ledgers. One of the chairs along the opposite wall was occupied by a light-skinned woman in a long dress made of forest green material. She had deep blue eyes and angular features. The neckline of her dress was pushing the limits of decency. Her neck was adorned with a large onyx. The stone was set in silver and attached to a silver chain. She looked up at Isabel with some fleeting interest before staring once more out of the room's only window.

Isabel took a seat closer to the door and waited for her chance to speak with the King. After an hour's passing, she was the only petitioner left in the room. The scribe entered and bowed to Isabel before speaking. "King Alfonso sends his regrets that he cannot meet with you until evening Lady Montenegro," he said politely. Isabel was about to explain that she was the only daughter to Lady Montenegro, but then remembered that her mother was now Lady Barillos. She inclined her head and gave thanks to the scribe. "His majesty welcomes you to dine with him this evening. After this he will grant your audience."

"Inform his majesty that I am grateful," Isabel replied.

"Of course," the scribe answered. The bored way in which he said it gave Isabel the impression that he would relay none of what she had said. She left the palace and spent the afternoon talking to the various horse traders and stable masters in the city. As a whole, they were very interested in what she had to offer. Isabel guessed that they were eager to trick her now that her father had passed on. They did not realize that it would only be business as usual. The real challenge would wait until the following spring. All of them wanted to buy warhorses trained by Lord Rafael Montenegro, but how would they view those trained by a woman, even if she was his daughter?

Isabel returned to Castle Aljaferia as evening approached. The meal offered in the King's dining hall was just as sumptuous and extravagant as that which had covered the tables for the Feast of Saint Nicholas. Isabel was reminded suddenly of the pig's roasted carcass. It had so unnerved her the night she had performed before Alfonso's court. Something else had unnerved her as well, but now she could not remember it.

Many of the guests offered condolences on the loss of Lord Montenegro. Isabel accepted their sympathy with grace, even though it made her want to scream. The only fortunate part of it was that people didn't want to talk much after mentioning her father's death. This prevented the caddy insults and one-upmanship that the courtesans were so infamous for.

When the meal was concluded, Isabel met with King Alfonso in the same room where she and her husband had met him five months past. The King rose from the crimson couch where he was seated as Isabel entered the room. She closed the door and curtseyed low before him. "Your majesty," she said respectfully.

"Lady Montenegro," he replied with a nod. "How are you getting along?"

"Very well your majesty," she replied, "the best that can be done under the circumstances."

"I am very sorry about your father," he said. It was then that Isabel noticed the woman sitting behind him in the shadows. At first she thought it must be Queen Sancha. The woman looked back at Isabel and dispelled that notion. It was Petronilla, mother to both King Alfonso and to her husband Ramon.

"May God rest his soul," Isabel said, "but I have come to speak about your brother my husband."

"Yes," Alfonso said uncomfortably.

"That was not something that should have been passed to the scribe," Petronilla rebuked her. "Aragon is not yet aware of your marriage to my son."

"Forgive me," Isabel said, "but I did not speak his name."

"Nor do you have a husband in Montenegro," the Queen-Mother said with exasperation.

"You are right of course," Isabel admitted.

"What is it you wish to know," Alfonso asked?

"Anything," Isabel said quickly. "I have sent letters to him now for months without a single reply. Is he alive?

Tell me something. Tell me anything," Isabel said desperately!

"My brother lives," Alfonso told her. "I am certain of it."

"Oh praise be to God," Isabel exclaimed!

"As to your letters," he continued, "Italy is a hostile place presently."

"That is what the currier tells me," Isabel nodded.

"Your letters are being sent," Alfonso assured her.

"I have taken personal responsibility to make sure they are delivered," Petronilla added, "forasmuch as I can do from the palace."

"Thank you your majesty," Isabel replied.

"Of course," Petronilla nodded, "but there are several more things which complicate the matter."

"What are they?" Isabel asked.

"Ramon is, if I am not mistaken, is currently staging his own death. I suspect that it is he who does not send the letters back. If any were to be intercepted, it would ruin our little charade. This would cause quite a problem with Lord William and the French. I am certain that he does not want to get caught."

"But you know he is alive," Isabel asked hopefully?

"As I said," Alfonso answered, "he is alive."

"Shall I still send my letters? Will he receive them," she asked?

"It will take some time," Petronilla interjected, "but they will find their way to my son. From now on you should address him generally and not by name."

"My thanks to you both," Isabel said happily!

"We do what we can," Alfonso said with his hands held out.

"But mind you be silent on the matter," the Queen-Mother said forcefully.

"I will," Isabel promised. Her face was shining with relief and joy.

"Then we are concluded," King Alfonso said. Petronilla stood up from the shadows. Isabel curtseyed low and then left them together in the antechamber. She returned quickly to her carriage and the soldiers who waited there for her. She was so happy that Ramon was alive that she wanted to shout it from the rooftops! She could not do this, but would keep her secret from all but Pilar until his return.

The edifices of the Basilica del Pilar looked ominous in the darkness. The details of its domes and spires were lit from below by torchlight. The main door was open. Light flooded out from it onto the cobblestone square. "Stop the carriage," Isabel ordered. Her driver obeyed and one of the soldiers helped her down to the stones. "I wish to pray before we return home," she announced. "Remain here."

"As you wish," one of the men answered with a bow. Rodrigo bowed and smiled also, but then his eyes went back quickly to scanning those others who walked in the square. His alertness reminded Isabel of her father. Although she was overjoyed that Ramon still lived, the sight of the church had reminded her that his mortality yet hung in the balance. She was already praying for his safety, but felt the burden of her own sins upon her. It had been some time since she had last spoken to a confessor.

Evening masses were usually not held at the Basilica. So it was that Isabel entered into a mostly deserted sanctuary. The sanctuary itself was vast with high vaulted ceilings and more rows of pews than Isabel cared to count. The pews were made out of cherry wood and had been lacquered to a high gloss. A platform rose up at the front of the chamber. The platform contained a pulpit and an altar for laying out the implements of Holy Communion. Behind this, the wall was covered with an entablature made of gold. There were many bas-reliefs within it depicting various stories of the bible. Spreading out from either side of this were bigger-than-life reliefs of the saints. They all stood in much the same position with their hands folded and heads looking down toward the parishioners.

There were three men seated together in the pews closest to the front of the sanctuary. Two of these personages were dressed in the garb of priests. The one sitting farthest to the left wore the red robes and accoutrements of a Cardinal. Another man was standing in the row ahead of the first three. He was a person of considerable musculature and appearance. He was dark skinned for a Spaniard and very handsome. Black hair hung to his shoulders and he had a neatly trimmed beard and moustache on his face. He was covered from neck to toe in thick leather armor. The hue of the armor was a dark brown like the bark of a maple tree. Over this he wore a scarlet surcoat on which were the gold embroidered images of a cross, a sword, and an olive branch. A steel buckler was attached to each of his arms just below the elbow. A large scabbard hung from the man's waist but there was no weapon inside it. Isabel assumed that he would have removed it before entering the sanctuary. The look on his face was one of intensity as he addressed those who sat before him. "And that is why we have to act now," he whispered loudly as Isabel made her way to the confessional booth.

"Patience is a virtue Hector," said a deep bass voice from one of the men seated.

"Not if it results in death," the man called Hector shot back!

"Hold," the deep voice interrupted him. "We are no longer alone." Hector looked down over the pews at Isabel. Turning his face more toward her revealed the scar that ran from the corner of his left eye, across his cheek, and to the corner of his chin. His gaze made her feel uncomfortable and Isabel hurried to her destination. She closed herself inside.

The confessional was a simple affair. Dark cherry wood walls with a bench built into one of them. A lattice work of iron covered the small window that led to the adjacent booth for the priest. After several minutes, Isabel heard the open and shut of the door on the other side. Isabel could not discern the man's face but she could see that he was a Spaniard and that his robes were crimson. "Bless me father for I have sinned," Isabel said through the grate.

"Tell me your sins," echoed the deep voice of the confessor.

"I have had the wicked thoughts about my mother's new husband."

"You find this man attractive," the man asked?

"No," Isabel replied with disgust, but she softened her tone when she remembered who she was speaking too. "No, it is not like that. I feel that he has deceived my mother."

"What lies has he told?"

"It is not a specific lie father. He himself is a lie. I know him to be a man of no principle and that his trickery will ruin our good name."

"You know this for certain?"

"I do."

"Then tell me what it is that drives you to penance?"

"I have many times wanted to kill him."

"I see," the confessor replied. Isabel could almost sense him frowning. She sat uncomfortably waiting for the man to go on. "You know that murder is the greatest sin forbidden by God," he said.

"Yes father," she replied.

"As Cain slew his brother Abel and Abel's blood cried out from the ground…"

"Yes father."

"You know that to commit sin in your heart is the same as to have committed it in the flesh?"

"Yes," Isabel answered. "I do not know what it is…the way he looks at everything…something evil in his face. I am afraid of what will happen to my mother."

"Give me your hand," the deep voice commanded. Isabel was not sure how to respond. She hesitated. "Put your hand upon the grate," the man instructed her.

"Yes father," Isabel agreed. She had been expecting to receive her penance. The confessor should have given her some number of Hail Mary's and Our Father's to recite until her soul would be purged of sin. His request was strange, but Isabel complied. She placed her palm tentatively on the iron lattice work. The man's hand quickly joined hers. She could feel one of his cold fingers touching the flesh of her palm through a break in the iron.

"Our father, who art in Heaven," the confessor began. Isabel joined in The Lord's Prayer and their two voices became one. Halfway through the recitation, Isabel became suddenly faint and had to brace herself with her other hand to avoid crumpling into the wall of the confessional. "...the kingdom and the power and the glory," the man concluded, "forever and ever...amen."

"Amen," Isabel echoed, but she could not stand for the dizziness.

"Kill him," said the deep voice of the confessor from the other side.

"What," Isabel asked in disbelief?

"Kill him," the man replied. "The Lord commands it."

"This is not happening," Isabel said as she rose to her feet. Her faintness was quickly evaporating. Surely whatever lurked on the opposite side of the confessional was not a man of God!

"For the sake of your mother," it continued relentlessly, "do it!" Isabel threw open the door to the confession booth and fled toward the entrance of the sanctuary. She could hear the priest's door opening and closing behind her. She looked over her shoulder as she neared the entryway but the man was not pursuing her. The very same cardinal that had so unsettled her after her performance before King Alfonso's court now stood next to the confessional. He wore the crimson robes and hat common to his office and leaned upon a silver staff with a crucifix atop it. This time he was not obscured by shadows but stood under the almost complete illumination of a massive chandelier. The cardinal's face was now revealed in hideous clarity. It may have been handsome once, but where his eyes had been, now only scarred sockets remained. One sickeningly long finger was pointed out toward Isabel. "Do it in God's name," the cardinal shouted! Isabel fled out of the Basilica.

"We go now," she screamed as she swiftly approached the carriage. Without assistance, Isabel climbed up inside and slammed the door shut! "Ride," she shouted at the top of her lungs! The carriage rumbled quickly away from the Basilica and over the bridge crossing the River Ebro. Isabel did not look back.

CHAPTER III

It was very late when Isabel returned to Montenegro's Keep. She told no one what the Cardinal had said, not even Little Grandma. In the first place, she would have had to admit to her own dark thoughts in order to tell about the confessor. Then she would have to convince whomever she told that a man of the cloth had actually instructed her to commit murder. It was unbelievable and likely to get her into trouble.

Isabel did not bother to wake her mother but went straight up to her bedroom. Once she had changed into her nightgown, she crossed over to stand by the window. The courtyard was mostly dark with few torches for illumination. She could barely make out the gleam of metal from the guards on the Keep's walls. A shiver coursed through the girl's spine, but it was not the night air. It seemed that her father's death had turned the whole world upside down. How could a cardinal of the Holy Church command her to kill? Surely Lord Barillos was not admirable, but that was not enough reason to destroy him. Isabel tried to imagine that she was mistaken about what the cardinal had said but she could not lie to herself.

In the morning, Isabel dressed herself in a simple white gown. She was passing by the entry hall on her way to the private dining room when she noticed something amiss. The walls were bare. The great tapestries depicting her father's military victories were nowhere to be seen. "You," Isabel called after a serving woman on her way to the kitchen, "come here."

"Yes my lady," the woman answered. She hurried over to where Isabel was waiting. Picking up the grey folds of her dress, the woman curtseyed and averted her eyes down toward the floor.

"Where are my father's tapestries?"

"His lordship had them taken down," the woman replied hesitantly.

"For what purpose?"

"He has taken them to Zaragoza for cleaning my lady."

"Where is his lordship," Isabel asked with unconcealed suspicion?

"He is with the tapestries Lady Isabel," the woman answered.

"Of course he is," Isabel frowned. She couldn't imagine why her mother's new husband would want to glorify her father. "Thank you miss," she said curtly.

"Is there anything else my lady wishes," the servant asked politely?

"No," Isabel replied. "That will be all." The woman curtseyed once more and Isabel nodded her dismissal. The serving woman went back toward the kitchen while Isabel walked slowly into the midst of the entry hall. She stood there for several moments before her thoughts were suddenly interrupted.

"Pilar," Alejandra screamed from upstairs, "Pilar come quickly!" Isabel rushed up the stairs and reached the landing in time to see Little Grandma disappearing into her mother's bed chamber. Isabel ran after her. Lady Priscilla was moaning in pain when her daughter came through the doorway. Little Grandma had one hand held to the woman's forehead. Priscilla's eyes were closed and her face was pinched up with agony. Alejandra stood closer to the wall behind the older woman. Her face was streaked with worry. "You do not have a fever," Little Grandma told Isabel's mother.

"It hurts," Priscilla groaned!

"Where does it hurt?" Pilar asked.

"My stomach…ahhhh…all the way down," Priscilla answered raggedly. Pilar opened the woman's nightgown and ran her hand over her stomach, pressing down gently at intervals.

"Is it there," the old woman asked? "Is it there?"

"All over," Priscilla replied and then cried out once more.

"Oh my," Pilar said with amazement written all over her face!

"Ahhh," Priscilla moaned!

"There it is again," Little Grandma exclaimed!

"Oh.., oh," Priscilla said. Her breathing began to slow down and she sighed with relief as the pain abated.

"Lady Priscilla," Pilar said excitedly, "you are with child!"

"I knew it," Isabel's mother breathed. Isabel was too stunned to speak.

"Why did you not tell me," Pilar asked?

"Manuel was convinced that I had some sort of stomach ailment. He seemed so sincere in trying to pamper me that I believed it too."

"You cannot talk to a man about these things," Pilar chided.

"I know...I know," Priscilla answered, "but I thought that my womb had dried up."

"Do you think Lord Barillos will be pleased," Isabel asked flatly? The idea that her mother should bear a child by that man was less than appealing.

"If it is a boy," Priscilla answered. That stung, but Isabel did not think her mother was trying to be intentionally hurtful.

"You are very far along," Little Grandma said. "You barely show at all!"

"It was the same with Isabel, remember," Priscilla said smiling. "When will I conceive?"

"Any day now," Pilar answered as she took the other woman's hand.

"So soon," Isabel's mother asked? "I hope you are wrong. The child will be sickly if it should come so fast."

"Lady Priscilla," Pilar said with tears in her eyes, "I felt your baby's feet. He is too big already."

"Do you mean...," Priscilla asked hopefully?

"That is exactly what I mean," Pilar replied.

"How wonderful," Priscilla cried! Pilar cried with her but they were happy tears.

"He will be a child of Montenegro," Pilar said proudly.

"Little Rafi," Priscilla wept. "Rafael would have been so happy."

"You mean it is my father's child?" Isabel asked as she realized what the older women were talking about at last. "Oh mother, that is wonderful!"

"Yes," Priscilla agreed tearfully. "Praise be to God." They were all overflowing with joy and talked at length about the coming child who Priscilla was convinced would be a son. Little Grandma was planning dozens of little outfits in her head that had yet to be sewn. After speaking excitedly to one another for some time, Isabel's mother needed to sleep.

Pilar and Isabel were still talking animatedly as they walked down the hallway toward Isabel's room. In the midst of her happiness, a sobering thought occurred to the young heiress. "What are we going to tell Lord Barillos," she asked seriously?

"Nothing," Little Grandma replied as the joy drained from her face as well.

"We have to tell him something," Isabel said as they entered her room.

"It is true," the elder woman agreed. "We will let him believe the child is his."

"Until when," Isabel asked?

"I do not know," Little Grandma replied, "at least until he has made it out of the womb."

"How do you know it will be a boy?"

"Only God knows," Pilar replied, "but in this case a girl would be better." The old woman began to remove Isabel's clothing so that she could go to bed.

"What do you mean?"

"Men can be strange," Little Grandma replied evasively. "One never knows how they might react."

"He would not do anything to a child would he," Isabel asked nervously, "or my mother?"

"I suspect not," Pilar replied, "but my conviction is not strong enough to speak freely of it. Just follow my example if you please."

"I will," Isabel replied as the change over from dress to nightgown was completed. The older woman's implications were disturbing indeed. She could not imagine anyone wanting to hurt a child, but she decided to heed the warning.

✝   ✝   ✝

The next afternoon, Isabel was up in her mother's room knitting baby clothes with Little Grandma and Lady Priscilla. They were all interrupted from their work by the loud crash of breaking glass from downstairs. "What goes on down there?" Priscilla demanded as she looked up from her needle craft.

"I will find out," Isabel said with irritation. She rose from where she had been seated on her mother's bed and placed the half finished hat on the small table next to it. She left the room and made her way quickly down the stairs. It was easy to tell where the noise had come from because she could hear Manuel loudly berating one of the servants in the hall.

"You clumsy pig," Lord Barillos shouted angrily! There was a mumbled apology followed by a cry of pain and surprise from the offender. "Hurry up," Barillos snarled, "and mind you get every last piece. Otherwise, I will have you searching on your bare feet."

"Yes my lord," the servant replied desperately. Isabel practically ran to reach the dining room. She entered the chamber to find her step- father standing menacingly over the servant. The serving man was down on his knees collecting shards of crystal in one hand and holding them protectively with the other. An overpowering stench of alcohol washed over Isabel as she drew closer. Lord Barillos clothing was mussed and wrinkled as if he had slept in it. It was not at all the bearing of nobility.

"What is the meaning of this," Isabel demanded? Thinking that Isabel was addressing him, the servant replied.

"It was but an accident Lady Isabel," he said fearfully as Manuel hulked drunkenly over him. "I swear it shall never happen again!"

"Is my lord well," Isabel asked rudely? The bite in her voice was lost on her drunken step-father.

"I should say not," Barillos slurred as he pointed one finger shakily up into the air for emphasis. "This dog ran into me. I was knocked into the table…quite roughly. My hip will surely bruise from where it struck the corner."

"How tragic," Isabel said sarcastically.

"It was…it is," Barillos agreed. "I tried to catch myself on the table and this is what happened!" Isabel nodded with a frown. "Keep working you imbecile," Lord Barillos shouted! The servant lowered his head still farther toward the floor and obeyed the best he could. "I should have you whipped for your stupidity alone!" The drunken lord raised a hand as if to strike down at the man but Isabel cut him short.

"My lord," she said sharply.

"What," Barillos asked loudly? He swayed on one foot but steadied himself on the table.

"My mother has been eagerly anticipating your return. Will you not go up to see her?"

"Your mother," Barillos said perversely as if a sinful thought had just occurred to him. He was no longer interested in the crouching servant. "I will go to her now."

"Very good," Isabel said with a bitter taste in her mouth. "Let me deal with this man!"

"Yes, you take care of im'," Barillos slurred as he tottered over to the eastern stairwell.

"Finish what you are doing and then return with a broom," Isabel instructed once the drunken Manuel was leaving.

"Yes my lady," said the male servant nervously.

"Relax," Isabel sighed, "our new lord is an idiot." The servant did not comment but hurried to finish his task. Isabel left him to it and went back up the stairs and from there into her mother's room. Manuel was cavorting around and acting like a fool when she arrived.

"My wife is with child," he bellowed! "It's going to be a son," he told Isabel as he wobbled next to her. There was a tone in his voice that seemed to be daring her to dispute with him. Isabel had no such desire. "This calls for a drink," Manuel shouted! Priscilla winced but kept on smiling as she lay in her bed propped on several pillows. Barillos was sloppy and reeked of spirits. He was nothing like Isabel's father had been. "Fetch us some wine," he told Alejandra.

"Right away my lord," Alejandra said quietly as she curtseyed.

"Make sure there is enough water in it," Isabel muttered as the chamber maid passed her by. She did not know whether Alejandra had heard her or not, but she hoped that she had. Barillos continued his sideshow until the woman returned with the wine. He stumbled about; shouting, singing, and kissing Priscilla and Isabel with his putrid breath. There was a rancid stench emanating from his body.

Alejandra held the bottle of wine in one hand and a silver tray with several glasses in the other. She set the tray on the table by the bed and began pouring from the bottle. Manuel snatched up an empty glass before the serving woman could get to it. She looked up at him with uncertainty. "Pour the wine," Barillos said as he held his glass out toward her. "Careful not to spill," he warned as she filled his glass. "Be sure to bring the rest up to my room after," he said with a revolting smile. Alejandra nodded and stepped back quickly. She passed the glasses out to the rest of them. Priscilla declined.

"A toast," Barillos shouted. He didn't even seem to notice that Priscilla was not holding a glass at all. "To my future son," he exclaimed!

"Here here," Pilar managed to say before Isabel and the two chamber maids raised the glasses to their lips. While the women were sipping delicately, Barillos drank as though he were involved in a contest to reach the bottom. Manuel fell unceremoniously to the floor when the last drop had gone down his throat. The glass did not break but slipped from his hand and rolled along the floor a short way.

"My lord," Alejandra asked nervously. Manuel began to snore. Priscilla closed her eyes and put a hand to her head.

"Take him up to his room," she said with exasperation. "Get some of the soldiers to help you carry him."

"Yes my lady," Alejandra replied respectfully. Isabel walked over to where her step-father was sprawled out. Spittle was forming and reforming on the side of his mouth as he slumbered on. Isabel tapped his boot with her shoe.

"Time to go," Isabel said crossly. There was no response. Without thinking, she dumped the rest of her wine onto the unconscious man's face. Little Grandma gasped in shock. Isabel should have been worried also, but her anger was stronger. Fortunately, her mother had not seen what had just transpired. For Manuel's part, Isabel might as well have offered him a blanket. There was no reaction from Lord Barillos.

A few short minutes later, Alejandra returned with several of Montenegro's soldiers. The men carried the drunken lord out of the room and up to his bed. Isabel could not help but feel ashamed for her mother.

At dinner that evening, Isabel was forced to dine alone with Lord Barillos as her mother did not feel up to eating. They ate in silence. Barillos would let a groan escape his lips every so often. He still looked quite ragged from his ordeal. Isabel glared at the wretched man as she ate. Barillos finally noticed her irritation. He looked back at her and spoke. "What is it," he demanded? "Have you something to say Isabel?" Isabel was careful to compose herself before speaking.

"I was just wondering where the tapestries are my lord," she said neutrally.

"What tapestries?"

"The tapestries my lord," Isabel reminded him, "the very same that you took to be cleaned in Zaragoza."

"What do you want with them?"

"Not much," Isabel replied, "only to know where they have been stored so that I may have them hanging in their proper place by morning."

"They are...still in Zaragoza," Manuel struggled.

"Is something wrong my lord?" Isabel asked him.

"No. The tapestries are old and must be treated with care. The cleaning is going to take some time longer than I had planned."

"I see," Isabel said unconvinced.

"I am to return for them soon," Manuel explained.

"Well," Isabel said as she finished her plate, "I will leave my lord to his rest. I can see that you are ailing."

"Yes, thank you," Barillos replied and held his forehead with one hand. "We will speak more tomorrow. I give you leave." Isabel stood and curtseyed slightly. One of the servants pushed her chair in as she left the man to eat alone. Over the next few days, Manuel played the part of the loving husband. It was not long, however, before he was making his way back to get the tapestries. Later that same day, a cry went up from the servants in the kitchen. Isabel hurried down to see what was causing the commotion.

"Where is it?" the voice of the head cook echoed loudly out of the kitchen. "I will know where it is right now!" The first thing Isabel noticed as she entered was the red faced cook yelling at one of the younger females who worked in the kitchen. The rest of the kitchen staff looked on in fearful silence. They all wore long white aprons over their simple clothing. The females had their hair tied up with white scarves as well.

"What is this," Isabel demanded? "What is it that disturbs my rest?"

"This girl has stolen from your mother Lady Isabel," the cook said accusingly.

"I have taken nothing," the girl insisted!

"What has she stolen?" Isabel asked.

"Almost all of the silver," the cook exclaimed: "bowls, trays, teapots, cutlery…the list goes on!" Isabel frowned. The things the cook listed seemed like a rather large amount for one girl to carry. Surely she would know that these things would not go unnoticed.

"How certain are you of this," she asked the man?

"There could be no one else," he explained. "Marta was the only one in the kitchen yesterday evening. When we came in this morning, the silver was gone!"

"I would never steal from Montenegro," Marta declared!

"Come with me," Isabel told her sternly. "The rest of you go back to your work. My mother will have her breakfast on time." There were murmurs of assent as Isabel left the kitchen. The girl Marta followed nervously behind her. They went to her father's study and Isabel closed the door. She seated herself behind the table and left the girl to stand. "Tell me what you have done," Isabel said as she looked up.

"I have done nothing my lady," Marta answered sincerely.

"You were the last one in the kitchen."

"I was my lady."

"Where is my mother's silver? Tell me now!"

"The…the new lord of Montenegro took it all out."

"Why was the head cook not informed?"

"Your father..," Marta began.

"He is not my father," Isabel corrected her.

"Lord Barillos made me swear to silence."

"Did he?"

"Oh please do not tell his lordship," Marta pleaded! "I beg of you. He promised that I will be flogged and put out if I ever speak of it. I have no other place to go." The girl was now starting to cry.

"Be not afraid," Isabel told her. "I will find the truth of this matter."

"I have not stolen my lady. I swear to it!"

"I know," Isabel replied. "Come now. We will return to the kitchen."

"As my lady wishes," Marta said as she curtseyed before the table. They returned to the kitchen. Isabel paused in the doorway while Marta entered with apprehension. All eyes were on the serving girl.

"She is not a thief," Isabel told them. "I will suffer no one to treat her as one." This last she stated pointedly while staring at the head cook.

"Yes my lady," he answered. His eyes were lowered in deference as he did so. Isabel left them to their tasks and went back upstairs to see her mother. Priscilla had managed to get herself up onto one of the couches. Isabel's mother was knitting a tiny tunic for the new baby.

"Mother," Isabel said as she entered the room, "we have a very serious matter to discuss."

"I think I know," Priscilla sighed, "but do go on."

"Most of the silver has been stolen," Isabel reported.

"Surely not," Priscilla said with alarm. "Most of those things were passed down from my mother!"

"I know," Isabel said with disgust. "The servants point the finger of guilt at Marta."

"Marta is incapable of such a thing," her mother disagreed. "She was born here."

"Marta," Isabel continued, "when pressed, revealed the culprit to be your husband."

"Manuel," Priscilla asked in disbelief?

"Yes," Isabel confirmed, "and I believe her."

"Why would he do such a thing?"

"I do not know, but he took our tapestries to Zaragoza over a week ago and has returned without them."

"Those tapestries contain the only images I have of Rafael," Priscilla said angrily.

"Manuel said that they are still being cleaned. That is why he has gone back again."

"I am sure he will bring them back soon," Priscilla reassured herself.

"But now he has stolen the silver as well," Isabel interjected, "and he takes it with him to Zaragoza." Her mother had run out of arguments. Priscilla frowned but said nothing. "I will have him followed," Isabel said. "We shall soon discover what goes on in the capital."

"Who do you have to send," Priscilla inquired?

"Someone I trust," Isabel said.

"Be sure they act with discretion," Priscilla warned. "I do not want to bring shame upon our family."

"Leave it to me," Isabel said. "The last thing I would do is bring shame to Montenegro."

"I hate this," Priscilla said unhappily.

"As do I," Isabel agreed. She kissed her mother on the head and left the bed chamber. As she walked down the corridor, Isabel went down a list of names in her head that she thought she could trust. Out of these, she narrowed further to those who might be capable of accomplishing the surveillance. "The less they know the better," she decided aloud while descending the spiral stairs. With that said, she returned up to her room.

Isabel could not go to Zaragoza herself. It would surely attract attention. She briefly considered trying to disguise herself as a man, but rejected that too. Her cover would be blown should she have to speak to anyone. To travel alone to Zaragoza as a woman would present a host of other dangers that she did not care to imagine.

Captain Pascual was trustworthy, but as the commander of the army; his face would not go unrecognized by her step-father. Little Grandma was too old and a woman besides. She groaned in frustration and then walked over to her window. Perhaps the cool breeze might help clear her mind.

Looking out toward the battlements, she noticed one of the archers peering down at her. He noticed her eyes on him and bowed slightly. It was Rodrigo, the man who had carried her father home despite the danger. She waved to him and smiled. When she lowered her hand, Rodrigo turned his attention back over the walls. It occurred to her then that she had found the man she was looking for. She hurried from her room and laid a hand on the shoulder of one of the guards patrolling the hallways. "Fetch me Rodrigo," she told the man.

"Of course my lady," the guard replied.

"Send him up to the aviary. I will see him at once."

"I obey," the man answered. He turned around and hurried toward the western tower which would connect him by bridge to the battlements. Isabel headed east to the spiral stairs leading up to the aviary. The pigeons became noisy in anticipation of food as Isabel entered. This time she had not brought any with her. However, it did occur to her that their ruckus would prevent eavesdropping.

The Heiress of Montenegro was quickly joined by Rodrigo and the man she had sent to bring him hither. "Here is Rodrigo the Archer as you requested," the other man said with a bow. Rodrigo bowed also.

"Thank you soldier," Isabel said graciously. "You may leave us now." The guard bowed once more before leaving them alone in the top of the east tower. "Shut the door," Isabel told Rodrigo. His face looked somewhat apprehensive.

"Will no one else be joining us my lady?" the archer asked as he obeyed.

"No one," Isabel confirmed. "I have a task of the utmost importance and I will let no one else hear of it."

"I am honored," Rodrigo said proudly.

"Wait until you have heard," Isabel warned. "I want you to follow Lord Barillos to Zaragoza."

"Does my lady anticipate danger?"

"No. There is a thief in the house. Surely you have heard?"

"I overheard something from the servants."

"I suspect that Lord Barillos and this thief are one and the same man," Isabel said gravely. She realized then that meaning to tell as little as possible had turned into telling everything. It was too late to go back, however.

"Surely not," Rodrigo shook his head. Isabel then told him the story of the tapestries and the missing silver. His eyes were filled with disbelief which turned to anger when Isabel spoke finally of Marta's revelation.

"Why would she make such an accusation," Rodrigo asked? "She could be beheaded if my lord were to learn of it."

"Why," Isabel repeated the man's question, "because she is naïve to such things and because it is the truth. If she were smart enough to lie, she would also be smart enough to choose a different person on which to lay guilt."

"You are wise," Rodrigo agreed, "but what good will it do for us if I do reveal Lord Barillos to be the thief? Everything in Montenegro now belongs to him."

"Firstly; it will stop me from having to punish an innocent," Isabel answered. "As for what else that information may be used for...leave it to me."

"When shall I depart," Rodrigo asked eagerly?

"As soon as you can make yourself ready," she told him. "I will inform Captain Pascual that you will be away for a time."

"Yes my lady."

"See that you are not recognized," Isabel continued.

"I will," Rodrigo promised. "I will be worthy of this great trust you put upon me."

"Farewell then," Isabel smiled.

"My lady," Rodrigo said respectfully. He bowed to her and then left her alone in the tower. She went down then to the courtyard where the soldiers were sparring with each other. Captain Pascual was overseeing their efforts and making corrections when necessary.

"A word with you Captain," Isabel said as she approached behind the man.

"Lady Isabel," he said. The captain turned toward her and bowed slightly. "I did not hear you coming."

"Come and speak with me," she told him.

"Of course," he replied. "Continue," he shouted at the men. He then followed Isabel into the keep and up to her father's study. Isabel did not enjoy lying to the man but it seemed the wisest course of action. It was a believable story she told and Captain Pascual did not seem to notice the deception. She told him that she was sending Rodrigo to take an urgent message to Zaragoza. The letter would then be taken to a distant relative who was at war in Genoa. "I wish you would have told me," Captain Pascual sighed. "I have much better riders than Rodrigo."

"But none that I so trust," Isabel explained.

"I understand," he nodded.

"Excellent," Isabel said. "I felt I should tell you so that he would not be missed..."

"My thanks," the captain replied. Isabel nodded. "Shall I return to the yard then my lady?"

"Yes...go," she answered. Captain Pascual bowed and left in a hurry to get back to his men. Rodrigo did not return for nearly seven days.

Once he had come back to the barracks, Rodrigo removed his uniform in favor of his plain brown tunic and breeches. It was an easy decision because it was the only other set of clothing he owned. His cloak was a darker brown than the rest. His horse and the saddle bags full of provision were provided by Lady Isabel. She had even given him a bed roll for the journey. The blanket looked more comfortable than the one he had in the barracks. He took also his dagger, a quiver of arrows, and the longbow that rarely left his hands.

Rodrigo rode hard out of Montenegro. He caught up with Lord Barillos several hours later. He had to slow down and cling to the tree line until the carriage was once more out of view. He did not want to arouse suspicion. A man on horseback would logically pass them by. Rodrigo did not want to get that close for fear that someone might recognize him. His fears were unfounded but he remained cautious nonetheless.

Since he knew where Barillos was bound and he could travel much faster, Rodrigo decided that he would follow by night. They would be less likely to see him as long as he kept to the woods by day. His intuition served him well and he overtook the carriage on that same evening. The firelight in the distance gave him plenty of time to take precautions. He slowly rode his horse into the trees and traveled in a wide arc around his targets' campsite. He thought there would be trouble when he heard the guards conversing as he snuck by. "Did you hear something," one of the men asked?

"I cannot be sure," answered the other, "a wild animal perhaps?"

"It must be," the first man agreed nervously. None of the guards were motivated to go searching through the dark woods. Rodrigo waited until they were once more relaxed before the fire. He then continued at a stealthy pace. He would have been much quieter if not for the horse that he led on a rope behind him. If the guards heard him, however; they made no indication of it.

After some time, Rodrigo circled back to the road. He rode until the sky turned grey to signify the approaching dawn. He led his mare far into the trees and tethered her to one of them. The bedroll was just as comfortable as it appeared and it was not long before he found sleep. He was awakened on occasion by the sounds of the forest, but it did not take him long to bed down once more. He did not hear the sound of the carriage wheels until midday. He could not see the road clearly but he was certain that it was the carriage of Lord Barillos.

Rodrigo sat up and froze as he heard the wheels crunching on the hard packed earth of the path. His mare made a slight nickering noise but that was all. The carriage moved on without incident but Rodrigo was unable to fall back asleep. He followed the trail slowly for several hours from the safety of the trees. Once night fell, he brought his horse out to run.

Before long, the great city of Huesca came into view over the tops of the trees. He slowed down as he entered and traveled slowly down the main road. There were few people out late at night save the occasional patrol of the guard. The city was mostly dark except for its inns and taverns. Rodrigo had been given a small amount of money. He was contemplating whether or not to get something hot to eat when he saw Barillos' carriage parked in front of a large two story structure. There was a covered walkway which led around the top floor and Rodrigo could see several doors leading in.

There were two people on the walkway. The first was a well-dressed man who carried a wooden mask over his face. The second was a young woman dressed in a white nightgown that left little to the imagination. Her eyes were darkly shadowed and even from far away, Rodrigo could see that her cheeks were dusted crimson. The man was laughing and carrying a drink in his free hand. The woman pressed her body up against his playfully and helped herself to a drink from his glass. She whispered something in the man's ear. With their bodies still touching, the woman turned around. She pushed back suddenly with her hips and set the man off balance. She giggled and he roared with laughter as he stumbled after her. The woman opened one of the doors and the man tottered in. She followed and closed the door behind her.

Barillos carriage was guarded by two of his henchman. None of the soldiers of Montenegro looked at these men as equals. They were little more than ruffians. Rodrigo kept his head down and his face averted as he led his horse up to the house of ill repute. He tied the mare to the hitching rail that nearly ran the length of the building. There was a large man leaning against the wall behind the rail. He had a leather collar around his neck and a footman's mace hung from his belt. From the shape of his tunic, Rodrigo guessed that the man was wearing leather armor beneath it. "Welcome to the Fox and Cat," the man said gruffly as Rodrigo tethered his horse. Rodrigo simply nodded. He ducked under the rail and handed the man a coin from his belt pouch.

"Keep an eye on my horse if you would my friend," Rodrigo said.

"Enjoy yourself," the man grinned as he pocketed Lady Isabel's money. Rodrigo walked slowly across the wooden porch. He could see a small wooden sign hanging from an iron post over the entryway. A fox was depicted on the sign in pursuit of a white cat. The two animals were running nose to tail in a circle. It was only because of normal association that one would perceive that the fox was chasing the cat. Rodrigo could see both scenarios. He entered the main door of the brothel with his hood obscuring most of his face. His need for secrecy did not seem out of place here.

No one seemed to take much notice of the hooded man as he moved through the tavern. Manuel Barillos was seated at the center table along with several other men. There was a high stakes game of dice being played and many of the prostitutes were competing for the attention of the gamblers. Judging by the other men's clothing, they were merchant class at best. Manuel was clearly the wealthiest man at the table. "Another bottle of wine," the gambling lord called loudly!

"My lord is generous," a man with a waxed moustache and goatee said disapprovingly. He had long black hair and his fingers were covered with expensive rings. There were two rough looking men behind him and a dark skinned beauty in a provocative red dress sitting on his lap. Manuel's men sat at the table behind their lord. Lord Barillos looked as happy as a pig in swallop! He had a pile of money on the table before him and a whore sitting to either side. Their desire for his money could easily be mistaken for a lustful wanting of the man himself. Rodrigo suspected that one of the prostitutes was already going to work from the placement of her hand below the table.

When the bar maid came by, Rodrigo quietly ordered a tankard of ale. He was approached by two different whores. He explained to each of them that he was waiting for someone who would be joining him soon. It was not difficult to turn them away with such a large amount of coinage being displayed on Lord Barillos' table. "This is Manuel's night now," Lord Barillos told the man with the waxed moustache. "I hope you have come ready to play!"

"You may want to keep that bottle of wine for when your luck runs out my lord," the man joked.

"Not tonight Mateo," Barillos said grandly. His eyes rolled back for a second and he had to grip the table for balance.

"Steady girls," Mateo chuckled. There was laughter from the other gamblers and a sly wink from the woman who was probably dirtying her fingers under the table. She had dark hair and a most indecently cut blue gown. It had no sleeves and the neckline only concealed her areola from view half the time.

"Oooh," the woman sighed as she leaned her upturned face in toward Manuel. He grabbed her roughly and kissed her as his hands pawed over her breasts. There were cheers from the other men at the table, all save Mateo who had work to do. Rodrigo watched as the man quickly dumped his dice out of the wooden cup and into the hand of the dark skinned girl on his lap. There was another pair of dice which he retrieved from an open pouch on his belt. He quickly placed these in the cup and then made a grand show of shaking the dice to get Lord Barillos' attention.

"Shall we raise the stakes," Mateo asked innocently?

"Are you so fond of losing," Barillos laughed.

"My big man will take everything," the whore in the blue dress boasted. Rodrigo noticed the smile she shared secretly with Mateo.

"What have you got," Manuel challenged?

"You know," Mateo replied, "I'll give you back your wife's tapestries if you win, but if I triumph than you forfeit all the silver you've got in your carriage."

"I suppose you'll want all my winnings too," Barillos laughed?

"Well you still owe me on account," Mateo said calmly.

"I've been up all night," Barillos chuckled, "but I am no fool."

"And..," Mateo prodded.

"If I win, you will also give me Sara as my new chamber maid."

"Sara brings me a lot of money," Mateo said hesitantly.

"If you lack the bravery," Barillos began.

"Let us toss the dice now," Mateo shot back! "I shall take your wager!" Sara whispered something in Manuel's ear and a perverse smile covered his drunken face.

"You will regret it," Barillos declared! "Come now my little flower," he invited the prostitute called Sara. "Give me some luck." He held the wooden cup toward her and she leaned down close to it. She slowly pursed her lips and blew into the cup. Sara smiled seductively at Barillos as she raised her head back up. He chuckled and grinned back at her. Shaking the wooden cup dramatically over his head, Manuel cast his dice down onto the table. "Pair of fours," he cried excitedly, "beat that!" Mateo groaned and pounded his fist on the table for show. He then let the weighted dice tumble out of his own wooden cup. Rodrigo could not see how the dice had landed, but he could guess the result by the shark's smile that covered Mateo's face.

"You lose," Mateo said with satisfaction.

"Impossible," Barillos screamed! His face was now scarred with anxiety and disappointment.

"Bad luck my friend," Mateo said consolingly as he pulled Barillos' coins across the table with both hands.

"Let us roll again," Manuel practically begged.

"You have nothing to put up my lord," Mateo reminded him.

"I have the horses that draw my carriage," Manuel said loudly, "and the carriage itself!"

"Be at peace," Mateo said. "My lord has had too much to drink. Let us talk again tomorrow. We can play again then if you desire."

"I am going to win the next toss," Barillos insisted. "I can feel it!"

"Of course my lord," Mateo agreed, "but we will throw tomorrow. Fear not. Please accept the room as my gift for the evening."

"You are a good man Mateo," Barillos said emotionally. He was deep in his cups.

"Sara," Mateo called out to the blue garbed whore, "take my friend Manuel up to his room. Make sure he is well cared for."

"My pleasure," Sara replied. Although she was speaking to Mateo, her eyes were locked on the new lord of Montenegro. She led the drunken Manuel to a large wooden staircase leading to the second floor.

"Are you going to take care of me Sara," Manuel asked suggestively?

"Come on," she answered. She led Manuel onto the walkway and out of Rodrigo's view.

"Good work," Mateo congratulated the other men seated at the table. "Now let us drink Lord Barillos' wine!" The men laughed as the bottle was passed around.

"How did you know this would succeed," one of the men asked?

"I always know a mark when I see one," Mateo said smugly. He raised his glass and the others followed suit. "To our new friend," he said contemptuously.

"Here-here," one of the other men bellowed. This set the entire group to laughing. Rodrigo had seen enough. He placed some coins on his table and left the Fox and Cat behind. Mateo's men were already unloading Lady Priscilla's silver when Rodrigo came outside. He thanked the man who had kept watch over his horse and rode off into the night. He did not journey on to Zaragoza, but turned in the opposite direction toward Montenegro.

Everything Lady Isabel feared was true and there was more besides.

Rodrigo was angry. He considered going back to Huesca and taking the silver by force. Fortunately, he had the presence of mind to realize that the opportunity was already past. Perhaps he could have stolen Barillos' carriage and made off with the silver if he had planned it from the start. Priscilla's valuables were now somewhere inside the Fox and Cat.

Rodrigo was not a large man, nor was close combat his specialty. He was only an archer, (a very good one to be sure), but not someone accustomed to brawling. The other problem was that a dead man could not report back to Lady Isabel. He had promised not to disappoint her. Rodrigo's anger helped him stay awake that night as he rode swiftly back toward home.

CHAPTER IV

Isabel was watching as Captain Pascual trained the cavalrymen in the open field next to Black River Village. It was the same field where the war with Morera had taken place. She would have liked to join in the training, for it reminded her of her father. She could not be seen in public wearing men's clothing, however, nor was it seemly for a woman to pursue such skills.

It was early in the day when Rodrigo approached on horseback. Lady Isabel was sitting on a comfortable divan that had been set below a white canopy. When Rodrigo dismounted, she rose and walked out to meet him. "Rodrigo," she said questioningly, "what brings you back to me so soon? You should be just arriving in Zaragoza today."

"Shall we speak in private my lady," Rodrigo suggested?

"Yes," Isabel agreed. "Leave your mount with the others." She gestured toward the cavalrymen who were watching and resting while the rest simulated mounted combat on the field. Rodrigo did as he was instructed and then followed her back into the shade of the white fabric. Isabel did not resume her position on the divan but remained standing.

"I know that my early return is cause for some confusion," Rodrigo began, "but my lady's instructions have already been fulfilled."

"Tell me," Isabel commanded.

"My lady's suspicions are confirmed," he told her, "but it is not to Zaragoza that my lord travels."

"Where is he?" Isabel demanded angrily.

"At a brothel in Huesca," Rodrigo replied with eyes downcast. "It is called the Fox and Cat. He has lost the tapestries in a game of chance and now the silver as well."

"What else does my lord do at this brothel?"

"He drinks to excess and indulges himself in other ways as well. Allow me to spare you the sordid details. I am sure my lady can imagine what goes on in such a place."

"Spare me not," Isabel replied, "but tell me plainly."

"He disgraces his marriage vows to Lady Priscilla with the basest of harlots. My lord does not wait to hide behind closed doors, but does such things in the common room as would make your mother's blood boil!"

"Cretinous pig," Isabel cursed!

"I am sorry," Rodrigo said. He was ashamed for her and for all of Montenegro.

"No Rodrigo," Isabel replied. "You have done well and have my thanks."

"Thank you my lady," Rodrigo answered with a bow.

"Report back to Captain Pascual."

"What shall I say is the reason for my early return?"

"Say that you gave up the letters to a rider in Huesca as I commanded you. If he has more questions, than send him to me."

"I will do as you say."

"Good day Rodrigo," Isabel concluded.

"Good day to you Lady Isabel," he replied. Rodrigo bowed low and then left Isabel beneath the white canopy. She returned immediately to Montenegro's Keep by carriage. She was in a foul temper by the time she stormed up the stairs to her mother's room. "Leave us," Isabel told Alejandra and Little Grandma as she entered the room. The two chamber maids picked up on her anger and left without even a ghost of an argument.

"Isabel," Priscilla said disapprovingly as they left, "what have I told you?"

"Our lord is at a brothel in Huesca," Isabel interrupted.

"He is what?" Priscilla asked with a horrible edge to her voice.

"He lies," Isabel explained. "He tells you that he goes to Zaragoza only to spend more time with the whores in Huesca!"

"Tell me you are lying," Priscilla hissed!

"Do you wish to be deceived?"

"Perhaps I do," Isabel's mother replied, "but tell me the truth instead."

"Your husband has gambled away the tapestries of father's greatest triumphs. He stole your silver and has lost it in games of chance as well."

"What more?"

"He does things in the common rooms of the Fox and Cat that bring shame to us all. His fornication is a public spectacle and he treats your marriage vows as filthy rags!"

"Oh," Priscilla said as he she had just been injured. Her face was filled with shame and hurt.

"I am sorry Mama," Isabel said, "I should have chosen my words with more thought."

"It would amount to the same thing," Priscilla said.

"What are we going to do?"

"What can we do?" Priscilla asked forlornly. "All that I have is given to Manuel. Now even that is gone."

"Let me deal with him," Isabel said hatefully.

"No my daughter," Priscilla said as she touched a hand to Isabel's cheek. "Do not let such thoughts blacken your heart."

"It is blackened already," Isabel replied.

"Perhaps we are fortunate," Priscilla said. "Since he is so open with his indiscretions, I may be able to petition the Holy Father for an annulment. It will certainly be conceded."

"Annulments are rarely granted," Isabel thought out loud.

"They will grant this one," Priscilla said furiously. "I will show them how his foolishness affects the safety of the northern border. There can be no alternative! They may not care what happens to Lady Priscilla but they will be mindful of what could befall the entire nation. Just wait until I get my claws into that man!"

"I am eager to see him pay," Isabel agreed.

"I should have never married again," Priscilla swore. "God knows that my heart belongs to Rafael."

"Everyone knows," Isabel said. She could not keep herself from becoming emotional. "I miss him so much!"

"I miss him too," Priscilla said. She held Isabel close until her grief subsided. They planned then for the day that Lord Barillos would return.

† † †

It was nearly a week after Rodrigo's arrival that the new lord of Montenegro came back from Huesca. His carriage was meant for a team of six horses, but was now pulled by two very tired looking animals. Isabel was just about to retrieve Santiago from the private stable when she saw the sad spectacle of her stepfather's return. The young woman paused in the entryway to watch as he stepped out of the carriage with its depleted team of horses. His henchman parked it in the carriage house next to that of Lady Priscilla. The horses would then be taken to the stables while Barillos remained in the keep.

Isabel caught up to the man as he entered the main doors. "Welcome home my lord," Isabel said as he passed. There was a sardonic edge to her voice that she had failed to suppress. Barillos grunted and continued walking toward the east hallway. Isabel hurried up to her mother's room so that his arrival would not go unnoticed. Priscilla was sleeping as Isabel came up, but the knowledge of Manuel's return made her instantly alert. There was a set to her jaw and a smoldering anger in her eyes that Isabel knew all too well.

"I wish to sit up now," Priscilla said. Alejandra moved quickly to assist her mistress and propped several pillows behind her back. Priscilla let out a sigh of disgust once she was situated. "Invite my lord to come and join us," she told Alejandra.

"Yes my lady," Alejandra replied. She quickly left the room to deliver the request. Isabel started to leave as well but Priscilla halted her.

"Stay here with me," Priscilla commanded. "You have more of a right to know what goes on in my house than Manuel ever shall!"

Thank you mother," Isabel replied as she walked over to stand by Priscilla's bed side. After several minutes, Alejandra returned with a sorry looking Lord Barillos behind her. His hair was disheveled and his clothing looked very similar to how it had appeared on his last return from Huesca. There was nothing jovial about him this time.

"Where are the tapestries," Lady Priscilla asked without preamble?

"They are not yet finished," Manuel lied.

"Truly?"

"It is the truth," the man replied with feigned anger. "I grow tired of them wasting my time!'

"Who are they," Priscilla demanded. "They should be flogged for their laziness!"

"An excellent notion my love," Barillos agreed. Isabel thought she saw relief in the man's eyes. He probably thought his lies were still a secret.

"Who are they," Priscilla asked again?

"It is...it is a group of rug merchants in Zaragoza. Despicable men they are and lazy to a fault!"

"What are their names?" Priscilla asked pointedly.

'Their names dearest," Manuel struggled to ask?

"Yes Manuel, their names. Surely you have not given some of our most prized possessions to men who do not even have names?"

"Of course not," Barillos agreed.

"So...who are they?" Priscilla needled him.

"A...a group of rug merchants," Manuel began. He was looking up at the ceiling as if the script for his next deception would magically appear there.

"You said that already," Priscilla shouted! Her anger startled him and he looked down at her with surprise written on his face.

"Calm down my sweet," he said. "I will not let these men harm your tapestries."

"Where are the tapestries," Priscilla asked furiously?

"I know that Zaragoza is far away," Barillos said.

"Where are the tapestries?" Priscilla screamed!

"I will have those imbeciles punished," Manuel promised. He furrowed his brow to show displeasure.

"I see only one sloth in need of a whipping," Priscilla said from between clenched teeth. "Leave us," she said then to Alejandra. The chamber maid curtseyed uncomfortably and left the room. Isabel shut the door behind her.

"At least your daughter understands the rules of decorum," Manuel told Priscilla. "Well done," he said to Isabel. "In her delicate condition, your mother has forgotten her tongue as well as her wits!"

"Preserving my lord's reputation is no concern of mine," Isabel replied acidly. Barillos glared at her and then at her mother in the bed.

"What is the meaning of all this?" he demanded.

"What happened to my silver?" Priscilla shot back.

"How should I know?" the man retorted. "I have been away in Zaragoza."

"That is a lie," Priscilla told him.

"A woman," Manuel said condescendingly, "even a lady, is in no position to make such accusations!"

"A real man has no need for deceptions," Priscilla insulted him. "How was your stay in Huesca?"

"How did you…" Barillos blurted out. "I made no stay in Huesca, only passed through. What is all this meddling?"

"I had you followed," Isabel spoke up.

"You what," Barillos asked incredulously?

"I do not waste time repeating myself," Isabel stated.

"You are a disgrace to my house," Priscilla seethed!

"I," Barillos began, but Isabel's mother was finished allowing him to speak.

"My mother's silver, the tapestries, the only images of my dead husband; you have taken them all and pissed them away in games of chance!" Return what you have stolen or God himself will not save you from my fury!"

"I am your husband," Barillos shot back!"

"Get out," Priscilla screamed! "I never want to see your face again until you bring back what is mine!"

"You are hysterical Priscilla," Barillos admonished. "Now calm yourself lest I be forced to lock you away."

"You do not have that power, Manuel," Priscilla answered. There was challenge in her eyes.

"I am lord of Montenegro," Lord Barillos thundered! "Guards!"

"Call them off," Isabel said calmly.

"Why?" Barillos scoffed. "Perhaps you both need to be locked away until you realize who rules here." A half-dozen guards burst through the door to Priscilla's room with swords drawn. One of them quickly shielded Isabel and her mother as the others scanned the room for danger.

"Is there an intruder," one of the guards asked. He was out of breath and he gripped his sword in both hands.

"Lock these two harpies in the tower," Lord Barillos commanded. The soldiers were hesitant to obey. The looks on their faces ranged from confusion to contempt.

"Does my lord truly wish to know who controls the army?" Isabel asked menacingly. The mood in the room had changed and now the guards were all staring suspiciously at Isabel's stepfather. "My lord has taken too much to drink," she announced to the room. "We thank all of you for your swift response, but there is no danger."

"How dare you?" Manuel spat.

"Sheath your swords," Isabel commanded. The soldiers slowly obeyed. "Wait for me in the hallway," she told them. "I shall join you shortly."

"Yes my lady," one of the men said as he bowed his way out of the room, "my lady Priscilla, my lord..." Then they were gone, but not so far as Manuel might have liked. Isabel smiled icily at her stepfather as the door closed. Lady Priscilla regained her composure as well.

"You have only succeeded because my men are not here with us," Manuel threatened, "but it will not always be so."

"Your band of ruffians is of little concern to us," Lady Priscilla said with a regal calm.

"Have a care not to threaten my mother again. It will be rewarded with the quick and merciless deaths of your men," Isabel said with hatred and disgust, "all six of them."

"Be at peace my daughter," Priscilla said. She looked then back at Barillos. "Depart from me now Manuel," she ordered. "Do not return without those things you have so foolishly squandered."

"What if I cannot regain them," Manuel asked wretchedly.

"Then I will petition his holiness the Pope for an end to our marriage. It too is a lie."

"It was a lawful marriage," Manuel replied nervously.

"That will hold little meaning once I explain to the Crown of Aragon how your foolish ways will drain our coffers," Priscilla told him. "Montenegro's Keep is a vanguard against the French and all of Aragon's enemies who might come in from the north. It cannot be so ill used."

"What can I offer them in exchange," Manuel implored her?

"Nothing from Montenegro," Priscilla replied. "Look to your own estate."

"The estate is all I have," Barillos cried! "There is nothing there, not even servants to keep up the place!" Lady Priscilla shook her head.

"You are a charlatan of the worst kind," she said heavily. "Sell your estate then…and bring back my things."

"It may not fetch a good price," Manuel said. It seemed as if he were grasping for anything at all.

"Bring back my tapestries and I will be satisfied," Priscilla sighed. "I can live without the silver if I must." Isabel frowned.

"I love you," Manuel said sorrowfully. "Please forgive my indiscretion. I am your husband. Soon we will have a child."

"You are every woman's husband," Priscilla snapped back! Her anger was quickly returning.

"I love only you," Manuel insisted.

"You have made a mockery of me with the lowest daughters of Huesca," Priscilla shouted!

"It was a mistake," Barillos admitted, "but our child…"

"It is not our child," Priscilla screamed!

"You have been unfaithful then," Manuel said accusingly?

"No you imbecile," Priscilla retorted. "The child is heir to the true lord of Montenegro!"

"He is my son," Manuel disagreed.

"He will not be your son," Priscilla told him loudly. "The baby comes any day now. He could not possibly be your descendent and praise be unto God for that!" Manuel looked as if she had been struck a blow, but there was nothing he could do about it. "Get out," Priscilla said coldly. "I care not what you must endure to make this right. Bring back the treasures of Montenegro or sleep in the dirt."

"I will bring them back," Manuel whined. His eyes were reddening with the onset of tears.

"Get out," Priscilla said again. Manuel hesitated. His eyes begged her for mercy.

"Better do as she says," Isabel told him. Manuel looked at Isabel with such hatred in his eyes that she thought he would strike her. Instead, he slunk away from her mother's bed chamber like a whipped dog.

"See that he leaves," Priscilla told Isabel after the door had shut behind the man.

"I will," Isabel promised. She went out into the hallway where the soldiers were waiting for her. "Help

Lord Barillos prepare for his journey," she commanded them.

"Yes my lady," they answered.

"No time to waste," she continued, "my lord is in a hurry to depart." The soldiers hurried down the stairs to obey the only child of Lord Montenegro.

✝   ✝   ✝

While Lord Barillos was far away, Lady Priscilla became increasingly bed-ridden. Little Grandma stayed with her from morning until night. Even in the dark, she was never far. Alejandra temporarily became Isabel's chamber maid. She was not unpleasant or rude, but it felt different not having Little Grandma around.

Isabel was walking along the battlements one afternoon when she spied a carriage ascending the steep path up to the keep. A cart was being drawn behind the carriage. As the small caravan approached the stone bridge spanning the gorge, Isabel recognized the carriage as belonging to her stepfather. There was a grayish tarp over the cart, but Isabel could see the rolled up tapestries sticking out of the back of it. She found it strange that the carriage was now being pulled by donkeys instead of horses.

It had been a fortnight since Isabel had seen Manuel. She went down the wooden stairs along the wall so that she might meet up with him in the courtyard. He did not appear drunk which was a relief. He was helped down by one of his bodyguards. There was an air of anxiety amongst the men that Isabel found out of the ordinary. Barillos himself looked like a cornered cat. "Welcome back my lord," Isabel said neutrally.

"It is good to be back," Lord Barillos said with a nod. "Has the child been born yet?"

"Not yet," Isabel answered.

"Very good," the man said with a sigh of relief.

"What is good?"

"I wanted to be here for the birthing," Manuel explained. "Your mother will need me."

"Even knowing that it is my father's child," Isabel asked suspiciously?

"She is still my wife," Manuel said with reproach.

"I will summon some men to hang the tapestries in the entry hall once more. Have you brought the silver as well?"

"No. I was unable to," Manuel said with obvious embarrassment.

"My mother will be eager to see that you have brought back the tapestries. She is in her room with Pilar."

"I will go to her," Manuel said nervously.

"Excellent," Isabel said. She looked at the cravenly man with disgust plainly written on her face. More than anything, it made her sad. Her father would never have been so fearful of her mother's anger. He would never have broken her trust either. "You are a wretch of a man," Isabel muttered to herself after Lord Barillos had gone inside.

She spent the next several hours having the servants re-hang the tapestries just so. Isabel found that she was very particular about it now that her father was gone. She was sure that the servants were glad to be rid of her once she gave them leave.

As she was being served dinner in the private dining room, Isabel saw Little Grandma heading slowly toward the kitchen. "How is my mother?" Isabel called out to her through the doorway. The old woman paused and then moved farther into the opening to answer.

"She sleeps now," Pilar said. There were grey crescents under the old woman's eyes and she looked haggard. "She will go into labor soon I think."

"Will she be well," Isabel asked with concern?

"All will be well mija," Little Grandma smiled wearily.

"Can I see her?"

"Look in on her if you wish," the old woman replied, "but be careful not to wake her. Your mother needs her rest."

"I will be careful," Isabel promised as she rose from the table.

"I have to get something to eat," Little Grandma said.

"You look like you need some rest as well," Isabel said. "Lay you down when you finish eating. "I will watch her. I shall call you the instant you are needed."

"I shall try," Pilar said hopefully. The old woman made her way toward the kitchen while Isabel headed for the eastern stairwell. Isabel had barely begun to ascend the stairs when she heard her stepfather's desperate cries coming from her mother's room.

"Pilar," Manuel screamed, "Pilar!"

"Little Grandma," Isabel shouted!

"Coming child," the old woman shouted from down in the kitchen. Isabel did not wait, but ran up the stairs to her mother.

"Somebody help," Lord Barillos cried out! "Somebody help us!" When Isabel rushed into the room, Manuel was bent over her mother who was thrashing about on the bed. There was a basin of steaming hot water on the floor next to it with several rags inside the water. Priscilla's face was pink and still wet from the washing it had received.

"Push Mama," Isabel said as she ran to her mother's side, but it was not the labor that was causing her pain. Priscilla was grasping at her throat and making ragged choking sounds. Her eyes bulged from their sockets as she fought for breath! "Little Grandma... hurry," Isabel cried with alarm!

A blur of movement caught Isabel's eye. Down by her feet was one of the white tunics that she had knit for the baby. Some of the water must have splashed on it because there was a large wet spot right in the center. What had attracted Isabel's eye was a grey mouse that had run out from beneath the bed. The mouse started chewing on the baby clothes where the water had spilled on it. It was missing an eye and had a deep scar across its snout where a cat may have opened up its flesh. When the mouse finally saw Isabel with its remaining eye, it scampered quickly under the bed and dragged the tiny tunic with it.

"What goes on," Little Grandma cried as she came to Priscilla's side. "Oh my God, oh my God!"

"Help her," Isabel shrieked, "do something!"

"She is choking!" Pilar screamed. "Sit her up...sit her up!" Isabel dragged her mother to an upright position and held her while Little Grandma beat her hand on the choking woman's back. Isabel noticed Manuel standing back away from the bed. He looked worried but did not move to assist in any way. Her mother was making the most awful coughing sounds. When she did draw breath it was raspy and painful. Isabel desperately slapped her mother's back. Priscilla coughed twice more and then let out a horrible gagging sound, which ran out of steam as her eyes rolled heavenward. Her head slumped forward and she became dead weight in Isabel's arms.

"Mama, Mama!" Isabel screamed as she continued to beat on her back. Little Grandma put her hand on Priscilla's neck, but just briefly.

"Oh no," Pilar cried. "Lay her down." Isabel laid her mother back on the pillows while Pilar pressed her ear to Priscilla's breast. Isabel looked on hopefully, but the grimace of pain on Little Grandma's face told a story of despair.

"Mama," Isabel sobbed. She stretched her hand out to touch her mother's cheek.

"We have to save the baby," Little Grandma said tremulously.

"My mother," Isabel said forlornly.

"Get out of here Isabel," Little Grandma shouted. "Fetch me Alejandra now!" Isabel looked at her mother once more and then ran as if in a dream. The confused faces of the servants seemed alien to her as she screamed at them for help. She saw one of the serving women running upstairs with a knife from the kitchen clutched in her hand. It was unreal.

Isabel paced back and forth from the entry hall to the kitchen. There was nothing for her to do. The soldiers would not let her into her parent's room. No amount of her hysterical screaming would move them. Finally, Captain Pascual took her by the shoulders and led her up to her room. He stayed and listened to her tearful begging. He held her close as her body was wracked with anguished sobs.

"Hold the knife steady!" Pillar's screeching voice echoed from across the hall. "Breathe," Little Grandma shouted! There were slapping sounds as the old woman kept shouting that same word over and over. "Oh no," Little Grandma wailed, "no! Breathe little Rafi…breathe for grandma," she begged wretchedly! Isabel covered her ears and closed her eyes as Little Grandma's wailing filled the keep. She rocked back and forth until her own weeping joined in the discordant symphony. Captain Pascual's eyes were filling up with tears also but he tried to remain strong. He was lying to Isabel and telling her that all would be well.

"When Isabel looked up from her sorrow, Little Grandma stood in the doorway like some ghastly apparition. Her white dress was soaked in blood and her arms were coated up to the elbows. Her chest began to hitch, though no sound issued forth. "I am sorry Isabel," she finally sobbed. "Oh my God, I am so sorry!" Isabel ran to the old woman and grabbed her by the shoulders.

"My mother," Isabel asked desperately? "My mother…my Mama is alright?" Little Grandma could only shake her head.

"Priscilla is gone," Pilar said in a very small voice.

"No," Isabel moaned as her face was pulled tight with grief.

"I..," Little Grandma sobbed, "I could not save Little Rafi." Isabel let out an inarticulate cry as the old woman continued. "I could not save him. God forgive me I could not!" The two women held onto each other. It did not matter that Pilar was covered in blood. Dirtying her dress was the least of Isabel's concerns. She found herself praying to God even though she knew it was too late. Her mother was dead and the line of Rafael Montenegro was broken.

† † †

The funeral of Lady Priscilla was held in much the same fashion as that of her husband several months earlier. The Church of the Greater St. James was filled with white lilies and swaths of turquoise cloth. There were two coffins, one much smaller than the other. Manuel had spared no expense at his bride's death. He had suggested that they bury her at her family's cottage in Zaragoza, but Isabel refused.

"My mother and her son will lie down with my father," she had said, "so that they may awaken together in the Resurrection." Some might consider it a loss of face that Lord Barillos had conceded to his step daughter's wishes, but the new Lord of Montenegro had much to be concerned with. The least of his concerns was his own personal shame.

Lord Vasquez came up from Zaragoza and his entire family accompanied him. Catherine retained her composure at the funeral but her eyes were red with crying. David tried very hard to be brave until Aunt Imelda wept openly. He then could not help but join her.

Manuel made an impassioned speech before those assembled. Isabel could not remember a single word of it. What did this cowardly man know of love? Nevertheless, Lord Barillos wept louder than they all when the coffins were lifted up for the funeral procession. The march went up and down the main street of Black River Village before returning to the graveyard behind the church. The priest said a long prayer over the dead. He espoused Lady Priscilla's many virtues and the innocence of her child. He prayed that the Lord would watch over all of Montenegro and that He would guide Lord Barillos through the storms ahead. Lastly, he prayed for Isabel.

There was a feast laid out in the keep that night, but Isabel could hardly stomach it. Aunt Imelda invited Isabel to come down with them to the Summer Cottage for a time. Isabel tearfully agreed. She would be glad to leave. Every sight she looked upon inside Montenegro's Keep brought memories. These memories bore with them the bitter truth that her family was no more.

Manuel did not question Isabel, but kissed her on the forehead when she bid him farewell the next morning. It was awkward, but Isabel thought that Lord Barillos had his own grief to contend with. At Isabel's request, both Alejandra and Pilar accompanied her to Zaragoza.

They spent the next several weeks at the cottage and Isabel was in no hurry to return. She sent word to Captain Pascual to secure her dowry chest in the secret passage behind her father's bed. A letter came back to assure her it was done. David was an almost constant shadow, but even he knew to leave Isabel alone when she needed solitude. Catherine was uncharacteristically kind toward Isabel. Her aunt and uncle were never too busy to console her either.

One summer afternoon, the three cousins had gone out to the pond for a swim. Once there, they stripped themselves down to their undergarments. Isabel and Catherine sat on the wooden dock. David, (with his boundless energy), went immediately into the water to play. "You should come home with us," Catherine said as they watched David's antics a short way off.

"Are you serious Catherine," Isabel asked? This was not at all the cousin she was used to.

"Of course," Catherine smiled. "We are cousins you know, even if we did fight pointlessly over a man."

"He was not very likeable," Isabel chuckled.

"No," Catherine agreed mischievously, "and not much of a man either."

"Catherine, you are positively awful," Isabel said with amusement.

"It was awful," Catherine groaned dramatically. This set both women to giggling.

"How fare you now?" Isabel asked.

"Look at me," David cried! He dove under the water. His legs came up above the surface and kicked several times in the air before falling back under.

"Bravo," Isabel called out to him.

"I'm running upside down," David exclaimed!

"I see you," Isabel replied across the water. Catherine answered Isabel's question once David had gone underwater again.

"I am betrothed to Jean Pierre. He is the son of Duke Adhemar of France.

"I have never heard of him," Isabel admitted.

"I suppose not," Catherine replied. "When Jean Pierre's father and older brother die, I will be made a duchess."

"Are you pleased?" Isabel asked.

"It is a good match," Catherine replied. "I will be well cared for."

"When is the wedding?"

"At the beginning of spring," Catherine replied.

"Will it be here in Zaragoza," Isabel asked? "I would want to attend."

"I should be pleased for you to be my maid of honor," Catherine sighed, "but the wedding will be in Narbonne."

"I shall do my best," Isabel promised.

"It is a long way," Catherine said. "I will not be offended if you cannot come."

"That is wonderful," Isabel smiled. "I am happy for you!"

"And you," Catherine inquired.

"Still wondering," Isabel answered. It wasn't exactly a lie.

"Will you come and stay with us?" Catherine asked once more.

"Oh I would like that Catherine, but I am afraid that I shall have to go back to Montenegro," Isabel sighed.

"Whatever for," Catherine asked? "You are no relation to this Lord Barillos. Do you suppose he will miss you?"

"I do not think that he would," Isabel said wryly.

"Forgive me Isabel," Catherine implored her. "I did not mean to be so coarse."

"It is nothing," Isabel answered sadly. "I would not miss him either."

"Then why stay?"

"Manuel is an imbecile," Isabel explained. "He cannot possibly handle Montenegro without me."

"You were always so stubborn," Catherine said as she looked out over the water.

"It is the truth," Isabel insisted. "The man can barely ride a horse!"

"Is he that bad?"

"Worse," Isabel confirmed. She wanted to tell Catherine just how reprehensible her stepfather had been, but she did not want to bring shame on the memory of her mother. "He is neither brave nor strong. I think my mother must have felt sorry for him."

"That is too bad," Catherine agreed. Isabel saw a twinkle in her cousin's eye before she spoke once more. "You know that we live much closer to the crown than you do cousin?"

"I know," Isabel said suspiciously.

"There are many young lords in Zaragoza this time of year," Catherine said as she pushed Isabel playfully. Isabel laughed out loud.

"That is just what I need right now," Isabel said sarcastically. "God forbid!"

"You really should be considering it," Catherine said seriously.

"Of course you are right," Isabel sighed. She could not tell Catherine that she had already wed. "I will come next spring…after your wedding."

"Oui oui, I'll wager a pretty mademoiselle like you might find a suitor or two in France as well," Catherine joked.

"I might," Isabel chuckled, "but I must first put things in order at home."

"Alright," Catherine groaned. "I shall just have to wait until next year to play the matchmaker, but you mustn't wait a day longer!"

"I will not," Isabel said sadly as she looked out over the water. "The river of time flows but one way."

CHAPTER V

Isabel was loathe to leave the Summer Cottage and her cousins behind, but she could not stop worrying about what might be going on in Montenegro. Her apprehension only grew as she traveled closer to her homeland. With increasing frequency, she saw heavily laden carts traveling southward toward Huesca. These were not merchant's carts. They belonged to families who were dragging along all their earthly possessions behind tired looking animals. She thought she recognized one of Montenegro's kitchen servants riding up on a pile of trunks, but she could not get a second look.

"Slow down," Isabel shouted out the window to her driver. The man reigned in the horses and slowed them to a walk. There was a somber mood among the peasants traveling southward. They seemed like so many lost souls, wandering without a destination. As her carriage traveled further north, Isabel saw a man with a long bow walking beside the convoy of uprooted families. The closer he came, the more certain Isabel was that she had seen him before. The archer was wearing simple, brown, peasant's garb, but he stood tall like a soldier.

"Rodrigo," Isabel called out to him. Rodrigo looked up quickly. His eyes fell downward when he saw who it was that had addressed him.

"Stop the carriage," Isabel commanded. She got down quickly and ran over to where Rodrigo had paused to wait for her.

"My lady Isabel," he said sadly as he bowed at the waist.

"Where are you going?" Isabel demanded. "Your place is in Montenegro!"

"It is," the archer agreed, "but Montenegro has changed."

"What has he done?" Isabel asked with terrible apprehension. 'What has Lord Barillos done?"

"It is too awful to speak of," Rodrigo replied. "Come with us Lady Isabel, for we are all peasants now."

"Has Montenegro fallen," Isabel asked incredulously, "to what army?"

"Montenegro has fallen in on itself," Rodrigo replied morosely. "I am your most loyal servant Lady Isabel, but my mother and sisters are hungry."

"We have never had famine," Isabel disagreed.

"Please come with us," Rodrigo implored her. "I hope to find work in Huesca…or Zaragoza if they will not have me. I am an excellent hunter. I promise that you will not starve."

"No Rodrigo," Isabel said emotionally. "We are going back to Montenegro. I will right this wrong, whatever it may be!"

"I cannot go back," Rodrigo said sadly. "Farewell my lady." He began once more to plod south along with the mass of peasants.

"Come back here," Isabel cried after him!

"Come with us," Rodrigo called back with a wave of his arm.

"I command you to stop!" Isabel yelled at the slowly moving herd. The peasants looked at her but made no move to obey. "Stop," she said quietly. Summoning her courage, Isabel stalked back to the carriage. "Take me home," she ordered sharply.

"Yes my lady," the driver answered. He helped her up into the carriage and then climbed back on top. Isabel's anger grew with every turn of the wheels toward Montenegro.

It was nearly sundown when they reached Black River Village. Many of the shops and houses had been boarded shut. Her father's horses should have been grazing in the cool hours of dusk, but Isabel could only spot three or four animals. "Go," Isabel said furiously! The driver pushed the team of horses hard up the mountain and across the stone bridge that led into the keep.

Isabel was helped down out of the carriage by her soldiers. She didn't even spare them a second glance before storming through the main doors of her home. She could hear raucous laughter and boisterous voices coming from the dining hall. Two soldiers stumbled down the hallway toward her. They leaned on each other and reeked of strong drink.

"Who is this little flower," one of the soldiers asked as he leered at Isabel. They wore the uniform of Montenegro, but Isabel had never laid eyes on either of them. They certainly did not conduct themselves in a manner befitting one of her father's men.

"Open your lips again and I shall have you beheaded," Isabel said icily, "now be gone from my sight!" The men looked with confusion at each other and then back at Isabel. She glared contemptuously down at them.

"We beg your pardon," one of the soldiers said hastily. Both men departed in haste, whispering to each other and shooting nervous glances back at Isabel. She strode angrily into the dining hall to find a scene of debauchery. Many ruffians in the garb of Montenegro's soldiers were filling themselves with strong drink. There was much food weighing down the tables, but the guests seemed to be drinking more than eating. There were several women mixed in with the 'soldiers.' They did not carry themselves with dignity. There was none to be had. These women were dressed in revealing clothing which paraded their flesh before the hungry eyes of the men.

One such brazen whore had straddled a soldier who was sitting at one of the tables. His tunic was pulled to one side and his hose were around his ankles. The woman's skirt was bunched up around her hips and she rocked back and forth in the pleasure of their fornication.

The sound of Manuel's laughter carried over the noise of the revelers. Isabel's eyes quickly found the spot where her stepfather sat. There was a dark haired woman in his lap who was playfully nibbling at his bottom lip. She threw her head back and smiled down lustfully at him. The whore lowered the cloth of her blue dress to reveal one caramel colored breast. Manuel began to suckle like a babe.

"I have returned from Zaragoza," Isabel shouted over the tumult. Silence washed over the room. Even Manuel looked up sheepishly from the woman's breast that was thrust out toward him. "I can see that you are all in mourning over Lady Priscilla's death!" The whore pulled her blouse up and there was color rising in her cheeks. "Get out," Isabel shouted! "Return to your barracks. There is no one manning the battlements and you are all worthless with drink. Go now!" The men slowly began to rise. "Take these swine with you," Isabel commanded. One finger was pointed at her father's harlot.

"No one is going anywhere," Lord Barillos said loudly as he stood from his chair. The whore, (Sara), was forced to stand as well. "My men obey me!"

"Your men have defiled my father's house," Isabel retorted! "Look at this filth!"

"Lady Isabel," Manuel replied angrily, "my men will only obey you at my leisure. Now get you up to your room lest I have you taken there forcibly. The soldiers of your father are no longer here. This is my domain now!"

"You disgrace..." Isabel began.

"Do as I command," Manuel shouted over her! "Your room or the tower... Make a choice!" Isabel made a sound of disgust and turned away from the horrible scene.

She found Pilar and Alejandra in her room already. They had finished unpacking her things and were talking to each other in hushed tones when Isabel came through the door. "Please close the door my lady," Alejandra requested. There was such fear in the woman's voice that Isabel complied immediately.

"Welcome home," Isabel said sarcastically as she slammed the door shut. Little Grandma handed Alejandra a key. The younger chamber maid hurried over to the door and locked it behind Isabel. "What is the meaning of this Alejandra? It is time to sleep for the night."

"Oh please let me stay," Alejandra begged. "I am afraid to

go out among those men." Isabel sighed.

"Of course you shall stay," Isabel said. "A lady needs all the help she can get."

"Thank you," Alejandra said with relief.

"We cannot stay here," Little Grandma said quietly.

"This is our home," Isabel protested, but she knew that the old woman was right. "What goes on? What do the servants say?"

"Lord Barillos is throwing away the wealth of Montenegro," Pilar said worriedly. "He refused to pay your father's soldiers and now they have left to the four winds."

"Even Captain Pascual," Isabel asked with disbelief?

"They say he was the first to leave. Some of them suspect foul play but there is none to confirm it. Captain Pascual had no family after the war with Morera. Others say he left because there was nothing to tie him here."

"How could Montenegro be impoverished already," Isabel asked? "Is it possible?"

"Lord Barillos sold most of the horses to the Count of Huesca," Alejandra reported. "This is the wealth that now funds his extravagance."

"Not the horses," Isabel cried! "They are the life's blood of Montenegro! Did none of the soldiers resist?"

"Marta tells me they had no choice," Alejandra replied. "What could they do against the might of Huesca? Their commander had disappeared and Lord Barillos is not a man to entrust a war too. The Count of Huesca took what he had rightfully paid for. Even if they had resisted, there would have been repercussions from Zaragoza. It is all a great disaster!"

"Oh my God," Isabel said. Her voice was stricken and she had to sit down.

"We cannot stay here," Little Grandma reiterated.

"No," Isabel agreed. "We will go back to the Summer Cottage by the first light of morning."

"Does not the house in Zaragoza belong to Lord Barillos as well," Alejandra asked worriedly?

"No," Isabel replied.

"The Summer Cottage belongs to Lady Priscilla's brother in law, Lord Vasquez," Pilar explained. "Lord Barillos cannot touch it."

"Let us speak no more of this," Isabel quieted them. "I will go and inform the last of Montenegro's soldiers that we shall soon depart. The two of you stay here and make ready."

"Yes my lady," Alejandra replied. Pilar simply began packing. Isabel quietly left her room and walked quickly to the stairwell. She walked softly down the spiral stairs that ran along the wall of the east tower until she reached the ground floor. The men who accompanied her carriage to Zaragoza were in the process of feeding the horses when Isabel entered the stables.

"Be quiet," Isabel whispered loudly before the formalities could begin. The five soldiers looked anxiously at her as one. "We are leaving just before dawn," she told them. "Do not go inside the keep. Make your beds here inside the carriages. You should all be invisible."

"What goes on inside the keep," one of the men asked?

"Lord Barillos has replaced all of your brothers with his dogs. It is as I feared. You six… Were there not six of you?"

"There were my lady," the man admitted. "Francisco deserted us on the road from Huesca." Isabel shook her head.

"Thank you all for your loyalty," Isabel said with sincerity. "You are the last of Montenegro. Choose one of you to stand vigil while the rest get some sleep. Manuel's brigands are drunk inside my father's house. Once they fall asleep, we will begin moving out my belongings. I will send Pilar to inform you when it is time."

"We will do as you command," the man promised. There were murmurs of assent from the others as well.

"What of our families," a second man asked?
"Two of you go down to Black River Village and wake them," Isabel decided. "Help them pack everything quietly and make sure their carts are on the road and ready to go before first light. The rest of us will catch up in the

carriage."

"Yes my lady," the men echoed. There was a brief exchange among them as to who should go down to the village. Based on the size of their families, they chose the two men with the largest number of people to care for. These two, at Isabel's command; took fresh horses from the sepia colored mares that had once pulled Lady Priscilla's carriage. Isabel suspected that Manuel now used them for himself. They were finer than anything he might have left.

After the riders departed, Isabel returned quietly to the keep and made her way back up to her room. She watched as her chamber maids finished packing the trunks for the coming journey. "The two of you must sleep now," she told them. "I will remain awake until we have departed."

"I do not know if I can bring myself to sleep," Alejandra said.

"You must try," Isabel told her. "I will keep watch over you."

"Thank you my lady," Alejandra answered. The two women shed their outer clothing and lay down to sleep in Isabel's bed. Isabel sat on the bench under the window overlooking the courtyard. Pilar snuffed out the candle beside the bed and plunged the room into darkness.

The hours of that night seemed to stretch on forever. Isabel alternated her gaze from the door to the window. She waited for the sky to lighten which would tell her it was time to depart. Listening to Alejandra's heavy breathing and Little Grandma's snore did not help Isabel's resolve to stay awake. She caught herself closing her eyes several times and had to stand up to avoid unconsciousness. Eventually, the sounds of the drunken soldiers died out. They were soon replaced by the chirping of a cricket in the courtyard below.

Isabel was about to wake her servants when she heard the sound of many footsteps coming up the stairs. "This is the way," she heard her stepfather's voice clearly from the hallway. The handle of her door jiggled back and forth loudly and Isabel gasped! "Wake up," she whispered loudly to the sleeping women!

"It is locked," a man's drunken voice said irritably.

"Of course," Manuel slurred, "but I have the key. Get out of my way." Isabel had forgotten about the master key. It only made sense that Lord Barillos would have it now. She frantically shook both of the slumbering chamber maids.

"Get up! Get up!" she said out loud as the scraping noise of the key echoed in the room. No sooner had Isabel's servants opened their eyes than chaos erupted all around them! Isabel had just enough time to see Manuel grinning like a jackal from between the shoulders of the men in front of him. The torchlight from the hallway illuminated the large figures of Barillos' men storming into the chamber.

Isabel fought desperately to keep Manuel's men off her, but she was quickly overpowered by the two who grabbed her arms. She vaguely registered the cries for help coming from her servants. She felt cold iron shackles biting into her flesh as the two men forced her arms into position and held her face down on the bed. Pilar was subdued almost immediately and Alejandra fared little better.

"Leave now!" Isabel yelled at the top of her lungs. "Leave now!" She hoped that the soldiers below would hear her and obey.

"Lady Isabel," she heard one of her men shout back.

"Leave nuh..," she yelled before a large, sweaty hand clamped over her mouth.

"Get them to the tower," Manuel said. His voice was both petty and triumphant, like a child who had just succeeded in getting one of his siblings into trouble. "A week's confinement should teach you some manners," Manuel told Isabel as her face passed by his. She and her chamber maids were dragged bodily up the western stairwell.

The thick door to the prison tower was opened and the three women were shoved inside. Isabel's heart sunk when she heard a clashing of steel from the courtyard. Some of her men, (maybe all three), had chosen to fight. They would die for their loyalty.

Three of Manuel's thugs removed the women's shackles while the rest mobbed around the doorway with swords drawn. Isabel was pushed roughly to the floor and Alejandra was shoved into a wall before the men departed. Isabel could hear the sound of the iron bar sliding into place on the other side of the door. "Get to the courtyard," Manuel shouted! The sounds of their boots echoed through the opening in the bottom of the prison door as they hurried down the stairs.

There was a horrible gurgling sound from below. Isabel rushed to the opening facing the courtyard. It was the worst of all possibilities. One of her soldiers already lay dead on the cobblestones. His blood drained quickly from the place where a sword had punctured through the side of his neck. The other two fought bravely, but they were soon overpowered by Manuel's reinforcements that seemed to arrive from all directions at once. Isabel could watch no longer. She turned back to where her two chamber maids were huddled together on the floor. The older woman was comforting the younger. Isabel sat herself down against the side of the fireplace.

"I told them to run," Isabel said aloud. No one answered her; not Alejandra, not Pilar, and certainly not God. After several hours of troubled and uncomfortable sleep, Isabel picked herself up from the unyielding stone. She looked into the empty fireplace on the east wall. There was no wood stacked beside it. Isabel wondered if this was because of the season. There would be little need for extra warmth in the summer time, at least during the hours of daylight. She spied the rack which should have contained the implements for tending a fire. It too was barren. The doors to the iron-barred cells on the west wall were locked shut. There were two ragged looking bed rolls in each. The rest of the chamber was empty. The cold stone floors were slightly damp from the outside humidity.

Montenegro's Keep seemed unusually quiet that morning. There was no training going on in the courtyard and no bustle of the servants from within. Even the sounds of the watchmen were missing. One opening faced the river. Isabel could not see a single man on watch from any of the other three openings. There had always been soldiers up on the walls for as long as she could remember, even on the Sabbath Day. The battlements were as empty as the cages that hung suspended on iron bars out each of the four openings of the tower.

The other two women slept. Little Grandma had propped herself against the iron bars of one of the cells. Alejandra slept with her head on the older woman's thigh. Isabel was very hungry, but there was no sign of food either present or forthcoming.

Pilar was the first to awaken with a loud snort. She rubbed her eyes and looked around the room. Her confusion quickly turned to fear when she realized where they all were. "Isabel," Pilar called out questioningly?

"I am here," Isabel replied from her place by one of the openings.

"Are you hurt?"

"No," Isabel replied. "No one has been here since they locked us in."

"Wake up," Little Grandma told Alejandra. "My old bones are killing me." The younger woman groaned and picked herself up from Pillar's lap. Alejandra winced as she rubbed the soreness out of her left shoulder. "I shall start a fire," Little Grandma announced as she used the bars of the cell to help herself to a standing position.

"There is no wood," Isabel said. "We shall just have to wait for the sun."

"Why would they take the wood pile?" Little Grandma wondered out loud.

"They have taken everything," Alejandra said dismally.

"I am surprised they left the pulley system intact," Isabel said. "That was to be Eubasio's escape route after he would have finished my murder."

"Perhaps we could borrow his idea," Alejandra said as she hurried over to the opening facing the river. Isabel came over and joined her there. On either side of the pulley were long ropes containing wooden buckets at intervals. The spaces between the buckets were about the length of a man. The pulley was run by a long iron crank that was attached to the floor inside. Two chains ran up from the crank and into the bottom of the pulley. The chains would turn the wheel from the inside while the ropes drew up the buckets from without. The rushing waters of Black River washed over the jagged rocks below. It was a long way down.

"That current looks strong," Isabel frowned. "Perhaps he had not thought this through."

"I suppose not," Alejandra reluctantly agreed. She was staring over the rocks to the place where Black River became a waterfall. The water plunged down into a gorge that surrounded the keep on three sides. "What will happen to us?" Alejandra asked after some time.

"Only God knows," Isabel said. "We shall have to wait out the week before we flee Montenegro."

"Yes," Alejandra agreed, but her voice lacked conviction. It wasn't until later that afternoon that food was brought up for the prisoners. The door opened and a soldier with dark brown hair stepped inside. He wore a long beard and his hair was pulled back into a short ponytail. He carried a large wooden bowl with a ladle lying inside of it. Isabel could see three or four other soldiers in the hallway behind the man. The soldier set down the steaming bowl of brown colored gruel on the prison floor. His face bore an amused grin.

"Where is the rest of it?" Isabel asked.

"That is all," the man replied.

"There are no spoons," the heiress complained, "no bowls either. Surely Montenegro is not without such things."

"That is what my lord instructed me to give," the soldier explained, "no more and no less."

"It is not acceptable," Isabel told him.

"Then do not eat," the soldier smirked. He stood back to his full height and grinned at Isabel before leaving the way he had come. Isabel sat down before the bowl. The steam coming off the food bore an odor that reminded Isabel of pig slop. She curled her nose and got to her feet once more.

"I am not putting that in my mouth," Isabel shuddered. Little Grandma sighed and then made her way over to the gruel. She wrinkled her nose also, but picked up the ladle nonetheless. "What are you doing?" Isabel demanded. "We do not have to subject ourselves to such indignity!"

"How often are we to be fed?" Pilar asked before taking her first sip.

"How can I know such a thing?" Isabel asked with irritation.

"You cannot," the old woman replied before taking another sip from the ladle. "None of us can."

"She speaks the truth," Alejandra said as she joined Pilar on the floor by the wooden bowl.

"I will not eat that mess," Isabel said emphatically. She watched as Little Grandma finished what was in the ladle and then passed it on to Alejandra. The younger woman dutifully choked it down.

"Come and sit with us," Little Grandma invited. "Lord Barillos' men do not seem to do anything with regularity...other than drink themselves senseless. I trust they will not remember us often." Isabel reluctantly took her place around the bowl and then came her turn with the ladle.

"It is not as bad as it smells," she remarked.

"It is much worse," Alejandra said. The corners of her mouth turned up and then they all shared an uneasy bit of laughter.

"We do what we must," Pilar said when their laughter had died. They finished the bowl and left it sitting by the door. They did not receive another meal that day. The three women spent the next few days praying and talking about what might happen in the days coming. These talks were not pleasant and they were all agreed that they would leave as soon as the opportunity came. Isabel assured them that her uncle would take them in. Perhaps they could take up permanent residence at the Summer Cottage.

On the evening of the fourth day of their confinement, Lord Barillos paid them a visit. He was accompanied by several armed guards. His eyes were glassy, but he did not reek of strong drink yet. Isabel ascertained from the disheveled look of her chamber maids that her own appearance was probably lacking as well. "I have decided to release one of you," Lord Barillos announced.

"I do not understand why either of my servants must be locked in with me," Isabel retorted. "Surely they have done nothing to displease you."

'That is the truth," Manuel agreed, "which is why I am releasing Alejandra presently.

"But not Pilar," Isabel queried?

"No," Manuel confirmed.

"Why ever not?" she asked him.

"Pilar is your chamber maid," Lord Barillos replied. "This is your chamber," he said as he waved his arms expansively over the room.

"You should let me go," Isabel said unhappily. "This is unjust. You know that it is."

"My decision was one week," Manuel replied, "or have you forgotten?"

"How could I possibly forget?" she replied. Alejandra stood up from where she had been sitting on the bed.

"I beg my lord's pardon," she said nervously.

"What is it," Lord Barillos asked?

"Might I stay here with Lady Isabel as well," Alejandra asked meekly?

"You do not want to stay in here," Manuel disagreed.

"Oh but I do my lord," Alejandra insisted, "I am my lady's chamber maid also."

"No Alejandra," Lord Barillos said firmly. "We do not have enough help as it is. You are needed."

"Yes my lord," she replied. Alejandra lowered her eyes and curtseyed. As she walked out, the younger maid looked desperately back at Isabel and Pilar. She looked like a child being taken away from her parents for the first time.

"I will see the two of you in three days," Lord Barillos told those who would remain.

"Yes my lord," Pilar replied tersely. Isabel simply glared at the man. Manuel left the prison tower followed closely by his guards. The guards locked the door behind them. "I wish she were not so timid," Pilar thought aloud.

"Why?" Isabel asked.

"We will pray for her," Pilar said uneasily. Isabel's question was ignored. Little Grandma closed her eyes and whispered a prayer to St. Michael.

It was much later that night when Isabel was awakened by the sounds of many footsteps coming up the stairs. The key turned loudly in the lock of the heavy prison door. The door opened and six of Barillos men walked into the room. They had the uniform of Montenegro's soldiers, but Isabel would never think of them as such.

Little Grandma was awakened by the sound of the lock. So it was that they were both standing by the time the last soldier shut the door and locked them all in together. "Lord Barillos commands that you be placed in cells," one of the men told them. He had salt and pepper gray hair and crooked teeth that were discolored yellow at the tips. There was the sound of a challenge in the man's voice. It was as if he were daring them to resist. Little Grandma walked obediently into the cell closest the door to the stairwell.

"No," Isabel argued. "We have done nothing wrong. We have not tried to escape. What you propose is senseless."

"It is not my job to make sense," the man with the crooked teeth said, "only to obey." He grinned as one of the other guards locked the old woman inside her cell.

"This is ridiculous," Isabel said accusingly.

"Will your ladyship go on her own or will she need help," the man asked? His veiled threat was not lost on Isabel.

"I will go," Isabel said reproachfully. She maintained her poise as she crossed the chamber and entered into the next cell. Before she could even turn around to face them, the guards had already locked her inside.

"By the way," the crooked toothed man added gleefully as the others crossed toward the door. "Your serving girl is doing a great job! We are all satisfied with it." He winked at Isabel and then shut the main door to the tower prison as he left. A short time later, there was a commotion outside the chamber. As the participants came closer, Isabel could make out what was being said.

"Do not touch me," Alejandra cried!

"Move it along," a gruff man's voice barked!

"No," Alejandra shrieked! "Stay away from me!"

"You're going to your cage woman," the man said. "We have no more use for you!"

"I go," she said tremulously. "Just stay back there." The door opened and the young chamber maid hurried in. She shut the door even before the guards could do so. They locked it from the outside and there was the sound of boisterous laughter as their footsteps receded downward. Alejandra remained facing the door. It was dark once more in the prison except for the moonlight which cast a sickly glow in through the towers openings. Alejandra's form was little more than a shadow. By the way the serving woman was shaking, Isabel was certain that all was not well.

"Alejandra," Isabel whispered. "What has happened? What have they done to you?" Alejandra let out a whimper but did not turn to face the other two women.

"Are you hurt?" Little Grandma asked, but it seemed like a rhetorical question. The shadow was nodding her head up and down.

"I..," Alejandra began, but she could not continue. She whimpered again and then really began to cry. She leaned on the door as the sobs wracked through her body.

Nothing Pilar or Isabel said would elicit a response. "You were right," Alejandra said when she finally managed to stop crying. "We cannot stay here!" This last was said with grief rising in the woman's voice until she was weeping once more.

"What happened?" Isabel asked, but it was no use. Eventually, the woman's sobbing fell silent. She turned away from the door and walked across the chamber. Little Grandma gasped as the young woman came out into a swath of moonlight. The fabric of her dark colored dress had been rent asunder, leaving a wide gap down the front of her skirt. She had been stripped of her undergarments, leaving her naked from the waist all the way to her bare feet. There appeared to be a dark shadow under her left eye.

As Alejandra walked closer and closer to the opening facing the river, Isabel began to be filled with a sense of dread. "Alejandra stop," Isabel called out sharply! "What are you doing?"

"I have to leave," Alejandra replied nervously.

"No," Pilar almost shouted. "Get away from there!"

"I must go," Alejandra reiterated. She stretched herself out along the iron bar of the pulley until her hand reached the rope. She let out a terrified cry as her legs fell off and she swung downward. There was nothing that either of the others could do to help from their cells.

"I have to go," Alejandra said from out of sight.

"She made it," Pilar said with relief. "She must be on the pulley rope." Indeed, there was no telltale sound to suggest that the woman had fallen. It was not long, however, before Isabel was startled by a blood curdling scream that quickly receded into the gorge. "Oh my God," Pilar wept, "she's gone over!"

"No," Isabel moaned!

"She wasn't strong enough," Pilar said sorrowfully. There was nothing left to say. They could not even console each other as they were locked in separate cells. Their beds were straw mats, topped by threadbare blankets. Isabel tried to get comfortable as the straw poked through at her.

When at last she slept, Alejandra's scream followed her into dreaming.

† † †

Isabel could not tell whether it was she or Little Grandma that was first to awaken. She lay in silence on the straw for some time before rising. Little Grandma was lying on her back and staring at the ceiling. Her eyes were blank and haunted. The old woman looked over when she noticed that Isabel was sitting upright. Her expression did not improve. "Did you sleep," the older woman asked vacantly.

"A little I think," Isabel replied, "and you?"

"I am not certain."

"Isabel sighed and stared despondently around the empty prison, now made emptier still by Alejandra's tragic escape. "Do you think we should have called the guards?" Isabel asked.

"Do not be foolish Isabel."

"They might have saved her," Isabel argued without conviction.

"She is with God now," Little Grandma replied as she made the sign of the cross. "It is better this way."

"How can you say that," Isabel exclaimed? "Alejandra is dead!"

"That is enough," Pilar scolded! "What if they had saved her Isabel? What then?"

"I...I do not know," Isabel said shakily.

"Yes you do," Pilar argued and then she looked away to hide her own tears. Isabel swallowed a lump in her throat.

"Sorry Little Grandma," she said in a very small voice. Little Grandma just shook with grief. Isabel wanted to ask what would happen to them, but she realized the question would be pointless. The old woman didn't know either. "I wish we would have gone to stay with my uncle," Isabel finally said.

"Me too child," Little Grandma said without looking back at her, "me too." Some time later, the prison door banged open and a single guard came through. He was carrying a familiar wooden bowl with an equally familiar gruel steaming inside of it. He paused in the doorway and looked around the large chamber. The more he looked, the more panicked his expression became.

"Where is the other one," he asked? His eyes scanned the room in nervous confusion. Neither woman answered him. "Where is the other woman?" he asked more forcefully.

"Gone," Little Grandma answered simply.

"Gone?" The man quickly searched through the room but there was only the one possible hiding spot. Alejandra was not in the fireplace. "Captain," he yelled, "captain!" Moments later he was joined by a second guard.

"What are you screaming about," the second guard demanded?

"The servant girl has escaped," the first exclaimed! "Where is Captain Lozano?"

"Here," the older man with the crooked teeth said as he pushed his way into the room.

"Captain," the first man said breathlessly, "the other serving woman is gone!"

"Where did she go," the older man snarled?

"I do not know Captain," the guard replied. "She has escaped!" The crooked toothed man grabbed the first guard by the scruff of his neck and wagged a finger in his face accusingly.

"You left the door open you imbecile? What do you think Lord Barillos will do to you because of this?"

"I did not leave it unlocked!" the man insisted. The captain slapped him across the face and then shoved him to the floor.

"Where is she," the older man roared? "How did she escape?"

"Alejandra has cast herself into the river," Little Grandma said hatefully. "Your claws will never touch her again."

"What," the crooked toothed man asked with disbelief? He went to the opening by the pulley and stared down into the raging waters below. "Damn," he cursed. The second guard quietly joined the older man.

"She could never have survived that," the second guard said. "What shall I tell my lord?"

"The truth," the captain replied unhappily. "What else is there?" The two men walked toward the main door of the prison. The first guard picked himself up off the floor to depart also.

"Release us," Isabel demanded. "Open these doors now!" The crooked toothed man just shook his head.

"She must be daft," he told the other two men and then the door slammed behind them. Isabel pounded her fists on the bars and yelled after the men. All she accomplished was sore wrists and a hoarse throat.

"It is enough," Little Grandma said after several minutes of Isabel's hysterics. "Save your strength. The soldiers had been in such a hurry to leave that the bowl of gruel had been forgotten on the stone floor. Isabel never imagined that she would long for such a revolting substance, but that was exactly the case. The gruel was cold and thick by the time Manuel Barillos paid them a visit. He was accompanied by two of his men.

"I have decided to release you early," he said neutrally, "to mourn Alejandra's death."

"Look what you have done," Isabel shouted! Little Grandma gave her a fierce look and held one finger up to her lips.

"I have done nothing," Manuel replied calmly. "Perhaps mercy is not the correct reaction for you."

"Your men raped her Manuel," Isabel screamed! "You know this is true!"

"It is true," the man agreed as if they were discussing the weather or an interesting species of squirrel.

"Have you punished them?" Isabel asked sharply. "Only death would suffice and not even that is enough!"

"I have punished them," he replied. Isabel noticed that his left eye was twitching as he said this last. Lord Barillos was lying. "There is no call for execution."

"They raped her," Isabel shouted!

"And they have been flogged," Manuel replied angrily. "You act as if my men had killed her. She killed herself!"

"It is the same thing," Isabel spat!

"Be still Isabel," Little Grandma whispered loudly.

"I will never let you get away with this," Isabel promised.

"You know Isabel," Barillos sneered, "you are very much like your father was; strong and quick to anger, but not very intelligent."

"How dare you speak his name," Isabel shouted?

"Well," Barillos replied condescendingly, "a smarter girl would have kept her mouth shut. Even this old servant woman would agree with me, no?"

"She is very upset my lord," Little Grandma said with her eyes looking down at the floor.

"You see," he continued, motioning one hand at the more servile Pilar. "Now you will have to mourn the girl's death here."

"Let us go," Isabel said angrily. "We only wish to leave this place forever. You have ruined Montenegro! We will go to Lord Vasquez and trouble you no more."

"How curious," Manuel said with amusement. "The daughter of Lord Montenegro has decided to tell a lie. Really Isabel, stick with things you are good at. Lying is not one of them."

"I do not lie," Isabel seethed, "but you are the master of it!"

"You are correct," Manuel said proudly. "You told the truth when you promised revenge. I would be a fool to release you now."

"Oh no," Little Grandma said quietly. Manuel spied the bowl of gruel on the floor and motioned to it with one hand.

"Take that mess and give it to the old woman," Lord Barillos said. "My daughter needs to learn humility."

"I am not your daughter," Isabel muttered. Manuel ignored her. One of the soldiers picked up the gruel and carried it over to Little Grandma's cell. He set it on the outside but let the ladle hang inward so that she might eat through the bars. Little Grandma began to eat right away for fear Manuel would change his mind.

"Well I suppose that we are concluded," Lord Barillos said with false disappointment. Little Grandma put the ladle down for a moment in order to entreat him.

"Do not leave my Lady Isabel to rot in prison my lord," she humbly requested. "Have mercy."

"She is only receiving what her foolish tongue requested," Barillos answered. "Unfortunately, you must both pay the price." Little Grandma just averted her eyes at the floor. She did not beg him further. Isabel was silent also. She had realized too late that she should have held her tongue. Lord Barillos and his soldiers left them alone.

"No words passed while Pilar ate the gruel. When the bowl was half empty, she pushed it out and away from the bars. It was a great effort for the old woman to get down on her stomach and shove the bowl to midway between the cells. She was panting when she sat up once more. Isabel lowered herself down and then stretched her own arm out until she reached the bowl. If it had been full, Isabel surely would have spilled it. She slowly pulled it back until it was resting against the bars of her cell. Pilar tossed the ladle over and it clanged loudly against the iron cell. Both women looked worriedly at the prison door.

"Eat quickly," Little Grandma hissed. Isabel obeyed and downed her portion of the gruel in little time. The guards did not come. "Push it back," the old woman said when Isabel had finished. Isabel picked up the bowl and tossed it instead. The impact of the wood on the iron bars was not as loud as the ladle had been. "Shhhh," Little Grandma hissed!

"I just wanted to make it easier for you," Isabel whispered.

"Toss me the ladle," Pilar replied. "It doesn't matter now." Isabel slid it across the floor instead. The ladle still made a clang when it struck the iron. Little Grandma picked it up and set it once more inside the bowl.

"I am so ashamed," Isabel told Pilar. "Please forgive…"

"Do not speak to me now," Pilar interrupted her. "There is nothing to be done for it!" Isabel felt like a fool. She went to the corner of her cell farthest away from Little Grandma. From there she could look out the opening with the pulley system and see Black River rushing over into the gorge.

"This is all my fault," Isabel said brokenly. Little Grandma said nothing. Left with only the sound of the water for company, Isabel began to despair.

CHAPTER VI

As the days dragged on, Isabel watched Black River Village's slow transformation into a ghost town. Montenegro's Keep felt just as empty. Her father, her mother, Alejandra, her brother who had never been born; they were all dead. She blamed herself for Alejandra's death and feared what might become of Little Grandma.

Little Grandma's reassurances that they would be released were delusional at best. Isabel tried being respectful, but it did nothing to change her stepfather's mind. Though she hated to admit it, Manuel Barillos was right. She would have ruined him had he released her. It was an undeniable fact.

Isabel could do nothing but watch from the tower as the glory that was Montenegro disintegrated around her. She even heard some of Barillos' men talking worriedly to each other about the lack of money. Everyone who had worked Black River Ranch had moved on. Their families went with them. Without the horse trade, the shops were forced to close their doors. Only a few families of farm folk remained. They could not leave their land, but would probably have to do so if Manuel continued to increase taxes.

One night, the prison door opened and two soldiers entered in. One of them bore a burning torch. The carried a chain with a pair of shackles on either end. Manuel stumbled in behind them. He carried a wooden goblet of wine in one hand. With the other he leaned on the wall to stay upright. "Bring Ish-abel," he slurred.

"Why the shackles," Isabel asked suspiciously?

"I think you should have your bed," Manuel smiled. "A lady should shleep in a bed."

"Why the shackles," she reiterated?

"I cannot have you running off," Manuel said as he shook a finger at her. "I'm not shtupid!" The two guards came into Isabel's cell. One of them was making ready with the chains.

"Get that thing away from me!" Isabel shouted as the men closed in. She struck at them with her fists and squirmed to free herself from their grasping hands. Ultimately, it was an exercise in futility. In little time they had shackled her wrists and ankles. A chain ran down the front between the two sets of shackles. The length of it was short enough that she could barely raise her hands away from the front of her thighs.

The two men wearing soldier's uniforms led Isabel out of the tower with their lord capering behind them. "A nice warm bed for you," he giggled. Isabel glared at him. She would not let her fear show.

"There is no need for these chains," she told him.

"We will see," he said in a sing-song voice. Isabel was half led and half dragged into her room with its familiar bed. The breeze from outside lightly tossed the dark blue curtains of the canopy and the lighter ones beneath. All of her things were laid out exactly as she had left them. There was, however, one immediately noticeable difference. A thick, iron chain was attached by a manacle to one of the bedposts. The opposite side of the chain had a smaller shackle. This smaller one was quickly attached to Isabel's right ankle, replacing those they had forced on her in the tower.

"Why must you keep me like a dog?" Isabel asked her stepfather. "What have I done to you that you hate me so?" Manuel's face looked ashamed and he could not immediately answer.

"It is for the best," he finally mumbled.

"What about Pilar," Isabel asked? "I need her."

"Not yet," he said. "I just need you to be good. Much depends on your hospitality so…be nice Isabel. Can you do that?"

"You are drunk," she told him. "I know not what you are saying."

"Maybe that is best," he replied, "guards." He sharply motioned for his men to follow and the three of them left quickly. Manuel cast a guilty glance over his shoulder as he retreated. The door was closed then, leaving Isabel alone. The chain was long enough that she could walk around most of her room. She could not travel far enough to reach the door, however. She found that she could sit on the bench by the window and see outside by looking over her shoulder. It was an improvement from the prison cell, but she worried what might be happening to Little Grandma. Why had Lord Barillos separated them?

Minutes later, the guards returned with a large wooden tub. The tub was filled with steaming hot water. "Lord Barillos wishes for you to be more comfortable," one of the men said.

"Will you remove the chain," she asked him?

"We cannot," the man replied.

"Then leave me be," Isabel said with irritation.

"Yes my lady," the man replied. The two guards made for the door and closed it behind them. Isabel waited for some time before entering the bath. She wanted to be sure no one was coming back. The water felt marvelous on her sore muscles. Isabel used the soap and the small cloth they had left to wash the filth from her body. As good as the water felt, she could not relax for the constant reminder of captivity clamped over her ankle. She was a prisoner and her release was not assured.

Isabel used a larger cloth to dry herself off and changed into a pastel blue nightgown from her armoire. She lay down in her bed but left the candles burning. It was a relief to her bones to finally lie down here, instead of the filthy straw mat that she had been sleeping on. Cool air blew in from the window and her skin felt smooth and clean.

As Isabel's eyes were growing heavy, she was jolted back to wakefulness by the sound of a key rattling in the door. "Are you certain?" a man's voice said from outside.

"Without a doubt," her stepfather assured him. "You will be the first." The door opened to Manuel who held it open for the taller man behind him. This other was dressed in the garb of nobility. A burgundy tunic was secured by a black leather belt with a gold plated buckle. Black hose covered the man's legs and his shoes were adorned with similar buckles. He wore a burgundy hat which flopped over to one side. Isabel could not see his eyes under the shadow of the hat, but the corners of his mouth were turned up in a grin.

"My lord," she said sharply as she rose from her bed. Manuel sighed and looked over at her.

"This is Lord Guillermo from Castille," he told her. "Remember what I said before."

"I am not properly dressed," Isabel said angrily, but Lord Barillos shut the door. She was alone with the stranger. She finally saw Lord Guillermo's eyes as he came closer. He leered at her with undisguised lust. Isabel's mouth suddenly felt dry and she backed up a few steps. "Come no closer," she said tremulously.

"Come now," he said as if he were talking to a friend. "You do not wish to lose your home do you?"

"Stay back from me," Isabel warned.

"Lord Barillos owes me a lot of money," the man grinned.

"He should pay you then," Isabel replied.

"Oh he is," Guillermo chuckled. "Get over here."

"No," Isabel replied. Her heart was pounding like a rabbit.

"Just relax my lovely," the man said soothingly. "You might even find this pleasurable." He took off his hat and dropped it on top of her bed. Isabel had retreated to the other side of the canopy, but there was little room between them.

"Take off that gown," Guillermo invited as he removed his belt. He set it neatly on the foot of the bed next to his hat.

"You get out of here right now," Isabel exclaimed! She could hear the trembling in her voice and cursed herself for showing weakness. Guillermo pulled his tunic up over his head and let it drop to the floor. Isabel's skin crawled as the man's chest was revealed with its dark black hair. The groin of his hose left nothing to the imagination. The black material was pulled taught with arousal.

"I see this going two ways," Guillermo said arrogantly. "You will either beg me to stop or beg me for more." He looked at her and his eyes seemed to penetrate right through the fabric of her nightgown. He strode forward like a rooster strutting atop a barnyard fence.

"Do not dare..," Isabel began.

"You can beg me to stop if that is how you want it," Guillermo said. Then his body was in motion. He rushed around the bed toward her. His eyes were wide and he was grinning like a marionette! At the last moment, Isabel noticed the black leather belt folded in half on her bed. Guillermo grabbed her by the left shoulder as she snatched up both sides of the belt with the opposite arm.

The belt made a loud smacking noise as Isabel strapped Lord Guillermo across his cheek. "You bitch," the man cursed! No sooner had the words left his mouth than Isabel whipped him across the other cheek with a reverse stroke. He lost his grip on her arm after being hit the second time.

"Get out of my house," Isabel screamed as she lashed his face mercilessly with the belt! Lord Guillermo raised his hands instinctively to ward off the painful blows. It was at that moment that Isabel brought her knee up hard into his bulging crotch.

"Help," Guillermo grunted as he doubled over in pain. He was trying to get back up and guard the stinging flesh of his face at the same time. Seeing the opening, Isabel brought the belt down hard across the exposed flesh of his neck. Guillermo cried out and lost his footing. He caught himself on the bed but Isabel did not slow her attack. She strapped his hands so hard that she lost hold of one side of the belt. Unfortunately for her would-be rapist, it was the buckle that swung free.

One strike from the buckle and Guillermo's hands dropped free of their protective position over his face. With her free hand, Isabel pulled the leather belt down through the hand holding the strap. She re-tightened her grip on the mid-section of the belt to give herself more control over the buckle. Guillermo rose half way to a standing position before she brought it down hard across his forehead. A stripe of blood appeared where the side of the gold buckle had impacted. "Guards," Guillermo cried desperately as he was beaten back to his knees!

"Scream as loud as you like," Isabel snarled! The belt buckle's edges were quickly painted crimson as she beat Guillermo about the head with a frenzy of blows. Barillos' men rushed into the room. Isabel managed to lash out with the buckle only once more. It crashed into the side of the first man's eye before the Heiress of Montenegro was overcome by the mob.

They pushed Lord Guillermo clear of danger and slammed Isabel down onto her bed. One man was holding her face in the pillow as the others attached manacles to her wrists and ankles. This time they secured her wrists behind her back. Isabel nearly lost consciousness as one of the guards smothered her face into the pillow. He flipped her over onto her back once the manacles were all in place. Isabel inhaled sharply as the blood drained from her face. "Miserable swine," Isabel screamed at them! "God holds a special place in hell for each of you!"

"Shut her up," Lord Barillos said from the safety of the doorway. Isabel had not seen him come in, but how could she have? "Wait," he said to Guillermo as the man pushed past him toward the door. Guillermo's face was a mess of blood and bruises.

"This was not the agreement Manuel," the man said with an injured tone. "You lose everything!"

"Give me some time with her," Manuel called after Guillermo as he walked away down the hall. "I can make it better!"

"I shall give you a fortnight," Guillermo called back. "You had better fix this!"

"I will my lord," Manuel shouted anxiously. Isabel had been lying in stunned silence, but she found her voice once more.

"Curse you Manuel," she raged. "My father should have killed you years ago!" Manuel ignored her and left in pursuit of Lord Guillermo. His guards left the room also. Isabel continued to her tirade long after the door was shut.

† † †

The next morning, several of Barillos men came and released Isabel from her bonds. Her wrists were painfully sore from having slept on them the night before. Her tail bone felt like someone had gone to work on it with a mallet! The guards pulled her up to a sitting position. Isabel winced and groaned as the pain coursed up her spine and into her neck.

The men brought her a large hunk of bread to eat with her gruel. It was small consolation for the close encounter of the night before. The thought of food as a reward made Isabel sick to her stomach. She forced herself to eat nonetheless. Her meal was finished by the time her loathsome stepfather entered her bed chamber. Isabel glared at him but said nothing. She hardly knew where to begin! Lord Barillos coughed uncomfortably before speaking. "You should not have done that to Lord Guillermo," he chastised her.

"I wish you would die instead of talking to me," Isabel told him.

"You do not understand what is happening," Manuel replied.

"Yes I do," Isabel retorted!

"No," Manuel disagreed. "I owe Lord Guillermo a lot of money…a lot of money." Isabel could hear the fear in the man's voice as he said this.

"He told me," she said with disgust.

"If he is not satisfied, Montenegro's Keep could be lost."

"Do I seem to be someone who wishes your rule to last forever?" There was a biting sarcasm in Isabel's tone and Lord Barillos' face darkened.

"I thought you would be this way," he said angrily. "You only think about yourself!"

"You disgust me," Isabel answered.

"Fine," Lord Barillos huffed. "I suppose you are in need of some persuasion."

"I wish you would die!" Isabel screamed at him. Manuel shut the door hard as he exited the room. Isabel covered herself with the bed sheets and sat nervously awaiting what might come next. She was watching the handle of her bedroom door when an ear-splitting scream came to her window from above! It was a woman's scream. "Little Grandma," Isabel called out fearfully as she hurried over to the window. Another scream sliced through the air. This one was even more agonizing than the first. Little Grandma," Isabel cried! No answer came from the prison tower. Isabel could only imagine what they might be doing.

No one came to see her until later that evening. The crooked toothed captain came in with the usual wooden bowl of gruel. This he placed on the small table by the side of Isabel's bed. Once he had done this, Isabel could see that there was a white cloth napkin in his hand. This napkin he placed gingerly beside the bowl. "What is this for?" she asked unhappily.

"Lord Barillos wishes for you to have it," the man said with a hideous grin. He then left the room. Isabel scooted herself over to the small table and looked. The napkin had been sloppily wrapped over a silver spoon.

"What is this," Isabel thought out loud, "another cursed reward?" She pulled the bowl closer to her and then reached down to uncover the spoon. Isabel gasped as the contents of the napkin were revealed in their entirety.

There was a small, bloody lump of flesh resting beside the spoon about half way down the handle. There were roughly circular blood stains in several places on the inside of the napkin where the severed end had touched cloth. Isabel reached out with one tentative finger and jabbed into the side of whatever it was that had bled on the white cloth. The lump rolled over revealing a blood soaked fingernail. It was some time before Isabel could quiet her screaming.

Several hours later, Lord Barillos entered the room with six of his guards. The captain was among them. Isabel's eyes were red from crying and she began to shake when the men entered. She pulled the sheets tight around her as they looked on like a pack of wild dogs. The men smelled of alcohol. Some of them were carrying short chains with manacles on either end. "Put her down," Lord Barillos commanded. His dogs fell upon her, forcing her limbs one by one into the restraints. They secured the other ends of her shackles to the bedposts.

Isabel was left lying spread-eagle on her back. Her heart beat like a hammer. Manuel staggered over to the bedside and flashed her a wicked smile. "How do you like this," he asked?

"Do not do this," Isabel said desperately!

"Poor little Isabel," Manuel sneered. "The rod of nobility is too good for you, no? Perhaps you will enjoy wallowing around in the mud instead."

"I beg of you," Isabel pleaded, "do not do this!"

"I do not plan to do anything," Lord Barillos chuckled. "She is yours," he told the old crooked toothed man.

"We thank you for your generosity," the captain grinned.

"You cannot allow this," Isabel exclaimed!

"Wait until I am gone Captain Lozano," he told the crooked toothed man.

"As my lord wishes," the man chuckled.

"No," Isabel cried! "Do not leave!" Her pleas fell on deaf ears as Manuel closed the door behind him.

"Take off your clothes men," Captain Lozano said. "We have work to do."

"No," Isabel cried once more! The captain laughed as he and his men began to discard their clothing. Isabel writhed and jerked on the bed in an effort to free herself. She could no more break the bedposts than she could snap the chains.

"Do you think she will squeal as loud as the servant girl," one of the men asked?

"I hope she does," another chuckled as he roughly fondled her breast through the material of her nightgown.

"Stop this," Isabel shouted!

"Get your hands off of her boy," Captain Lozano barked! Isabel felt a small and senseless glimmer of hope which died when the man spoke again. "You know that I get to go first," the old man said as he loosened his belt. Isabel could not help but look on in horror as the crooked toothed man removed his undergarments and unsheathed his old and withered meat.

"No...No," she kept saying, but her consent was of no concern to anyone in the room. Her voice grew louder as the older man approached.

"Ha," he said as he bounded up onto the sheets. Isabel sobbed as she thrashed about on the bed.

"Get her Captain," one of the younger men urged, but the man needed no encouragement. His eyes traveled hungrily over Isabel as he took a kneeling position between her legs.

"Give me a blade," the captain said. One of the younger men handed him a dagger. Lozano grabbed hold of the bottom of Isabel's nightgown and cut a long gash down the center of it.

"Help," Isabel screamed! The Captain gave back the dagger and then grabbed both sides of the fabric around the cut. He flexed his arms and rent the nightgown all the way up to Isabel's breasts.

"Now we shall have some real fun," the crooked toothed man said as they all feasted their eyes on her uncovered flesh. Isabel kept screaming. Some part of her mind kept expecting her father to break into the room and rescue her. There was no one coming. Her suffering continued long into the night.

† † †

Isabel awakened the next morning feeling like a discarded pile of refuse. Someone had removed her manacles in the night, but the clamp around her right ankle had returned. Her stomach was tied in knots. Her calves and thighs were sore from the abuse. Her innermost parts hurt worse still. Her mind was numb as she sat up and looked at the familiar sight of her bedroom. There were surely good memories here, but they were now as spoiled as curdled milk.

A strangely dressed servant brought her the usual bowl of shit and set it on the bedside table. The woman's clothing was so revealing that it reminded Isabel of the whorish attire on the wenches from Manuel's party. It then occurred to Isabel that this was one of these very same prostitutes. She stared blankly at the woman carrying the gruel. After her night of shame, she found that she could not even summon the smallest bit of revulsion for the whore. The old Isabel would have been contemptuous. Now there was nothing.

The woman left as quietly as she had come. She looked sympathetically at Isabel. This made the heiress very uncomfortable. Isabel looked at her bed sheets until the other woman was gone. She discarded her ripped nightgown and found another to replace it. The new one was made of a soft white material. Isabel was not concerned with the color or beauty of the gown, however. She just wanted to cover herself. She did not eat and it was nearly two days before she did so again. No one came to see Isabel for some time. A guard came in to check her food on occasion, but that was all.

Many days later, two of Barillos men brought the wooden bathtub into the room once more. "Lord Barillos commands that you bathe yourself," one of the men said.

Isabel did not reply. The men left the room, but Isabel took her time before getting in the tub. Once in the water; she washed herself vigorously, but soap would not wash away the stain of her shame. After washing herself several times over, Isabel began to cry. Why was Manuel allowing her to bathe? The last time she had done so it was in preparation for Lord Guillermo.

Her inner thighs were bruised from where the men had punched them. Even after the bath, Isabel felt as if she were covered in filth. Her mind was a mess as well. That night, Barillos came to visit her. He remained in the safety of the doorway. Isabel's chain would not allow her within arm's reach. Knowing this, she stood at the opposite side of the room facing him.

"Well," he said, "Lord Guillermo will be coming back tomorrow evening." Isabel did not reply. "I expect you to be a good girl and give him what he wants."

"You will have to chain me up again," Isabel said with disgust. "I do not do such things willingly."

"This time you will," Manuel said smugly.

"I will not!"

"Yes Isabel," he smirked, "or do you want Pilar to suffer?" Isabel looked up with dread. "She has plenty of fingers left. When those run out…we shall find something else, no?"

"I wish you would die," she said under her breath.

"You keep saying that as if it matters," Manuel sneered. "When the time comes, you will obey." Isabel said nothing. She cried silently once the man she hated had left her alone in the bedroom.

When the time drew near, Lord Barillos sent his whore up to Isabel's room. "My lord wishes for me to help you prepare," the woman said. It was the very same whore that was now assigned to bringing Isabel her food.

"To help me prepare," Isabel repeated in a deadpan voice. She allowed the prostitute to comb out her blue-black hair. There was no need to change out of her nightgown.

"Sara is my name," the woman said as she applied red powder to Isabel's cheeks. Isabel ignored her. "It will not be so bad," Sara said. "You will become accustomed to it in time." Isabel felt herself wanting to cry again. She turned to anger instead.

"Do not speak to me," Isabel snapped! "I must endure enough already!"

"Suit yourself," Sara said sourly.

"This is not my choice," Isabel retorted. "Do not presume that we are the same. What is happening now is forced upon me. The rest of you are lower than the dirt!" Sara stopped trying to make up Isabel's face then. She stood up and looked down at the heiress once more before leaving.

"No one chooses to be a whore," Sara said with an injured tone, "but I forgive you."

"Spare me your generosity," Isabel shouted after her as she left the room. Sara did not answer but only kept walking. Isabel tried to keep on a brave face, but she could not stop her tears from falling when she thought of what the night would bring.

The time that Isabel feared finally arrived without fanfare. Lord Barillos came into the room with Lord Guillermo in tow. "Good evening Lady Isabel," Manuel said cheerily. Isabel was sitting on the bed. She could not answer. She looked down at the bed as her face burned with shame.

"You are sure about this," Guillermo asked apprehensively.

"She has learned her lesson Lord Guillermo," Barillos assured him. "Remember Isabel," he warned, "Pilar will pay for your every mistake."

"I know," Isabel muttered.

"What was that?" Manuel asked.

"Have you no pity," she asked as she looked up at her stepfather?

"For you," he asked? "No. I do not…and even less for Pilar." Isabel just looked back down at her bed sheets. Out of her peripheral vision, she could see Lord Guillermo approaching. He was not wearing a belt this time. Manuel left the room but did not close the door. Apparently, no indignity was too great that he should not inflict it upon her.

Isabel tried not to watch as Lord Guillermo undressed. She would not look at him. She could not. She shivered uncontrollably as he removed her nightgown. She saw his lustful grin out of the corner of her eye as she felt his filthy hands upon her breasts. "You are going to be a good girl, are you not?" he asked her. Isabel cringed.

"Just do what you came to do," she forced herself to say. Guillermo pushed her roughly down onto her back. Then he was upon her. Every instinct in Isabel's body cried out for her to resist, but she could not risk more harm to Little Grandma. It was sickening. She tried to imagine that it was her husband, but this was nothing like what she had shared with Ramon. It was like a rat forcing itself into an open wound.

CHAPTER VII

*"Wherefore is light given to him that is in misery, and life
unto the bitter souls; which long for death, but it cometh not;
and dig for it more than for hidden treasures; which rejoice
exceedingly and are glad when they can find the grave?"*
Job 2:20-22

Time crept forward like an assassin stalking his victim through a darkened street. Isabel lived in constant fear. She had before thought that Manuel was weak-willed. She had assumed that he was tragically enslaved by the allure of gambling. It was more than that. Lord Barillos was a man consumed by evil. He had a vindictive nature and her suffering gave him pleasure. Every day she prayed for deliverance. Some days she prayed that God would kill him.

After several weeks of degradation, Manuel decided that he would let Isabel roam free. Isabel assumed that Barillos did this because he thought he had broken her spirit. She was wrong. "You will be free to move around the Keep," he proclaimed. "Do not imagine that this changes anything. You will still bed whosoever I command you to bed. Failure to obey me will bring swift punishment upon your chamber maid. She will remain in prison."

"She is only an old woman," Isabel said with her eyes lowered in deference. "The things you force me to do…Is this not enough for you?"

"More than enough," Manuel replied gleefully, "but I must ensure that you will continue to obey. Therefore will Pilar be under constant guard. She will pay the price for your disobedience. If I ever find that you are not in the Keep, your precious Little Grandma will be executed! Isabel cringed visibly eliciting a wide grin from her captor. "Do not think to leave," he continued, "not even to the courtyard. Know that her death will not be quick. I shall let her suffer first…as you have suffered!"

"Do not do such a thing," Isabel pleaded. "It is too much for her."

"I know," Manuel answered smugly. "It is a bit much for me too, but I am certain that I can find those who would be willing to bed her."

"There is nothing good in you Manuel," Isabel said as she shook her head. He shrugged his shoulders and held his hands out to show his lack of concern. He then went on talking as if their conversation was the most natural thing in the world.

"Perhaps the candles will have to be snuffed out. That will save money actually!" Barillos let out a little chuckle at his joke before he called the guards to release her. Isabel's hatred was written all over her face. She could not take her eyes off her stepfather as his guards unshackled her. "I know," he said with amusement. "You wish I would die." Isabel exhaled loudly as her body shook with impotent rage. Barillos laughed out loud. "Say it if you want to," he taunted. Isabel remained silent until Manuel and his guards were gone. She closed the door and wept.

It became one of Isabel's duties to feed Little Grandma. She was more than willing to do it. She knew that there was no one else who would be so attentive. At the same time, she was quite cognizant of the reason why Lord Barillos had commanded it. He wanted her to see...and not just that her chamber maid was still alive, but to witness what she had endured already. Isabel's heart broke every time she saw Little Grandma's finger. The left pinkie was a nub that now ended at the second knuckle. The tip was black and crusted over with scabs. Little Grandma always tried to hide her left hand because she knew how it upset Isabel. It was no use. The Heiress of Montenegro did not need to see the severed finger in order to know it was there.

"You should run away mija," Little Grandma told her one night when the guard had stepped out. They were both locked in the tower for the moment. Little Grandma was confined further to her cell.

"I cannot," Isabel said sadly.

"Yes you can," Pilar disagreed. Isabel looked up with red stained eyes.

"They will kill you when I am gone. Lord Barillos assured me it will be done the moment I cannot be found."

"I am an old woman," Pilar sighed. "I have lived long enough."

"Do not say that," Isabel cried! "I will find a way to free us both."

"Nonsense," Pilar answered. "You must flee now while you are unchained. Who knows when Lord Barillos may change his mind?"

"You will be killed!" Isabel protested.

"It is of no matter," Pilar said forcefully. "Do you suppose that I want to remain locked in this prison?" She reached a hand through the bars and touched Isabel's cheek. "Do not be sad my Isabel," the old woman said comfortingly. Isabel could not help but feel the absence on the end of the woman's finger as she did so. "I am ready to meet God."

"I know," Isabel answered, "but it is more than that."

"You wait until that man is getting drunk with his whores," Little Grandma told her, "then make haste. Do not leave by the bridge. Someone will see you. The tunnel behind your father's bed is the way to escape!"

"But..." Isabel disagreed.

"Mind you to replace the panel," Pilar said.

"Little Grandma, I..."

"Just do as I tell you," the old woman interrupted. There was a scraping noise from outside the prison door before it opened once more. The man who entered was not the same guard who had locked them in.

"That is enough talk," the new guard said sharply. "Be on your way," he told Isabel. The heiress closed her eyes and exhaled to quiet her anger. This was not how she had been treated when her father ruled.

"Go Isabel," Pilar encouraged. She was talking about more than just leaving the room.

"Yes," Isabel agreed, but her heart was not in it. She opened her eyes.

"I love you," the old woman mouthed silently. Isabel forced herself to smile and then left Little Grandma with the guard. Isabel was free to go where she pleased and so she made her way up to the top of the other tower. There was still a glorious view of the countryside. From that height, it was easy to pretend that Black River Village was still thriving.

Isabel spent little time outside her room. Any time she was not in her chamber was spent in one of the two towers. Her ability to move throughout the keep did not guarantee that she would not suffer the predations of Manuel's guards or the guests he often brought up from Huesca. She found it wise to stay out of view.

The aviary was a good place to think. Isabel knew that something had to be done. Obedience to Lord Barillos would not result in her eventual freedom. The scandal that would follow her release would likely ruin him. Little Grandma wanted her to run away. The brave old woman was willing to suffer death because of it. She did not realize what horrors would be inflicted upon her. Isabel knew them intimately.

Isabel looked over at the pigeon coop. Many of the birds were missing but there were a few left. One pigeon stood out from the rest. Here was the catalyst for Isabel's plan. The pigeon with the green ringed eyes was from Queen Petronilla's birds. She could use him to send a cry for help! She looked back out of the opening of the tower and frowned.

There were several men on the battlements. One of them might see the messenger depart. She doubted that any of them had the skill to shoot it down, but it would be at least a day before the letter was delivered. It would be several more days before anyone might come to her rescue. She would have to release the pigeon at night.

There was also the matter of parchment. There was none to be had in her room and certainly there was no ink either. Manuel would not approve of her writing. Isabel planned to steal the ink and parchment and hide them away in the aviary tower. Her room would not be safe. She would send the letter to the Queen-Mother. The Crown of Aragon would have to respond. They would see what had happened in Montenegro. They would also see Pilar and her severed finger. Isabel would tell them everything. Lord Barillos would surely hang!

Isabel returned to her chamber. There was a small seed of hope in her heart. The more she thought about it, the more it grew. That night, Lord Barillos and his guests were making merry in the dining hall again. Isabel secretly made her way into her father's study. Those things she needed were not hard to find. She hid the parchment and the inkpot in her clothing. The quill she palmed up her sleeve.

Isabel walked quickly back to the eastern tower. If anyone had been about, they might have noticed the nervous expression on her face. They would have stopped her and the plan would be a ruin. Fortunately, the so-called soldiers were drinking and whoring with the rest of the guests in the dining hall. She wasted no time. She softly closed the door to the aviary and quickly penned her letter by moonlight.

To the Queen-Mother, Petronilla of Aragon,

Please help. I and my chamber maid are held captive inside Montenegro's Keep. Lord Barillos has drained my father's land of wealth. His foolish ways have resulted in the desolation of Black River Village. He has inflicted all manner of senseless evils upon me. He cut off my servant Pillar's finger and now holds her hostage. He threatens to kill her if I leave or disobey him in any way. I pray God that you will receive this letter and act with all haste.

Signed,
Lady Isabel Montenegro

The writing was very small and confined to a thin strip of parchment that would be secured to the pigeon's leg. Isabel carefully folded it and then tore off the excess. She cursed. There was nothing to secure the letter with. She picked up the cage and slid the pieces of parchment underneath. They would be safe and hidden between the table and the bottom of the coop. She put the inkpot back into her clothes and snuck out with the quill back in her sleeve. She returned these items to the study and then went quickly back to her room. The clinking of glasses and the sounds of laughter echoed up from the stairwell.

It had been some time before Isabel had felt hope. She was so worried that her plot would be discovered that she forgot to be fearful of other possibilities. A bad night of gambling for Manuel would mean agony and humiliation for Isabel.

After several hours of lying awake, Isabel heard voices outside her door. One of them belonged to her stepfather. "We are done negotiating," Lord Barillos said. "The price was already agreed upon."

"You lost the bet," the other man said. His voice was high and nasal like a prepubescent child.

"I did lose," Manuel agreed, but the price was agreed upon. Your wager was put up against a night with my daughter."

"But you made it seem like she is a virgin," the man said sulkily.

"I never said she was," Barillos retorted.

"But you made me believe it was so..." the other man whined. Isabel felt sick all over. The two men were haggling over her as though she were a slave at auction.

"Look," Manuel said with irritation, "what you believed is not my concern! If you do not want to lie with her, than go back to the dining hall."

"It is only that I thought she was pure," the man explained.

"Well and good Master Cruz," Barillos replied, "as long as you understand that it is a forfeiture. I do not owe you money simply because you have changed your mind."

"Let me look at her," the whiny man sighed.

"Oh God," Isabel whispered, "let him find me horrible to look upon. She pinched up her face in hopes that she would appear deformed. The door opened. Manuel stood side by side with the fat, slovenly creature called Cruz. She redoubled her efforts, curling her lip and crossing her eyes.

"Well," Manuel asked uncomfortably?

"She is older than I thought," Master Cruz thought aloud, "but I like the chain. I will take her."

"No," Isabel moaned. The fat man licked his lips and walked over to the bed. Manuel walked away, leaving the door open once more.

"Do not cry little one," the man said in a voice one would use for a baby. "Papa is going to take care of you. Yes he is. Yes he sure is!" The way the man spoke was more revolting than his doughy rolls of flesh that soon became slick with perspiration. Isabel would have gladly suffered death than be subjected to such corruption, but Manuel had turned her unswerving loyalty into her greatest weakness. She could not be the cause of such evils as he had promised for Pilar. Isabel was trapped.

Several days later, a very unhappy looking Sara came up to Isabel's room. "Lord Barillos desires your presence at dinner this evening," she said. Isabel turned back from the place where she had been standing and staring out the window. The day was dying and Montenegro's Keep was slowly being enveloped by shadows.

"I will be there," Isabel said uneasily.

"How marvelous," Sara replied sarcastically. She turned around and stalked angrily from the room. Isabel wondered what had happened to cause the sudden change in the woman, but she was more concerned with whether there would be guests at the keep that evening. She had not seen any arrivals that day but there was no telling if someone would come later.

Isabel chose the most unattractive clothing she could find. It was the same attire she normally used to train horses. She even wore the pantalones instead of a proper skirt. "What is this?" Manuel asked when she came down into the dining hall. There were only two places at the table, one at each end. Barillos sat in the high-backed chair meant for Rafael. The other was clearly meant for Isabel.

"I would like to check on the horses after dinner," Isabel replied. That was not the reason for her dress, but it became also true as soon as she had said it. She wanted to see what was left.

"There are few remaining," Manuel told her. "You are not allowed in the courtyard anyway." Manuel sighed with exasperation. "Perhaps I will allow you to clean out Santiago's stall."

"Has he starved," Isabel asked with dread?

"No," Manuel replied. "He is fed but no one can get close to that animal. No one will ever buy him and the stall is filthy!"

"He will let me in," Isabel assured Manuel, "if you will permit it."

"We shall see," he answered. "Bring out the food!" Manuel clapped his hands together as he finished speaking. A very sour looking Sara entered from the kitchen. On one hand she carried a silver tray laden down with food. There was roast beef and tiny roasted potatoes. There was also a selection of breads and some steamed asparagus. The prostitute served Manuel. He then directed her to serve Isabel also. This she did begrudgingly. She glared at Isabel before returning to the kitchen.

Much of the meal passed in silence. Manuel kept looking at Isabel as if he meant to say something. Isabel did not wish to hear it, whatever it might be. In the meantime, she had another agenda. She spread the white cloth napkin over her lap, but she had no intention of keep her stable clothing spotless. As she held her fork with one hand, she quickly stuffed the napkin into her pantalones with the other. Manuel did not seem to take notice.

Lord Barillos had something to say. Inevitably, he began to speak. "This has not been the best time," he said heavily. Isabel kept eating to avoid conversation. She was trying to figure out what she would use to cut the napkin into tiny strips. "I only do what I have to for Montenegro. I hope you understand that," he told her.

Isabel paused with her fork half way to her mouth. Anger burned through her mind. Manuel's delusional apology was even more offensive than his insults. She fought to stem the tide of angry words that threatened to spew forth. "You do understand Isabel, do you not?" he asked.

"I understand what will befall Pilar if I do not obey your commands," she said neutrally.

"That would not be necessary if you understood. I do not want Montenegro to be taken away from us. I know that you do not want it either," he told her. Isabel exhaled audibly and closed her eyes for a time before speaking.

"Is it not enough that I obey, however revolting it may be? Must you also have my sympathy," she asked? "Were there even a shred of goodness in you Manuel, you would release us."

"I cannot," he replied uncomfortably.

"Then what is it," she asked? There was fury rising in her voice as she spoke. "What more do you want from me?" Isabel shouted across the table!

"Quiet yourself," Manuel pouted. "You do not want me to call the guards."

"Call them," Isabel screamed! "There is nothing more that you can do to me! You have taken all that I have."

"Guards," Lord Barillos shouted! Isabel could hear the sound of the men approaching.

"No need to call your dogs," Isabel said hatefully. "I will go. If you are seeking for sympathy, than I suggest you find it in the arms of one of your whores. I am certain that they will humor you until your detestable friends grow tired of me!" The guardsmen hurried into the room. Isabel held up a hand dismissively as if she were still in control. "I go," she told them. They did not try to stop her as she walked through them and straight to the main doors of the keep.

"Where are you going?" Manuel demanded.

"To muck out Santiago's stall as I was commanded," Isabel called back testily.

"Go with her," Manuel told his men. "See that she does not try to escape." They followed Isabel out to the private stables located within the keep. Manuel had not lied about the lack of horses. Only Santiago and two of Priscilla's sepia colored mares remained. There were three donkeys and many stalls with no animals in them at all.

Santiago startled when Isabel came into view. He flared his nostrils and stomped at the filthy floor of his stall. "It is alright," Isabel said soothingly. She held a hand out toward the old stallion. The guards stood congregated at the entrance. Isabel thought she saw one of those who had defiled her among them. She looked away. She would not be able to calm Santiago if she were not calm herself. "It is I," she told the horse. "It is Isabel."

After a tense standoff, Santiago ambled forward. His cheek brushed against Isabel's outstretched hand. She scratched his face through the thick grey fur that covered it. The horse leaned down further as Isabel continued scratching. Santiago picked up his head and nickered softly as he stared out at the yard with longing. "I know boy," Isabel said. "I want to run too."

Isabel picked up a shovel from the wall and ducked into Santiago's stall. She mucked it out and then cleaned the stallion's hooves with an iron pick. She got a large comb and brushed the dirt out of his fir. The horse closed his eyes and seemed to enjoy the attention. Isabel found that she was able to forget her troubles for a time. Eventually the guardsmen decided that it was enough. "Time to go back," one of them said.

"Alright," Isabel replied with disappointment. "Allow me to put the tools back." It was a small indulgence and the guards permitted it. As she was hanging the tools back on the walls, Isabel noticed that one of the long thick hairs of the horse's mane had come loose onto the comb. She pushed the horse hair down into the neck of her tunic. She would have to find it inside, but it would surely not make it past the leather belt she wore at her waist.

Isabel removed herself from the stall and followed the guards back to where the others were waiting. These men escorted her back into the main doors of the keep. She returned to her room and made herself ready for bed. She put Santiago's long, black hair into her armoire for safekeeping and then blew out the candles that lit the bed chamber. She lay awake in the darkness for some time before putting her plan into motion.

When the moon had risen high enough to shine through her windows, Isabel rose and made her way over to the armoire. She removed a long, wooden comb used for holding her hair back. She broke off several of the tines of the comb to create sharp edges. With these new tools, she frayed the stolen napkin until she was able to rip off a thin strip from the side of it. She took this and the hair from her armoire and snuck out into the hallway. Remaining close to the walls, Isabel crept through the shadows and into the stairwell that would take her up to the aviary.

Isabel froze and pressed herself up against the wall of the tower stairs as she heard footsteps approaching from the hallway below. Fortunately, Lord Barillos' men did not enter the tower. The Heiress of Montenegro was even more careful as she crept up the rest of the stairs. Once in the aviary, she lifted up the coop and retrieved her letter from beneath it. She rolled it up as tightly as she could and tied it together with a piece of the napkin. She knotted Santiago's hair around the cloth and set it on the table.

Isabel spoke in soothing tones to the pigeons until she had caught the one with the green rimmed eyes. She secured the tiny letter to the bird's right leg by means of the thick hair from Santiago's mane. She eyed her handiwork critically. It would hold. She wished that she could send a letter to her uncle instead, but the letter had already been written.

This would be the only opportunity she would receive. Isabel took it. Alone in the darkness, Isabel carried the pigeon to the opening in both hands. Once there, she gently tossed him up into the night sky. The pigeon flew quickly away from the keep. Isabel closed her eyes and prayed that God would let the message be delivered. It was difficult to say a prayer now that so many had gone unanswered. Isabel held on to this last fragile hope. Surely, God would have mercy upon her this time.

Over the next few days, Isabel spent as much of her waking time as possible inside the aviary tower. One sunny afternoon, she saw her salvation. Like the dove that descended upon Christ in the water, the messenger pigeon flew low over the walls and landed upon Isabel's outstretched finger. There was a tiny wooden tube attached to the bird's left leg. Isabel excitedly removed the parchment that had been rolled up inside of it.

To Lady Isabel of Montenegro,

Your letter was received. I come presently to sit in judgment of Lord Barillos. If you are harmed further before my arrival, I will consider it as an admission of his guilt.

Petronilla of Aragon

Isabel silently gave thanks to God as she carefully rolled up the parchment and placed it back into the tube. She kept it in her hand in case she might need it again. Just as she was about to depart for her room, the door to the tower swung open. Captain Lozano was standing there with his arms crossed over his chest. "I saw your little friend flying in," the crooked toothed man said accusingly.

"Where is the message?" Isabel stood tongue-tied. Lying was not her strong suit.

The captain came menacingly toward her. "Give me the letter you little bitch," he threatened, "else I will have to teach you a lesson again!"

"Touch me not," Isabel shouted! "I will give you the letter!" She thrust the wooden tube out at him. He snatched it out of her hand with a satisfied smirk.

"Come with me," he growled as he grabbed her by the arm. "Lord Barillos will want to read this." Captain Lozano practically dragged Isabel down the stairs to her father's study where Manuel was poring over his accounts. He shoved Isabel into the room and followed quickly after.

"What is the meaning of this interruption?" Lord Barillos demanded as the captain slammed the door behind them. Isabel rubbed her arm where the man had laid hold of her.

"I found her in the east tower," Lozano answered as he placed the wooden tube on the desk. "A pigeon brought her this my lord." Manuel narrowed his eyes at Isabel before he picked up the tube. He carefully removed the letter and spread it out on the desktop. His face darkened as he read. When finished, he looked up at Isabel with venom in his eyes.

"Lock her in the tower," Manuel snarled! Before Isabel could react, the crooked toothed man had shackled one of her wrists and twisted her arm behind her back. He forced her down over the desk. The pain shooting up her arm was excruciating!

"Give me the other arm now or I shall break the one I have," Captain Lozano threatened.

"Any injury you do to me will be revisited upon you a hundred fold," Isabel exclaimed! Her face was stuck in a grimace as the crooked toothed man pressed it into the surface of the desk.

"Some things do not leave marks," Captain Lozano said as he ground his crotch into the back of Isabel's dress. "Now give me your arm or I shall take something sweeter!"

Manuel grabbed Isabel's other wrist and assisted his captain in shackling her. "Get up whore," the captain barked as he jerked Isabel to her feet.

"Take her away," Manuel ordered. "Do not touch her. We need her unharmed...for now."

"Very well my lord," the man huffed. He dragged Isabel out into the hallway and up the tower stairwell. "You get away this time," he said as he herded her up the steps.

"You will hang if the Queen-Mother finds that I have been hurt," Isabel threatened. The captain led her up into the top of the prison tower. From there he dragged her into her cell.

"Get in," Lozano told her when Isabel did not move fast enough. He shoved her through the cell door opening and she nearly lost her balance. In the meantime, she could hear the iron door being locked behind her. "Back up to the bars if you want me to free your hands," the crooked toothed man said with irritation.

"Rot in hell," Isabel cursed him!

"You do as I say unless you want me to embarrass you in front of the old woman," he told her.

"You would not dare!"

"Oh but I would," the captain grinned. "I have not forgotten how it was to be inside of you."

"I will see you hang," Isabel promised.

"Maybe," the crooked toothed man agreed, "but if not...you know what comes next!" Isabel glared daggers at him. The captain smirked back at her. "I will come back later to see if you still want to be in those manacles." Isabel spat on the ground toward him, but it fell short. Lozano smiled at her then. His eyes seemed to promise the horrors to come. He left Isabel and Little Grandma locked in their respective cells and slammed the prison door as he went out.

"I told you to escape," Pilar said accusingly. "Now look what has befallen you!"

"Not now," Isabel answered.

"Why not now," Pilar demanded? Isabel forced herself to calm down and forget about the captain's threats before she answered.

"We are saved," she said. "I sent a message to Aragon by pigeon. The Queen-Mother is even now traveling to Montenegro to sit in judgment!"

"The Queen," Pilar asked with disbelief? "She is coming here?"

"No," Isabel replied. "Sancha is queen now. I am speaking of the former queen, Petronilla of Aragon!"

"What did you tell her? I mean how did you convince her to come?" Little Grandma asked.

"I told the truth," Isabel answered, "and now she comes!"

"Praise be to God," Pilar exclaimed as she clapped her hands together!

"Shhhhh," Isabel said with one finger raised to her lips, but she was smiling also.

"Sorry," Pilar said. Her face was radiant.

"The Queen-Mother said that if they hurt as again, it will be considered an admission of guilt," Isabel whispered.

"Praise God! What a relief!"

"Yes," Isabel agreed.

"We must be careful not to upset them though," Pilar cautioned. "Who knows what they might do if Lord Barillos starts to feel desperate?"

"It is the truth," Isabel replied. The two women kept their mouths shut for the next few days. Food was delivered with much greater regularity. The quality of it went up considerably as well. Isabel's manacles were removed, but not by the captain of the guard. Isabel would not let any of those who had harmed her come near. The crooked toothed man unhappily complied by sending one of the others to release her. They could ill afford for Isabel's wrists to be bruised when Petronilla would hold court.

Isabel was awakened one morning by the sound of trumpets, heralding the arrival of Petronilla of Aragon. From the corner of her cell, she could see down into the courtyard. "She comes," Isabel said excitedly as the first of the royal soldiers came through the gate! Two men in brightly colored costumes came behind the first ranks of soldiers. Each of these men carried a silver trumpet in his hand and blew several long blasts to announce the coming of her majesty. After the men on foot came several rows of mounted cavalry. These gave way to a team of eight white horses drawing a black carriage.

Isabel immediately recognized the crest of the House of Aragon engraved upon the door of it. The grooves in the wood had been inlaid with silver. A young man carrying the yellow and scarlet flag of the nation rode close behind. More ranks of horsemen brought up the rear.

The courtyard was quickly filled with the soldiers of Zaragoza. Pilar couldn't see from her cell, but Isabel excitedly relayed every detail! She could not see the main doors of the keep, but it was logical to assume that Barillos and his dogs were gathered in front of it. The carriage came to a stop with its door facing toward the keep. The heralds closed in with their silver trumpets as two soldiers came forward with a large bolt of red cloth. The two soldiers rolled out the cloth toward Montenegro's Keep so that Petronilla's feet would never touch the earth.

The Queen-Mother stepped down from the carriage with the assistance of the man who had been driving it. She was garbed in a beautiful violet gown with long sleeves and a very high neckline. Peacock feathers stuck out from the neck of her gown and extended far past her shoulders. A white, cloth head covering concealed all but her face with its powder whitened skin and aristocratic features. Her blue eyes stared imperiously at whoever was gathered in front of the keep. A golden crown rested upon her brow. The sunlight gleamed upon its metal arches.

"Her majesty, the Queen-Mother," one of the heralds shouted!

"Petronilla of Aragon," bellowed the other! "Make way for her royal majesty!" Petronilla seemed to glide over the red cloth that stretched out before her. She was flanked closely by her soldiers. She moved then out of Isabel's vision. Isabel could hear Lord Barillos welcoming her. Whatever was said afterward was too quiet to hear.

Isabel could faintly detect the bustle of servants and guards below as Lord Barillos' men scrambled to accommodate the Queen-Mother. "It is finally over," she sighed. Little Grandma just smiled.

CHAPTER VIII

Later that morning, a sober-looking Captain Lozano released the two women from their cells. They were escorted to the dining hall by armed guards. The tables had been set up like three sides of a rectangle. Petronilla sat at the high backed chair in the middle of the center table. She was surrounded by men-at-arms and her various servants. Lord Barillos, Captain Lozano, and several others of Barillos' men sat at the table on the left. The prostitute, Sara, was dressed in the simple clothes of a washer woman. Her usually displayed assets were now covered by a plain brown dress and a white apron. Her hair was covered by a white scarf. The men were cleaned up also. Their boots and armor were not polished to perfection, but they were polished. They had bathed and their hair was actually combed.

Manuel wore a light green tunic and white hose. His hair was slicked back with oil and he wore a silver circlet on his brow. Rafael's signet ring was prominently displayed on his right hand and a gold cross pendant hung on a chain about his neck. It did not escape Isabel's notice that the guards seated at Barillos table were the very same ones that had inflicted their lusts upon her.

Isabel stared at Barillos and his men as she and Little Grandma were seated at the table on the right. They were the last to sit down and the only ones present at their table. As soon as they had done so, a man in the white robes of a priest came out into the midst of the tables. He had a glossy green collar piece that fit over his neck, hung down over his chest, and extended to his knees. He had black hair that was mostly covered by the conical shaped hat common to important members of the papal clergy.

"We are gathered here under the presence of Almighty God," the priest began, "to hear the trial of Lord Manuel Barillos of Montenegro. Justice will be handed down by none less than her majesty, the Queen-Mother, Petronilla of Aragon. May the light of God's unfailing wisdom shine down upon her and this noble gathering. I,

Bishop Delgardo Royo, will act as the mouthpiece of her majesty. Bishop Royo walked around Isabel's table and seated himself in the empty chair to the right of the Queen-Mother. "You are all reminded that those who speak before her majesty are under a solemn vow of truth. Any deliberate falsehoods will be punished swiftly and without mercy. Refusal to answer any questions will be seen not only as an affront to her majesty, but also as an admission of guilt."

Bishop Royo stood then and addressed those assembled once more. "Let all those who swear to tell the truth before God stand now with me." Isabel was the first to get up out of her chair, but all present did as the priest had invited them. "Then we are all sworn before God and the Queen-Mother," the bishop concluded. "You may be seated."

Once everyone had resumed their seats, the bishop spoke once more. "I call first, Lord Manuel Barillos, to the floor." Lord Barillos stood slowly and walked out into the midst of the rectangular area between the tables. His bearing was firm and confident. So much so, that he was barely recognizable as the coward Isabel was accustomed to. "You stand before her majesty with many accusations leveled against you my lord," Bishop Royo said. His voice was loud and carried even to the back of the dining hall. "Do you wish to confess your sins before I read the accusations?"

"There is nothing to confess your eminence," Lord Barillos answered.

"Very well," Bishop Royo answered. "You are charged with the unjust imprisonment of one of Aragon's nobility...Lady Isabel of Montenegro. You are further charged with the unjust imprisonment of her servant Pilar. These charges are accompanied by the needless torture of an old woman. Above all, you are today accused of negligence; specifically, the ruination of Aragon's northernmost province. Your depletion of Montenegro's resources has left Montenegro under-manned and vulnerable to a French invasion. If found guilty of one or all of these crimes; your sentence may include forfeiture of land, loss of station, and imprisonment. Do you understand?"

"I do," Manuel answered.

"Are you Lord Manuel Barillos responsible for any of these crimes for which you are accused?"

"I am not."

"You are now granted the opportunity to plead your innocence before her majesty," Royo told him.

"Thank you your eminence," Manuel replied graciously. "Let me first respond to the ruination of Montenegro. When Lord Montenegro passed on, his widow placed Lady Isabel in charge of the stables and the business of horses. This was due to the fact that Master Aquinas had died tragically in the war with Morera. Also, the widow Montenegro had little knowledge of horses. I myself am equally ignorant of the horse trade. When Lady Priscilla became my wife, I acquiesced to her wish to leave Lady Isabel in charge. It did seem prudent at the time."

"When my late wife died, Isabel foolishly sold off most of the horses and then retired to a cottage in Zaragoza belonging to her uncle, Lord Vasquez," Manuel continued. "Isabel had been given her mother's signet ring in order to handle the business of horse flesh. So it was that she was able to sell off such a large number of the animals without my knowledge. It was a devastating blow to the herd. Unfortunately, I had little choice. The horses were already paid for. The knights who purchased them were making haste to Italy. I could not deny such noble men those things which they needed and had rightfully purchased." Isabel ground her teeth. She was so furious she could barely contain herself as her stepfather continued his tale.

"So now I am left to pick up the pieces of this unfortunate situation," Manuel said sadly. "If I have failed your majesty, it is only because I was moved upon to put trust in my wife's only child." Isabel glared at Lord Barillos. "As to the matter of unjust imprisonment," Lord Barillos said, "the chamber maid Pilar is a thief and was caught stealing silver from the kitchen." Little Grandma gasped with disbelief. "This is the reason that the end of her finger was removed, as a reminder to never steal again and as a lesson to anyone else with such ideas. A Lord must rule his subjects," Barillos concluded. "That is all that I have to say your majesty."

"You have not answered all of the accusations my lord," Bishop Royo reminded Manuel. "Did you unjustly imprison Lady Isabel of Montenegro or no?"

"The imprisonment was just," Manuel sighed, "but I beg of you. Do not make me explain the circumstances before this court. It will bring shame to my house."

"You are required to answer all questions," Bishop Royo answered.

"Recant this accusation Isabel," Lord Barillos pleaded. He looked quite pathetic as he stared at her with desperation in his eyes. His performance garnered no sympathy from Isabel.

"I will not," Isabel said icily.

"Please…I beg you to change your mind."

"I will not recant!"

"Just answer the accusation my lord," Father Royo said with exasperation.

"You leave me no choice," Lord Barillos fumed! "The reason that I imprisoned Lady Isabel was to curb her fornications!"

"Liar," Isabel shouted as she rose to her feet!

"Sit down," Bishop Royo barked! "You will speak when spoken too or you will be thrown in prison!"

"Forgive me," Isabel said as she stared at Manuel with hatred in her eyes. She seated herself and watched as her stepfather continued his little dance of deception.

"I do not have witnesses for all of my daughter's indiscretions," Manuel said, "but I do have a substantial amount. Most of these are confessions of guilt. I suspect that she has bedded several members of Huesca's nobility. However, I am keenly aware that her lusts are not confined to men of breeding." Isabel's face was red with anger and her countenance darkened with every word that came out of

Manuel's mouth. "I wish I could say that her wickedness was only something played out with men, but that would be a lie." Barillos then buried his face in his hands and pretended to weep. "Oh Isabel; what have you done to us," he sobbed? Petronilla made a motion with her hand for Lord Barillos to sit down.

"You may sit down Lord Barillos," Petronilla said.

"Thank you your majesty," Manuel sniffed as he bowed to the Queen-Mother. He walked quickly over to the chair he had left behind and seated himself once more. Isabel was furious and even Little Grandma was seething!

"I call now Lady Isabel Montenegro to the floor," Father Royo proclaimed. Isabel stalked out into the middle of the tables. She could scarcely wait to open her mouth. "You are accused of fornication with both nobility and commoner alike. You are accused of lying before God and her majesty in regards to Lord Barillos. You are further charged with the ruination of Montenegro. If found guilty, your fate will lie in the hands of Lord Manuel Barillos. Do you understand?"

"I understand," Isabel replied coldly.

"Do you wish to confess your sins," the bishop asked?

"I have done nothing for which I must confess, save that which Lord Barillos has forced upon me!"

"Are you, Lady Isabel, responsible for any of the crimes of which you are accused?" Bishop Royo asked?

"No," Isabel responded. "It is all lies!"

"You are now given the opportunity to plead your innocence before her majesty."

"My servant Pilar is not a thief," Isabel said from between clenched teeth. "She is the oldest servant in this house and has served Montenegro longer than anyone else. She would not be so foolish as to steal. At her advanced age, no one else would take her if she were forced to leave. The silver was stolen by Lord Barillos to pay his gambling debts to a brothel in Huesca. The horses were sold by Lord Barillos for the same reason. I was in charge of the stables as he says, but I had already left for Zaragoza when he himself sold off the animals."

"As to the matter of my fornication..," Isabel paused. She fought back the tears that threatened to overtake her.

"Go on," Bishop Royo prompted.

"I was raped," Isabel said with emotion, "by every soldier sitting at that table. I was raped by several other men that I had never seen before." Barillos just shook his head sadly and looked down at the floor.

"After Lord Barillos sold off the horses," Isabel explained, "the whole of Black River Village became almost instantly desolate. His gambling worsened even as the number of people he could tax dwindled. With nothing left to offer his creditors..." She was trying very hard to hold back the tears but could control them no longer. "He offered me," Isabel cried. "I fought the first of them off. Lord Guillermo was his name. He was from Castile. As punishment for my refusal, I was tied to my bed while those six men forced themselves inside of me!" Isabel pointed her finger accusingly at the men at Barillos table. Their eyes found other things to look at. Captain Lozano was the only exception. He grinned and crossed his arms over his chest.

"A fortnight later," Isabel continued, "he brought Lord Guillermo back. He imprisoned Pilar and threatened to kill her if I did not obey. Just to make sure, he cut off her finger and had it delivered in a napkin next to my evening meal." Isabel swallowed hard.

"Oh Isabel," Manuel said sadly.

"You are reminded not to speak," Bishop Royo interrupted. Manuel fell silent as Isabel spoke once more.

"He will never stop your majesty," she said as she looked up into the eyes of Petronilla. "Even still, he gambles away my father's wealth and offers me as payment. When they grow tired of me, Montenegro will be no more. If you have any love for my father, than you must depose him." Petronilla shifted uncomfortably in her seat but did not look away. "Let Montenegro be ruled by someone else, someone capable." She looked then at Manuel. "If it remains under the rule of this cretin lord, Montenegro will fall." Manuel glared stonily at her as she looked back at the Queen-Mother. "I beg of your majesty… Do not believe his lies. He has already turned his own estate into a hovel and seeks to do the same here. Do not allow this reckless evil to continue!" After a moment of silence, Bishop Royo spoke.

"Is that all my lady wishes to say?" he asked.

"It is," Isabel replied. She curtseyed and started to make her way back to the table before the bishop stopped her.

"Remain where you are Lady Isabel," he said. Isabel turned round and retook her position in the center.

"As you wish, your eminence," she replied, curtseying once more.

"We shall now hear the words of the witnesses," Bishop Royo said. "In that Lord Barillos was allowed to speak first, Lady Isabel will call her witnesses first. Lady Isabel…" Royo gestured with one hand indicating that it was Isabel's time to speak.

"I call my servant Pilar to the floor," Isabel stated.

"What will Pilar tell us," Royo asked?

"She will tell you the horrors we have endured. She will tell you that my soul is intact even if my body is destroyed. She will tell you how Lord Barillos has gambled away the wealth of our house. She will tell of his guilt."

"Very well," the bishop answered. "Come forward Pilar. You may be seated my lady."

"Thank you your eminence," Isabel replied respectfully. She looked at the old woman encouragingly as Pilar came out to stand before Petronilla's court. Pilar held nothing back. She told how Barillos had stolen the silver. She told of how he had stolen the tapestries and then lost them as well. She spoke about how Rodrigo had followed him to Huesca and witnessed the squandering of Montenegro's wealth. She even told how he had made a public mockery of his marriage vows to the deceased Lady Priscilla. She showed them what remained of her little finger and explained how the Captain had cut it off as a lesson to Isabel."

"What about the accusations of rape?" Royo inquired when Little Grandma paused to catch her breath. "Can you tell us anything about this?"

"Isabel never told me about it, but..," Little Grandma shuddered. "At night, I heard screaming."

"You heard Lady Isabel screaming," the bishop asked?

"Yes."

"How can you be certain?"

"I have been with her since birth," Little Grandma replied. "Hers is the most familiar voice to my ears."

"What else did you hear?"

"Laughter," Pilar said as she swallowed a lump in her throat.

"Who was laughing?"

"They were," Pilar answered as she gestured toward the men at Barillos table.

"Those men," Royo inquired? "How are you so certain it was they?"

"Isabel does not lie," Pilar answered confidently.

"So you are not certain if these particular men are the same ones that you heard laughing?"

"When you ask me that way," Little Grandma replied with irritation, "I suppose that I am not."

"Did the soldiers ever tell you why they removed your finger?"

"Captain Lozano said it was to teach Isabel a lesson."

"It was not to punish you for stealing?"

"No. I have never stolen from Montenegro!"

"Have you stolen elsewhere?"

"No," Pilar retorted. The bishop was obviously getting under her skin.

"I see," Royo said expansively. "So you are not a thief, you believe everything Lady Isabel tells you, and you are certain of nothing...except that you heard screaming at night. Does that sum it up?"

"I also heard laughter," Pilar said indignantly.

"Ahh yes, I had forgotten the laughter," Royo said. "Now with this laughter…the screams…could they have been screams of passion?"

"No!"

"Lust perhaps?"

"Never!"

"Thank you Pilar," the bishop smiled. "You may now sit down." The old woman stood confused for a few moments. She looked upset and Isabel could see that there was more that she wanted to say. Instead, Pilar curtseyed and returned to her seat. She was, after all, a servant used to following the commands of those in higher station.

"Will my lady call someone else?" Royo asked.

"There is no one else who will speak the truth," Isabel answered.

"Then please be seated," Royo told her. Isabel curtseyed and did as she was asked. "Very well," the bishop continued, "Lord Barillos…please call your witnesses."

"Thank you, your eminence," Barillos responded. "I call first Captain Lozano to the floor." The crooked toothed man stood up from his seat.

"What will Captain Lozano tell us?" Royo inquired.

"The truth," Lord Barillos answered. "Whatever he sees fit."

"Very well," Royo answered, "come forward captain." Lozano bowed low and then walked to the center of the tables. He gave Isabel a little wink before turning toward Lady Petronilla and Bishop Royo. "Captain Lozano," the bishop said loudly, "do you have any sin which you desire to confess before this court?"

"No," the crooked toothed man answered.

"Very well… You and your men are charged with the rape of Lady Isabel. Are you guilty of this crime?"

"No," Lozano answered, "not I."

"Then tell us what happened."

"Lady Isabel says she was raped. There is more to it than that," he said conspiratorially.

"So you did commit fornication with her," Royo asked?

"Not I," Lozano replied. He cracked his knuckles and then launched into his tale. "I heard the same sounds that Pilar heard one night. It was very alarming to me and I did rush to Lady Isabel's room to discover the matter! What I saw there would be an affront to her majesty to describe."

"Try to get your point across, captain," Royo encouraged.

"Those five soldiers sitting at my table were engaged in the most shameless acts of fornication with Lady Isabel." The men at Barillos table really started looking uncomfortable when it seemed that Lozano would sell them down the river.

"Did you also engage in these acts?"

"I did not."

"Surely, you must have exacted some punishment from them. Why are they not executed already?"

"That was my first thought your eminence," Lozano replied seriously, "but it was all so strange."

"Speak plainly," the bishop told him.

"As I watched all this taking place," Lozano replied, "Gomez was begging for help, even as he was…thrusting himself into her. He was crying out to God for help and saying that he could not stop. Then he started begging me to take him off!"

"What did you do?"

"I took him off of her," Lozano answered with wide eyes. "I had to do something. She tried to entice me to commit adultery with her as well. She waited until we were alone as I was taking her up to her cell."

"Did you," Royo asked?

"I did not, but I had my men severely flogged for having done so," Lozano reported. "Still, it made no sense to me. I was going to hang them all until each of them told me a remarkably similar story."

"What story," Royo prodded?

"That they did not want to do such things with her. She forced them."

"How were they forced?"

"Witchcraft," Captain Lozano said confidently. "How else would five honest, God-fearing men perform this awful crime?

"Witchcraft is a serious accusation Captain," the bishop warned.

"I know not whether she is a witch or possessed of the devil," Lozano said, "but I pray that your eminence can cast it out!"

"Why do you think that Lady Isabel is possessed of a devil?"

"When I or one of my men goes to feed her in her cell, it seems to us that she is of two minds. Often times, she acts in a most sinful manner. She touches and exposes her most private parts while trying to tempt someone to come into the cell with her."

"And other times," Royo questioned?

"Other times she seems more like herself. She is very angry and confused during these times. She accuses my men of rape. She does not remember having tempted them."

"What about her screams?"

"Her screams," Lozano asked?

"Yes. Would you say that she is screaming in horror or ecstasy?"

"Ecstasy at first," Lozano said as he pretended to shudder, "but it was definitely horror by the time I broke it all up."

"You swear to this?"

"On the names of all the saints," Lozano replied. "That is why I have also brought Sara, the washer woman, to testify."

"Shall I call her now my lord," the bishop asked Manuel?

"Certainly," Lord Barillos agreed.

"Please be seated Captain," the bishop invited. He looked then at Sara. "Come forward woman," he said unkindly.

"Yes, your eminence," Sara replied. Her voice sounded like that of a timid child. She walked nervously out to take Captain Lozano's place. The crooked toothed man sat down as Sara got to the midst of the floor.

"What is your name woman?" the bishop asked.

"Sara…it is Sara your eminence."

"Have you ought to confess?"

"Yes."

"Well," Royo said with shock, "here is a surprise!" He looked around the room as if Sara's willingness to confess were some great joke. "Tell me your sins, child."

"I did commit fornication," Sara said with color rising in her cheeks.

"With whom," the bishop asked interestedly?

"With Lady Isabel," Sara said in a choked voice.

"This mockery has lasted long enough," Isabel shouted as she rose from her seat!

"You are commanded by the Queen-Mother to sit down Lady Isabel," Royo thundered! "Do so, or else I will have you removed!" Isabel swallowed her anger and carefully reseated herself. "Do you swear before God and her majesty that this is the truth?" he asked Sara.

"I do," Sara gulped. "I do swear it."

"You vile and wicked woman," Royo hissed!

"Please," Sara begged, "it was not in my power to do otherwise."

"Really," Bishop Royo scoffed? "Tell us what happened that you could do nothing other than commit an abomination!"

"I was serving her food and she…she looked at me," Sara began. "I heard a voice in my head but…it was not the voice of my lady."

"What did the voice say?" Royo asked thoughtfully.

"It commanded me to lie down on the cell floor. It threatened to kill me if I disobeyed. Then..." Sara broke off as if the memory was too much to bear.

"Then," Royo prodded.

"Lady Isabel did things to me...unspeakable things! I was so scared. I did not move for I knew that I would die. It was Lady Isabel that committed the fornications...but it wasn't her."

"Speak more plainly," Royo interrupted her.

"I saw a vision," Sara said.

"What did you see?"

"I saw the Devil," Sara moaned. "The Devil was taking me as if I were one of his harlots!"

"The Devil made you his whore," Royo exclaimed! Sara whimpered and nodded her head yes. Isabel crossed her arms in disgust. Predictably, the five soldiers told similar tales of how Isabel had bewitched them. They did not see visions, however. Bishop Royo became quite animated. The collaborating stories of witchcraft seemed to have whipped the clergyman into frenzy! "We have heard all the evidence," Bishop Royo said finally. "Lord Barillos, have you anything to say before the Queen-Mother passes judgment?"

"I have nothing more," Manuel answered.

"Lady Isabel," the bishop asked? Isabel stood before addressing Petronilla.

"Lord Barillos has ruined every province under his rule. I did not know him before he came to Montenegro. The truth is self-evident. As for these contrived tales of witchcraft, they are but the desperate lies of these fearful men who await your majesty's judgment. I have nothing more." Isabel curtseyed and seated herself once again.

"Very well," the bishop replied. He sat down in his chair next to the Queen-Mother and conversed briefly with her in whispers. He then stood up to address the room. "The Queen-Mother will now pass judgment...all rise." Everyone stood up from their seats then except for Petronilla.

"You may be seated," Petronilla said. There was the scraping of many chairs as everyone sat back down. She closed her eyes and sighed heavily before speaking. When she opened them, she was looking directly at Isabel. Isabel's heart sunk. She had seen that look before. It was the same guilty countenance that had been on Manuel's face before he had let his creditors defile her!

"Do not do this," Isabel found herself saying out loud.

"Silence," Bishop Royo hissed! Lady Petronilla looked away from Isabel then. She was resolved.

"I declare Lord Manuel Barillos to be innocent," she said with no hint of emotion.

"No," Pilar cried!

"He has acted honorably as a steward of Montenegro and a member of Aragon's nobility," Petronilla continued. Isabel closed her eyes as if doing so would make everything go away. "I declare Captain Lozano to be innocent. He has acted honorably as a member of Lord Barillos' guard. He has risked much in admitting what he knows to be the truth. The rest of you, to include Lady Isabel, are to be locked away in prison. There you will await an inquest by Bishop Delgardo Royo. May God have mercy on your souls. Take them away."

"How can you do this," Isabel cried? "You know what the truth is!" The soldiers of Petronilla laid hands on Isabel and Pilar as the heiress continued to make a plea for the Queen-Mother's integrity. "Aragon cannot afford to lose Montenegro," she implored. "Get off me," she shouted as the guards twisted her arms behind her back. "This is a mistake!"

"Silence you," one of the guards said as he put shackles over Isabel's wrists. He then dragged her unceremoniously toward the door. "This is because of my husband," Isabel shouted as realization dawned upon her! Petronilla did look at her then. The Queen-Mother's face was haunted with guilt for a split second before she concealed it.

"Take her away," Petronilla commanded. Isabel was dragged screaming back up to the prison tower. Her accusations fell on deaf ears as she was thrown into one of the cells. Pilar and the whore, Sara, were thrown in with her. The five of Barillos men were led into the other cell. There they willingly gave up their weapons before being locked inside. The prisoners were made to stand against the bars of their respective cells while Petronilla's soldiers removed their shackles. Once freed, they were left in the tower with no guard to watch over them.

Pilar sat with her back against the wall. She looked down at the floor with a lack of expression. Sara sat fearfully in the corner nearest the door. Isabel paced furiously to and fro across the stone floor. One of her passes brought her close to Sara and it was more than she could bear. "You stupid cow," Isabel shouted down at Manuel's forgotten whore!

"My lady," Sara began, but she was cut short by Isabel kicking her in the side of the head. Sara crumpled and put her arms up to shield her face.

"How dare you make up such miserable lies?" Isabel spat down at her.

"I have to do what Lord Barillos says," Sara pleaded. "He will kill me!"

"Shut your mouth," one of the guards in the other cell told Sara.

"Not if he is locked in prison you imbecile," Isabel shouted!

"Let her alone," Pilar cautioned.

"You foul woman," Isabel cursed. "I should pull your hair out piece by piece!"

"Let her alone," Pilar said more forcefully! Isabel snarled as she turned away from Sara and stalked over to where Little Grandma sat. She dropped down beside her and crossed her arms over her breasts. The heiress exhaled sharply as she stared up at the ceiling. This was to avoid having to see anyone. She was too angry to lay eyes upon them.

Petronilla and her retinue left for Zaragoza later that afternoon. There were no trumpets to signal their departure. Isabel wondered why they would leave so early. Was there not an inquest to be held? Her confusion was laid to rest that evening when Bishop Royo entered the prison tower. He was accompanied by two red robed acolytes. He had discarded his ceremonial finery for a plain black robe with red ties across the chest of it. He was also accompanied by two of Lord Barillos guards.

"What happened to that woman's face," Royo inquired as he gestured toward Sara. Sara put a hand up to cover the purple bruise that ran along the top of her left jaw line. "Why are these prisoners not guarded?" he demanded of one of Barillos men. There was a mumbled reply from the guard. Royo just shook his head. "Bring her to me," he commanded.

The two soldiers went to the door of the cell holding the women. One of the guards remained at the entry while the other went in to fetch Sara. The whore kept her eyes averted from Isabel, but she hurried to put the bars between them. Bishop Royo beckoned the soldiers with a wave of his hand and then departed with his acolytes. The soldiers followed, moving Sara along between them.

Sara did not return. The soldiers did. This time there were three of them. One stood guard while the other two escorted the male prisoners out of their cells one by one. They were all taken from the tower, presumably to speak with Bishop Royo as well. Eventually, Isabel and Little Grandma were the only prisoners left. They took the old woman next, leaving the heiress all by herself. When Pilar was brought back, her face was as white as a sheet! She looked at Isabel with terrified eyes as she was led to the cell that had been occupied by Isabel's rapists. Isabel wondered what had happened to scare Little Grandma so badly.

"Come to the bars," one of the guards told Isabel. She did so. They had her turn around so that they could replace the shackles over her wrists. The door was then opened and they led her to her mother's old sitting room. It was not as she remembered it. The couches were now soiled by spilled drink and God only knew what else.

"Place her on the couch there," Bishop Royo told them. The soldiers obeyed and propped Isabel up so that she could sit in relative comfort. On the table between the couches were a quill and a small inkpot. A wooden scroll case sat next to these. Royo sat across the table from Isabel. "Remove her bonds," he ordered. The soldiers did so as he gave them further commands. "Wait outside the door in case my lady needs to go back to her cell," he said. The soldiers bowed then and left the two of them alone in the dirty sitting room. Once the door swung shut, Bishop Royo began to speak once more. "I have no desire to hurt you, Lady Isabel," he said reassuringly.

"I see through you," Isabel replied. "You needn't pretend that you have my best interest at heart now that her majesty is gone. You were against me from the start."

"Oh good," Royo said mirthfully, "that will save us a great deal of time."

"So what do you want to ask of me," Isabel inquired sarcastically? "Have I consorted with a devil or made a deal with Belial? Do I have the mark? Have I ever flown aloft on a broom or turned someone into a toad? What could you honestly desire to know?" Bishop Royo laughed out loud. "At least one of us is amused," Isabel said acidly.

"I know you are not a witch," Royo chuckled. "I also know that you have never been possessed of a devil."

"Then why not release me?"

"That is what I intend to do," the bishop replied as his merriment died down. "Firstly, I need you to sign this," he said as he removed a rolled piece of parchment from out of the scroll case. He held it out to her.

"What is it?" Isabel asked apprehensively as she took the parchment.

"You can read, I trust?"

"I can," she replied as she unrolled the parchment. What was written there was not at all to her liking.

I, Lady Isabel of Montenegro, do hereby confess to having consorted with a devil. In the beginning, it deceived me. I believed that it was an angel of the Most High God. By the time I discovered its true nature, it was too late. I know that my womb has been tainted by evil. Any children I might bare could likewise be tainted. For this reason, I regretfully consent to an annulment between myself and Ramon Berenguer, the Count of Provence. I will spend the rest of my life atoning for my great sin. May God have mercy on my soul.

(There was a space left blank for her to sign before the letter was concluded.)

I have received this confession on the fourth day of the sixth month in the year of our Lord 1184 at Montenegro's Keep.

Delgardo Royo
Bishop of
Zaragoza

"This is a confession of guilt," Isabel said angrily.

"I knew you could read," Royo said with mock approval.

"It is a lie."

"Yes."

"You said that you believe me."

"I do."

"What sort of game are we playing?"

"Now you understand," Royo exclaimed! "You have but two options. This is one of them."

"What is the other," Isabel asked suspiciously?

"If you sign the confession," I will have you released into the care of Lord Vasquez."

"But by signing I agree to dissolve my marriage," Isabel said angrily. "I do not agree to this!"

"That is not really part of the choice."

"You cannot force me to sign," Isabel told him. "Even if you do… I will talk."

"I do not have to force you," Royo grinned. "If you will not sign the confession, I will conclude that you are but a wicked woman who is consumed by her lusts. The Holy Church will still approve of the dissolution of your marriage. The only difference is that I will leave you here at the mercy of Lord Barillos."

"You are a man of the cloth," Isabel said with disgust. "Have you not taken a vow to tell the truth before God?"

"God is only a story to keep the peasants in line," Royo replied. "Surely you know this."

"The vows I took with my husband are sacred," Isabel answered. "I will not break a promise before God so that Petronilla of Aragon can have her way!"

"You are making a terrible mistake," Bishop Royo said as he stood up from the couch where he had been sitting. He held his hand out to her. "May I have the confession back if you will not sign it?" Isabel dropped the parchment on the table. Royo leaned over and retrieved it. "Last chance," the bishop warned as he returned the confession to the wooden scroll case.

"Burn in hell," Isabel cursed him.

"I will consider it," Bishop Royo said with amusement, "but not yet." He clapped his hands together and shouted for the guards. Barillos' men rushed in and forced Isabel back into her manacles. "Take her away," the bishop shouted! "Her wickedness knows no bounds! She tries to persuade even me to commit fornication!"

"Move witch," the guard growled as he forced Isabel from the room.

"God will not forget you Delgardo," Isabel seethed!

"Depart from me, oh daughter of Babylon," the bishop shouted piously back at her! Then she was being hauled up the stairs to join Little Grandma in prison.

CHAPTER IX

By the time the door to the prison tower was closed once more, Isabel was in tears. "What happened down there?" Little Grandma asked.

"Bishop Royo was going to release us, but only if I would confess to witchcraft," Isabel cried.

"God knows you are innocent mija," Little Grandma said comfortingly.

"I should have lied," Isabel said sadly. "I could have told the truth once we were safe at my Uncle's cottage!" Pilar put an arm comfortingly around Isabel's shoulders.

"Do not blame yourself," the old woman told her. Petronilla, (may she burn in hell), is a liar. This is only because she does not want you married to her son."

"That must be why Papa was against it. I should have listened to him."

"How could you have, Isabel?"

"I suppose that you are right," Isabel agreed. They sat together without speaking for some time. Little Grandma hummed softly and stroked Isabel's hair. Though Isabel could not consciously remember the songs Pilar chose, they were the very same ones that the old woman had used to lull baby Isabel to sleep. The two women were still leaning against each other when Lord Barillos' guards entered the room.

"Come to the bars, Lady Isabel," the first guard said gruffly. The other came to stand next to their cell and held the manacles up in his hands.

"What is this about," Isabel wanted to know?

"You are to be returned to your bedroom," the first man explained. "I think that we should do this the easy way, no?"

"I will go," Isabel promised. She approached the bars and turned around. She held her hands back so that the guard could place the manacles over her wrists. She felt the cold steel on her flesh before the door to the cell was opened. The shackles were only attached to her right wrist, however.

"Face me," the second guard commanded as he came into her cell. Isabel did so. He quickly held her wrists together in front her body and snapped the manacles over the left wrist as well. He then attached a length of thick chain to the smaller chain that held the manacles together. Using the chain as a lead rope, he pulled Isabel from the tower and led her down to her room. He took her to her bed and unlocked the chain from her ankles. The chain, now holding only her wrists, he ran up over the top bar which connected the two posts at the foot.

"You do not have to chain me," Isabel said. "I will not run away."

"Lord Barillos commands it," the guard replied simply. He yanked down hard on the chain and Isabel gasped as her arms were wrenched upward. Such were her bonds that Isabel could only stand if on tiptoe. The guard wasted no time in wrapping the long chain around the bottom of the bed posts. The chain links formed a triangle with Isabel nearly hanging in the center of it.

"Let me down," Isabel shouted, but her captors only left the room. Her arms became sore quickly, especially around the shoulders. She discovered that if she knelt on the edge of the bed, than she could relax her arms or her legs, but not both at once. Every noise she heard from the hallway terrified her. She fearfully awaited her stepfather's punishment.

After what seemed like a very long time, Isabel heard the door to her bedroom open and then slam closed. "Give it to me," she heard Manuel demand of whoever had entered with him. "You have caused me a considerable amount of trouble," Manuel said. "You have been a very…bad…girl."

"You never told me that I was forbidden to write letters," Isabel replied. Her answer sounded ridiculous, even to her own ears.

"Yes," Manuel conceded, "so I suppose I shall let your Little Grandma live…this time. I am going to punish you instead."

"Thank you," Isabel forced herself to say. She had to be strong for Little Grandma's sake.

"We shall see how you feel about it when I am through," Manuel sneered. He jabbed the handle of a whip into Isabel's cheek. She could feel the pressure of it on the back of her jawbone. "You thought to take my position," he said threateningly. Isabel could feel her heart beating. She was afraid but she would not give her stepfather the satisfaction of knowing it. She did not gratify him with a response either. "You are nothing," Manuel sneered!

Isabel cringed as Barillos began to undo the laces on the back of her gown. His touch made her skin crawl. His hands were soft like a woman's. She could feel the edges of his fingernails scraping over her back as he worked furiously to uncover it. When finished, he grabbed hold of her hair and yanked her head back. "No one is ever going to come for you again," he breathed in her ear. His lips brushed against her earlobe as he spoke. His hot breath made the hairs on the back of her neck stand on end.

Isabel's head snapped down as Manuel released his hold on her blue-black hair. She could hear, (rather than see), him walking back toward the door. The footsteps stopped then. There was a loud crack as the whip landed on her exposed skin! The stinging pain forced her to arch even further. There was a fresh jolt of pain as she lost her footing and hung suspended by the chains for a moment. A tickling sensation began near her left shoulder blade as if there were something tiny crawling on her skin. If she could have looked, Isabel would have known that it was the trickle of her own blood.

Lord Barillos lashed out at her again and again until Isabel's back was covered in red stripes. She could not tell which was louder; the sound of her screams or the growling cries of exertion from her tormentor. Barillos finally came around the side of the bed until he stood inside her line of sight. He tossed the whip down on top of the royal blue blanket. She watched as the shadows around the whip deepened immediately. This was an illusion. The reality was that Isabel's blood was staining the fabric around the spot where the whip came to rest.

There was a fresh sheen of sweat on Manuel's brow and the gleam of excitement in his eyes. He withdrew a pair of sheers that he had stuck in his belt. He opened them wide so that the candle light reflected off the sharp edges. Barillos then walked down the side of the bed toward a struggling Isabel. "This will only hurt if you move," he chuckled.

Isabel twisted and threw herself about in her chains, but it was ultimately futile. Manuel cut up the side of each of her sleeves. Isabel's resistance resulted in several small cuts on the sides of each of her arms. After the sleeves were cut, the top of Isabel's dress fell down in ruins. Isabel struggled in vain as her breasts were exposed to the balmy air. Her back felt like it was on fire!

Lord Barillos stepped back to admire his handiwork. "This is what happens when you defy me," he said as he stared down at her. "Do it," he said coldly, but his eyes were looking beyond her.

"I have waited for another little piece of this," Captain Lozano said as his rough hands rode up the sides of Isabel's dress. It must have been he who had handed Manuel the whip.

"No," Isabel cried! She began to weep as the crooked toothed man pulled the skirt of her dress up to her waist. She struggled in her bonds but she knew it was a useless fight.

"Does my lord wish to leave," Lozano asked as he loosened his belt?

"Not this time," Manuel answered smugly. He crossed his arms and leered at Isabel as the captain rubbed his naked crotch all over her backside. Lozano pushed her forward until her knees were resting on top of the bed. He followed her onto the mattress to prevent her from moving away.

"You know what is coming, yes," the crooked toothed man asked lustfully? More revolting than Lozano's assault on her body was the look of complete perversity that covered the face of her stepfather. Isabel could sense Manuel's sickening desires as his eyes roamed over her breasts and drank in her agony like an irresistible wine. She cried out from the pain and revulsion that filled her. Below this was fear. The thought of Manuel doing the same to her as his captain did was terrifying! She felt that it would break something inside of her. Then she would never stop screaming.

They unshackled her wrists and let her broken body drop down onto the bed once the crooked toothed man was spent. Her feet were left in chains so that only the top half of her rested on the mattress. Fortunately, Barillos had been content merely to watch the horrible scene play out. It had been enough…this time.

Isabel wept into her pillow. She looked up again and again in fear that Lord Barillos might return. The door was open but her stepfather never came back that night. Isabel began to realize why the door had been left open during her previous torments. It had been done with the sole purpose of allowing Manuel to watch the atrocities unfold.

That night, Isabel prayed for her own death. It was a desperate prayer. At its core was a horrible realization. The heiress prayed for death because she knew that she would never take her own life. This was not from a fear of damnation. She could imagine no worse hell than this. Isabel was too afraid of how Manuel had promised to defile Pilar. This was what stood between her and suicide. The Lord would not answer her.

Barillos men unshackled Isabel's feet in the early hours of morning. Even the slightest of movements caused her pain. They carried her up to the prison tower and laid her unceremoniously on one of the filthy bedrolls inside Pilar's cell.

Isabel slipped in and out of consciousness. She vaguely remembered Little Grandma asking for a salve.

Isabel's head was feverish and her entire body was in some state of disrepair. She woke in darkness. The guards had pulled the other bedroll in from the cell they had kept her in before. Pilar was now sleeping upon it. A jar of salve that smelled like camphor rested next to the old woman's feet. Isabel cried when she saw Little Grandma's resting face. Here was someone who would take care of her to the end, even though it was Isabel's fault that they were in the awful predicament. She reached out a hand and rested it on Pilar's arm. Sleep finally came but it was not without dreaming.

"Kill him," said the cardinal that Isabel had met in the Basilica Del Pilar. He stared down at her with his scarred and empty eye sockets. In the dream, Isabel lay upon the ground with the cardinal crouched over her.

"I will not kill," Isabel sobbed. "I cannot."

"Do it in God's name," the cardinal growled. His canine teeth were long and sharpened. Blood filled his mouth and began to leak out after he was done speaking. Isabel cried out in horror and saw no more.

Isabel was left alone for several days while Little Grandma tended to her wounds. Worse than the physical ailments were the memories of what had happened. She felt guilty for having committed so many sins, mainly pride. If only she had lied her way to freedom. She and Little Grandma might then be safe. If only… If only she had listened to the disfigured cardinal! If she had killed Manuel, then her mother would still be alive. Priscilla would have born her father's son. What if the deformed clergyman had given her a command directly from God? These dark thoughts fed on themselves, like a snake devouring its own tail.

One morning, Isabel and Pilar were awakened at dawn by the sound of the prison door being thrown open. Captain Lozano entered. One of the younger soldiers came immediately behind. The younger man was struggling to carry a large wooden bucket filled with steaming water. For a moment, Isabel thought they might expect her to bathe with a sponge or something. Providing her with a bath was not the reason for the visit, however.

"Drop it there," Lozano ordered. The younger man nearly did drop the bucket as he lowered it to the floor. His strength ran out at the last few inches, causing some of the water to slop out. "Be careful," the crooked toothed man snapped!

"Yes sir," the young guard replied nervously. Captain Lozano then looked at Isabel with an amused expression playing on his face.

"You are to be released from your cell," the crooked toothed man said with a grin.

"There is no purpose to me bathing before being subjected to your filth," Isabel said angrily.

"Such a temper," Lozano laughed, "but I have not come to draw you a bath. The Queen-Mother has stripped you of your status."

"What?"

"You are now a peasant like me," the captain explained, "and since you are a peasant; it is the will of Lord Barillos that you be made to work like one."

"No, no, no," Little Grandma interjected. "Whatever it is that my Lord requires, let the burden rest upon me."

"How noble," Lozano sneered, "but my Lord insists that you are to remain here. Isabel will work."

"I am more accustomed to such work," Pilar insisted. "Do not subject my lady to this."

"Be at peace," Isabel told the old woman. "I have endured much greater humiliation than this."

"But...," Little Grandma began.

"It is nothing," Isabel assured her as she walked to the door of their cell.

"Good," Lozano said as he unlocked the door. "Today you will be washing floors. You can get hot water from the kitchen. Start with Lord Barillos' bed chamber and work your way down."

"I will," Isabel agreed. "Just let me go to my room and get some proper clothing."

"I suppose," Captain Lozano conceded. "Take that bucket to my Lord's chamber," he told the guard.

"Yes sir," the young man said regretfully. He picked up the handle of the bucket in both hands and hauled it off toward the stairs. Isabel left the tower and made her way down to her bedroom. The captain did not at all seem concerned that she should be going by herself. Why would he? She donned a plain white blouse and the brown pantalones that she used normally for the stables.

Isabel crossed the hallway and entered what had once been Lady Priscilla's bedroom. It was a relief to see that Lord Barillos was not present. The young guard had not bothered to wait for her. She would have only herself to move the heavy bucket. There were several dark cloths inside the hot water.

The Heiress of Montenegro removed one of the rags and squeezed the excess water back into the bucket. She could not do it all at once for the steaming water that hurt her fingers. After several tries, Isabel was satisfied. She moved from one section of the floor to the other, sopping up the dirt that had settled there. Her fingers grew pink from the hot water, but her hands were desensitized after a time. She focused herself on the work. It was oddly comforting because it allowed her to think about something other than her own misery.

The water in the bucket darkened every time Isabel put one of the rags back into it. By the time she was cleaning the floor next to the bed, the water had become opaque with the accumulated dust. She was down on her knees scrubbing when she found it. Isabel stretched her arms farther and farther in front of her until she was all but lying on the floor to clean below the bed. She caught sight of a white rag out of her peripheral vision. The rag was hidden far underneath. It was doubtful that anyone would find it, but Isabel had become dedicated to her chore. Cleaning her parents' room made her imagine that they would come back to it at any moment. Her father would wonder what she was doing. Her mother would be angry. *"What are you doing crawling all over the ground like a servant?"* Isabel could almost hear the voice of her mother.

Isabel had to lie all the way down in order to reach the rag below the bed. She was barely able to hook it with her middle finger. It was with considerable effort that she pressed her water-logged finger down on the cloth and dragged it toward her. Once the rag traveled closer, Isabel was able to grasp the fabric and pull it all the way out.

There was a tiny skeleton lying in the dust that had collected on top of the white cloth. Isabel blew away the dust. She coughed as some of the particles entered her nose and mouth. The skeleton was revealed to be some kind of rodent. There was a hole chewed in the center of the cloth. Isabel picked up the white cloth and held it close to her face so that she might get a better look at the bones. She looked at each bone of the rat's tiny leg with a morbid curiosity. Moving her gaze to the head, she noticed that the rat's front teeth were long and curved down over its lower jaw.

Isabel caught her breath as she looked up at the top of the rodent's skull. Down the center of its face was a hairline crack. This crack no doubt came from a grievous injury, a cat's claw perhaps. It would have assuredly left a scar. This was the same rat Isabel had seen under the bed the night of her mother's death.

Isabel lowered the cloth down and let the rat skeleton tumble off onto the floor. She could then see something else about the cloth that demanded her attention. The fabric around the hole was discolored yellow. Her first thought was that the rat had relieved itself, but that did not seem quite right. She brought the cloth back up to her nose and inhaled deeply. The fabric around the hole did not smell like blood or urine as would be expected. It was a bitter odor that reminded Isabel of crushed almonds.

"Oh my God," Isabel cried! The rag dropped from her hand and settled over the rat skeleton like a burial shroud. The cloth had somehow caused the death of the rat, but the animal was not its only casualty. It was poisoned. That much was certain. Isabel thought back to her mother's last day living. Had not Lord Barillos been cleaning her face with a wet cloth when Isabel had first entered the room? He had not been concerned about her mother having a fever. He had been trying to remove the smell of the poison from her face.

Isabel worked like the Devil. In her mind, the dirt was her stepfather. With the wet cloth, she was trying to remove the stain of him from Montenegro. Her sorrow for the death of her mother became a bitter hatred that settled upon her heart like a stone.

By late afternoon, Isabel had worked her way down to the dining hall. Her knuckles were raw and her fingers were water-logged and tender. She was about a third of the way done with the room when Lord Barillos came in. He was accompanied by two of his guardsmen. Manuel seated himself at the head of her father's table and rang a small silver bell. The guards stood watch along the wall behind him. Isabel looked away. She could not bare the sight of him!

"You did a splendid job upstairs," Lord Barillos complimented her. Isabel moved her entire body so that her back was to him as she cleaned the floor. "I should have had you on your knees weeks ago," Manuel quipped. Isabel scrubbed harder. One of her knuckles started to bleed from the abuse.

"I wish you would die," Isabel whispered to herself. Then she set into the floor with a vengeance. She watched as the work aggravated the cut on her knuckle and made it bleed all the more.

"I have news for you," Barillos said through a mouthful of food. "A letter came from the Queen-Mother." Isabel paused in her work but did not get up from her hands and knees, nor did she look back at him. "To Lord Manuel Barillos, and so on and so forth," he began. She could hear the rustle of parchment in his hands. "I must express my deepest sorrow for the loss of your wife, Lady Priscilla, and the shame now brought upon you by your daughter. Please inform Isabel that she has been stripped of title and that her marriage to my son has been declared void by the Holy

Church. I will spare you any further humiliation by not requiring either of you to be present for the annulment."

The world seemed to grow very small as Isabel listened to her stepfather reading Petronilla's letter. "I have sent word of Isabel's wickedness to my son in Genoa. Her betrayal cut him to the quick." Isabel closed her eyes and tried to keep her body from shaking as grief washed through her. "Count Berenguer has agreed to the annulment, though his duty to Aragon prevents him from being present. By the time you read this letter, the declaration will have already been made in front of the cardinals and the Bishop of Aragon," Barillos read. Isabel trembled uncontrollably as her step father read the letter of her ruin.

"If you have no further use for her," Manuel continued smugly, "I would encourage you to send her to the Convent of the Angels in Pamplona. That would be the best place for one such as she." Manuel walked over to the place where Isabel was crouched as he read. "You wouldn't be interested in the rest of it," he told her. "She apologizes for my troubles and assures me that I will find another bride one day. Is that not kind of her?"

Isabel would not speak. It was all she could do not to rise up and attack him like a rabid animal! Barillos paused several feet behind her. "I do not think you would want to live in a convent," Manuel said. "Perhaps you might consider me as a future husband?" Isabel clenched her hand around the rag until she could feel her nails digging into flesh.

"I should sooner die," Isabel replied hatefully.

"No other nobleman will have you," Manuel explained. "I am your only hope."

"I have work to do," Isabel said tersely. She then began to scrub the floor furiously.

"Oh calm down Isabel," Manuel chuckled. "I do not want to marry you!" Isabel scrubbed harder. "I do not need to marry you." There was an odd note to the man's voice as he said this last. "Men," Manuel said as he motioned his guards over with one finger. Isabel saw the boots of one of the men walking around the tables to get to her location. The second guard was circling around the other way. Before she could react, her step father grabbed tightly on to her hips and knelt quickly between her legs. He pressed the bulge of his trousers roughly into the seat of her pantalones.

Isabel lost her balance. She shrieked loudly as her shoulder dropped onto the stone floor. Manuel lost his grip as she rolled over onto her back. As her body turned, Isabel brought up her right foot and kicked Lord Barillos in the mouth with the back of her heel! There was a very satisfying 'thud' as Manuel's head was rocked to the side.

There was no time to survey her handiwork. Isabel knew that if she continued to fight Lord Barillos, then she would soon be overpowered by his guards. That meant that she would be shackled and that meant that she would have his filth inside her. She had reached her breaking point. "Get her," Lord Barillos shouted as Isabel scrambled toward the door. He got up off his knees while the two guards gave chase.

Isabel ran out of the room and down the corridor toward the entry hall. She could hear the sound of boots pounding down the stairs from the archway on her left. She kept running. Isabel paused in the center of the chamber, unsure of where she should flee. Lord Barillos and his men were in hot pursuit from the west. She turned toward the east hall but saw four men running toward her from it.

Having no other choice, Isabel ran into the courtyard. The drawbridge was down. The way to the stables was clear. Isabel briefly wondered if she might have time to hide in the carriage house or the hayloft before she was discovered. "Stop," Manuel shouted as Isabel struggled to make up her mind. She looked fearfully back over one shoulder. Manuel was standing in the entryway to the keep while his guards slowly advanced.

"Isabel," Pilar yelled down from the prison tower, "get to the stables and get out of here!"

"Shut your mouth old woman," Barillos barked! "Get back inside," he roared at Isabel, "lest you be responsible for her death!"

Isabel was defeated "I will come back," she sobbed wretchedly.

"That's a girl," Manuel said triumphantly. His guards were getting ever closer.

"Go Isabel," Little Grandma shrieked!

"I cannot," Isabel wept. "You do not understand what he will do to you."

"I will make it slow," Barillos promised with a sneer. Little Grandma was standing by the tower opening facing the courtyard. Isabel could see the old woman closing her eyes and making the sign of the cross.

"Isabel," Pilar shouted as she opened her eyes. Isabel looked up at her. "I love you!"

"I love you too," Isabel cried. She knew that the guards would have her in just a few short moments. Then her stepfather would take everything. Pilar forced a smile and backed up into the shadows of the tower.

"God forgive me," Little Grandma screamed as she cast herself over the edge! Isabel watched in horror as the old woman plummeted head first toward the cobblestones. There was an audible crack as her head made impact with them. Her body flopped down after so that her feet were splayed out toward Isabel. Blood covered the top of the old woman's forehead and leaked down over her face. Little Grandma made two short gagging sounds, her chest hitched and then she breathed no more. Isabel's wailing scream echoed into the gorge surrounding Montenegro's Keep.

The guards had paused in disbelief. "Do not let her escape," Manuel shouted at last! Isabel ran. She felt the pressure on her blouse as one of the guards grabbed at her sleeve. She tore out of his grasp and bolted toward the entrance to her father's private stables. Panicked and disoriented, Isabel ran blindly inside. The sounds of the boots behind her drove her to run ever faster. She practically fell into the wooden posts that bordered the stall at end of the stable. This was where they kept Santiago. Isabel ducked quickly through the rails.

Santiago whinnied loudly and backed up several steps at the sudden intrusion. Manuel's two guards were standing several feet away from the rails. One of them had put a hand on his sword. Isabel looked up at her father's horse and saw that he was looking at her also. His eyes were wide and spooked. "Do not hurt me Santiago," Isabel said softly. Her voice was shaking.

Barillos and several more of his men had gathered around the entrance to the stables. "Get her out of there," Manuel said angrily! "I do not pay you for nothing!" Santiago looked at Isabel for several more seconds before making a nickering sound with his nostrils. He looked then out at her assailants. He stomped his hoof against one of the rails and it left a circular indentation in the surface of the wood.

A terrible calm came over the Heiress of Montenegro as she realized what course she would take. Isabel undid the latch on Santiago's stall and pushed the gate out wide. There was a creak as the hinge swung out. The barrier between the warhorse and the guardsmen was eliminated. "Stay back," Isabel warned them. The guards seemed to actually heed her warning. The one drew his sword, but both began back-stepping toward the exit. Santiago's nostrils flared and his eyes seemed to rivet themselves upon the man who had drawn steel.

Using the side rails of the stalls for a leg up, Isabel mounted the massive stallion and held on tight to his thick black mane. She was not accustomed to riding without a saddle, much less a horse of his size. The situation left her no choice. It certainly helped that she was wearing pantalones instead of a skirt, however. "We are leaving now," Isabel said loudly. The other guard drew his sword also and held it out before him with trembling fingers.

"What are you idiots waiting for," Manuel shouted? "Do as I command!" Isabel could feel the horse's muscles tensing below her.

"Ha," Isabel said softly as she tapped the heels of her bare feet on the horse's flanks. Santiago took two steps forward and then bolted toward the man who had first drawn his sword. The horse reared up on his hind legs without making a sound. The guardsman tried to draw back his arm in order to strike at the beast, but he was not quick enough. Isabel dug in with her knees and held on for dear life as Santiago brought one massive hoof down on top of the man's head! The skull shattered inward before the guard could even scream.

As soon as the warhorse was down on all fours again, he whirled around and kicked backward with both legs. Isabel had to lean back to avoid being thrown. One of the horse's hooves missed its mark, but the other struck Barillos' man squarely in the chest. There was a crunch of bone before the guard was knocked into the air. The man landed in a sitting position. His spine slammed hard into the wooden rails of the stall behind him. One rail struck his lower back and the other impacted on the back of his neck. The man's head lolled to one side, though his eyes were still open and fearful. "I…I cannot move," he said desperately. The sword lay useless on the ground beside him, much like the fresh corpse of his fellow guard.

The men around Lord Barillos stared at their murdered fellows with wide eyes and jaws hanging down. Manuel looked more fearful than any of them. Santiago pranced around to face the guard who had meant to attack him from behind. "Oh no," the paralyzed man moaned, "no-no-no!" Santiago whinnied loudly and made a quick burst forward. Isabel lost her hold on the horse's flanks and had to drop off as he reared up once more. The warhorse struck down at the guard's exposed throat with an already blood-soaked hoof. The sharp, iron-shod edge ripped a half moon-shaped opening from one side of the man's neck to the other! Blood gushed down from the man's crushed esophagus and onto the collar of his shirt. Isabel could see his broken spine sticking up out of the wound.

The young woman wasted no time in grabbing her father's saddle from the hook on the wall. The saddle blanket was nowhere to be found, but the bit and bridle were hanging close by. Santiago back-stepped toward the wall and placed his enormous body protectively in front of Isabel.

"Kill it," Lord Barillos screeched! His men drew their swords and began to advance with tentative steps. Here was something they would not be able to intimidate. Isabel threw the saddle over the horse's broad back and tightened up the strap as quickly as she could.

"Stay out of our way," Isabel said menacingly. The men paused and looked nervously at each other, at Santiago, and then back at the man who would send them to their deaths. The grey warhorse dipped his head so that Isabel could more easily put the reins on him. He flared his nostrils and looked eagerly out at the rest of the men who would dare to stand against him.

"Do as I have ordered you!" Manuel shouted in a high pitched voice. "I will have the heads of the cowards among you!" Isabel led Santiago over to the dead man that the warhorse had broken on the rails. His gaping neck wound was already attracting flies. She felt a wave of nausea, but steadied herself on the animal's flank. The soldiers had resumed their slow and fearful advance.

Isabel picked up the sword that had fallen from the dead man's hand. It felt heavy and terrible in her hands. An image of her father came to her mind. He was sitting on Priscilla's deathbed with his forearm held up and his hand clenched in his fist. *"You are Montenegro,"* said the voice of memory. Isabel grabbed hold of the back of the saddle and the sword with one hand. She put her bare foot in the stirrup and grabbed the saddle horn. Quickly hoisting herself up, she held the long sword in one hand and the reins in the other. The warhorse stomped at the stable floor and flared his nostrils in anticipation.

"You will never make it out of here Isabel," Manuel threatened. "Get down from that horse or I will make it much worse for you. Do it now!" Isabel stared at him with a cold hatred gleaming in her eyes.

"After all you have done Manuel," she said condescendingly, "death would only be a favor to me."

"You are about to get your wish," he retorted.

"No," Isabel corrected him, "not today." She pointed the sword toward her stepfather and spoke in a loud voice. "Let no enemy of Montenegro draw breath on my father's land." One of the younger men was trembling as his gaze traveled between the two corpses and the massive grey stallion between them.

"I give up," the youngest guard decided out loud. He dropped his sword and turned to flee.

"Ha," Isabel shouted! She dug in with her heels and slapped Santiago's left flank with the reins. The horse had little need for encouragement. He burst forward like a coiled spring! Isabel swung down with the sword at the first man who approached on her right side. The guard quickly brought his own blade up to parry, but overshot his mark. The arc of Isabel's blade went low and sliced through the flesh of the first man's wrist. There was a loud clang as the bleeding man's sword hit the floor. His newly opened wrist clung to the rest of his arm by a thread and he cried out in shock and pain.

Santiago nearly crushed Isabel's leg as his form hugged the wall. She had to bring her sword in close as the warhorse charged toward the second enemy. He trampled over the man and left a bloody mess in his wake! Lord Barillos screamed and made a break for the safety of the keep. As fast as his legs pistonned beneath him, Manuel could not outrun a horse. Santiago leaned forward and broke into a full gallop. "Ha," Isabel screamed once more as she spurred the warhorse on. Manuel zigzagged to the left at the last second. This put him on the side of the horse opposite from Isabel's sword. As Santiago's head came forward of the fleeing lord, he leaned over and bit savagely into the man's shoulder. Manuel cried out as he was lifted off the ground by the horse's powerful jaws. Lord Barillos' legs bicycled uselessly before Santiago tossed him aside. A huge gobbet of flesh was ripped off in the horse's teeth as he flung the man away.

Manuel dropped to the ground with an agonized cry. Blood flowed freely from the open wound. The man's bones were visible through the blood and meat. "Help," Manuel cried out! Santiago's momentum carried him forward. Several archers were running out onto the battlements. Isabel could also see one of Barillos' men working the crank close to the front gate. Her step father stood with difficulty and then limped quickly toward the door of the keep. One hand held the opposite arm just below the open wound as if the entire appendage might fall at any minute.

Santiago started toward Manuel, but Isabel quickly redirected him toward the drawbridge. There was no time for revenge. "Ha," she cried out! Santiago thundered toward the only escape route. Isabel quickly switched the reins into her right hand and transferred the long sword into her left. "Go," she screamed as the gate began to rise up.

She could have tried for a daring leap over the gorge, but Isabel found that there was a much more practical solution. She held the sword out straight as Santiago charged forth. Barillos' guard was still desperately trying to raise the gate when Isabel buried the long sword into his back! The weapon was wrenched from her grasp as she and the warhorse sped past.

The drawbridge fell down with a crash as it impacted the stone bridge that crossed over of the gorge. Isabel took Santiago's reins in both hands and spurred him on to a run. His hooves thundered down the trail toward Black River Village. The young woman had never felt so alive as the wind of freedom washed over her.

Part III

Suffering

CHAPTER I

Isabel did not look back as Santiago galloped swiftly through the village and out to the main road that led south out of Montenegro. If she had looked, she would have seen the cloud of dust that meant she was being pursued. Fortunately, there was someone to see it for her. There was an older woman in a plain brown dress that stood by the steps of the church. She had one hand up to shield her eyes from the sun as she looked up toward the keep. "They are coming my lady," the old woman shouted as Isabel rode past!

Isabel did not look back but changed her course toward the river. She rode down past the shipping warehouse and plunged her horse into the water. She quickly discovered that Black River was too deep to cross even on horseback. She dismounted to relieve some of the weight on Santiago and then swam back toward shore. With the reins, she led the horse toward shore as well. Together, they rode swiftly down the river.

The stallion's legs kicked up water as he charged forward. Isabel threw several glances back over her shoulder but her enemies never appeared. She slowed her pace once she had gone around the ledge of Lover's Rock. Even beyond the rock, she kept to the shallows by the riverbank. She did not want to leave a trail for her pursuers.

In little time, Isabel came to the river bend. She could see the tattered sails of a boat sticking up out of the forest beyond the opposite bank. As she came closer, she could see that the vessel had gone to ground between two trees. She could not imagine how fast the boat had been going to penetrate so far into the woods. She guessed from the weather-beaten look of the hull that it had been there for some time. Tree branches were beginning to form a canopy over the deck which was now overgrown with moss.

She had not heard anyone giving chase. So it was that Isabel reasoned she had run long enough. She brought Santiago up to the grassy shore just past the bend in the river. She got down onto the bank and led her horse back to the running water. Santiago dipped his head and began to drink. Isabel squatted down and brought handfuls of water up to her lips as she looked up river for any signs of danger. This was not something her father had taught, but rather a lesson learned from reading scripture. When Gideon brought the children of Israel down to the river to drink, God had him divide them into two groups. Those who lapped the water like dogs were considered unfit to serve in the army. Those who knelt down and brought the water up with their hands were considered more able. (Judges 7:5) Isabel did not want to be surprised in such a vulnerable position. When she had drunk her fill, she remounted the grey stallion and traveled slowly downriver.

As the sun began sinking low over the trees, Isabel's stomach reminded her that she had more problems than just avoiding capture. She didn't know the first thing about surviving in the wild. She kept looking hopefully into the woods as if something recognizable as food would conveniently present itself.

When darkness fell, Isabel brought Santiago up into the shelter of the trees. She dismounted and removed the saddle from off his back. The night was warm and balmy. Her undergarments were still damp in places from her earlier swim. It was fortunate that the sun had dried her outer clothing already. Isabel stripped down while the stallion grazed contentedly on wild grass. "You like it better out here," Isabel asked? Santiago made a wuffling sound and continued to munch on the wet shoots that grew by the bank of the river. "Me too" Isabel sighed. She put her blouse and pantalones back on and hung her damp undergarments over a tree branch.

She lay down in the grass further up from the bank where the earth was not quite so moist. She used the side of her saddle for a pillow. It wasn't exactly comfortable, but it kept her head up out of the dirt. The moon was partially obscured behind two grey clouds. It seemed to stare down at her with a half formed face. The call of an owl echoed from somewhere in the trees.

Isabel was not afraid to sleep in the woods. She imagined that the presence of her father's warhorse had much to do with that. Nevertheless, it was some time before she was finally able to sleep. She had been running on pure adrenaline, but now the weight of the day's events sunk down upon her.

Little Grandma was dead. She would never be able to erase the bloody memory from her mind. She prayed for God's mercy. Surely, he would have compassion for what the old woman had done. Could such a selfless act still be considered a mortal sin? She made a thousand excuses in her mind, but the Holy Church's position on suicide was simple. Isabel began to cry silently as she looked up into the night sky. Little Grandma was in Hell. She had sacrificed everything for Isabel…even her soul.

The dew that formed in the grass made Isabel's clothing wet and uncomfortable by morning. The back of her blouse and pantalones were soaked and the sides were damp. There was an ache in her stomach and her head felt thick with sleep. She rubbed her eyes and stood up. There was a large, red mosquito bite on her ankle and several more on her forearms.

Isabel looked frantically around for her father's horse, but he was nowhere to be seen. "Santiago," Isabel called out nervously. "Hello…Santiago…" A nickering sound came out of the trees. Isabel walked in the direction of the noise until she saw the stallion with his head lowered to the grass. He looked up and raised his ears as she came closer. Once they made eye contact, Santiago went right back to grazing. "I guess I should have tied you up," Isabel said out loud. She wondered if she could tie a knot that would hold the massive beast. There was no lead rope attached to his reins. In any case, she was glad that the horse had not run off.

Her stomach ached, but there was pain far worse that Isabel had already endured in Montenegro. She traveled downstream until there was no more daylight. She had stopped several times for food and water, but only Santiago was able to eat anything. Isabel was very hungry by the time she bedded down that night. Her stomach audibly expressed its displeasure.

Isabel slept with her head higher up on the saddle. It would not improve her comfort level, but she hoped that she would not be so wet in the morning. She decided not to tie Santiago up by his reins. Were she to succeed in securing him to the wood, than he would not be able to protect her if she were attacked in the night. In that case; the best she could hope for would be that her knots did not work, making the entire exercise pointless.

By the morning of the third day, Isabel was starving. She felt worse waking up than she had going to bed. It was as if she had barely slept at all. Nevertheless, she saddled Santiago and continued her journey. Black River fed into the Ebro. Here, Isabel turned toward the west and continued.

By late afternoon, she could see the tallest buildings of Huesca looming over the trees. She was famished and the sight of civilization was most welcome. She spurred Santiago into a canter, but quickly halted the horse as the docks and sailing ships of the city came into view. This would be the first place Manuel's men would search for her. Entering the city would attract attention. Many of Lord Barillos' friends would be inside. No matter how much food might be available, Isabel had no money. Huesca was not the place to look for charity.

Instead of continuing down toward the docks, Isabel backtracked until she felt it was safe. She led Santiago into the forest and made her way to the main road. She could hear the sounds of traffic as she came closer to it: the creaking of wheels, the crack of a whip, and the grumbling of the travelers. "Woe," Isabel said softly. Santiago stopped. His ears were pricked up as he looked in the direction of the road. Though the pangs of hunger were unbearable, Isabel decided she must wait until dark. She did not want to expose herself by crossing the road. So it was that she waited in the dense underbrush with only her horse and some hungry mosquitoes for company.

The plants around her had jagged edges and prickers which made silence even more of an effort. Isabel looked down at these plants with frustration. That was when she really noticed them. She was standing in the midst of a huge blackberry patch. Santiago looked back at her with what she fancied was a disapproving stare.

Isabel was very quiet as she moved from one spot to another. In each place that she hunkered down, the young woman quickly and voraciously devoured every small piece of fruit she could lay her hands on! She was so hungry that she failed to give thanks to God until after her belly was full. The stuffy feeling in her head lifted, but her fingernails were stained purple from feasting.

Isabel had to return to the river to relieve herself, but there was plenty of time left in the day. She used her undergarment to form a crude bundle which she filled with berries. There were stains forming on the cloth where the juice leaked through, but that hardly mattered. She waited until dusk gave way to darkness. The noise of the travelers on the road to Huesca had given way to the sounds of the forest at night: the hoot of an owl, the howling of wolves in the distance, and the ever present whine of the insects. Isabel rode forward and out of the dark forest. The two fugitives were illuminated by the moon's glow for several seconds before being swallowed by the trees on the opposite side of the path. They did not stop until Isabel felt that they were far enough away to avoid notice.

Isabel woke up the next morning in a foul state. Whatever she had slept in had not been kind to her skin. Her flesh was red and itchy. She started to scratch her arm, but that only made it worse when she stopped. Using a church tower for reference, Isabel circumvented the city of Huesca and finally made it back to the River Ebro on the opposite side. Santiago drank deeply from the flowing water as she removed his saddle. Isabel undressed and lowered herself down into the river. The water was cool and soothing to her irritated flesh. She remained in the currents for some time while Santiago grazed along the bank. Isabel sunk below the surface of the water and closed her eyes. Being submerged below the surface of the river was very relaxing. All sound was drowned out and the world seemed very far away.

Isabel spat out a small amount of water and inhaled deeply as she came up for breath. She would have happily gone back under except that she saw eyes watching her from the forest. The shape of a grey wolf materialized out of the trees. Santiago had already noticed the intruder. He was standing at attention with his backside facing the water.

A second wolf came to stand beside the first and a third appeared farther down the bank. Santiago reared up and whinnied loudly before stomping his feet down hard onto the mossy earth. The wolves did not retreat. The first two advanced on the grey warhorse's left flank while the last wolf crept up from the right. The wolves snarled and barked menacingly while the horse turned frantically back and forth. He seemed to be trying to face all three of them at once.

As the wolves closed in, Isabel swam quickly toward the shore. She stood waist deep in the water when next she came up for air. The wolves were stalking ever nearer to her father's stallion. Their heads were held low and their teeth were barred. Santiago faced the two wolves with an occasional glance back at the one by itself. His nostrils flared and his eyes were wide with fear.

Isabel splashed noisily in the water as she ran toward her companion. "Get out of here," she shouted. The wolves took notice of the newcomer. Their hackles were raised and they growled at her. One made several snapping motions with his teeth. Isabel's heart was pounding. She briefly imagined what it would be like to be eaten alive. Would it be quick? She suspected that it would not. One of the hungry beasts might lockjaw around her throat, slowly closing the air off to her lungs and draining out her blood. The other two might busy themselves with ripping open her stomach and devouring her insides.

Swallowing her fear, Isabel bent down and grabbed a smooth, fist-sized stone from beneath the water around her feet. She heaved the rock with all her might at the wolf that was creeping up on Santiago from behind. The rock struck the wolf broadside just behind its shoulder. The beast snarled and turned its attention toward the girl in the water. Isabel grabbed another stone and threw it hard. It bounced off the side of the animal's forehead and left a small cut behind. The wolf yelped and bolted toward the safety of the trees. Isabel hurled another rock into its hindquarters as it ran off into the forest.

Santiago suddenly charged toward the remaining wolves. He held his head low to the ground with his lips curled back. One of the wolves turned tail and ran. The other bounded off to the right and then leapt at the side of the stallion's neck. Santiago wheeled around in time to slam the side of his head into that of his attacker. No sooner had the wolf landed, than Santiago sank his teeth into one of the beast's hind legs. The wolf cried out sharply as bone snapped and the warhorse launched him into the air. The other wolves circled around to help their fallen comrade, but must have thought better of it. As they looked on, Santiago pounded the fallen wolf into a blood-soaked mass of fur and bone on the riverbank!

Isabel continued to shout and throw rocks, but the other two wolves had had enough. They disappeared into the forest. Santiago continued to mangle the fallen wolf long after it had drawn its last breath. "That is enough Santiago," Isabel said loudly. The horse ignored her command and continued to pummel the corpse until he was satisfied. Once the stallion had calmed down, Isabel saddled him and continued her journey south. She would be more comfortable when the dead wolf was far behind them.

It was still two days journey to the Summer Cottage. However badly she wanted to gorge herself on the berries she had collected, Isabel only ate a few at a time. She did not eat enough to remove the hunger that ached within her. She drank large amounts of water in attempt to trick her stomach for short periods of time.

On the last day of her journey, Isabel was famished! She laid her head on Santiago's neck, only lifting it occasionally to make sure they were still headed downstream. So it was that she passed by her destination. It did not dawn on her until she could see the Basilica del Pilar in the distance.

The refugee from Montenegro was only steps away from the stone bridge that would lead her to safety when she heard the thundering of many hooves. This sound was known to Isabel and it jolted her fatigued body into vigilance. Her mind began to panic as she imagined a detachment of riders from Montenegro. They would surely take her back to a hell which she had become intimately familiar. "Ha," Isabel shouted weakly. Santiago began to trot forward. She dug her heels into his sides and the horse's pace increased to a canter. This quickly became a run. "Go faster," Isabel said desperately, but Santiago did not run fast enough.

As the horses charged past them, Isabel realized they were without riders. It was a beautiful sight and Isabel began to laugh as her fear melted away. She had to pull hard on the reins to prevent Santiago from following the mustangs that dashed along the river bank. The herd whinnied and nickered to each other, kicking up river water as they went.

"Woe…woe," Isabel said. Santiago finally halted. His ears were perked up and his eyes were fixated on the herd. He nickered and stomped one hoof into the dirt. "You want to go with them," Isabel said with realization. She almost lost her balance dismounting. Her body was weak with hunger. With effort, she undid the buckles on the saddle and let it fall off. She did the same with the harness. Part of Isabel told her not to be so foolish. She would need a horse to complete her journey to the cottage. This was overridden by the deep longing that she sensed in the warhorse. This was where he belonged. "Go," she told him. Santiago looked back at Isabel with uncertainty. "Go Santiago," she sad more forcefully. The horse tossed his head. "Ha," Isabel screamed as she slapped his broad side with one hand.

Santiago charged forth. In no time at all, he had overtaken the herd. The broad shouldered stallion was soon lost to Isabel's sight. Eventually, only a thin cloud of dust remained to mark the horse's passing. "You are free Santiago," Isabel said. Tears mixed of joy and sorrow fell down. She could not save Little Grandma, but at least Santiago would not die trying to protect her.

Isabel made her way back to the bridge and walked slowly across on her bare feet. She clung to the side for support. Her journey could not end tonight. She would have to wait until morning to complete the trek to the cottage. Tonight, she hoped to find mercy from the church.

The end of the stone bridge on the Zaragoza side was lit by many torches. There were several of the city's guards gathered around the landing. She could not hear what they were saying to each other until she drew closer. "Who goes," one of the soldiers called out?

"It is only I," Isabel called back. Her mind was thin with hunger and it did not occur to her that the answer was insufficient.

"It is a woman," one of the other guards told the first.

"What business does she have outside the city in the middle of the night," asked the first?

"Come here woman," the second guard commanded.

"I seek refuge," Isabel said at last.

"Where are you coming from," the first man asked?

"From Huesca," Isabel half-lied. "Please… I have had almost nothing to eat in a week's time. Help me to the church…I beg of you." The guardsmen looked at each other and then nodded their unspoken decision.

"Lean on me," the first guard offered as they came to her. Isabel almost collapsed as she did so. She was faint with hunger. She could not remember much of that first night.

The two soldiers had taken her to the basilica. She was handed over to a stalwart woman in the black and white habit of a nun. This woman helped her into the back of a cart and from there into a simple complex of buildings outside the city. Several other nuns had joined the first as she helped Isabel to sit down at a wooden table. They brought her a hunk of bread and a warm bowl of luke-warm porridge. It was probably left over from their evening meal. Isabel ate ravenously.

After the food, the sisters took Isabel's clothing. She remembered the feel of the sponge and the warm water on her skin, but little more. It was, therefore, a complete surprise to Isabel when she awakened in a simple straw bed with clean white linens.

The night gown that covered Isabel's body was soft from wear. She could not remember having had it put on. She felt blessedly full however. Though Isabel was the only one in bed, the chamber she awakened in was filled with them. The beds were all neatly made and had a trunk sitting at the foot of each one. "So here you are awake," said a woman's voice from close by. Startled, Isabel quickly turned her head. There was an older woman with grey hair and dark eyes working the floor of the sleeping hall with a worn out broom. Her back was stooped over her work and her fingers were curled with arthritis.

"Where am I," Isabel asked? "Why is there no one else here?"

"The sun came up long before you did," the old woman explained. "The other sisters are busy elsewhere."

"What is this place?"

"You are inside a convent. We are the Sisters of Santa Maria del Pilar."

"Thank you for your generous hospitality sister," Isabel said gratefully.

"Thank God," the old nun shrugged. "I am Sister Genevieve, but you can just call me Veva."

"Sister Veva," Isabel repeated.

"Yes," Veva replied, "now get you out of bed."

"May I have my clothes," Isabel said meekly.

"There are clothes in the trunk at the foot of the bed," Veva said as she began sweeping again.

"Thank you," Isabel replied. She rose and walked around to where the wooden trunk sat. She opened it easily and found a plain black dress inside. "Will you...help me to put it on," Isabel asked uncomfortably when Veva made no move to assist her. The heiress was not used to dressing herself. That had been Little Grandma's duty.

"I have work to do," Veva snorted.

"Alright," Isabel said with uncertainty.

"Just pull it over your head girl," the woman sighed. Isabel put the dress on backwards the first time, but managed to get it right on her second try. She was about to close up the trunk when Veva stopped her. "Cover your head," the elder woman said curtly. "This is the House of God."

"Forgive me," Isabel said with confusion.

"Here," Veva said as she pulled out a white cloth head covering from the trunk. She put the scapula over Isabel's head and then loosened her dress so that she could tuck in the rest of the white material which extended down over her bosom. Once done, Veva tightened the dress and pulled up the black hood. She looked critically at the finished product. "That is good," the old woman decided.

Isabel closed up the trunk and looked expectantly at Sister Veva for direction. "Follow me," the old woman sighed. She left the room and Isabel followed. She was led down a narrow hallway filled with unmarked wooden doors. Sister Veva stopped abruptly and knocked on one of the doors. "Come in," said the voice of a woman from the other side. Veva held the door while Isabel entered in.

The Mother Superior's attire was much like the others. The only difference was the white frock that covered her shoulders and a wooden cross that hung on a chain from her neck. She was sitting at the head of a large table. There was a leather-bound book open before her. The pages contained a list of names and dates. Beside this was a quill resting beside a stoppered bottle of ink.

"I was told you were seeking refuge," the woman said.

"Well yes," Isabel replied timidly. "I suppose that I am."

"Who are you?"

"I am...I was Lady Isabel of Montenegro."

"Speak more simply," the mother superior said. She looked up from the book and revealed a face that was wrinkled with age. It was obvious that she was once beautiful. To Isabel, she looked like the image of a saint.

"I was stripped of title," Isabel said. "The church annulled my marriage to the Count of Provence, but it is all a terrible mistake!"

"That will be enough," the mother superior said. "I know who you are now."

"I just want to be on my way," Isabel said nervously. "I am bound for my Uncle's estate north of the city."

"I will give you leave if you insist," the aged woman replied," but I strongly urge you to remain here with us."

"But..."

"Servants of Lord Barillos have already been here asking after your whereabouts," the Mother Superior said. "You came here seeking refuge. I can assure you that none will touch you within these walls."

"What if they come again," Isabel asked with fear?

"Men are not allowed here," the old woman explained. "I have no desire to give you over to them."

"Why would you not?"

"They told me that you had run away because Lord Barillos would not let you run free with the men of Montenegro."

"I would never!"

"I know," the aged woman interrupted. "The reason I know is in the manner of your arrival. A real strumpet might have traveled to Huesca at the most. She would not have endured starvation in order to come here. Also, what more senseless place to go than a convent if you seek to lead a life of fornication?" Isabel breathed a sigh of relief

"I will stay here if it pleases you," she said. "I am not as common as they have painted me. It is just that...Lord Barillos...he forced me to do such things... It is all a terrible lie what has befallen me."

"You may call me Mother Serena," the old woman told her, "or simply mother."

"Thank you mother," Isabel replied respectfully.

"You are quite welcome child," Mother Serena replied. "Sister Veva will give you something to occupy your time while you are here. You will need to take a Christian name for yourself. Do you know what it might be?"

"I am not certain."

"You may have until evening to think on it. I have to account for all my sisters. I am sure that you would not wish for me to write your birth name into my book."

"That is the truth," Isabel agreed.

"Sister Veva," the mother superior beckoned.

"Time to go child," Veva said as she came behind Isabel.

"Mother," Isabel said. "There is one more thing if it is not too much to ask a question?"

"What is it," Serena asked?

"To be a sister...I am married to Ramon Berenguer of Provence and..," Isabel struggled.

"You were married," Serena corrected her.

"Yes...That is true isn't it," Isabel said sadly.

"Be at peace," Mother Serena said. "I will not force you to take vows. You may take them as the spirit moves you."

"Thank you mother," Isabel said genuinely. The wrinkled woman nodded and then Sister Veva was hurrying Isabel out of the room.

"What can you do," Veva asked as they walked back up the narrow hallway.

"Well," Isabel hesitated.

"Peel potatoes," Sister Veva inquired?

"I have never done such a thing in my life," Isabel said indignantly!

"Well you had best tell me what else you can do," Veva retorted, "or peeling potatoes shall be a joy that you will soon experience."

"I can write," Isabel said quickly.

"Spanish," Veva asked, "or something else?"

"Both Spanish and Latin," Isabel answered.

"You can read too?"

"Of course," Isabel replied with a raised brow. "You cannot have one without the other."

"Do not get haughty with me," Veva scolded!

"Forgive me," Isabel said confusedly. She was not accustomed to taking orders from anyone but her parents.

"God forgives and so do I," Veva replied dismissively.

"There isn't much I can't do with horses," Isabel added. "I ran my father's stables after his death."

"That's handy," Veva replied. "We do not possess any horses."

"Oh…I am a singer of some skill. I used to perform before my father's court. I was once even summoned to appear before the Crown of Aragon."

"That we can use," Veva said with interest. "Our last choral director, (God rest her soul), has been taken back to the Lord. It has been a long time since we have had a choir. The sisters will be so happy!"

"I will be glad to be of service," Isabel answered. She could not help but smile with the old nun.

"I will speak with our mother about your fluency in Latin. I am sure it will be of use to her," Sister Veva said. Isabel nodded. "In the meantime," the old woman said grandly as she opened the doors to the kitchen, "these potatoes cannot peel themselves!"

"You said," Isabel began.

"I know," Veva replied as she gently pushed Isabel into the kitchen. Two other nuns were already immersed in a pile of potatoes. "I also said it will be a joy," the old woman said.

"Which means what," Isabel asked angrily?

"You knew that it was not a joy, true?"

"It is the truth," Isabel replied hesitantly.

"Then you should have also known that you would be doing it anyway," Veva concluded.

"But…"

"No buts," Veva interrupted. "Sister Maria and Sister Guadalupe will help you." The sound of the kitchen door shutting behind Sister Veva was loud. Isabel was left to wonder how the old woman had duped her into this.

"There is a knife over there on the table," Sister Guadalupe said while gesturing with her own knife. That was how it began. When the three sisters finally left the kitchen, Isabel's fingers were dreadfully sore and they smelled like damp earth. She wondered why the other two women had not deigned to speak with her. She had tried to initiate conversation several times. There were only meager results. The other women used as few words as possible and usually just grunted. If either spoke an entire sentence, it invariably had something to do with the potatoes. If nothing else, the silence gave Isabel time to decide on a name.

The evening meal was more than enough. While Isabel could barely remember eating the night before, she savored every morsel of the lamb shanks and potato soup she was given that day. After a delicious meal, she was called back to the office of the mother superior.

Serena was sipping the last of her soup with a wooden spoon when Isabel and Sister Veva arrived. "Isabel," Mother Serena began, "I expect for you to determine which sisters are best suited to a choir by tomorrow evening. All the sisters will meet with you in the chapel after the morning chores are completed."

"It will be my pleasure," Isabel smiled.

'Teach them all you can. I am not certain how long we will have you with us."

"I will," Isabel agreed.

"Though I have nothing for you to do today," Mother Serena continued; "I may call upon you from time to time to assist me in the drafting of letters. Sister Veva tells me you are versed in Latin."

"I am."

"Very good," the mother superior said. She looked then into Isabel's eyes. "Have you come to a decision?"

"A decision," Isabel asked?

"The name you will take," Serena clarified. "Have you given it much thought?

"I have," Isabel replied.

"What is it?" Mother Serena opened the leather-bound book once more. She opened the ink bottle as well. Serena dipped the white quill in the bottle and held it poised to write. She looked up at Isabel expectantly.

"I shall be called Magdalena," Isabel told her.

"Why do you choose that name," Mother Serena inquired?

"Because I have sinned," Isabel replied solemnly. The room was silent then except for the scratching of the quill on parchment.

CHAPTER II

Isabel remained cloistered with the Sisters of Santa Maria del Pilar for almost three months. She was able to incorporate the majority of them into the choir who had the desire. The only exception was Sister Veva who sounded like an old frog. After six weeks of practice, the sisters began to perform at the Catedral de Seo. They performed behind a screen which kept the eyes of men from seeing them. While this was a matter of protocol, it also served to protect Isabel from the eyes of those who would betray her to Lord Barillos.

Many of the younger nuns were in the habit of complaining about the strictly regimented life at the convent. For Isabel, it was a Godsend. There was almost always something that needed to be done from morning till night. If she was not conducting choir practice; there were meals to be prepared, clothes to mend, laundry to do, rooms to clean, and several masses to attend throughout the day.

Isabel wished that she would have been able to take her dowry chest when she left Montenegro. She would have loved to share the Biblia Sacra with Sister Veva and the others. There was nothing that Isabel owned from her old life and nothing to remind her of a childhood long gone. Even the clothing she had worn during her escape had been ruined on the trip. She was happy that it was at least safe from Lord Barillos, even if she would never see her things again.

She had written several letters for the Mother Superior. Most of them were simple correspondence between Serena and Father Lorenzo of the Catedral de Seo. One particular evening, Isabel had been called to Mother Serena's office to write a letter of great importance. She sat patiently at a small table waiting for the aged nun's dictation. A black quill was poised in Isabel's hand.

"How to begin," Serena said out loud as she paced to and fro in front of the table. Her face looked vexed. "To his grace, Count Ramon Berenguer IV…" Isabel caught her breath as the old woman continued. "God be with you. I am writing you this day to inquire as to the whereabouts of my grandson, Philippe Verdura. As you know, he is the only heir to his father's line. Though his intentions are pure, he is a disobedient child who has gone off to fight against his father's wishes. Please send him with all haste back to Aragon. I will receive him at the Convent of Santa Maria del Pilar and deliver him back into his father's care."

"I pray that God will watch over you," Serena continued. "We who are here in Zaragoza are looking forward to your safe return." Isabel tried to conceal her sorrow as she wrote the letter but did a poor job of it. "What is the matter child," Mother Serena asked with concern?

"It is nothing," Isabel said as she wiped a tear from her cheek.

"Now see what I have done," Serena scolded herself. "I was so worried about Philippe that I forgot what it is that this man means to you. Forgive me."

"No no," Isabel said as she dried her eyes. "I can do this. I want to do it."

"That is the end of the letter," Serena said. "If you will just add the closing so that I might sign it."

"Yes mother," Isabel nodded. The quill scratched loudly on the parchment as Serena came over to stand behind her. She handed the quill to the mother superior and the elder woman signed the bottom of the letter. Serena looked down at Isabel as she lit a red candle for the seal.

"Would you like to send something as well," Serena asked?

"That could cause a lot of trouble," Isabel said, but her voice was hopeful.

"I might be just old enough not to care," Mother Serena smiled. "Besides, I will simply fold your letter inside of mine. No one will be the wiser. Would you like to write?"

"More than anything," Isabel replied quickly. Serena gestured toward the blank sheaf of parchment and smiled. Isabel moved the finished letter aside and pulled a fresh sheet. She dipped her quill into the inkpot. After a short time, she wrote.

To my love, Ramon...

I cannot imagine what horrible lies your mother has sent you or the pain that you must have endured. I have never betrayed our love. What has befallen me was done against my will. After my father's death, my mother was wed to Lord Manuel Barillos. He murdered her secretly with poison. My father's unborn heir was killed also.

Lord Barillos gambled away all the wealth of Montenegro and sunk himself in debt. When his money ran out, he used me to pay his creditors. I attempted to kill the first man he sent to my bed. After this, he locked Little Grandma in the prison tower to ensure my obedience.

I will spare you the horror of what they did to my body. I was able to get a message to your mother by pigeon. She traveled to Montenegro to sit in judgment. Instead of saving me, Petronilla condemned me for a whore and worse.

The men who have befouled me are now free because I had supposedly bewitched them into their vile acts. Bishop Delgardo accused me of witchcraft and then offered me a Devil's bargain. I could either confess to consorting with devils or be found guilty of fornication. Either would result in the end of our marriage. I was too foolish to lie so that I might escape.

Since I would admit to neither charge, they left me as a prisoner to Lord Barillos. Your mother stripped me of title and the Holy Church dissolved our marriage with neither of us in attendance.

God will never forgive me for the deaths I have caused by my pride. I have escaped Montenegro and am now cloistered in the Convent of Santa Maria del Pilar in Zaragoza. I cannot ask for your forgiveness. There were many times when I could have escaped. Little Grandma begged me to do so.

I hope this letter finds you well and I pray that you will remember only those times we shared that were pure and beautiful. I will surely be taking the vows of chastity in the coming days. Mother Serena and the other sisters have been very good to me. I wish that I could turn back time and save what has been lost. Please know that my heart is now, and will forever be...yours.

Isabel

The letters were sent by ship the very next morning. As the carrier departed the convent, Isabel closed her eyes and prayed. If only God would watch over Ramon, then perhaps this time he would receive her letter. It was more than she could pray for that they be reunited, but she carried a small hope in her breast.

Six weeks later, Isabel's prayers were answered. A letter was delivered to the convent. It arrived in a wooden scroll case that was engraved with the crest of Berenguer. It was brought by one of Ramon's officers. "Pepito," Mother Serena cried when the man had removed his helmet.

"Grandma," the man said happily as Mother Serena embraced him. The broad shouldered young Philippe was grinning from ear to ear. "I bring this letter from the count," he said as he handed her the scroll case.

"Read it to me," Mother Serena commanded as she handed the case to Isabel. Isabel nearly ran over to snatch the scroll case out of the old woman's hands. She opened it and placed it on the table before removing its contents. The tiny knife on the desk made short work of breaking the wax seal of Berenguer. There was a smaller scroll tied with red string inside.

Isabel unrolled the first piece of parchment and read aloud. "Here is the prodigal grandson you requested," she read aloud. "I know that you will deliver him safely to his father. God be with you always. Signed...Ramon Berenguer the Count of Provence."

"What does the other one say," Mother Serena asked? Isabel untied the string and unrolled the second sheet of parchment.

"It is for me," Isabel said with emotion.

"You may retire child," the aged nun smiled.

"Thank you mother," Isabel said excitedly. She hurried to the sleeping hall and sat herself down on the bed wherein she slept. She carefully opened the letter as if it were an ancient script that might crumble at the slightest touch.

My dearest Isabel...

I knew it was not true what my mother said. At the same time, I never imagined that she would betray me in such a manner. Stay within the safety of the convent.

By the time you read this, I will be only a few short weeks from returning to the Crown of Aragon. I come back for you my love. I will marry you again...a thousand times if needs be. Wait for me.

Love Always...
Ramon

Isabel hugged the parchment to her breast and wept. It had been so long since she had felt hope. She reread the letter several times just to make sure that she was not dreaming.

For the next ten days, Isabel felt like she was walking on air. No amount of work in the convent could dampen her spirits. Late in the afternoon of the eleventh day, word came that Count Berenguer would be returning. Mother Serena gave Isabel leave to go to the Basilica del Pilar and meet him. There were the celebratory sounds of trumpets as Isabel approached the main road that came in from the bridge over the River Ebro. She could see a dust cloud approaching from the north. "Ramon," she breathed as she came to join the throng of citizens.

The people of Zaragoza were already lining up along the main thoroughfare. The trumpets sounding at the Basilica were being answered from the Catedral de Seo and Castle Aljaferia farther off. Isabel's heart felt light. She could scarcely contain her excitement as the banners of

House Berenguer and the Crown of Aragon began to materialize out of the swirling dust. The priests inside the basilica began to work the bell tower. Soon there was a throng of people gathered in the square and all along the main road. Isabel was able to make her way to the front where she waited anxiously for her husband.

A cheer rose up from the crowd as the first soldiers set foot on the bridge. Isabel noticed that she was not the only young woman waiting for her husband's return. She saw the same excitement and longing in other faces as well. The noise became deafening as Aragon's army crossed over and set foot in Zaragoza. "Esteban," a young woman in a simple brown dress shouted happily. "Mi amor!"

Esteban, (who was two ranks in from the edge of the formation), broke into a grin as he saw the young woman waiting for him. There was a dent in the young man's helmet. The side of his face was covered with dirt and there were dark stains on his clothing. Tears stood in the eyes of the woman who adored him as the procession marched on toward the Crown of Aragon.

Then came the cavalry. The horses looked even more exhausted than the men. The mounted officers followed behind the rest. This was the moment for which Isabel had been waiting so long. Among the officers, she first recognized Captain Quintero riding on a black charger. He was waving to the crowd, but the smile on his face was strained. Isabel looked at the others. Their faces were grim. This was not the look of triumphant heroes returning home.

Behind the officers was the carriage of Count Berenguer. Ramon was not visible. It would have made more sense for him to ride out where the people could see him. As Isabel was trying to figure out how she would catch her husband's attention, she noticed the standard bearers as if for the first time. She could see the yellow and crimson flag of Aragon carried by one rider. The flag of Provence was held aloft by another. A third rider carried the standard of House Berenguer. There was yet one more rider coming behind the others. He carried a long pole with a cross piece toward the top. From this hung a solid black banner. The man who carried it looked beaten. He hung his head and did not spare so much as a single glance for the welcoming crowd.

A cart was being drawn by two black mares behind the carriage. A hush fell over the crowd as its contents came into view. The sight of the ornate, cherry wood coffin was like a knife to Isabel's heart. This scene had become all too familiar to her. Her throat was choked with grief but she would not cry out. Tears slid from her eyes as she fell in behind the coffin with many other women of the city. The edges of the wood were inlaid with gold and the flag of House Berenguer was draped over it. Isabel did not need the lid open to know who was inside. She knew.

Isabel followed silently along as the wailing funeral procession wound through the streets of Zaragoza. It ended at Castle Aljaferia. The army was greeted by more trumpets, pealing the sounds of victory. The jubilation of the palace courtesans was cut short by the sight of the coffin.

The King and Queen were standing at the top of the steps that led into the castle proper. Petronilla stood on the other side of her son. The nobles were gathered in the walkways around the grand courtyard. Captain Quintero and several of the other officers dismounted and walked up toward them. The officers kneeled until King Alfonso invited them to rise.

The mourners melted away, all except Isabel who stood oblivious to the outside world. Ramon was dead. With a strangled cry, Petronilla ran down the steps toward the funeral cart. Six soldiers were bringing the coffin down so that it could be interred in the family crypt. The lid of the coffin was divided into two parts. No sooner had the men set the coffin down and removed the flag, than did the Queen-Mother fall down sobbing on top of her son's final rest. Petronilla opened the top portion of the coffin in order to see his face.

The skin of Isabel's dead husband was ashen and decay had already set in on the journey home. She had to look away as the sound of Petronilla's screams filled the courtyard. As four of the officers took part in folding the flag, two more gently pulled the hysterical queen-mother from her youngest son's coffin.

Isabel did not look back until she heard the lid closing once more. Petronilla was being held up by Ramon's officers. Her face was a streaked mess of tears. Queen Sancha remained on the steps, but the king came forward to collect his mother. He took her into his arms. Petronilla buried her face in Alfonso's chest and wept.

Isabel watched as they carried the coffin into the castle. Petronilla regained some of her composure, but still leaned heavily on her son's arm. Isabel started to follow the bearers of the coffin, but was cut short by the queen-mother's hand resting lightly on her shoulder. "Thank you for coming sister," Petronilla said tearfully, "but you may return now to the convent." Isabel looked then over at the woman who had stopped her. She could see the light of recognition in Petronilla's eyes. "Oh my God," Petronilla cried as her face pinched up with grief. The older woman's hand fell off Isabel's shoulder as she began to weep once more.

"I go," Isabel said flatly. She did not curtsey, but simply turned around and exited the courtyard. No one called her back for the affront or attempted to stop her from leaving. She did not stop until she had come once more inside the walls of the convent. Isabel walked to the sanctuary and knelt down in front of the altar. She then wept then louder than they all.

Isabel quieted herself when she felt the presence of another behind her. She dried her eyes and stood up from the sanctuary floor. "What is it, child?" Mother Serena asked. "What has happened? Was the count not pleased to see you?" Isabel turned slowly to face the older woman.

"If it pleases you," Isabel said sadly. "I should like to be considered as an initiate."

"I am sorry Isabel, but you should spend more time in prayer before asking this of me," Serena said. "What did the count say?"

"Nothing," Isabel said as her face pinched up once more.

"He did not even acknowledge you?"

"My Ramon is dead," Isabel wept! "I tried to wait for him. It was not my fault!"

"Come here child," Serena said as she put her arms around the sobbing Isabel.

"He is dead," Isabel cried into the older woman's habit. "I have nothing. All is lost!"

"Fear not," Serena soothed. "We will care for you for as long as you desire."

"I am sorry Mother," Isabel cried. "The things I have done...I understand your decision."

"I did not say that you are unacceptable Isabel," Serena replied as she held Isabel close. "Come to me again on the Lord's day. You should have had ample time to think upon it by then."

"Thank you mother," Isabel said in a very small voice.

"There is no question that we would welcome you Magdalena, but I need you to be certain of your desire to ask."

"Yes mother," Isabel agreed as the old nun led her back to the dormitory. "I shall pray upon it."

"Good," the mother superior said as they came into the long hall with its many beds. "Try and get you some sleep." Isabel nodded and walked slowly to her bed. Serena departed while Isabel changed into a nightgown provided her by the convent. As was customary, Isabel put the nightgown on over her habit and then removed the habit itself. This was the time to say her evening prayers, but Isabel could not bring the words to mind.

"Everyone I love dies," Isabel whispered heavenward. "It is more than I can take." No answer came down from on high. Isabel lied awake for some time until the rest of the sisters laid down as well. Eventually, the only sounds were the breathing of the other women as they slept.

Choir practice was cancelled by Mother Serena that week. She told Isabel to spend more time in meditation and prayer. This also gave the bereaved widow some much needed solitude. On the third day of her grief, Isabel was summoned to the sanctuary.

Mother Serena waited up near the altar. A veiled woman in a black gown sat upon the front pew. "Here she is your majesty," Serena said as Isabel walked quietly up the aisle. "I will take my leave." The veiled woman stood and turned around toward Isabel as Serena left by the side door. As she drew near, Isabel could see the face of Petronilla beneath the thin, diaphanous fabric of the veil.

"Why have you come," Isabel asked with an utter disregard for the old woman's station? "Do you wish to deliver me back to Montenegro?"

"This is not the reason for my visit," Petronilla said. Her face was aged even further by the death of her son.

"You shall have to have me killed if you wish me to go back to that place," Isabel said hatefully.

"I have come to beg your forgiveness," the queen-mother implored.

"What difference would that make," Isabel scoffed?

"Let me explain so that you may understand," Petronilla offered. Isabel stood in the center aisle of the sanctuary with her eyes on her dead husband's mother. She neither discouraged nor encouraged the older woman to speak. "When I discovered that you had secretly wed my son," Petronilla began, "I went straight away to a trusted friend for advice. I went to Lord Enriquez of Morera. He said he would take care of everything. He promised to make you go away but I did not know that he meant to kill you!"

"My death would only have been a joyous relief for your majesty," Isabel replied scornfully.

"But I did not mean for them to take your life," Petronilla insisted!

"I wish now that they had," Isabel said flatly.

"I believed Lord Barillos because it served my purpose," the old woman admitted. "The Crown of Aragon could not be sullied with common blood. It would be scandalous!"

"Was that how you comforted yourself," Isabel asked? "How could you? I was an innocent girl," Isabel said accusingly.

"Let me find atonement," Petronilla pleaded. "I am sorry. I will restore your title. I am more than ready to be generous."

"Do whatever you will," Isabel scoffed. "It will not bring back my husband."

"I know," Petronilla sobbed. "It is all my fault that he is dead!" The queen-mother wept for her lost boy, but Isabel was not moved to comfort her. Eventually, she took out a bundle wrapped in brown cloth and handed it to Isabel.

"What am I to do with this," Isabel asked skeptically?

"Just open it," Petronilla said. The cloth was filled with scores of letters. Each of them bore the seal of Berenguer. Isabel opened the first of them.

My dearest Isabel,

I have arrived in Nice. It is to be less than a week before we are together again. How my heart yearns for you!

Lord William has become my enemy. As soon as I set foot in his palace, he once more put forth the idea of marrying his daughter. I declined. He kept badgering me for a reason as if my refusal was not sufficient. Finally, I told him. I am going back to Zaragoza to there be wed to Lady Isabel of Montenegro!

Lord William began making all sorts of accusations and sent me out from his estate like some kind of criminal. No matter. I am eager to be rid of this place. Praise be to God, my love. We shall very soon be reunited!

Love Always,

Ramon

"He was almost here," Isabel said sorrowfully.

"Yes," Petronilla agreed, "but they killed my Ramon ere he left Nice."

"France is at peace with us," Isabel said.

"They are saying it was an act of revenge from Genoa," Petronilla said sadly, "but I know what has happened. Lord William had my son killed in such a way that he could remain blameless." Why did the queen-mother suspect such an act, Isabel wondered?

"Was it the same way you killed my father," Isabel asked with furious realization? "Was it the same way that his servant Eubasio was to kill me?"

"Forgive me, forgive me," Petronilla sobbed.

"Forgive you," Isabel shouted? "You should die! I should kill you where you stand! You cannot begin to imagine what I have suffered because of your wicked meddling!"

"Oh please do," Petronilla cried wretchedly! "I deserve to die."

"I am not like you," Isabel answered. "Far be it from me to grant you the mercy of death. No. Live Petronilla. Live and remember my face. This face loved your son so purely that nothing could cause it to wane! I would have made him happy," Isabel cried. "I would have fulfilled his every wish."

"No," Petronilla cried!

"Yes," Isabel interrupted her. "You would have seen me as a thorn in his side. It would have given you something to gossip about with the other hags in Alfonso's court, but in your heart you would have known. You would not have been able to avoid seeing how selflessly I would have served him." Isabel's voice was breaking and she began to weep as she continued. "I would have been a good mother. It was to be a beautiful family! Now it is nothing and now…now you bring me this worthless apology?"

"I am sorry," Petronilla said brokenly.

"God compels me to forgive you," Isabel said from behind clenched teeth, "and so art thou forgiven."

"Thank you Lady Isabel."

"It is Magdalena now," Isabel snapped. "Hold off on your gratitude. It is just as futile as your apology and twice as worthless as my forgiveness!" Petronilla could not voice a reply. Isabel continued on mercilessly. "Every day you will try to banish me from your memory, but you shall not succeed. Look well upon my face Petronilla, for you will recall it every time that you recall his. You will pray for your own death, but God will curse you with a long life. You will sleep with blood on your hands forever!"

"This is more than I can bear," Petronilla wept. She walked quickly out of the sanctuary. Isabel did not follow. She could not. Once the queen mother was gone, Isabel wept also.

As requested, Isabel spent much time in meditation and prayer. Her decision to become a nun was not a difficult one. She had been pondering it for weeks already. Before she learned that her husband would take her back, Isabel had already made the choice. The death of Ramon only reinforced it all the more.

Queen Petronilla reinstated Isabel's title and declared her innocent of the charges brought against her in Montenegro. This information was given to her in the form of a royal edict delivered by the Mother Superior. "This changes nothing," Isabel said with disgust as she finished reading it.

"The Queen-Mother also wishes you to know that Lord Barillos has been commanded to execute the men whom you named as your rapists," Serena told her.

"Manuel has not the courage to execute them. He will just let them escape," Isabel said. "What of those who defiled me after she left me there to die? What a worthless exercise of royal power!"

"At least you need not fear being captured," Serena noted. "Now that you have been declared innocent, you may travel safely to Lord Vasquez and see the rest of your family. So you see that some good has come out of this?"

"I do see," Isabel admitted, "but I no longer wish to go to my uncle. Shall I live a normal life? Shall I find another husband? No. I wish to stay here…with you and the rest of the sisters."

"It is not yet the Lord's day," Serena reminded her."

"My mind is already made up," Isabel replied. "I wish to serve God. I will ask once more on Sunday, but it will only be a formality. I have known that this is the path God wishes for me to follow for quite some time now. Ramon's return seemed like such a blessing," she sighed. "It was not the gift I imagined it to be. I am grateful to you for having had the chance to write to him that one last time."

"It was only God pushing me in the right direction," Serena answered modestly.

"That is exactly what it was," Isabel agreed. "God knew that my Ramon would be killed, but at least he gave me the comfort of knowing that his love for me never died."

"I cannot help thinking that he might have lived if not for the letter," Serena said sadly.

"We go as the spirit moves us," Isabel told her. "You cannot bear blame for what has happened. It was not your kind act that killed my Ramon, it was Petronilla's madness. I must thank Him for giving me a love so pure, even it if was but for a little while."

"You will be reunited in heaven," Mother Serena said.

"Yes," Isabel agreed. There were tears in her eyes but she managed a smile. "I believe we shall."

Normally, prayers in the convent were conducted by the mother superior. On Sundays, Father Hernando from the Catedral de Seo would hold mass. He would read the liturgy in Latin and then perform a short sermon. The sisters would then receive communion. Following the service, Father Hernando would take the nun's confessions.

On this particular Sunday, Mother Serena took the pulpit once the priest's message was concluded. She looked out over the sisters who sat side by side in their pews. "There is one among us who wishes to join our order," she said. "Let that woman stand now and come here to me." Isabel stood up as the others looked on. She walked up the aisle to join Serena. The mother superior and Father Hernando came down from the pulpit and escorted Isabel to stand before the altar. There was a long prayer recited in Latin by the priest before Serena spoke again. "Magdalena wishes to join our sisterhood and dedicate her life in service to Christ."

"Amen," the sisters said as one.

"The life of a sister is not an easy one," Serena continued. "The Sisters of Santa Maria del Pilar have made solemn perpetual vows of poverty, chastity, and obedience. The vow of poverty leads us to emulate Christ, he who left a rich life in paradise to be born in the squalor of Earth. Our sisters lead lives in which they have no desire for personal gain. What is earned by our community is used for the good of all. Through the vow of poverty, a sister is freed from the world of material possessions so that she may devote her time to serving others."

"Christ," Serena went on, "who was free from sin, did not defile himself with the sins of the flesh. The vow of chastity forbids a sister to marry or engage in any other sort of romantic behavior. This vow frees us from the demands of being a wife. In this way, we can give all of our love to God."

"Like Christ," the old woman continued, "a nun seeks the will of God. The vow of obedience binds us to follow the orders of our superiors in the Holy Church. As a member of our community, she will search for the will of God through thoughtful conversation and prayerful reflection. Let us all endeavor to be exemplars of these vows while Magdalena makes her decision to walk closer with God. Lead her in the paths of righteousness, strengthen her when she is weak, and lift her up should she fall."

"Amen," the sisters said as one.

"Welcome to the Sisterhood of Santa Maria del Pilar," Mother Serena said happily. "Go now and sit among your sisters."

"Praise be to God," Isabel said meekly. Isabel saw warmth and welcoming joy in the eyes of the women as she went to sit down once more. Father Hernando recited several verses in Latin and then drank from the chalice that sat atop the altar. He then invited the sisters to come forward.

They came by rows, filing out from each individual pew and then kneeling in a line before the priest. Father Hernando walked down the line of sisters and gave them the Eucharist before a new line came to take the place of the first. Isabel closed her eyes as she received the host and then made the sign of the cross. After all had partaken in Holy Communion, the priest said a prayer in Latin which ended the mass.

Some of the sisters gathered in the garden after the service was concluded. It was a beautiful place with great lengths of ivy covering the stone walls. A stone fountain rose up out of the center of the enclosure. The statue that rose out of the fountain was of Santa Maria del Pilar with her face raised up toward heaven. At her feet were several cherubs who poured water out of large clay pots into the pool below. There were stone benches facing the fountain on all four sides and white roses grew around its base.

The sisters there were all congratulating Isabel on her decision. Some gave condolences on the loss of her husband as well. "Sister Magdalena," Father Hernando said as he walked out among the nuns. Isabel looked back from the conversation she had been having.

"Yes father," she asked?

"Walk with me sister," the priest invited.

"Of course," Isabel agreed. They walked out of the garden and into the grounds of the convent.

"Your work with the choir has been very beneficial to our church," Hernando said. "The nobles have been especially generous of late." Isabel only nodded. "Now that you are planning to stay, I wonder if you are familiar with liturgical drama."

"I am," Isabel said wistfully. "My father took me to Teruel when I was a little girl. It was the most beautiful thing I have ever seen!"

"Was it," the priest asked?

"Oh by far," Isabel confirmed as she remembered.

"The Catedral de Seo would be blessed if you and your sisters would perform such a drama. Can it be arranged?"

"Nothing would please me more," Isabel breathed! "Alas, there are many things which we would need for it."

"Such as…"

"Wood for the set, paint, fabric for costumes, swaths of red cloth, an actual cross perhaps…"

"Send me the list of your desires," the priest interrupted. "I will be happy to fulfill them."

"I will," Isabel replied happily.

"What will you play?"

"The Resurrection," Isabel answered. "I remember it well."

"Who will play the virgin do you think?"

"Sister Guadalupe has a very pleasant voice."

"Why not yourself," Hernando asked? His stare was making Isabel a bit uncomfortable, though she could not understand why.

"Who will direct the drama if I am a player," she questioned?

"I am certain that you could do both. You are ideal for the role."

"What do you mean?"

"Your appearance is more…statuesque…than the other sisters," the priest smiled.

"I shall consider what you have said," Isabel said, but she had no intention of doing so.

"I must insist," Hernando replied. "I have heard of your talent as have many of the nobility of Zaragoza. "If

God hath blessed you with such a gift, it is only righteous to share it with others."

"I have dreamed of such a thing," Isabel admitted, "when I was young and the world seemed so wonderful."

"You are still young," Hernando remarked. Isabel said nothing. "Sister Magdalena," he said as he stopped her with a hand on her arm. Isabel turned to look the man in the eyes. "I have heard of your sorrow."

"Yes," Isabel said uncomfortably. "What has happened has happened. It is my cross to bear."

"Not completely," Hernando said comfortingly. "I will always be available to hear your confession and console your spirit."

"Thank you father," Isabel said.

"Laying yourself bare before God will provide the healing your soul needs most," the priest continued. "Do not neglect yourself in this."

"I will not," Isabel smiled. It seemed that this priest was genuine and her reservations before were just her own senseless fears. "Let me visit with you next week," she said. "I will be more ready to talk then."

"Mind you not to forget," he cautioned.

"I am certain that you will remind me if it comes to that," Isabel chuckled, "but I will not forget."

"Good," Father Hernando answered. "Fare thee well, sister. God be with you."

"And also with you father," Isabel replied. She did go to confession the following week. She confessed her sinful desire to murder Manuel Barillos. She placed blame for the atrocities she had suffered upon her own shoulders. In the course of her confession, Isabel told Father Hernando everything. The priest seemed particularly interested in learning how her stepfather had manipulated her into committing such abominations. He asked many questions until Isabel had described every horror that had transpired in great detail.

Father Hernando prescribed a number of catechisms and instructed Sister Magdalena to seek the Lord in prayer for better understanding. When Isabel left the confessional booth, she felt as if a great weight had been lifted from her. She recited the Lord's Prayer as well before going to bed that night. When that was done, she prayed for understanding and wisdom.

As Sister Magdalena knelt with her forehead pressed down onto her mattress, she was overcome with a feeling of peace. Somehow, she knew that the soul of Little Grandma was safe with God. If she had been asked how she knew this to be true, Sister Magdalena would not have been able to explain it.

CHAPTER III

After the passing of three months, Magdalena was asked to take her first vows. These were simple vows of poverty, chastity, and obedience. They would later become permanent if she was resolved to give up everything for Christ. Mother Serena said that it would be several years before Isabel would take the solemn perpetual vows that would seal her to God forever. To Isabel, it seemed like a foregone conclusion. Many of the other nuns knew it too, but they stood on their traditions.

The liturgical drama of the resurrection was beautiful in every way. Though it was a great deal of work, Isabel took the part of the Virgin and directed the others at the same time. She poured every once of emotion into the songs she sang in the Catedral de Seo that first night. Though she had never had a child of her own, death and loss were intimately familiar to her. When the Virgin was mourning the loss of her son, Isabel was really mourning the loss of those she had loved.

The liturgical drama became quite the spectacle in Zaragoza. The coffers of the Catedral de Seo grew fat with coins. Isabel soon added more dramas to the repertoire of the Sisters of Santa Maria del Pilar. The story of Ruth was told, the Immaculate Conception, and the parable of the widow. For a time, Isabel experienced contentment.

It was late in October when Sister Magdalena was summoned to the office of the mother superior. Serena was there, along with Father Hernando. "Come and sit down," Serena invited. Isabel sat in one of the chairs which faced the older woman's desk. Father Hernando was half sitting and half leaning on the corner of it.

"Yes mother," Isabel inquired.

"The Lord has work for you elsewhere sister," Father Hernando smiled.

"He does," Isabel asked apprehensively. I thought I was to remain here with the Sisters of Santa Maria del Pilar."

"I am certain that you will return here in time," Hernando assured her, "but first I must ask that you go the Convent of the Angels which is outside the city of Pamplona."

"What can I do there?"

"Sister Raquel has passed on to the Lord," the priest replied. "Now there is no one to care for the orphans. There are other sisters there, (to be sure), but you are the best choice."

"Who will take my place," Isabel inquired? She was not overjoyed at the prospect of leaving.

"Sister Guadalupe," Mother Serena answered. "I think she would be the best replacement."

"You're probably right," Isabel agreed.

"If her tongue is not sharp enough, then we still have Sister Veva," the older woman chuckled.

"That will keep them in line," Isabel noted, "but why have they chosen me seeing as I have never raised a child?"

"The Cardinal said it was more important to find a sister with a pure heart," Hernando explained. "I naturally thought of you."

"You are too kind," Isabel said respectfully.

"It is only the truth," Hernando smiled. "I know that you will miss Zaragoza, but these children really need someone who will care for them.

"I am eager to meet these little ones," Isabel relented.

"I knew you were the one for this," Father Hernando said excitedly. "Did I not tell you that she was the one Mother Serena?"

"You did indeed," Serena replied. Isabel could see that the mother superior was just as unhappy about her leaving as she was. "Go with God child," she said to Isabel. "You will depart immediately after morning prayer."

Isabel said her goodbyes to all of the other sisters. They were all sad to see her go, particularly those who were involved in the liturgical dramas. She left Sister Guadalupe in charge of the choir and Sister Veva promised to ensure that the others would live up to their vows of obedience.

There was nothing to pack but one change of clothing. It was strange to Isabel not to have servants bustling about to ensure that all of her dresses and other things were ready to go. Here in the convent, she had only the clothes on her back and one extra habit to wear while she laundered the first.

After the candles in the sleeping hall had been snuffed out, Magdalena was yet awake in her bed. She would miss the Sisters of Santa Maria del Pilar. She would miss Mother Serena most of all. She could have remained there forever and been content. She was worried about her new position in the Convent of the Angels. Her only interactions with young children had been with her cousin David. She hoped that the orphans would accept her and that she would be able to bring some joy into their little lives. She pondered how terribly abandoned an orphan must feel, especially if they were very young. That night, Isabel promised God that she would love them as if they were her own children. In so doing, she would teach them to love Him.

† † †

It had been planned that Father Hernando should accompany her to Pamplona. A simple donkey-drawn cart awaited her outside the back of the convent. A swarthy looking man in a grey tunic and trousers stood beside it. His muscular arms were covered with thick black hair. The hair on his head was shaggy and long. Isabel approached with hesitation. She had not been this close to a man, (other than a priest), since her escape from Montenegro. Noticing her discomfort, the man spoke in a soothing tone. "Father Hernando will not be able to accompany us," he told her.

"Surely he knows that I am not to be in the company of men," Isabel exclaimed! The peasant man sighed and looked down at the ground. He waited for some time before speaking again.

"I was once a slave," he said without looking at her. "Before that, I was a man."

"I do not understand," Isabel said irritably.

"I am a eunuch," the man said with embarrassment, "but you may call me Armando."

"Sister Magdalena," Isabel replied.

"My thanks sister," Armando said politely. "If you will take your place in the cart, then we can be on our way." Isabel nodded. She walked around the other side of the cart before climbing up onto the wooden bench toward the front of it. The bench was old and uncomfortable. It needed to be sanded down by the looks of it. Armando seated himself beside her. He picked up the stick that rested on the bench between them. Attached to the stick was a leather cord. From the end of the cord, a fresh carrot was tied.

"What is that," Isabel asked, indicating the strange device with one hand?

"My burro does not work for free," Armando chuckled. He picked up the stick and dangled the carrot in front of the donkey's face. Immediately, the cart began to move forward.

It was a long journey to Pamplona. At night, they slept in the back of the cart. Armando offered to sleep on the ground, but Isabel insisted that he sleep in the cart also. She remembered how she had woken up soaked from the dew on her trek down the River Ebro. Out of respect, Armando slept with his back to her.

The Eunuch was a pleasant traveling companion. He told her the story of how he had been captured in war. He told her of his years in bondage and his eventual escape. Armando kept a woodsman's axe beside him in case they were attacked. Fortunately, he was not provided with a chance to use it. Isabel did not discuss her own tragedies. This did not present any awkward silences as Armando was content to do most of the talking.

On the second day of their journey, they had stopped in the afternoon to rest the donkey and stretch their legs. It was a good opportunity for the two of them to eat as well.

Before long, there was the sound of wheels on packed earth as another cart approached. This one was drawn by a brown work horse and the back of it was enclosed in a cage of iron. The man who drove the cart wore a black hood with cut outs for his eyes. His clothing was black also and he carried a sword at his belt. Several similarly attired men rode behind the cart, presumably to guard its contents.

The prisoners were all women. They were dusty from the road and their faces looked haggard from lack of sleep. Their dresses were common and most were ragged from overuse. The collar of one dark haired woman's blouse had been ripped down the front so that more of her bosom would be available to the eye. Another prisoner's skirt was rent up the side almost to her waistline. The entirety of her left leg could be seen through the opening. These women's faces were hard; all save for the tiny blonde haired girl who sat huddled in the back corner. Her countenance was filled with fear.

"I wonder what all these women have done," Isabel mused aloud.

"They are harlots," Armando explained. "Do not suffer yourself to look at them!" Isabel quickly looked at the ground. She only raised her eyes again once the prison cart had traveled far from view.

"Where could they be going," Isabel asked?

"I know not where they go now," Armando answered, "but we both know where their paths will end."

"In hell," Isabel agreed. "I cannot understand why any woman would willingly subject herself to such evils."

"Nor I," Armando agreed.

"The girl in the back of the cart seemed afraid. Perhaps she will repent."

"Let us pray so," the eunuch replied, "but she may fear only for her body. The soul is another matter entirely."

"It is the truth," Isabel agreed. They traveled in silence for some time before Armando continued his mostly one sided conversation. Like Isabel, he had sought refuge from the church after his escape. His condition made him an ideal candidate for transporting and guarding women.

What started as a speck on the horizon, gained in size and clarity until it became the city of Pamplona. The Convent of the Angels was situated on the main road leading in. It was surrounded by fields of grain on three sides. An olive orchard ran along the opposite side of the wide dirt road. Grey clouds were rushing overhead. Soon the sun became obscured by them. There was a flash of lightning in the distance followed by a peal of thunder. The downpour was immediate! By the time the travelers reached the front gates of the convent, their clothing was soaked through.

The walls of the convent were made of a dark wood with a grayish tinge to it. The wood was made even darker by the water running down. Pamplona was no longer visible through the sheets of rain that fell to earth. The walls were arranged in a large rectangular shape. Facing the road was a cobblestone square that indented into the rectangle. Large iron gates stood on either side of the square. The center wall contained an ironwork grate fashioned to resemble thorn covered brambles. Next to the grate was what appeared to be a small wooden cupboard with iron handles.

Over the high walls, Isabel could see the top floor of a large structure on her left and the twin bell towers of a church on her right. Everything else was concealed by the cloister. "Follow me," Armando shouted over the rain. Isabel grabbed her change of clothing and hurried after the eunuch. Once they got closer, Isabel could see a flat leather cord that hung down from a square shaped recess in the wall. Armando yanked down on the cord several times which rung the bell on the opposite side of the wall.

Even though Armando was ringing the bell constantly, it still took some time before it was answered. "I am here, you can stop now," a woman said loudly through the grate! Isabel could make out the black and white cloth of the nun's habit and the broken up image of the woman's face. "State your business," the nun said.

"I have brought Sister Magdalena from the Convent of Santa Maria del Pilar in Zaragoza," Armando shouted back.

"Have you purchased any lamp oil?"

"No," Armando replied. "I do not have a lamp. Why do you ask me this?"

"It is nothing," the nun answered quickly. "Wait a moment." Isabel could hear doors opening and closing on the other side of the cupboard before the other woman spoke again.

"The key is in the pass-through sister," the nun told Isabel.

"Thank you sister," Isabel replied. She opened up the wooden doors and retrieved a large steel key from out of it. She could see that the back of the cupboard had doors which would open to the inside of the convent. There was also a locking mechanism on the inside of the outer doors to prevent burglars from using it as a crawl space. Although the burglar would need to be small indeed to fit.

"Your service is ended," the nun told Armando as Isabel closed the cupboard doors.

"Of course," Armando replied. "Where may I find lodging?"

"Go to the monastery," she answered. "The priests will find lodging for you there."

"In Leyre," the eunuch asked?

"Leyre," the woman confirmed. "Go with God."

"Thank you sister," Armando replied. "Farewell Sister Magdalena," he said with a hint of regret.

"Farewell," Isabel said in return. While the eunuch went back to his donkey cart, Sister Magdalena unlocked one of the iron gates which led into the convent. She could hear the animal braying its displeasure as she locked herself in. Isabel waved once to Armando, but he was too busy trying to get his stubborn animal to take him where he could get out of the rain. The sound of the donkey was quickly lost behind the droplets falling on the roof above.

The gate led directly into the cloister. The ceilings were vaulted and there were crenellated arches stretching up the walls like the claws of giant crabs. The arches and baseboards were of the same black hue as the floors. The walls were the unfinished grey of the outside. There were open archways along the inner walls of the cloister. Through these openings, Isabel could see a large white building across the soaked lawn. Lights burned from within but there was no one outside. The cloister wrapped around the lawn and then continued until it had connected with the far side of the building. From there it would continue on to enclose the rest of the convent as well.

"Greetings sister," said a female voice from behind Isabel. She turned around to see a nun much younger than most of those she had met in Zaragoza. The woman could not possibly have been more than twenty years of age. Her face had a cherubic appearance with rose colored cheeks and a mouth which formed a perfect cupid's bow. A strand of her dark hair had fallen down below her scapula and barely came into view over the left side of her forehead. She had bright blue eyes and a small pointed nose.

"Peace be with you sister," Isabel said.

"And with you," the woman replied. "I am Sister Clara. Follow me and I will introduce you to our mother."

"Of course," Isabel replied. She fell into line behind the other woman and followed her closely.

"This convent is dedicated to the four archangels," Clara said as they walked, "but it should have been dedicated to Mary of Magdalene…a woman with whom I am sure you are intimately familiar."

"What do you mean?"

"You are her namesake are you not?"

"I am," Isabel said with shame.

"We all are," Sister Clara added. "Fear not, there are much worse places that one can end up."

SISTER MAGDALENA

"Much worse," Isabel agreed. She followed Sister Clara around the circumference of the lawn until there were no more archways. They continued on by torchlight until they arrived at an iron door which led into the side of the white building Isabel had seen when she came into the convent.

"This is the infirmary," Clara explained as she opened the door with a massive brass key. "This is also where our more…difficult girls are kept." Isabel nodded uncomfortably as the door creaked open. The hallway that Sister Clara led her into was lit by a row of small windows that ran just below the ceiling. The illumination was made even dimmer by the grey clouds and the rain.

It looked more like a prison than a place of healing. Rows of iron cells lined both sides of the walk. Many of them were empty, but a few were occupied. Isabel guessed that each cell could have housed two, or even three people. However, no cell contained more than one. The prisoners were invariably female and all wore dresses made from a drab brown material.

One girl stood up worriedly as the nuns approached. It was the same innocent looking prisoner from the cart that has passed Isabel and her eunuch escort. Once Sister Clara came into full view, the woman looked intently down as if studying the floor. Sister Clara paused and narrowed her eyes at the young woman. After a few uncomfortable moments, she continued walking and Isabel followed.

The next woman had come up to the bars and was holding one loosely in each hand. She looked out at Isabel with a wild desperation. "You have to help me sister," the woman exclaimed! "You have to get me out of this place!" Before Isabel could think of a suitable reply, Sister Clara's hand shot out and grabbed the first two fingers of the woman's right hand. Clara's knuckles visibly tightened and she twisted her hand down to one side. "It hurts," the woman cried out!

"Not as bad as it will hurt next time," Clara promised. There was a cruelty in the other woman's face that Isabel would never have expected when they first met by the gates. The prisoner was driven to her knees by the great pressure inflicted on her fingers. Clara finally let go. The prisoner clutched her injured fingers while Clara berated her. "Now keep your whore's mouth shut! It is what brought you here in the first place." The prisoner nodded her head and looked fearfully up at the nuns outside her cell. The rest of the prisoners they passed did their best to look anywhere else but at the nuns.

The two sisters passed through another locked iron door and into a plain room with stairs leading up the side of the far wall. Another set of stairs built below the first went down to a lower level. There were three more doors at the far end of the room, one on each wall. There was one more door to Isabel's left before she came to the foot of the stairs leading up. "That one leads back into the cloister," Sister Clara said as she pointed to the door on Isabel's left. "The door at the far end leads to more cells. The other two go to the other prison halls. Our beds are upstairs."

"What is below?"

"Our mother, Sister Maria Elena will surely explain it to you upstairs," Clara replied. "This is not the place." The other woman began to climb the stairs with Isabel following behind her. The stairs opened into an unadorned hallway with a large window on the opposite side. Plain wooden doors lined the hallway. Each had a number marked on the door in black charcoal. "You will be in bed four," Clara told her. She pulled out a ring of keys and selected the one that would open the door to Isabel's new home. The inside of the room was dimly lit by the window in the north wall. There was a small and uncomfortable looking bed to one side. The other contained a stool and a small table with a lantern resting upon it. There was a trunk hidden in the corner behind the head of the bed. "You may put your belongings there," Clara said with a finger pointed toward the trunk. Isabel untied her bundle and spread the habit that had been wrapped around them out over the small table.

"My habit is still wet," she explained, referring to the one on her body.

"No time to waste," Clara said. "Our mother will speak with you now."

"Coming," Isabel sighed. She left her habit behind and followed Clara back to the end of the hall leading to the stairs. The door that Sister Clara opened was marked '1'. Inside was a small office with a desk and several book shelves along the walls. There were doors leading out to the right and the left. Due to the placement of the windows, Isabel could see that the right door led onto the roof. There were not many books in the shelves. They were mainly filled with scroll cases and sheaves of parchment.

The mother superior was well advanced in years. She was a plump woman with heavy jowls and loose, wrinkled skin. It seemed to take her some considerable effort to look up at them. "Come in," she smiled.

"This is Sister Magdalena from Zaragoza," Sister Clara announced.

"How wonderful," Maria Elena exclaimed! "The children will be so happy. You are dismissed Sister Clara."

"I shall not be very far away," Clara said sharply.

"I imagine not," the old woman sighed. "Peace be with you."

"And also with you mother," Sister Clara said tensely. She turned and left the room, closing the door loudly as she went. Mother Maria Elena flinched from the noise of the door. She recovered quickly and looked happily up at Isabel.

"Sister Magdalena," the older woman began.

"Yes mother," Isabel said respectfully.

"Have you never cared for children before?"

"I never have," Isabel admitted.

"Are you disappointed?"

"I am sad to be away from Mother Serena and my sisters," Isabel said, "but I am eager to serve the Lord."

"You are disappointed then."

"No," Isabel disagreed. "I have made a vow to God that I will care for them as if they were my own."

"We shall see," Mother Maria Elena said. "Have Sister Clara get you some dry clothing and then show you around your new home. Lastly, I wish for you to meet the children."

"Where will I find her?"

"She is lurking about in the hallway no doubt," the old woman said irritably. "You should have no difficulty."

"Those women," Isabel said cautiously; "what have they done that they should be locked behind bars?"

"What have they not done," Maria Elena sighed. "All of our girls come from the worst of backgrounds. Most of them were harlots before being taken to us. All have engaged in fornications the extent to which I prefer not to imagine."

"I see," Isabel answered. What Clara had said at the gate now started to make sense.

"Most girls live in the dormitory. Those who misbehave or are afflicted in mind are housed here in the infirmary. The others are made safe by their being here and they are safe from themselves. Sister Clara is in charge of the infirmary," the old woman added. "She can tell you better than I."

"I will ask her," Isabel replied.

"You have leave Sister Magdalena," the mother superior said at last. "Go with God and welcome to the Convent of the Angels."

"Thank you mother," Isabel replied. She turned around then and left the office of the mother superior. The doorway to room '7' was ajar. Sister Clara came out of it before Isabel could pass by.

"Now you have met our mother," she said as she shut the door behind her. "What do you think?"

"I think I should pass on to you what she said," Isabel replied neutrally.

"Please do," Clara said.

"It is only that she wants me to have dry clothing and she requests that you show me where everything is."

"I will of course obey," Sister Clara said sweetly. "Isabel thought she detected some insincerity in the woman's voice. "You have already seen our rooms," Clara began. "There are nine of us now that you are here. The girls outnumber us by about five to one so be alert. We must project strength if we are to remain in control."

"I understand that perfectly," Isabel assured her.

"Excellent," Clara nodded. "You and I may get along after all."

"That girl you disciplined earlier," Isabel ventured. "What did she do?"

"She attacked Sister Laura inside the mill," Clara replied. "Do not let their innocent young faces fool you!"

"I will be more cautious," Isabel agreed.

"I will show you the mill first," Clara said. Isabel looked back once at her room. She wondered why they were not tending to the matter of her wet clothing as the mother superior had commanded. She followed Sister Clara through the door by the stairs that led back into the cloister. After this, they came to an archway which led into the alley between the infirmary and an even larger building. The rain was still flattening the grass and forming great puddles within it. The sisters continued on through the cloister along the back of the compound.

The farther they walked, the stronger came the smell of baking bread. Small rectangular shaped grates were placed at intervals along the inner wall of the cloister at waist level. "Come and see," Sister Clara beckoned as she knelt down by one such grate. The smell of the bread became overpowering as Sister Magdalena brought her face up to it.

On the other side, Isabel could see a wooden trough raised up on poles from the floor. Two unhappy looking girls in brown dresses were kneading the dough inside of it. Beyond this, Isabel could see large, wheel-shaped stones on the ground. Two of the brown clad girls sat cross legged around each of these mill stones. With their hands, they moved the stone lids in a clock wise motion. The air coming through the grate was hot and the women's dresses were soaked through with sweat.

"The girls know about these peek holes," Clara said as they both stood up again, "but they never know when one of us might be watching." She stood up then and beckoned Isabel to join her. Clara then led Isabel farther down the back of the cloister.

The next archway that they came too looked out on a cobblestone walkway which spanned the length of the convent. The mill and the infirmary were on the right side. Two smaller buildings were placed along the left. Their rooftops were connected by stone bridges with small statues of angels placed at the center of each on top of one of the hand rails. Over the top of the first building on the left, Isabel could see that the second had an upper story which was a smaller rectangle on top of the wider base. "This is the dormitory," Clara said. "The closer building is the dining hall and the kitchen together. If you look out to the left of the archway, you will see our chicken coop. Beyond that is the garden."

Isabel poked her head out into the rain long enough to see the coop and the rows of herbs and vegetables that were now saturated from the downpour. The coop was very small and one would have to duck down to go inside of it. She could hear the sounds of the chickens from within.

From her vantage point, Isabel could see over the dining hall to the large grey chapel that dominated the far side of the convent. Its two bell towers loomed imposingly over the rest of the compound. Their shadows fell down over the smaller buildings. Isabel came in out of the rain. She wiped her face with one hand. Her clothing was still quite wet from her journey.

"Ready to move on," Sister Clara asked impatiently?

"Yes," Isabel answered. She wondered if Clara would remember that she needed to change. They continued through the safety of the cloister to the church. Isabel noticed more grates which would surely allow one to secretly observe the girls as they worked in the garden. There was also an archway that provided an alternative access to it.

"That door leads behind the sanctuary," Clara said as they rounded the next corner. "You can also get upstairs from there. Uriel's bridge leads from the second floor of the church over to the girls' dormitory. At no time are any of the girls to be on the bridges or rooftops. We severely punish those who disobey." Isabel nodded. Clara continued on, pointing at the grates as she spoke. "No one is to speak during mass but the priest. If it is a prayer meeting, than it is only the nun who leads that should be heard."

"I see," Isabel said. They continued around the chapel until they came back to the front of the convent. Double doors opened from the sanctuary directly into the cloister. Stained glass windows lined the upper walls of the vaulted sanctuary. The pews were long wooden benches with no backings. A portion of the floor at the far end was raised up perhaps a foot from the rest. Upon this platform was a plain wooden pulpit and a large table for communion.

There were four recessed alcoves in the wall behind the pulpit which began about six feet from the floor and continued all the way up. Each alcove contained a statue of one of the four archangels; Michael, Gabriel, Rafael, and Uriel. Hanging between the centermost alcoves was a statue of the crucified Christ. It was fashioned of marble and the detail was so fine that one could actually see the tears falling down his cheek. "How beautiful," Isabel said reverently.

"Yes," Clara agreed. "I remember thinking the same thing when I first saw it." There was a bitter edge to the woman's voice that prompted Isabel's next question.

"Was it very long ago," she asked?

"It was," Clara replied, "but let us get you back to your room and out of that wet clothing."

"Thank you," Isabel said. "It has become quite unpleasant." The cloth was clinging to her skin and rubbing it raw in some places. Sister Clara led her around that portion of the cloister that encompassed the two iron gates. They walked quickly past the first gate to avoid the possibility of someone outside noticing them. There was no one there in the pouring rain, however. Magdalena guessed that it was force of habit on the part of the other sister. As they rounded the corner to that portion of the wall with the grate of iron vines, Isabel could see the back of the pass-through cupboard and the bell which Armando had used to summon Sister Clara.

The inner wall of the cloister behind the grate consisted of many open archways facing the lawn in front of the dormitory. In the center archway was a stone well built half in and half out of the cloister. They hurried past the next gate and on around to the infirmary. They walked once more through the prison hall. There were no cries for help this time.

"I will go and fetch you a dry habit," Sister Clara said as they came up into room '4'. "You should disrobe." Before Isabel could answer, the other woman shut the door loudly behind her. The former heiress removed her habit and then the white scapula beneath it. Her skin was still damp and the rain outside did nothing to help her gain warmth. She did not want to sit on her bed and get the blanket wet, nor did she wish to leave an embarrassing print of her backside on the room's one wooden stool. Isabel shivered as she crossed her arms over her breasts.

Without so much as a knock, Sister Clara abruptly entered the room with a dry habit and a towel. "What are you doing," Isabel asked angrily? "Surely you knew that I would be unclothed."

"Of course I knew," Sister Clara smiled as she closed the door softly. "I was the one to suggest it."

"Could you not knock and then hand it through the smallest crack of the door," Isabel asked rhetorically? She snatched the habit and the white scapula from Sister Clara and immediately set to covering her nakedness.

"You are so sensitive," Clara chuckled. She didn't even have the decency to turn away while Isabel dressed herself!

"I find your behavior to be revolting," Isabel said crisply. "This shall be the last time you enter my quarters."

"Your quarters," Clara scoffed? "It is but a closet with a bed in it."

"Nevertheless," Isabel said reproachfully. Her stony glare told the other woman more than words.

"Perfect," Sister Clara said sarcastically; "another one who thinks herself too good for us. You know Sister Magdalena, it is written that pride goeth before a fall."

"And that is why I shall lead the way to the orphans," Isabel answered quickly. "You may follow behind me." Sister Clara was momentarily speechless. Isabel's arm hit the side of Clara's as she left the room, but she made no effort to beg her pardon. It made no sense to apologize for an intentional act.

"You cannot get in without the key," Clara reminded Magdalena as she hurried after her. Isabel's stride was much longer than Sister Clara's.

"I know this," Isabel said without looking back.

"How do you expect to get in then," Sister Clara demanded. To Isabel, she sounded like a petulant child. Sister Magdalena turned around then and stared at the smaller woman.

"Let me explain it for you," Isabel said. "Mother Maria Elena instructed you to get me dry clothes and then show me around the convent. Instead, you let me suffer in my soaked habit until you had finished the tour. You took a vow of obedience, no?"

"Of course I did," Clara retorted with one hand placed upon her hip.

"Then you must take me now to meet the children. Those were your orders from the mother superior. If you cannot keep up with me, then I will of course wait at the door." With that, Isabel turned and went down the two flights of stairs that led to the orphans' chamber. The second staircase led down to a small foyer with a locked door on either side. The door on the left was much more heavily reinforced than its counterpart. Sister Clara did have to catch up, but it was not by far.

"To your left is the sanitarium," Clara said irritably. She removed a small key ring from the larger one she carried with her. "The smaller key is for your cell. The larger will take you inside the orphans' living area. Sister Eva is inside. You will replace her." Isabel took the keys and began opening the door on the right. "You have much to learn Sister Magdalena," Clara said ominously.

"Thank you sister," Isabel replied without so much as a glance back at the other nun. She let herself into the orphanage and closed the door quietly behind her. The room she found herself in was lit by oil burning lamps. There was a fireplace at the far end of the chamber but it was not lit. Five small beds were spaced along one wall. The opposite wall contained five recessed alcoves with cribs in each.

Only two of the cribs were occupied: one by a sleeping infant, and the other by a young boy of perhaps three years of age. The little boy stood up in his crib when Isabel entered the room. He had a full head of brown hair and the most hopeful eyes she had ever seen. They were dark brown with long lashes.

Three older children were sitting between two of the beds. Isabel could only see the tops of their heads over the bed sheets. There was a boy with black hair and another blonde. The tallest of the three was a girl with auburn pigtails. In addition to her hair, Isabel could see the pale skin of her forehead.

As it turned out, all of the children were pale. It was an unfortunate side effect from living far from the sun. The last inhabitant was Sister Eva. She was sitting on a rocking chair in the center of the room with some knitting in her hands. She stood up almost immediately when Isabel had come in. "Sister Magdalena," Eva asked?

"I am she," Isabel replied."

"Sister Clara gave you the keys, I trust?"

"She did."

"Praise God," Sister Eva said with relief. "My work here is done."

"Will you not stay long enough to show me what to do," Isabel implored her? "I have never had a child before."

"If its hungry…feed it. If it's dirty…clean it. If it's bothering you…put it to bed. Simple," Eva said callously.

"Well I…" Isabel began

"Put Gabriella in charge if you must leave the room for any reason," Eva said.

"Who is Gabriella," Isabel asked? The older girl stood up from between the beds. She wore a brown dress like the condemned women above. She could not have been more than nine years old. Her eyes looked older than her small frame would suggest, however.

"I am Gabriella, sister," the young girl said politely. She waved one tentative hand in the air. The two boys who sat around her peeked up over the bed with uncertainty. It was hard to see them clearly in the shadowy space between the beds. The boys wore brown tunics and pantalones made from the same material as the dresses. Isabel guessed them to be around five or six years of age.

"Hello Gabriella," Isabel said warmly. "Who are your friends?"

"This is Raul," the girl said motioning to the dark haired boy.

"I am Liz," the blonde boy said as he waved his arm enthusiastically over his head.

"His name is Lysandro," Gabriella corrected, "but that is what we usually call him."

"Hello," Isabel said. "I am Sister Magdalena."

"A pleasure to meet you sister," Gabriella said. Lysandro repeated Gabriella's salutation. Raul mumbled a greeting as he looked down at the floor. "Let me show you the others," Gabriella offered as she walked across the room. Lysandro began marking the floor with a white piece of chalk as Isabel followed the older girl.

"Esmeralda is asleep," Gabriella whispered as they passed the baby. She was clutching onto a rag doll with both hands and her mouth was open in a perfect little 'o' shape.

"She is a pretty one," Isabel said as they passed, "a pretty name as well."

"You like it," Gabriella asked? "I like it too. I wish it was my name. That is why I chose it for her."

"You chose it," Isabel asked?

"Yes, she did not have a name. Sister Raquel just called her the baby, but I call her Esmeralda. When Sister Eva took over, I just told her it was her name. You will not punish me will you?"

"No," Isabel replied. "There is nothing wrong with what you did. A child needs a name and you chose the perfect one." Gabriella beamed.

"This last boy is called Aaron," she said.

"Down," Aaron asked hopefully?

"Yuck," Gabriella said as she pinched up her face. "You pooped Aaron!"

"No poop," Aaron disagreed, "down?"

"Yes you did," Gabriella insisted. "You went poop."

"Yuck," Aaron said.

"Come on," Isabel said as she reached her arms out toward the boy.

"No," Aaron exclaimed as he backed into the corner of the crib.

"He wanted to get down a moment ago," Isabel said with confusion.

"He is scared of you," Gabriella explained. "Let me."

"Alright," Isabel said as she took a few steps back. "I did not mean to scare him."

"The other sisters," Gabriella began, but then she bit her lip.

"Yes," Isabel prodded?

"Well, it is just that they did not seem to like us very much…Aaron especially."

"Why do you say that?"

"I am sorry sister," Gabriella said as she took Aaron out of the crib. She set him down and he immediately ran toward the other boys!

"Liz," Aaron called out as he ran toward them, "Raoo!"

"Why would they not like a little boy?"

"He is a Jew," Gabriella explained, "at least he was." The girl put a smile on her face before she spoke again. "Now he will be a Christian like us though, won't he sister?"

"Of course," Isabel affirmed.

"Leave the chalk alone Aaron," Raul scolded as he drew his hand away from the smaller boy's.

"It's my chalk," Aaron said indignantly as he reached out again. "Its mine!"

"Let's go Aaron," Gabriella said as she scooped him up from the floor.

"It's my chalk," Aaron sobbed!

"You can play with the chalk in a moment," Gabriella said as she carried the toddler over to a large, free standing cupboard. "Right now you stink!"

"In a moment," Aaron called out excitedly. He seemed much happier with this answer. Gabriella set Aaron on top of the cupboard which rose to just below the height of Isabel's waist. There was a small basin of water on top of it. Gabriella laid Aaron down on his back easily enough. Then came the task of changing the diaper cloth. In the meantime, Aaron made raspberry noises with his mouth and grinned from ear to ear. The girl changing him could not help but laugh.

"Is he always so happy," Isabel asked?

"He is when the nuns are away," Gabriella said. "He is too loud for them. He is quiet otherwise." Having finished changing the boy's diaper, she set him down on the floor. Aaron looked up uncertainly at Isabel as he walked past her and then ran toward the other boys.

"My chalk, my chalk," Aaron cried out excitedly!

"Gabby," Raul said plaintively.

"Oh let him play with it for a moment," Gabriella scolded. "You know how quickly he loses interest."

"Alright," the two older boys said in unison. Raul handed Aaron the chalk.

"My chalk," the toddler exclaimed triumphantly! He showed it to Gabriella by holding it high above his head.

"Yes Aaron, that is your chalk," Gabriella agreed. The boy then began to scribble on the stone floor. He made buzzing noises with his mouth as he did so. Unlike the other boys, Aaron wore only a tunic and his diaper. "He came here when he was a baby like Esmeralda," the girl told Isabel. "That is why he is so happy. He doesn't know anything else." Gabriella disposed of the dirty cloth in a bucket with a lid that sat in the corner by the cupboard. "One of the women will come down in the morning to take it away," she explained to Isabel who was wrinkling her nose. Isabel nodded.

"How is it you all came to be here?"

"Shhhh," Gabriella said with a finger held to her lips. "I shall tell you later tonight," she whispered, "once the others are sleeping."

"Alright," Isabel agreed. She spent the rest of the day learning how to take care of children from a nine year old girl. Gabriella was very patient with them, but she could be stern when it was called for. It was clear to Isabel that these children looked to her as a mother figure.

It took little time for the children to warm up to Isabel once they realized that she was actually interested in them. By days end, they were all playing a game that Isabel's Little Grandma had played with her when she was a child. It was a variation of hide and seek in which Isabel would pretend to be a monster as she looked for the children. If found, she would tickle them mercilessly! Isabel was shambling around the room with her arms held above her head. "Here comes the tickle monster," she said in a deep voice. The children, (who would hide in the cupboard or beneath the beds), would often give themselves away by laughing before they were caught.

Isabel had an extra portion of food brought down so that she could share her evening meal with the children. She would have stayed longer, but Sister Eva arrived and insisted that she come to Vespers with the other nuns. Gabriella was telling the rest of the children a bedtime story from memory as Sister Magdalena shut the door behind her.

CHAPTER IV

Isabel and Sister Eva entered the sanctuary as the mother superior was leading the other six nuns in prayer. Both sisters dipped their fingers in the marble basin of holy water that was mounted to the wall by the entrance. After genuflecting and making the sign of the cross, they made their way up to where the others were seated. Filling the rest of the pews were the brown garbed women who had come to the Convent of the Angels by no choice of their own. Isabel guessed that there were perhaps forty of them.

After the last prayer was said, one of the sisters led the prisoners out of the sanctuary. Another followed behind them. The rest of the nuns congregated up toward the front of the chamber. Isabel was among them. "Let us all welcome Sister Magdalena to our order," Maria Elena announced.

"Nice of you to join us," Sister Clara said. It was obvious that she spoke in reference to Isabel's late arrival to Vespers and not to her coming to the Convent of the Angels.

"I am Sister Laura," one of the nuns said. She moved closer and clasped hands with Isabel. She had an old scar that ran in a horizontal line across her chin.

"A pleasure to meet you sister," Isabel replied as Sister Laura backed away. She was greeted next by Sister Esperanza and Sister Roberta.

"You have already met Sister Clara and Sister Eva," the mother superior said. "Sister Consuela and Maria Castellanos are taking the penitents to their dormitory. Sister Laura is in charge of the mill. Sister Roberta runs the kitchen. Sister Esperanza handles the gardening. Sisters Consuela and Maria manage the dormitory. Sister Eva will resume her duties in the church. Sister Clara is second to myself and is in charge of running the infirmary."

"Sister Magdalena will be watching the orphans," Maria Elena told the other sisters. "Let us make her feel welcome in our home."

"We missed you at dinner Sister Magdalena," Clara said. "Was there any trouble?"

"Not at all," Isabel replied. "The children need supervision, especially at meal time."

"Who is acting up this time," Eva asked as she rolled her eyes heavenward. "Was it the Jewish child?"

"He is to be a Christian now," Isabel said curtly. "His name is Aaron." Sister Eva nodded noncommittally.

"He tries my patience," Eva said with a sigh.

"I find the children quite easy to care for," Isabel replied, "all of them."

"All is the better," Sister Eva said with relief. "Praise be to God." The other sisters shared looks with Sister Eva and each other that told Isabel that they were all in agreement. Father Hernando had been right to send her here.

"I have to make sure they're in bed," Isabel said with a frown, but her displeasure was not with the children. She was gracious as some of the sisters offered more words of welcome on her way out of the sanctuary, but she left quickly. As relieved as Sister Eva was to be away from the children, that was how happy Isabel was to get away from the other nuns.

When Isabel let herself back in the children's room, there was only one lamp still burning on top of the cupboard. All of the children were in bed and all but Gabriela were sound asleep. The oldest child sat on top of her sheets looking up at sister Magdalena with expectant eyes. Isabel quietly crossed the room and seated herself next to her. "They are all asleep," Gabriela whispered.

"I see," Isabel nodded her approval, "you'll make a very good mother someday."

"I would like that I think," the girl replied. Isabel could see that her complement made Gabriela feel proud of herself. "I will tell you where we come from now, if that is your wish."

"Tell me," Isabel whispered back. Gabriela sighed and looked up at the ceiling as if collecting her thoughts.

Isabel was struck again with how much older the child's face appeared.

"This year will be my fifth come Christmas," Gabriela began "my mother was a prostitute in Pamplona."

"I'm so sorry," Isabel said with genuine sympathy "that must've been hard for you."

"Not really," Gabriela smiled. "Sometimes I think this is worse. I miss her very much. Mama did what she had to do. She always put me in another room. I heard things, but..." The girl sighed. "What choice was there?" Isabel had no answer and so the girl continued. "She didn't let the men touch me. There were other girls at the bordello not so lucky. Mom used to tie ribbons in my hair and tell me how I was the most precious girl in the world. She used to say that we were going to go live in the country when she had enough money."

"Where's your mother now?" Isabel asked.

"Upstairs I suppose," Gabriela said. "I do not know. We came here when the convent was still being built in some places. The sisters separated us right away. They said it was best for me. Mama kept getting in trouble just for talking to me. Sometimes she was whipped. Sometimes she did not get to eat. Nothing worked. That is why they put me down here."

"That is horrible," Isabel said! "Why would they do such a thing?"

"I guess they think I will grow up to be a prostitute if she talks to me. I won't though. Mom said she would kill me if I did what she did." Gabriela smiled bitterly. "She just wanted me to be happy because she wasn't."

"She sounds like a good mother," Isabel said

"She is," Gabriela agreed.

"I will make sure you get to speak with her," Isabel promised.

"The others won't let you," Gabriela said.

"We shall see," Isabel replied. "Tell me about the others."

"Raul was born here," Gabriela said. "He was a baby when I arrived. His mother used to get in trouble too. She just wanted to hold him, but Sister Raquel wouldn't let her. I guess they let her suckle him for about a year, but then they put him down here with me. I heard his mother screaming outside the doors."

"That is awful," Isabel said.

"Will you keep a secret?" Gabriela asked seriously.

"I swear," Isabel said as she made the sign of the cross.

"She said.., it is your fault I was with child," Gabriela whispered. "Now you will not even let me see him?"

"How could that be," Isabel asked incredulously?

"I do not know," Gabriela whispered, "something bad though."

"Indeed," Isabel agreed.

"Poor Liz still doesn't know what happened," Gabriela said sadly. "He was Aaron's age when he came to us. All he knew was that they took his mommy way. He comes from somewhere else I think."

"Ahh," Isabel nodded.

"Sister Raquel told me that Aaron's parents had him outside marriage. His mother was a Jew and his father a Christian. The father refused to claim him and the mother was arrested for trying to steal horses."

"What happened to his mother?"

"I do not know, but I'm certain that she is not here."

"Why not?"

"Sister Raquel said that no one would ever see her in Pamplona again. It seemed like maybe something bad happened to her."

"What about Esmeralda?"

"I do not know anything about her," Gabriela admitted, "but she is my baby now."

"She is beautiful," Isabel smiled.

"Where do you come from Sister," Gabriela asked?

"It is late now Gabriela," Isabel replied. "I may tell you another day."

"All right," Gabriela agreed. "Goodnight sister," she crawled under the covers and Isabel tucked her in.

"Goodnight child," Isabel said. She bent over and kissed the girl on the forehead before blowing out the lamp. She left the room quietly and returned to her own bedroom on the top floor. Isabel knelt by the side of the bed and prayed that God would watch over the children and their mothers. As she settled herself into the covers, Isabel couldn't help thinking about how awful it must be to be separated from one's own child. How could the nuns expect these women to repent if they would not let them see their children? As she drifted off to sleep, Isabel heard the sound of the bed creaking in the room next to hers. There was another sound also. It was the sound of a woman's voice but it was muffled by the wall. It could have been speech. It might be someone crying. Isabel couldn't tell, but she paid it no mind.

The next morning found Sister Magdalena in the office of the mother superior. "You must understand sister," Maria Elena said firmly, "your duty is to protect the children, not to reintroduce them to evil." The conversation was not going as Isabel had hoped.

"These children need to see their mothers," Isabel replied with exasperation, "even if it is only a little while."

"Their mothers must first be reformed."

"Gabriela's mother has been here for nearly 5 years," Isabel almost shouted! "How long must she suffer?"

"These women are whores sister," Maria Elena explained, "and Flora is far from penitent."

"Mother," Isabel implored, "do you not think she would be more receptive to the message of salvation if she could see her daughter? The woman should see us as the name of our convent implies. What we are doing now can only breed hatred for God and the church!"

"Sister Magdalena," Maria Elena shouted, but then she was overcome by a fit of choking coughs. Isabel moved quickly to beat her hand on the old woman's back, but Maria

Elena pushed her way. At that moment, Sister Clara came swiftly into the room.

"What goes on here," Sister Clara demanded?

"Take Sister Magdalena out of my office," the mother superior croaked. "Instruct her that the children are not..." Maria Elena released another fit of coughing before continuing on. "They are not to have contact with the harlots."

"I will make sure she understands," Sister Clara promised. Isabel scowled. "Follow me Sister Magdalena," Clara ordered. Isabel looked once more at the mother superior before she left the room. Though she could not see her own face, she was certain that her expression was less than respectful.

"Go to your room," Clara said sharply!

"I'll not have you in my room again," Isabel replied angrily. "You must have forgotten."

"I have no time for your petty desires," Sister Clara snapped. "Get you to your room or be locked in a prison cell!" Isabel stalked back to her room. She turned around and blocked the doorway to prevent Clara from entering. The smaller woman stood there sizing her up. Clara must've decided not to force the issue. She berated her from the hallway instead. "You will not be long for the sisterhood if you cannot keep your vows," Sister Clara rebuked her!

"I have not disobeyed," Isabel argued.

"The mother superior is weak with age," Sister Clara said. "You would hurry her into an early grave with your obstinance. Do as she tells you sister. Argue with me if you must, but the outcome will be no different. Save yourself some time and obey."

"The children need their mothers," Isabel said from between clenched teeth.

"You are their mother now," Clara shouted! "Get you down and tend to them."

"It has been..," Isabel began.

"Enough," Clara interrupted her. "It is not a suggestion sister. Do as you're commanded!"

"Yes sister," Isabel said with restraint. She closed the door to her room and headed toward the stairs.

"I'll be watching you Sister Magdalena," Sister Clara threatened. Isabel continued down the stairs without a reply. She could not. She was afraid that once she started talking, she wouldn't be able to stop. In this foul temper, there was no telling what else she might do. How could the nuns be so blind? They were so focused on being in control that they must've forgotten the convent's original goal. To keep a child from its mother was not in any way godly!

The children immediately picked up on Isabel's mood. They looked up at her with wide and questioning eyes as if they were at fault. "All is well children," Isabel said when she saw there worried faces.

"Down," Aaron called hopefully from his crib.

"You want down," Isabel asked as she came to the edge of his bed. Aaron held his arms up and smiled. She lifted him up out of the crib and set the child down on his little legs. Aaron began talking and gesturing toward Isabel but none of his words made any sense. "I do not understand you mijo," she laughed. Aaron ran over and jumped on Raul's back. The older boy pulled him off and tickled him mercilessly. Their laughter was infectious and soon the whole room was giggling.

As she lay in her own bed that night, Isabel heard the same creaking and sobbing noises coming from the room next to hers. She tried her best to ignore it, but the noises became louder still. With a groan of discontent, Isabel rose from her bed and opened the trunk at the foot of it. She was wearing her white nightdress and she now donned the light-colored scapula that would cover all but her face.

Isabel was worried about Sister Consuela who occupied the room next to hers. She wondered what it could be that made her cry every night. Not wanting to wake the other sisters, Isabel softly opened her door and stepped out into the hall. The sobs were quite loud now and it seemed that Consuela might actually be in some sort of physical pain.

The door to room number five had been left open a crack. It was from this vertical slit that the moaning came along with a sliver of lamp light. Through the slit Isabel could see Consuela's bare leg with the white of her night dress below it. Something did not seem quite right. Isabel leaned in closer to peek through the opening.

It was not pain that caused the other woman's fussing. She was not even sister Consuela. It was Clara who sat on the bed with her legs spread wide. She hiked up her skirts both black and white over her waist. The sobbing moans were her cries of ecstasy. What Isabel saw next gave her a sick feeling in her stomach. Sitting next to Sister Clara was the room's proper occupant. Sister Consuela held her skirts up as well and was quite obviously pleasuring herself. One of the so-called penitents was down on her hands and knees with her face buried in Sister Clara's exposed sex.

The door creaked slightly. Isabel drew back, but not before she saw the brown clothed woman looking back at the door with alarm. Isabel hurried into her room and shut the door behind her. She at least had the presence of mind to shut it quietly, so as not to give herself away.

Isabel removed her scapula and placed it under her pillow. She lay there nervously with her eyes closed. Her reaction should have been outrage, but what she had seen so sickened her that she had no desire to speak of it. Not one of the three women she had seen gave her any reason to believe that they were being forced. This was something altogether different. Isabel made the sign of the cross over her breasts and prayed silently as she heard the door to room five swinging wide on its hinges.

"Who is there?" Sister Consuela's voice called out. There followed some hushed tones the Isabel could not discern.

"I'll take her back to her cell," Sister Clara whispered loudly. "Get you to bed." The door to room five shut loudly. Isabel could then hear the two sets of footsteps descending the stairs. She remained awake until she heard Clara returning. The door across the hall opened and closed before Isabel heard nothing more.

Isabel recited prayers and did her best to purge the memory of the abomination from her mind's eye. Was nothing sacred?

†   †   †

Isabel did not go to the mother superior the next day as she had decided the night before. She had learned from her torment in Montenegro that it was far more prudent to keep her mouth and her tongue in check. She worried that the perversity she had seen was far more widespread.

The nuns prayed no less than five times a day. Isabel did her best to act as if nothing had happened. Unfortunately, the mere sight of the nuns involved made her skin crawl. She suspected that they knew.

"I have decided to sleep with the orphans," Isabel told them all after evening vespers. She hoped that none would question her. This was why she waited to speak until all were present. The guilty would not dare to argue in front of the innocent, but who were the innocent?

"Do you find that proper sister," Maria Elena asked?

"We would not sleep with the women in their dormitory," Sister Eva added.

"The baby needs more than a nine-year-old girl can provide," Isabel explained. "I already must leave them several times a day for prayer."

"You do not care for prayer," Sister Clara asked rudely?

"That is not it at all," Isabel replied. "It is only that I am afraid to leave the children alone for such long periods of time. Even if nothing is amiss, I am certain that I will sleep better knowing that they are safe."

"What say you Sister," the mother superior asked Clara?

"Let her do as she says," Clara said scornfully. "She may even be right."

"You may sleep with the orphans Sister Magdalena," Maria Elena said. "We will see how it is as time passes." The old woman looked at Clara for a reaction. The uncertainty in the eyes of the mother superior spoke volumes as to who was in command. This also made Isabel aware of how futile reporting the incident of the night before would have been.

As Sister Magdalena walked back through the cloister, Sister Clara fell into step beside her. "You look pleased," Clara said sarcastically.

"I am," Isabel replied in a neutral tone.

"I just wanted to be clear on something," Clara continued. "Like Sister Eva and Maria Castellanos, you have yet to take your solemn perpetual vows. As a novice, you may be called upon by any full sister to assist her as she sees fit."

"Is there something you would like me to do Sister Clara?"

"Not especially," Clara replied. "You are helping the convent by caring for the children. Focus on that."

"I am quite focused," Isabel told her.

"I also expect no more disagreeableness from you. One needs to know her place."

"Of course," Sister Magdalena nodded.

"Good," Clara said with satisfaction. "I shall see you tomorrow."

"Good evening," Magdalena said finally. Sister Clara quickened her steps and left Isabel behind. For her part, Isabel had no desire to remain in Clara's company. She also had lost her desire to confront the other nun. Any strife Isabel cooked up between them would be sure to affect the children. It might even be dangerous to them. Above all, Isabel wanted the orphans to remain safe from harm.

For the next several months, Isabel kept to herself during prayer services. When asked, she would relate that the children were doing well. She might also relate some small bit of information on how one of them was improving, but the other nuns didn't seem to care about the particulars. It seemed right that she should say something, however.

Gabriela was greatly disappointed when Sister Magdalena told her that she would not get to see her mother. "Thank you anyway sister," the child said sadly. "I was sure that they would not permit it."

On Sundays, Father Benigno would hold mass inside the sanctuary. Benigno was well advanced in years, but his eyes held a youthful vitality. After taking confessions, the priest would meet with Maria Elena to discuss the running of the convent. Isabel noticed that Sister Clara invariably accompanied them during such meetings. Father Benigno would also drop by from time to time during the week to check on the mill or the infirmary. Mostly he came alone, but sometimes he had other men of the cloth with him.

As Sister Clara had suggested, Isabel focused her attention on the children. Though she did not have a bible to read from, Isabel knew most of the stories well enough. The going was slow, but she was using ink and parchment to teach the older children how to read. It would have been easier if she'd had a bible or another book, but the results were promising. Aaron could not read as well as the older children, but he had mastered his letters in only a few weeks time.

During the hours of darkness after the children had gone to bed, Isabel would try and formulate a plan for getting the children out of the convent entirely. She would have to work out how they would be reunited with their mothers later. Isabel wanted to give them a life that might resemble normalcy. It was not good for them to be shut away from the sun. How pale they were.

Every day, Isabel would travel outside the orphans' room. During these times she would attend prayer with the other sisters or acquire some food for the children. Months passed. Isabel was walking through the cloister one day when everything changed. The leaves of the trees inside the convent were made all the more beautiful with the rusted colors of autumn.

It was Sister Magdalena's habit to enter the infirmary through the second set of doors that opened on the stairwell down to the orphan's room. On one particular day, she varied in her routine. For some inexplicable reason, she went through the first set of doors which led into one of the prison halls. The prisoners did not say anything to the black and white garbed nun as she traveled up the walkway between the iron-barred cells. Isabel paused when she reached the cell of the woman whose fingers had been twisted by Sister Clara. What gave Isabel pause was how remarkably similar in appearance this woman was to Gabriela.

"You must be Flora," Isabel said as she came over to the edge of the bars.

"Yes sister," Flora said apprehensively.

"Your daughter is well," Isabel whispered. "She loves you very much."

"Is she safe," Flora asked desperately as she rushed over to stand by the bars?

"She is," Isabel confirmed. "Keep your voice down."

"Pardon me," the woman whispered.

"She takes care of the other children like a mother. You have reason to be proud."

"Will you tell her," Flora asked hopefully? "Will you tell her how proud I am?" Isabel nodded and smiled. "Please let me see her…even for a moment!"

"You have to behave first. Repent. Whatever it is that Sister Clara wants you to do, that is what you need to accomplish. If you do that, I may be able to sneak you down to see her."

"You do not understand," Flora said. "I have done nothing wrong!"

"You struck Sister Laura in the mill," Isabel reminded her. "That is why you are imprisoned."

"No-no-no," Flora shook her head. "It is not any wickedness of mine that keeps me here. It is…" Flora's words were cut short by the sound of a door opening from up the hall. Sister Clara entered and turned a suspicious eye on both of them. Isabel looked quickly back at Flora and spat out the first thing that came to mind.

"Do they never bathe you," Isabel asked rudely? "Keep you to the back of your cell when I pass. You smell like the slop of a swine herd!"

"Sorry Sister," Flora said, taking Isabel's cue. She backed slowly toward the wall as she spoke.

"Turn your head when you speak woman," Isabel said with disgust, "or do not speak at all!" By this time, Sister Clara had joined Magdalena outside Flora's cell.

"Did she open her mouth again," Clara asked?

"I wish that she had not," Isabel groaned.

"What have I told you about speaking," Clara demanded of the prisoner?

"I did not speak first sister," Flora pleaded. "I was just…standing here."

"Is it the truth," Clara asked Isabel? Her eyes were sharp and penetrating.

"It is the truth," Isabel replied. "She was standing so close to the bars that her stench curdled my stomach! How could I not say anything?"

"How indeed," Sister Clara asked with a grim satisfaction? Her eyes bored into Isabel before she looked back at Flora. "Cleanliness is next to Godliness," she said sweetly, "and we should never be ungodly should we?"

"No sister," Flora replied nervously.

"Do not worry," Sister Clara grinned. Her face was like a hungry vulture poised over a carrion feast! "Sister Magdalena will return presently to help you remember to keep clean."

"I shall return," Isabel promised sternly.

"Come now sister," Clara purred. "Let me show you where the lash is kept."

"Lead the way," Isabel replied in a tone that she hoped sounded properly cruel. Sister Clara was only too pleased to oblige her. She led Isabel to a pair of black doors and opened one. Clara held the door while Isabel entered in. Like most rooms in the convent, the misericord had little in the way of decoration. A wooden crucifix hung on the wall opposite the door. In the center of the room was a prayer bench which rose only inches from the ground. In front of this was a hard wooden platform with stocks built over the top of it. The holes in the stocks faced upward and were positioned such that the captive would be able to clasp their hands together in prayer.

"Here it is," Clara said as she gestured toward the long whip which was coiled around a peg in the wall. She grasped the handle and several of the coils before removing it. "You will know how to use this, will you not?"

"I will," Isabel lied.

"Let me see," Sister Clara said as she thrust the handle out toward a reluctant Isabel. The handle was warm to the touch and Isabel's flesh recoiled from it as though it were a venomous snake! Nevertheless, she grabbed onto the whip tightly. "Give it a try," Sister Clara invited, "just to make sure it isn't too long for you."

"Give it a try," Isabel asked?

"Yes," Clara responded impatiently, "just strike at the misericord for practice." Isabel did her best to swing the whip at the stocks over the prayer bench. It struck the top without much gusto and then slid off onto the ground. The whip hung limply from Isabel's unsure hand.

"Are you not going to crack it," Clara asked? Isabel tried several more times, yielding results little better than the first. "Give me that," Clara finally said with disgust. She wrenched the whip from Isabel's hand. "Like this," Clara said loudly as she whirled the weapon over her head and then swung down at the misericord. At the last second, Clara pulled back sharply. This caused the whip to make a loud snapping noise. Sister Clara cracked the whip several more times for good measure before handing it back. "You are a liar," Clara told Isabel as she roughly shoved the lash into her hands.

"I certainly am not!"

"You have never used a whip."

"I have…seen it used," Isabel struggled. "I did not think it was that difficult."

"Not the same," Clara admonished her. They spent the next hour or so in practice. It only took half that time for Isabel to master the whip, but Clara seemed to really be enjoying herself. Isabel was sure that it was her discomfort that was exciting the other woman. "I think you are prepared sister," Clara said at last.

"I think so," Isabel agreed, "but I do not think it is necessarily the best medicine for her ailment."

"Nonsense," Sister Clara shot back! "The woman needs to keep herself clean."

"How could she possibly?"

"Now Sister Magdalena," Clara said sharply; "we cannot afford to be inconsistent. We must do as we say."

"We must," Isabel agreed, but her heart spoke otherwise. She followed Clara back into the hall which contained Flora's cell. Flora was huddled along the back wall. Her eyes were filled with fear.

"I see the problem," Sister Clara said as she pointed toward the floor of the prison cell. "Her straw mat is moldy. Give it here." Flora picked up the mat from the floor and brought it quickly forward. She then handed it through the bars to Clara.

"Here it is sister," Flora said with her eyes on the floor. Isabel noticed something small and dark within the straw, but she could not be certain what it was.

"Yes, yes," Clara said impatiently. "Give her the one from the empty cell," she told Sister Magdalena. Isabel walked into the cell to the left of Flora's. She bent down and picked up the other straw mat. She could not see what the difference was between the two, however. Just as she was about to ask Sister Clara, she heard the clang of the cell door and the jingling of keys as the other nun locked her in.

"What are you doing," Isabel cried as she turned sharply around? Sister Clara stared coldly through the bars that separated them.

"What I should have done long ago," Clara answered. "Take this rot," she said to Flora. The prisoner dutifully took back her straw mat and then retreated back into her cell. She looked relieved as if the mat were important to her. The nun then looked back at Isabel. "The real question is what are you doing Sister Magdalena?"

"Open the door," Isabel demanded, but her voice lacked confidence.

"I am going to inform Mother Maria Elena that you have broken your vow of obedience," Clara said, "then we will decide what is to be done about it!"

"I have done nothing wrong," Isabel replied nervously.

"Do you see that grate in the wall behind you sister," Clara asked smugly? There was indeed one of the small vertical grates at the back of the cell that Isabel now occupied. Isabel was left speechless. Sister Clara must have heard everything. "Lying only adds to your sins," she said. With that, she turned and left them alone in the prison hall.

Being locked in a cell set Isabel's teeth on edge. Her mouth was dry and she could not shake the feeling of impending horror. Her mind was flooded with all of the evils she had suffered at the hands of Lord Manuel Barillos. "It is not so bad sister," Flora said reassuringly. "They will not keep you long."

"Yes, thank you," Isabel said uncomfortably. She tried to compose herself but could not stop her hands from shaking.

"They will never let me go," Flora said, "but you have to get loose so that you can save my Gabriela."

"Save her," Isabel inquired? "Does she need saving?"

"She will," Flora nodded, "and it will not be long."

"What do you mean?" Isabel suddenly put a finger to her lips as she remembered the grate. She crept over to it and peered through. Satisfied that they were alone, she beckoned Flora closer to the bars that separated their two cells.

"You are different," Flora whispered as she approached the bars. "I can feel it, but the others…"

"Yes," Isabel prodded?

"Sister Clara and the rest of the nuns here are wicked. Even Father Benigno shares in their evil!"

"Tell me," Isabel urged. She peered once more through the grate before speaking again. "I need to know this."

"When I was arrested, the constable in Pamplona turned me over to the Convent of the Angels. He said that they would teach me to be a respectable Christian woman. Yet all I have learned is that this place is a secret brothel for men of the cloth."

"That cannot be true," Isabel gasped, but she could see no hint of deception in the other woman's face.

"It is true," Flora insisted. "That is the reason they keep me in prison, so that I cannot tell the other women."

"And the nuns allow this to go on," Isabel asked with amazement? "Why do they not tell anyone?"

"Because we are all here at the whim of Father Benigno; at any time he could cast us out into the streets!"

"On what grounds," Isabel asked?

"Any that he can imagine," Flora replied. "The church has always taken the word of men over that of women."

"Sister Clara seems not to be upset by the goings on at all."

"She is the worst of them," Flora whispered.

"What makes her so angry," Isabel whispered back?

"Clara…Sister Clara," Flora corrected herself. "Sister Clara came here just after I did, but she was a penitent back then."

"What was her crime?"

"Like me," Flora sighed, "she had done the same things as I. We were both housed in the same brothel for a time. She thought she was better than me. She thought she was better than everyone to tell you the truth. She did not like that I would not sell Gabriela to the men who came. She said that I was a worthless whore who felt special because I had found one little thing to be proud of. She was right now that I think on it." Flora's eyes were starting to moisten as she spoke.

"I do not think you are worthless," Isabel said comfortingly.

"You are very kind," Flora smiled. "Gabriela has always made me proud. As long as I could keep her safe, I felt that I was worth something after all."

"I know how you feel," Isabel said sympathetically.

"This place has changed all that," Flora said sadly. "I can no more keep Gabriela safe than I can walk through these bars. I have not seen my daughter in four years!"

"I will keep her safe," Isabel promised.

"Yes," Flora agreed. "You can get out of here! When they are done punishing you, then..."

"I only have keys to my room and the children's room," Isabel sighed. "That is all."

"You must find the keys to the gate," Flora whispered. "Leave me here, but get my Gabriela away from this horrible place!"

"There are five children in my care," Isabel whispered back.

"Then all of them," Flora said vehemently, "before they come of an age to attract attention!"

"Perhaps I might escape long enough to send word to the Sisters of Santa Maria del Pilar in Zaragoza. Mother Serena would know what to do. She is very wise."

"Yes," Flora whispered sharply! "Please do that before they hurt my baby!"

"It is wrong for them to keep the children so," Isabel frowned.

"Oh if only I could see her again," Flora sobbed. "It would be the happiest day of my..." Isabel cut the other woman off with a finger raised to her lips. Her eyes bulged out as she did so to communicate a sense of urgency. Isabel had heard footsteps. She rose from the grate and walked to the other side of the wall before sitting down again. Flora backed away from the wall and lay down on her straw mat.

The footsteps grew louder and then stopped abruptly. When they started up again, the sound became fainter as it receded down the hall. "Must have stopped for a look," Flora said nervously. Isabel only nodded, keeping the finger raised in front of her mouth.

Some time later, Sister Clara and Sister Laura entered the hall where Isabel and Flora were kept. Laura held a torch aloft in both hands. Following behind the nuns were two richly attired priests. These men looked around furtively as if they might be caught at any moment. Father Benigno was the last to enter the hall. He shut the door that led out into the cloister and followed behind the others. His face was not the least bit nervous. His eyes shown with anticipation and a devilish grin played on the corners of his lips.

Flora rose from the miserable mat she had used as a bed and approached the bars. "Do not speak," she whispered to Isabel as she made her way forward. Flora put her hands together and stretched them out toward the front of the cell. Sister Clara reached her hands in toward Flora's. In the nun's left hand was a pair of manacles which she quickly latched around the prisoner's wrists. Not a word passed between them. That was the most monstrous part of the whole thing. It was a routine that Flora had come to accept.

What Isabel saw and what she remembered of her own torment caused her heart to race and her muscles to shiver. Father Benigno frowned as his eyes came to rest upon her. "Sister Clara," he inquired; "why do I see a nun of this convent imprisoned along with the penitents?"

"She had a plan to smuggle Flora into the basement to see her child," Clara reported. "It was against the direct commands of myself and Mother Maria Elena."

"And that is all," the priest asked?

"Yes father," Clara answered.

"Who is she," he asked?

"Sister Magdalena of Zaragoza," she replied. She spat out the word Magdalena as if it were something rotten in her mouth!

"Come hither Sister Magdalena," Father Benigno called out. Isabel pretended to be asleep. "Wake up," the priest said much louder. There was but a moment of indecision. Isabel decided to obey. She reasoned that they would be compelled to come in her cell if she did not. The imprisoned nun got to her feet and came forward.

"Yes father," Isabel asked? Her heart pounded as Clara led Flora out of her cell and down the hall.

"Is it true what Sister Clara said of you," he asked?

"It is true," Isabel admitted.

"How would you know what she said if you were sleeping," the priest asked pointedly?

"I was not sleeping," Isabel said, "that is…I was afraid."

"You mustn't be afraid of me sister," Father Benigno smiled. "Perhaps this punishment is too severe."

"I will release her in the morning," Sister Clara called back with irritation.

"We shall see," he replied with a grin. "But come now, we must put the woman Flora to the question."

"Of course father," Clara agreed. She paused in the midst of the hall so that she might look back and address Isabel. "She is accused of witchcraft," Clara said. "Quite fearsome…do you not think so Sister Magdalena?"

"I do," Isabel answered. She understood what it was that the other woman really meant. It was not that one should be afraid of witches so much as they should fear being accused of witchcraft. Flora was led in chains to the room which contained the misericord. Father Benigno and Sister Clara entered with her. Someone shut the door and Isabel could hear a wooden bar being lowered on the other side. It was impossible for Isabel to hear anything with clarity except the crack of the whip and Flora's pain filled screams! The screaming continued after the whipping stopped. These cries were morbidly familiar to the former

Heiress of Montenegro. She was certain she knew what went on behind the closed door. It was impossible for Isabel to shut out the noise even when she put her hands over her ears. It was equally impossible for her to push back the dreadful anticipation that infected her thoughts.

Isabel was playing possum again when the other two sisters led Flora back to her cell. They locked her up once more and removed her manacles without incident. The door to the misericord was ajar. Isabel could hear the sounds of coins being poured into someone's hands inside. "Very good my brothers," she could hear Benigno saying. Moments later, he was leading them back out into the cloister. Once Flora had lowered herself down onto the mat, Sister Clara and Sister Laura left as well.

Flora shivered in the far corner of her cell. When they were alone again, she rose up to her knees and began to dig her fingers into the straw. "Flora, what are you doing," Isabel whispered?

"I cannot protect Gabriela," Flora moaned. "There is nothing I can do. She finally pulled a thin vial out of the straw. There was a dark colored liquid inside.

"Do not fear," Isabel reassured. "I will get back to her tomorrow."

"It no longer matters," Flora said as she removed the tiny cork from the top of the bottle. She took a very small sip of the contents and then replaced the cork.

"Of course it still matters," Isabel disagreed. Flora crawled over to the bars between their two cells.

"Here," Flora said as she handed the vial through. "You will need this now." Her voice was weary. "Nightshade," the woman said as she rested her head against the bars. I smuggled it in years ago thinking I would use it to escape. This was not the escape I had planned, but I will be gone soon enough."

"That is fatal poison," Isabel exclaimed with alarm!

"Yes," Flora agreed as her head slipped a few inches farther down the bars. "God forgive..," she started to say, but then slipped into unconsciousness. Isabel smacked the bars with her free hand in a futile attempt to wake the woman up. She tried slapping the woman's face and even pinching her ear! Flora was unresponsive. Her breathing became more and more shallow until it stopped.

"Oh no," Isabel moaned as she backed away from the bars. She sat herself down on the straw mat, not able to pull her eyes away. The corpse of Gabriela's mother was slumped against the bars. Her eyes were closed but her mouth was wide open as if trying to give voice to her final scream. Isabel's heart pounded. She wanted to call someone, but she was afraid of whoever might come. She quickly removed her black nun's habit and hid the vial within its folds. Using the habit as a pillow, she laid down on her mat with her face pointed toward the empty cell.

By morning, Isabel only knew that she had been down for some time. She could not be certain as to whether or not she had slept. It did not feel so. She looked over at Flora's cell once more and felt suddenly nauseous. The position of the corpse had not changed. However, there was now a fly crawling about on the dead woman's left eyelid and another on her tongue. Isabel really did scream then!

Sister Clara was standing in front of Isabel's cell in a flash! "What," Sister Clara demanded? There were dark circles under her eyes.

"Ahhhhhh," Isabel moaned as she pointed toward the dead woman with one finger.

"Oh my Lord," Sister Clara exclaimed as she made the sign of the cross. She pulled the key ring from the cord around her waist and unlocked Isabel's cell door. "Come out," she said. "I am sure you have now been punished enough."

Isabel came quickly out of her cell. Her eyes were continually drawn back to the corpse, which was now made more real by the presence of sunlight and the insects. "Shield your eyes," Sister Clara said. She then pressed Isabel's key into her hand. "Get you back down to the orphans. Sister Laura and I will handle this." Isabel had no need for a second invitation. She fled from the prison hall and down the stairs in the chamber beyond.

"My children," Isabel said with relief as she came back into more familiar surroundings. Lysandro was holding Esmeralda who grabbed onto his index finger with her tiny fist. The other children were gathered round.

"It's a baby," Aaron said knowingly.

"Sister Magdalena has come back," Liz exclaimed!

"Sisser," Aaron shouted as he ran into her arms!

"We were hoping you were still here," Gabriela smiled. She took Esmeralda so that Lysandro could join the other two boys who were already embracing Isabel.

"I was ill," Isabel told them. Her eyes were wet with tears. "I would never leave you!" Gabriela walked over with the baby and Isabel put a hand on each of their faces. The three boys were hugging her from all sides. "You are all my children," Isabel said with emotion.

Soon the children and their caretaker were back to playing games and learning to read and write. Sister Magdalena had invented several games designed to help the children in this regard. The activity allowed Isabel to push the thought of Flora to the back of her mind. She could not look too long upon Gabriela, however. The resemblance to her dead mother was nearly perfect.

Later that night, Isabel tossed and turned in her bed. Knowing what was happening within the Convent of the Angels made it impossible to fully relax. Why had Gabriela's mother killed herself? What had changed after so many years of imprisonment that would cause Flora to abandon hope? These disturbing thoughts were interspersed with images of the flies crawling on the dead woman's face. Sleep was long in coming.

CHAPTER V

As Isabel tried to retain some semblance of calm, the thought of what might happen to her children preyed on her mind like a devouring beast. She spent the next two days in indecision. How could she discover what had provoked Flora into taking her own life? There was no one in whom she could place her trust.

On the morning of the third day, Isabel felt sick to her stomach due to a lack of sleep. It occurred to her that being ill might give her the opportunity she needed. Perhaps the information she was searching for could be found in the quarters of the other nuns. If nothing else, she hoped to find the key that would facilitate her escape.

At Morning Prayer, Isabel complained of nausea and begged permission to rest in bed. Mother Maria Elena granted her request. Isabel left the sanctuary and returned to the upper level of the infirmary. All of the other sisters had locked their bedroom doors. The Mother Superior had forgotten. Maria Elena's door stood ajar and Isabel slipped quietly inside.

Papers and account ledgers were spread out over the old woman's desk. There seemed to be nothing of import. However, Isabel did locate the master key after some searching. It was hidden in the top drawer of the desk behind a false back. The sound of footsteps ascending the stairs cut Isabel's search short. She shut the desk drawer and hurried out of the office. The key was held tightly in her hand. Leaving the door to her bedroom open, Isabel hurried to her bed and lay down. She hid the key beneath her pillow.

Isabel let her eyes droop and tried to appear suitably wretched when the mother superior passed by. Maria Elena looked in on her and frowned. "Do you need for anything Sister Magdalena," the old woman asked?

"I just need to rest mother," Isabel replied weakly.

"Take off your habit and make yourself more comfortable," the old woman advised.

"Oh yes," Isabel agreed as though she had not thought of it. Maria Elena stood in the doorway for a few more seconds. Satisfied, she continued on to her office. Isabel could hear the old woman moving things around on the desk and she feared that her theft would be discovered. She waited nervously in her bed until the mother superior went back down the stairs to attend the second prayer of the day.

After Isabel was certain that the woman had left, she crept out of her room and back up the hall. She was about to reenter the mother superior's office but the door was locked. Isabel inserted the master key and let herself in. The papers and ledgers on the desk revealed nothing. They were mostly accounts and lists of goods kept inside the convent's walls. "There must be something else," Isabel whispered to herself.

The top drawer of the desk contained parchment and writing utensils. There was little else. She opened the second drawer and found that it was filled with coins. As Isabel prepared to open the final drawer, a creaking noise startled her up from her search! "What are you doing in our mother's private things," Sister Clara demanded as she came into the room?

"I...nothing," Isabel gulped as she closed the bottom drawer back again.

"Nothing," Clara smirked? "You did not seem the sort of woman that would steal."

"I have taken nothing," Isabel said. The master key felt like a lead weight in her closed hand.

"You are trying to discover our secrets," Clara said with realization in her cruel eyes. "You should not want to know them I think, but now you will." She walked swiftly from the room, leaving Isabel momentarily alone. Isabel's heart was beating rapidly within her breast. It was time to run. She would have to save the children from outside the walls of the convent. Surely the Holy Church would condemn this place! There would not be another chance to possess the master key. "Sisters," Clara yelled on the other side of the door. Isabel dashed forward. Sister Clara had to be silenced in order for her to escape. "She is in our mother's rooms," the other nun screamed!

No sooner did Isabel open the door than she saw three sisters rushing toward her. Sister Clara and Sister Laura were in front and she thought it might be Eva behind them. She turned and fled out the door which led to the roof. She dashed across the top of the building and onto the bridge which led to the dormitory. "Do not let her escape," Sister Clara shrieked as Isabel ran past the statue of the Angel Michael.

Two more sisters came running out of the dormitory's second floor access. Isabel ran like the devil to reach the other side of the bridge before the nuns could close her in. "Faster," Sister Clara screamed from behind! The two from the dormitory increased their efforts. It was going to be close.

Isabel jumped to her right before being very nearly cut off at the end of the bridge! The other nuns stumbled into each other and Isabel thought she might taste freedom. Yet; as she landed, the toe of her shoe became wedged in the crack between the dormitory roof and Michael's bridge. The flat, stone surface of the roof rushed up to meet her. Isabel brought her hands up at the last second, absorbing only part of the impact. Her vision swam. She could feel something warm and wet on the side of her head. Stars danced in her vision as the nuns fell upon her like a pack of hungry jackals.

† † †

The details of Sister Magdalena's struggle were hazy to her at best. The sisters' fists and hard shoes had rained down from all directions. Eventually, Isabel had lost consciousness. When she awoke, she had been stripped of all clothing and locked in the stocks of the misericord. The stone floor was cold and unforgiving to her bare legs. The muscles of her body were sore and bruised. The face of Christ seemed to stare disapprovingly down at her from the wall.

Isabel could feel the manacles on her ankles, though she was unable to see them. She could hear the chains drag across the floor whenever she moved either of her legs. Her movements were restricted. The stocks and chains would only allow her to move from a kneeling position to one that more resembled a crawl. Her mind began to close in on itself as she understood her predicament.

Hours later, the door to the misericord creaked open. "What have we here sister," Father Benigno asked as he came into the room. Isabel looked back over her shoulder and saw Sister Clara following behind the priest.

"Our Sister Magdalena stole the mother superior's key and was planning to escape," Clara answered sweetly. "We mustn't allow it father."

"We cannot have that," Father Benigno agreed.

"Shall we talk to her first Papi," Clara asked as she put her arms around the priest's torso from behind. Father Benigno grabbed one of her arms and spun Clara around to face him. He kissed her roughly on the mouth. Isabel had to look away.

"Whatever you want," the older man replied after a sharp intake of breath.

"Whatever…I…want," Clara said mischievously. She walked around the misericord until she stood between Isabel and the crucifix, blotting out the image of God. "Hello Magdalena," Sister Clara said with amusement. "I knew you would be here eventually." She shot the priest a knowing look and then smirked back down at Isabel.

Sister Magdalena was gritting her teeth to hold back the fearful sobs that threatened to break free of her mouth. "You are an abomination," Isabel said! Her voice was thick with emotion.

"I know you saw me," Clara said conspiratorially. "Why did you not tell?"

"Who would I tell," Isabel asked hatefully?

"Oh she is a smart one," Father Benigno chuckled.

"She is not so intelligent," Sister Clara grinned. "Is that not why they sent you here sister," she asked sarcastically, "to watch the children?"

"Now now sister," Benigno chided. "Let us not reveal everything."

"We have to reveal something," the nun said suggestively. She reached her hands up underneath the back of her black hood. "You have been a rotten little girl Magdalena," she said as her fingers played with the strings that held her dress together. The black outer garment loosened to Clara's touch. She pulled down her sleeves then and removed it entirely.

Isabel flinched as she felt the priest's hand caressing her outer thigh. "She is very shapely isn't she," he commented?

"Very," Sister Clara said lustfully as she pulled down the material of the white dress that made up the habit's undergarment. "I am going to punish you sister," she promised as her small breasts came free of the white cloth.

"God will punish you," Isabel answered. She was trembling in her bonds.

"He will not," Clara said darkly. She pulled the white dress down past her ankles and stepped out of it, naked except for the black hood and the white scapula beneath it. Isabel cried out as one of her legs was yanked back across the stones! The manacle was pulled all the way back to the steel ring set into the floor. The priest inserted an iron rod through the chain behind it which locked Isabel's leg into the crawling position.

"You have taken vows," Isabel cried as Father Benigno took hold of the other chain. He yanked it back also and locked the other leg in place. "You have taken vows," she shouted once more!

Sister Clara burst into laughter, but there was no mirth in it...only cruelty. "Pray to him if you want to," she jeered as she gestured back toward the crucifix. She ran her hands over the side of her breasts and down over her hips as she walked languidly over to the place where Isabel was restrained. "See if he answers your prayers," Clara taunted as she ran her fingers over and through her exposed sex. "You can pray all night Sister Magdalena," the other nun breathed, "but this is what you are going to worship!"

"Oh that's my little girl," the priest chuckled perversely. Sister Clara removed her hand from her crotch and slapped Isabel across the face. It was not a hard hit, but the wetness left behind made the flesh of her cheek crawl with revulsion! The priests hands rubbed up and down her thighs and then to the small of her back.

"Pray to him," Clara said mockingly as she strode back to where Father Benigno was kneeling. Isabel did pray in an attempt to retain her sanity.

"Our father who art in Heaven," she whispered to herself. Father Benigno grabbed her by the hips and roughly forced himself upon her. "Hallowed be thy name," Isabel moaned. Try as he might, the priest could not seem to penetrate her as she twisted and bucked in her bonds.

"This is not working," the priest said with irritation.

"Let me help," Sister Clara offered.

"Thy Kingdom come," Isabel whispered desperately. She could feel the other woman getting down on her knees beside her. Clara's bare flesh rubbed against Isabel's as she moved. "Thy will be done." She was trying to block out the moans of pleasure coming from her tormentors. Clara's moans sounded like she had a gag over her mouth. At intervals, she would inhale deeply and then start all over again. "Give us this day our daily bread," Isabel whispered. She was trying so hard to shut out all that went on around her. She would not look back, but focused instead upon the cross.

"Now try," Clara said huskily as she brought her head up. She grabbed Isabel's thigh with one hand and spread her open with the other. "Forgive us our sins," Isabel cried out as the priest defiled her! Clara removed one hand from Isabel's backside but left the other which dug painfully into her leg. By the sound of things, Sister Clara had found something else to do with her free hand.

"Do not worry Magdalena," Clara said, bending over so that she could breathe into Isabel's ear. She pulled Isabel's hair down to the other side to keep her head from thrashing about. "You just think that you do not like this."

"No," Isabel screamed!

"Can you feel your body betraying you," Clara asked? She exhaled loudly before running her tongue around the bottom of Magdalena's earlobe.

"No, God no," Isabel shrieked!

"Yes," Clara purred. "Your whore's body is betraying you now isn't it?" Father Benigno grunted and moaned as he continued to violate her. "She loves it," Clara told the man. "The whore loves it!"

"She loves it," he mumbled. Sister Clara stood then and stepped one leg over Isabel's prostrated form. She bent over and braced her hands on the stocks next to Isabel's. Isabel tried to bash her head up at the other woman, but she could only hit her by slamming her head sideways into Clara's arm.

"My whore's body loves it too," Sister Clara told her. The priest removed himself from Isabel before standing up. Isabel could no longer focus on the crucifix. Praying was just as futile. She pinched her eyes shut as the sobs wracked her body. Sister Clara's breasts barely brushed against Isabel's back as the priest took the other nun willingly. Their cries reached a crescendo before Sister Magdalena's captors removed themselves from their position over her.

Clara walked back into view in front of the misericord. Her body glistened with perspiration and her voice was thick. "You are going to do whatever I tell you Sister Magdalena," she said.

"I will do nothing that you ask," Isabel sobbed!

"Alright," Clara sneered, "but whatever you will not do for me, that I shall take from Gabriela."

"Please," Isabel begged as panic filled her mind. "She is only a child. Have mercy upon her!"

"You are going to do what I tell you," Clara said smugly as she came closer.

"I will," Isabel cried wretchedly. "I will do what you say."

"I know," Clara said as she ran one finger down Isabel's tear stained cheek. "I know all about you." It seemed like an eternity before the suffering of that night was ended. There was not an inch of Isabel's flesh that was left undefiled, and nothing so profane that they would not inflict it upon her.

When Sister Clara finally unshackled her ankles, Sister Magdalena was broken in spirit. Her mind was so busy trying to erase the horror of that night that she could not speak beyond a moan. They had to help her to put her clothes back on. The fabric of Isabel's habit felt foreign over her now soiled flesh. "You will stay with the children now," Clara told her as they led her down the stairs to the orphanage. "I have taken your key, but you will not need it again."

"The children," Isabel struggled. "They will wonder why I do not go to mass."

"We will put you in your cell during masses," Clara said. "One such as you need not befoul the sanctuary." Isabel did not answer as she shuffled along between Father Benigno and Sister Clara. Tears fell from her eyes as she went. She had escaped Montenegro only to find a new torment. "Now Sister Magdalena," Clara said patronizingly, "I need not remind you to be silent about this."

"The children must be protected," Isabel said in a low monotone.

"Precisely," Clara agreed. "You will be a good girl for us," she snickered. Isabel nodded her head and wiped the tears from her face. Clara handed her a small hooded lantern which she took weakly in one hand. Father Benigno then opened the door to the orphanage and Isabel walked quietly inside. The door was closed behind her and she could hear the lock falling into place.

The children slept…all except Aaron who lifted his head up from the bottom of his crib. The sound of the door lock set him to crying as the room was immersed in darkness. Isabel made her way quickly over to him. "Aaron," Gabriela called out? Her voice was heavy with sleep.

"It is all right Gabriela," Isabel whispered as she set the lantern down on the cupboard. "I have him."

"Alright," Gabriela replied as Isabel picked the sobbing boy up out of his crib. "Goodnight sister."

"Goodnight mija," Isabel replied. She held Aaron close and made soft shushing noises in his ear. He wrapped his tiny arms around her neck and nuzzled his head in to lie atop her bosom. Isabel carefully seated herself in the rocking chair and gently rocked the small boy to sleep. It took an amazing amount of self control to keep her body from shuddering as the tears fell from her eyes. Eventually, Isabel took Aaron back to his crib and laid him softly down among the blankets. She crawled into one of the unused children's' beds. Her body shook as the grief overtook her at last. Isabel cried silently into her pillow as the children slept safely in their beds.

✝   ✝   ✝

The months dragged on. With Flora dead, Isabel became the new slave to the lusts of the clergy. Usually it was the same two who had defiled her that first night, but there were others. Every few days, a priest would come. Money would be exchanged and more humiliation would be poured out upon Isabel's abused flesh. Worse still were the nights when Sister Clara would come alone. It was very hard to retain a positive demeanor with the children during the day, but that was exactly what Sister Magdalena did. She made up her mind that they could not know.

In the nights that followed, Isabel was horrified to discover that Clara and Laura were not the only nuns in the convent so given to abominations. They all were. Some of the sisters were content to watch. Some desired more. It seemed to Isabel that these sessions were more about dominance than any physical gratification.

The Festival of Saint Nicholas was fast approaching. Isabel was determined to create good memories for her children. After the children would go to sleep, Isabel made presents for them. She used the sheets of the one unoccupied bed to make a new rag doll for Gabriela. There was nothing to create much detail with, but the form was right. She made a second doll for little Esmeralda.

Sister Magdalena took apart the flimsy wooden frame of the spare bed. Using the straight edge of an iron cross that hung on the wall, she whittled down the bed posts until they vaguely resembled the short blades used by the Roman Legionnaires. These treasures she hid in the crawl space below the small dresser used for changing and holding the children's clothing.

No tree would be brought in for the orphans, but Isabel had them draw one on the wall with chalk as Christmas drew near. The children became very excited as the holiday approached. Aaron, (who now spoke in simple sentences), was most excited of all.

Isabel loved them all dearly. "I will give them Christmas," she would often think to herself. It was this goal that kept her going. When the pain and the cruelty were over, making the children's presents kept the young woman from going completely mad.

On the eve of Christmas, Isabel had convinced the nuns to give the children a little something special for dinner. It was the least they could do, but even still they had made Isabel pay for it with the world's oldest currency. That did not matter. What mattered was the happy looks on their faces as they ate roasted chicken and fresh broccoli. For desert, they had a cherry pie. Aaron became so delighted with the pastry that he could scarcely sit still. "More pie please," the toddler kept saying after Isabel had told him what it was. Isabel and Gabriela both gave up a bite of their desert to satisfy the child. When there was almost nothing left, Aaron had pushed all the scraps together to put the last bite of pie filling onto his fork. He was just about to put the pie into his mouth when he paused. "Baby pie," he told Sister Magdalena. His eyes seemed thoughtful.

"Is that a baby pie, Aaron," Isabel asked him?

"Baby pie," the three year old said seriously. He took his fork and walked over to where Gabriela sat with Esmeralda in her lap. "Baby pie," Aaron said happily as he held the fork out to the infant. Isabel nearly wept for the little boy's beautiful heart!

"Aren't you my good boy," Gabriela swooned. "Here Aaron, let me give it to her." She took the fork from his pudgy fingers and carefully fed the last of the desert to the baby in her lap.

"Baby pie," Aaron exclaimed as if it were the most amazing thing in the world! Esmeralda ate quickly while the other children smiled down at her. She burped loudly and that set the others to giggling. Gabriela patted Esmeralda's back and held her over one shoulder until two more burps came out.

Once they were all in bed, Isabel entertained them with stories of Saint Nicholas bringing presents to the children all over the world. "How will St. Nicholas get all the way down here," Lysandro asked with suspicion?

"Through the chimney," Isabel answered.

"He has never come before," Raul noted.

"Well that is because no one told him that you were all down here," Isabel explained, "but he is sure to come this year."

"Why," Raul wanted to know?

"Because I told him," Isabel answered as if it were obvious. Gabriela was too old to fall for such tricks, but she kept silent just the same. Isabel told the children that they had to be sleeping in order for St. Nicholas to visit. She had to reiterate this several more times before they finally slept.

The next morning was beautiful. Isabel had set their presents out below the chalked drawing of the tree. She woke to the sounds of their excited shouts. Esmeralda decided to teethe on her doll, but that hardly mattered to Isabel. It was little time before the boys were play fighting with their new swords. She overheard some friendly disagreements between Raul and Liz over who was dead and who was the hero of Spain. Aaron was unconcerned over these particulars. He laughed as he waved his sword wildly around the room.

"Thank you Sister Magdalena," Gabriela said as the boys were playing. There were tears in the young girl's eyes. "Thank you so much!" Isabel could not speak as her own tears threatened to come forth. She embraced Gabriela and held her close.

"Merry Christmas Gabriela," Isabel said. It was perfect. Despite what Clara and the rest had done to her, despite what might lie ahead; Isabel had succeeded. Her children were happy and safe. This was everything.

✝   ✝   ✝

Three days later, Isabel found herself once more inside the stocks and chains of the misericord. Sister Clara was not there with her. No one was. This meant that they had another customer, another priest, another Godless cretin. It was all the same. She tried to fight the panic that always overtook her, but it was no use.

The sound of the door opening startled her. The chains scraped lightly over the stone floor as her muscles tensed. "Would you prefer to be alone," Sister Clara asked? "Yes," a man's voice replied. It was somehow familiar.

"Enjoy yourself father," Clara chuckled as she shut the door.

"Oh my God, what have they done to you," the man exclaimed after several seconds?

"Who...who is it," Isabel asked nervously? "Who's there?" The man did not reply, but walked around until he stood in front of her.

"Father Hernando," Isabel gasped! She was so ashamed to be seen like this, but the sight of the familiar face sprung hope within her as well. "What are you doing here?"

"I was wondering the same thing," he answered. "I came to see how you were doing and this is how I find you." Isabel tried to move her forearms in closer to conceal her naked breasts, but the stocks were not designed for freedom of movement.

"Help me," Isabel said desperately. "I need to get out of here!"

"I will not leave you alone sister," Father Hernando said with concern. He knelt down and put his arms around her. The priest leaned in closer so that they she could lean her head on his shoulder. "There-there," he said consolingly.

"There are children," Isabel said, "five children. They are trapped in the basement. These evil women…they do not even allow them to come out into the sun! You have to help us father!"

"Wait," he interrupted her. "Calm down and tell me what has happened so that I can ensure that those who deserve punishment will receive it." Isabel really did try to calm down. She knew that this was important, but the more she told of her ordeal, the more she could not control her weeping. It was humiliating to be seen in such a state. "I am here now," Father Hernando told her as he wiped a tear from her cheek.

"I..," Isabel began to speak but she could not finish.

"What is it sister," he asked?

"I am just so happy that you are here. I thought…I thought…"

"There is the Sister Magdalena I know," Father Hernando said as he looked down at her tear streaked face. "So innocent," he sighed, "so trusting." There was an odd note in the man's voice that made Isabel catch her breath. She stopped weeping and pulled her head back away from him. Father Hernando had not come to save her. The perverse smile that covered his face as he looked down at her was all the confirmation she needed.

"Not you too," Isabel said quietly. Father Hernando shrugged as he stood up from the stone floor.

"Why do you suppose I sent you here," he asked with amusement?

"You're disgusting," she answered miserably.

"Did you believe that laughable story about how the children needed someone with a pure heart?" Hernando rolled his eyes heavenward.
"They did need someone," Isabel retorted!

"Perhaps," Father Hernando replied, "but it is no concern of mine." He winked at her and then began to take off his tunic. "I have heard that they turned you into a very accommodating whore," he said cheerfully. "Naturally, I had to come and see for myself before the last of your girlish innocence was used up." Isabel spat on the ground near the man's feet. He barely seemed to notice.

Once free of his clothing, Father Hernando put his hands on his hips and looked down at her. "This will be such an indulgence," he said lustfully as he walked toward Isabel. His arousal could not have possibly been more noticeable. The priest trailed one hand down the small of her back as he moved toward the rear of the misericord. "There," he said once he had knelt down between her legs. "Is there anything you should like to confess?" As he spoke, Father Hernando rubbed himself all over her most intimate parts.

"Revenge is not mine," Isabel said as her body shivered with fear.

"It is not," the priest agreed. "I knew you would be good for this," he sneered. "You told me everything I needed to know!" Isabel moaned with revulsion. She twisted her hips to try and get away from the man, but her bonds allowed so little movement. "If you would do anything for an old servant woman," he chuckled, "than how much more for a group of babes?"

"No," Isabel screamed! She tried to move this way and that but she could not stop the priest from forcing his way inside. Father Hernando became quite animated;

grunting, pawing, and calling out God's name as he filled her with his corruption. There was no pleasure in it for Isabel. Her body did not betray her as Sister Clara had often suggested. The touch of Father Hernando was like that of a reptile!

Father Hernando's emotional betrayal made this rape far worse than those which had come before. Isabel's skin still crawled with loathing after the priest had spent his lust. She felt as though her body were an open cistern, filled to the brim with waste.

Sister Magdalena forced her mind to go numb before returning to the children. If only they would give her a bath, but washing would not be enough. She paced slowly through the darkness for some time after being locked once more in the orphan's chamber. A single candle guttered in its holder on top of the small dresser.

Isabel was about to lie down and try to get some sleep when she heard noises coming from the fireplace. There were still a few coals burning in the ashes at the bottom of it. She came to the mouth of the fireplace and leaned her head in very close to the opening.

The noises became clearer until Isabel realized she was listening to the voices of men. She leaned her head all the way inside. The heat from the dying embers was uncomfortable, but not so hot that she would have to back out. "You have something that no one else has," Father Hernando's voice echoed down from above.

"It is a great risk," Father Benigno said apprehensively. "How long until they are here?"

"Ten days," Hernando replied.

"That soon?"

"Yes," Father Hernando agreed. "This is the only convent I know of that could offer children." Isabel's heart nearly stopped as she realized what the men were discussing!

"And these clergymen who are coming," Benigno asked, "this is what they prefer?"

"The compensation will be rich indeed," Hernando said greedily.

"You needn't keep reminding me," Benigno retorted. "You give the children to them if that is what they want. It will be worth a lot of money to us."

"We will make a good lot of gold," Hernando agreed. There was more that was said, but the priests were starting a fire. Isabel could not hear them over the crackling of the flames above and the hiss of the wood as the heat devoured it.

"Oh dear God," Isabel whispered to herself when she could hear no more. "No," she exclaimed! "This cannot be!" She rocked back and forth in front of the dark fireplace. The smell of the burning wood drifted down to her. "No, no, no," Isabel moaned. She held her arms tightly over her breasts as she rocked. There was nothing left to hold onto. This was why Flora had committed suicide so many months ago. Gabriela would be defiled. All of the children would, and there was nothing that Isabel could do to stop it.

Isabel could not sleep that night. Her mind was sorely troubled. For the children, the joy of Christmas had yet to wear off. All of them were still happily playing with Isabel's hand-made toys. She had to look away from them to conceal her terror and grief.

Later that afternoon, as Isabel was changing Aaron's diaper cloth; it occurred to her what she must do. There was yet one more item hidden in the space below the dresser. The mere thought made her sick to her stomach, but she could see no alternative. She bent down next to the dresser and shoved one side out from the wall. "What is wrong," Gabriela asked from the rocking chair where she was tickling Esmeralda's face with one of the rag dolls? The baby laughed and squealed every time the doll brushed her skin.

"I thought I heard a rat," Isabel lied as she fished underneath the dresser with her hand.

"Stand back," Raul said with his wooden sword held high in the air. "I shall protect you!"

"Stay back," Isabel shouted at him!

"You should not look with your hand sister," Gabriela said worriedly. "It might bite you with its dirty little teeth!" Isabel's hand finally closed over what it was that she was looking for. She quickly palmed the vial and shoved it further up her sleeve.

"You must be right," Isabel replied. "Why don't you boys push back the dresser for me?" Raul and Liz hurried over and pushed the dresser back to its proper place. Aaron ran over to help as well, but he only succeeded in pushing on Raul's backside. The older boys kept looking down for the rat, but of course there was none to be found. "*I am the rat*," Isabel thought. Her hands were shaking and she felt that she would scream with every second's passing. She could not allow herself to lose control. Isabel passed what remained of their time together in silent agony. She wanted there to be another way, but there was only this. She could not let her children be defiled.

Dinner was served late. It came in a large bowl with a wooden ladle. There were several smaller bowls so that each of them could have their own meal inside. The food was a simple combination of mutton stew and bread. Before they ate, Isabel had the children put their toys back in the dresser. She held the baby so that Gabriela could put her doll in as well. While the children obeyed her command, Isabel uncorked the vial and dumped its deadly contents into the stew. The hair on her neck tingled as she did so and a wave of nausea passed through her. She quickly hid the vial on the floor beneath her crossed legs.

The children gathered round Sister Magdalena as she prepared their last supper. They looked up at her with perfect trust. It was heart breaking. She ladled out the tainted stew into each of their bowls including her own. "Time to say thanks," Aaron said.

"Yes," Isabel agreed. "Let us all fold our hands and bow our heads." The children obeyed except for Esmeralda who was too young to understand. Isabel's eyes were open. The children looked like little angels with their heads bowed in prayer. "Oh God," Sister Magdalena said tremulously. "We give thanks for your blessings. Thank you for this…food." Her voice was breaking up. "And thank you for these wonderful children," she sobbed. Gabriela opened her eyes and looked up. Sensing that something was wrong, the girl intervened.

"Say the blessing Aaron," Gabriela said before bowing her head once more.

"Thank you God for Sisser Magalena," Aaron prayed, "and the food we are gonna eat…amen!"

"Amen," Gabriela smiled.

"Amen," Aaron shouted triumphantly.

"Aaron wait," Isabel almost shouted, but he was already working his spoon like a shovel.

"What is it," Gabriela asked with alarm.

"It is," Isabel said in defeat as she watched Aaron devouring the poisoned food; "it is only that he should not eat so fast."

"Slow down Aaron," Gabriela said.

"It's very good," Aaron said happily. The other boys began to eat also and Gabriela and Isabel soon joined them.

"What is the matter Sister Magdalena," Gabriela asked with concern? Isabel nearly choked, but she managed to swallow what was in her mouth before speaking.

"It is nothing," Isabel replied.

"Nothing," Gabriela asked skeptically as she took another bite.

"Well," Isabel said with tears in her eyes. "I have wonderful news for all of you."

"What is it sister," Lysandro asked with a mouthful of food?

"I'll tell you after dinner," Isabel said. She forced excitement into her voice as she spoke. She stopped eating then. She had forgotten about the baby. Isabel dipped her hand into the stew and began to feed Esmeralda with her fingers. The infant greedily sucked the drops and ate as fast as Isabel could keep it coming.

When they had finished their last meal together, Isabel tucked each child into bed. The children were very tired. Esmeralda was already asleep when Isabel put her down in the crib. *"Perhaps she is dead already,"* Isabel thought to herself with sorrow.

"What is the good news," Gabriela asked drowsily from between the sheets?

"Well," Isabel said as she sat down on her own bed, "we are leaving this place."

"What," Raul asked?

"Where are we going," Lysandro wanted to know?

"There is a very rich man who will be taking all of you in," she told them.

"Me too," Aaron asked hopefully?

"Of course you too Aaron," Isabel replied. "This man lives in his own palace. He has plenty of servants so none of you shall want for a thing."

"You mean we will just play all day," Lysandro asked excitedly?

"Yes," Isabel answered. Her voice was choked up and her eyes were heavy with the coming sleep.

"Why does he want us," Gabriella asked?

"He is an old man," Isabel answered, "too old to have more children, and that is why you will all get to live with him."

"What about you," Gabriela asked? "Will you not be going with us?"

"I will have to convince the old man," Isabel said as the weight of her own mortality sunk down upon her.

"You will convince him," Gabriela said confidently as she drifted off to sleep.

"Does he have ducks," Aaron asked hopefully?

"Yes Aaron," Isabel answered. Her voice was thick with emotion. "There will be lots of ducks, more than you can even imagine!"

"We will catch some of them," Liz told the younger boy. He closed his eyes then also.

"I want to catch ducks too," Raul said sleepily. "We could all three catch them."

"Ducks," Aarons smiled. "Prayer is before bed," he mumbled after a few seconds.

"Our father who art in heaven," Isabel prayed.

"Father in the heaven," Aaron echoed.

"Hallowed be thy name," she continued.

"I love Jesus," Aaron told her. It was the last thing the three year old boy ever said.

"He loves you too Aaron," Isabel cried. "Jesus loves you too." Her eyes darkened and Sister Magdalena saw no more.

CHAPTER VI

Isabel's body fell slowly through a formless black void. Far below her was a fiery pit. The tortured cries of the damned rose up from the inferno. Her heart felt like it would explode inside her chest! Her feet began to tingle as the flames licked closer to her bare flesh. She could hear the sound of her own screaming echoing in her ears. Then there was nothing.

Sister Magdalena opened her eyes. Her vision was still clouded. She could make out the white pillow and the sheet beneath it. Everything beyond this was a blur. Her throat was thick with phlegm and her head felt as if it had been weighted down to the pillow. She brought up one weak hand to rub her eyes.

Raul's bed was closest to her and she could see the line of his dark hair coming up above the sheet. Isabel sat up and was immediately nauseated as a wave of vertigo washed through her. She groaned as she picked herself up off the bed and held one hand to her forehead.

Although the pounding ache in her head did not diminish, her senses sharpened immediately as she remembered the terrible thing she had done the night before. It had not worked. She began to fear for the children again immediately. At the same time, there was the relief that she had not killed them. The stew must have diluted the poison. "Time to wake up," she called out hopefully. She walked closer to Raul's bed and reached her hand out toward the sheet. "Raul," she said. She held her breath as she pulled down the sheet. She was about to say his name again when her eyes were filled with the most horrible vision imaginable!

Raul's skin was ashen. His mouth was opened wide and his eyes stared blankly out from their sockets. There was an unpleasant odor as well…very faint, but noticeable. "Oh God no," Isabel cried out as her fingers tore desperately at the flesh of her neck. She looked around at the others. None moved. She ran from one bed to the next; tearing off sheets, shaking dead bodies, and weeping as she felt their cold faces. Aaron had rolled sideways. His eyes were closed, but his face was pressed up against the side of the crib. Isabel ran to his crib. "It's alright Aaron," she sobbed. "I've got you. I've..," but as she lifted his head away from its uncomfortable position, there was no warmth to be felt in his little cheek. Aaron hung lifelessly in her hands.

The child's corpse fell back down into the crib as Isabel lost her ability to stand. She fell to the floor, weeping and pulling out her hair in front of Aaron's crib. She could not rise for some time as she sobbed wretchedly into the stones of the floor. Sister Magdalena looked back over her shoulder once. The poison vial had found its way out from its place underneath her pillow. She must have moved it on accident during the night. This vial might be able to grant her the only wish she had left.

It was a foolish hope. Isabel tipped up the vial and managed to drip the last of the nightshade onto her tongue. She swallowed it immediately, holding out hope for some time that her end would come. It did not. Isabel became desperate. She tapped on the vial with her free hand until her fingers hurt. She stuck her tongue into the top of the vial as far as it would go. She sucked on the opening so hard that her lips became sore with exertion and her gums bled. "No," Isabel screamed! She threw the worthless vial at the wall where it shattered into dozens of sparkling shards.

"Damn you," Isabel cursed the broken glass! "God damn you!" The sounds of Isabel's wailing filled the room. Moments later, the door to the orphanage burst open. Sister Clara and Sister Roberta came swiftly into the room.

"What goes on here," Clara demanded?

"Damn you," Isabel screamed at her!

"Get a hold of yourself sister," Clara shouted! "You will wake the..."

"They are dead," Sister Roberta interrupted. Her face was white and her voice was filled with the horrible realization.

"What," Clara asked incredulously? Then she looked closer. "What have you done," she asked rhetorically?

"You cannot hurt them," Isabel moaned. "God forgive me you cannot…"

"Bitch," Clara screamed as she backhanded Isabel across the face!

"You cannot hurt them," Isabel said again as she rocked back and forth on the floor.

"Come on," Clara ordered Sister Roberta as she backed away from the weeping Isabel. The nuns backed out of the room and locked the door. Isabel was left among the dead. She saw Gabriela's arm hanging limply off the side of her bed and this set her to wailing again.

When the nuns returned, there were six of them. It mattered little. Isabel did not even try to fight. They had her locked in manacles in little time. Once she had been bound, the nuns hauled Sister Magdalena off to a prison cell. As fate would have it, it was the same cell that Gabriela's mother had occupied. After Clara removed her bonds, Isabel collapsed into a miserable heap. She cried at the top of her lungs and could not pick her head up from the stone floor. Sister Clara's jaw was set in a permanent frown as she banged the door closed. "What are we to do now sister," Roberta asked nervously?

"I do not know," Clara answered, "but she stays in here from now on."

"Damn you," Isabel shrieked at them! "Damn all of you!"

"Let us go," Clara told the others. They followed her out and left Isabel to curse herself.

✝   ✝   ✝

Clara sent the nuns back to their work areas under strict orders not to share what had happened with anyone who did not know already. She did not trust Roberta to keep silent, and guessed that all of the sisters would know by lunch time. The mother superior was talking with Sister

Esperanza in the cloister outside the mill when Clara pulled
her aside. The penitents would normally have been stooped
over among the vegetables in the garden, but there was no
use tending the barren fields of winter. In the cold season,
Esperanza and her girls helped Sister Laura in the mill.
They left Sister Esperanza to her duties and traveled
together to Maria Elena's office. "I have grave news," Clara
said once they were closed inside.

"What could it be," the mother superior asked
nervously?

"The children are dead," Clara told her.

"Impossible," Maria Elena exclaimed!

"Sister Magdalena killed them," Clara said flatly.

"What…how?"

"She poisoned them. They are all dead."

"That cannot be," the mother superior disagreed.
"Where would she get poison?"

"I do not know, but she has," Clara said impatiently.
"They are dead I tell you!"

"What will we do," the older woman asked
worriedly?

"What can we do? Father Benigno is not scheduled to
arrive until supper."

"We could send him a message," Maria Elena
suggested.

"There is no one to send," Clara said with
exasperation. "There is no one working the grain fields at
this time of year. We cannot send any one of us out of the
cloister. Someone might see them."

"But this is an emergency," Maria Elena practically
whined. "A sister may leave to get help in an emergency."

"That is true," Clara agreed, "but what explanation
would she give? The children are dead."

"That is a good reason for an emergency," the mother
superior said.

"I remind you mother that most of those children are
not even supposed to exist. Two of them are the bastard get

of Father Benigno himself. In fact, only one of them was not fathered by a clergyman."

"What will we do? What will we do," the old woman asked nervously?

"No one can know about those children," Clara said seriously.

"This is God's punishment upon us for our wickedness," Maria Elena said fearfully.

"Pull yourself together old woman," Clara barked!

"We are being punished," the old woman said as if she did not hear the other nun. "We have sold their innocence for gold and now they have been killed to spare them the fate we had in store. We will burn…"

"Do shut up," Clara interrupted her.

"We will though," the old woman said with certainty.

"You are useless," Sister Clara said in disgust. "Why don't you stay up here in your office and cry while I figure out what must be done?" With that, Clara stalked out without a backward glance. Maria Elena made no move to stop her.

Sister Clara spent the rest of the day tying herself in knots. She was very irritable and did not hesitate to take out her frustration on the penitents as they went about their labors. Physical violence was only a temporary salve for her anxiety, however. It did nothing to quiet the doomsayer in her mind. Father Benigno had told her that one of the men who came for the children was a cardinal from Byzantium. Byzantium was very far from Pamplona. The cardinal would not be pleased that his trip had been in vain. Father Benigno and Father Hernando had gone to Leyre. They would certainly be back by nightfall for another go at Sister Magdalena, but by then it would be too late. There was no way to know exactly when the cardinal would arrive, but there was certainly not much time left. Clara would have to lay the blame on Sister Magdalena and hope for the best.

As expected, the two priests returned to the convent for the evening meal. Sister Clara made sure to be the one to open the gate when she heard the sound of the bell tolling from the church. One of the penitents was already scrambling to reach the gate, but Clara shooed her away. "Get back to work," she hissed at the brown garbed prisoner! The woman averted her eyes and hurried back to the dormitory where she had been scrubbing floors.

"Sister Magdalena has ruined everything," she told them as she unlocked the iron gate. She would not answer their questions until she had led them up to Maria Elena's office. The two men were as worthless as the mother superior when it came to planning a course of action. Father Hernando wanted to hurry back to Zaragoza, but it was already approaching dark. There was a storm brewing as well. Dark grey clouds spread quickly across the sky as the nuns and priests bickered back and forth inside.

Father Hernando was adamant about returning to Zaragoza and the Catedral de Seo at first light. For the Convent of the Angels, he offered no help or advice. The Cardinal was scheduled to arrive the following afternoon according to Benigno. In the end, he resolved himself to Sister Clara's plan, paltry though it was.

At the request of the mother superior, Father Benigno held mass that evening after the penitents were asleep in their dormitory beds. Maria Elena wept silently as the priest placed a communion wafer on her tongue. Sister Clara just shook her head and prepared herself for the coming day. Whatever their punishment, Clara was determined that she would find a way to get herself out of it. She could be very persuasive when the need arose.

The rain had increased as the darkness deepened. It was falling in great sheets by the time the nuns were gathered inside the sanctuary with Father Benigno. Father Hernando sat alone in the back corner. Sister Clara guessed that the younger priest would have run back to Zaragoza in the dead of night if not for the storm.

For the partaking of the wine, Father Hernando walked up the aisle and joined Father Benigno behind the table which contained the host and the chalice. Father Benigno lifted the vessel high above his head and began to pray. "I desire, Oh God, humbly to offer thee the sacrifice of a troubled soul and a contrite heart," he said. The sound of the rain hitting the roof of the sanctuary was quite audible over the hollow prayer.

There was another sound below the steady clatter of the rain. As Father Benigno concluded the prayer, Sister Clara realized what it was. It was the tolling of a bell. "Someone is at the gate," she announced as the priests were drinking from the chalice. Clara stood up from the pew where she and her sisters were kneeling. Father Benigno looked down nervously toward the front of the sanctuary. Father Hernando looked as though he might jump out of his skin! A cardinal could demote them in an instant. He could reassign them to any number of miserable parishes or worse.

Sister Clara was worried about the more dangerous possibilities. What if this cardinal decided to expose them? There would be no better way to cloak his own dark desires than to condemn them for theirs. They might be defrocked, excommunicated, or worse. All of these troubling thoughts ran through the nun's head as she hurried through the cloister to the front gates. Rain water was pouring off the roofs of the convent's buildings. It formed great puddles in the grass. Some were wide enough to resemble small ponds.

Lightning crashed in the distance and threw stark illumination onto the darkened convent. The statue of the Angel Michael was briefly visible in the azure glare of the lightning. Clara shivered as an icy wind howled into the walls of the cloister.

The iron gate finally came into view. There were no travelers huddled next to it and Clara briefly wondered if they were waiting at the opposite gate. There was the roll of thunder overhead and then a second bolt of lightning lit up the night! A dark carriage was stopped in the square between the two gates. A man in a heavy cloak sat on top of it. His head was held down against the elements and his hands clutched the reins as the freezing winds battered his hunched form.

Clara came up to the iron bars of the gate to welcome the visitors. She was about to cry out for them to come inside when another flash of lightning revealed that there were two men standing in the cobblestone square as well. They were several yards in front of the carriage and faced the iron vines through which the nuns did their business with the outside world.

Unlike the driver of the carriage, these other two men stood tall. They were bothered not at all by the wind and the freezing rain. The man closest to Sister Clara was tall and gaunt. He wore a black, hooded robe and leaned upon a silver staff. The staff bore an iron statue of Christ on the cross at its apex. On the other side of the black robed man was a shorter individual with a red surcoat and long, dark hair. His elbows were guarded by steel bucklers and he carried a two-handed sword. The point of the blade rested on the cobblestones and he gripped the cross piece with both hands.

The robed man brought his other hand over to join the first in gripping the staff. He stretched out his fingers as he did so. These fingers were so long that they bordered on the grotesque! Sister Clara's voice caught in her throat. She did not understand why she should fear these men so greatly. Certainly the one was a cardinal, but that did not explain her terror. She had gone so far as to place the key into the lock of the iron gate, but then she stood as if paralyzed. Her heart pounded in her breast.

Another stroke of lightning revealed that the cardinal was looking right at her! There was a strip of black cloth tied over his eyes which would make it impossible for him to see. Nevertheless, Clara knew that she was being examined. She felt naked before him. The man spoke then. His voice was deep and devoid of inflection. "Are you going to let us in?" His hollow voice carried even over the pounding rain.

"Yes," Sister Clara found her tongue at last. Her body was finally moving as she fumbled open the lock. Clara pushed the gate outward then to allow them entry. The robed man caught the gate before she could push it all the way open. His pale fingers wrapped around the iron like sickly worms that had never seen the light of day. Clara could not help but let out a startled gasp. The two men were now inches from the gate! She had not seen them move from the center of the courtyard. She rationalized that it must be a trick of the storm.

"Are you not going to inquire who we are," the hollow voice of the black robed man asked?

"Well…of course I will," Clara said nervously, "as soon as I get you gentlemen out of the rain."

"How kind," the cardinal answered. He opened the gate and held it for the other man. The shorter man had black hair that hung past his shoulders and a thick scar which ran across the line of his cheekbone below his left eye. He stared at Sister Clara as she let him pass. His eyes were dark and predatory.

Next came the black robed man and the silver staff with its image of the crucifixion. This is my traveling companion, Hector Del Toro," the gaunt man said as he entered. Once in the torchlight, Clara could see that the warrior's surcoat was a deep crimson and had a gold crest emblazoned upon it. The crest depicted a cross with an olive branch on one side and a sword on the other. There was something written in Latin around the edges of the crest, but Clara could not read such things.

"A pleasure to meet you," Sister Clara said to the warrior. "I am Sister Clara." Hector nodded but did not acknowledge her further.

"I am Cardinal Eustachius," the robed man announced in his deadpan voice. "You should be expecting me."

"Yes, your eminence," Clara replied quickly, "but we were expecting you tomorrow afternoon."

"I grow tired of waiting," the cardinal replied. "Take me now to see Father Benigno."

"Yes, your eminence," Clara said again. She wanted to walk swiftly to obey, but the cardinal's pace did not match his demands. He leaned upon the staff and held onto Hector's broad shoulder with his free hand. As they approached the main doors of the sanctuary, Sister Clara saw Father Hernando walking quickly away through the cloister beyond. He looked back once but only increased his steps. Hector whispered something in the cardinal's ear and then strode rapidly to overtake the man.

"Proceed sister," Cardinal Eustachius said as he wrapped his long, icy fingers over her shoulder. Sister Clara led the man slowly into the sanctuary. "Describe what you see," Eustachius said as they entered.

"All of my sisters are here," Clara said uneasily. Father Benigno is returning the communion chalice to the reliquary."

"Who else," the hollow voice inquired?

"No one else you eminence," she replied.

"Where is Father Hernando?"

"He is in the cloister," Clara answered uneasily. "Your man is fetching him I think."

"You assume correctly," the cardinal replied. "Send the rest of the nuns to their chambers," he said loudly.

"Yes, your eminence," Father Benigno said. He gestured to the nuns and they took their leave in little time. Sister Clara turned to follow them, but the cardinal's hand tightened painfully over her shoulder.

"Not just yet," Eustachius said quietly. "I have need of you." He released his grip and gently prodded Clara to move forward.

"Welcome to Pamplona, your eminence," Father Benigno said as he came down from the platform on which the communion table rested. "I hope your journey was as pleasant as it was swift." Eustachius extended his long hand out to the priest. Father Benigno shook the cardinal's hand. He tried to take it back, but the cardinal's elongated fingers would not release him.

"Let me look at you," Eustachius said as he pulled the man closer. Father Benigno was compelled to stand there while the blind cardinal ran his grotesque fingers over his face. His long index fingers eventually came to rest on the man's temples. The muscles in the cardinal's hands tightened as he pressed firmly in. The father let out a strangled cry but stood obediently in place. Eustachius sighed heavily when he finally drew away. "Where are they," the cardinal asked pointedly?

"Well," Benigno replied nervously, "the children…that is…they…"

"Where are they," the cardinal said slowly as if he were teaching a child. At that moment, the doors of the sanctuary were thrown open. Father Hernando stumbled and nearly fell as Hector shoved him back into the sanctuary.

"Good evening your eminence," Hernando said as he gained control of himself. Hector shut the large wooden doors behind them.

"Come here to me father," Eustachius' deep voice echoed across the sanctuary. Hernando cringed when the blind man began to feel all over his face with his misshapen hands. "What? Stop it," Hernando said fearfully as the cardinal's fingers dug into his temples.

"Take me to the children," Eustachius told Father Hernando a short time later.

"I cannot your eminence," Father Hernando replied as he rubbed at his temples.

"You cannot?"

"They are dead your eminence," Father Benigno said.

"Dead," Eustachius began softly; "they are dead?"

"They are," Father Hernando admitted with eyes downcast.

"How could you let this happen," the cardinal asked? There was anger rising in his voice.

"It was..," Father Benigno began.

"I have traveled all the way from Constantinople," Eustachius shouted! "It is a long journey," he finished in a whisper.

"The woman who was caring for them went mad," Benigno explained. There was a whining quality to his voice that reeked of desperation and fear. "She poisoned each and every one of them."

"I will speak with her," Eustachius said menacingly. "Who is she?"

"Her name is Sister Magdalena," Benigno replied. Clara could hear the relief in the man's voice as he shifted the blame.

"Take me to her," the cardinal whispered.

"Sister Clara can take you, your eminence," Father Benigno said. "She is in charge of the infirmary and the prison halls.

"Very well father," Eustachius replied. A sardonic smile played upon his lips as he spoke once more. "Go you both to the gate and let my carriage enter into this place," he told the priests.

"Right away," Father Hernando exclaimed as he jumped up to obey! "The driver must be freezing!"

"I will speak with both of you later," the cardinal told them.

"Of course your eminence," Father Benigno replied.

"We would be honored," Father Hernando added.

"Doubtless you would be," Eustachius replied contemptuously. "Lead the way sister." Clara led the blind cardinal out of the sanctuary. Hector remained with the priests. "Why do you think this Sister Magdalena would kill children," the cardinal asked as they made their way through the cloister?

"I do not know your eminence," Clara replied. "Perhaps she has lost her mind."

"Perhaps," the blind man echoed back, "but why would she do that?"

"Do what, your eminence?"

"Lose her mind," the cardinal clarified.

"It is beyond me," Sister Clara answered innocently.

"What is it you are afraid of sister," Eustachius asked as they rounded the bend.

"Nothing at all your eminence," Clara lied. There was something very unsettling about the long fingered man that clung to her shoulder.

"Though the night is cold, I can smell your sweat," he whispered into her ear. "Your heart beats too quickly."

"I..," Clara struggled.

"Are we close sister," the blind man asked?

"Yes," she answered. Sister Clara opened the door to the infirmary's prison hall and led Cardinal Eustachius inside.

Isabel sat with her back propped against the wall of her cell. Her eyes were closed from exhaustion but she was not sleeping. Her body would not stop shaking after the terrible thing she had done. Her eyes came open with the sound of the lock. Sister Clara was holding open her cell door for a man in black robes. The man seemed both terrifying and familiar to her, but she could not place him. "Return to your quarters sister," the black robed man said. His deep voice carried the hint of an Italian accent. Sister Clara bowed slightly and turned toward the exit.

"Give me your key," the man ordered. Clara retraced the few steps she had taken and reluctantly handed over the master key. "Go now," the man said as he put the key into a small sack that hung from his belt. Clara hurried out of the prison hall. "Tell me," the man said, "why have you shed innocent blood?"

"What concern is it to you," Isabel asked sardonically?

"We have come all the way from Constantinople to act on their behalf," the blind man frowned.

"You are he who has come for the children," Isabel inquired?

"I am Cardinal Eustachius," the man replied.

"You are an abomination to God," Isabel cursed him! "The children are forever beyond your reach!"

"You will hang for your crimes," Eustachius said thinly.

"I will gladly pay that price," Isabel said defiantly. "I would barter my own salvation to keep them out of your diseased clutches!"

"We came not to hurt the children," Eustachius explained, "but to save them."

"You are lying," Isabel said with growing panic. The weight of what the cardinal was suggesting was more than she could carry.

"I have heard your voice before," Eustachius said. "Do you not recognize me child," he asked after several minutes had passed. He slowly undid the knot of his blindfold and let it fall down onto his neck. The cardinal had no eyes within his sockets. They had been burnt out long ago. Now only scars remained. Isabel moaned softly as she recognized the man who had commanded her to destroy Lord Barillos. *"Do it in God's name!"* he had said. He bent down closer until their faces were nearly touching. Isabel recoiled in horror!

"You have destroyed the children," Eustachius growled! The points of his sharpened canine teeth were visible when he spoke. Isabel wept uncontrollably. She had not spared the children from the horror of being defiled. She had deprived them of a beautiful life far away from the Convent of the Angels. The cardinal grabbed her roughly by the head. The pain was immense as his fingers dug into the flesh of her temples. In that instant, Isabel was no longer locked in a cell.

Isabel hovered over the Convent of the Angels as if in a dream. She watched herself arriving as the eunuch departed. Time seemed to speed up until everything was a blur. There was Isabel meeting the children for the first time. Next came a vision of Aaron jumping up and down in his crib.

"Well, it is just that they do not seem to like us very much, *"Gabriela said, "Aaron especially." There was then the vision of the fly crawling around on the dead woman's eyelid.*

"You are all my children," Isabel told the bodies clustered around her.

"Can you feel your body betraying you," Clara asked. She exhaled loudly before running her tongue around the bottom of Isabel's earlobe.

Isabel's next vision was of the chalk drawing of a Christmas tree that she had made for the children. Esmeralda was teething on her doll while the boys fought valiantly with their crudely carved wooden swords. "Thank you Sister Magdalena," Gabriela said as the boys were playing.

"Did you believe that laughable story about the children needing someone with a pure heart," Father Hernando asked with amusement?

"We will give them the children if that is what they want," Father Benigno's voice echoed down from above.

"I love Jesus," Aaron told her.

"He loves you too Aaron," Isabel cried. "Jesus loves you too." Aaron hung lifelessly in her hands.

When the cardinal removed his fingers from Isabel's flesh, she could still taste the poison on her lips from that horrible night. She was crying again. Aaron was gone. They all were. "What would you have me do with her," asked the man with the scar across his face. He had a dark complexion and wore a crimson tunic with a gold embroidered crest. The warrior must have come in during Isabel's visions. She remembered him also. It was this same man who had been with the cardinal back in the Basilica del Pilar.

"Leave her where she is," the cardinal answered. "There are more deserving souls to shepherd here."

"We will come back for her," the scarred man inquired?

"That much is certain," Eustachius replied. They left Isabel locked in her cell as they set out to punish the wicked.

✝   ✝   ✝

Sister Clara had gathered all the important personages of the Convent of the Angels in the office of the mother superior. They could hear the sounds of Sister Magdalena's wailing from below. Clara found these pain filled cries to be comforting. It meant that the cardinal was blaming her for the loss of the children.

As Clara was explaining this theory to the others, the door opened. Enter Cardinal Eustachius and his scarred protector. "Close the door," the blind man said softly after both had entered in. Hector obeyed and then stood with arms crossed in front of the exit. The hilt of his two-handed sword rose up from behind the shoulder of his tunic. "You have not kept your promises," the cardinal told them. There was no attempt to disguise his animosity. He had not bothered to wrap the cloth around his eyes either. The sockets were cauterized and filled with scars and blackened flesh for them to look upon.

"The cardinal does not travel so far to be robbed of his prize," Father Hernando admonished the others. There was a long and uncomfortable silence in the room. The cardinal replaced Hector del Toro in guarding the door. The scarred warrior then walked about among those who were gathered. He would stop every so often to inspect something; a ledger, a duck feather quill, a rosary which lay on the desk, etc... Finally, Cardinal Eustachius spoke.

"The blame rests with you," the blind man said as he pointed one pale finger at Father Hernando. While Cardinal Eustachius was speaking, Hector balanced the point of his sword in the grate of the fireplace. He left the weapon sticking out at an angle from the hot iron.

"How could I have possibly known this would happen," Hernando pleaded?

"You sent her to us," Father Benigno rebuked him. "None of this would have happened without your Sister Magdalena!"

"What about the poison," Hernando said accusingly as he looked toward the sightless emissary from Constantinople?

"What about it," Benigno growled?

"Such things are not allowed in the convent," Father Hernando said pointedly. "How is it then that Sister Magdalena acquired enough poison to kill five children?"

"You speak as though I put the poison into her hands," Benigno scoffed.

"That would be ridiculous," Father Hernando retorted! "This is not a matter of purposeful wrongdoing, but of incompetence."

"I am not incompetent," Father Benigno shouted as he pounded both of his hands down on top of the desk! Hector drew a long dagger from its scabbard and twirled it round until the point was once more facing the floor. "...and I will not be insulted by the likes of you," Father Benigno shouted! No sooner had these words left the man's lips before the blade of Hector's dagger pierced down through the flesh of Benigno's left hand. The dagger bit deep into the wood of the mother superior's desk. Maria Elena cringed back in her seat with strangled cry. Father Benigno cried out as his blood welled up around the blade.

Father Hernando's mouth gaped open at the scene that was being played out before him. He did not know whether to run or remain where he was. His indecision was rewarded by Hector's iron shod boot smashing down into the top of his kneecap! Hernando collapsed to the floor as several of the bones in his leg were shattered. "Gentlemen," Hector said quietly. His voice was like the hiss of steel on leather. "Let us not raise our voices."

"Ahhhhh...ahhhhh," Father Benigno moaned as he tried to pull out the dagger with his free hand. The slightest movements of the blade made him wince in pain and quickly remove his hand from the hilt of the blade which held him fast to the desk.

"My leg," Hernando cried fearfully, "I cannot move my leg!"

"Talk softly when you address your superiors," Hector admonished them. Father Hernando swallowed hard. His breathing was coming fast and shallow. Father

Benigno grit his teeth and bore the agony of the blade. Hector placed one hand gently upon the hilt of the dagger. Benigno's eyes bulged out as the warrior's gnarled fingers closed slowly around the weapon.

"No," the old priest pleaded, "no I beg of you." In one deft movement, Hector pulled the blade free of the desk and the priest's punctured hand. Father Benigno cried out more from fear than from any physical pain.

"Shhhhh," Hector said with one finger raised to his lips. "The cardinal speaks."

"This convent is condemned," Eustachius announced gravely. "The stench of corruption is like a plague upon this place. You are all to be put to the question."

"Oh my God," Mother Maria Elena said tremulously. "This is all my responsibility!"

"Save your confession for later mother," the cardinal suggested. "There will be time." This last was said in an ominous tone which caused the elderly woman to tug nervously at her chin. "Hector," Eustachius said at last, "take them."

"You are all under arrest," the warrior said quietly. He did not look at them but stared into the fire as he spoke. "You are given the opportunity to surrender."

"The alternative is less than desirable," the blind man promised. Hector pulled the two handed sword free of the grate and held it out in front of his body with both hands. The last few inches of the blade were glowing red from the fire. He moved then over to the fallen form of Father Hernando. He raised the sword high over his head which caused the younger priest to cower and whimper like an animal.

Without hesitation, Hector swung down and amputated Father Hernando's lower leg with the massive blade! He then pressed the red hot metal of the sword tip into the open wound. Hernando howled in pain! He tried desperately to wriggle away from the searing hot metal as it burned into the injury. He managed to roll over onto his stomach so that he could use his hands to crawl away.

Before the priest could get very far, Hector pressed his foot down onto the younger priest's tail bone. Hernando thrashed about and screamed as the metal cauterized his flesh. Pinned as he was, the one-legged man could not break free.

Clara watched all of this in morbid fascination. She had certainly forced people to do things against their will. She had severely punished those who disobeyed or those who struck her fancy. This was a whole new level.

Finally, Hector released the sobbing man from under the weight of his iron-shod boot. Father Hernando scrambled into the corner of the room where he managed to prop his back up against the wall. His chest heaved as he looked fearfully up at Hector. The scarred warrior placed the tip of his blade down onto the floor where it scorched the wood. He leaned upon the hilt, holding onto the weapon with both hands. His dark brown eyes traveled from one person to another, daring each of them to act. "Imprison them all," Cardinal Eustachius commanded.

"If they resist your eminence," Hector inquired?

"Break them in pieces," the cardinal replied. He then took two steps to the right to open a clear path to the door.

"You and you," Hector said as he pointed first at Father Benigno and then at Sister Clara; "help this wretch to his cell." Father Benigno hurried to obey, ensuring that his injured hand would be on the side away from Father Hernando. Sister Clara stared in awe at the cardinal's guard. She came quickly out of her reverie as he spoke and moved to help. "As for you," the warrior told Maria Elena, "lead the way."

"Yes," the mother superior said as she rose shakily to her feet, "yes."

"Now," the warrior barked! The mother superior flinched from the sound of his voice, but quickly hurried to the door. Father Benigno and Sister Clara held up the amputee who hopped on his one remaining leg between them. Hector followed.

It was slow going down the stairs. Father Benigno almost lost his balance at one point and was forced to grab the rail with his injured hand. Hector placed them in separate cells along the same wall. They were not in the same prison hall which contained Isabel's cell and the misericord, however.

Hector stood silent sentinel until the cardinal arrived with a man none but Sister Clara had yet seen. Even her view of him had been obscured by the rain. This other man's blonde hair was shaved into a ring that left the top of his head bald. He wore the white robes of a priest with a black belt and black lining inside the hood. He had a pointed nose and cunning eyes. A smile played at the corner of his lips as if he were privy to a great secret which gave him pleasure. The cardinal followed this young man closely. The long fingers of his left hand were anchored tightly to the younger man's shoulder.

"Corral the rest of the sisters," the blind man commanded as he removed his hand from the white robed priest.

"Follow me," the young man told Hector. "I have seen one of the nuns rattling the gate."

"Lead the way Father Salvatore," Hector said while motioning with one hand. The two men departed, leaving the cardinal to pace up and down the cell block. He paused in the center of the room and turned his twisted sockets toward the prisoners. He steepled his pale fingers before his chest and began to speak.

"You have all been deliberately misled," Eustachius told them. "Rumor had reached my ear in Constantinople about the goings on at this place. Several of the whores in Pamplona have spoken to one of my agents. These women had all at one time been incarcerated here. I have been in Pamplona for several months already."

"I knew nothing of this," Father Hernando said desperately!

"You are all guilty," the cardinal said in disgust. "Some of you are more revolting in the eyes of God than others. I have little interest, therefore, in your confessions. Repent, for in a little while…you shall see God!" After a moment of silence, the blind man continued. "One woman confessed to me that she had strangled her newborn son. Why would she do this?" He moved his head as if he were looking at all of them in turn. His face finally rested in a way that suggested he was looking at Father Benigno. "Because it was your son," he snarled, "and she believed that such an unholy union could only produce an abomination!"

"What is it to you," Father Benigno asked from his cell? "We all know why you came here, regardless of the reasons you gave to the Holy Church!" The cardinal smiled and raised his face toward heaven. "The letter," he chuckled. "The letter was but a ruse to ascertain the depths of your depravity. You are right, however, when you say that everyone knows."

Eustachius reached into his robe and pulled out a piece of rolled parchment. The seal had already been broken. The cardinal held this up as he continued speaking. "An answer revealed before the Holy See… So," he said as he dropped the letter onto the stone floor, "here am I."

"I did not know about the children," Father Hernando exclaimed!

"We shall see," the cardinal said gravely. He stretched out his bony fingers toward Hernando's prison cell. He continued to hold them out as he walked slowly forward.

"Please," Father Hernando begged, "I had no part in this!"

"Repent," Cardinal Eustachius hissed as his fingers wrapped all the way around the bars of the amputated priest's cell, "for the end cometh!" Sister Clara, (who was in the cell next to Hernando), was afforded another glimpse of the blind man's razor sharp teeth as he spoke. The upper and lower canines extended well beyond the rest and were sharpened to fine points.

After this, the cardinal let go of the iron bars and began to make his way up the row of cells. One hand trailed along the bars. The sounds of Eustachius' footsteps and his fingers skipping along over the bars were the only audible noise in the prison hall. When he reached the end of the cells, the cardinal passed through the doorway leading out into the cloister. The last visible sign of his presence were his pale fingers curling around the door frame before it closed.

Moments later, the doors at the opposite end of the cell block opened. The white robed priest came first and held the door open for the cardinal's guard. There were screams and shrieks for help coming from outside. Hector came in dragging a length of rope behind him. The other end of the rope was tied securely around Sister Eva's ankles. She bucked and twisted and clawed at the walls, but the nun was no match for the powerful man who dragged her roughly across the stones. The bruises on her face, her bleeding knuckles, and broken fingernails were a testament to the futility of her struggle. Clara guessed that Sister Eva's clothing hid still more bruises and scrapes.

Hector dragged the screaming woman into the cell next to that of the mother superior. He hauled her inside and cut the rope with his long dagger. Eva was on her feet in an instant. Her face looked like a spooked rabbit. Before the nun could decide whether to escape or run to the back of her cell, Hector raised up his hand and slapped the side of her face with force! The strike of his palm sent Sister Eva to the floor. She was barely able to spin around and absorb some of the impact with her hands.

"Rise up again," Hector said challengingly. He stood over Sister Eva until he was satisfied that she would not try to run. Her fearful eyes darted about her cell for a few seconds, but then seemed to turn in on themselves. Eva laid the side of her face down on the stones as a tear spilled out over her cheek. Sister Clara saw that Eva was looking at Father Hernando in the cell next to hers. It must have been the sight of his blackened stump that finally killed her spirit.

"Something the matter sister," Salvatore asked mockingly as he leered down at Sister Eva?

"Come on," Hector growled! "I do not wish to be about this all night!" The two men left as quickly as they had come. It did not take long for the rest of the nuns to join their sisters in prison. Most came willingly. Sister Laura, however, was brought in with one man holding each of her arms. Her face was bruised and her eyes were swollen shut. Blood leaked out of one nostril and down into her mouth. Sister Clara noticed a small amount of blood at the corner of Hector's mouth. There was no sign of a cut, however.

Sister Laura was shoved into her cell. She put out her hands quickly to avoid slamming into the opposite wall. Hector locked the cell door behind her with the key given him by the cardinal. Sisters Esperanza, Roberta, and Maria came willingly to their respective cells. Sister Consuela came unconscious. There was no evidence of violence on her flesh, save for the thin strip of blood on the side of her left wrist. Hector carried her into a cell and dumped her unceremoniously onto the floor. That her head landed on the straw mat seemed fortunate considering the alternative.

With the business of capturing the nuns concluded, Salvatore left the prison hall. Hector remained to watch over the prisoners, though it was hardly necessary. After a short time, Eustachius was led back in. Salvatore guided the blind man to the spot where Hector stood and waited while the cardinal transferred his long fingers to the warrior's broad shoulder. "Watch over the penitents my son," the cardinal told the white garbed priest. "Hector and I will handle this wretched lot."

"I obey," Salvatore replied. Clara thought she detected a hint of disappointment in the young man's voice. Nevertheless, the younger clergyman exited the prison hall and went back out into the cloister. When the door closed, Eustachius began to speak once more.

"We shall start with the mother superior," he decided. Maria Elena paled and looked to be on the verge of fainting.

"Come out," Hector said as he opened the old woman's cell. The mother superior did as she had been ordered. "Get you to the misericord," he commanded. Maria Elena left the prison hall and entered the chamber which would take her to the next. Hector came immediately behind her with the cardinal attached.

"What do you think will happen to us," Sister Laura asked once the others were gone? Her voice was small and terrified.

"We shall have to wait and see," Sister Clara replied. They waited for what seemed like forever…and then the screaming started. The mother superior was never returned to her cell. Hector opened up Father Hernando's cell next.

"The cardinal will see you now," the warrior said as he advanced on the cowering priest.

"I…I did not know," Father Hernando protested. "I swear it!" Hector did not answer. He bent over quickly and grabbed the priest's good leg in his weather-worn hands. The cardinal's guard then threw the crippled man effortlessly over one shoulder. Hernando's cries ended in a grunt as his stomach landed on top of Hector's crimson tunic. The young priest continued to profess his innocence all the way out of the east hall. Minutes later, the screaming began again from the misericord.

After the passing of an hour, Father Hernando was carried back into his cell. It would have been better for the remaining sanity of the others if he had not been returned. The first thing Sister Clara noticed about him was that he had been stripped bare of clothing. The next was that he had lost consciousness. Bright red lines traveled horizontally across his thighs where they had been tied painfully together. These red lines were evident on his torso as well and all the way up to his neck. The warrior's arm obscured the priest's most intimate parts from view.

Hector's face was grim and devoid of emotion. This was far more disturbing to Sister Clara than the impish glee which marked the face of Salvatore. She understood that there was pleasure in cruelty, but Hector's deadpan expression and set jaw reminded her more of the prisoners who toiled endlessly in the mill. There was no joy. There was no sorrow. There was only work to be done.

Hector dropped Father Hernando off in a sitting position against the back wall of his cell. The priest's head slumped to one side, but was caught by the bars bordering the cell that had recently housed Maria Elena. Clara detected a strange odor coming from the unconscious man.

Father Salvatore and Hector moved next into Father Benigno's cell. The older man gave some token resistance, but it was only the protest of one who is already defeated. Benigno went from shouting, to crying, to begging in little time as he was hauled off to the misericord.

There was no way to know the lengths of time between Father Benigno's agonized wailing. Neither was there any way to know how long each fit of screaming lasted, but it was a long time. Father Benigno was returned in much the same way as Father Hernando; naked and unconscious, his body had been wrapped tight with rope also. Clara saw the deep burn marks on the man's inner thighs as Hector passed by her cell. She watched closely as the man was set down in his cell once more. She wished that she had not. His genitals had been burnt and blackened beyond recognition!

The nuns were weeping in fearful anticipation of who the strangers might choose next. Outwardly, Sister Clara remained calm. Inside, her mind was shrieking! Clara's cell door was the next to be opened. "You need not drag me," she said bravely. "I will go."

"Go then," Hector said curtly as he held the door open wide. She went. Out of her peripheral vision, Sister Clara noticed the priest called Salvatore ogling her. Perhaps she would find a way out of this yet.

"The cardinal will hear your confession," Hector told her as he followed close behind. The sound of his heavy footfalls rode above all else. Sister Clara was more than familiar with the walk to the misericord. She had taken countless victims there to be punished. After seeing those who had now returned from thence, Clara was now experiencing real terror.

Fortunately, Sister Clara had a plan. It was this plan that allowed her to walk confidently amongst her captors. She knew what all men wanted. She would give it to them. The thought of being at the mercy of three fearsome strangers made her heart race. Below this was a perverse excitement. They intended to break her, but Sister Clara would bring her captors to their knees!

The first crack in Sister Clara's resolve was the crumpled form of Maria Elena in the far corner of the room. The only thing visible of the mother superior was the black of her habit and the flesh of one exposed hand. The flesh was wrinkled and now devoid of life. Clara steeled herself and looked back at the men who had followed her to the misericord.

Father Salvatore closed the door and stood by it with arms crossed. A smirk covered his face. "Take the habit off," Hector commanded. "You are unworthy of it."

"Yes," Clara agreed, "I am not worthy." She took her time undressing, running her hands over the fabric of her dress before removing it. Clara was no stranger to the art of seduction. She could see the lustful eyes of Salvatore lingering upon her. She made eye contact with him several times. Her flirtatious gaze and sinuous movements had no effect on the warrior, however.

Sister Clara removed all of her clothing except the black and white head covering. As she rose to her full height, Clara exhaled loudly and ran her tongue around the inside of her bottom lip. She crossed her arms and cradled her breasts in her hands as she moved toward the two men who blocked her way to the door. "What shall I do now," she asked as she pushed her breasts up invitingly. Salvatore was breathing heavily. His eyes were transfixed upon her naked form.

Sister Clara gave the younger priest a smile which promised to fulfill his every perverse desire. She walked slowly and languidly toward Salvatore, but it was the warrior whom she encountered first. "All of it," Hector snarled as he ripped the black hood from her head! Clara nearly fell as she was jerked forward. She was left with only the white scapula for a head covering.

Hector tossed the black cloth on the floor and looked impatiently at his captive. The dark skinned Spaniard terrified Clara, but she was determined to escape the fate of the other prisoners. She would be punished differently…in a manner more pleasing to her. "You are so rough," she told Hector. "Can you not see that I need to be touched differently?" Hector took one menacing step forward. He grabbed Clara by the arm and raised his other hand. The nun was able to remove the scapula before he could rip it from off her head. Her dark hair was long and it spilled down her back when freed from the scapula. Nuns were supposed to shave their heads closely, but this was not the only rule that Clara had been breaking. "Here it is," she said. Her voice was low and sultry.

Hector snatched the scapula from Clara's hand and shoved her roughly toward the misericord. She was barely able to catch herself on the stocks as she fell. "On your knees," Hector snarled! Clara obeyed. She assumed the same humiliating position that she had so recently forced Sister Magdalena to take. The warrior quickly manacled her ankles while Salvatore approached her from the front.

Clara looked up lustfully at Father Salvatore as he locked her wrists into the praying position. His face burned with desire for her. "I really need to be touched differently," Clara said as she moved her hips slowly up and down toward the man who was chaining her ankles. "I'll never tell anyone," she whispered to Salvatore, "never!"

"Get out of here," Hector barked at the young priest! "Inform the cardinal that the next prisoner has been prepared."

"Yes, I..," Salvatore stammered. "I will bring him immediately." He exited the misericord and slammed the door behind him.

"Are we alone now," Clara asked after the younger man had gone. There was no reply from the cardinal's guard. Clara looked back over one shoulder at him. His eyes were like granite, but Clara was determined to break him. She arched her back and pushed her hips back to invite him in. "Touch me Hector," she breathed. "I want to be touched." Hector snorted in derision and left her alone with the corpse of Maria Elena.

Time passed. Sister Clara shivered slightly. There was nothing to look at but the cross or the dead mother superior's withered hand. She turned her head in the other direction. She would not let herself be shaken. The younger priest, Salvatore…he was but one step away from fornication. Once he fell, the others would be forced to look the other way. She would be released…but would that be enough? Clara's innermost parts tingled as she imagined Hector taking her. He would need a bit more prodding, but it was not beyond her ability. Suddenly, the door opened.

"I will call for you," the cardinal said. Clara turned her head back in time to see the door to the misericord closing. She was alone with Cardinal Eustachius. His burnt out sockets seemed to stare down at her as he crossed slowly over to the place where she was bound. Chained as she was, Clara could hardly seduce a blind man. Her shapely form, her smoldering eyes, and her lover's mouth; these were all things that existed only in the world of sight.

Sister Clara shifted her weight in an attempt to find some relief for her sore muscles. She knew that she should say something to this man. Perhaps she could raise his blood with words alone. Try as she might, she could not bring herself to the task. Eustachius seemed less like a man and more like a creature that had crawled out of a dark pit. His twisted sockets, his horribly pale skin, and his grotesquely elongated fingers made him resemble a monster out of a child's nightmare.

The cardinal's footsteps echoed faintly in the room as he approached. The man stopped and Clara could hear him sniffing loudly from behind her. The thought of his hideously deformed fingers on her skin was not appealing, but Clara was aware that her life hung precariously upon the cardinal's whims. "I feel so helpless," Clara heard herself saying. Her voice was full of lust, despite the fact that the thought of the man touching her made her want to scream. However, there was something fundamentally wrong with Sister Clara's mind. The thought of her own helplessness filled her head with a perverse anticipation.

"What is that smell," Eustachius asked?

"You know what it is," Clara smirked. The cardinal took in a very long and slow breath through his nose. He exhaled heavily.

"I'm down here," Clara breathed. "I am all chained up for you."

"Is that the stench of your arousal," the cardinal asked as he came to stand in front of her. Clara opened her mouth to say something more, but Eustachius spoke again before she was able. "Is that the quagmire of filth between your legs?" The deep shadows inside the cardinal's eye sockets seemed to stretch back into oblivion. "Let me illuminate for you," he said as he bent down toward her.

Clara gasped as the disfigured man positioned his face mere inches away from hers. He opened his mouth exposing gums that had receded up with age. His teeth were stained with blood and his canines were sharpened to perfection. A carrion stench came from within his mouth. Fresh blood clung to his gums in crescent shapes that spanned from one tooth to the next like the webbing between the toes of an amphibian. This creature had already feasted upon the others and now it had come for her. "The only thing that excites us is the taste of your warm blood," Eustachius said in a low rumbling voice. A horrible scream arose in Clara's lungs and issued out of her mouth. It would be but the first of many.

CHAPTER VII

The cardinal's pale fingers came toward Sister Clara's face like so many tentacles. His head was cocked to one side as if examining her. Clara moaned with fear and revulsion when the cold appendages began to feel all over the flesh of her face. His index fingers eventually found their way to the nun's temples. His nails suddenly and painfully dug into the woman's flesh. Something warm and wet trickled out from the places where they had broken skin.

Clara's skull felt as if it would rip in two! Her life flashed before her eyes, revisiting each of her sins and revealing the rot within her. Clara was sobbing when the cardinal finally removed his horrible hands from her flesh. "The time to repent is now," the blind man said as he held up a straight razor in one hand.

"No please," Clara cried out, "do not kill me!"

"You will wish that I had," Eustachius promised. "There is salvation in death."

"Please," Clara cried desperately, "I repent!"

"Your sins are many," Eustachius told her. "You will burn far from the sight of God." With that, the cardinal rose and moved around to Clara's side. He knelt down and ran one grotesque hand over the flesh of her back. She felt the cold metal of the razor and then the stinging bite of the blade as it penetrated her skin!

"What do you want to know," Clara shrieked? "I will tell you whatever you need to know. I swear it!"

"There is nothing more to discover," the cardinal replied without emotion. His voice was deep and hollow. He worked methodically with the straight razor, making several precision cuts along the top of her back. Each series of cuts resembled an inverted V. Clara sobbed and moaned as the cardinal cut thin red lines into her flesh. "Repent," he told her as he pinched the loose flap of skin between the first v-shape.

"I repent," Clara sobbed!

"You are afraid," the cardinal said. "I can smell your fear, but…" His fingers tightened, causing the skin flap to tear slightly at the bottom of the V. "You do not repent," he said absently.

"I do," Clara tearfully insisted. "I…"

"You do not," the cardinal hissed! He yanked down hard on the flap of skin. The force of his hand tore a strip of flesh all the way down the length of Sister Clara's back! The pain was unbearable! The sound of her screaming echoed off the walls in the chamber. Eustachius let go of the bloody strip of flesh in his hand. It hung down over Sister Clara's waist like the loose strap of a dress.

Clara cried out when the cardinal touched her again. He slid one long, revolting finger down through the length of the open wound. "Please," Clara begged, "no more… I have sinned!" There was a smacking of lips as the cardinal sucked the woman's blood from the tip of his pale finger.

"Yes," Eustachius said zealously. He brushed his fingers over her temples once more. There was a feeling of tremendous pressure in her skull that subsided as quickly as it had begun. "No," the cardinal decided reproachfully, "God is not finished with you!" He placed his hands on the nun's bleeding back. His fingers crept across her flesh until they rested on the second v-shaped cut.

"Please no," Sister Clara cried, "please no." There was a ripping sound followed by a howl of pain as Eustachius ripped another strip down the length of her spine!

"Time is of the essence," he said in his deadpan voice once Clara's screams had quieted. "This is but a small taste of what awaits you beyond the Land of Flesh." The cardinal continued his horrible ministrations until the strips of Clara's flesh had all been peeled down to her waist. These strips came to resemble the tail feathers of some freakish bird once they were all in place. Her wounds were bleeding profusely.

Eustachius slowly removed an iron from the room's only fireplace. He held the glowing point out away from his body. "This pain will be immense," he promised. He then pressed the hot metal into the first of Clara's wounds. The pain radiated out over her entire back and caused the muscles of her shoulders to seize up. The sound of her own screaming resounded in her ears. Sister Clara eventually lost consciousness, but her new found fear of damnation followed her into dreaming. Clara dreamt of fire.

† † †

Isabel sat huddled in the corner of her cell. She could hear the awful sounds coming from the misericord as, one by one, her captors were led inside. None departed on their feet, but were carried out by the cardinal's guard. Isabel could not tell whether any of them were dead or unconscious. The smell of blood and burnt flesh permeated the air.

When all of the others had been used up, the cardinal and his men came back for Isabel. "On your feet," Hector said gruffly as he unlocked her cell door. Isabel rose nervously to face her new captors.

"You must atone for your great sin," Eustachius told her. "We came to save the children, but you have destroyed them." Isabel began to shake violently as she was overcome with sorrow. "You will dig their graves," the cardinal said. Isabel could not speak, but she nodded her head up and down. "Go and sin no more," Eustachius said as he made the sign of the cross toward her.

"Follow me," Hector said. He turned on his heel and led Sister Magdalena out into the cloister and then to the garden. The air was still moist with the passing of the rain. The warrior pointed to the far side of the field where a shovel had been planted into the earth. Lying in a row against the cloister wall were the corpses of the orphans. "Do not delay," Hector ordered. He pushed her forward toward the dead.

Isabel's choked sobs became louder as the children's faces and distinctive features began to materialize out of the dark. Here was Gabriela, her face bloated and the smell of decay emanating from her body. There was Lysandro and Raul. Last were the little ones, Aaron and Esmeralda. The stench of the grave was overpowering and flies were already gathered for the feast.

Isabel vomited into the vegetable garden. She leaned upon the shovel for support. When the turmoil in her stomach receded, she set herself to her penance. She buried each of the children in a shallow grave. Their faces seemed to stare up accusingly at her from the ground. She tried to pray for forgiveness as she worked, but her words seemed meaningless. Her children were murdered. Their blood was on her hands. Gabriela's eyes suddenly opened while Isabel heaped dirt upon her. "I forgive you," the corpse said, "but God will not." Her eyes closed and her head slumped to the side. Isabel screamed in terror, but there was no one about to hear her.

"I am going mad," Isabel thought to herself. After a time, Isabel began her work anew. She worked until well after the break of dawn. Her hands were blistered and raw from her toil. Not knowing what else to do, Isabel made her way to the sanctuary. She found Father Salvatore there with several of the older prisoners gathered round. He was instructing them on how to stack wood for a charnel pyre. He looked up at Isabel as she entered.

"Peace be with you," the young priest said.

"And with you father," Isabel replied by rote.

"Get you to bed Sister Magdalena," Salvatore told her. His face looked haggard as well. "You have suffered enough this day."

"Yes father," Isabel agreed. She returned to the infirmary and traveled up to the nun's quarters. The door to her old room had been left open and she went gratefully inside. She lay down and was asleep in minutes.

When Isabel awoke, it was well past nightfall. She put on the clean nuns habit from the trunk at the foot of her bed. She ventured out then onto the roof of the infirmary. As she came closer to the edge, she could see that the garden had become a staging ground for the largest pile of wood she had ever seen. It was stacked nearly to the height of a man and stretched across the yard in back of the dormitory. The pyre had five poles rising up in a line through its center. The poles were positioned at long intervals from each other. As Isabel came onto St. Michael's bridge, she could see that Sister Eva was being bound by the dark skinned warrior to the first of the stakes. He used a length of rope to secure her body into position.

The brown clothed prisoners were gathered round the pyre. Some shouted condemnations while others were content to watch in silence. Isabel ran down to join the throng as the condemned were bound, one by one, to the charnel pyre. Several of the penitents held burning torches in their hands.

As Isabel made herself part of the mob, she noticed that each pole was being fitted with one prisoner on each side. The only exception was Sister Clara. She occupied a pole to herself at the far end. Father Benigno and Father Hernando were tied onto the stake immediately to the right of Clara.

The purposeful way in which Hector del Toro walked up and down in front of the wood pile reminded her of her father. This was the same way in which Rafael would stride across the battlements of Montenegro. He would stare at each man he passed as if he could see all of their shortcomings made manifest upon their faces. It was the same with the cardinal's guard. He tapped a footman's mace into the palm of one hand as he walked.

Father Benigno flinched away from the warrior's gaze. His face flushed with embarrassment which quickly turned to anger. "You will never get away with this," he yelled at Eustachius who stood silently inside the archway that led into the cloister. The cardinal's elongated hand rested on Father Salvatore's shoulder. The blind man seemed to look away from the shouting priest, but Isabel noticed that he was cocking the side of his head toward the man…listening. "I have powerful friends in Rome, the condemned priest yelled! Hector paused. "You will all be killed for this," Benigno threatened. The Cardinal remained silent.

When the mace came down once more into Hector's hand, he grabbed it tightly by the haft. He held the weapon close to his chest as he turned around. The warrior walked purposefully up onto the charnel pyre until he stood face to face with Father Benigno. "You will not…be able to run…far enough," Father Benigno stuttered. His voice had lost its confidence.

"Have you anything else to say before your body is consigned to the flames," Hector asked somberly. Father Benigno tried to articulate a reply, but fear held his tongue. "Any last words," the warrior inquired," a confession perhaps?"

"I..," the priest began nervously. No sooner had that single syllable left the man's mouth before Hector was in motion. The warrior lifted up the mace in both hands until it was on an even plane with his neck. He then smashed the haft cross-ways into Father Benigno's mouth! The sound of splintering bone was audible to Isabel from where she stood amongst the penitents. The force of the blow broke Benigno's jaw and left his teeth a shattered ruin. The priest let out an inarticulate howl of pain as blood gushed out from his gums and down over his chin. "Tell it to God," the warrior said coldly.

Isabel had to look away. Her gaze fell upon the cardinal. Beneath the mutilated eye sockets, his mouth turned up in a satisfied grin. The smile was brief, but not so quick that it escaped her notice. Isabel shivered as she looked back at the pyre. Hector was coming back down from atop it. She could still see the blood of Father Benigno on the haft of the man's weapon.

Without warning, Hector snatched a torch out of the hands of one of the brown clad prisoners. He then stalked back toward the far side of the garden closest to the chicken coop. As her eyes followed his progress, Isabel noticed a dark bundle lying on the wood between two of the stakes.

Her eyes were drawn down to one corner of the black cloth. Here she saw a withered foot sticking out. The bundle could only be a nun's habit. This was what was left of Maria Elena.

When Hector reached the coop, he turned around to face the cardinal. Though nothing was said, Eustachius seemed to know that all was in readiness. His sepulchral voice began to chant a prayer in Latin. "We stand before God in the face of evil, he proclaimed once the prayer was concluded. "There shall be no forgiveness for the unrepentant. They will burn until their bodies are consumed and their souls shall continue to burn in perdition."

Eustachius raised his right arm then and slowly lowered it back to the ground. Hector's arm lowered also, and with it the torch. "Repent," the cardinal shouted as the flames touched the bottom of the pyre, "for the time of judgment is upon you!" Isabel heard the crackling of the logs as the flames spread over them toward flesh. The Mediterranean breeze was cold and damp that morning. Because of this, the spread of the fire was slow in coming. Nevertheless, the fearful cries of the condemned began long before fire touched skin.

Sister Eva and Sister Consuela would be the first to go. Eva alternated between begging God and her nightmarish captors for deliverance. Sister Consuela was reciting the 23rd Psalm. Sisters Roberta and Maria Castellanos were tied to the next stake. Maria's lips were trembling as she looked down at the encroaching fire. Roberta was saying something, but weeping made her words incomprehensible. Sister Laura and Sister Esperanza were keeping their eyes closed as if that alone would stave off the inferno. Where their two hands were close enough on the stake, they held on tightly to one another. Esperanza's lips moved silently in prayer as Laura sobbed uncontrollably.

Father Benigno was tied to the next pole. Isabel could not tell whether he was moaning in fear of the flames or from the agony of his mangled face. She could not see the face of Father Hernando who was tied behind the other priest. Having only one leg, he had been tied in a sitting position atop the pile of wood. The last stake contained only one victim. Sister Clara was alone.

✝   ✝   ✝

Clara's knees felt as though they would give way at any moment. Bound as she was to the stake, it hardly mattered. The rough wood pressed painfully into her already burnt back. Cardinal Eustachius had cauterized her wounds and burnt off the bloody strips of flesh with the fire iron. Time seemed to crawl in the torch lit garden of the convent. Whether the condemned started by praying, weeping, or cursing God; they all ended in the same fashion. Their agonized screams echoed far into the night.

As Sister Eva and Sister Consuela were blackened by the fire, Clara could see the flickering shadows dancing over the statue of the Angel Michael. The Angel carried a flaming sword in one hand. His right foot crushed the devil that lay defeated beneath him. The face of the angel appeared malevolent as it stared down at the condemned souls who were bound to the charnel pyre. The smell of burnt flesh drifted down to Clara as her sisters' shrieking filled the air.

Sister Clara was given the opportunity to watch others die many times before she herself succumbed to the flames. First they would try to pick up their feet from the increasingly hot wood. Cries of terror would become howls of pain as the tongues of flame licked up toward their flesh. She stood stoically waiting for the end. Her mind, however, was in frenzy. Panic overtook her as she watched Sister Esperanza's face blackening and peeling away. Father Benigno was screaming as the flames overtook him. Hernando was already a blackened corpse below the others.

"I curse God," Sister Clara yelled defiantly!

"You cannot curse God," Cardinal Eustachius answered her without emotion. His voice boomed across the garden. "It is the Lord who curses you." Then the flames were upon her.

†   †   †

After some time, the bodies of the condemned were nothing more than charred bones chained to the fire blackened stakes. The prisoners, who had gathered for the spectacle, now lost their fervor. Silence had descended over the mob. There was nothing left but the ghastly remains of their tormentors and the dying embers. "You are all free to leave this place," Eustachius said at last. "Those among you who wish to stay may do so. More God-fearing sisters will join you in a few short days. This house is now cleansed." For a moment, the brown clothed women did nothing. Then, one by one, they began to scatter. Isabel expected some looting as the women departed, but this did not occur. The fear of the cardinal and his men was too great.

Many of the women left the Convent of the Angels forever, but just as many remained behind. Isabel could not help but wonder why they stayed. Was life outside even worse than imprisonment? Isabel joined in with those who were leaving. She removed both the black hood and the white scapula that covered her head. Her blue black hair spilled down over her dress. It had grown back during her months in bondage and now hung to the middle of her back. She cast the nun's head coverings onto the cobblestones of the courtyard as she departed the convent.

"Sister Magdalena," Hector called out to her. Isabel turned around to face him. He had picked up the hood and scapula and now held them in his left hand. Several yards behind the warrior came Father Salvatore and the cardinal. Eustachius' pale fingers gleamed in the moonlight. His elongated hand rested on Salvatore's shoulder.

"I have betrayed my vows," Isabel told them. "I am not worthy to wear such things."

"Come with us," the cardinal invited her. "We journey now to Zaragoza."

"I cannot return to the church your eminence," she said as she shook her head. "There is too much blood on my hands."

"We will take you as far as the summer home of Lord Vasquez," the cardinal said as the trio came closer. "You may leave us there."

"I..," Isabel said indecisively.

"I promise that you shall arrive safely," Hector assured her. Again, Isabel was reminded of her father, though this man was surely something darker.

"Thank you," Isabel told the warrior, "and thank you, your eminence."

"You will go with us," Eustachius said. His voice was so devoid of inflection that Isabel could not tell whether it was a question or a command. Nevertheless, she agreed. The agonizing guilt she felt was great, but Isabel wanted to see the Summer Cottage, even for a little while. Salvatore held the door of the carriage open while Hector helped the blind man inside. He next held a hand out to Isabel. She took the warrior's offer of help and allowed herself to be lifted.

The walls inside the carriage were covered in black leather. The seat cushions were made of burgundy colored velvet. Unlike the other coaches Isabel had ridden in, this one had no windows. There was a small rectangular opening by the bottom of the wall across from the door, but it was clearly meant only for ventilation. If any light were to come through, it would extend only a few scant inches beyond the carriage wall.

Once Hector was inside, he shut the door, plunging the interior of the carriage in darkness. Isabel could hear the boots of Father Salvatore as he climbed on top and took the reins. She had to reach down and grab hold of the seat as the carriage jerked to a start. As they traveled away from the convent, the cardinal's pale foot was briefly illuminated by torchlight. After this, the only focal point was the sliver of moonlight coming in from the rectangular vent.

It was more than a little disconcerting for Isabel to be stuck with two men in complete blackness. At any moment, they might make a grab for her. She would never see it coming. She wanted to ask them why the carriage had been so designed, but she was inexplicably afraid of the answer.

There was a great deal of motion in the carriage. This could have meant that the road was poorly kept. By the sound of the horses' hooves, however, Isabel knew it was the speed at which Father Salvatore was driving them. The noise and bouncing of the wheels abated after some time. Salvatore slowed the horses down to a walk. "I know you," the voice of Eustachius sounded in the darkness.

"I believe so your eminence," Isabel said nervously.

"Lady Isabel of Montenegro," the cardinal said.

"I was," she replied. "I suppose I am again."

"Did not the Lord call to you sister?"

"I have broken my vows of obedience many times over," Isabel said into the darkness.

"How?"

"I...killed my children," Isabel answered. Her voice became thick with sadness. "I destroyed those who depended upon me most of all."

"You have sinned."

"Yes," Isabel replied, trying to stem the tide of sorrow before she drowned in it.

"Is this your reason for forsaking God?"

"I am not worthy to be a nun," Isabel said tremulously. "I am not even worthy to be spat upon."

"None are worthy in the sight of God," Eustachius said. Isabel could not answer. She wept silently. Her face was pinched up with agony, but she would not open her mouth to let it go. In her mind, she was not even worthy of sympathy after what she had done. "Sleep now sister," the cardinal told her, "and get your rest. We shall have need of you on the morrow." Isabel carefully laid herself down on the velvet cushion. She groped out with her hands to find the wall before doing so. She was the only person on her side of the carriage. The darkness made her feel as if she were blind also.

Sleep was not easy in coming, but exhaustion finally won out. The next thing Isabel knew, Father Salvatore was shaking her awake. The door of the carriage was open. The sky outside was grey in the early hours before dawn. "Wake up my Lady," the young priest urged. There was a strange quality of desperation in the man's voice that made her sit up quickly.

"What is it," she asked with alarm?

"Come on now," he replied. "Let me help you down." Cardinal Eustachius and Hector were still sitting across from her. The cardinal's face was unreadable. Hector was staring out at the grey sky. Was that apprehension in his eyes? Isabel could not know what worried the man, but she allowed Salvatore to help her quickly down from the carriage. He quickly closed and locked the door before breathing a sigh of relief.

"I do not understand," Isabel said as the first rays of sunlight broke over the mountains to the north. "What is the matter?"

"All is well," Salvatore replied evasively. "The cardinal tells me that you once bred horses."

"I did," Isabel agreed, but her suspicion was up.

"So you know how to ride then?"

"Of course I do," she replied.

"Very good," Salvatore said, "then you will not mind taking turns driving the carriage?"

"I suppose not," Isabel said. "Is that why you woke me so early?"

"It is," the young priest confirmed, "but let us break bread first. The horses must rest for a bit."

"They do look tired," Isabel noted. Father Salvatore opened up a large sack from the rack on top of the carriage. From this, he withdrew a round loaf of bread and a flask of water. They shared this simple meal in silence while the horses grazed along side the road. When enough time had passed, the two of them climbed up onto the top of the carriage and sat on the driver's bench. Isabel took the reins. She had never driven a carriage before, but she assumed that it would not be much different from riding.

"Just continue north up this road," Salvatore told her.

"What will you do?"

"Sleep," he replied. The priest laid himself down over the rest of the bench beside her. He had a large knapsack that he used as a pillow and a heavy blanket. He tucked himself into a fetal position. Still, his feet hung off over the side of the bench. "You can wear this coat," Salvatore said as he pointed one finger behind him. There was a heavy brown coat lashed to the back of the seat. Isabel untied the coat and put it on. She drove the carriage north. True to his word, Salvatore was soon snoring loudly.

Isabel held her hands back inside the long coat sleeves to protect them from the cold winds. The ground on the sides of the road was still wet with dew. Isabel could smell the tree bark as she traveled. Though she tried to focus herself on driving the horses, Isabel could not help but think of the dead. The faces of the children kept rising to her mind. If not the children, Isabel remembered Little Grandma's head dashed against the stones. She had gained her freedom, but at such a cost. It could have been different. "If only I had been more courageous," Isabel whispered. She tried to tell herself that she had only done what she knew, but it was no consolation.

At midday, Isabel stopped the carriage to rest the horses. They did not seem to be tired, but Isabel knew that they had traveled all night and into the morning. Father Salvatore slept on. Isabel let him. She climbed down off the carriage and unyoked the animals. She left the reins on them though, in order that they should not wander too far.

Isabel tried to open the door to the carriage but it had been locked. "Your eminence," she called out? She rapped lightly with her hand and waited. Salvatore sat up quickly.

"What do you think you are doing," he sputtered?

"The horses need to rest," Isabel explained. "I thought the cardinal and his guard would like to stretch their legs."

"Fool girl," Salvatore cursed as he climbed down from his perch! "Do not think to disturb Cardinal Eustachius again!"

"I only thought…"

"No," Salvatore interrupted her as he carefully inspected the door. "The cardinal knows we are stopped. If he wishes to get out, he will do so. Do not disturb him again. He is probably sleeping!"

"I am sorry," Isabel said as she backed away.

"Very good," Salvatore replied irritably. For their afternoon meal, Isabel and Salvatore had bread again. This time there was a bit of cheese as well. Eustachius and Hector remained inside for the entirety of the day. Only when they had stopped for the night did they leave the dark interior of the carriage.

"Are you still uncovered sister," the cardinal asked as he stepped out onto the soft earth.

"If you please," she answered him; "I am simply called Isabel your eminence."

"I remember her," the cardinal said as Hector and Father Salvatore gathered wood for a fire. Isabel did not know if she should respond or not. "The first time was at the court of King Alfonso. Do you recall?"

"I do," Isabel replied. She remembered that his mutilated face had given her nightmares.

"You sang so beautifully," the cardinal said nostalgically. "It was very convincing."

"I should have listened to you," Isabel said sadly. The cardinal sniffed at the air and then directed his gaze toward the fire that was just beginning to feed on the wood pile that his men had constructed. Hector was putting a small piece of flint back into a metal box.

"Lead me to the fire," Eustachius said as he wrapped his fingers over her left shoulder. Isabel dutifully took the man over to a large log that Hector had rolled into their campsite. She was careful to hold on to the strange man until he had seated himself. Isabel then sat down on the log next to him. "What did I say that you should have listened?" the blind man asked when they were all settled in?

"Kill him," Isabel said bitterly. "You told me to kill Manuel Barillos."

"You did not," Eustachius said flatly.

"No," Isabel agreed. Her throat was constricting as her tears threatened to resurface.

"I should have come to Montenegro," the cardinal told her.

"This is my fault, not yours," Isabel disagreed. "I should have done as God commanded."

"Are you still uncovered," Eustachius asked again?

"I am," she admitted. The cardinal did not say anything further, but Isabel could feel his disapproval. She went to sleep in the carriage and left the men to talk around the fire. The shadows of the camp fire danced over the cardinal's disfigured face. The light did not penetrate into his sockets, however. Isabel fell asleep quickly that night. She was tired from driving all day. She was exhausted also on a deeper level where consciousness was a chore.

In the darkest hour of night, Isabel came awake. One of her legs was hanging uncomfortably off the side of the bench and her thigh muscle had become sore from the odd position. She drew the long coat closer around her face like a blanket. She then tucked her sore leg back up on the bench and rubbed her cold foot against the opposite leg.

The door to the carriage was kept shut against the cold. It was impossible to know who was in the carriage with her, but Isabel wondered. There would never be room enough for all four of them unless two were to sleep on the floor. She dared not get up to find out, lest she should step on one of the men.

"Vincente's men have taken residence in the Catedral de Seo while we were gone," Hector said from outside.

They are insidious," Eustachius cursed. The crackling of the fire had long since ceased.

"I told you we have to act," Hector grumbled.

"It is not as simple as you believe Hector," the cardinal's monotone voice replied.

"What could be simpler than giving me leave to destroy them?"

"Word would travel back to Samael in Constantinople," Eustachius disagreed. "We would all be executed."

"It is only a matter of time before the Architects move against us in open war," Hector said. "Vincente's bloodline must be severed. We cannot conspire in the shadows forever. Every day that we fail to act is another day that they grow stronger."

"There is a truce," Eustachius reminded the warrior. "We have trade agreements and in some cases have allied with them against the Children of Mo'lech. The Convocation will not give us license to destroy the Architects. Your thirst for blood…"

"This has nothing to do with thirst," Hector snarled! We made a pledge to root out heretics and destroy them. Shall we break our vows to God or to Samael?"

"Have patience my son," Eustachius assured him. "I loathe the Architects as much as you… more perhaps. When we crush them, however; it must be a complete victory."

It will be too late," Hector replied, "or will you not be moved until they take the Basilica as well?"

"Enough," Eustachius said firmly. "My mind is made up." That was the end of it and Isabel heard nothing more. She kept expecting the two men to come into the carriage to sleep. It was too cold to be outside. If they ever did enter in, Isabel was not awake to notice it.

The strange pair was inside the carriage when Isabel awakened. Father Salvatore was shaking her again and herding the young woman out into the cold. He shut and locked the door to the carriage as if his life depended upon it. The second day's journey was much easier than the first.

Instead of leaving all the work to Isabel, Salvatore traded off with her. Since their journey brought them up from the south, they traveled through Zaragoza before reaching Isabel's destination. They went first along side the castle of King Alfonso and the Crown of Aragon. Aljaferia loomed imposingly from the rolling hill that lifted it up over the plains. They traveled next through the marketplace and from thence past the splendor of the Basilica del Pilar. Lastly, they went over the stone bridge where Isabel's escape from Montenegro had ended.

It was well into the afternoon by the time the carriage rumbled up the path to the Summer Cottage. The huge sycamore stood silent sentinel on the road up. A cold wind ripped through the trees and bit into Isabel's face and hands. There were no flowers blooming in the fields and many of the trees were bare of leaves.

Tears fell from Isabel's eyes as they approached. She should have brought Pilar and Alejandra to this place long ago. Now she was alone. So many of Isabel's fond memories were here. "Happy to be home," Salvatore asked?

"I am," Isabel lied. She wondered if her aunt and uncle would take her in. They would surely cast her out if they knew the things she had done! Isabel chuckled wryly. She remembered a time when her bickering with Catherine seemed like the hardest thing in her life. How naïve she was back then.

She parked the carriage in front of the wooden porch around the far side of the house. Servants came out to greet her but Isabel did not recognize them. They took the chests and sacks on the back of the carriage into the house. Others waited to take the carriage and the horses to the stables. Father Salvatore refused to open the carriage, however. He assured the servants of Lord Vasquez that the cardinal would not wish to be disturbed while praying. Salvatore informed them that he would stay with the carriage until the cardinal was ready. This was markedly odd, but none of the servants were inclined to question a distinguished guest from the Holy Church.

Isabel was led to her room by a female servant. It was very much as she remembered it; two canopy beds, two armoires, the dressing platform and the vanity with its sheet of reflective metal. She looked at the distorted image of herself in it as the woman left her alone. The black dress she wore was meant to be part of a nun's habit. Now it more resembled the garb of a peasant girl attending a funeral. Isabel looked at her dark reflection and thought of all those who were gone. She turned her head away. The last thing she wanted to see was herself, even if the image was distorted.

The woman who brought Isabel to her room had mentioned that they would be eating soon, but Isabel was far from hungry. Tears slid down her cheeks as she sat upon the bed. She looked down at her hands…a lady's hands. To Isabel, they appeared monstrous. Every groove and crevasse in the surface of her palm seemed to be a thin disguise for what lay beneath.

Suddenly, Isabel could not bear to be inside the cottage any longer. How dare she find safety after all that had transpired? It was hideous to contemplate what she would tell Catherine or Aunt Imelda. Would she give them the truth? Lying was not one of her talents. What would she say then? *"If not for me,"* Isabel imagined herself saying, *"my parents, my chamber maids, and five innocent children might still be alive. Perhaps by taking me in, some of you will die also."*

Isabel left the cottage but there was nowhere she could run in order to escape herself. She could hear the voices of the dead whispering in the trees that lined the path out to her sanctuary. She wanted it to be her imagination. *"I was their mother,"* Gabriella said accusingly. *"You killed my babies. You killed us all!"*

"I love you Isabel," Little Grandma sobbed.

"You were never meant to marry Ramon," Rafael told her. *"We are all dead because of it."*

"No," Isabel wept as she walked through the whispering trees.

"It could have been Manuel's child," her mother said sadly. *"He never would have known the difference. I just wanted to be loved."*

"Coward," her father said accusingly.

"No," Isabel cried. She held her hands up over her head as if to ward off the voices that assaulted her from all directions. She had come to the edge of the pond. It was the dead of winter and her whole body shivered from the cold. Her coat was still lying on the bed inside the Summer Cottage.

Looking up at the now deserted gazebo made Isabel sick with grief. She caught her breath as an image of her dead husband shimmered into existence inside. His skin was pale and sallow and his neck had been slit from one side to the other. There was dried blood below the wound and his shirt was stained through. His eyes were closed but his mouth hung wide open. Dirt had crusted around his teeth and covered his tongue. Ramon's body was slumped down onto one of the gazebo's benches. His position was very similar to that of the guardsman whom Santiago had killed on the rails of her father's stable.

Without warning, Ramon's head lifted up from the place where it lay on the back of the gazebo. Dirt fell out of his mouth as he turned his milky, white eyes upon Isabel. The moan that came out of her was a wretched and fearful sound. *"I was almost home,"* the corpse of her husband croaked. *"You killed me!"* He suddenly jumped up from the bench and vaulted through the window of the gazebo. The dirt filled revenant was coming right toward her! Isabel sobbed uncontrollably as she put her hands over her eyes. She heard a splash as Ramon's corpse hit the water. She moaned in agony as her mind disintegrated in terror. She could only huddle there like a child and pray that the monster would leave her alone.

When Isabel at last uncovered her eyes, there was no one around. She stood in the water up to her ankles. She was shivering violently. Isabel saw the faces of the dead looking up at her from below the water. These faded slowly, leaving indiscernible shadows behind. She walked forward. Her teeth chattered as the freezing water traveled ever higher onto her form. The pain to her muscles was sharp and immediate as she descended. The Heiress of Montenegro did not pause to reconsider. She would pay for her sins. Even the fires of the inferno seemed preferable to the mental anguish she know felt. It seemed that the wall between the living and the dead had thinned and Isabel could no longer tell truth from fiction. She continued on into the dark water.

Finally, there was nothing left of Isabel but a bit of blue black hair floating on the surface of the pond. Then that too disappeared. Her vision dimmed as she took the water into her lungs. Her pain finally subsided as her flesh went numb. Isabel sunk into the depths of her sanctuary until only blackness remained.

Part IV

Beyond Death

CHAPTER I

Isabel awakened on the bank of the small pond. The mud below was freezing and the cold had soaked through to her bones. The left side of her neck felt numb. She opened her eyes to darkness. Her vision was clouded from the water and debris that had collected in her eyes, but she sensed that someone was knelt over her.

Convulsions coursed through Isabel's body as her life expired in the mud. She could hear men's voices as if from very far away. A blessedly warm liquid filled her mouth. It seemed to come from a tear in the softest water skin her lips had ever felt. Where the liquid came from was not important. It flowed quickly down her throat and seemed to spread warmth throughout her entire body. It was easily the most intense pleasure she had ever felt.

Isabel closed her eyes and sucked greedily at the torn skin until it was taken away from her by force. "It is enough," said a deep, deadpan voice from the dark above her. She gasped as the feeling subsided. It was quickly replaced by an awful hunger.

"I starve," Isabel said weakly.

"She is one of us now," said another man's voice, "for good or ill." Isabel recognized the voice. It was the Cardinals guard.

"Hector," Isabel inquired? She rubbed her eyes and looked again.

"She wakes," Cardinal Eustachius said as Isabel's eyes came into focus. The sky was dark, but Isabel could see his face as clearly as if it were bathed in moonlight. This made no sense to her. The Cardinal's face should've been obscured in shadows. Perhaps it was the moonlight reflected off the surface of the water.

There was something dark and wet at the corner of Eustachius' lips. It had a metallic odor that Isabel found strangely compelling. Noticing the young woman's tension, the Cardinal wiped the corners of his mouth with one hand and then sucked whatever it was from his long index finger.

"I starve," Isabel said again. Mindless of the mud, Eustachius slid his arms below and lifted her up. His fingers wrapped around her left hip and one side of her torso below the arm. His arms were thin but surprisingly strong. Hector led the way back to the cottage and Eustachius followed. "How do you know where to go when you cannot see?" Isabel asked uneasily.

"The sound of Hector's boots," Eustachius replied. There was little comfort in his answer because it did not explain how he would be able to keep from tripping. The grounds of the summer cottage couldn't possibly be familiar to the man. Nevertheless, he carried Isabel all the way inside without stumbling. Even stepping up onto the wooden porch did not shake him!

"Wake up whom you must," the cardinal told Hector. "A bath must be drawn."

"I shall take care of it," Hector replied as he pulled out one of the wooden chairs by the breakfast table. It grated noisily along the floor. Eustachius lowered Isabel down into the seat with Hector to guide him.

"Have them make me something to eat," Isabel said eagerly.

"No," Eustachius said loudly! "You have had enough."

"I am starving," Isabel insisted. "There is plenty of food I assure you."

"You nearly drowned," Hector explained. "If you eat now, you are likely to throw it all up."

"I feel better now," Isabel argued. "Have them get me something."

"No," Eustachius interrupted as Hector left the room, "you may eat when we arrive at the Basilica."

"I cannot wait until tomorrow," she said crossly. "I am hungry now!" She was so confused. Had she dreamed of drowning herself? That would explain the voices.

"That is why we are leaving tonight," the cardinal told her.

"I have no plan to return to Zaragoza your eminence," Isabel said as respectfully as she could.

"You will bathe as soon as the water is prepared," the cardinal said. "Find something to wear from your room upstairs. Be sure that whatever you choose will cover your head until we can get another habit for you."

"I am no longer worthy to..," Isabel began.

"Silence," the cardinal interrupted has he held one pale finger toward her. "Your desire to forsake your solemn vows has less to do with your worth and more to do with cowardice!"

"I am no coward," Isabel said angrily!

"Look at you," the cardinal said with disgust. "It is because of your cravenly act that we sit here together this night. Bravery is in your blood, but when it counts... You do not measure up."

"I will remain here," Isabel said tersely.

"I told you to kill Lord Barillos," Eustachius rebuked her, "and yet he lives. How many of those you love must suffer and die before you will do as God commands you?"

"I..," Isabel faltered.

"Spare me your excuses," Eustachius continued on mercilessly. "That woman in the convent, Gabriela's mother... Did you suppose that she gave you the vial of poison in order to kill the children?"

"I do not know why she gave it to me," Isabel answered. "I thought she meant that I should kill myself."

"Why could you not have prepared a special treat for the nuns and priests whom Hector destroyed? It could have been a gift...from the children."

"I did not think..."

"Correct," the cardinal cut her off "you were so worried about having to face the children after they had been violated that you murdered them. Thinking is exactly what you failed to do. Is it not?"

"Yes," Isabel admitted. "I thought it was the only way."

"And now here we are," the cardinal concluded. "You were going to drown yourself if you didn't freeze to death first. This ultimate act of cowardice would've secured your place in hell! You are fortunate that I intervened."

"Why," Isabel wept. "I was better off dead!"

"I saw you," Eustachius said flatly. I saw the strength of will within you when you sang before the court of Alfonso. I saw it again at the Convent of the Angels. You have a selflessness that is almost Christ-like." Isabel could only look at the floor. "I see you Sister Magdalena, but your lack of decisiveness makes a coward of you. You know what must be done in your heart. You have always known. Now the Lord calls you to do it!"

"What must I do," Isabel asked meekly?

"Follow me," Eustachius said, "and I will show you the way to do God's will, however unpleasant it may be."

"I will go where you lead me," Isabel agreed. "I will keep my vows." The conversation was cut short by the arrival of two bleary eyed servants who went straight into the kitchen to stoke up a fire to boil water on. The sight of the servants going to the kitchen reminded Isabel how hungry she was. "You'll have to excuse me your eminence," she told the cardinal.

After several seconds of silence, Isabel rose from the table and made her way up to her room. The servants had already set up the porcelain tub in the middle of the room by the vanity. In years past, Isabel would have waited for a female servant to remove her clothing. Life in the convent was not so pampered. She removed her black dress which was filthy with mud, and laid it over the back of the chair in front of the vanity. For the sake of decency, she left on her white undergarment.

It struck Isabel as odd that she was not freezing. Her hair was still damp, her clothes even more so. In the middle of winter, she should have felt much worse. "Perhaps I am sick," Isabel mused aloud, but then why did no one come to cover her with a blanket? For all the reasons that would suggest she should feel cold, the only thing Isabel felt was a ravenous hunger.

After the passing of time, servants arrived with buckets of steaming hot water. After the men left, Isabel removed her undergarment and placed it with the rest of her wet clothing. She tested the water with one hand. It wasn't nearly as hot as it appeared. She climbed into the tub and lowered herself gratefully into the warm water. The water was soothing, but it would have been better if they had let her eat something. She felt so ashamed of herself for wanting to forsake her vows. It was as Cardinal Eustachius had said. If anything, she should be even more dedicated to repentance and doing the will of God.

Taking a hot bath had always made Isabel feel relaxed and sleepy. Not this time... The water felt quite refreshing, but she was not in the least bit drowsy. Perhaps it was the knowledge that she would soon be traveling to Zaragoza.

A female servant brought up some towels and began to set them on the bed. "I am done," Isabel said as she rose from the water.

"Yes my lady," the young woman answered with averted eyes.

"Just hand them here," Isabel said before the woman could come further. Having a servant dry her off was a thing of the past. The servant girl did as she was commanded. She curtsied and left the room once Isabel had taken the towels from her.

Isabel wrapped one towel around for long, blue-black hair and used the other to dry off her body. There were many beautiful dresses to choose from. Isabel selected the crimson and black dress with the embroidered crest of Montenegro upon it. She took the towel off her head and dried her hair. She spent a good deal of time brushing it out. There were so many memories in the attire she had chosen. Isabel was suddenly overcome with emotion. She felt a tear slide down her cheek and raised a hand to wipe it away.

When Isabel removed her hand, there was blood on her finger. If only to confirm her suspicion, Isabel tasted it.

It was blood, and it had streaked all the way down her face. "Something really is wrong with me," Isabel thought uneasily. She grabbed one of the towels and sunk part of it into the bathwater. With this, she cleaned her face. She felt her eyes several times and examined her fingers for more blood. There was none to be found. She wondered if she were cut somewhere, but digging her finger deeper into her eyes seemed intuitively foolish.

Instead of the triangular shaped hat that was meant to complement her dress, Isabel wore the black diaphanous shawl from her wedding gown. The carriage was already prepared. The main doors leading into the breakfast room stood open when Isabel came down. Hector was pacing to and fro by the table. He paused when she entered and looked at her. The man seemed at a loss for words. "Are we going them," she asked politely?

"We are," he said gruffly as he looked away from her. "Come." Hector strode outside and held the carriage door open for her. Father Salvatore was sitting on top once more. The cardinal's robes could be seen inside the opening of the carriage. As Hector helped her up, Isabel's eyes met those of Father Salvatore. It was only for a brief moment, but long enough for her to see that his face was a twisted masque of hatred. She wondered what she could have done to offend him so.

For some time, the carriage was silent except for the turning of the wheels. "It is so much brighter in here," Isabel said with confusion. The faces of Hector and Eustachius were plainly visible to her even in the almost complete darkness of the carriage. There was no sense in it.

"You must be prepared to do God's will," the cardinal said.

"I am," Isabel said.

"We are not taking you back to the Sisters of Santa Maria del Pilar," he explained in his deadpan voice.

"Why not," Isabel asked? She was now more confused than ever. Hector's eyes seemed to glitter in the unnatural dark. "Is there another convent?"

"Because of what you have done," the cardinal said, "you may not go back to them."

"What will I do?"

"You are with us now," Hector said.

"Yes," Eustachius agreed. "God has another plan for you."

"Where are you taking me," Isabel inquired?

"To the Basilica del Pilar," the cardinal replied. "I will have another habit brought for you from the convent."

"What can I do in the Basilica for your eminence," Isabel wondered aloud?

"You will see," Hector grinned. His white teeth gleamed in the darkness and Isabel saw that his canines were sharp and pointed as knives! Surely, this was a trick of the light; but what light?

"First you must be properly dressed," Eustachius said. "Let us pray together, for the burden of God's work is heavy." Hector bowed his head and closed his eyes. Isabel did likewise. The cardinal began to recite scripture in Latin.

They arrived at the basilica in the dead of night. Isabel stepped down from the carriage into the moonlit cobblestone square. There was a delicious aroma coming from inside the edifice, but Isabel could not identify it. She wrapped the black mantilla tighter around her slender form and followed the men into the open doors to the sanctuary. There were candles lit up by the altar, but their flames were guttering and the illumination was dim and filled with shadows.

"Leave her in the confessional," Eustachius told the younger priest.

"Of course," Father Salvatore replied. There was a bitter edge to his voice. While the cardinal and his guard traveled down the grand corridor on the left, Isabel was led into the confessional booth. "Stay here," the father told her before slamming the door shut. She could hear him cursing under his breath as he walked away.

Isabel sat waiting. The fragrant odor was stronger now, and it was coming from somewhere in the church in the direction that the cardinal had gone. She kept expecting someone to enter the other confessional booth, but no one did. Eventually, Father Salvatore opened the door and tossed a nun's habit and scapula in at her. "What shall I..," Isabel began. She had meant to ask what to do with her dress, but the young priest rudely interrupted her.

"Change your clothes," he snapped before shutting the door loudly on her once more. Isabel wondered what she could have done to vex the man so. She quickly removed her dress and replaced it with the black and white garb of a nun. Her eyes kept returning to the grate. She did not want any priest to see her unclothed. Fortunately, no one came.

When Isabel had finished changing, she folded up her dress and carried it in both hands. She exited the confessional booth to find Eustachius and Hector waiting in the pews. "Ready to go sister," Eustachius asked?

"I am ready," Isabel said confidently.

"Then follow," he replied as he stood up from his seat. Hector stood also. The three of them traveled together into the grand corridor. Hector led the way to a door unlike the others that lined the hall. It was a huge stone door with a darkly colored handle. The Cardinals guard took a long, iron key out of his belt pouch and stuck it into the opening below the handle. There was a loud noise as the lock turned over. Hector opened door and held it as Isabel and the cardinal entered.

Eustachius held on tight to Isabel's right shoulder which made her lead the way down the steep spiral that led to the dungeons. "Down the stairs," he whispered as if it were not obvious. Isabel walk slowly so as not to trip up the blind man, but she had a feeling that he only held on to her for show. The delicious smell became overpowering once Isabel was in the stairwell, but it was accompanied by the screaming of those who were chained below. She heard the heavy door close behind her. There was a strong desire to increase her stride, but Isabel resisted it.

The stairwell ended in a dark tunnel with black, uneven walls that seemed to be carved from the rock itself. Flickers of light came from the small windows set into the iron doors that broke through the rock's surface at intervals. Mortal eyes would have required the assistance of a torch to navigate through the winding cavern. Isabel, (though she knew it not), and those with her had no need for such things.

Isabel had no desire to look into the rooms she passed. The screaming of their occupants told the story well enough. The tunnel opened up into a large cavern with another tunnel leading farther down on the opposite side.

Heavy chains were attached to the ceiling of the cavern. From those chains, men were suspended in various states. Some were shackled by their wrists while others hung upside down by their ankles. Most of these unfortunates were already dead and in varying states of decomposition. Maggots feasted upon the eyes and lips of one victim. His mouth seemed to be open in a frozen scream as the larva devoured his decaying flesh. Other corpses had only begun to attract flies, while still others were little more than bones and the ragged remnants of the clothing they once were.

The most wretched of the chained men were those who still drew breath. They hung with fear-stricken eyes. Some stared at the dead who dangled around them. Others made a concentrated effort to look only at the floor. One man had his eyes pinched shut while he mumbled useless petitions to God, Jesus, and whatever Saints might spare him from suffering.

One chain hung lower than the rest. Its victim was hung upside down over a large copper basin. His limbs were thin and malnourished, and his eyes were rolled into the back of his skull. His throat had been freshly cut and the blood drained down over his face. What little was left dripped slowly into the copper receptacle below.

Isabel's stomach growled, but she pushed away the thought of food. She reasoned that she must truly be starving in order to feel hunger in the presence of the mutilated dead. A large open table stood in the center of the room. Manacles were attached to each leg of the table, where they could then be stretched to the four limbs of a human being. A dark and uneven stain covered the center of the surface.

Two large fire pits were sunken into the stone floor. The blazing fires within them provided illumination for the torture chamber, along with a great deal of heat. Those prisoners still alive were covered in sweat.

Two iron posts rose up in the far corner of the chamber. Between them was a man dressed in rags. His beard was unkempt and hung unevenly down to the middle of his threadbare tunic. His eyes were likewise concealed by the shaggy hair that hung down over them. His body was covered with the marks of the lash. Some stripes bled. Others were little more than bruises. A long whip hung over his neck, almost as if to taunt the man. His head slumped down and his chest moved rhythmically as he slept.

"See the man bound between the posts," Eustachius asked as he held on to Isabel?

"Yes," she replied.

"Take me to him," the Cardinal requested. Isabel led the blind man over to the prisoner. Hector followed behind them. "This man's name is Esteban," the cardinal said. "He was betrothed to a young woman of breeding. He conspired to lie with her before the consecration of marriage."

"He is being punished for fornication," Isabel asked? "Is that the only reason he is here?"

"No," Eustachius smiled as Isabel placed his hand on one of the iron posts. "His betrothed needed more than his sinful desires to stray from the will of God. Esteban told her that he had dreamed a dream." The cardinal carefully removed the whip from the man's neck by lifting it up over his head. His grotesque fingers tightened around the handle as he walked several steps back from the posts. Isabel backed away also. "In Esteban's dream, God had told him that he and his future bride would give birth to the next pope. The Lord told him that they must not wait until after the wedding, for the child needed to be born in the spring."

"She believed him," Isabel asked incredulously?

"To the shame of her father," Eustachius agreed. "She did. Esteban did not marry her as he had promised. Ruining one man's daughter was not good enough for this man. We found him courting another here in Zaragoza. Though she had not yet fallen, he had told her a similar tale. We took him, but it is not for his lecherous ways that Esteban now stands bound before you."

"Then what," Isabel asked? Eustachius brought up his hand and the whip whirled over his head.

"For blasphemy," Eustachius snarled as he cracked the whip down onto the prisoner! The lash fell upon Esteban's face and tore a thin strip of blood in his cheek as the cardinal snapped it away. Esteban awakened instantly and cried out with a combination of shock and terror! "Are you ready to repent," the cardinal asked as he ran the whip through his hand. Blood remained on his thumb and index finger as the whip departed.

"I have already repented," Esteban said wretchedly! Isabel was drawn to the fresh blood like a moth to flame. She reasoned that she was feeling pity for the man. He had sinned, but was all this necessary? She told herself that she might help him by tending to his wounds.

"What are you doing sister," Hector asked? There was a gleam in the warrior's eyes that Isabel found unsettling. They were like the eyes of a circling vulture.

"He has repented," Isabel said as she put one slender hand upon his face. "I will help him." Blood seeped out of the man's wounds and onto Isabel's thumb.

"Help him," Hector encouraged her! Something horrible awakened in Isabel. Her pangs of hunger became worse than ever. She could see the veins below the man's skin. They were pulsing with blood. She felt a slight tingle in her gums as her reason fled.

Sister Magdalena's fangs flashed in the torchlight. "No," Esteban screamed in horror! "I repent! Please, do not…" Isabel could smell fear and it made the allure of the man's blood all the more intoxicating. She tore into the flesh of his face like a ravening beast! She gorged herself on the blood that flowed freely from his wounds, but even this was not enough. In her impatience to feed, Sister Magdalena ripped chunks of flesh from Esteban's already injured face. The man's wailing resonated in the chamber, and it was joined by the others who looked on. Finally, Isabel locked her jaws around the man's jugular and tore out his throat entirely! She sucked greedily from the wound as her victim convulsed beneath her. The prisoner slumped down in his chains as his life slipped away. Isabel remained until she had consumed every drop.

CHAPTER II

"More blood," Isabel growled! Her fangs were lowered and her face was covered with it. Her whole body was still tingling from the feast and her hunger would not be sated. Eustachius motioned toward the copper basin with one pale finger. Isabel wasted no time in closing the distance between her and the basin. She got down onto her hands and knees and drank deeply. In the far reaches of the woman's mind, she was appalled by what her body was doing. It was very much like a pregnant woman who is compelled to eat dirt or some other unsavory substance. She was powerless to resist.

The blood inside the copper vessel was nourishing, but it was not intoxicating like that which Isabel had drained from the chained man. She was still hungry after consuming all of the dead man's blood, but it was more manageable. As she lifted her head up from the basin, she saw the cardinal and his guard standing over her. Beyond them, she could see what remained of her first meal. Isabel nearly swooned as the gravity of her actions settled upon her like a lead weight.

"Look at her," Eustachius said disapprovingly. His empty eye sockets seemed to stare down at her.

"She is covered in it," Hector sneered. Isabel moaned and wiped her face. She cried out in horror when she removed her hands and saw the blood that covered her fingers.

"You are an abomination," Eustachius shouted!

"No, no," Isabel said as she cringed upon the stone floor. She could not even begin to explain what she had done.

"Cast out the drinkers of blood," the cardinal continued. "They are an abomination unto God and have no place among you!"

"I could not stop," Isabel cried!

"Look at her," Hector exclaimed with convincing shock, "her tears... She cries blood!"

"She is cursed by God," Eustachius said. His voice had resumed its usual lack of inflection. Isabel wept. She remembered her discovery in the bathtub of the summer cottage. Here was the explanation she had feared.

"Damned for eternity," Hector agreed solemnly.

"Make it stop," Isabel pleaded. "I am still hungry."

"And so shall you ever be," Eustachius declared without mercy.

"I repent," she said fearfully.

"It is too late for repentance," Hector told her. "You are dead already."

"What," Isabel asked incredulously? "I am not dead. I..."

"Cast out from the light of God's mercy, cursed to dwell in darkness; you exists beyond death," Eustachius said with condemnation in his voice. "You will forever hunger for the blood of man. You shall drink and never be satisfied."

"What have I done," Isabel cried?

"Even after all the wickedness which your hands have wrought, merciful God would have forgiven you. When you walked into the water, the line was drawn. You have turned your back upon salvation," Eustachius said.

"Will I burn," she asked with fear?

"No," Hector answered.

"Your soul belongs in purgatory," the cardinal answered, "but God hath sent us to deliver another fate." Isabel looked questioningly at the blind creature that stood before her. From her vantage point, she could see that his canine teeth were sharpened like those of his guard. She had not imagined this in the carriage. Hector seemed to sense her thoughts and he grinned. His sharp canine teeth were then fully revealed to her. "You will suffer perdition on earth," the cardinal promised, "for God hath allowed me to make you one of us."

"An abomination," Hector added.

"A vampire," Eustachius said flatly. "Follow me." "Destroy the prisoners," Eustachius told Hector as they left.

"They have seen too much. They should have repented by now."

"I obey," Hector replied. He turned around toward the damned. Isabel could hear the fearful cries of the prisoners as they departed. These cries quickly turned to screaming. The tunnel slowly descended into the earth. After a time, there was no light to guide the way, but the unnatural eyes of the undead had no need for it. Eustachius guided Isabel through a thin crack in the wall that led down to a small chamber. In this chamber were three heavy marble coffins and a lighter one made of wood placed there as an afterthought.

"Remain here this day," the cardinal told her. "Your place of rest is the grave. Pray to God, for your need to repent is great."

"But I am damned already," Isabel said sadly.

"Perhaps," Eustachius agreed, "but even the devil could be saved were he to beg for God's mercy. How different than are we? If you suffer death again you will know, but too late." Isabel thought on this. She was about to ask the cardinal something more but when she turned back, he had already gone.

Isabel opened the lid of the wooden coffin which made a loud creaking sound. There were cushions lining the bottom of it. She could not discern what color they were, however. The lack of light rendered everything in shades of gray.

Sister Magdalena knelt down over her deathbed and prayed for forgiveness. It seemed unlikely that God would forgive the horrible creature that she had become. Exhaustion later drove her into the coffin. There were tears of blood dried upon her cheeks as she closed herself inside. Sister Magdalena slept far from the light of day. Isabel was dead.

Sister Magdalena awoke to the sounds of the other vampires rising from their marble coffins. She pushed back the lid of her own, and pulled herself up. Hector and the cardinal were rendered in black and white in the darkness. "Are you awake my daughter," Eustachius asked?

"I am," Isabel replied as she stepped out of the coffin.

"Today I will teach you what you are."

"An abomination," Isabel said under her breath. Hector smiled sardonically.

"It is more than that," Eustachius told her. "The vampire is cursed by God. You are such a creature; but you are fortunate in that you will soon be part of the greatest organization of the undead on earth, the Convocation of Saints. We of the Convocation continue to worship Christ and do his will on earth. As I told you, even the Devil himself could attain salvation through repentance. We are such devils, Hector and I. I am its grand inquisitor. Hector has been assigned to protect me. It is our duty to root out blasphemers and heretics. These wretched souls must be driven to repentance."

"We are devils upon the earth," Hector said. "It is not our place to provide comfort. Once the sinner is delivered unto us by God, they will surely die."

"But we must do everything in our power to open the way to salvation before we allow them to expire," Eustachius added. "As members of the clergy, it is against our nature to kill. That is the other reason Hector accompanies me, to act as executioner. God waits for the faithful and the damned. Hector has the unsavory task of sending them hither."

"It is my burden," Hector agreed solemnly, but Isabel did not detect any regret in his countenance.

"What of Father Salvatore," Isabel asked? "He is not with us."

"No," Eustachius frowned. "Father Salvatore is not yet one of us. It is his place to protect our bodies by day, for we are cursed to remain in darkness. We cannot move about in the sun and the curse compels us to slumber."

"Beware the light of the sun," Hector cautioned. "It will burn like the fires of the inferno."

"You will drink the blood of man to sustain you," the cardinal said, "but you need not kill them. You must exercise restraint in your consumption."

"I will never allow myself to do that again," Sister Magdalena vowed.

"You will drink the blood of man," Cardinal frowned. "If you do not, your hunger will drive you to murder!"

"I will," she said uncomfortably. "I will drink then… if I must."

"You must," Hector said.

"There are many horrible things that your curse will require of you my daughter," Eustachius said. "God has willed it that you be mine. As my child, you will be called upon to drive men to Christ through suffering."

"Surely there are better ways to guide someone to salvation," Isabel disagreed.

"There are," the cardinal agreed, "but some men cannot repent without a taste of perdition. I am certain that you have met men such as this."

"I have," Isabel admitted. She thought bitterly of Manuel Barillos. There was nothing good in him.

"It is these men whom God sends to my hands. This is my burden," Eustachius said sadly. "It is a yoke that we will now share."

"It is not in me to do such things," Isabel said uneasily.

"You have brought this fate upon yourself," Eustachius rebuked her. "God sent us to give you a second chance at redemption. This is your punishment child! It is a hard road, but far preferable to damnation and the torments of hell!"

I will do what the Lord asks of me," Isabel said humbly, but she cringed inside to think of what that might be.

"Come," Eustachius said as he walked toward the tunnel out of the crypt. "The blood that now flows in you is the same as that which is in me. I will show you how to read the minds of men like an unraveled scroll." Isabel followed the cardinal out of the abysmal crypt and from thence into the torture chamber.

The corpse of Isabel's first victim still hung limply between the iron posts. She could see his teeth and gums through the jagged opening inside of his cheek. His face was covered with patches of missing skin that Isabel had torn off with her teeth. His throat was a gaping hole that was now collecting flies.

One of the flies flew up from Esteban's torn throat and lit on his exposed gums. Isabel's eyes focused on the insect. Her vision narrowed for a moment and then she was looking at the fly with crystal clarity. She saw the creature vomit onto the ridge where the dead man's teeth and gums met. It then used its long mouth to consume the milky white fluid that it had regurgitated. "Sister Magdalena," Hector said sharply. Isabel's vision returned to her immediate surroundings.

"Forgive me," she said with confusion. The cardinal was already standing at one of the doors in the far tunnel which lead back up to the basilica. Hector, it seemed, had come back to fetch her.

"Come" Hector said curtly. He turned and walked quickly toward the door where Eustachius was waiting. They had to duck in order to enter into the torch lit chamber. The cardinal followed. The iron door sounded loudly as it clanged against the jam. A young man lay spread-eagled on the rack in the center of the room beyond. His four limbs were tied to metal wheels, and from there back to a circular crank that would stretch all of them at once.

The young man had long, black hair and an underdeveloped mustache that showed his age. He was handsome and his flesh was unscarred. He was looking over at them with a mixture of defiance and fear. He wore nothing but a loincloth of white linen. His arms and legs were stretched tight, but the real pain had yet to begin. "Just observe for now," Eustachius whispered. He then walked over to the side of the rack. "Why are you here," the cardinal asked?

"I was captured in the grove," the man answered.

"In the grove," Eustachius echoed; "but why are you here?"

"They brought me here," the young man said with confusion. The cardinal's hand shot out so quickly that Isabel didn't even see it move. His pale fingers pressed hard into the sides of the man's cheek, giving the prisoner a comical, fish-faced appearance. It was no laughing matter, however.

"Pay very close attention," Eustachius said with clenched teeth. "I am asking you what you were doing in the grove. Why did they arrest you? Why are you here?" The prisoner tried to respond but his words came out unintelligible. Eustachius shoved the young man's head away as he released his grip. The pink imprints of his fingers were still visible on the man's cheeks.

The prisoner took a deep breath once he was free of those grotesque fingers. "I wasn't with the rest of them," the prisoner said desperately. "I do not know those people. I am innocent. You must let me go. I had no part in this!"

"What were they doing," Cardinal asked?

"They worshiped an idol in the grove. Surely it was witchcraft but I had no part in it!"

"What brought you there?"

"What br…" the prisoner stammered. "I was… I was hunting in the woods. I came upon the grove at almost the same time as the soldiers."

"You were unarmed," Eustachius said. "Why did you not think it prudent to bring a weapon?"

"There was no…no need," the prisoner replied nervously.

"Do you often hunt with your bare hands?"

"No, of course not," the man insisted!

"Then why did the soldiers find no weapon upon your body?"

"I… because..." The man struggled.

"Because you're lying," the cardinal concluded.

"No please... I swear."

"Do not swear," Eustachius warned, "for surely your sin will find you out."

"I am not a witch," the prisoner cried! The cardinal began to slowly run his fingers over the man's exposed skin. The prisoner trembled. After some time, Eustachius finished his examination.

"You are wealthy," the cardinal said. It was not a question.

"Yes," the young man said with a mixture of hope and relief. "My father is always willing to donate to the church, and..."

"It was only an observation," the cardinal said as he shook his head. "Your flesh is smooth and without any imperfection. You have never worked, nor have you suffered, but you will tonight."

"My father will pay!"

"You will pay," the Cardinal disagreed calmly. He reached one hand blindly out and patted it on the prisoners arm, then the rack, and finally the metal crank. His fingers curled around it and pulled hard. The wheel was turned 180° and very rapidly. The prisoner cried out as the pressure in his limbs increased. Eustachius leaned in very close to the man's face before speaking again. "Confess it," the cardinal urged. "I am listening."

"I am innocent," the man cried! The last syllable became a scream as the cardinal cranked hard on the wheel. Isabel flinched as the prisoner cried out.

"Come here Sister Magdalena," Eustachius invited. He moved around to his victims head and placed his index fingers gently upon the man's temples. "Come and see." The cardinal exhaled sharply as he increased the pressure of his fingers. The prisoner shuddered under the blind man's touch.

Eustachius retained his position by the young man's head for quite some time. The man himself moaned and thrashed upon the rack, but it did him little good. The cardinal's hands seemed to shiver for a time, but it was not very long. "He lies," Eustachius said when he finally removed his pale fingers. "Break him!" Hector stepped forward, but the cardinal stopped him with one grotesque hand splayed out over the warrior's chest like some monstrous spider. "Sister Magdalena," Eustachius clarified. Isabel walked forward with hesitation. She put one hand on the crank and paused.

"How can you know that he lies," she asked? "Hunting is not outside the realm of possibility."

"With his bare hands," Hector scoffed?

"He could have dropped his weapon when he was arrested," Isabel said.

"He refers to the place of demon worship as 'The Grove.' He does not call it a grove," the cardinal explained. This implies a certain familiarity. He is lying."

"He could be telling the truth," Isabel insisted.

"Come here," the cardinal said again. "Place your fingers upon the prisoner's temples." Isabel did so. "Now I want you to close your eyes and think about what this man might have been doing in the grove." Isabel closed her eyes and tried to imagine what might have occurred. She guessed that he had been involved in the idolatry, but that was hardly mind reading. "Concentrate," Eustachius said sharply. "You must rip it from his mind. He will resist you but you must prevail if justice is to be done!"

"I have done nothing," the young man cried again as he thrashed his head about!

"Pretend that the lives of your remaining relatives depends upon it," Eustachius shouted at her! Isabel grabbed hold of the young man's head and held it firmly in place.

"Be still," she said with irritation. The prisoner did not yield. Isabel pressed her index fingers hard into the man's temples as she closed her eyes. Her nails dug into his flesh until they drew blood. "Stop moving," she snarled! When Isabel opened her eyes, she was no longer in the torture chamber below the Basilica.

Sister Magdalena hurtled through a dark tunnel that was segmented by jagged rings of crimson light. Her body was ejected out into the air over a thick forest. She could see a clearing in the canopy afar-off, but it was covered in a dense fog. Her speed decreased dramatically and she floated down toward the earth like an autumn leaf.

Isabel's feet touched ground and she made her way toward the clearing. The features of the forest were blurred as if she were in a dream. She looked down at her dress and saw that it was black no longer. The nun's habit she now wore was an iridescent white with tiny pearls sewn throughout. As she came closer to the fog shrouded area, the young man from the torture chamber stepped out of the mist. There was fear in his eyes and for a brief second, Isabel saw blood covering the lower knuckles of his fingers. "Go away," the man said. "No one wants you here!"

"Get out of my way," Isabel commanded him.

"These are my secrets," the young man said nervously. You cannot..."

"I will devour you," Isabel growled at him!

"Please no," the young man begged as he cowered on the ground at her feet. As Isabel walked toward him, his body quickly dissolved into the mist. She stretched out her hand toward the fog and it quickly dissipated as if burned away by the sun. The clearing in the grove of trees was then revealed to her sight.

On each side of the clearing were six figures in coarse black robes. They were of all shapes and sizes and some were obviously female. They wore grotesque wooden masks which covered the top half of their faces. Each mask was meant to resemble a demonic bull. The artistry and skill, (or lack thereof), of the individual cultists made each of them unique.

At the far side was an altar built of piled stones from a nearby creek. The stones were smooth and flat on either side. Another black robed man emerged from the trees behind the altar. He carried a lead rope which was attached to a slender young woman in her bed clothes. Her blonde hair was long and unkempt, and she looked down at the ground with resignation.

Although this last man was wearing a mask like the others, Isabel somehow knew that he was the very same man now imprisoned by the cardinal. His mask became transparent as she looked upon it and the young man's face could be seen beneath. He led the girl up to stand behind the stones of the altar. Looking closer, Isabel could see that the top of the altar was covered with bundles of rolled straw. The straw had been coated with black tar. Isabel could smell it as clearly as if she had been standing by the altar.

In the next instant, Isabel was standing on the opposite side of the stones from the young man whose spirit she was invading. "Behold our sister Ana," the young man called loudly across the clearing. He seemed to look through Isabel as if she were not there at all. "She comes to spit in the face of God by offering her soul to the God of the grove!"

"The God of the grove must be fed," the twelve cultists chanted in unison.

"Not since the time of my grandfather has our God come in the flesh. Ana's offering will surely bring him to us this night."

"An offering a blood," the cultists chanted.

"But not of blood only my brothers and sisters... the God of The Grove will come for her soul, and consume it!"

"Praise be to Mo'lech," the robed figures said as one.

"Behold," the young man said dramatically with an exaggerated wave of his arm, "the sun dies in the western sky."

"The power of Christ fades," the cultists replied.

"Lay you down upon the altar Ana," the young man commanded, "for his time draws near!" The roped women crawled dutifully up onto the tar soaked straw and lay down upon it. The young man pulled her across the stones until her legs hung off one side of the altar. He removed the long lead rope and kissed her. She pushed up her neck to kiss him in return. When the young man stood once more, tears had welled up in the eyes of the sacrifice. "Give me your hands," the priest demanded! Ana held her hands up toward him. He bound them together roughly with the rope. He then pulled them back over her head until her forearms were bent over the side of the altar.

The young man ran the length of rope first to one ankle and then the other. From thence, he returned to her wrists to complete the circuit. The tension of the rope was so great that the girl could barely move. "Come now my sisters," he said. Four of the cultists moved up to the altar and took position at each of its corners. They simultaneously lowered themselves into a kneeling position facing the stones. Each female cultist laid a hold of one of the sacrifices limbs and held fast.

Drawing a long knife from his belt, the young man cut down the center of the woman's nightgown. Isabel's heart quickened as she remembered her ordeal in Montenegro. The woman shuddered and her breathing came fast as the knife cut through her gown and exposed her flesh to the gathering night.

The young man continued the tear in the fabric until he had rent it in twain. He folded the two halves of the nightgown over, revealing her naked form to the cultists who looked eagerly on. When finished, the priest held the blade high in the air. "With this blade we make the offering of blood," he cried! He reversed the blade and then plunged it down into the meat of her thigh. She cried out in pain as the steel entered her skin but fought the urge to scream.

Leaving the dagger buried in the woman's thigh, the young man pulled open his robe, revealing his own nakedness to the onlookers. "With our lusts, the soul will be made ready for our God," he shouted!

"Prepare the sacrifice," the cultists chanted. Without removing the dagger from the woman's leg, the young man forced himself inside of her. Blood flowed freely from around the blade as he thrust himself into her again and again. Ana was sobbing and crying out with pain as the young man defiled her innermost parts.

The young man lay down atop the sacrifice and panted heavily when his lust was spent. Rising back up, he held both hands heavenward. "You are a dog and worthy of this fate," he proclaimed. After his voice echoed back from the trees, the young man spat in the woman's face.

"What are you doing," she sobbed? The young man said nothing. He walked around behind the altar and lifted his hands once more.

"Come my brothers," the priest shouted into the night. Isabel looked on in horror as each of the male cultists took their turn in defiling the sacrifice. Each man would first remove the blade and then raise it high into the air.

"Praise be to Mo'lech," the others would say in unison. The holder of the blade would then plunge it deeply into one of Ana's limbs. After this, he would force himself inside of her, pounding relentlessly until his arousal was sated. Then the next cultists would come, and the next, and the next. The females who held the woman encouraged the men as they raped the sacrifice. The woman holding her right leg was licking up and down the length of one leg as the blood flowed freely.

When each of the men had finished with her, Ana was weeping and covered with blood. Each of her limbs had been pierced deeply with the dagger and her blood flowed down onto the stones. "We bring you the offering of blood," the young man cried out as he ripped the dagger free of her left arm! She screamed and continued weeping as the cultists responded to the young man's declaration.

"Praise be to Mo'lech," they chanted.

"Call to him," the young man shouted down at Ana!

"I am scared Carlo," she sobbed.

"No," the young man growled as he slapped Ana across the face. "You will destroy the power of the ritual!"

"I want to go home," she cried. "I want to go home!"

"Call to the God of the grove," Carlo shouted, "or you will be alive when we invoke his fire!"

"No," Ana whimpered.

"Do it," Carlos snarled.

"Praise be to Mo'lech," Ana said weakly.

"That's right," Carlo said with a psychotic gleam in his eyes. "Do it just like I have instructed you."

"I... I offer my soul... Carlo, I am frightened."

"Praise be to Mo'lech," Carlo screamed as he raised the blade high! Its bloody point was turned down toward Ana's flesh.

"No," Ana shrieked, but it was too late. Carlo brought the long dagger down swiftly into the flesh of her throat. Her mouth opened and closed spasmodically as her blood poured down from the wound. Carlo twisted the blade in all directions until there was a gaping hole in the woman's neck. Ana was dead.

Sister Magdalena could watch no longer. She turned her face from the atrocity and was suddenly hurtling through the dark tunnel once more. One of the jagged rings began to expand until it was large enough for a man to crawl through. A black skeletal hand reached up out of the crimson light. It was followed by a fire blackened skull and the rest of the bones below it. Isabel slowed down as she floated over the animated skeleton. She could see the ethereal form of the woman surrounding the charred bones.

"Help me," the apparition croaked. "I'm afraid."

"I cannot help you," Sister Magdalena replied.

"Please," Ana said fearfully. "I do not want to go to hell. I am scared."

"I cannot help you," Isabel repeated.

"But you are a nun," Ana wept. "You have to help me!"

"It is too late," Isabel said finally. Suddenly, her body was flying away from the girl's spirit.

"Come back," the ghost shrieked from behind her! The jagged rings rushed by with increasing speed until Isabel's vision was crimson blur. When she found herself back in the chamber below the Basilica, Isabel felt disoriented as if she had just been thrown from the back of a horse. She removed her fingers from Carlo's bleeding temples and stood slowly. She looked around the torch lit chamber and saw that the other two vampires were waiting patiently beside her. Father Salvatore now stood in the entryway with the iron door ajar.

The shadows on the younger priests face lengthened and receded with the flickering of the flames. A smoldering anger creased his countenance and his hands shook with jealous rage. "What are you doing," Salvatore demanded of the cardinal?

"Is it not obvious," Eustachius replied without emotion?

You are teaching her Dominion over Spirit," he spat, "her?" Eustachius crossed his arms, wrapping his long fingers around his thin shoulders as he looked across the room at his servant. "Not even Hector has been given such a gift," Salvatore said incredulously!

"It comes naturally to her," Eustachius replied. "It is the will of God."

"Hector," Salvatore pleaded, "you are several centuries old. Is this not an affront?"

"I am content to do as the Lord wills," Hector replied stonily.

"You are not content Hector," Salvatore nearly shouted! "You are lying! You cannot be content to exist as the Cardinals hound. You do whatever he says. You believe everything he says. Eustachius is not God!"

"Is that what this is really about…thrall," Hector asked contemptuously?

"You do not need him," Salvatore said with one accusing finger pointed at Eustachius. "You are every bit the man that he is. He is blind and helpless, but still you serve his every whim. Why Hector? Why have you made yourself even more blind than he?"

"Perhaps you could ask the Lord himself," Hector said threateningly. One hand reached back toward the massive sword that hung over his shoulder. Salvatore cringed in fear but recovered quickly.

"No," Eustachius said with one hand grasping the warrior's tricep. "Do not barter your salvation for one man's words." Hector released his grip on the sword and let his arm drop back down.

"Salvation," Father Salvatore scoffed. "You really are deluded!"

"You shall never receive the blood Salvatore," Eustachius said. "Be gone from my house."

"You promised," Salvatore screamed! "I have done everything you asked."

"Not everything," the cardinal disagreed.

"Who has protected your sleep for the last generation," Salvatore asked? "I have! That is twenty-six years of obedience, twenty-six years! Now you give this woman, this outsider, the gift that is rightfully mine?" The man's face was red and tears were threatening to fall from his eyes.

"Your heart has never been in the right place," Eustachius replied. "You are too focused upon temporal power Salvatore. Yours is the sin of greed. You do not wish to serve God; you wish to be served as God."

"It is the same thing that you do," Salvatore retorted! "I have done everything you asked in order to attain it. I deserve the blood, but you have squandered it on this suicidal whore!"

"You are done speaking in my house," Eustachius said. He motioned with one grotesque hand toward Hector. Salvatore took a step back.

"I do not deserve this," the younger priest said fearfully.

"You will leave now Salvatore," Hector said coldly, "as a whole or in pieces."

"I will go," Salvatore said. His voice was choked with emotion, "but you will see me again!" Hector snarled and drew the sword quickly from its scabbard. Firelight danced on the massive blade.

"Let him go," Eustachius said loudly. Father Salvatore fled up the stairs and out of the dungeon.

"He will endanger us," Hector said from behind clenched teeth. "Let me do what must be done."

"No," Eustachius commanded. "Murder is not God's will."

"He will betray us," Hector snarled!

"As for me and my house," Eustachius said finally, "we will serve the Lord. Salvatore will find his reward. We shall not hasten it."

After a long silence, Hector sheathed his blade and turned to Isabel. "What did you see," he asked her? He walked slowly over to join her by the rack as she answered him.

"He is a witch," Isabel replied shakily. Everything that happened in the grove was at his behest."

"That isn't true," Carlo pleaded.

"It is true Carlo," Isabel replied emotionally. The mere sight of the man made her flesh crawl!

"What? How do you know my name," the young man asked nervously?

"The Lord reveals all Carlo," Eustachius said as he walked over to the wheel that controlled the rack. He cranked the wheel sharply to the left, eliciting a loud grunt and some fast, shallow breathing from the prisoner. "Is there not something you wish to confess," the cardinal asked?

"You already know," Carlo said tensely. "Just kill me and be done with it!"

"Hector will kill you tomorrow," Eustachius informed the man. "You have little time in which to repent."

"I will not repent," Carlo retorted!

"I will meet you later in the sanctuary," Hector told the cardinal. "I wish to pray."

"Go in peace," Eustachius replied. He moved away from the crank and knelt down by the prisoners head. "You will face all manner of torments in hell my son," he whispered. "You will here receive a taste of the pain which awaits therein."

"I serve the God of the Grove," Carlo said defiantly.

"Sister Magdalena," Eustachius invited, "take the wheel. This blasphemer must be prepared to face judgment." Isabel came forward and placed her hands upon the wheel that controlled the tension of the ropes.

"As the ropes tighten," Eustachius whispered to the prisoner, "you will feel incredible pain in your thighs and shoulders. The bones of your limbs will separate from their sockets. If the break is not clean, then the jagged edges of bone will puncture your insides."

"Let me go," Carlo said nervously. "My father will pay."

"As the wheel continues turning," Eustachius continued, "you will actually hear your skin stretching out and ripping. If you do not die of shock, you will experience the agony of your limbs being completely separated from your body. You will believe. All that will be left is to wait for death. You will pray that it comes soon, but a far worse fate awaits you beyond death."

"My family has money," Carlo pleaded. Eustachius rose back up to his full height.

"Help him to repent sister," the cardinal said.

"I will," Isabel replied, "but how will I know when it is done?"

"The secrets of his heart shall be open to you," the cardinal replied. "Simply do as I have shown you."

"I will."

"Can you do all that God requires?"

"I can," Isabel answered. What she had seen in Carlo's mind disgusted her. He needed to be punished, and the nature of the vampire at its base is monstrous, no matter how the soul of the man or woman so made resists the urges.

"We shall see," Eustachius said as he went up the stairs. As soon as she heard the cardinal close the door at the top of the stairwell, Sister Magdalena cranked the wheel hard. Carlo screamed as the pain course through him.

"I am not going to stop," Isabel told the priest of Mo'lech. "You believe you should entreat me not to turn the wheel, but in actuality; this will be what you should most desire."

"Have mercy," Carlo said desperately.

"My fingers will be Ana's fingers," she replied as she tightened her grip. "What mercy do you suppose she would have for you?" Isabel cranked the wheel before the man could voice a reply. He cried out once more. "You should pray for forgiveness from God," she warned him, "otherwise you shall experience such horrors as this for all eternity." It was as if the voice coming from Isabel was not hers at all, but some other thing's.

"God forgive me," Carlo screamed! His chest rose and fell rapidly as he was fearfully trying to see the crank out of his peripheral vision.

"You would say anything if only I would stop," Isabel mused aloud. "You do not repent."

"I do," Carlo insisted. "I have sinned. I have sinned."

"I wonder," the nun said as she walked slowly to the side of the rack over the man's head. She put her index finger down once more onto his temples. She closed her eyes and dug her nails once more into his already bleeding flesh.

In an instant, Isabel was flying through the dark tunnel once more. She came to rest in a dense thicket. Thorn covered vines made movement impossible. There was no sky here, only darkness. Isabel peered through the thorns and saw a man huddled beneath them. The man was Carlo. He was naked and covered with small, bleeding cuts. He looked fearfully up at the sky that was not.

The distance between Isabel in Carlo closed rapidly, though she did not move at all. "What are you doing Carlo," she asked him?

"I am hiding," the man said nervously.

"From whom," she asked?

"God," Carlo replied fearfully.

"God is coming soon my son," Sister Magdalena told him. "You would do well to repent. Your sins are many and terrible. Are you not ashamed?"

"Hardly," the man scoffed! "I just need to hide. Mo'lech will come!"

"And then," Isabel inquired?

"Then shall I stain the altar with the blood of one hundred sacrifices," Carlo said with a psychotic zeal!

"Mo'lech will not save you," she told him.

"I just need to hold on," Carlo disagreed. Isabel turned away from the priest and traveled back through the tunnel to the Land of Flesh. Her captive was praying in a language she did not understand. However, she did recognize the name of his God when it escaped his lips.

"Pray louder," Isabel mocked him as she cranked the wheel! Carlo screamed and then continued his prayers in earnest. The wheel became very easy to turn as Isabel use the entirety of her new strength. In her mind, it was Manuel Barillos on the rack and how she made him pay! The sound of the wheel and Carlos screaming drowned out the popping noises which signified the separation of his bones.

So dedicated to this man's pain was she, that Isabel did not stop until his left leg completely separated from his body! Carlo convulsed as blood foamed up out of his mouth. It was more than his mortal frame could bear.

The sight of the blood awakened Sister Magdalena's hunger and she quickly sunk her fangs into the dead man's throat. When this was exhausted, she bit into the inner thigh of the severed limb and drained the blood from it also. Her feeding was interrupted by the cardinal's large, right hand cuffing the side of her head.

"You have killed," Eustachius roared! The leg fell out of Sister Magdalena's hands and onto the rack.

"He would not repent," Isabel shot back! Her senses were sharpened by the fresh blood and her nerves were on edge.

"The night is far from over," Eustachius rebuked her. "There was still time!"

"He was praying to a demon," Isabel countered.

"Then you have assuredly damned him to hell!"

"Do you not find it to be a just reward," Isabel asked pointedly?

"It is not our place to kill Magdalena," Eustachius said angrily. "This is not your first time knowing such a thing either."

"You said Hector would kill him tomorrow whether or not he repented."

"I did indeed."

"Then what real difference is there?"

"Do not question me child," the cardinal barked! "Get you up to the confessional and repent! You have committed murder."

"As you command," Isabel said tersely. She stalked from the room and shut the iron door hard when she came up into the Basilica. She traveled down the grand corridor until she arrived at the sanctuary with its high vaulted ceilings. As she entered, Isabel saw Hector walking swiftly down the center aisle. His countenance was grim and there was a dreadful resolve in his dark eyes.

Without a word, Hector strode out of the Basilica and into the dark streets of Zaragoza. Isabel stood there for several seconds. Though she could not know what his intentions were, Isabel sensed that something was afoot. Eustachius would need to be informed.

CHAPTER III

Hector's boots fell heavily on the cobblestones as he made his way through the slumbering city. The streets of Zaragoza were very familiar to him. He no longer needed to use the bell tower of the Catedral de Seo as a reference point. The immortal warrior knew exactly where his destination lay.

The rear entrance to the cathedral was a tunnel leading through the bottom of the massive stone wall surrounding the church and its grounds. There was a man standing at either side. These men wore white tunics and grey hose below thick leather armor. Each man carried a shield the size of a barrel top and had a sword hanging from his left hip.

The vampire could hear them speaking to each other from far away. The two guards were commiserating about their respective wives which could most adequately be described as harpies. Hector did not smell fear. This was good, for it meant that they were less likely to be on the alert. A stealthier individual might have looked for a quieter way, but stealth was not in Hector's repertoire. Violence would suffice.

Torch sconces were set into the wall at several intervals inside the tunnel. The firelight spilled out of the tunnel and into the street beyond. There were only about ten meters between Hector and the guards when one of them finally noticed his presence. "Hail stranger," the closest guard said as Hector approached. The vampire briefly considered making up a story to lull the humans into a false sense of security, but Hector was not a man of words.

The important thing that caught Hector's eye was the scabbard of the man he was closing in on. The strap that normally held the weapons handle in place was undone. Perhaps this man had loosed the blade as a precaution against just such a situation as this. "Are you lost," the other guard asked?

Hector did not answer. He quickly grabbed the first man's sword and released it from the scabbard. In the same movement, he balled up his offhand and slammed his fist into the unsuspecting man's face. There was the gratifying feeling of bone shattering beneath skin. The man crumpled against the wall and fell to the ground as his killer stepped toward the second guard.

The other man had removed his blade only halfway out of its scabbard when Hector stabbed him through the throat with his partner's sword. Blood oozed out around the blade and the man made a gurgling sound as he struggled for air. Hector stepped sideways and ripped the sword free of the man's neck with both hands. The second guard fell to the earth with half of his neck severed.

Hector returned to the first man and cleaved his head from his shoulders. He dropped the blade and picked up the severed head by the hair. He then stalked quickly toward the iron gate and kicked it free of its hinges. The cardinal's guard paused as he came into the grounds of the cathedral. The smallest sliver of moon was visible beyond the bell tower and the night sky was filled with stars. This area was deserted, but he could hear the alarmed voices of the men inside. There was a white, stone statue of the Christ rising out of some well manicured shrubs. Rain water had smeared the face of the statue which gave the illusion that the Nazarene had been crying.

Hector looked up at the cathedral. Only one of its many windows shed any light to the outside. The warrior sniffed at the air. The savory aroma of fresh blood was coming from the direction of that same window. It was situated on the fourth floor at the back of the cathedral and had a balcony overlooking the city.

The physical prowess and strength of the elder vampire had grown over eight centuries into an unstoppable force that younger vampires could only dream of. Eustachius would not be pleased. Hector was not prone to disobedience, but he believed that the alternative would be much worse. Salvatore was surely giving the Architects information on his master's resting place. Eustachius did not rule the city in name, but he was the main reason that Zaragoza remained in the hands of the Convocation. The Architects would not dare to attack an elder who had walked the earth for over a thousand years.

Salvatore's betrayal would change things. The Architects would send their thralls into the Basilica to drag Eustachius and his brood screaming into the light of day. Hector had known for some time that this day would come. Salvatore had merely hastened it. There was a slight chance that the warrior was wrong. Perhaps Salvatore would not betray them. However, Hector had survived for so many generations by always trusting his instincts. In matters of bloodshed and betrayal, it was always better to strike first.

Hector made the sign of the cross toward the statue of Christ and then disappeared. It is not exactly correct to say that he disappeared, however. The vampire ran toward the cathedral at full tilt! So fast was he, that no mortal eye would be sharp enough to detect his advance.

Hector launched himself into the air toward the fourth floor balcony. Just before impact, he tossed the guard's severed head through the opening and into the brightly lit chamber. Small cracks appeared where his boots landed. The wheel was now in motion. Hector drew the massive sword from the hanger on his back and walked inside.

Two chandeliers filled with white candles were the source of the light that had emanated out into the night. A set of heavy, wooden double doors provided the only natural exit from the room. A massive, claw footed table rested below the chandeliers. Hector's prey were gathered around the table and Salvatore was among them. They had risen from their chairs to see the spectacle of the head which had unceremoniously been tossed on the surface of the wood before them.

One of the vampires had spilled his wooden goblet out onto the table. The blood which had been inside was now a dark puddle on the table which was slowly dripping off one side. There were other goblets still upright and it was from these that the smell came. The decapitated head sat in the midst of the table like a macabre centerpiece for the feast.

The godless Architects were dressed in the brown robes that rightly belonged on men of the cloth. Hector only vaguely recalled some of their faces from the few encounters he had had with them. Eustachius had done all of the talking of course. The salient point was that their leader was not present.

"You're not welcome here," one dark-haired man said loudly. There was a nervous edge to his voice that marked his cowardice. "Guards," he shouted! The double doors opened, and two men dressed similarly to those who were already dead outside entered the room. One of the guards carried a French halberd. The other wielded long sword and shield like the others. To their credit, these men did not look fearful.

"Wait," Salvatore said uneasily. "Hector is a good man. He can be reasoned with."

"Hold," the dark-haired man said with one hand held up. The guards paused. One man had gone around the right side of the table. The other, the one with the French blade, stopped himself halfway around the left side. "Tell us," the dark-haired man said to the cardinal's guard. "Will you speak with us?"

"You can talk if you want to," Hector replied dismissively.

"Join with us," Salvatore offered. "Eustachius can be defeated." Hector just shook his head. "You call me thrall, but you are the slave Hector," Salvatore nearly shouted! "Even now, the great cardinal sends you to do his dirty work while he rests safely inside the Basilica."

"I am not here at Eustachius' command," Hector grinned. "His wish was that you all be allowed to fester within this great city awhile longer."

"Keep him away," the dark haired man said loudly! The vampires, who were dressed as cathedral guards, began to advance toward Hector once more.

"You came of your own accord," Salvatore asked in disbelief? "You always do as the cardinal commands."

"Not always," Hector replied. He was no longer looking at the traitor. He choked up on his sword and assumed a half crouching stance in preparation for the guardsman's attack.

"This is the House of God," the dark haired man said in a last effort to avoid what was coming.

"You have turned it into a den of thieves," Hector replied calmly. "I bring the scourge." The vampire with the long sword was now within striking distance. It seemed that Hector was watching the guard on the far side of the table, but he was also watching the closer man out of his peripheral vision. When the architect guard raised his sword to strike, Hector exploded into motion!

Hector let go of the two handed sword with his right hand and used it to grab his opponent's wrist. The sword was left in his stronger and more dominant left. He yanked his enemy's arm out wide before chopping it off at the shoulder. The guard's long sword clattered to the floor as the elder vampire used the freshly severed appendage as a weapon of opportunity. Hector clubbed the man across the face with his own bloody shoulder before tossing it aside.

Hector returned his offhand to the hilt of the sword and brought a powerful overhand slash down toward his enemy's head. The guardsman brought up his shield to block the attack, but he did not possess the strength to stop the elder's momentum. There was the ring of steel on steel as Hector sword crashed down on the top lip of the man's shield. The shield was knocked down along with the arm of its bearer. The blade of the two handed sword cleaved down through bone and divided the man's head and neck neatly in half. The cardinal's guard drew the sword away as he took a step back and swung it high over his head. Before the younger vampire's body could hit the floor, Hector removed both halves of his head with one powerful strike! The skin shriveled as the vampires flesh resumed its actual age.

The guardsman with the halberd was now running around the table to close with Hector. Salvatore fled along with several of the others. This group ran out the double doors, leaving the rest to their fate. The false monk closest to Hector had picked up a knife from the table. Hector grabbed the man by his brown hair and slammed his face down onto the heavy wooden surface. Using the table as a chopping block, Hector decapitated the vampire quickly with his sword.

Hector blocked the downswing of the halberd in the nick of time as he sidestepped away from the table. While the two weapons were still touching, Hector kicked hard into his enemy's right hip. The remaining guardsman cried out as his legs gave way and he fell backwards over the table. The cardinal's guard quickly brought his sword up and used it to wrench the halberd from the man's grasp as he fell. Hector grabbed his opponent's weapon with his left hand and impaled the younger vampire through the heart with the spike on the bottom of the pole-arm. In so doing, the last guardsman's paralyzed corpse was connected securely to the table.

Several more of the Architects were put violently to the sword before Hector realized there was a problem. Those who had fled when the melee began were going to escape. The resting place of Eustachius would become known to the Architect Council. Those who resided currently in Zaragoza would not be enough to force their way past the defenses of the Basilica, but more would come.

Hector had been in the Catedral de Seo many times before the accursed architects had infested the capital. Because of this, he knew that all staircases within the structure would lead directly or indirectly into the sanctuary. He ignored the fleeing vampires for the time being, and ran back out onto the balcony. He hopped up on the railing and then stepped off into the drop.

Once on the ground, Hector ran at superhuman speed around the cathedral. Ignoring the sentinels who guarded the main entrance, Hector rushed through the open doors and into the sanctuary. The grey stone interior swept up beautifully into several different vaults in the impossibly high ceiling. High up along the sides of the sanctuary were small balconies meant for the rich. It would not do to place the gentry down with the unwashed masses of Zaragoza.

Several of the 'monks' who had fled the meeting room were now running into the sanctuary with fearful expressions. They might've been lucky enough to see a blur of color before Hector's blade cleaved the first vampires head from his shoulders. His next victim was divided in half at the waist. He fell to the ground screaming as blood and entrails slithered out of his torso and onto the sanctuary floor.

Some of the Architects died like men. Others begged for mercy. In the end, their fates were one. The only exception was Father Salvatore. The traitor had managed to escape during the carnage.

Hector's anger urged him to begin the hunt. He wanted very much to rip out the traitor's throat and feast upon his warm blood. Wisdom dictated otherwise. Such an open display of his nature would attract the wrong kind of attention. Mortals were weak, but they could be truly dangerous by the light of day.

Tracking Salvatore by scent would have been quite easy in the wild. Here in Zaragoza, his smell would be drowned out by the myriad of other humans who took residence there. While the Cardinals guard was contemplating his next move, he heard a very small grunt. The vampire whom Hector had split apart above the waist was now desperately trying to reach across what was left of his body. His fingers stretched out toward a nearby pew but could not make contact.

Hector always felt more comfortable when he had a purpose. This turn of events provided him with one. He had little chance of catching Salvatore before he would betray them all to Vincente. However, there were still many of the vampires in the cathedral who might be able to heal themselves.

The elder vampire quickly turned toward the architect who had alerted him. Blood was pooling fast around the younger vampires gaping wound in the entrails that had also found their way to the floor of the cathedral. Hector realized that his fallen enemy was trying to flip over so that he might crawl to some dark place and perhaps avoid destruction. "Oh Jesus," the wretched thing on the floor cried out!

"Never too late to pray," Hector said as he lifted his sword high with both hands.

"Our father who art..." (thunk) the Architects praying was cut short by the descending blade. Hector's sword bit wood as the other vampire's head rolled underneath a nearby pew. His flesh rapidly decayed and shrunk around the bones.

Before leaving the cathedral, Hector returned to the conference room and made sure that all of the undead within had been sent to receive their eternal rewards. When the butchery was concluded, he ran out onto the fourth floor balcony and jumped. He soared high into the air and cleared the walls of the cathedral. Eustachius would need him now. The cardinal's guard landed hard on the cobblestones of the road outside. Some of the rock cracked beneath his feet and he hit the ground running.

Isabel nearly tripped over herself as she ran down the spiral stairs that led into the dungeon. Eustachius was in the midst of opening up one of the cell doors when she burst out into the poorly lit tunnel. He cocked his head toward her but said nothing. "Your eminence," she said eagerly. She was surprised that the exertion had not left her breathless. Isabel was not yet accustomed to the fact that she had no need to breathe. "Hector is gone!"

"Is that why you have rushed down here to speak with me," Eustachius asked?

"Yes," Isabel said, "but..."

"Hector has duties that lie outside the dungeon sister. It is nothing to worry yourself over"

"Does he have duties outside the Basilica your eminence," she asked? Eustachius frowned and said nothing for several moments. He sighed and clasped his hands behind his back.

"Rarely," the cardinal said at last. "There was something about him," Isabel said. "His eyes..."

"Was it murder," the cardinal inquired?

"I do not know," Isabel answered.

"You do know," Eustachius corrected her. "That is why you could not wait to tell me."

"You must be right," Isabel agreed. "What are we to do now?"

"Nothing," he answered. "Once Hector gets something into his head, there is little that can be done to dissuade him."

"Will he kill Salvatore?"

"It will be more than that I think," Eustachius said gravely.

"We should go after him," Isabel said.

"No," the cardinal shook his head "he will come back to us."

"As you wish," Isabel agreed reluctantly.

"Let us wait for him in the Bell Tower," Eustachius suggested. Isabel nodded her head in acquiescence and followed the blind man to the stairs. "Lead the way," he said when they came out into the corridor. He put one hand upon her shoulder to give off the illusion of dependence.

"I do not know the way," Magdalena whispered. "Take me to the balcony overlooking the sanctuary," Eustachius whispered back. There were not many humans roaming the halls of the Basilica at night except for the occasional group of guards. These men traveled in groups of two or three and saluted whenever the cardinal passed by.

Once upon the balcony of the cathedral, Eustachius directed Isabel down the side corridor which led to a series of private balconies for the nobility. In the archway at the end of the corridor leading to the bell tower, Isabel could see the thick, hemp rope hanging down as she approached. The air grew colder once the two of them made their way inside the tower. Wooden stairs traveled up the sides of it. The sound of the howling winds grew stronger as they made their ascent. The stairs ended at a series of wooden platforms which surrounded the huge iron Bell on three sides. The other side gave way to the stairs.

Sister Magdalena and the cardinal stood together in silence for some time. The nun looked down over the city while Eustachius listened. Hector finally appeared at the far end of the cobblestone square below. He did not move furtively, but carried himself like a king. His back was straight as he walked with a purpose to the main entrance to the Basilica. "He comes across the square," Isabel reported. "I hear him," Eustachius replied. "He is alone."

"Yes," Isabel replied. Then she realized that it was not a question.

"Let us go down to meet him."

"I will go first," she replied

"Then I will follow," Eustachius said in turn. He placed a hand on Magdalena's arm before she led him out of the tower, through the balconies, and finally into the sanctuary. Hector had already entered and was walking swiftly toward the western corridor when Sister Magdalena and Eustachius came down. "What have you done," the cardinal called after him. Hector stopped and turned around.

"Your eminence," he said.

"I smell blood," Eustachius said disapprovingly. "You have disobeyed me."

"Salvatore escaped," Hector reported. "I put the rest of them to the sword. We have to move."

"Did I not tell you to leave Salvatore to his fate?"

"I found him with the Architects," Hector replied. "They were planning to destroy you and asked for my help. I cannot always do as you say your eminence, especially if it goes against my oath to protect you."

"Vincente is dead," Eustachius asked eagerly?

"He was not present with the rest," Hector replied.

"Salvatore will run to him," Eustachius said.

"And he will send the mob to bring us out of the darkness and into the sun," Hector concluded.

"It will take more than the knowledge of my resting place to storm the Basilica," Eustachius returned.

"It does not matter," Hector said. "We would be foolish to believe that the Architects have no spies within these walls." Eustachius steepled his fingers below his nose as he mulled this over.

"Have the coffins buried in the cemetery across the river," the cardinal decided. "Salvatore's new masters will not be pleased when he leads them to an empty tomb."

"Where shall we make our beds," Sister Magdalena inquired?

"Where we must," the blind cardinal answered. "We are going to Constantinople."

"We are long way from the great city," Hector reminded him.

"We will go by sea," Eustachius said. "Fetch Javier and Felipe. We will need men to guard our sleep. We'll take the river and book passage to Italy from the coast."

"This will take some time," Hector frowned.

"Make haste," the cardinal replied. "We have very little of it."

"I will make it so," Hector promised. He pounded his fist on his chest in salute and then set off into the city.

"What would you have me do," Isabel asked?

"Gather your clothing," the cardinal replied. While Isabel went to the dungeon to gather her things, it seemed that there were servants or guards hurrying about do the cardinal's bidding all over the cathedral. Isabel had barely collected her other habit and the black and crimson gown she had worn from the cottage when a contingent of guards bearing torches entered the crypt and carried away the coffins.

Isabel wrapped the gown inside her habit to avoid any appearance of abnormality. In little time, the three vampires were boarding a medium-sized sailing vessel with the two thralled guards. The thralls accompanied the three of them down to an enclosed cabin in the hold of the vessel. Once the vampires were safely inside, the two thralls posted themselves as sentries at the room's only door.

The boat launched almost immediately and was soon speeding down the River Ebro towards the ocean. The vampires were forced to feed discreetly from their thralls and a story was concocted about the three of them falling ill. This kept the mortals away from their resting place and prevented them from becoming curious. They docked in Amposta and transferred there to a larger ship that would take them across the Mediterranean Sea. On the last day of the trip, Javier transferred Isabel from her bed to the inside of a wooden box that seemed to be made for just such a task.

Sister Magdalena awoke to the sound of her resting place been pried open. The tingling in her gums meant that her fangs were lowering in preparation for whatever danger might be on the other side of the box. Thankfully, it was only Eustachius' thralled guard Felipe. "Are you well sister," he asked apprehensively.

"I am," Isabel replied us her body began to relax. Felipe extended an arm to help her up and she accepted it. At the same time, Javier was engaged in prying open Hector's crate. When the elder was released, both thralls set to work in freeing their master. Eustachius inhaled deeply after he was helped to his feet.

The chamber in which Isabel found herself was filled with the smell of earth and the stale odor of decay. There were many rectangular receptacles for coffins set into the walls. Some of them were empty, while others were filled with the bones of the long dead. "We are home," Eustachius told her. Hector moved his neck from side to side and then stretched out his arms.

"Where are we," Sister Magdalena asked?

"In the catacombs below Constantinople, the center of power for the Convocation of Saints," Eustachius told her.

"We are safe here," Hector added.

"Tonight I will present you to Samael; the first vampire to serve in the shadow of the cross.

"What shall I say to him," Sister Magdalena asked?

"Just be respectful and answer truthfully should he ask anything of you," the cardinal replied.

"His Holiness can sense deception," Hector warned. "Nothing angers him more than being lied too."

"All is the better that I do not lie," Isabel answered.

"Stay with her," Eustachius told Hector. "I will have Javier take me to the rest of the elders."

"We will remain here until the bell tolls," Hector promised. "May I suggest that Felipe go with you also your eminence?" Eustachius nodded his approval. "Sister Magdalena will be safe with me."

"Very well," Eustachius said. "Let us go to the inner sanctum," he told his thralls from the Basilica. The white clad guards guided the cardinal to the marble door that led out of the crypt. It took both of them to move one of the heavy doors. Isabel stood in silence with Hector for several minutes after they had gone. Torchlight flickered off the bones that lay in the crypts along the walls. Hector walked quietly over to the doors of the crypt and closed them softly.

"You have to take this audience seriously," Hector said when the door was shut completely.

"Do I give the impression that I think it of no consequence," Isabel asked?

"To make a new vampire amongst the Architects, one has only to seek permission from their elders. A vampire of the Convocation of Saints does not seek permission."

"What are you trying to tell me?"

"Initiates to our society are brought here to be judged worthy of the blood."

"I see," Isabel said. "Why are you telling me this?"

"To make sure you are accepted," Hector replied.

"What must I do?"

"Samael seeks initiates with conviction above all else. Do not fall into the trap of courtly etiquette. Vampires of the Convocation are not meek."

"Even though his station is above mine," Isabel asked?

"You can be respectful without being weak," Hector explained.

"I will heed your warning," Isabel said gratefully. Some time passed before she spoke again. "Why are you helping me?"

"It does not matter," Hector replied curtly. Several minutes later, the sound of a bell tolling could be heard from above. "It is time," Hector said anxiously. "Follow me." Isabel followed him through the torch lit catacombs until they came to a stone wall which contained a massive set of doors carved from the rock itself. These doors stood open and the murmuring of many voices could be heard from within.

Set into the cavern floor about an arms length from the edge of each door was a rectangular slab of granite that rose up to the height of Isabel's waist. Each slab was topped with a white marble rendering of an angel. In front of these were large brass bowls in which fire burned up and licked the sides of the stones. The feet of the statues had also been fire blackened in places.

The statue on the left had one arm tucked in close to its body and the other raised toward the heavens. Both hands were stretched out in supplication and the Angels face was stricken with anguish. The statue on the right covered its face with both hands as if weeping. The fires below gave these angels a malefic appearance. Isabel wondered if this was by design.

The stone doors opened into a long hall which led to another set of doors opening inward. The walls were lined with tapestries, some of which depicted the Saints. Wooden benches filled with votive candles set on the floor in front of each depiction. In front of these were smaller benches with leather cushioning for the knees. The most luxurious of the tapestries were those that hung at either side of the doors leading to the inner sanctum. The tapestry on the right Isabel recognized as the Angel Michael driving the Devil back into Hell. Michael carried a flaming sword in his right hand and was stepping on the neck of another angel with black reptilian wings and grey robes which were soaked with blood.

The tapestry on the left depicted the same black winged angel hovering over a host of others who also were grey robes. The faces of these angels were filled with rage and they carried an enormous variety of obsidian bladed weapons. As Isabel drew closer, she could see that the eyes of the angel who hovered over the rest were pure white and shone like stars. She could also see that there were brass plates set into the wall beneath each of the tapestries. Each of these plates was engraved with swirling characters from a language that she did not understand.

After passing through the second set of double doors, Isabel walked down the center aisle of the sanctuary between two rows of marble pews. Torches burned in their sconces which were set into the walls of the chamber. The figures who occupied the pews stared at her with cold eyes and a uniformly monstrous demeanor.

Beyond the pews were too ornate tables weighted down with golden, jewel encrusted goblets and long knives that were equally as extravagant. Past these communion tables was a raised shelf of rock. Staircases had been carved on either side and were guarded by men in white robes with black executioner's hoods. In their hands, the strange looking guards held broadswords with their points resting on the cavern floor.

Atop the platform was an exquisitely carved throne of white marble. Massive wings of a like material spread out from the sides of the throne. A man sat upon it wearing long heavy robes the color of charcoal. He had the chiseled features of nobility and his head was adorned with a platinum circlet. His eyes were completely white and had no discernible pupils. The firelight reflecting off the man's circlet created the illusion of a halo.

Beyond the throne was a steel manifold which covered most of the far wall. Behind this was a roaring inferno inside the largest fireplace Isabel had ever seen. It was half again as tall as a man and wide enough to fit a carriage inside with a team of horses.

Eustachius rose from one of the front pews as Isabel came closer. Hector came over from where he had been standing along the wall and led the Cardinal to the center aisle. "Stand here with me," Eustachius said quietly as he gestured with one hand. Isabel took her place beside her maker and faced the throne. She was soon joined by Hector who took up position on the other side of her.

When the man on the throne stood, Isabel could see that he rivaled her father in height. He was not nearly as muscular as Rafael had been, but no less imposing. Eustachius knelt down before the man and Hector followed suit. Isabel joined them. "My son," the grey robed man said to the cardinal. "It has been too long since you walked among us. Stand and be recognized." Eustachius rose to his feet and turned round to face the pews for a moment. Whispers rustled through the assembled vampires as he turned his mutilated eye sockets toward them. "Praise God," someone said aloud. Eustachius turned back toward the platform.

"Hector del Toro," the grey robed man continued; "your presence is an honor to those gathered here tonight."

"Thank you great one," Hector answered respectfully. He also turned briefly toward the audience so that they might see his face.

"Who is this woman that you bring before me," the man asked as he stared critically down at Isabel?

"This is my daughter," Eustachius answered. There were gasps and whispers among those assembled behind them. "Sister Magdalena," he finished. Isabel did not curtsy.

Instead, she inclined her head in deference to the man above her.

"Sister Magdalena," the grey robed man repeated, "is this your true name?"

"It is the only one I have left," Isabel answered.

"Well then sister, welcome to the Convocation of Saints. I am Samael." Isabel bowed her head once more but did not respond. "Tell me Sister Magdalena," Samael continued. "What besides your pathetic desire to end your own life and my son Eustachius' pity makes you worthy of the blood?" Isabel was momentarily struck dumb by the barbed question. She could feel the eyes of the others boring into her from the pews as well. As she regained her composure and prepared to speak, the answer came.

"Must I be worthy of a curse," she asked? The crowd sat in stunned silence. Surely Samael would not suffer this woman to denigrate the blood.

"She is finished," a man's voice said quietly. Samael glared down at her. His lips parted but Isabel was quick to preempt him from speaking.

"In the years preceding my death, my life became a ruin," Isabel said. "I have no desire to describe to you the unimaginable horrors that were inflicted upon me, nor do I wish to list those whom I love who are now dead. It was my desire to hasten the hellfire which I knew to be my destiny."

"Your last living act was one of cowardice," Samael said accusingly.

"It was not cowardice," Isabel disagreed. "Suicide is largely a sin of the godless. For who but the godless could end their own life, knowing that they will soon languish in the fires of the inferno? It seems to me that a man who commits such a sin must first convince himself that hell is but a tale to be told. I have never stopped believing," Isabel said vehemently, "and my existence beyond death has only strengthened my faith in Him. You and all those gathered beneath you are free to decide whether I should be one of you, but you cannot dispute that which God hath already preordained." Murmurs traveled through the crowd but Samael held up one hand to quiet them.

"It is God's wrath which hath cursed me to suffer perdition on Earth. It is His will that I shall drive men to Christ through suffering," Isabel declared. "The torments which God commands me to inflict are as abhorrent to me as the abomination which I have become, but this is my penance."

"I see now why Eustachius chose you sister," Samael said. "You are welcome among the Convocation of Saints. Go now with your maker and be one of us."

"Come my daughter," Eustachius said proudly as he placed his elongated right hand upon her shoulder. "Take us back to where I was sitting before," he whispered. Isabel lead the blind man back to the front pew on the left side of the sanctuary and Hector followed after them.

Once all three were seated, there was again the tolling of the bell. The sound emanated from an archway off to the right side of the rock shelf which contained Samael's marble throne. From her vantage point, Isabel could see another man dressed in a black executioner's hood in white robes like the others. A huge rope hung down from somewhere beyond her vision and the hooded man was pulling it down with both hands.

There were whispers among those assembled and Hector looked back over his shoulder at the entrance to the underground sanctuary. Isabel followed the older vampires gaze to a beautiful young man who walked slowly down the center aisle. His face was soft and free of blemish. His long eyelashes made him look somewhat androgynous, but no less striking. The ghost of a smile played upon his lips and his blue eyes were filled with eagerness.

As the young man approached the rock shelf, a slightly older man stood from the front row on the right side of the sanctuary. Both of these men had long, brown hair and cream colored robes which hung down to their ankles. The older man had a green cassock that covered his collar and hung down in a thin strip over the center of his chest.

"Father Giancinni," Samael said when the two vampires were standing side-by-side together. "I expected to see you here some time ago."

"It has been too long great one," Giancinni agreed. "I would have come earlier, but there was important work to be done in Ravenna. The Judaizers were gaining too much influence with the mortal flock."

"No other concerns father," Samael inquired, "preparedness perhaps?"

"No great Samael," Father Giancinni answered. "All is as it should be."

"Of course it is," Samael answered contemptuously. He gestured with one hand toward the initiate.

"This is my son Lucian," the father reported.

"Lucian," Samael repeated the word as if tasting it. The younger vampire bowed deeply at the waist.

"I am he," Lucian said as he stood back to his full height.

"You are two years dead," Samael said with irritation.

"I am great one."

"It was not a question."

"A thousand pardons your Holiness," Lucian said nervously.

"Make it ten thousand," Samael retorted.

"Ten thousand pardons you're…"

"Enough," Samael cut him off. "So tell me Lucian, what have you accomplished in two years time?"

"I..," the initiate stuttered. "I have memorized most of the Divine Liturgy and... I do not understand great one. What do you want me to say?"

"Whatever comes to mind," Samael's eyes widened with sarcasm as he spoke.

"I have not made any other major accomplishment, but I have been striving."

"Striving for what," Samael inquired?

"Well... To learn the rest of the liturgy and... More about God and... My place in the world beyond death... Great one..," Lucian struggled. Samael shook his head in disapproval. Isabel noticed that Father Giancinni was fidgeting with one side of his robe.

"That is the whole of it then," Samael finally asked?

"It is great one," Lucian replied.

"He has only one accomplishment after two years dead," Samael told those assembled, "but it is not an accomplishment because he has failed to completely memorize the liturgy." He looked back down at Lucian once more before speaking. "Worthless," Samael said rebukingly. "You have accomplished nothing!"

"Yes great one," Lucian agreed.

"Why did you give him the blood Father," Samael demanded? "I am at a loss."

"He shows great potential you're Holiness," Giancinni replied nervously. "He is eager to learn all there is to teach."

"And he is obedient, is he not," Samael asked knowingly?

"Unquestioningly so," Giancinni agreed.

"Naturally," Samael scoffed. "God needs strong souls to fight in his army. How will you assist the Convocation of Saints in defeating the children of Mo'lech?"

"I am not a man of war," the initiate replied fearfully.

"Suppose you are all alone and one of the accursed Children were to come for you," Samael said. "What then?"

"I will happily accept death if that is God's will," Lucian replied.

"Look child," Samael said angrily; "I am asking you a question. Let me make it plain for you. What is it that makes you worthy to be a part of this convocation?"

"I am not worthy," Lucian said with his eyes cast deferentially toward the floor of the cavern.

"Revolting," Samael tisked!

"He has great humility," Father Giancinni said desperately! His voice was almost a wine.

"So you are unworthy Lucian," Samael asked finally?

"Not even to touch the hem of your garment your Holiness, but I will strive to become worthy," Lucian replied reverently.

"If you have so little faith in yourself, then why should anyone here believe in you?"

"I will humbly obey and do all that is required of me," Lucian answered. His maker's anxiety was starting to rub off on him.

"There is nothing that I shall ever require of you," Samael said coldly.

"I am so sorry Lucian," Father Giancinni said quietly. His voice broke with sorrow.

"I declare this Child Lucian to be unworthy of the blood," Samael said loudly. His voice reverberated in the chamber. "Let none speak his name again and let God judge among the living and the dead." A moan escaped the father's lips as Samael finished speaking.

There was a rush of wind in the chamber. Suddenly, the hooded guards who had been standing at the stairs were now behind Lucian. They each grabbed a hold of one arm and held fast. In their free hands, they carried the broadswords which were now poised to either side of the initiate's neck.

"Dust thou art," Samael said gravely. The hooded guards levitated up into the air carrying the failed initiate with them. The third vampire wearing an executioner's hood came out from the bell pull into position in the center aisle of the sanctuary. He held out both hands with his palms facing the backs of the hovering trio. "... And unto dust shalt thou return."

There was a sound like a great stone being dropped into water and Isabel could actually see the air rippling out from the third vampire's outstretched hands. The other two let go of Lucian's arms. The beautiful young man fell down for but a moment before an invisible force slammed into him from behind. The young man was hurled into the fire at terrifying speed! Father Giancinni covered his ears to drown out the wailing of his child on fire.

Samael looked dispassionately down at the petitioning vampire as a sob escaped him. "Put your hands down to your sides," Samael barked! "Hear and remember it well." Giancinni obeyed and his body trembled as he looked on. Lucian's screaming stopped and his bones fell onto the wood pile as Samael continued. "You knew that I would destroy him!"

"I did not know," Father Giancinni cried!

"You knew," Samael shouted! "The next time you make such a pitiful mistake, have the courage to correct it yourself."

"I did not know," the weeping vampire insisted.

"Your hands are stained with that young man's blood," Samael said with disgust. "Get out of my sight."

"Yes great one," the father said in defeat. He turned and took his walk of shame down through the midst of the sanctuary. No one said a word as he left. Samael sat back down on the winged throne. He held one hand up toward the gathering of the undead as Father Giancinni reached the entrance to the sanctuary.

"No more," the gray robed elder said wearily. "This meeting is adjourned. I will say no more initiates this day." The vampires rose quietly from the pews and made their way out. Isabel followed Hector as he guided Cardinal Eustachius out of the sanctuary. Felipe and Javier brought up the rear. Isabel would never forget the image of Lucian's burning corpse or how close she herself had come to death.

CHAPTER IV

Positioned as they were in front of the sanctuary; Sister Magdalena and her elders were among the last to leave. They had only taken a few steps outside when Samael called after them. "Eustachius," the gray robed vampire said. "Tarry here awhile with me." The cardinal stopped and inclined his ear back toward the throne. "There is trouble brewing in the southern reaches of France."

"Hector," Eustachius said without turning his head. "I must speak with Samael. Stay with the Convocation's newest member."

"I will," Hector agreed. Eustachius nodded and whispered in Felipe's ear. The thralled guard led his master back into the sanctuary. Seconds later, the hooded executioners appeared and closed up the doors. The last of the undead departed through the midst of the fire lit statutes, leaving Hector and Isabel alone in the hall of tapestries.

"These tapestries are so beautiful," Isabel said, gesturing toward those that hung beside the sanctuary doors. "I do not recognize them in relation to the scriptures." She ran her hands softly over the tapestry with the gray robed angel with the gleaming eyes.

"These tapestries tell the history of our people," Hector said. "This one is called the Great Deception. The angel with black wings was Lucifer who is now called Satan. He convinced a third of the angels that God was unjust and could be defeated. In that era, the Angels were called the True Children. This tapestry shows Lucifer leading them to war." Isabel marveled at the artistry. The tapestries were so exquisitely rendered that one could almost believe that Lucifer's army would march right out of the cloth.

"This one looks familiar," Isabel said. She ran a finger over one of the angels at the head of the column. He was gesturing with an obsidian sword as if to drive his army forward.

"He does," Hector agreed. "The angel you see there is Samael."

"This is the leader of the Convocation of Saints," Isabel asked with wonder?

"The very same," Hector answered. "Samael was once the general of Lucifer's army."

"How could he then be over such a faithful group as this?"

"Remember what our maker told you Sister," Hector said. "Even the Devil could be saved were he to repent and serve God. After the fall, Samael rebelled against Lucifer. He and his followers came here to Italy while Satan and his angels remained in the Holy Land."

"This one reminds me of Michael and the Dragon," Sister Magdalena said as she walked to the other side of the doors.

"It is," Hector agreed. "This one is a more accurate representation of Lucifer than the caricatures which you have seen. The horned monstrosity is a myth constructed by man."

"Will I find you here also," Isabel asked?

"Hardly," Hector replied. "I was born to a woman here on earth."

"How long ago," Isabel inquired?

"A very long time," Hector replied. "It was over eight centuries ago when Eustachius gave me the blood."

"Show me the rest," Isabel suggested. "I am eager to know more."

"I can think of no better way to spend time waiting for our maker," Hector agreed. "Follow me." The cardinal's guard led her to the far right corner of the hall. They stopped before a tapestry which showed a powerful looking black man standing in front of a snow-covered mountain. The mountain seemed to rise up out of a bowl shaped gorge which was lined with ice.

The Black Man wore nothing but an animal skin over his waist. His eyes were pure black without even a hint of white at the edges. His face was cruel and his sharp teeth were plainly visible as he seemed to sneer down at the viewer of the tapestry. Upon closer inspection, Isabel noticed that the snow around his feet was littered with a garden of bones. The skulls were rendered in exquisite detail. Their canine teeth were longer and sharper than the rest. Unlike the other tapestries, this one had no prayer bench in front of it. "What does the plate say," Isabel asked as the brass below the tapestry caught her eye?

"There is not a literal translation for it in Spanish," Hector told her, "but it most closely means, 'The Traitor'."

"Who is he?"

"Mo'lech was one of the True Children during the War in Heaven. He fled leaving the rest to die."

"Perhaps he saw the error of his ways," Isabel thought out loud.

"No," Hector disagreed. "Mo'lech does nothing out of contrition. This tapestry shows the Dark One in Ice Wall. He lured most of the True Children to his frozen kingdom at the edge of the world. He deceived them into believing that he would be able to free them from their earthly prisons. He then destroyed their bodies and bound their souls to the mountain."

"Mo'lech," Isabel said. "Samael mentioned his children."

"With whom we are at war," Hector finished for her. "The Children of Mo'lech are spread throughout Persia and the Holy Land. Their spies range even further."

"Why are you at war," Isabel asked? "Is it because of the betrayal?"

"That was what started it," Hector replied, "but there is no longer a choice in the matter. Mo'lech has commanded his children to destroy all others. We must fight."

"Are they so many that the Convocation is in peril?"

"There are many more vampires among the convocation."

"Why does the convocation not crush them then," Isabel inquired?

"It is not so simple," Hector replied. "Where we rule openly, the children of Mo'lech rule from the shadows. This makes them harder to find. Because of the Dark One's blood, they all possess Dominion over Fire; something that we vampires are extremely vulnerable to."

"Not only sunlight," Isabel asked?

"No," Hector answered. "Bones cannot move without muscle. A burnt vampire is just as helpless as one who is staked, if not more so."

"I will remember what you have said," Isabel said as she walked to the next tapestry. It was much more familiar to her than the last. This tapestry was an image of the great flood. Toward the top of it, Isabel could see a wooden Ark being buffeted about on a stormy sea. Below the surface, the water took on progressively darker shades of blue to denote depth. As her eyes traveled down the tapestry, Isabel began to see the shadows of men drowned beneath the waves. The farther toward the black abyss her eyes traveled, the more monstrous became the shadows of the dead. Some of the corpses had strange features such as horns, tails, or claws. Others were gargantuan in size. All were misshapen in some way. "What are these creatures," she asked? "Are they demons?"

"They were the Nephilim," Hector answered, "the offspring of forbidden unions between angels and human beings."

"The fallen angels you mean," Isabel said.

"No, the fallen angels cannot bear children."

"This cannot be true," Isabel shook her head. "Heavenly Angels would not profane themselves with the sins of the flesh!"

"And the children of God went in unto the daughters of men," Hector recited.

"I have read that passage," Isabel nodded, "but I supposed that it meant the faithful who were chosen of God went in to the daughters of idolatry."

"God did not choose the people until Abraham," Hector explained. "You must not change the words of scripture. The children of God can only refer to his angels. Humans would be the children of Adam. The fallen angels are children of Lucifer."

"I see what you mean," Isabel agreed.

"It was not merely the wickedness of man that caused the flood," Hector continued. "The Nephilim had powers similar to the Angels. This combined with the sinful hearts of men made them an abomination unto God, even as we are abominations."

"Why does God not destroy us," Isabel asked?

"No one knows," Hector said. "Some suggest that the fallen must be allowed to work evil upon the world in order to prove the folly of their rebellion from God. This does not explain why those of us who were born on Earth are allowed to exist. It is a great mystery."

"This is the first time I have heard you speak at any length," Isabel said. "You surprise me with your wealth of knowledge." Hector only smiled.

"Look here at the bottom of the tapestry," he said as he pointed downward. Below the black abyss was a layer of brown that Isabel had not noticed because the candle flames obscured it. She saw bodies cocooned in the earth below the water.

"Are those the vampires," she asked?

"Precisely," Hector said approvingly. "To hide from the sun, Lucifer and his children buried themselves beneath the earth and waited there until the flood waters receded. By night they would swim up to feed from the dead and then return to the bosom of the earth." After a few moments, Hector moved onto the next tapestry. Isabel followed. "Here we see the children of Israel and the golden calf," Hector said. The image portrayed was of many people gathered around an enormous bonfire. Israelite tents could be seen in the background and beyond them rose the mountain of Sinai. There was a large cloud over the top of the mountain and a fire seemed to burn within it. The faces of the Israelites were filled with awe. The golden calf seemed to hover in midair in front of the bonfire.

"Why does the calf float," Isabel wondered aloud. "Does the artist imply that the idol had divine powers? This is heresy!"

"That is not all what the artist conveys Sister," Hector responded. "Look closer at the fire." Isabel looked into the rendering of the flames and gasped as she saw what the elder vampire was referring to.

"There is a man inside," Isabel said as she traced her finger over the black shadow within the fire. The shadow of the man held a hammer aloft. It reminded Isabel of the blacksmith in Montenegro. This was the same stance of the man who was engulfed in flames. "Did they burn him," Isabel finally asked?

"They tried to," Hector replied. "This tapestry shows the night when the calf was made. The man inside the fire is Mo'lech. While Moses was in communion with God on the mountain, the Dark One came to tempt the Israelites away from Him. In anger, the Kohathites threw him into the fire. Mo'lech spoke to them out of the flames. He eroded their faith and claimed that it was he who had delivered them out of Egypt. From within the flames, Mo'lech fashioned the golden calf and then caused it to float out of the pyre and come down amongst the people."

"Why did the Lord not destroy Mo'lech," Isabel asked?

"God was with Moses on the mountain," Hector answered. "When Moses came down, the Israelites were drunk with wine and fornication. Several thousand of them had been enthralled. It was these thralls that the Levites destroyed to purify God's people."

"What of Mo'lech?"

"Just as he fled from the War in Heaven, Mo'lech abandoned his thralls to the wrath of God and his servant Moses."

"Why is it that I have never read of vampires in Scripture," Sister Magdalena asked? "They seem to play an important role."

"Virtually all references to our kind were removed by the Council of Nicaea."

"Why?"

"At the behest of Samael and the elders of the Convocation," Hector explained. "We serve God, but in our veins runs the blood of devils. Try and explain this paradox to mankind and you will quickly find yourself the target of an angry mob. That is why our secret must be kept."

"I understand," Isabel nodded. The tapestries appeared to have been worked by the same hand. So it was that Isabel immediately recognized Mo'lech as they came to the tapestries on the opposite wall. In the next rendering, he sat upon a throne of gold and ivory. He wore only a golden loincloth and sandals. He looked down with contempt at those who were knelt before him, a man and a woman.

The man was dressed in scarlet robes. His fingers were covered with jeweled rings and his wrists with bracelets. He bowed low upon his knees and offered a crown in his outstretched hands. The hair on his head was gray with age.

The woman was covered only from the waist down by a light green loincloth that fully revealed the sides of her legs. Her skin was dusky and her hair dark. There was a small gold chain that traveled from her nose to her left ear, and her features reminded Isabel of the Saracens. She leaned down over the man so that the dark flesh of her breast brushed against his robe. Her slender arm stretched down toward his neck and held it down with her hand. "What is this," Isabel asked after a time?

"The Fall of the House of David," Hector replied. "The man on his knees is King Solomon. The woman is Naamah, a princess of the Ammonites whom he took for one of his brides. See how she makes him prostrate himself even lower before Mo'lech? For the secrets of vampirism, Solomon betrayed his covenant with God. This tapestry reminds us that even the wisest of men can be led into evil."

"See how he looks down at them," Isabel said thoughtfully.

"It shows his hatred of mankind," Hector added. "It was only a few short weeks after Solomon received the blood that Mo'lech destroyed him, thus assuring his damnation."

"How horrible," Isabel said.

"Let me now show you the crucifixion," Hector said, motioning with his hand to the next tapestry. At first, Isabel believed that it was of a poorer quality than the others. There was no appreciable color to it. The image was rendered in black, white, and shades of gray. Christ was upon the cross. His head was slumped down and his eyes were closed. There was a wound in his side where the centurions spear had pierced it. Another Christ-like figure was depicted below the cross. This form was pure white and clothed in robes. The second figure stretched his hand out toward the mob surrounding the cross.

Most of those gathered stumbled about with their eyes closed and their hands outstretched as if they had been struck blind. The rest were in various states of agony. Many of these unfortunates were missing limbs and bleeding profusely from what remained of their appendages. One of these was missing both legs and his face as well. Only one man stared in awe at the ethereal figure of Christ below the cross. This man had fallen upon his knees and folded his hands in reverence. "What is this," Isabel asked in fascination?

"It is finished," Hector read from the golden plate beneath. "After the death of Christ, a great storm blew in from the west. The clouds blotted out the stars and the wind extinguished the torches of the mob. It was then that the Holy Ghost came down unto Lucifer and the fallen who had gathered there to revel in what they believed was a victory. The Holy Spirit stretched out his hand against them. Every one of them who had come to Calvary was then liquefied through the power of God. Their remains seeped into the earth and their spirits were expelled from the Land of Flesh."

"Who is he who prays before the cross," Sister Magdalena asked?

"Only Samael was spared," Hector said with reverence. "God the Spirit spoke to him and allowed him to live that he might spread the message of redemption to all those who exist beyond death."

"I cannot believe this," Isabel said with amazement!

"I only speak the truth," Hector assured her.

"No, no," Isabel said quickly. "It is only that I have just been in the presence of one who came face-to-face with Christ."

"It is a lot to take in," Hector said apologetically. Before they could move on to the final tapestry, Eustachius entered in from the sanctuary.

"We are leaving," Eustachius announced.

"So soon," Isabel inquired? Eustachius ignored her.

"We go to the Chapel of the Cross in France," he said. "There is no time to waste."

"Is the Chapel in danger," Hector asked uneasily?

"I have passage already paid for on the Sofia. Get on the boat," Eustachius commanded. "Samael has sent our things ahead of us."

"I am ready," Hector said with a dutiful nod.

"The ferryman is already waiting," the cardinal told him. With that, Eustachius walked quickly toward the door. Hector hurried to join him and took his hand to preserve the illusion of the cardinal's helplessness. Over the centuries, Eustachius had become so attuned to sound and the motion of the air that his lack of sight was of little consequence.

Isabel hurried to follow them, but not before stealing a glance at the final tapestry. The figure portrayed was horrible to behold. He was tall and gaunt and his skin was as pale as snow. His eyes, like those of the other fallen Angels were of one solid color...gold. His chest was bare and his only clothing was a long black loincloth secured by a leather belt. His mouth was open wide revealing rows of thin, spine-like teeth. His fingers ended in golden claws. His body was devoid of hair and golden wings lay down over his back. These wings were fanned and insectile in appearance.

The tapestry showed the side profile of the pale creature. His far hand held a golden trumpet out at arm's length as if he were protecting it from the viewer of the image. His closer hand was stretched out toward Isabel and his face was filled with menace. A cloud of locusts swirled around the creature and seemed to fly out in the direction his hand was pointing. These locusts had faces like men and long tails that ended in stingers such as one might see on scorpions.

There was no time to wonder over the tapestry as Sister Magdalena was herded along through the tunnels of the underground cathedral. In little time, the three vampires came to a huge cavern which contained a subterranean river. A wooden dock stretched out from the cave floor over the water. Chirping sounds echoed loudly in the chamber. A monk in a hooded black robe carried a pole that would propel the barge upon which he was standing. Without words, Eustachius and his children boarded the wooden vessel and the ferryman began to guide it down the river.

The tunnel narrowed and they passed beneath the low hanging ceiling of stone. The new cavern which the ferry passed into was a man-made cistern. Greek style columns made of marble insured that there would be no collapse. The ferryman poled through the cistern for some time before coming to another dock. This one was made of stone. It was flanked to either side by huge stone heads. The heads had snakes instead of hair and their features were feminine. One of the stone carvings had been placed upside down and the other was turned on its side. The upside down head was of a greenish hue. The other was violet in color.

The ferryman remained there until all three passengers had left the barge. Still no words passed between them as he departed back into the farthest reaches of the cistern. Eustachius led them along a wooden path which hugged the wall of the cistern until it led out into a quarry of stone. Man-made steps led up out of the quarry and into a dense forest.

As much at home in the wild as in the cathedral, Eustachius led them through the trees until they came to a secluded cove. Soldiers waited for them in a large rowboat that had been dragged a short way onto the beach. In the silvery, moonlit water of the cove was a much larger vessel, presumably the Sofia.

One of the soldiers called out in Italian and Hector answered in kind. It sounded like some sort of greeting, but Isabel was not versed in their dialect. The soldiers helped Eustachius and his brood onto the boat and then rowed quietly out to the waiting ship. A rope ladder was tossed down from the starboard side of the Sofia. One by one, the vampires ascended. Hector went up first and then assisted Isabel and the cardinal up onto the deck.

The sailors were spread out here and there along the ship. Some stood while others leaned against the sides or were perched in the riggings. "Your rooms are prepared your eminence," said a bearded man with a white bandanna wrapped around his head.

"Thank you Captain," the cardinal answered. "Your punctuality is greatly appreciated."

"Take them below," the Captain said gruffly. Two of the sailors immediately approached and led the vampires to the stairway that would take them down into the belly of the ship. "Raise anchor," the captain said loudly as Isabel made her way down toward a pair of wooden doors leading into the hold.

Their rooms consisted of a bedroom and a storage room. There were only two beds in the chamber, but none of them would be sleeping there. There was also a large open table with seven chairs bolted to the floor around it. There was a wooden cabinet set into the wall behind the table and two large port holes that let in the moonlight. The actual sleeping area was the storage room which contained several trunks and three heavy marble coffins. The door to the storage area could be barred from the inside. Here there were no port holes.

Eustachius sat at the one chair that was positioned at the head of the table. "Come and sit down," the cardinal said as he motioned to the other chairs. Hector sat on the far side of the table so that he would be facing the door. Sister Magdalena took the first seat she came to. "You have questions no doubt," the cardinal said. "We have had little time to talk since your death."

"I do," Isabel admitted.

"I will hear them now," Eustachius said. After taking a moment to collect her thoughts, Isabel spoke.

"When I journeyed into Carlo's mind, I passed first through a tunnel..," Sister Magdalena trailed off. She was not quite sure how to articulate her question.

"In order to enter the soul of another," Eustachius said, "one must first be free of the Land of Flesh. The soul leaves the body and travels through the Land of Spirit and into the soul of another. The tunnel is simply a sheath which protects you from the dangers of the spirit world."

"Something came through," Isabel said fearfully.

"Something came through," Eustachius asked? His brows furrowed over mutilated sockets.

"It was...the ghost of the woman that Carlo had sacrificed to Mo'lech," Isabel replied. She explained to the older vampires how Ana had begged her for help.

"Your soul is naturally attuned to those who exist beyond the Land of Flesh," the cardinal replied in reverence. "I sensed the presence of many spirits when I first saw you in the court of King Alfonso."

"You are a medium," Hector said respectfully.

"A medium attracts spirits because the door to his or her soul is always open," Eustachius told her. "Have you ever heard the voices of the dead?"

"Not until I buried the children," Isabel remembered, "and again when I went out to the pond. I heard many voices. They were…accusing me."

""In what way, Eustachius acquired?

"They were the voices of those who died because of me. I saw a vivid image of my dead husband. He was like some foul revenant come back to take me to hell!"

"Tell me," the cardinal encouraged her. Isabel related the story of her suicide and the spirits that had plagued her. When she had told everything, Eustachius spoke once more.

"Those were not the spirits of your loved ones," he said. "The Fallen that have not attained a physical host, those whom you know as demons; are also attracted to the soul of the medium. Have you ever experienced such a possession?"

"No," Isabel replied. "My family has always served God."

"Your faith is strong. Spirits can always access a medium's dreams. Has this happened to you?"

"I am not certain," Isabel replied. "I have had many terrifying dreams. I would pray to Jesus Christ and then wake up."

"When you were burying the orphans, your soul was weakened by your desire to take your own life. This allowed the demons to manifest, but I suspect that they had been following you long before this." Isabel nodded her head. The things Eustachius was saying were disconcerting but held a certain kind of sense.

"Why have I not heard them since," she asked?

"Because I have been protecting you," the cardinal replied. "I will teach you how to fortify yourself against them."

"I will learn diligently," Isabel promised.

"Once the spirits contact you, the door can never be fully closed again. You will suffer their attentions until the end of time. I hope you have the strength."

"God willing," Isabel said as she made the sign of the cross.

"What else," Eustachius asked after a moment of silence?

"Well," Isabel struggled for a moment, "there was one more tapestry in the cathedral that I was curious about."

"Which one was it," the cardinal asked?

"The tapestry of Apollyon," Hector supplied. "I did not have time to tell her of it."

"Well then do so now," Eustachius said with a motion of his hand.

"She is your child," Hector said deferentially. "You would tell it better than I."

"Tell her," Eustachius said again.

"The Angel Apollyon holds the key to the bottomless pit. When it is opened, all of the afflictions of the apocalypse will be unleashed upon man. The creatures in the tapestry are the demon locusts which are said to be in thrall to Apollyon. I am not certain why Samael keeps that image in the main hall of the cathedral. Perhaps it is to remind us that while we are immortal, our time on earth is limited," Hector explained.

"Very astute," Eustachius said with approval. Their discussion continued long into the night. The cardinal taught Isabel many things during the voyage to France. Self control was even more important aboard ship. If one were to take too much blood and kill one of the sailors, suspicion would be aroused. The cardinal taught her to control the lowering of her fangs and how to use her own blood to heal the puncture wounds made by her teeth.

It was also during this voyage that Eustachius taught her the rudiments of Dominion over Air. It was a struggle, for the powers of the air did not come naturally to her as did those of the spirit. The souls of Felipe and Javier provided a training ground for Sister Magdalena to develop her Dominion over Spirit. Isabel wanted to travel into the soul of the cardinal, but he forbade her. "It is too perilous," Eustachius said, but on this he would say no more.

By journeys end; Isabel could barely move a spoon across the table, but her maker seemed pleased. It was daylight when their ship docked in the French port. The village of Saint Cyprian was bustling with activity while the vampires slumbered in coffins placed inside the carriage which would carry them inland to Languedoc.

The cardinal's children were escorted by a heavily armed contingent of soldiers on horseback. The windows of this new carriage were able to be opened, unlike the one they had in Zaragoza. Isabel pulled back the wood panels which covered the window nearest her, and secured them to special housings built into the walls of the carriage. The French peasants looked fearfully out from the inns and taverns which they passed.

For Isabel, their fear had a delicious aroma that stirred her senses. Disgusted by her desire for their blood, she made the sign of the cross and closed up the carriage window until they had left St. Cyprian altogether. Soldiers escorted them through the city and several leagues farther down the road toward Languedoc. A smaller path led off the main road into the wilderness.

In the midst of a broad meadow was a wooden chapel that resembled the longhouses which Isabel had read about in the stories of Roman conquests against the barbarians of the North. The only difference was that these poles only lifted their structures a few scant inches from the ground. Also, there was a large wooden cross built into the apex of the roof over the entrance and stained glass windows along the sides. Torches burned in iron sconces set to either side of the door. Four iron spikes rose up several feet from around the edges of each sconce. Grim faced monks stood below these flames with arms crossed. More torches burned from within, illuminating the narrow windows which line the sides of the building.

The carriage stopped and the monks who stood by the door moved quickly to help the vampires down. From this distance, Isabel could see the chain shirts peeking above the neck lines of the monks' robes and scabbards which were sometimes visible below the hems of their garments as they walked. Most of these warrior monks were stationed inside the chapel standing silently along the walls. Isabel noted that not one of them stood in front of a window.

The chapel itself was a simple affair with roughly cut pews which contained no backings or padding of any kind.

There was a crude pulpit in the front of the chapel. Behind this was a small wooden column upon which rested a silver reliquary.

Isabel noticed that Eustachius and his bodyguard became more uncomfortable as they approached the pulpit. Hector's fists clenched and his face pitched up into a grimace. Eustachius put one hand to his forehead and exhaled audibly as they drew near. Isabel saw that there was something on top of the pulpit. Resting atop two iron crescents which were built into the surface was a thick length of wood which ended in a jagged point on one side. The object was about 2 feet in length and as thick around as one of Magdalena slender wrists.

Hector and Eustachius knelt reverently before the pulpit of the secluded chapel. After a moment, Isabel joined them and bowed her head also in prayer. The hushed sounds which emanated from her elders let her know that they were in considerable pain: a sharp intake of breath here, a stifled cry there.

Isabel felt no such pain, to the contrary; kneeling there in the chapel, she was overcome with a feeling of peace and the pangs of hunger left her completely as she prayed to God. When the cardinal rose, so too did his children. "Let us go down," Eustachius said. His voice was strained. Hector stepped around the pulpit and opened the reliquary. He pulled down on a goblet which was connected to a lever inside the wooden column.

There was a loud creaking noise as a large piece of the wooden floor swung downward, revealing a wooden staircase. Eustachius was the first to descend and Sister Magdalena followed him. Hector brought up the rear and motioned to one of the monks as he walked down the stairs. "Close it," he commanded.

The warrior closest to the reliquary moved quickly toward it. As the three vampires came down to a wooden landing, the floor panel raised back up and sealed them in. The landing was nothing more than a narrow walkway which led to another staircase leading down. Heavy wooden doors were set on either side, and there was torch sconces set into the center of the back wall. "The chapel guards sleep in these chambers," Eustachius told Isabel as they continued to the second staircase.

The second landing was even smaller the first. A single wooden door faced the stairs coming down. A torch was set into the wall facing third stairway down. Eustachius opened door and waited while Isabel and Hector entered in. As Isabel passed by the third stairwell, she saw another door at the bottom of it. There was a window in the door and firelight danced behind it.

The chamber which the Cardinal led them into was a crude study. Bookshelves lined two of the walls. There was a long table by the east wall with simple wooden chairs set around it. Eustachius grabbed the torch from outside the door and set it into a sconce located inside the chamber. The silence in the room was only broken by the crackling of the flame. "I did not wish to speak of the cross fragment where ears might hear," Eustachius said. "We will deal with the Catharists in time, but we are here to protect our holy artifact. You felt its power in the sanctuary, did you not?"

"I did," Isabel replied. She was hesitant to explain to them how it had affected her so much differently.

"This shard of the true cross was recovered by Samael after the crucifixion," Eustachius explained as he crossed the room. "It is said that a vampire who is truly penitent may find an escape from the curse through the power of the cross."

"So one of our kind could be human again," Isabel asked?

"For a brief moment only," Eustachius said reverently. "The vampire must have faith and offer himself as a sacrifice to he who bears the cross fragment, but the bearer must be innocent when he drives the fragment into the heart of the penitent."

"How many have offered themselves," Isabel asked?

"Not many," Eustachius said sadly. Finding a true innocent is all but impossible."

"As likely as finding a vampire with true faith and repentance," Hector added. "I have no doubt that I am a sinner."

"You are a good man," Sister Magdalena disagreed. Hector smiled wryly.

"Sadly, Hector is right," the cardinal said. "But the cross gives us hope that God will one day provide for even such as we to be saved."

I dare not imagine such a thing," Isabel said.

"Hector," Eustachius said, "go to your men and hold communion."

"It has been some time," Hector said he started toward the door.

"Do it quickly," Eustachius called after him. "Time is not a luxury." Hector nodded gravely and left the cardinal's study.

"Hector will give communion," Sister Magdalena said in confusion.

"It is different for us," Eustachius explained. "The chapel guards are enthralled to him and so the sharing of blood must be his."

"And they all will drink," she inquired?

"They must all partake," Eustachius confirmed.

"What lies beneath us," Isabel asked?

"The dungeon," the cardinal replied, "and below that our graves." Isabel nodded. There was a silence in the room for a few moments before the sounds of men chanting in Latin echoed down from above.

While waiting for Hector's return, Isabel begin perusing the leather bound tomes that filled the shelves on the back wall. There were Bibles in several languages, but it was the more obscure titles the peaked her interest: the Gospel of Samael, the Key of Solomon, and other titles written in languages long dead. "Bring something to the table Sister," Eustachius invited.

"Your eminence," she asked?

"Read it out loud," he said. As Isabel reached for the Gospel of Samael, she was interrupted by the unmistakable sound of steel on steel. The sounds of battle ensued and she could hear the men shouting up above. The cardinal stood quickly as Isabel turned round. "They are upon us," he whispered!

"Who is," Isabel asked as she moved toward the door?

"The Architects," Eustachius said as he walked quickly after. He took a key from a chain on his neck and handed it to her. "Wait for us in the dungeon," he instructed.

"I will go with you," Isabel disagreed.

"No," the cardinal nearly shouted as he locked her arm in a vice like grip. "You are too young to the blood. Do as I command you!"

"Yes, your eminence," Isabel said nervously. She took the key and walked down the final staircase. As she turned the key in the last door, she couldn't help remembering words she had often heard her father saying to his men. "It is better to die on your feet than on your knees." Isabel frowned and shut the door behind her.

CHAPTER V

Hector walked quickly up the stairs. He felt behind the torch sconce until his fingers brushed over the loose panel. There was a scraping noise as the large floor panel swung down to allow him into the chapel. "Gather the men," he told the monks as his chest cleared the plane of the floor. One of the warriors walked quickly past him as Hector came up the stairs. The elder vampire opened the reliquary and grabbed a golden chalice from inside. He carried this vessel in both hands as he walked out into the center of the chapel. The power of the cross fragment was not unbearably painful from this distance, but it could not be ignored.

Hector waited while the guards who slept below were roused from their slumber. These men filed up the stairs in the brown robes common to all. Unlike the others, they carried no blades and wore no armor. Among them was Gerard, the French man who acted as commander in Hector's absence. He had piercing blue eyes that looked alert even after being roused from sleep. The small finger of his left hand was missing, given long ago in defense of the Chapel of the Cross.

The men gathered around Hector, forming a circle in the chapel which stretched out into the pews. After a time, Hector bowed his head. The man did likewise. Almighty God," Hector prayed, "your servants are gathered here in your presence to be joined in Holy Communion." He placed the chalice at his feet and drew a dagger from its sheath. He then held the blade to his wrist. "This is the blood of the Old Testament," Hector said as he cut deeply into his flesh. Blood welled up from the wound before he held it down over the chalice. Blood drained loudly into the golden vessel. "The blood of God the Father, passed down to us through his servant Samael. The men sang in Latin while Hector's blood filled the golden vessel.

The wound in Hector's wrist closed and he returned the dagger to it´s sheath. He knelt down and picked up the chalice in both hands. His voice joined the others as the handed the cup to Gerard. The Frenchman put the vessel to his lips and drank. Gerard passed the cup to the man on his right and the process repeated until every man had partaken of Hector's blood

As the men were preparing to resume their positions, Hector heard the distinctive whistle of arrows coming from outside. A scream erupted as a score of arrows bit into the wood of the chapel. "They are upon us," one of the door guards shouted as he hurried inside. There was a bloody shaft sticking out of his forearm.

Without the need for orders, the warrior monks threw off their robes and drew a wide variety of bladed weapons. Those who had been sleeping charged down the stairway to arm themselves. "Do not come outside unless I give the order," Hector shouted! "Stay clear of the windows!" He strode quickly toward the main doors. He would gauge the threat before letting the enemy know how many soldiers they would be facing.

Hector walked out the main doors of the Chapel of the Cross and descended the stairs down to where wood met earth. Miguelito, one of the younger thralls, had been pierced through the forehead with a broad tipped arrow. Judging by the way it had forced itself through the young man's skull, it must have been fired from a long bow. Hector's exterior was calm and nonplussed. He would grieve for Miguelito later.

Suddenly, the night air was alive with the whistling of arrows all aimed toward the cardinal's guard. Without a moment to spare, Hector invoked his Dominion over Air to create a sphere of tempestuous wind around him. Leaves and small debris were thrown up from the ground surrounding the vampire. The arrows veered sharply to the right when they came into the tempest. Some were broken while others impacted the ground or the wall of the chapel. Hector rested the blade of his sword on the grass beneath him as the high winds howled and his dark hair was tossed in the breeze. He waited. Many more of the shafts were deflected by the sphere before the enemy archers decided to conserve their ammunition.

Three men on horseback emerged from the trees in advance perhaps twenty paces from the tree line. Coming behind the horses, was a ring of French soldiers. Hector guessed they were at least fifty strong and maybe as much as one hundred counting those who were still hidden by the wilderness.

The horse in the center was ridden by a man in gray hose with a navy blue tunic bordered in white. Bronze plates were attached to his forearms, calves, and thighs. By the shape of the tunic, Hector surmised that there was a breastplate beneath it. His long brown hair hung down in waves from the conical helmet which protected the top of his skull. He had pale skin and sunken features around deep set eyes and thick brows. The men riding beside him were standard-bearers. One carried the flag of Languedoc, the other bore a blue-and-white standard which was likely to be their commander's colors. Their standards were held downward, while a white flag was held up to invite parlay.

Hector did not move. Finally, the horses came forward at a slow walk. At the last possible moment, Hector released the winds back to their proper course. "Hector del Toro," the enemy commander said smugly. "We have come for your master. Stand aside and let justice prevail."

"His eminence has done nothing wrong," Hector replied. "Be on your way."

"The Convocation of Saints is displeased with the slaughter at the Catedral de Seo. We have come to arrest the traitor Eustachius."

"You are not of the Convocation," Hector scoffed. "Who are you that I should listen?"

"I am Jean Baptiste," the commander replied, "and I come to carry out the will of Vincente."

"Tell your master I would not be moved," Hector said.

"It is the will of the Convocation," Jean Baptiste said condescendingly.

"Samael would give no such order. We have just come from Constantinople. Why not kill his eminence there where he was vulnerable?"

"Your great Samael, as he calls himself, has agreed to look the other way while your master's blood pays for that of our kinsman. There are over one hundred men here to remove you from my path if needs be."

"It was I alone who killed your fellows in Zaragoza," Hector replied.

"Surrender than, and we will spare your master," Baptiste offered. There was sarcasm in his voice. The eyes of the cardinal's guard darkened.

"We will inflict such suffering upon those of you who remain that you will wish you had fallen upon your own swords," Hector promised.

"You shall not live to regret those words," Baptiste replied. He turned his horse around and galloped back to the rear. He standard bearers followed. Hector used all of his will to encompass the Chapel of the Cross as he had encompassed himself. The effort left him weak and he staggered back. He regained his strength by biting into Miguelito's neck and consuming the dead man's blood. He carried the fallen monk's body inside as the enemy arrows were deflected by the massive sphere. The grass flattened around it as the wind rushed over.

Hector laid his fallen thralls body on top of the closest pew. "Make ready," he told the others. He walked quickly to the rear of the sanctuary and saw that the cross fragment had been concealed. The top of the pulpit was built on a crossbar which allowed the surface of it to be inverted. Nevertheless, Hector could still feel the power radiating from the artifact.

The French soldiers shouted out their battle cry as they stormed through the doors of the chapel. Hector held his sword tight into his body. His knees were relaxed and he took a half crouch stance as he waited. The French were nearly upon him before his thralls rushed in from both sides.

There was enough room in the center aisle to fit three men abreast. Hector swung at the first man's sword with such force that it flew from his fingers. The elder vampire jumped toward the man in the center. This man's attention was held by the massive blade and so he was unprepared for the fist that smashed into the side of his skull. His body crumpled sideways into the soldier next to him. Hector drove his sword through both of these men's stomachs in one thrust.

There was a sharp pain as the man who had lost his sword thrust a dagger into Hector's left armpit. Leaving the sword in his injured arm, the cardinal's guard reached back and tore off the man's helmet by the chinstrap. While his enemy was still shocked over the loss of his helmet, Hector used it to bash his face in!

As the dead man fell, the dagger went with him and Hector's wound quickly healed itself. Hector snarled as he began to whirl his blade in a figure eight pattern. He moved relentlessly forward. His blade moved so rapidly that blood sprayed out from either side of it like the wake of a sailing ship. Blocking Hector's onslaught was futile as none in the chapel had the power to withstand his unnatural strength.

Having practiced this maneuver many times, Hector's thralls moved back away from the center aisle as he plowed through the enemy. Those who managed to dodge to the right or left were quickly impaled on the monks' blades. Mortal blood covered the center of the pews and splashed onto Hector's allies as well.

If Jean Baptiste had told the truth about the size of his army, Hector assumed that nearly half of them were now dead. The sound of the boots coming up the stairs behind him meant that Gerard and the others would now joined the fray.

Hector charged out onto the field of battle far ahead of the thralls who came behind him. The enemy soldiers passing through the supernatural wind were thrown several yards to the right as they crossed through. Many of them fell to the ground, but just as many of them managed to stay on their feet. Hector returned his sword to its sheath and charged toward the enemy.

The sphere dissipated as Hector ran through it. Everyone else seemed to move in slow motion as he ran within inhuman speed toward the enemy commander. Baptiste hurled down his spear toward Hector as he closed in. The cardinal's guard narrowly avoided the spear by dropping to his hands and knees.

Wasting no time, Baptiste drew his thin sword and charged forward. His stallion reared up and brought its iron shod hooves to bear on the crouching vampire. Hector leaped to the left in time to avoid the horses attack. While still in the air, the elder vampire reached out with both hands and seized the stallion's right front leg. As his feet hit earth, Hector twisted the animal's limb inward at the ankle. He then shoved the horse's calf violently free of its knee!

Hector spun away and drew steel as horse and rider toppled to the ground. The momentum of the horses fall caused Baptiste to be thrown sideways toward the cardinal's guard. He began the melee with an overhand strike. Jean parried with his rapier, but the force of the attack nearly knocked it from his grasp. Before Baptiste could mount a counterattack, Hector kicked him hard below the rib cage which sent the younger vampire flying back toward the tree line. His spine crashed into the stout trunk of a sycamore tree. The enemy commander fell to the ground.

Hector plunged his sword into the horse's neck which ended its pitiable screaming. Its mouth bit at the air as it choked out its last breath. Four of Baptiste's soldiers charged forward to protect their master. Hector seemed to disappear for a moment as his body moved too swiftly for human eyes. In seconds, Baptiste men lay on the ground in pieces. One had been stabbed through the heart. One was beheaded. Another had lost a leg and was screaming at the sight of his own bloody stump! The last soldiers face was a mask of pain. He had been divided below the rib cage.

The cardinal's guard opened his mouth and inhaled deeply. The power of his blood caused that which poured out of the divided man's stomach to be drawn through the air and into the elder vampire's mouth. Some of this blood still covered half of Hector's chin as he turned his predatory gaze once more upon Jean Baptiste.

The younger vampire had picked himself up off the ground. There was an audible crack as he shifted his bent spine back into place. All around them, Hector's thralls were joining in battle with those of Baptiste's army who remained. While many of the enemy soldiers had also partaken of vampiric blood, it was not as potent as that which flowed in Hector veins. Also, Baptiste´s men had only recently been enthralled. Hector´s thralls had served for much, much longer. The results were telling.

"Stand down," Baptiste shouted across the din. "I will not be killed by the likes of you Del Toro!" To Hector, the enemy commander looked ridiculous.

"I have no intention of killing you," Hector said menacingly as he choked up his grip on the two-handed sword. "Last chance to destroy yourself..."

"Come on," Jean shouted challengingly as he moved into a half crouch. Hector sprang forward and there was the ring of steel on steel as their deadly dance began. The slower and weaker Baptiste was forced to devote all of his efforts toward parrying Hector's whirling blade. One of Baptiste's parries knocked Hector's blade aside for a moment. Jean seized the opportunity to make a lunging thrust toward the elder vampire's heart. Hector deflected the blade with his own sword but only succeeded in redirecting it into the upper portion of his right leg.

Hector barred his fangs and roared as he lashed out at his enemy. Using the cross piece of his sword as a weapon, the cardinal's guard smashed it into Jean's left eye with both hands. The force of the blow staggered the younger vampire. His eye was a bloody mess, but it was quickly knitting itself back together and he did not lose hold of the rapier.

Hector swung down quickly with his sword and severed Baptiste's arm just above the elbow. The younger vampire snarled as he tried to retrieve the blade with his remaining hand. The other was rapidly decaying on the ground. Baptiste nearly regained his rapier before Hector severed his remaining arm at the shoulder. He kicked the surprised commander in the kneecap which drove him to the dirt. Hector chopped down with the two-handed sword and relieved Baptiste of his legs also. "Have mercy," Baptiste cried out as Hector raised the sword high over his head. The cardinal's guard reversed the blade and drove it down through the younger vampire's heart.

Hector left the two-handed sword sticking up out of Jean Baptiste's chest. He picked up his enemy's rapier and joined his thralls in crippling those who remained. After Jean Baptiste was felled, many of his soldiers tried to flee the battlefield. Few escaped. When it was done, Hector and his warriors gathered up the dead from the blood spattered field. Their brothers were set aside for proper burial. The enemy were piled in great heaps and set to burn.

Jean Baptiste, and those of his soldiers who had the misfortune to survive, were taken to the lowest level of the Chapel of the Cross. There were fifteen of them in all. Wounds that would have killed normal men were slowly healing due to the blood that kept them in servitude to their master. If Baptiste were to be given enough blood, he might have regenerated his lost limbs, but there would be no such offering.

Hector placed Baptiste's limbless body on top of the stone table which sat in the middle of the torture chamber. The rest of the men he had placed in cells. The dungeon below the Chapel of the Cross was a simple affair. The heavy iron doors at the bottom of the stairs led into a hallway that was lined on either side by a row of five iron prison cells. The prison hall led into a torch lit cavern. The chamber had only one man-made wall which contained a large fireplace and many iron pegs. These pegs contained a wealth of metal implements both mundane and grotesque.

Four iron stakes had been pounded into the floor in the center of the cavern. Each state contained a short chain attached to a steel shackle. The stone floor between the stakes was stained with the blood of those who had been restrained there. An anvil had been placed near the fire for the forging of weapons and other implements. The molds were stacked in the corner behind it.

At Hector's command, an iron pot was filled with tiny brass ingots and then suspended from an iron framework which had been set into the fireplace. While he waited for the brass ingots to melt, Hector placed the body of Jean Baptiste on the floor between the stakes. He placed one iron shod boot on the enemy commander's stomach and yanked the two-handed sword free of his heart. As the wound slowly closed, Hector sheathed the sword on his back. He could see Baptiste men looking on from their cells. Fear was etched into their faces.

As Baptiste opened his eyes, Hector was collecting the tools necessary for what he was about to do: a small auger with a wooden handle, a flat iron funnel, an iron ladle with a bucket of water, and a steel, claw-like device known as the 'breast ripper'. All of these he placed on the stone floor next to Baptiste.

Jean's eyes were darting rapidly around the cavernous torture chamber before Hector knelt down over him. "I.., I need blood," Baptiste said nervously.

"You do," Hector agreed as he picked up the breast ripper. He began to fit the steel claws around the enemy commander's right peck.

"Hector," the disapproving voice of the cardinal echoed out of the prison hall. Hector looked back at Eustachius whose figure was dimly illuminated by torchlight. "Are you about to engage in the work of an inquisitor? It is not your place."

"This has nothing to do with repentance," Hector replied as he pushed the breast ripper's claws down into Baptiste's flesh. The enemy commander grunted sharply as the steel claws entered his body. "The architects must understand that they are not to attack this holy place again."

"The prisoners will live I trust," Eustachius questioned?

"They will live," Hector affirmed.

"Do what you must," Eustachius said flatly. He turned back then and left Hector to his work. Once he heard the iron doors close again, the cardinal's guard turned his attention back down to the crippled vampire below him. Hector took a firm grip on the handle of the breast ripper which was attached to the claw by a thick chain.

"I can tell you whatever it is that you need to know," Baptiste said nervously. Hector yanked down hard and ripped a huge gobbet of flesh from Baptiste's chest. The younger vampire screamed loudly. There followed some tortured moans from Jean, accompanied by the gasps and cries of terror from the other prisoners. The Architect's blood went to work immediately, healing the wound in the space of a minute.

"You should save your blood," Hector said as he fitted the breast ripper onto the freshly healed skin of his enemy.

"Just tell me what you want to know," Baptiste said as he grit his teeth. His fangs were lowered and his eyes were wild with fear.

"You have nothing to interest me," Hector answered. With that, he ripped off the chunk of Jean's chest once more. The younger vampire cried out as blood and flesh were ripped from his body! Hector stood and moved over to the fireplace. He waited for some time until the brass had melted inside the iron pot. Baptiste was entreating him for mercy, but Hector was deaf to his supplications.

The cardinal's guard removed a heavy piece of cloth from the mantle and used it to lift the pot out of the fire. He carried this over to the place where Baptiste lay and set it up beside him. He then beckoned to one of his thralls who were guarding the prisoners. "Go and fetch Sister Magdalena," he told the man, "and be quick about it."

"I am already here," Sister Magdalena spoke from the darkness.

✝   ✝   ✝

As Eustachius had commanded her, Isabel hid herself in the dungeon during the battle. When Hector's men came down to deliver the prisoners, she had pressed her body into a dark corner of the torture chamber. Only when Hector entered with the mangled body of Jean Baptiste did she realize that the cardinal's guard had led the men to victory. Not knowing what to do next, Isabel had remained in the corner…watching.

"I did not see you there," Hector said uncomfortably. Isabel guessed that the elder vampire was not accustomed to being surprised.

"What is it that you wish for me to do," she asked?

"Come here," Hector said with a motion of his hand. "You must get accustomed to this sort of work."

"I obey," Isabel replied as she came over and knelt beside him.

"Hand me that auger," Hector ordered. Isabel did so. "Hold what remains of his left arm," he instructed. She grabbed Baptiste's stump with both hands and held it up toward the cardinal's guard. Hector held the shaft with his fingers and worked the crank handle with the opposite hand. The point of the metal implement he placed squarely on the exposed bone.

Baptiste began screaming as Hector's hands moved at a feverish pace to drill a hole into the center of the bone. This process was repeated in quick succession upon the other three severed limbs. Once the holes were bored, Hector immersed the ladle in the cauldron of molten brass. The ladle had a small triangular protrusion which resembled the lip of a pitcher. This protrusion allowed Hector to pour the brass into the holes he had drilled into Jean's bones. Isabel held the screaming vampire in place while the cardinal's guard worked with awful precision. She would have preferred to leave the awful work to others, but this what she believed she deserved for her sins.

When the brass overflowed, it formed caps around the broken ends of Baptiste's bones and seared the meat around them. Hector would quickly pour cold water on each individual bone as soon as this took place. Steam rose into the air along with the wailing of the once proud commander. "Sister Magdalena," Hector said as he ladled up another bit of molten brass.

"Yes," Isabel replied, but her attention was on the brass which had now solidified over the vampire's bones. She looked at the man's face but could not summon any sympathy. It occurred to her that every man whom she tortured reminded her in some way of Manuel Barillos.

"The cardinal will be displeased that you are doing this. This has nothing to do..."

"I know," Isabel answered. "It has nothing to do with repentance."

"Yet you are still here," Hector pointed out.

"The shedding of blood on holy ground is an affront to God," Isabel explained. "So you see; this has everything to do with repentance."

"Hold this funnel into his eyes," Hector said as he knelt down on Baptiste's chest. He placed one hand on the prisoner's forehead to keep it steady.

"Please," Baptiste begged. "My eyes... You cannot."

"The pain will help to cleanse your soul," Isabel said as she placed the funnel against Baptiste's left eye. His eyelids pinched shut reflexively.

"Amen," Hector said solemnly as he poured the brass down into the funnel. The molten metal burned through Baptiste eyelid in little time and destroyed the eye below. "The water," Hector said forcefully above the sound of Baptiste's agonized wailing! Isabel took the pitcher and poured it down over the vampires brass filled socket. It took a great amount of water to solidify the brass and cool it enough to halt the damage being done to Baptiste's brain.

When Hector and Magdalena poured brass into Baptiste's right eye, he was no longer coherent. The tortured sounds he made were those of a dumb animal. Some of the prisoners were already weeping and they had yet to be touched.

Over the next several hours, Hector mutilated the remaining prisoners with Isabel's assistance. Five of the prisoners had both legs amputated and the wounds cauterized shut with hot irons. The other ten had their eyes burned out so that they bore some resemblance to Eustachius.

Jean Baptiste was sealed inside a wooden box. Once the mutilated prisoners were taken out of the chapel, this box was placed on a litter which Hector attached to one of the enemy's horses. "Return from whence you came," Hector commanded them. "Those of you, who have eyes to see, lead your brothers. Those of you with legs to walk, carry those who will see for you."

"We have no weapons," one of the men said pleadingly. "How will we defend ourselves from highwaymen?"

"That is beyond my concern," Hector said.

"If you are killed, it will be God's vengeance for desecrating this holy place," Isabel told them.

"Tell them of your suffering," Hector concluded, "and tell them it will be as nothing when compared to those who dare to come after you." It was a wretched mob that departed from the Chapel of the Cross that night. Sister Magdalena and Hector watched them go.

"What will they do," Isabel asked as the last refugee disappeared into the darkness of the trees?

"If they make it back to their Architect masters," Hector replied, "then we will be attacked again."

"You do not think this lesson is one they will learn," Isabel asked?

"I think it will give them pause," Hector said, "but they will come again in time." Hector sighed. "Let us go in now to Eustachius. He will have words." As Hector had guessed, the cardinal was angered when he learned that Isabel had assisted in torturing prisoners. However, her justification of it as punishment for desecrating holy ground was enough to placate him.

✝   ✝   ✝

It would be six years before the Architects dared to attack the Chapel of the Cross again. In the time between, Eustachius and Isabel devoted their time to the Cathar Heresy. Like anyone involved in the practice of torture for extended periods of time, Isabel became numb to the pain of her victims. It was only as she lay sleeping in her coffin by day that her conscience came to call.

Over the years, Sister Magdalena became disenchanted with the persecution of the Cathars. These heretics believed in God as a duality. They thought of the God of the Old Testament as evil. This evil God was balanced by Jesus Christ, the benevolent God of the New Testament. The Catharists' idea that God was evil was blasphemy in the eyes of the church. It had fallen to Eustachius, (and others like him), to save those who would repent and kill those who would not.

In time, Isabel realized that the persecution of these heretics only strengthened their blasphemous beliefs. Furthermore, many of them were kind and caring individuals who endeavored to be righteous. Much to Eustachius' displeasure, she would often refuse to participate in torturing the majority of those who were captured and brought to the Chapel of the Cross. Only if the Catharist was guilty of other grievous sins would Sister Magdalena do her duty. This caused much contention between maker and child. Hector wisely remained silent on the matter.

On the night of the final attack, Sister Magdalena and Cardinal Eustachius were embroiled in an argument over the treatment of a particular prisoner. Gisele was a Baker's wife, a woman with child, and a Cathar heretic. In the six years past, Isabel had only shown her disapproval by abstaining from torturing those she deemed unworthy of it.

With Gisele however, she could not ignore the innocent child inside the woman's womb. This was the final straw which led her to outright mutiny!

"The child is innocent," Isabel screamed! "Even you must admit to that." Her voice echoed loudly off the rock walls of the torture chamber below the Chapel of the Cross. A pregnant woman lay naked in the midst of the stakes on the dungeon floor. Her limbs were manacled to each post. Her stomach was swollen with the child that was condemned along with her. There were small cuts on her inner thighs where the cardinal had terrified her into submission. Her eyes were sick with fear and she looked up imploringly at Isabel.

"Shirk your God-given duty elsewhere," Eustachius said without emotion. "There is work to be done." Hector stood uncomfortably along the wall by the fire.

"The child is innocent," Magdalena hissed!

"The woman is a recalcitrant heretic," Eustachius said angrily. "You recall we set her free. Here she is again, only two short months later. Having known the truth..."

"Do not quote scripture at me as if I am ignorant of it," Isabel interrupted! "I have borne witness to the scores of recalcitrant heretics which you have commanded Hector to destroy. They did not believe in the Roman Catholic Church; not before, not when you set them free the first time, and not when you put them to death for falling back into heresy."

"They were given the truth," Eustachius said.

"One cannot know the truth if they do not in their hearts believe it."

"Go upstairs sister," Eustachius said. "Your presence is not required."

"I will not leave," Isabel said firmly. "I will not allow this abomination to continue!"

"You dare to challenge me," the cardinal asked with contempt?

"The child must live," Isabel said, "and the prisoners, whose only sin is Catharism, must live to understand that what they believe is wrong."

"We were sent here to deal with the heretics," Eustachius spat, "or have you forgotten?"

"It is not I who has forgotten," Isabel retorted. "We were sent here to protect the Cross fragment."

"Branding yourself as a sympathizer for heresy could incur serious consequences," the cardinal threatened. "Speak with care."

"God damn you," Isabel cursed!

"Lock her away," Eustachius shouted. Hector sighed and stood up from the wall he was leaning upon. "Stay away from me Hector," Isabel cried! "I will not be locked away, not ever again!" Hector frowned and started toward her.

"You are worse than a murderer Eustachius," Isabel said with one finger pointed accusingly toward the cardinal. "How many have you destroyed when they are as yet unrepentant in these six years that I have been by your side? How many hundreds more before that? The unrepentant are damned!" Hector gently placed his hand on Isabel's shoulder. She jerked away and continued her tirade. "How many souls will you send to Hell before you are satisfied," Isabel screamed?

"Take her away," Eustachius snarled! He almost sounded desperate.

"Alright," Hector sighed, "let us do this with dignity sister."

"There is no dignity here Hector," Isabel said tremulously. "Take comfort in this your eminence; the soul of the child will be the only one of your victims to ever ascend into heaven." The cardinal nearly staggered as the logic of Isabel's words finally hit home.

"Enough," Hector said he grabbed Isabel roughly by the shoulder. His fingers were strong as a vice and his bones were hard as iron.

"I have sinned," Eustachius said. Hector paused. "Let her go," the cardinal added as he dropped down onto his knees. Hector released his grip. "I have sinned," Eustachius wept, "and I have led my children astray."

Suddenly, the sound of steel on steel echoed from the other side of the iron doors. Hector's head turned sharply toward the exit. "Soldiers," the cardinal's guard exclaimed! "Stay with him," he told Isabel. As soon as these words departed his lips, Hector disappeared from sight. The iron doors slammed open bringing the sounds of battle even closer.

Eustachius started quickly toward the now open doors to the dungeon. Isabel walked beside him. He did not command her to stay behind as he had done in the past. Sister Magdalena would not have obeyed in any case. They walked swiftly toward the stairs and whatever awaited them above.

CHAPTER VI

There was a wet, choking sound from the stairs above just before the bloodied corpse of one of Hector's thralls fell down into Isabel's view. He seemed to stare wide-eyed at her in death. Seconds later, a French soldier armed with a halberd stepped over the freshly made corpse. His weapon was wet with blood and his vampiric nature was evident. Blood covered the man's chin and his fangs were lowered. He was illuminated by the torch on the wall directly behind him. "Here he is," the French vampire shouted up the stairs. Isabel could hear his fellows responding as the enemy began to walk slowly down towards them. "Just give us the fragment your eminence," he sneered. "Your safety will then be assured."

"Fool," Eustachius retorted. "None of you can touch our sacred artifact!"

"We've brought a child with us," the vampire sneered. "I suggest you cooperate." Another Architect dressed in the garb of a French soldier joined the first. This one carried a saber.

"We will never surrender such a holy relic to the godless," the Cardinal returned!

"Well," the second vampire smiled as he twirled his sword slowly in front of him. "Vincente wants you alive."

"He said nothing about the woman," the first soldier grinned as he repositioned the halberd and continued his descent.

"Be gone," Isabel shouted as she stretched out her hand against them. Over the years she had resided in the Chapel of the Cross, she had learned the reason for the oddly crafted torch sconces therein. She now made use of it. There was a sound as of a great weight plunging into water. The air rippled out in front of Isabel's hand like the simmering heat of the desert. The first vampire was launched into the air over the top of him who followed behind. The halberd dropped to the ground as its wielder was impaled through the heart by one of the four iron spikes that stuck up from around the torch. Isabel's victim could not scream as the fire burned through the flesh of his back and set his clothing ablaze.

The second vampire sprang down the stairs with his saber raised high. Eustachius stretched out his grotesque fingers toward the assailant. Again, there was that strange plunging sound. This time, the sword was ripped free of its owner's hand and flew back toward the unfortunate who was being consumed by fire on the wall.

Eustachius made a halting motion with his hand and the blade froze in mid-air. The remaining Architect looked fearfully back at the weapon. The cardinal made a turning motioned with his fingers as if he were spinning dial. The saber began to move in slow circles, increasing rapidly in speed until it was a metallic blur.

The enemy vampire looked back and forth between the cardinal and the blade. His eyes were stricken with fear and indecision. Eustachius made a beckoning motion with his hand and the saber flew quickly toward its owner. The spinning blade sawed through the vampire's neck and continued toward the cardinal. Isabel had just enough time to see that the enemy had lost his hands also. Just before being decapitated, the vampire had brought those hands up reflexively to shield his face. His body turned to ash seconds after hitting the stairs. The body of the other was now completely engulfed. Isabel knew that when the flames consumed his heart, this first adversary would be ash as well.

The saber slowed down dramatically as it approached the cardinal. The arc of its last swing placed the handle easily into his outstretched hand.

"Come," Eustachius said. Isabel followed him swiftly up the stairs. The secret entrance to the basement stood wide open. The bodies of the monks littered the stairway along with the piles of ash that were once the undead.

"Back you dogs," Hector shouted from above! Isabel and her maker hurried up to join him. The pews of the sanctuary lay in splinters and the floor was strewn with the dead. The last of the attackers who had come in the first wave lay dead at the warrior's feet. The entrance to the Chapel of the Cross had been destroyed by catapult as had the wall and most of the roof surrounding it.

A small army was gathered back by the tree line. There was not a beating heart among them. The Lords of the Night rode on horseback. They were surrounded by several ranks of infantry. The riders bore no standards and there was no indication of who their leader might be. Hector suddenly cocked his head to one side. His face contorted in rage. "He is here," the cardinal's guard snarled. Then he was gone. The speed of his departure blew back dust and splinters of wood in his wake.

"We must stay together," Eustachius shouted, but it was too late. Isabel retrieved a long sword from the wreckage. She stood by Eustachius and waited. "There is no shame in fleeing my daughter," Eustachius said. "We will surely die here."

"We shall not die on our knees," Isabel replied. "We will stand together."

As the last vampire's head was cleaved from his shoulders, Hector's concentration was disturbed by a most loathsome sound. Far-off behind enemy lines, Hector's preternatural hearing detected a familiar voice." "The Cross fragment is hidden in the pulpit," Salvatore told his new master.

Knowing that Salvatore was betraying them to the Architects kindled Hector's anger and his heart was consumed by the darkness within. "He is here," the cardinal's guard snarled. He burst into motion and ran at superhuman speed toward the offensive sound of Salvatore's voice. As he crashed into first rank of infantry, Hector could see the traitor fleeing into the trees. Severed limbs and decapitated heads flew up from the enemy as Hector sliced through them.

With his eyes on the prize, Hector cut through those soldiers who stood in his way. He could hear the tumult of the shocked men behind him as he nearly flew into the forest. He was heedless of the branches that scratched him before being broken off by his momentum. Salvatore's dirty blonde hair was visible through the trees as the man fled. His head was no longer shaved as it had been in the past. His clothing was different as well. He wore a red doublet and white hose.

The sight of his prey made Hector run even faster. A short spear buried itself in the earth beside his feet as he ran. The cardinal's guard turned around in time to see a man with ashen skin and black leather armor leaping down at him from the trees. His head was clean-shaven and a blue, swirling pattern was tattooed up the right side of his face. He carried a small, curved shield in one hand and a thin saber in the other.

Hector parried the sword just in time. With his offhand, he delivered an uppercut to his enemy's stomach which flipped the assassin upside down and sent him flying through the air.

Another man identical to the first emerged from the trees. The only differences were that the second man carried crescent shaped blades attached to a long chain and his tattoo was on the left side of his face. He swung the chain slowly over his head as he advanced.

"Kill him," Salvatore yelled triumphantly from deeper in the forest! Hector held his sword low in one hand and waited. He was forced to divide his attention between the two assassins. "Those are Vincente's best warriors Hector," Salvatore taunted. "You're going to die a failure. Eustachius will soon follow. I know you can hear me Hector!"

Hector did not answer. Vincente's assassins grinned like fanged jackals as they made a wide circle around the cardinal's guard. As he looked from one enemy to the other, the one carrying the sword and shield disappeared. Hector quickly looked back to see that the other assassin had vanished as well.

Silence descended. Hector turned in slow circles, his eyes scanning the forest floor. After a few scant seconds, he saw a crescent shaped indent appear in the dirt to his left. Another appeared forward and to the right of the first. Hector averted his body so that his side was facing the approaching footsteps. At the last second, he lashed out with his sword. Hector swung the weapon in a broad arc toward the invisible foe. A thin line of blood appeared in the wake of the blade. The body of the sword wielding assassin shimmered into existence around the wound. He hunched over in pain as his blood worked to heal the deep wound in his stomach.

Hector lifted up his sword to finish the job and inadvertently parried the crescent shaped blade swinging toward his head. The chain wrapped several times around Hector sword before its wielder yanked back with all of his strength. The Architect failed to wrench the sword from Hector's powerful grasp, but he did force the cardinal's guard to face away from his injured twin.

Hector used his strong hand to grab hold of the chain while gripping his sword in the other. He ripped the chain from his assailant's hand and then whirled around to parry the sword strike which he intuitively knew would be coming. Predictably, the slash was aimed at his neck and not his heart which was protected by his breastplate. Steel rang on steel and echoed through the trees. Hector used his strength and the momentum of the parry to drive his enemy's sword to the ground.

The assassin managed to step back quickly enough to avoid losing his blade. However, because he was forced to stoop down to do so; the Architect's face became a target of opportunity for Hector's powerful right hook! Though the vampire's blood would allow him to heal, the force of the blow shattered his jaw and knocked him on his back.

Hector quickly took a knee as he whirled to face his other adversary. At the same time, he swung out with his sword at an upward angle. The other twin was now armed with a long dagger which he held high above his head. His offhand was held out to block whatever might come. His intent had been to paralyze Hector by burying the dagger in the warrior's skull. Unfortunately, his attack was ill-timed.

The two-handed sword cleaved diagonally through the assassin stomach. He fell to the forest floor in pieces with his stomach leaking blood out on top of his boots. With superhuman speed, Hector removed the chain from the base of his blade and picked up the long dagger in his right hand. The sword he wielded in his more powerful left.

"Time to die," Hector told the twin whose body was still whole. The older vampire snarled and sprang forward. Sparks flew from their weapons as the undead began to fight in earnest! The cardinal's guard fainted with his sword, bringing it up for an overhand strike that he pulled at the last second. The assassin stumbled to the left as he moved to block an attack that never came. The blade of the dagger flashed in the moonlight before being buried to the hilt in the Architect's chin. The tip of the blade punched out the top of his skull. Hector let go of the dagger and his enemy dropped to the earth. With both hands, Hector raised his sword and decapitated the tattooed vampire.

The cardinal's guard returned to the already defeated twin. This vampire's stomach and most of his pelvis had reformed during the battle. It was not enough. Hector quickly cut the man's head free of his shoulders and walked away from the rapidly deteriorating corpse.

"You cannot hide from me Salvatore," Hector called out. He swung his blade in a slow circle before choking up on the hilt with both hands. "Nowhere to run," Hector sneered as he scanned the trees. "You've run out of friends. It's time to reap your reward."

Hector sniffed the air as he came slowly forward. He thought he detected the smell of man off to his left and altered his course in that direction. A mild acidic smell joined the rest. Hector paused. A thin stream of liquid poured down over one of the trees roots and formed a tiny puddle. "Come on out," Hector said condescendingly. "You should not worry over much about wetting yourself.

Everything you have will be set free in death." A moan escaped Salvatore's lips as he realized he had been discovered.

The traitor took several steps out from the tree he had been hiding behind. One leg of his white hose was wet and beginning to stain. "Let me go," Salvatore begged. "You know that I cannot stand against you." His body was shivering with fright.

"You would have done well to consider that before Judas Iscariot," Hector admonished.

"I am unarmed," Salvatore said desperately! Hector laughed out loud.

"What would you do were you armed?" Hector took another step toward the traitor. Salvatore cringed. "Oh very well," Hector said with amusement. He tossed his sword to the ground at Salvatore's feet. "Do your worst," the elder vampire taunted! Salvatore's hands shook as he picked up the sword from the forest floor.

Hector's sword was much too big for the former priest. Salvatore's musculature was ill-suited to the rigors of war. Nevertheless, he picked it up in both hands and stood there trembling. "They did not give you the blood. Did they, Salvatore," Hector asked? His voice was dripping venom.

"Not yet," Salvatore said with injured pride.

"Take a firmer grip on that sword," Hector cautioned. "When I take it away from you, you will have waited too long." Salvatore began to cry wretchedly as Hector closed in. The cardinal's guard paused within arms distance of Salvatore. Eustachius' former thrall trembled.

"Here is your big chance," Hector said as he spread his arms out wide. In the next second, the vampire's larger hands were placed firmly over the top of Salvatore's. He stared into the traitor's eyes as he crushed his fingers against the hilt of the two-handed sword. Salvatore screamed in pain as one by one, the fingers of his hands were shattered by Hector's iron grip!

Hector's sword dropped to the ground when its owner let go. Salvatore's hands were a broken and bleeding mess. Hector moved quickly to place the thrall in a headlock. "Do you wish to open your mouth," the cardinal's guard snarled? He forced the fingers of one hand into Salvatore's mouth. The fingers of his other hand he jammed in as well so that his palms were facing in opposite directions.

Salvatore bit down with his teeth and broke through the skin of Hector's fingers. He could not hope to damage the vampire's bones, however. Hector was centuries-old. "Do you wish to open your mouth," the vampire asked again? Salvatore cried out in terror as Hector began to widen his jaw, ignoring the damage to his own fingers.

"Do you wish to open your mouth," the elder vampire roared? He broke Salvatore's jaw apart and ripped the top half of the man's head from the rest of his body! He growled ferociously as he tossed the grisly remnant to the ground. Hector fed greedily from Salvatore's gaping wound. He dropped the husk to the earth and then ran back toward the Chapel of the Cross.

Through the shattered remains of the church's front wall, Isabel could see the Architect army approaching. The sound of their boots moving in unison could be felt vibrating below her feet. The twenty or so men who were mounted road slowly behind the foot soldiers. Isabel kept expecting them to charge, but the Architects moved with the slow assurance of victory.

Infantrymen began to form in ranks over the demolished pews. The riders brought their horses to a halt behind them. One of them was a boy of perhaps seven years of age. He carried no weapons and looked around nervously at the mounted warriors who surrounded him. One of these warriors carried the lead rope to the young boy's mare in his hand. With the other, he removed his helmet and looked down at Eustachius with satisfaction.

This Architect was a tall and muscular man with Icelandic features. He had blond hair worn long down his back and a full beard which covered his neck. His blue eyes were sharp and reflected a calculating intellect. "You know why we have come," the blue-eyed man said.

"Vengeance," Eustachius answered.

"Vengeance," the man asked mirthfully? "Vincente is not nearly so passionate. We come for the artifact."

"You will not have it," the cardinal told him. "Go back to your master, Ulric."

"I have with me this young boy," Ulric grinned with a nod in the direction of the child. "How are you called boy?"

"I am called Luc," the boy answered with a thick French accent.

"Luc's father owes us a debt," Ulric said jovially. Luc here wants to do his part in order that we do not have to exact the price in blood. Is that not right, Luc?" Luc nodded his head vigorously. "Give me the Cross fragment Eustachius," said Ulric, "then perhaps I will allow you to flee into exile."

"You shall never take this most holy relic," the cardinal said angrily.

"You're resistance will end in death," Ulric chided. "All of your thralls are dead. Even your precious Hector del Toro cannot save you. I have already seen to that!"

"You are lying," the cardinal told him.

"Am I," Ulric asked? "Where is he? He should be by your side, now more than ever." The cardinal frowned. "Prepare to rush," Ulric screamed! As one, the infantrymen drew their swords. They held their shields out in front of them and hefted their blades up over their heads. "Stand aside," Ulric said menacingly! Isabel and Eustachius stood their ground. "Take the boy to the pulpit," Ulric instructed one of the other riders. "The fragment is hidden below the surface of it." The other vampire dismounted and then helped Luc down from his horse. Hand in hand, they walked up the center aisle.

Isabel held one hand in a halting motioned toward the Architect who was leading the boy toward them. "Do not tempt God's wrath," Isabel warned him. Ulric began to laugh.

"The last stand of Cardinal Eustachius and his misguided children," the enemy commander sneered. "Save your dramatic proclamations woman," he told Isabel. "My historians will only record how you groveled and begged for mercy."

Seeing that the vampire approaching her was perfectly aligned with one of the torches that burned on the wall behind her, Isabel unleashed the power of her blood upon him. She made a beckoning motion with her empty hand. There was a plunging sound in the air before the approaching vampire was catapulted over. Luc was knocked to the ground when the Architect lost his grip on the child's head. The vampire flew over Isabel and impaled himself on the iron spikes that stuck up from the torch sconce. His clothing began to catch fire and there was the smell of burning meat.

"Rush," Ulric screamed! The infantry charged forward with fangs barred and blades held high. Without a thought for her own safety, Isabel pulled the lever inside the pulpit to bring the artifact around to the top. She pulled the shaft of wood out through the iron housing which secured it to the pulpit. The artifact felt warm to the touch but it did not burn her.

"Stay back," she commanded! The vampires shied away. Some dropped their blades and others curled into a fetal position. They could not look at her. Eustachius staggered to his knees.

"Magdalena," her maker said confusedly; "what are you doing?"

"Destroy her," Ulric bellowed! With great effort, some of the infantrymen continued their advance. Several of the riders drew crossbows and began to knock bolts. Isabel would never be able to fully explain how she knew what to do; only that it was God's will.

Power coursed out from the holy artifact and infused every molecule of Isabel's being. Her body glowed like the sun as she held the fragment aloft. The Architects hissed and cried out as their flesh began to sizzle. "Oh Lord," Eustachius said reverently as his flesh began to peel away, "I am ready to come home. Forgive me my sins." His eyes could not turn away from Isabel.

"In the name of God," Isabel shouted. Her voice seemed to echo from everywhere at once. "Get thee back to Hell!" Fires erupted in the sanctuary is the bodies of the undead spontaneously combusted with holy flame!

"Retreat," Ulric shouted as fire blossomed up from his chest. The child fled the Chapel of the Cross, narrowly avoiding the burning corpses which howled in agony around him. Isabel looked down then at her maker. Eustachius knelt by the pulpit. His entire body was engulfed in flames. His now skeletal hands were clasped together in prayer.

"*End this,*" Eustachius spoke into her mind. "*Drive the cross into my heart. I am ready to see God!*"

"God is merciful," Isabel said as she walked toward him as if in a dream. It was her voice but not her words. She thrust the glowing fragment through the cardinal's fire-blackened rib cage and into his heart. The screams of the Architects filled the air around them. A blinding white light erupted from the artifact. Silence fell upon the ruined sanctuary as Isabel dropped to her knees. Images of Cardinal Eustachius' life flooded her mind.

Here was a bloody battlefield and his victory over the Goths in ancient Rome. Then came a broad shouldered man dressed in the garb of a Caesar. The Emperor commanded that Eustachius should celebrate his victory by giving thanks to the pagan deities of Rome. "Thou shalt have no other gods before me," Isabel heard herself saying in Eustachius' voice.

The next scene was one of horror. A massive bronze bull sat in a courtyard before a temple made of white marble. The bull appeared to sit on its haunches and its left side opened on hinges like a gigantic door. Its insides consisted of many different compartments. Some of these contained animals for sacrifice. One contained a grain offering. Another was filled with flagons of wine. One of the larger compartments contained the decapitated head and the corpse of a prisoner who had been beaten and mutilated beyond recognition. Priests stood by while soldiers forced a beautiful young woman and her five-year-old son into the largest of the compartments. There was blood covering the chins of these unfortunate victims from where the priests had recently removed their tongues.

Isabel/Eustachius screamed as the soldiers shut up his wife and son inside the bull. The priest closed the door in the side of the idol and then set fire to the wood piled beneath. Isabel could feel the cloth gag in her mouth as she screamed and thrashed uselessly against her shackles.

The next scene was a dark cavern far below the earth. Samael stood over her. "It was the only way to save you," the elder vampire explained. "Trajan is satisfied that you are dead." Isabel and her maker screamed in derision and then dissolved into weeping. Sister Magdalena then saw a red-hot iron held in Eustachius' grotesque fingers. They were also her fingers. She screamed as she drove the glowing metal into her one remaining eye. The other had been burnt out already. The pain was immeasurable.

When Isabel's vision cleared, she was alone in the burnt out ruin of the sanctuary. All that remained of the other vampires were weapons, armor, and piles of ash that had once been their bodies. She rose shakily to her feet. The fragment of the True Cross was still held in her right hand and the flesh of her fingers gave off a faint glow.

Isabel knelt down and wrapped the artifact in the fabric of Eustachius' robes. She carefully took the bundle in her arms and rose to her feet. Standing at the edge of the ruined sanctuary, Hector stared at the carnage in disbelief. "They are gone," Isabel said.

"The artifact," Hector asked?

"I have it here in our makers robe," she replied sadly. Ashes fell from the bundle as she held it out toward the cardinal's guard. In an instant, he was standing before her. Hector grimaced as he looked down at the bundle. Whether from sorrow, or from the power of the cross; it was hard for Isabel to determine.

"He is gone," Hector said mournfully as he backed away from the aura of the fragment. "How did he die?"

"I took up the cross to prevent the Architects from stealing it," Isabel told him. "They were all burned. Eustachius asked me to drive it through his heart."

"And then," Hector prodded?

"I did as he asked," Isabel answered as she wiped the blood tears from her cheek.

"May God have mercy upon him," Hector said reverently as he made the sign of the cross. "Surely this is a sign that there is mercy even for such as we." He sighed heavily and there was silence between them for a time. "We stay here tonight," Hector said finally. "We will leave as soon as the sun sets tomorrow."

"Where are we to go?"

"Constantinople," the elder vampire replied. "The fragment must be taken back to the Basilica Cistern. We must get there safely before the Architects can recover."

"As God wills it," Isabel replied.

"Let us retire," Hector said wearily.

"Why must I destroy everyone I love," Isabel asked in a very small voice?

"No tears," Hector said as he wiped the blood from her eyes. "Come." The cardinal's guard offered his arm. Sister Magdalena leaned upon him as he led her down into the crypt. Hector laid her down in her white marble coffin. There was the scraping of stone as he closed her in.

When the two vampires rose, they set to work releasing the prisoners. There was no need for communication between them. It was the just thing to do. Isabel felt stronger than ever she had before. Eustachius'

sacrifice had greatly increased the power of her blood and given her dominion over all that her Maker had possessed.

Hector and Isabel gathered up what coins they could find from the church coffers and used them to book passage to Byzantium. By day, Isabel dreamed of her maker. Once back in Constantinople, they traveled down into the Basilica Cistern. There was no bell or other device to alert the ferryman of their arrival. They were thus forced to wait by the heads of medusa until other members of the Convocation departed.

When the ferryman did come, he seemed more than eager to be rid of them. He took the two downriver to the docks of the underground cathedral and dropped them off without a word. Everyone shied away from the pair as they made their way down to the great sanctuary. Some even cried out in pain when they passed by. Hector's teeth were set on edge, but he bore the agony of the artifact stoically.

Initiates and elders alike quickly opened the way to Samael's throne. The other vampires moved quickly through the pews until they were all congregated at the edges of the sanctuary. Samael stood up from the throne as Isabel and her companion approached. "What is this that you bring into my house," the ancient vampire demanded?

"It is the shard of the True Cross," Hector said reverently. He motioned to Samael's feet and then knelt down before him. Isabel placed the bundle down where Hector had directed her and then knelt beside him.

"Rise up," Samael said with irritation. Isabel and Hector obeyed. "Where is my son," he asked?

"Alas," the great Cardinal Eustachius is no more," Hector replied sorrowfully. Samael sat down upon the throne. His face was filled with pain.

"What has befallen him," Samael asked?

"Tell his holiness what has come to pass," Hector told Isabel. As Sister Magdalena related the tale of Eustachius' demise, Samael's countenance became more and more hardened against her.

"Only ash remained," she said at the story's conclusion.

"You came all the way across the sea to deceive me," Samael asked bitterly? "Why?"

"I tell only truth," Isabel swore.

"You are a liar," Samael said loudly as he rose up from the throne. Isabel began to speak in her defense, but the elder would not listen. "He told me of your rebellion…you who claimed that God had chosen you for just such a purpose!"

"Your Holiness," Isabel began.

"Tell me what you did to my son," Samael shouted! "You seek to disregard the mandates of God! Did you think I would not find you out? What was it Sister Magdalena? Did war bring you an opportunity for freedom?"

"Cardinal Eustachius commanded me to do it," Isabel answered with indignation!

"It is impossible for our kind to touch the artifact," Samael hissed! "Do not think to fool me with your concocted grief. You hated him! He told me so. Now you shall pay for your lies."

"It was his decision," Isabel screamed up at Samael. "Eustachius sought atonement for the hundreds of sinners he sent to Hell in the name of God!"

"Step away from this woman," Samael told Hector, "lest you be consumed!" Hector walked up closer to the shelf of rock that Samael stood upon.

"Your blasphemy is unwelcome in this holy place," Samael said ominously once Hector had moved away from Isabel. "May God have mercy…"

"You are the heretic," Isabel shouted! There was a collective gasp from the vampires who were now gathered at the back of the sanctuary. "You and the church," Isabel seethed. "Instead of spreading the message of Christ, you pervert the gospel by delivering it on the tip of a hot iron!"

"Destroy her," Samael thundered! Hector drew the two handed sword from his back and raised it to strike.

"Not you Hector," Isabel said tremulously. "Do not do this evil."

"I do the Lord's work," Hector replied calmly. He struck down with the sword, but instead of aiming for Sister Magdalena's neck; He used the blade to sweep the bundle of Eustachius robes toward her. The fabric opened up as it rolled forward and the cross fragment spilled out onto the ground. Isabel reached out with her hand and the artifact leapt into her waiting fingers. Samael screamed and staggered back as his flesh began to hiss like meat on a spit!

"You are the blasphemer," Isabel said loudly as the white, glowing aura of the cross crept up her arm. The flesh on Hector's face and arms began to bubble as he dropped to his knees. A cry of agony escaped his lips. Isabel let go of the artifact, but kept it suspended in the air through the power of her blood. She beckoned with her hand and the robe of Eustachius flew up and wrapped tightly around the shard.

"Praise be to God," Hector said as his skin began to heal. Samael and the rest were slowly healing as well.

"Come to me," Isabel said to the dark skinned warrior. Hector was beside her in an instant. His sword was drawn and he held it protectively in front of her.

"You will leave the shard of the True Cross here," Samael commanded.

"Do not tempt God's wrath," Hector replied fearlessly. "Can you all not see that Sister Magdalena has been chosen?"

"Stop them," Samael shouted, but none of the Convocation lifted a hand to obey. It was just the opposite as the rest of the vampires cowered along the walls of the sanctuary.

"Even you cannot stand against the power of the one God," Hector said as he and Isabel backed toward the exit. His eyes shone with zeal. Samael looked hatefully down upon them.

"You will pay for Eustachius," he told them. "I know not what powers you call upon Magdalena, but they come not from Christ. We are not fooled!"

"We go," Isabel said as they moved out through the double doors.

"God goes with us," Hector declared! He then grasped the stone doors which stood open before the statues of the fallen and slammed them shut with all his might! Cracks appeared in the surfaces of the doors as they crashed together. Hector grabbed Sister Magdalena up in both arms and fled. He carried her all the way out of the underground cathedral and the Basilica Cistern. There was no need to wait for the ferryman. Hector's feet flew over the surface of the water as he rushed Isabel far away from her enemies.

Hector was forced to stop in the forest surrounding the city of Constantinople. He was faint and leaned upon an oak tree for support. "You need blood," Isabel said. "Take mine." She held out her slender wrist. Hector dropped to one knee and accepted her offering. Isabel grimaced as her savior bit deeply into her wrist. The sensation became intensely pleasurable and she nearly swooned before Hector released her.

The wound in Isabel's wrist closed quickly. Hector gazed up at her with reverent adoration. There was a thin line of her blood still on his lips. "Tell me what to do," he said.

"Stand up," Isabel said. "I am the same as you." Hector used an oak tree to help himself to his feet.

"I will follow you to the ends of the Earth," Hector vowed. "No harm shall ever come to you."

"Thank you Hector," Isabel smiled. "I am honored."

"Where will we go," he asked?

"Home," Isabel replied. "I wish to go home."

CHAPTER VII

Hector, (it seemed), was a man of many resources. Sister Magdalena and her new protector journeyed out of Constantinople on a smuggler's ship. It was not an ocean-going vessel. They traveled along the coast until they reached the rivers that would carry them into inland Spain. They sailed up the Ebro by moonlight and came to the docks of Zaragoza as the great white orb reached its zenith.

In order to avoid notice from the Convocation of Saints, the vampires avoided the Basilica del Pilar altogether and traveled on foot to the Summer Cottage of Lord Vasquez. The servants regarded them with less suspicion once Isabel explained her lineage. A few of them recognized her, but even they sensed on some level that she had changed.

Isabel sent a letter to the Crown of Aragon that very night. She outlined her intent to retake possession of Montenegro. In the letter, she promised that after a year's time she would deliver three stallions to the crown. This was the tax agreed upon during her father's time. Several days later, a reply was delivered.

To Lady Isabel of Montenegro...

I expected never to hear from you again. The death of my son haunts me to this day and your letter made it seem as though he had just died. Words cannot express my grief.

In regards to your petition; I am sure that King Alfonso would be delighted to receive horses trained in Montenegro once more. However, we must first see whether or not you can restore it. Lord Barillos was a poor replacement for your father. Your childhood home changed hands several times due to border disputes. The damage done to Montenegro eventually became so great that another fortress was built to the north at La Vista Cascada. Most of the mountain people flocked to it. Montenegro is now home to but a few farmers and goat herders. There is little else. I hope that at last we can be reconciled. I loved Ramon as you did. What was Montenegro is yours. May God be with you and bestow his blessings upon you.

Petronilla
Queen Mother to the Crown of Aragon

"Give her majesty the queen mother my most sincere thanks," Isabel told the young man who had delivered Petronilla's message. The next evening, Isabel and her protector departed from the Summer Cottage and began the journey to Montenegro by carriage. It was not as well designed as Eustachius' carriage, but the windows could be secured after a fashion.

Isabel's plan had been to travel directly home. By the time she reached Huesca, however, hunger had one out. The driver of the carriage was one of Lord Vasquez' men. He waited with the horses while Isabel and Hector went in search of food. "We must be discreet," Hector cautioned. "I am certain that this feeding ground belongs to others."

"Nevertheless we must feed," Isabel told him.

"Agreed," the elder vampire replied. They walked down the main road of the city with its many inns, shops, and taverns. Most of the shops were closed for the night. As the two vampires searched for a likely vessel, providence provided them with one.

"God be with you Sister," a man's voice called out from a darkened alley. "Have you a coin or a crust of bread?" The voice was familiar and it set Isabel's teeth on edge. As one, the vampires change their course and walked quickly to the man who had asked for their charity. The flea bitten vagrant who sat wretchedly before them was dressed in filthy rags. His body was thin and malnourished and he stunk of sweat and urine.

The miserable looking man looked up imploringly at Isabel as she stood over him. Her pity turned quickly to a black hatred. Under the rags and layers of filth, this beggar was none other than Manuel Barillos. "You have seen better days," Isabel said flatly.

"It is true," Manuel said mournfully, "and if I told you how I once lived, you would never believe it."

"I might," Isabel replied. There was no recognition in Manuel's eyes. He was oblivious to the reunion.

"I was a Lord once," he said fretfully. "My fortunes are now gone and I sit here as the lowest of the low. Have you some coins or a small bit to eat?"

"I will do better than that," Isabel promised. If Manuel's mind were not so muddled with drink, he might have noticed the disturbing gleam in her eyes. "Let me help you up." She reached one hand down to Manuel and lifted him to his feet. Hector stood quietly behind her.

"You are strong," Manuel said with wide eyes once he had gained his feet. "Where are we going?"

"I shall take you to a place where you may eat your fill. It is a place designed for people like you. You will be fed. You will have a place to sleep away from the rain. All that you deserve will be given to you," Isabel promised.

"Praise God," Manuel said drunkenly! "Are there many people there?"

"No," Sister Magdalena replied, "but there shall be soon."

"Bless you Sister," Manuel exclaimed!

"God always rewards his children," Isabel said. Her eyes were cold as she led the man back to the carriage.

"Who is this man," Hector asked as he helped Barillos up into the carriage?

"He is to be our first penitent," Isabel told him with feigned happiness.

"I see," Hector said with sudden understanding.

"What is a penitent," Manuel asked as the vampires got into the carriage after him?

"What is it," Isabel asked as if she did not know?

"I do not know," Manuel said with irritation. "Do you have something to eat?"

"When we arrive you will be fed immediately," she promised. Manuel brightened up again at the prospect of food and then promptly went to sleep. His mouth dropped open and he began to snore. His flesh reeked of alcohol beneath his clothing.

"Disgusting," Isabel spat!

"You know this man," Hector asked?

"I do."

"I surmised as much,"

"What made you certain," Isabel asked?

"Begging is not something which requires atonement," Hector replied.

"His sins are many," Isabel said as she picked up the wretched man's arm. "I will explain it to you later." She bit into Manuel's wrist and took a small amount of blood. Hector took the opposite arm and did likewise. By periodically draining the man of vitae, the vampires kept Barillos unconscious for most of the journey. Having absorbed Eustachius' Dominion over Light through the power of the cross fragment, Isabel was able to conjure any illusion that her mind could /dream up. Manuel's homecoming would therefore be a memorable event.

There were still several hours left before sunrise when the carriage made its way to the mountain path to Isabel's childhood home. The walls of Montenegro's keep were damaged. Some parts were missing entirely, leaving nothing behind but jagged cracks through which one could see the deserted fortress of her father. The drawbridge lay open to any who would enter.

Crossing over the bridge, the carriage came to a halt inside the courtyard. Hector helped Isabel down. The battlements of Montenegro's keep were crumbling and overgrown with ivy. One of the two main doors leading into the keep itself had been broken halfway off its hinges. Manuel looked around in confusion as he prepared to come down from the carriage. "I know this place," he said slowly.

"Do you," Isabel asked? She grabbed the man by his collar and drove him down to the weed choked grass of the practice yard. Manuel's bones jarred as he fell to the hard earth below. "You should know it," she said as he spit dirt and bits of grass from his mouth, "for you are the cause of its ruin!"

"Why did you bring me here," Manuel asks nervously as he started to rise?

"Hand me your whip," Isabel told the driver. The young man looked nervously back and forth between her and the cowering man at her feet. "Now driver," she said forcefully! The man reluctantly obeyed.

"I am only a poor beggar," Manuel beseeched her. "Will you not let me go?"

"Get inside," Isabel said threateningly as she uncoiled the horse whip.

"What is this place," Manuel asked? Fear crept into his voice as he spoke.

"Montenegro," Isabel replied.

"I did what I thought was best," Manuel said. "I have already been stripped of title. Is this not enough?"

"Not by far," Isabel answered him from between clenched teeth. "Now get inside!"

"I must be going," Manuel decided. He began to turn toward the gate. In that instant, Sister Magdalena cracked the whip and left thick red welts across the man's neck. He cried out in pain and lifted one hand reflexively up toward the wound. Before Manuel could protest, the whip struck again. This time it left a thin line of blood running diagonally across the back of his hand.

"Get inside," Isabel screamed as she whipped Manuel mercilessly across the courtyard! He cried out for mercy but there was none to be had. As he climbed up the few steps that led to the main doors, the sting of the lash hit his left leg behind the kneecap and ripped out a line of flesh. Manuel stumbled down onto the stairs, nearly hitting his head as he did so. "Move," Isabel shouted! Before the fallen Lord could fully stand up, Isabel rushed forward and kicked him as hard as she dared in the chin. Barillos flew back and hit the door before collapsing to the ground. He lost consciousness while she looked contemptuously down at him.

† † †

Barillos woke up in darkness. The air was thick with humidity and his muscles were sore from lying on the damp stones. He cried out when he tried to roll over. The movement of his body broke several of the scabs on his back from the nun's whip. There was surely something familiar about this cruel woman, but he could not place it.

Moonlight streamed in from the four openings in the walls of the chamber. With great effort, Manuel lifted himself to a sitting position. He could see that there were three other cells in the prison tower other than his own. Rats skittered about in the darkness. Many of these vermin were feasting on the corpse of one of their dead brothers. Manuel could hear them chewing.

Manuel waited in terrified silence until the rise of the sun. Even then, the rats did not leave. Montenegro's Keep had been uninhabited for so long that the beasts had become emboldened. The sun rose and fell before anyone came to check on him. The majority of this time he spent trying to ascertain why he had been captured in the first place.

The gambling debts of Lord Barillos were considerable, but the Crown of Aragon had paid them when they stripped his title and gave Montenegro to Lord Jardin. Jardin had died in battle with the French. Montenegro had always been in question as far as which nation held sovereignty over it. The only reason it had remained under the Crown of Aragon for so long was because of the reputation of its former Lord. Rafael would never have let Montenegro fall. Manuel had no contention with the Holy Church. He wondered then why he was so hated by the nun and her stoic companion. He could not guess what they wanted from him.

After the setting of the sun, the door to the prison tower opened and the nun entered. She did not speak as she came closer to him, only looked down with eyes that were filled with a dark rage. A key ring rested over her left wrist like a bracelet. "Peace be with you sister," Manuel said when the silence became too oppressive.

"But not with you," the woman answered hatefully. She stared critically at Manuel for a time before speaking. "Stand up," she commanded. Manuel let out a whimper as he struggled to obey. Some of the scabs on his back reopened once more and his body was horribly sore from the stones.

"I cannot," Manuel whined as he held one hand to his lower back.

"If you do not stand now," the nun told him; "I will ensure that you will never do so again."

"Please," Manuel said. "I will rise." Though his body revolted against him, he managed to crawl over to the iron bars of his cell and pull himself up.

"It is time to eat," the nun said, placing emphasis on the last word.

"I am hungry," Barillos said hopefully. "Please sister, will you first tell me why I am being held in this place?"

"Montenegro," the woman clarified.

"This is Montenegro," Manuel said fearfully. "Why have I been brought here?"

"Eat first," the woman replied evasively. "It will become more and more clear to you as time passes." The nun followed Manuel down the stairs to the private dining hall. There was no need for her to give directions. Thick layers of dust collected on the table and the few chairs which remained. Most had already been looted.

"Sit you down," the nun commanded. She pointed at one of the chairs with a slender finger. Manuel was unsure whether the deranged woman would feed him or strike. Nevertheless, he sat. "When I have finished," the woman began. She paused abruptly as Manuel turned his head back toward her. A hard slap across the face sent his gaze quickly back to the table. "Do not look upon me you cretin," the nun hissed!

"I... I am sorry," Manuel replied nervously.

"When I have finished eating," the woman said again, "then will food be brought out for you." Her voice became louder as she bent down over his shoulder. Manuel's heart was beating hard in his chest as he forced himself not to look upon her. There was a flash of teeth in his peripheral vision before the woman bit deeply into the side of his neck.

Manuel cried out in surprise and fear, but his voice quickly subsided as the draining of blood took all his consciousness from him. The last thing he felt was the nun's fingertips pushing slightly on his temples. In the next instant, (it seemed), Lord Barillos was restored to his former glory. He wore a coat of brown velvet and his fingers sparkled with jewels. A great feast of roast pork had been spread out before him. A suckling pig sat on a platter with its hindquarters already carved out. An apple had been placed into its jaws. There were other platters of potatoes and fresh vegetables, rounds of cheese, and a freshly baked loaf of bread that still gave off steam. A flag of wine had been placed before him and his glass was full to the brim beside it. Manuel ate heartily. Each bit of food was more delectable than the one before.

Manuel looked across the table and saw Lady Priscilla looking at him with adoration. Her beautiful hair hung in a thick coil down over one shoulder and her blue eyes glistened. She was the picture of grace and beauty. Seeing her so happily smitten with him brought a pang of regret. Lord Barillos looked away from his wife. He saw that there was a strange figure sitting toward the center of the table. That chair had generally been used by Priscilla's daughter, Isabel. The woman who sat there, however, was dressed in the black and white habit of a nun. The shadows seemed to deepen around her as he looked on.

The nun pointed a finger at Lady Priscilla. Looking a second time at his former wife brought a much more macabre image. Priscilla's skin was rotting on her bones and had taken on an ashen grey cast. In her arms, the dead

Priscilla carried the corpse of an infant which was still attached somewhere below by a slimy umbilical cord.

Lord Barillos cried out in terror as the dead woman mashed the unresponsive corpse of her son against her decaying bosom. Manuel had stopped chewing his food which now tasted like revolting sludge. He gagged and coughed up what was in his mouth onto the plate before him.

On top of Lord Barillos plate was a rotten slab of meat which teemed with larvae. The maggots gorged themselves on the pork. They were not concerned when Manuel spit the mushy remains of their brothers on top of them. This realization made Manuel vomit. When he was finished retching, he smelled the thick aroma. He saw with rising disgust that the maggots were squirming about in his bile. The contents of the fallen lord's stomach disgorged once more, and he dry heaved over the plate when there was nothing more to give.

The nun had stood up from the table and was now walking down toward Lord Barillos without a hint of concern. Manuel looked up. "I have no money," he said desperately. "There is nothing to give you. I am sorry for whatever wrong I have caused."

"You say that as if it actually matters," Isabel said without sympathy. That was when Manuel recognized her at last. Isabel was quite a bit older now that six years had passed. Her cruel blue eyes seemed oldest of all. "Say it again if you like," she taunted him, "for I shall feel no regret over the horrors which I will surely inflict upon you!" She opened her mouth to laugh. Manuel cringed as he saw her sharp canines lowering down from the gums. "First, you'll promise anything if only to survive. Perhaps you will even dream of escape, but I... I will make you pray for death in the end!" Manuel began to weep as his hopes of gaining sympathy were extinguished. Isabel continued laughing at him. "Save your pathetic tears," she told him. "You have not yet begun to feel pain!"

† † †

Manuel awakened to find himself back inside the prison tower. He had been tied firmly to a chair with thick ropes which allowed him only the tiniest fraction of movement. He suspected that this chair was the same one he had occupied in the private dining hall. Manuel could only move his head and his fingers without impediment. His wrists were bound to the armrests of the chair. The rest of his body was lashed to the wood all the way down to his ankles.

The vampire Isabel emerged from the shadows of the tower's only exit. The white scapula of her habit reflected the moonlight. The cloth seemed to glow as she drew near to Barillos' cell. In her hand, she carried a well sharpened steak knife. Manuel could see his fear stricken eyes briefly reflected on the blade.

Sister Magdalena slowly removed the key ring from her wrist and stuck one of the keys into the lock of Manuel's prison cell. Her feet did not seem to move at all as she glided in toward him. "I am going to give you a list of names," she said. Her voice was almost soothing. "You are going to tell me where I can find the people they belong to."

"Why should I help you," Manuel asked with reservation?

"Do you honestly believe that you have a choice," the woman returned? Manuel shook his head but said nothing. "There is always a choice though, isn't there?" The nun smiled as she scraped the serrated edge of the knife along the flesh of her thumb. "It is quite sharp," she informed him. Manuel shifted nervously in his seat.

"Hold out your smallest finger," Sister Magdalena requested. Convincing himself that this would satisfy Isabel's vengeance, Manuel quickly pointed the pinky finger of his right hand outward. His hand was shaking. The nuns hand shot out like an adder and closed firmly around his outstretched finger. Her head snapped up quickly to look at him with those eyes that were both familiar and terrible.

"Do not hurt me," Manuel pleaded as the nun lifted up the knife and pointed the blade toward his finger. He tried to shake her grasp but it was impossible. Her grip was stronger than that of any man. She smiled sweetly.

"Where is Master Cruz," she asked him?

"I do not... I do not know where he is." Isabel tightened her grip on Manuel's finger and carefully inserted the knife below the fingernail. Barillos cried out as blood welled up from beneath the nail. Sister Magdalena shoved the knife in farther until the point of the blade pierced through the flesh at the back of the nail bed. She applied a slow pressure until the tip had extended a bit farther beyond the back of the nail bed. "Stop, stop, stop..," Manuel kept saying.

"Where is he," she asked with an eerie calm?

"I do not know which Cruz you mean," Barillos said as his breath came fast and shallow.

"You know," Isabel disagreed. With that, she twisted the knife hard! The steel pressed down into Manuel's nail bed and ripped the fingernail free of its housing. Barillos screamed in pain as he looked down at the mutilated finger. This made him cry out again. "Where is Master Cruz," Isabel demanded?

"He lives on the east side of Huesca." Barillos said desperately.

"That's better," Isabel said approvingly. "Tell me exactly where."

"I'm trying to remember the way," Manuel replied cheerfully.

"Shall I rip off another," Isabel asked as she grabbed onto the index finger of the same hand that had already been worked upon?

"No... Please," Manuel said. "I just need time to remember."

"I shall give you until tomorrow evening," Isabel told him. "Be ready for my return." She let go of his finger and glared down at him as she wiped the bloody knife on the fabric of his soiled tunic. "Here are the other names," she said, "Lord Guillermo of Castile and Captain Lozano, formerly of Montenegro… and I expect that you will have the answers by the time we speak again."

"I will," Manuel nearly shouted! Isabel nodded and then left the prison cell. She shut the iron door with a loud clang and locked it with the keys on her wrist.

"Remember Manuel," the nun said menacingly; "there are many parts of the body one could live without. You would be wise to avoid this lesson." She did not look back or wait for a reply, but departed from the tower. The iron reinforced door shut loudly and then Manuel was alone.

Barillos spent the better part of the day reminding himself where those chosen by the vampire were to be found. He desperately wanted to believe that she might release him afterwards. Would she not want to extract her vengeance more upon those who had defiled her? He had never succeeded in doing that. His mind wanted to block out what Sister Magdalena had said about praying for death. He could not forget her words, however; nor could he forget her cold eyes.

By evening, Manuel's muscles were cramped and sore from his bonds. His head ached from hunger and dehydration. His stomach growled. His bloodied finger was tender and he could feel every shift of the breeze on the exposed wound. He drifted in and out of consciousness. Someone had lit the torches which rested in sconces by the door out of the tower. When his vengeful stepdaughter returned, she brought with her the scarred warrior from the previous night. The man carried with him a small table which he placed immediately outside Manuel's cell. Isabel carried a role of parchment, an ink vial, and a goose feather quill which she placed on the table.

The nun held out her hand to the warrior who drew out a dagger from its sheath. He placed the handle into her outstretched palm and then returned to the table. While the man rolled out the parchment and uncorked the vial of ink, Sister Magdalena unlocked the cell door and entered. She carried the dagger casually down by her side, but Manuel could not take his eyes from it. "Let me explain what is about to happen," she said. "I will ask questions. You will answer them without hesitation. If you are a good little traitor, then I will release you from your bonds. Do you understand?"

"Yes," Manuel said eagerly, "I will tell you whatever you wish to know Isabel!" In a flash, the nun grabbed his index finger and pushed the tip of Hector's dagger beneath the nail. Manuel cried out in pain. "I will tell you what you want," Manuel sobbed!

"Never let that name cross your lips again," Sister Magdalena said angrily! "Isabel is dead. Now only I remain."

"I beg your pardon," Manuel said. His voice was strained. "I will never...aaaagh!" Sister Magdalena turned the blade slowly and ripped the nail from Manuel's index finger.

"Good," she replied. "See that you do not." Manuel's hand shook and he moaned as his gaze fell down upon the freshly uncovered nail bed. "Tell Hector where to find Master Cruz. Be as detailed as possible, but speak slowly so that he may write it all down." Manuel told everything she asked for and then some. While he was speaking, the nun rolled the dagger absently back and forth across her palm. Barillos had to lose several more fingernails before he learned to pace himself with Hector's writing. He gave very specific instructions on how to reach the estates of both Master Cruz and Lord Guillermo. He further revealed that Captain Lozano, (now simply called Oscar Lozano), had taken a job at the Fox & Cat in Huesca. Master Cruz and Lord Guillermo were known to frequent the place, though visits from the latter were less common. The rest of Lord Barillos men were either dead or scattered to parts unknown.

By the time the interrogation had come to an end, Manuel had only three fingernails remaining on his left hand. The right had been stripped bare. His fingertips were tingling from the abuse. "Will you release me now," he asked tentatively?

"I will release you from your bonds as promised," Sister Magdalena agreed, "but there is one more thing that I must take from you."

"I have nothing else," Manuel said nervously.

"That is where you are wrong," the nun said darkly. "You have much more to lose than you think." Isabel went to the table and inspected what Hector had written. She nodded her approval and then spoke to the man. "Deliver these men to Montenegro," she commanded him.

"I obey," Hector vowed. Isabel put one hand on his arm as he reached for the parchment.

"The ink must dry," she said. "It will only be a little while."

"Of course," the warrior agreed. "I shall wait." Sister Magdalena nodded and then glided softly out of the tower.

"Help me kind sir," Manuel said once the heavy door had fully closed. Hector said nothing. He did not so much as look up to acknowledge that Barillos had spoken. "I really have nothing to give," Manuel pleaded. "Please let me go!" Hector did look up then, but his expression was one of disdain. He spoke to Barillos as if explaining something to a particularly dense child.

"Your time on this earth is drawing to a close," the scarred warrior said. "Death comes swiftly to he who repents."

"I do not understand," Manuel whined.

"Repent," Hector repeated. "I have nothing further to say unto you." There was silence between them. After a short time, Hector rolled up the notes he had written and left Barillos alone in the tower.

Several hours later, Sister Magdalena returned with an armload of firewood. She came and went, bringing several more bundles of woods and stacking them by the fireplace. When she entered the tower for the last time that night, the nun carried with her an iron handled battle ax with two curved steel blades. She set this also by the fire.

She stacked the wood over the iron grate before lighting up the torch from the wall by the exit door.

"Will you let me go sister," Manuel asked after the silence became too much for him to bear? By this time, the fire was blazing. The shadow of the nun shimmered on the wall opposite the fireplace. She placed the blade of the axe into the flames so that it was propped up by the grate. Isabel then turned back to face him.

"Would you let you go," she asked scornfully?

"I have nothing," he replied. He wanted to lie and say that he would let himself go were the roles reversed. He wanted to try and convince her to forgive as Christ would forgive, but the words would not come. He knew that she would not believe him. "I told you everything," he said after another uncomfortable silence.

"There," Isabel said. "Now it is ready." She pulled the twin bladed ax from the flaming logs and walked purposefully toward Manuel. Something in her eyes made his stomach feel weak. He felt a warm trickle running down his right leg. "This is going to hurt," Sister Magdalena said as she raised the axe heavenward.

"No, no," Manuel cried. "You said you would let me go!"

"You once claimed to be a master of deception," Isabel hissed. "It would appear that you have lost your touch." She swung down then with the heated blade. The axe cut through the lower part of Manuel's calf and into the chair leg behind it. There was the hiss of burning meat as the blade cauterized the wound. The vampire held the red-hot metal firmly against Manuel's stump until the work was completed. Barillos heard screaming, but his mind had become so detached from shock that he did not at first realize that the voice was his.

Sister Magdalena moved behind him. She used the axe blade to slice through the knots of rope that held him to the chair. The nun then grabbed the backing and dumped him onto the floor. Manuel cried out once more as his knees hit stone. He barely managed to catch himself in time to prevent his face from smashing on the unforgiving surface. The chair landed on top of him.

"Leave if you can," Isabel said acidly. Manuel tried to rise up, but the pain was too great and his cramped muscles were useless. "Pity," Sister Magdalena said as she lifted his severed foot up from the prison floor. "I guess you will have to remain here." She locked the cell door once more and departed from the tower. Manuel Barillos was left sobbing on the floor of his prison.

†   †   †

Hector departed from Montenegro the following evening. He had compelled Lord Vasquez' men to stay for a few days. This would give him time to travel to the neighboring town of La Vista Cascada. There he hoped to obtain his own carriage. His money was dwindling, however. Sister Magdalena's request had provided Hector with a solution to this problem. He would take what he needed from those unfortunate men whom she had marked for capture.

So it was that the elder vampire did not journey to La Vista Cascada as planned, but traveled south to Huesca. He departed the carriage about a short distance outside the city and walked in the rest of the way. Hector approached the Fox & Cat only an hour or so before midnight. The dim torchlight on the second floor veranda showed a well-dressed man with a lion mask being led into one of the rooms by an improperly dressed young woman. Even from this distance, the vampire's preternatural senses could detect the foul odor beneath her skirts which marked her as a harlot.

Hector wrinkled his nose in distaste and started toward the entrance. There was a hitching rail along the front side of the building. Wheel tracks in the alley beside the tavern suggested a carriage house behind it. "You won't be bringing that blade in," a crooked toothed man said as he put up his hand in a halting motion. His other hand was wrapped around the sword which hung at his waist. Hector recognized the man immediately from Sister Magdalena's description.

"I beg your pardon Master Lozano," Hector said politely, "but I cannot surrender my blade. I must be able to defend myself."

"No weapons in here," Lozano began. He paused abruptly. "How is it that you know my name?" There was suspicion creasing the crooked toothed man's brow.

"I am a friend to Lord Guillermo of Castile," Hector lied. "He speaks very highly of you."

"He knows my name," Lozano said aghast?

"To be sure," Hector replied smoothly. "Is he here, I wonder?"

"Sadly no," Lozano said genuinely. "He only just left a fortnight ago."

"What a shame," Hector said with feigned disappointment. "Now I will have to journey all the way to Castile alone."

"What a pity," Lozano sympathized.

"Does your master have rooms to spare? My trip has been quite taxing."

"Where do you come from?"

"I am here from Rome," Hector replied. Lozano looked critically at the surcoat which marked the vampire as an agent of the church.

"I do not think this is the sort of place that the pope would approve of Sir," Lozano grinned.

"I am not a man of the cloth," Hector replied. "My guess is that you have food, drink, and whores, no?"

"We surely do," Lozano grinned.

"That sounds like exactly what I need," Hector said. "Come in sir."

"Hector," the elder vampire said.

"I do have to take that blade though my good man," Lozano said apologetically. "House rules."

"Master Lozano," Hector said. "I do not wish to disrespect you or your master at his own brothel.

Unfortunately, I have something of great importance for Lord Guillermo. I am under strict orders not to do what you are asking. But pray; tell me at what hour the Fox and Cat closes. I will return then to avoid any upset amongst your patrons.

"We close by the hour of midnight," Lozano said, "but I will have to ask Mateo still."

"Thank you my good man."

"Do not thank me yet," Lozano said. "I wish there was some way I could help you further."

"Actually there is," Hector answered. "Is Master Cruz here this evening? I have something for him also."

"You are from Rome," Lozano asked with amazement?

"Of course," Hector replied with his hands held out. "Is he inside?"

"I'll check for you," Lozano offered.

"You're a good man Sir," Hector said appreciatively.

In a few moments Lozano returned. "I did not think that he was here but I had to make sure. Do you know his estate?"

"I do," Hector smiled. It amused him how truly stupid mankind could be. What they would not do for a little respect, even if it were feigned.

"If you will wait, I could ask Mateo to let you in the back way," Lozano offered.

"I must speak with Master Cruz now," Hector said, "but I will check back with you when we are concluded."

"Very good," Lozano agreed.

"Farewell," Hector said with one hand raised.

"See you later," the crooked toothed man replied. Hector traveled some distance up the Main Street before pausing. He stood beside a lantern that hung from a wooden sign over the door to an inn. He read over the instructions which would lead him to Master Cruz' dwelling and then returned the parchment to its case. He set off in a generally eastward direction. The elder was eager to quench his thirst.

CHAPTER VIII

As Hector approached the estate of Master Cruz, he could see that there were few lights burning within. It was a massive structure of mahogany colored stone which could be seen across an enormous courtyard of manicured lawns and shrubs that had been formed into perfect circles. The shrubs lined the path up to the house and the side path which led to the carriage house. There were two guards stationed at either side of the main door. Torches burned on the outside wall behind them. These men were protected by leather armor and they carried long spears.

In days past, Hector would have simply carved a path to his target and destroyed anyone foolish enough to get in his way. After choosing to follow Sister Magdalena, however, he would not be able to take such direct methods. Sending sinners to hell, she said, was only serving the Devil. Thus, the elder vampire would have to rely on his wits and charm which had remained largely unused and dulled over the centuries as his power made them unnecessary. He hoped that these men would be as foolish as Lozano at the Fox and Cat, but it was a dim hope.

He passed the low wall built of stones that surrounded the estate and started up the path. The Cruz estate was four stories tall and had pointed roofs. The east wing was only two stories high and had a staircase going to the second floor from the outside. A small foyer was at the top of the stairs and torchlight burned from within its one small window. The door was located in a recessed alcove blocked from Hector's view. He did note the spear tip which stuck out at a slight angle from the alcove. There was at least one guard at this entrance. Underneath the stairs was an enclosed walkway with a door which led to the ground floor of the east wing. Hector did not see any men therein. Perhaps the entrance was guarded by the two men at the main door. There was no way to be sure. The only other lights in the dwelling came from the top floor. Surely this was where Hector would find the next penitent.

The guards at the door stiffened up as Hector approached them. They looked at him with wary eyes as he stopped just beyond the reach of their weapons. "It is late," one of the guardsmen said roughly. "What brings you here?"

"I have an urgent message from Lord Guillermo of Castile," Hector replied.

"Give me the message," the guardsman replied, "and I will deliver it."

"I cannot give it to you Sir," Hector answered. "It is here," he explained as he tapped a finger on the side of his head.

"Tell us what it is," the guardsman prodded as one of his brothers came out of the enclosed walkway below the stairs. Hector could see the second floor guard peering down over the railing as well.

"I was told that it was for the ears of Master Cruz and none other," Hector said firmly. The guard sighed.

"Go and tell Master Cruz that there is a messenger here from Lord Guillermo," the guard shouted up to the man on the second floor.

"I shall return," the other man called down. The first guard nodded as the other went inside. After some time, he returned to the top of the stairway. "Master Cruz will see now," he reported.

"You will have to leave the sword with us," the first guard said. Hector noticed that the man's voice had dropped several octaves to sound deeper. Hector stared the man in the eyes for several seconds. He could see the fear behind the stoic mask the guardsman was trying to project. The vampire reached his hand up to the sword hilt sticking out above his shoulder. He saw the humans' hands tightening on their spears.

"Easy," Hector said as he drew out the massive blade. He rested the point on the ground and offered the handle toward the first guardsman. The man took the blade quickly. Hector watched as the tension drained from his face.

"Go ahead upstairs," the guardsman said. "Tomas will show you the way."

"Thank you," Hector said. He turned and walked to the foot of the stairs. The guard called Tomas waited as the elder vampire ascended the steps. Hector was led into a foyer with wooden benches lining the stone walls. The vaulted ceilings ended in log cabin style roofing with cherry wood cross beams running between. Having taken the lantern off the hook by the door, Tomas led Hector through the lavish estate to Master Cruz' sitting room.

The floors were almost completely covered by expensive Persian rugs throughout the dwelling. The room where Hector first saw his target was no exception. There was a large fireplace on the back wall of the chamber. The flames licked up toward an iron manifold which stuck out several feet from the wall to catch most of the smoke. There were several plush chairs and a couch covered with soft, chocolate brown velvet.

Master Cruz had parked his considerable girth on the couch. His rolls of fat were covered by a white night robe and he wore a soft white head covering that seemed more appropriate for a matronly woman. There were four servants in the room; a girl and three boys, none of whom could have been older than eight years of age. They were all dressed in white loin cloths and sandals. The girl had a white scarf wrapped around the place where she would one day have breasts. All had dark hair.

Two of the boys were tending the fire. The girl was pouring a cup of hot tea from a silver tea set positioned on a small table beside the couch. The smallest boy was crouching down between the legs of Master Cruz with his head resting on the rug merchant's meaty thigh. He stared up at Hector with a hollow expression beneath his dark brown eyes. The faces of the other children were haunted as well.

Hector stomach turned and his anger kindled hot as he detected another odor below the smell of burning logs. It was the smell of fornication which had occurred recently.

"Welcome," Master Cruz said as he stroked the small boy's hair. "Sit down and make yourself comfortable."

"Thank you," Hector said curtly. He seated himself in one of the chairs facing the couch. It took every ounce of the vampire's self-control not to tear the fat merchant apart.

"What news from Lord Guillermo," Master Cruz asked in his nasal voice? Hector had been worried over what he might say to the rug merchant in order to lure him from his estate. Now his path was clear. In his centuries beyond death, Hector had learned there was no man easier to manipulate than one with a dark obsession.

"Lord Guillermo has been invited to the convent of Saint Genevieve in France. He wishes for you to accompany him," Hector told the man.

"What business have we at the convent," Master Cruz asked in confusion?

"The nuns at this convent may be the brides of Christ," Hector grinned, "but they are quite adulterous."

"I can find prostitutes here in Huesca," Cruz said in a whiny voice. "Why should I journey all the way to France?"

"Because there are several of the nuns who have given birth," Hector explained, "and they are eager to be rid of their children."

"Really," Master Cruz asked eagerly? "Does that mean that these children are not supposed to exist?"

"That is why Lord Guillermo thought you would be interested," Hector agreed. "You can do whatever you like with them. Best of all, the convent will likely give them away for free!"

"Surely they want to make a profit," Master Cruz said with suspicion.

"They do," Hector agreed, "but Lord Guillermo suggests that they can be easily coerced. He only asks that you pay him for the find."

"That is more than generous," Cruz smiled as he took the cup of tea from his servant girl. "Would you like some tea?"

"I am not thirsty," Hector lied. "Let us meet here tomorrow at dark and we can be on our way."

"I cannot leave that soon," the fat merchant whined. "I have business to conduct."

"What a shame," Hector said. "The convent will surely give the children to one of the other buyers."

"Other buyers," Master Cruz asked plaintively?

"But of course," Hector replied. "A deal such as this is attractive to many men of your taste, as I'm sure you can imagine."

"I will be ready tomorrow," Master Cruz said quickly. He sighed heavily and shooed the boy out from between his legs. He stood up with effort and had to catch his breath from the exertion. Hector rose also.

"A wise choice," Hector complemented him.

"Why must we travel at night," Cruz wondered aloud?

"Some of the other buyers are aware of this invitation," Hector said. "We do not want to be noticed."

"Would they hire men to attack me," Cruz asked fearfully?

"They very well might," Hector said gravely, "but that is why Lord Guillermo chose me to deliver the message."

"Lord Guillermo never told me he had friends in the church," Master Cruz whined.

"We all have our secrets Master Cruz," Hector said with one eyebrow cocked toward the children.

"It is true," Cruz agreed. "I will be ready tomorrow at dark."

"Until then," Hector said. He bowed to the revolting man on the couch and was then led back out of the house where his weapon was returned to him. Hector returned to the Fox & Cat where Lozano was waiting for him.

"I hoped you would come back in enough time," the crooked toothed man grinned. "Go around back to the carriage house. I will send someone to let Master Mateo know that you are here."

"You are too kind," Hector said as he bowed slightly. He turned on his heel and walked swiftly into the alley beside the brothel. Turning around the back corner of the building brought the carriage house into view. It was little more than a crude shelter with a roof and three walls covering a dirt floor. Black lines had been painted on the back wall to help drivers steer their carriages into their proper place. There was space for the carriages and stalls for the horses at the rear of each parking space. The carriage house was well lit by torches and lanterns and guarded by several rough looking men.

Hector waited until Lozano arrived. The crooked toothed man came out of the back entrance to the brothel after a short time. "Follow me," he said in a stage whisper. Hector obeyed and soon they were going up a narrow stairwell that connected the brothel to the dirt yard in front of the carriage house.

Lozano let Hector up the back way into a small windowless bedroom where a young woman waited in her nightclothes. The elder vampire handed Lozano a sack with the last of his money inside. "Will that be sufficient," he asked? The crooked tooth man nodded after a cursory inspection of the sacks contents.

"More than enough," Lozano said greedily! Hector was sure that the man would pocket the difference before it ever reached Mateo.

"Give my thanks to your master," Hector says he closed the door. He turned back toward the bed and saw that there was a prostitute there waiting for him. She had dark hair and smooth skin that had been scented with oils. She flashed him a sly smile and gazed up into his eyes. She let her eyes fall suggestively to his crotch before looking back up.

"You have me all night," she told him. Hector looked hungrily down at the woman which she surely mistook for a different kind of arousal.

"Let us make the most of it," he said as he came forward.

"Shall I blow out the lantern?" she asked, motioning to the candle which burned inside its iron and glass housing.

"No need," Hector said. "Why don't you come up out of that bed so I can have a look at you?"

"You want to see," the woman asked in a husky voice? She pushed her legs out and her feet fell down onto the wooden floor. She thrust her bosom up at him and rubbed her hands over the fabric covering her breasts. Hector could see her dark areola through the thin white fabric, but it was the vein on the side of her smooth neck that he was most interested in.

"Turn around," he told her.

"You want to untie the straps," she asked as she moved her hair aside?

"Indeed I do," Hector said as he rapidly closed the distance between them. He placed his hands upon her shoulders and pulled her close. The prostitute shoved her hips back into his crotch a split second before he tightened his grip and bit deeply into the side of her neck.

"Yes," the young woman sighed! One of the effects of the kiss was to produce ecstasy in mortals and vampire alike. It took very little time for Hector to drain her blood. He closed up the wound and then dropped her unceremoniously upon the bed. As he stripped off the woman's clothing to make himself seem more believable, Hector noticed how still she was lying there.

"Damn," Hector cursed as he felt the woman's neck for a heartbeat. This was a fine mess he had created. He still had no idea how he would convince Lozano to leave Huesca with him. Now there was a dead whore in his bed. His starvation on the journey from Montenegro lowered his ability to restrain himself. Hector looked down on the bed and the woman who lay dead upon it. He said a brief prayer for her soul and made the sign of the cross. He sighed heavily as he opened his eyes at the prayers conclusion.

Rising up from the floor, Hector pushed the bed across the room until it was completely blocking the door. He locked it as an added measure. Taking his sword from its scabbard, the vampire sat against the wall by the bed. He did not need to be comfortable. The sleep of the dead would overtake him as surely as the rising of the sun each morning.

The vampire awakened sometime later to sound of Lozano pounding on the door. "Wake up Sir Hector," the man shouted from the other side. Hector's head felt like it was being crushed under a lead weight and his joints were stiff. The sun had not yet set.

"Leave me be," Hector growled!

"You should've been out by noon Sir," Lozano said sternly. "Those are the rules."

"I paid more than enough," Hector shouted back! His eyes locked on the thin triangle of sunlight that came through the crack at the bottom of the door. He knew that his fangs were lowered because he could feel them brushing against his bottom lip.

"Uhmm," Lozano said with hesitation. "Is Lucia in there with you? She will be needed soon."

"Take it out of the money you are concealing from Mateo," Hector snarled!

"Let's not get angry," Lozano said nervously.

"I have paid you more than enough," Hector said again. "If you wake us again, I shall have to take account with your master. Now be gone!"

"Sleep well," Lozano said. "I will come back for you Lucia."

"She sleeps as well you fool," Hector shouted! "Do not come back until dark. I have no patience for you."

"I beg your pardon," Lozano said. His voice was getting fainter. Hector took a deep breath. By the time he let it out, the vampire was slumbering again. He awakened alone the second time. The corpse in the bed was already starting to stink, but had yet to attract flies. Hector stared at the dead woman on the bed. He rose from his place against the wall. Using his unnatural strength, the vampire lifted the woman up by one leg and chopped it off. The body fell back down onto the sheets while he cut the severed leg in half at the knee.

There was no mess to clean up. The woman had been drained of blood to the last drop. Hector worked methodically; removing each limb, and then separating it into two parts. Lastly, he lifted what was left of Lucia by her hair and decapitated her with one powerful blow.

The vampire gathered up the pieces of Lucia's body in the blanket covering the bed. He ripped off a strip of the blanket and used it to tie up the makeshift sack. He left by the stairway leading down to the carriage house. The guards noted his departure but they did not seem to be alarmed over the sack he was carrying. Perhaps if they could have seen it in the light, things might have been different.

Hector moved quickly through the city to Master Cruz' estate. The portly merchant was already overseeing the men who loaded his trunks onto the rack atop his carriage. "There you are," Master Cruz called out when he saw Hector approaching. "I thought you would have been here sooner," he whined.

"I am here now," Hector said in order to dispel any conversation about what he had been doing. "The sack is fragile," he said. "I'm going to need a trunk for it." Master Cruz paused for a moment.

"You heard the man," he said rudely to one of his servants. The servant was already busy with other luggage. "Get Sir Hector a trunk… immediately!"

"Yes Master," the man said. He half bowed as he turned around to go back into the house. While the carriage was being loaded, Hector worried about loose ends. Mateo would surely miss his prostitute if she were not there to earn money for him. The vampire could not risk being pursued. If they came upon Hector by day, it could be the death of him.

As Master Cruz' guardsmen lashed the last of the trunks to the top of the carriage, an idea began to form. "We need to stop by the Fox & Cat on the way out," Hector said.

"It is already dark," Master Cruz complained.

"I know," Hector sighed, "but it is necessary. Mateo's guard, Oscar Lozano, will be accompanying us."

"The old captain," Cruz asked? What business does he...?"

"Protecting you," Hector interrupted. "Do not worry yourself," the vampire said before the man could reply. "I will pay for him."

"Alright," Master Cruz agreed. In little time, they were in the carriage and headed toward the brothel. Hector had packed the pieces of the prostitute himself to avoid notice. His plan was a gamble, but the reasoning was solid. He would tell the tale that he had accidentally been too rough with the woman. Mateo would want a considerable amount of money for his prostitute's death. Hector would agree to pay it. He would inform Mateo that he would have to get the coins from the Convent of Saint Genevieve. A man like Mateo would be wary of tricks. Hector hoped that the brothel owner would send someone along to keep them honest. Lozano would naturally volunteer because he had an interest in Hector keeping his mouth shut about his embezzling. The risk was that they might instead attack. God would surely not begrudge self-defense, but Hector wanted to avoid the attention of the city guard and anyone else who might pursue him by day.

As he stepped out of the carriage, Hector realized another error. He had brought Master Cruz to the brothel. If things went badly, Mateo's men and the guards of Huesca would have a clearly identifiable target. Master Cruz' carriage was marked with his family crest both on the side door and the rear wall. Instead of worrying over what he could not change, the vampire walked straight to the door of the brothel. He left his sword inside the carriage to avoid any additional confrontations. "I need to speak with your master," Hector said as he approached Lozano at the door.

"He wants to speak with you also," Lozano frowned. "Hand over your sword."

"I left it in the carriage," Hector explained.

"Follow me," Lozano said. As the two of them walked past the tables inside, more of Mateo's men fell in behind them. Some of the patrons stared as they passed by, but no one said a word. Mateo met Hector in the dirt yard behind the Fox & Cat. In this way, the three guards who were surrounding Hector would be bolstered by the men who guarded the carriage house. Hector noted several old stains in the dirt which could only be blood. Apparently Mateo had conducted business here before.

"Master Mateo," Hector said politely as they came together.

"Where is my Lucia," Mateo said icily?

"Things got a bit out of hand," Hector sighed. "That is why I have come back here tonight."

"What do you mean by out of hand?"

"She requested that I choke her," Hector lied. "Unfortunately, I did not stop in time."

"You killed Lucia," Mateo said with rising ire? "She has never asked me or anyone I know of…to choke her. Why would she ask you?"

"That I cannot answer," Hector replied truthfully. "Nevertheless, this is where we are. I have already disposed of the body."

"Did you come here to die," Mateo asked menacingly? "That is what it looks like to me!"

"You do not wish to start a war with the church," Hector replied calmly, "nor does the church wish anyone to know that I was here."

"So what," Mateo snarled? "I care not for the church. Put this fool out of my misery!"

"Not so fast," Hector said quickly as the men drew their swords. "The only way you're going to win out of this is to let me pay you. The prostitute is dead, but what was she to you?"

"She was a good whore…young…"

"My master will be more than generous," Hector interrupted the man. "I will simply go back to the Convent of Saint Genevieve and explain what happened. I can pay you for the money you will lose on my account."

"How do I know you'll come back," Mateo asked sarcastically?

"Send someone with me to make sure," Hector offered. "I will even let your man carry my sword."

"I am listening," Mateo said begrudgingly.

"Send one of your most trusted men with me," Hector suggested. "I will pay your man at the convent whereupon he may return."

"What about my satisfaction," Mateo asked threateningly?

"I doubt it would be worth more than the money you will receive for your silence," Hector replied. Neither man spoke for a time.

"Let me take him," Lozano said with disgust. "I will make sure that he pays in one way or another." Hector silently gave thanks to God.

"See to it," Mateo agreed. "Leave now," he told Hector. "If you cross us, my man here will skin you alive." Hector had to restrain himself. He wanted to laugh out loud. Here the mice were threatening the cat!

"I understand," Hector said solemnly when he had harnessed his amusement.

"Pack your things," Mateo told Lozano. Mateo and his men kept a watchful eye on Hector until the crooked toothed man was ready. The vampire led them out to Master Cruz' carriage where he surrendered his two-handed sword.

"All will be well," Hector promised Mateo as he climbed inside. Lozano followed him with sword in hand. The convenient thing about having Master Cruz along was that Lozano was denied the chance to speak freely. He could not risk Hector informing the fat merchant about the money he was hiding from his master.

The route they took to the fictitious Convent of Saint Genevieve would lead them up through the Pyrenees and then down into southern France. Master Cruz tried to initiate conversation several times, but to no avail. The other two men watched each other with distrust. The obese merchant eventually slept. The sound of his snoring filled the inside of the carriage.

At some point while Cruz was sleeping, the eyes of the two warriors locked upon one another. Hector could see the challenge in Lozano's stare. Lozano absently fondled Hector's sword and looked meaningfully back at the vampire. Despite his best attempts to conceal his mirth, Hector broke out into laughter. "Do you find something funny," Lozano asked angrily? This only made Hector laugh all the more. In a flash the crooked tooth man had raised his sword up with the point held at Hector's neck. "That's a question," Lozano said menacingly.

"You're planning to kill me anyway," Hector grinned. "Do you think that I am not aware of it?"

"You just get the money like Master Mateo said," Lozano said. "Perhaps then you can keep your life."

"I am dead already," Hector answered glibly.

"You just keep your promise," Lozano said as he lowered the blade.

"I think you should get some sleep," Hector said flatly.

"What kind of fool do you take me for," Lozano scoffed?

"The kind of fool who will soon be asleep," Hector returned. He focused his will to create a vacuum around the crooked toothed man's head. Lozano gasped as the air was quickly drawn out of his body. "Sleep well," Hector said with a toothy grin. Lozano thrashed about as the flesh of his face darkened from red to violet. His eyes bulged out and he opened his mouth desperately to inhale. In moments, Lozano slumped to the side of the carriage, whereupon Hector dispelled the vacuum around him.

Lozano began to breathe again and the color slowly returned to his face. "Stop the carriage," Hector shouted! Master Cruz snorted and let out a whine before lying back down on the cushions of his bench. Hector opened the door.

Wind blasted him and he could see the dark forest rushing by. "Stop the carriage," he shouted out to the man who sat on top.

"Whoa," the driver called out as he pulled in the reins. The horses slowed down and soon came to a stop.

"Why are we stopping," Master Cruz whined as he rubbed the sleep from his eyes? Hector invoked his Dominion over Air once more, creating a vacuum over the obese merchant's head. Cruz made grasping motions at his neck as his face darkened from the lack of oxygen. It was a short-lived struggle. Hector released the vacuum and stepped down out of the carriage. Master Cruz slumped down on top of Lozano who was unconscious as well.

"You had better get down here," Hector called out with alarm! The driver scrambled to obey.

"What is it," the driver asked nervously as he climbed down onto the moonlit road?

"Something is wrong with Master Cruz," Hector said nervously. As the driver went toward the door to investigate, Hector wrapped his broad arms around the smaller man's torso and squeezed tightly. The man cried out and put up a good deal of resistance, but he was no match for the elder vampire's strength. Hector bit into the driver's neck from behind! He held him there in a bear hug until the loss of blood rendered him unconscious.

Hector jumped effortlessly up to the top of the carriage. He used his dagger to cut the ropes that bound the trunks. He leapt back down to the ground and quickly grabbed Lozano from his seat. He slammed the crooked toothed man down onto the dirt road and hog tied him with the ropes from the rack. Lozano woke up from the impact of his fall, but Hector moved too quickly. There was no opportunity to resist.

While Lozano spit out a mouthful of dirt. Hector cut what was left of the rope and divided it into two lengths. With these he hogtied first the driver, and then Master Cruz. He slung the bound men back into the carriage like gunnysacks. Hector searched through the trunks until he found Master Cruz' money. This trunk he put in with the prisoners. Everything else was left just a little way into the trees from the road.

Hector shut the men inside before leaping back to the driver's bench on top of the carriage. Hector bent the winds to his will and caused them to blow hard against the back of the carriage. He drove the horses as if devil himself was chasing them!

They reached Montenegro with only seconds to spare before the rise of the sun. Hector dashed over to the gate and furiously worked the chain crank until the drawbridge was closed. He then fled into the private stables. The blanket of sunlight was spreading part way over the straw behind him. Without a second thought, Hector leapt down into the well and sunk far below the water. The sun would not reach him there.

CHAPTER IX

Over the time of Hector's absence, Sister Magdalena haunted Manuel's dreams. She forced him to relive his sins and flooded his mind with horrific visions. She took only enough blood to keep her thirst at bay. For the first three days, Manuel's diet consisted of river water. Once he was sick with hunger, Magdalena added rats. These vermin were skewered and cooked on a spit before being given to him. She neglected to remove their heads, which made the meals that much more grisly.

Even a skilled inquisitor would have trouble torturing a man for days on end without doing much bodily harm. However, Isabel tormented the man mainly in his dreams. This eliminated the need for physical healing.

The vampires had made their lair inside the cavern beyond the secret passage from the master bedroom. Here they would be safe from the sun even if someone were to disturb their rest. They hid their coffins back with Isabel's dowry chest. This chest was back among the stalagmites that rose up out of the cavern floor. Isabel had no way of knowing why the chest was back in the secret passage out of Montenegro, she could only assume that Pilar or her mother had hidden it there before death. Her mother's wedding dress was gone, but the chest yet contained the Biblia Sacra that her father had given her when she was young.

On the evening following Hector's return, Sister Magdalena could hear the hoarse cries for help coming from the stables. She replaced the wall panel and then shoved the huge bed back over it. As a vampire, she needed no assistance to accomplish this task.

Isabel walked down through the east tower and made her way out of the keep. "Help us," a whiny, nasal voice brayed from inside the carriage!

"Quiet down," another man's voice said. "You do not know who might be out there."

"Help," the nasal voice yelled before breaking into a fit of coughing! Isabel could not sense where Hector was hiding, but she knew by the voices that he had succeeded. There was a great splashing sound as the elder vampire launched himself up out of the well. Water drained down from his clothing and boots as he landed on the dirt floor of the private stables. Hector's knelt down and ejected the water that had filled his body. Isabel drew closer and waited. She now recognized the voice of Master Cruz from the carriage.

"Guillermo is in Castile," Hector said when he had regained his composure. "I must go."

"Tomorrow," Sister Magdalena replied. "Today, I shall need your help with the prisoners."

"Help," Master Cruz wailed!

"Be quiet," said the voice of the crooked toothed man. How the sound of these men made Isabel's flesh crawl!

"Help," the obese merchant screamed louder!

"Shall we help them," Isabel asked? Hector nodded and walked around the door of the carriage. He opened it quickly and began tossing out the prisoners. Lozano grunted as he hit the earth, but that was all. The second man winced in pain at the impact of the dirt. Master Cruz screamed loudly as he fell toward the floor and began crying after he had struck ground.

"Who is this other man," Isabel asked?

"Master Cruz' driver," Hector explained apologetically. "I could not simply let him go."

"Take the money," Master Cruz blubbered from the floor. "Just let me go!"

"Where is it," Isabel asked?

"It is the mahogany chest with the steel bars on top of the rack," the obese man panted. Hector crawled quickly up onto the carriage and snapped the rope which held the one remaining trunk in place. He tossed it down and it landed heavily next to the fat man's terrified face. Master Cruz screamed in surprise but quickly bridled his tongue.

Hector located the key inside a pouch which hung from the fat man's belt. He carried it over to the chest and fitted it into the lock. "There is a small fortune here," Hector reported when he had opened the lid.

"Excellent," Isabel said approvingly. "We can use some of it to buy food for these miserable creatures."

"For the love of God sister," Master Cruz sobbed; "let us go. We only wanted to buy the children."

"What children," Isabel asked as her eyes narrowed?

"You know," Master Cruz wheezed, "the nuns' children. The ones you wish to be rid of." A sick feeling washed over Isabel as she remembered the children who had died in the Convent of the Angels. She regained her composure quickly, however.

"I had to tell them something which would entice them to leave Huesca," Hector explained. "This fat pig defiles children," he said with disgust. "That is why he has agreed to come here."

"I see," Isabel said with revulsion.

"Some of his child slaves were no more than eight years of age," Hector said. "The one boy could not have been over six."

"You do not understand," Cruz whined! "I wasn't hurting anyone."

"I saw their dead eyes," Hector told Sister Magdalena. "Salvation seems hardly possible for one such as he. Killing him would be a service to mankind."

"No; do not let him kill me," Master Cruz pleaded.

"That would be a mercy," Isabel said wryly, "but the time for mercy is at an end."

"Where in hell is this place," Lozano thought aloud?

"Right outside the door," Isabel answered meaningfully. There was silence for several minutes before she spoke again. "Imprison them," she told Hector. The elder vampire picked up the crooked toothed man and the driver by the ropes that bound their wrists to their ankles. Lozano grit his teeth and growled as his limbs were stretched. The driver cried out in pain as Hector hauled the two of them out of the stables and up to the tower.

"Did you come for the children," Isabel asked as she glided closer to the place where the obese man was hogtied? Master Cruz was sobbing wretchedly and could not articulate a reply. Isabel knelt down and placed her index finger is on the weeping man's temples.

The journey into Master Cruz' soul revealed horrors that would forever be etched into Isabel's mind. She saw the weeping faces of the children whom the obese man had defiled. She could feel how their sobbing filled the man with a perverse excitement. The images which she saw of Master Cruz' memories were so revolting that she could not remain within his spirit.

When Sister Magdalena returned to the Land of Flesh, she could see several drops of blood inside Master Cruz' hair. She reached a hand up to her face and discovered that she had been crying. The bound man was still sobbing and begging to be released. Isabel was deaf to his tears. She shook with rage as she rose to her feet. The abomination which this man had forced upon her was mild by comparison to the things he had done to small children.

Sister Magdalena levitated up into the air and then glided over to the tack wall of her father's private stables. The expensive things had long since been taken by looters, but there was still a few items remaining. She selected a small, curved horse pick that hung from the wall. The point of it had been dulled from use, and there was still a thin line of black crust on the tip.

Isabel slowly descended down to the stable floor. Her body turned around to face Master Cruz as she did so. The mere sight of him filled her heart with rage. "God give me the strength to preserve the wicked," she said as her feet touched ground. She knelt down before Master Cruz once more. "How could you hurt innocent children," she demanded?

"Please let me go," the fat merchant said with terror filled eyes.

"I want my mommy," Isabel said in the voice of a young boy that she had gleaned from her invasion of the man's soul. "I want to go home!"

"No," Cruz wailed in horror!

"Yes," Isabel replied in her own voice. "The Lord said; *whatsoever you have done to the least of these my children, you have done it unto me.*" Master Cruz moaned as the tears fell down from his squinty eyes. "You have been blind to their suffering," she said as she gently stroked the blubbering man's hair with one slender hand.

"Do not kill me," he begged her.

"God will open your eyes," she promised. Isabel let her fingers brush down from the man's hair to his face.

"My eyes are open," Master Cruz insisted! "Praise Jesus!"

"Praise Jesus," Isabel said soothingly. She pinched down onto the fat man's eyelid with two of her slender fingers. She pulled out the lid and carefully inserted the horse pick between it and the man's eyeball.

"I repent," he said desperately!

"Praise Jesus," Isabel said calmly as she shoved the point of the horse pick up and out through the top of Cruz' eyelid. Blood welled up immediately around the metal point as the fat man's screaming echoed off the walls of the stables. "Praise Jesus," Sister Magdalena shouted as she yanked the pick upward! The small implement was ripped clean of flesh. The left side of the eyelid hung down over the eye. The right side hung on by a thread. Blood leaked down from the wound and into his eye. Master Cruz made the most wretched, hitching cries as she peered down at him.

"Shall I take him," Hector asked from the stable entrance? Isabel had not heard him come in.

"Take him," she agreed.

"What shall I do about this?" he asked as he gestured one hand toward the bleeding mass that was Master Cruz' left eye.

"Let it bleed," Sister Magdalena said coldly. Hector grabbed hold of the rope that bound the sobbing merchant and carried him out of the stables as if he weighed nothing at all.

† † †

Lord Barillos woke up when Hector entered the tower. His head and right shoulder were sore from where he had fallen asleep against the bars of his cell. His body was weak from hunger. The men were imprisoned in separate cells. One cell remained vacant. The first man was not familiar to Manuel. The second was immediately recognizable. "Captain Lozano," Barillos asked in disbelief?

"What have you gotten me into Manuel," Lozano shouted?

"Still your tongue lest I remove it," Hector said as he untied the crooked toothed man. Lozano did as he was told. Barillos had never seen his former captain back down from any man. Nevertheless, Lozano looked up at Hector like a whipped dog. He did not even attempt an escape when the scarred warrior turned his back on him. Hector locked the door to Lozano's cell and left the same way he had come in. Barillos crawled over to the bars and looked up at the man who had once served him.

"How did you get here," Manuel asked?

"This is all your fault," Lozano said accusingly. "What in hell have you done this time?"

"It is Isabel," Barillos replied with fear.

"What," Captain Lozano asked angrily?

"The demon," Barillos explained, "the nun…it is Isabel!"

"You are drunk," Lozano retorted, but there was a nervous edge to his voice. A short time later, Hector returned to the tower carrying the bloated body of Master Cruz. He placed him roughly down on the floor of the last cell before cutting him free of his bonds. Manuel cringed as his gaze fell upon the other man's mangled eyelid. The man himself did not even attempt to rise up once Hector had freed him. Master Cruz cried softly on the floor as the vampire locked him in.

✝   ✝   ✝

The wealth which Master Cruz had brought from his estate in Huesca was indeed great. Apparently he did not believe the Cardinal´s guard in reference to the children being sold for next to nothing. Hector used a part of it to buy food for the prisoners. At Sister Magdalena's request; a feast was prepared for the remaining citizens of Montenegro. The nun had to make a pretense of eating behind a screen. Men were forbidden to look directly upon her. The farmers and fisherman who remained were wary of their new masters, even after Hector explained that the nun was Lady Isabel.

As the celebration continued into the night, the peasants became more and more receptive to the return of Montenegro's lost heiress. Isabel guessed that it was the influence of the wine. She could not have been more correct. It was not until much later that she would realize that Hector had put them all in thrall.

The elder vampire was very thorough. He made sure that every citizen had a glass. He even insisted on giving each of the children a small drink to join in the celebration. For the remainder of the evening, he filled the peasant's heads with visions of a glorious future. He would send the men to capture wild horses. He would buy breeding stock as well. These people knew that Isabel had been trained to breed horses by her father. Hector explained that he would train the stallions to war with her guidance. This was not entirely true, but most men would not feel comfortable riding a war horse bred and trained solely by a woman.

What Hector lacked in charm, he made up for with his vampiric blood. It took little time for the grey beards to start waxing nostalgic over the glory that was once Montenegro. Hector let them tell their stories. By the celebration's end, they were staring at the elder vampire with cult-like adoration.

The following evening, Hector left for Castile in the carriage of Master Cruz. He took several of the younger men to guard his rest. He could have waited longer, but he knew that it was important for Sister Magdalena to finish her task. "It is God's will that I help those who have defiled me to repent," she had said. "This is a part of my atonement for taking my own life."

Hector's adoration and respect for Sister Magdalena could not have been stronger. He had never thought it possible that a vampire could touch the cross fragment; and yet, she had done so. She had wielded it against her enemies and God had fought for her. This anomaly made Hector believe that redemption was attainable, even for a creature such as he. Isabel gave him faith.

The journey to Castile took several days. He ordered his new thralls to take the carriage off the path when they were within a mile of their destination. They hid behind a growth of thick brambles. The darkness would do the rest. "The man I will bring to you is an enemy of Montenegro," he told them. "He was one who had a hand in the war that caused its ruin." It was not exactly a lie. His thralls wanted to accompany him on the midnight raid, but he commanded them to remain with the carriage and await his return.

Of all the penitents, Lord Guillermo was the wealthiest. His estate was a keep which lay on a small hill to the north of Castile. It was surrounded by high stone walls with defensible towers on each corner. In the past, Hector would have gone over one of the side walls and cut a red swath to his target. According to Sister Magdalena's teachings, however; killing the wicked was sinful. This heretical idea made perfect sense to Hector. In fact, he had heard many holy men encouraging him to send sinners to hell in the past. What sense was there in that?

Throwing the idea of stealth aside, Hector walked confidently up to the gates of Lord Guillermo's keep. He assured himself that he would give the humans the opportunity to surrender and avoid bloodshed. The elder vampire was feeling quite proud of his newfound righteousness when a sentry called down to him from high atop the battlements. "Who goes there," the sentry asked sternly? The sound of his voice suggested that he was a young man.

"I come from the Holy Church," Hector shouted back. He did not think it prudent to give his name.

"It is the middle of the night," the sentry called down. "You may return by morning."

"I cannot wait that long," the vampire replied.

"My master will not appreciate your waking him."

"This is important," Hector replied.

"What business," the sentry inquired?

"Lord Guillermo stands accused of rape," Hector shouted up at him! "I have come to bring him to trial."

"By whose order," the second century scoffed?

"The Lord Most High," Hector replied. "Open the gate!"

"We shall not open to you Sir," the first sentry called down with amusement. "It would appear that the night air has robbed you of your wits."

"If you do not open the gate," Hector said, "then I shall have to enter by force!"

"I see no army," the second man jeered.

"Get you away from this place," the first guard barked, "lest I lose my patience and fill your breast with arrows!"

"Lower the gate," Hector said finally. The sentries knocked arrows into their bows and fired down at the vampire below. As the two arrows came toward him, Hector leaped up into the air and spun about. He deflected the first arrow with steel buckler on his right elbow. He would've deflected the other with the buckler on his left, but his timing was off. The point of the arrow pierced through his outstretched palm. After his feet touched ground, Hector surveyed the damage done. Blood covered the tip of the arrow and welled up around the shaft which stuck out of his palm. Placing the index and small finger of his right hand over the arrow and the other two fingers beneath, Hector applied pressure until the shaft snapped. He then pulled the remainder of the shaft quickly out of his wound.

"You had better get out of here," the second century warned. "Your luck will run out."

"The Lord decrees an eye for an eye," Hector shouted. "Surrender or make peace with God!" As Hector was speaking, the wound in his hand closed up. Out of his peripheral vision, he saw the sentries reaching back to their quivers. He flung one hand up toward the men, preempting their attack by exercising his Dominion over Air. The arrows in the second guard's quiver launched backward up into the air, spreading out as they did so. Hector made a halting motion with his hand and the arrows stopped. The two sentries looked up in disbelief as the shafts slowly revolved until their points were all facing downward. Hector chopped down with his hand causing the arrows to rain upon the terrified soldiers.

Hector left onto the battlements over the gate. The to sentries lay sprawled out on the walkway. Each of them was so filled with arrows that they were hard to distinguish from each other. Some of the centuries further down the battlements were now taking notice. They realized that something was amiss but had not yet identified it. Hector took the opportunity to kneel down over one of the arrow filled corpses and drink his fill. "Who is that man," shouted one of the other archers? "Alarm," shouted another, "alarm!"

Hector could not wait for the men to knock arrows. He held his hands out wide with his palms facing up and focused his will. "God forgive these men," Hector shouted as he pushed his hands up heavenward! Everywhere along the battlements, arrows flew up from quivers and levitated in midair. There was a moment's pause.

"The Devil is among us," one archer said in awe! An instant later, the sentries' arrows fell down upon them. Lord Guillermo's archers were killed to a man. Hector scanned the windows of the keep. He knew he did not have much time. Torches were being lid on the ground floor of the East wing. He could hear the sounds of the man bustling about inside. These would be Lord Guillermo's soldiers scrambling to arm themselves. Those who were armed were already rushing out into the courtyard. They ran toward the stairs that would bring them up to the battlements. Hector had no quarrel with these men.

The elder vampire ran west over the battlements in order to get a view of the far side of the keep. After a short distance, he saw his objective. There was a third-floor balcony that was twice as big as the others he had seen on the front of the keep. Mortals who held power were forever trying to attract attention to themselves with the biggest and most luxurious of everything. Hector could always follow the trail of arrogance.

Hector disappeared from the soldiers view as he used the power of his blood to quicken his steps. He vaulted off the battlements toward the balcony which he knew would lead to Lord Guillermo's bed chamber. There was the cracking of tile as Hector landed. All that stood between him and his target were heavy curtains to keep the wind out.

"What was that," a fearful voice inquired from behind the curtains. Hector pushed through them. Guillermo was wearing a white nightgown and sat holding up the lavish blanket of his bed so that it nearly touched his chin. He looked like a child suffering from bad dreams.

Lord Guillermo let out a short yell when Hector passed through the curtains. "Guards," he screamed frantically as Hector walked quickly toward him! Two soldiers, who had been posted outside the door, came immediately into the room. They held their swords out before them and carried round shields in their free hands.

"I do not wish to kill you," Hector cautioned the guardsmen. One of the men stood tensed to attack. The other frowned and looked over his shoulder toward the door. Hector watched this man's quick intake of breath which meant that he was preparing to shout. In less than the blink of an eye, Hector's fist was smashing into the man's stomach and robbing him of breath. The vampire crouched down on one knee, standing up again as he delivered an uppercut that knocks the soldier off his feet.

As the guardsmen somersaulted backward through the air, he let go of his armaments. While the round shield was still falling, Hector grabbed it in both hands and smashed it into the side of the second soldiers head! As the guards crumpled to the floor, Hector turned his attention to Lord Guillermo. "Stay back," the man said fearfully as he scrambled to his feet. The two of them were then standing on opposite sides of the bed. "Who are you," Lord Guillermo demanded?

"God hath sent me to punish you for your sins," Hector said. He barred his teeth and flexed his hands as he took one menacing step forward. Guillermo stepped back even though the bed was between them. "Start praying," Hector suggested. He jumped over the bed as if it were nothing and twisted Lord Guillermo's arm behind his back before the other man could react. Hector dropped his elbow down hard on the man's arm above the elbow joint. There was the crunch of bone and a howl of pain from his victim.

Hector bit savagely at the side of the Lord Guillermo's neck and drained him into unconsciousness. By this time, he could hear soldiers hurrying up the stairs. They were too late. Hector threw Lord Guillermo over one shoulder and dashed out onto the balcony. He made a short jump up with one foot and then used its opposite to launch himself from the railing.

Hector flew over the courtyard and landed on the battlements. Before Lord Guillermo soldiers could react, the elder vampire leapt down the other side and disappeared from view. He ran as fast as his blood would allow! Once obscured by the forest, he slowed himself to a mortal's pace.

"Open the door," Hector shouted as his carriage came into view. His thralls quickly obeyed and Hector shoved the Lord Guillermo inside. "Move out," he barked before joining his captive and closing the door. He placed manacles on the Lord's wrists and ankles. He then laid the man face down on one of the benches. The last penitent had been collected. Now there was only the journey home.

✝   ✝   ✝

Manuel Barillos woke with a start! His heart was pounding and his skin was covered in a cold sweat. There were tears leaking from his eyes and he could not stop the terrified moans which escaped his lips. As usual, Manuel awakened in one of the birdcages which hung precariously from the prison tower. It was late afternoon, but darkness was only a few short hours away. And while shivered involuntarily as he contemplated the coming night. With the darkness would come Isabel.

The dream which Manuel had been having left his mind in an unfettered panic! The most disturbing part was that he could not be certain which of his nightmares was real. He bit his index finger to keep from screaming as he remembered the images from the night before.

The flesh of my mother is not good enough for your Manuel," Sister Magdalena *asked with a hideous gleam in her eyes?* "Let us see how you will enjoy wallowing around in the mud!"

"I beg of you," Manuel heard himself saying. "Do not do this!"

"I shall not do anything," the nun said smugly. "He is yours," she told the crooked toothed man.

"We thank you for your generosity," the captain grinned.

"Get away from me captain," Manuel exclaimed!

"Wait until I am gone Captain Lozano," Isabel told the crooked toothed man. "This is no sight for a nun."

"As my lady wishes," the man chuckled.

"No," Barillos begged! "Do not leave!" His pleas fell on deaf ears as Sister Magdalena closed the door.

"Take off your clothes men," Captain Lozano said. "We have work to do."

"No," Manuel cried once more! The captain laughed as he and his men began to discard their clothing. Barillos writhed and

jerked on the bed in an effort to free himself, but the chains held him fast to the bedposts.

"Do you think he will squeal as loud as his stepdaughter did," one of the men asked?

"I hope he does," another chuckled as he roughly fondled Manuel's genitals through the material of his hose.

"Stop this," Manuel shouted! "You are my soldiers. Obey me at once!"

"Get your hands off of him," Captain Lozano barked! Manuel felt as if he were in control again. This small and senseless glimmer of hope died when the man spoke again. "You know that I get to go first," the old man said as he loosened his belt. Manuel could not help but look on in horror as the crooked toothed man removed his undergarments and unsheathed his old and withered meat.

"No...No," the former Lord kept saying, but his consent was of no concern to anyone in the room. His voice grew louder as the older man approached the bed.

"Ha," he said as he bounded up onto the sheets.

"No," Manuel shouted as he twisted around in an attempt to escape.

"Get him Captain," one of the younger men urged, but the Lozano needed no encouragement. His eyes traveled perversely over Manuel as he took a kneeling position between his legs.

"Give me a blade," the captain said. One of the younger men handed him a dagger. Lozano grabbed hold of the bottom of Manuel's left pant leg and cut a long gash up through it.

"Help," Manuel screamed in horror! The Captain gave back the dagger and then grabbed both sides of the fabric around the cut. He flexed his arms and rent the pant leg all the way up to Manuel's waist.

"Now we shall have some real fun," the crooked toothed man said as they all feasted their eyes on Manuel's nakedness. They seemed like a flock of vultures gathered for butchery. Manuel kept screaming. His men made sport of him and his suffering continued long into the night.

Manuel sat suspended in his cage, fearfully anticipating the coming night. The bars of his cage were just wide enough that he could extend his legs out to the calves.

Time seemed to fold in on itself. Every day began in the same manner. Manuel would awaken in the cage. Weak from hunger and terrified of the visions he had suffered the night before; Manuel would wait for Isabel.

After the darkness came, the nun would set out a feast. The meal would be placed upon a table which was positioned very close the opening from which his cage was suspended. In silence, she would cut up her meat, spread butter over bread, or pour herself a glass of wine. The aromas of the food would drift up to Manuel's nostrils and reawaken the pains of starvation. The former lord felt even more wretched here than he had as a beggar on the streets of Huesca.

When Sister Magdalena was done tormenting him with food, she would throw it out over the waterfall where it would eventually be swallowed by the dark water of the River Ebro. Most days, the prisoners were fed a thin gruel which barely sustained them. Some days they had nothing at all. During the night, Sister Magdalena would encourage them to repent. This was usually followed by some grotesque form of physical torture.

Manuel could not say how long he had been imprisoned in Montenegro. Surely it was a long time. He could not explain why his wounds and those of his fellow prisoners would heal so rapidly. Aside from hunger, the prisoners would generally wake up unharmed. Perhaps it was only his mind playing tricks.

Manuel would never know that the gruel contained a small amount of Hector's blood which greatly increased a mortal's capacity for healing. Sister Magdalena could have used her own blood, but she felt that doing so would be an obstacle to repentance. They should come to God on their own, not out of an obsessive need to please her.

Barillos was never certain when he was awake and when he was dreaming. Isabel tormented him with visions of the dead that seemed as if they were really happening. He was forced to relive each of the rapes he had caused to be inflicted upon her. For a long time, the other men did not wish to discuss his fears. Eventually, they admitted to having had the same dreams too. Like Manuel, they were unsure as to what was reality. They all remembered committing atrocities upon one another and they all recalled not having any control over their actions. Many times they were not allowed to speak of their own accord. The words that emanated from their mouths came from some other source. Only that man who was reliving the part of Isabel was able to speak and act freely.

At some point, the scarred warrior arrived with the last prisoner, Lord Guillermo of Castile. Lord Guillermo had already appeared in many of Manuel's more revolting nightmares. This made Manuel wonder if Guillermo had been there all along. In any case, he screamed just as loud as the rest of them.

The driver of Master Cruz' carriage did not escape the nun's ministrations. His was the sin of silence and apathy. He had turned a blind eye to Master Cruz' predations for years. Because of this, Sister Magdalena had used an iron from the fire to remove his eyes and damage his ears beyond repair. She fed on the driver's blood on occasion, but that was the extent of it. Isolation was his punishment.

The rest of them were whipped, scarred, burned, stretched on the rack, and subjected to whatever ills the nun's mind could devise. When the day was nearly upon them, Isabel would force each man to relive his sins beyond the wall of sleep. After what seemed like an eternity in hell, Isabel broke the routine. On that particular night, she was accompanied by the warrior Del Toro. Manuel could not explain, even to himself why he was so desperate to please this man.

"The penitents are quite obstinate," she told her companion. "They regret their fate, but not the actions which led them to it. They are slaves to lust. As long as this remains so, they will not repent. What must be done to open their eyes?"

"Leave it to me," Hector said gravely. The warrior left he room for a time while Sister Magdalena built up the fire. The flames were blazing by the time Hector returned. In his hands, he carried three coils of rope. Sister Magdalena seated herself at the small table while the warrior uncoiled the ropes down between the prison cells. Each rope was about three times the length of a man, but only as thick as an index finger.

The prisoners put up no resistance as Hector stripped them of clothing and wrapped the ropes around their bodies like so many cocoons. All that was left exposed of each man was his feet, groin, and head. Manuel could not resist being bound by the elder vampire. His limbs were cramped and useless after being stuck in the fetal position for so long. He could not understand why the others did not attempt to run. There was surely nothing to lose in trying. Once the prisoners were tied, Hector turned to face the fire.

"What is the meaning of this," Sister Magdalena said after a time.

"I will cure them of their lust," the warrior promised. "It will be only a little while longer." Barillos lay there listening to the crackle of the flame. He could not imagine what was going on in Hector's mind. Nevertheless, the power of the blood compelled his mind to invent foolish fantasies in which the scarred warrior would act as their unlikely savior.

When the fire had burned down, Hector retrieved the metal tongs from off the mantle and bent down to retrieve a burning coal. He held the glowing ember up close to his face to inspect it. Once satisfied, he turned once more toward Isabel. "I will show you what to do," he said. Barillos imagined that the warrior could use the coal to snap the ropes that held him. "Which of them do you wish for me to use?"

"Whomever you see fit," the nun replied.

"Get me out of here," Master Cruz implored the vampire who knelt down beside him. This made Manuel wonder if the others were having the same ridiculous thoughts that he was. Hector spoke coldly down at the helpless merchant. His teeth flashed in the firelight.

"We are the curse which God hath laid upon you for your wickedness." Slowly, the vampire began to lower the red hot coal toward Master Cruz' exposed groin. The obese man groaned like a frightened animal and began to thrash about in his bonds.

"Whatsoever ye have done to the least of my children," Isabel quoted; "ye have done it unto me." Hector steadied the thrashing man with one hand and continued.

"Behold God's vengeance," he said somberly. Hector roughly shoved the tongs down between Master Cruz' thighs. In all his years, Manuel had never heard such horrible wailing! He could hear meat sizzling and the acrid odor of burnt flesh. The fat man's agonized cries were joined by the terrified screams of those who would follow. Manuel could barely breathe as he awaited the inevitable.

Hector finally removed the glowing coal from Master Cruz' groin. He handed the tongs to Sister Magdalena. The nun walked gracefully over to the fireplace and traded her coal for another. This she carried back to the prostrate form of Lord Guillermo. There were flames reflected in her eyes even though she was facing away from the fire. Isabel knelt slowly down beside the man. Hector knelt down on the opposite side and held the man steady. The nun bent down until her face was almost touching that of Lord Guillermo. "I see this going one of two ways," she said hatefully.

"No," Guillermo sobbed. "Do not do this!"

"You can either beg me to stop," Isabel said, "or you can beg me for more." Guillermo whimpered as the tongs came closer to his most vulnerable parts.

"Behold God's vengeance," Hector said once more. Isabel inserted the coal between the man's thighs. Once again, the air came alive with the sounds of suffering. "That is long enough," Hector instructed after a time. Lord Guillermo was either dead or unconscious from the pain. He moved no longer.

"Let us not neglect the greatest of them," the nun said as she rose up from the floor. She went back to the fireplace and retrieved a hot coal for stepfather. Manuel was already hyperventilating when the vampires knelt down over him. The blood-born fantasies of Hector rescuing him were replaced with abject terror! "You shall pay most of all," Isabel promised. Her sharp fangs glistened as she bent closer to his face.

"Have mercy Isabel," Manuel heard himself saying.

"Mercy springs from love Manuel," she told him. "Everyone I love is dead."

"Behold God's vengeance," Hector intoned. Manuel was struck momentarily blind by the pain that coursed up through his body. The coal was placed directly beneath his testicles. These were consumed by the intense heat of the ember and the metal tongs which held it fast. Manuel could not imagine a more intense pain. His mind was wiped clean of thought as his flesh blackened. Yet, there was a greater pain than this. When the coal had burned its way through his testicles, then began a new plateau of agony. The odor of burning flesh was reinvigorated in the chamber as Manuel screamed his way into blessed unconsciousness.

CHAPTER X

As the months dragged on, Manuel witnessed the other prisoners attain Sister Magdalena's version of salvation. By what measure she judged, he could not imagine. Once Isabel was satisfied that a prisoner had repented, then Hector would come. For the vampires, salvation meant beheading.

One by one, Manuel watched as his fellow prisoners were decapitated. The driver of the carriage was the first to go. Dragged from his cell by the male vampire, the young man was thrown down on his knees beside the pulley system that brought water up from the river. Hector's sword sent the man's head tumbling down over the gorge and into the waters below. From his cage, Manuel had an unobstructed view of each and every execution.

Master Cruz offered no resistance when his time came. He did not cry as he had when first imprisoned. His eyes looked hopeful even after Hector's sword had traveled through his neck. Perhaps the monsters had convinced him that he would go on to paradise.

Weeks later, Lord Guillermo was led to the place of execution. He looked fearfully up at the warrior's raised sword as he knelt before the opening. Before Hector could bring down the blade, Lord Guillermo cast himself into the River Ebro. "He could have been saved," Isabel remarked to Manuel in a deadpan voice. There was no pity in her as Guillermo broke himself on the jagged rocks below.

"I have seen the error of my ways," Manuel told Isabel as she walked toward the exit. The nun paused, but did not look back. "I had become so prideful that I would have done anything to save face, even murder. I have betrayed everyone I have ever known." Sister Magdalena turned round to face the man who had destroyed everything.

"You betrayed my father did you not?" Her eyes narrowed up at him as she spoke.

"Yes," Manuel nodded.

"You were instrumental in the fall of Montenegro," she continued. "Were you in league with Lord Enriquez of Morera? Tell me the truth lest I rip it from your soul!"

"Yes," Manuel sobbed. "My estate was in ruins and Enriquez, he was a friend."

"A friend," Isabel scoffed, "a friend whom you owed a lot of money no doubt?"

"Yes," Manuel nodded. "He agreed to attack Montenegro and it was my part to marry Lady Priscilla. I was to pay off my debt to Enriquez in horse flesh."

"Enriquez could have sold all the livestock," Isabel noted. "Why would he need you or my mother?"

"He wanted Montenegro as a vassal of Morera," Manuel told her. "He would have profited from the trade of horses for centuries to come."

"So in essence, you killed my father as well," Isabel said.

"God forgive me," Manuel cried. "I am to blame for it all!"

"Yes you are," Isabel said with clenched teeth. She turned sharply and stalked out of the tower, slamming the door loudly behind her.

"Wait," Manuel called after her. "I repent," he said desperately. "I am ready to die!" As the nun's footsteps receded, the prisoner dissolved into weeping. Sister Magdalena did not return to the tower that night, or the next, or the next.

Several days later, Manuel awakened after nightfall. His sleep no longer followed a discernible pattern. His body was malnourished and sick from hunger. So fatigued was he that he did not even wake up when someone removed him from his cage.

The prison tower door slamming jolted Manuel awake in the chair they had placed him in. He sat before the table which was normally used to torment him with the sight of food that could never be eaten. He briefly pondered escape. Perhaps the door was left unlocked. If only he could get out in time, but his frail body told him otherwise. He could barely lift his head up from the table, much less escape from the keep.

While he waited to see what might befall him next, Manuel prayed for death. Enter Magdalena carrying a wooden plate and fork. She paused a few steps away from him to speak. The plate contained three very thin strips of meat. It was of a grayish hue which reminded Manuel of lamb. His stomach growled painfully as he looked on. "Perhaps I have been too harsh with you," Isabel mused aloud. "It may be God's will that you be given another chance to live."

"Praise God," Manuel said hopefully. His voice was small and unsure.

"Eat this meat," Isabel said as she placed the plate down before him. "If you can stomach it, I will give you more." There was a dark chili sauce spread lightly over each piece of meat on the plate. Manuel could smell the peppers. He took up the fork in his weak right hand and set to work. He was starving! Manuel would have preferred to eat faster, but his ruined muscles would only move so quickly.

"Thank you, Isabel," he said with effort when the plate was empty.

"I will get you more food," she said gently. "You deserve it."

"Oh thank you," Manuel said again. Sister Magdalena left the room with the wooden plate in hand. It seemed like an eternity until she entered the tower once more. She carried a sharp knife this time to go along with the fork. The cut of meat atop the plate was quite large this time. It was made from the same flesh as the first few pieces. Manuel could tell this by the grayish color of it. Manuel guessed it was a shoulder or a leg bone by the joint that curved over near the bottom.

Isabel sat the knife down beside Manuel's fork and then followed it with the plate of meat. She dropped the plate mere centimeters above the table. There was a sharp sound as the plate struck wood. Some of the juices slopped over onto Manuel's lap.

Manuel's intense hunger commingled with revulsion as his eyes fell upon the offering which had been set before him. The meat had been cooked slowly on a spit and was now sitting in its own juices. Manuel could see the reflection of firelight gleaming off the toenails. They were his toenails! This was not lamb. The grayish cast came from the months that his foot had been rotting in whatever place the nun had kept it.

"You do not have to eat it," Isabel said maliciously as she bent her face down close to his, "but if you do not…you will surely starve!" Manuel moaned in horror.

"Just kill me," he begged of her!

"You cannot choose to die Manuel," she said. "It is the same as suicide."

"Oh God," Manuel cried as he felt the bile rising to his lips!

"What will it be penitent," she demanded?

"I repent," he sobbed. "Oh God, I repent!"

"Then eat," Isabel said mercilessly, "for God will not grant salvation to one who starves willingly." Manuel cried like a small child. His tears fell down onto the macabre feast that had been placed before him.

"Please God," Manuel begged tearfully, but no deliverance came. He moaned in horror as he set about the grim task of cannibalizing his own flesh. Though his gorge rose several times, Barillos managed to strip most of the meat free of the bone and consume it. The worst part of it was that brief period of time when his stomach was welcoming the vile substance. He had been denied food for too long.

Manuel's head swam and nausea overtook him as he looked at the skeletal remains of his severed foot. "Behold God's vengeance," Isabel said. Barillos became violently ill then and disgorged the contents of his stomach all over what remained of the gruesome meal. The stench of the vomit and the sight of the newly covered bones made Manuel start to gag all over again.

"Praise God," Isabel said flatly when Manuel had no more to give. "You shall die after all. God forgive me, for I cannot kill you." She walked quietly from the room, leaving her stepfather to wallow in his own vomit. Moments later, Hector entered the room. Manuel prayed for forgiveness as the executioner approached. He dragged Manuel over to the place where the others had been killed.

The mercy of death was not granted to Manuel Barillos that night. Instead, Hector shoved him back into the birdcage. He was then suspended back in the usual spot over the river. Manuel wept and tore at his face with his hands when he realized that they meant for him to live.

The next morning, Manuel opened his eyes toward the sun. He stretched his legs out as far as they would go from the cage. This time they passed all the way through. "Oh," he said in amazement! He could hardly believe it! He laughed as he swung his legs freely back and forth over the water. It was a miracle. It was as if God had widened the bars for him. "Hallelujah," Barillos shouted down into the cascading water! He coughed weakly and then caught his breath. That was when he realized the truth.

This small freedom was not a blessing from God. His legs were free because of starvation. How sickly, like the legs of an insect they appeared to him. Manuel began to weep uncontrollably. He laid his head down on the cold iron bars...and soon gave up the ghost as weakness consumed him.

The next evening, Isabel walked up the stairs to the prison tower. She knew that she should call Hector to do God's will. Manuel had repented long ago. She paused on the stairs and drew in a breath to summon her companion. The command died on her lips. "God forgive me," she whispered as she continued her ascent.

Once in the tower, she immediately noticed how Manuel's legs hung down from the cage. She worked the iron crank which brought the cage back on the track of the pawl arm and into the chamber. Cranking the wheel as far as it would go placed the cage mere inches off the floor. The man did not cry out as one of his legs was bent at an odd angle beneath the cage.

"No," Isabel said with alarm. "You cannot die!" The cage spun round slightly, revealing the dead eyes and the gaping mouth of the man who had tormented her all those years past. "No," Isabel said forcefully. She opened the cage with a small brass key and grabbed Manuel by the temples.

Sister Magdalena focused her will but it was too late. She could not reach Manuel Barillos' soul for it had already moved on. What reward her stepfather attained in the afterlife she would never know. "No," Isabel shrieked as she dug her nails deeply into the dead man's flesh! She fell back away from the cage and collapsed upon the floor by the opening facing the river.

"God forgive me," she wept. Her tears of blood fell down to join the water from the mountains which cascaded into the river below. Isabel's face was contorted in rage as she looked back at Manuel's corpse. "You cannot die," she screamed! "I would resurrect you a thousand times, but to kill you again!" Of course, there was no response from the dead man. "I hate you," Isabel wept. "I hate you and all is lost."

It was a hollow victory in the tower that night. Manuel Barillos was dead. This did nothing to change the fact that Isabel's father was dead also. Lady Priscilla and her unborn son rotted together far below the ground. Ramon's body was a feasting hall for worms and Little Grandma was in Hell.

Isabel did not leave the tower until the sun forced her from it. The taste of vengeance was naught but bitter ash in her mouth. There was nothing left.

Sister Magdalena would come to lay claim to Montenegro and Black River Village under the auspice of her lineage. In time the horse trade would thrive again. The fortress would become a stronghold for the church while the new castle at La Cascada would take up the task of protecting the border, thus removing Isabel farther from the troubles of mortal politics.

The politics of the damned was another story. Cast out from the Convocation of Saints by Samael´s misunderstanding, she would exist an entity apart from the looming war between the Lords of the Night. The fear of her ability to employ the power of faith would sustain her untouchable status to the other vampire factions.

If they knew the truth, the Convocation of Saints would surely consume her. But the truth was obscured even from Hector. In the wake of Manuel´s death, Sister Magdalena´s faith had weakened. She knew that she would have killed her stepfather purposefully to send him to Hell, but grace had cheated her of that chance. So it was that the fragment of the cross began to affect her as well: the sinking feeling in her heart as she drew near, the burning agony if she were to actually touch it, the repulsion she could feel as palpable force anytime she was within the same room.

The artifact was sealed in a coffin and concealed in the caverns behind Montenegro. It would be lost to time, much as the Heiress herself. Several decades later; she would fall into a long sleep, leaving Hector as seneschal to take care of the affairs of state. Sister Magdalena would sleep far away from the pain of her losses. Centuries later…she would rise again.

† THE END †

Coming soon from the pen of Michael Converse..,

The Heretic

Chapter I

The Black Man opened his eyes. He was lying upon a huge disk crafted from black marble. His body was engulfed in the eternal flames that covered his resting place. The disc was suspended by four thick, iron chains that stretched up beyond the limits of mortal sight.

Mo'lech rose to his feet and looked around the vast cavern wherein he slept far from the burning sun. He could hear the underground river gurgling in the depths below him. "Rise," his deep voice echoed out into the darkness. Slowly and onerously, the chains began to carry the disc toward heaven. These chains were not driven by men or beasts, but by the souls of the angels which were bound there until the end of days. The fire which perpetually burned over the marble disc and protected the Dark One's rest was also so driven. The chains were gathered up onto long cylindrical cranks which were built into the ceiling of the cavern.

The disc rose up through the top of the cavern and came to rest in a small chamber which was barely larger than the disc itself. The men who had prostrated themselves around the opening were dressed in coarse white robes and turbans. With coal they had marked the front of their robes with the symbol of their master, the two-tined fork.

Mo'lech walked slowly out of the fire. These thralled cultists were called the Chemarim. Each of the Chemarim who were gathered around the pit had been chosen to remain there in prayer throughout the hours of daylight. They had been instructed that Mo'lech would only return from Hell if their blasphemous faith was strong. This was a lie of course. Mo'lech would come up from the cavern whenever he saw fit. It took very little to impress mankind, which was part of the reason why he held them in such contempt.

The white robed thralls quickly surrounded their master. They covered his loins with the golden cloth. They adorned his feet with golden sandals which had straps crisscrossing up to mid-calf. Over each of his massive biceps they fitted a gold circlet large enough to rest on a normal man's head. On his brow, they placed a golden crown. Set into the metal were nine spikes which rose up above the top of Mo'lech's head by nearly a foot. These spikes were crafted from ivory engraved with gold. Lastly they handed him an iron rod that was half again the height of a man. Most of it was plated in gold, except for the two-tined fork which made up the last two feet of the weapon.

The Chemarim who handed over the iron bladed pole arm was dressed much like the others. His robes were a deep crimson, which signified that he was one of the Dark One's children. This particular child was called Fahad Abdul Baqi. He was favored above the rest. His long black hair was drawn back into three braids which hung down over the back of his robe. He had firm, aristocratic features and cold brown eyes that had seen countless atrocities.

"Be gone from me," Mo'lech ordered the white robed supplicants. The fawning cultists continued to offer praises as they backed out of the chamber toward the tunnel leading out. Without warning, the Black Man grabbed the mortal closest to him by the wrist. "Your faith is weak," he said accusingly. "You have prayed to Allah!"

"No master," the wretched man whined. "I serve only the Dark.

"Liar," Mo'lech shouted! The prayers of the others grew louder as Mo'lech tore into the helpless man's neck with razor sharp teeth. After draining the human of blood, he cast the worthless corpse into the pit. "Be gone," he growled at the others! The lower half of his face was covered in the dead man's blood. The rest of the white clad Chemarim departed quickly. "What have you to tell me Fahad," the Black Man asked when the others had disappeared?

"The emissary from the French court comes to renew his fealty," Fahad reported.

"Is that all," Mo'lech inquired?

"No great one," Fahad replied. "Your spies have returned from Italy." Fahad sounded as though he had eaten something rotten as he spoke. He held the acrobats in low regard, considering them not worthy to partake of Mo'lech's blood.

"Send Kareem to me now."

"Here master," Fahad asked with obvious distaste?

"Where am I now," Mo'lech asked rhetorically?

"As you command," Fahad replied uncomfortably. He bowed low before the Dark One and then moved quickly out of the chamber. After some time, Kareem walked quietly down to join his master. Kareem was dressed in very loose brown clothing that concealed much of what he was carrying from view. His head and beard were clean shaven as a mark of disgrace but he did not seem to be a man of shame. There was a thin scar next to his left eye where a sword point had left its irreversible mark.

"You're man Fahad does not enjoy my company," Kareem smiled.

"He believes that he is second only to myself," Mo'lech explained. "Perhaps he worries that you threaten his position."

"I bring news from the west," Kareem said with a bow. "I believe the time is ripe to turn the so-called Lords of Night against each other." Mo'lech motioned with one hand to indicate his desire for the spy to proceed. As Kareem began to speak, the Black Man smiled.

✞

The year of our Lord, 1508 A.D.,
Twelfth day, Fifth Month. Daybreak.

Mercutio tightened the leather strap which held Persephone's saddle in place. The white mare was one of his father's geldings. Master Ambrosius would not be pleased to find either his horse or his son missing. Mercutio's father owned a vast orchard on the outskirts of Ravenna. The peaches which grew there were among the best that Italy had to offer. There was a wine press and a distillery there as well. The sweet wine produced by Master Ambrosius and his servants brought in the majority of the family's coins. Wealth was not a concern in Mercutio's household.

Mercutio and his two brothers wanted for nothing. That is, they should have wanted for nothing. From a young age, Mercutio had been instructed in the art of swordplay, tutored in strategy, and subjected to a rigorous regimen of physical exercise. As the second son, it was customary that he should bring honor to his family through military service. He had accepted his fate.

Mercutio was not jealous of his younger brother Fiorello. The lot of the third son was to join the priesthood, bringing honor to the family through service to God. Having no faith in the existence of God, or desire to abstain from the pleasures of the flesh; Mercutio was quite comforted that he had not been born last. Life without the pliant flesh of women would be unbearable. Nevertheless, he could not help but envy Dominic.

As the oldest, Dominic would inherit everything. Their father, Gianni, was never far from Dominic's side. He would give the oldest brother constant instruction on how to best manage the orchard and the bottling of the family's wine. At the dinner table, Dominic was always to sit at his father's right hand. However, there was no preference as to how the other two sons were seated.

Mercutio was not pessimistic by nature. He simply thought it unfair that he should have to risk his life for no tangible reward while Dominic would receive everything without significant risk. On the bright side, he had heard stories from his instructors about carousing in foreign lands that made soldiering sound somewhat attractive.

Like all sons, Mercutio had the desire to please his father, but he had several serious character flaws. He was an incurable thrill seeker. No danger ever seemed too great that he could not surmount it. He reasoned that he would eventually be killed in battle, so why not live life to the hilt? He was one of those men who must be the best at everything they ever attempt. The only thing he could be second at was birth order.., nothing else. If he ever met someone who seemed to be more skilled or talented than he, Mercutio could not rest until the tables were turned.

Mercutio had some respect for his parents. His tutors he held in higher regard, for they had all seen combat. However, he had no love for God or country. He looked forward to his future as a warrior, but only because it was an opportunity to prove that he was the best at it.

During his adolescence and teenage years, Mercutio spent much of his free time with the acrobats in Ravenna's theater district. He had seen the troupe perform as a small child. He had been amazed by their extraordinary balance and death-defying maneuvers. It was only his nature to want to master the art. The acrobats were from Persia. They only came to Italy in the warmer months to perform. They would take their earnings back to their families far away. These men from the east had made fun of Mercutio's clumsy attempts at first, but eventually agreed to train him…for a price.

Master Ambrosius would never have approved. Because of this, Mercutio lied to his father and presented the acrobats as warriors from the east. Since they already wore masks when performing in town, the ruse was successful. Mercutio was apprenticed to Kareem, the master acrobat, under the guise that it was Kareem the Moorish Master of Blades, which was arguably true.

After several summers of instruction, Kareem introduced Mercutio to a much more lucrative use of the skills he had been taught. Mercutio took to burglary like a fish to water! Nothing fueled his adrenaline more than creeping into someone's home in the dead of night. The risk of death and discovery was just as much a reward as the valuables nefariously obtained.

At first, Mercutio would serve as a lookout or be tasked with creating a diversion. As the acrobats put more and more trust in him, he would join them in their stealthy raids. Kareem taught and many other skills over the years: picking locks, stealthy movement, recognizing traps, and finding valuables that were deliberately hidden. Having no real need for money, Mercutio was content for Kareem and his brothers to divide the spoil mainly among themselves. The money he did take from the jobs poured into alcohol and loose women.

No job was too dangerous for the young Italian. In fact; the more danger… the better the thrill. Burglary was Mercutio's greatest vice. Deflowering virgins ran a close second. He had little trouble in fooling women. He had fine brown hair and amber eyes with gold flecks around his pupils. His body was well toned from years of physical training and he had a handsome face that encouraged trust. Mercutio wanted to squeeze as much fun out of life as he could before beginning his career as a soldier. He was convinced that he was the best, but as one old veteran had told him; war was not always about skill.

Persephone nickered softly as Mercutio undid the not which tethered her to an acacia tree. There was a noise from above and Mercutio turned to look. The fingers of the sun were just starting to caress the redbrick manor house from which he had come. The sunlight divided the color of the estate diagonally between red and pink.

Sounds had come from the opening of doors upon the second story balcony. These doors were made of an opaque, rose hued glass set in brass framing. Diana had come out in her nightgown. Her black hair was a bit disheveled and her feet were bare as she grasped the brass railing between them.

The young woman was beautiful, yet not so alluring as she had seemed the night before. She looked down at Mercutio with an injured expression that he had become accustomed to. There was little difference in the ending of this romantic interlude than in countless others. "Where are you going," Diana asked?

"Shhhh," Mercutio said he brought a finger to his lips. "Your father will summon the guards." The rest of their conversation was conducted mostly in stage whispers.

"But where are you going," she asked again?

"I am leaving," Mercutio said as though it were the most obvious thing in the world. "I must return home."

"Will you not come to meet my father this night as we talked about?"

"You talked about it," he answered with one brow raised.

"Do not say such things Mercutio," she said with emotion. "We are to be married. You know this!"

"I do not," Mercutio shook his head. "Let us agree that we have enjoyed each other and bid farewell."

"You leave me in ruins," Diana cried!

"Quiet," Mercutio hissed! "You are not ruined."

"I could be with child," she said plaintively.

"No," he disagreed. "The manner in which our love was concluded makes that impossible." He grinned then as he jumped up into Persephone's saddle.

"I am ruined," Diana wept. "If you will not be my husband, then no one will!"

"Someone will," he replied as he looped the lead rope over the saddle horn.

"I will be a disgrace," Diana said. "My husband will see that I am not pure when we consummate our marriage."

"You'll be fine," Mercutio assured her. "Men will forgive much for a pretty face."

"You rogue," she screamed! "I will be disgraced before any man who chooses me. What am I supposed to do?"

"I do not know," Mercutio retorted as he wheeled Persephone away from the manner house. Her scream would bring trouble in moments if he were not swift. "Baste yourself with pigs' blood," he shouted as he rode off.

"Bastard," Diana yelled as Mercutio made his escape. "You shall pay for this!" Mercutio laughed as the morning breeze washed over him. He vanished into the woods long before Diana could fully rouse anyone to pursue him.